HOPSCOTCH

"Cortázar's masterpiece. This is the first great novel of Spanish America . . . The astonishing moment when all the figures seem to have fallen into their right positions in the hopscotch court . . . [is] not only among the constituent scenes of a powerful anti-novel but, like deeply understood moments in life itself, rich with many kinds of potential meanings and intimations"

Times Literary Supplement

"Hopscotch, a . . . superb work, should establish Cortázar as an outstanding writer of our day . . . The dialogue is brilliant, whether the subject is literature, love, Mondrian, jazz or the fallibility of science. Individual scenes are superbly alive . . . the rapid-fire invention of the language makes every page sparkle, thanks to the translation by Gregory Rabassa, which gives a dazzling parallel . . . to Cortázar's stylistic magic"

DONALD KEENE, ***New York Times***

"The most brilliant novel in years . . . It is a spiralling, convulsive, exploding universe of a novel. It is the most powerful encyclopedia of emotions and visions to emerge from the postwar generation of international writers" **C. D. B. BRYAN**, ***Books and the Arts***

"Hopscotch . . . marks the true possibility of encounter between the Latin-American imagination and the contemporary world"

CARLOS FUENTES

"Everything that we take for granted . . . is subtly but ruthlessly brought to a crisis, and Cortázar does so in the midst of everyday life" ***Boston Globe***

"Here is literary cunning and accomplishment of a high order"

ROBERT NYE, ***Guardian***

"Julio Cortázar is one of the most distinctive voices in Latin American literature" ***Newsday***

JULIO CORTÁZAR lived in Buenos Aires for the first thirty years of his life, and after that in Paris. His stories, written under the dual influence of the English masters of the uncanny and of French surrealism, are extraordinary inventions, just this side of nightmare. In later life Cortázar became a passionate advocate for human rights and a persistent critic of the military dictatorships in Latin America. He died in 1984.

GREGORY RABASSA has translated some of the classics of modern Spanish and Portuguese literature, including *One Hundred Years of Solitude*, by Gabriel García Márquez. His most recent translation is *The Posthumous Memoirs of Brás Cubas*, by Machado de Assis. His translation of *Hopscotch* received the National Book Award for Translation.

"Cortázar is an original writer, circuitous and powerful . . . His method is to keep tight control over a world in which, just below the surface of charming, sophisticated social life, lies the unfaceable and unmentionable. At the centre of it, the narrator's voice is civilised, the main characters are eminently knowable and even nice, but the ice they walk on is thin"

ISABEL QUIGLY, *Financial Times*

"One gets to know a milieu, an atmosphere and a group of people with a closeness that is characteristic of only serious and lasting works of fiction . . . the reader is left with the conviction that Mr Cortázar has marked off a corner of the world singularly his own" THOMAS LASK, *New York Times*

Also by Julio Cortázar in a Harvill edition

BESTIARY: SELECTED STORIES

Julio Cortázar

HOPSCOTCH

Translated from the Spanish
by Gregory Rabassa

THE HARVILL PRESS
LONDON

First published with the title *Rayuela*, by Editoral Sudamericana Sociedad Anonima, in 1963
First published by The Harvill Press in 1967

This paperback edition published in 1998 by
The Harvill Press, 84 Thornhill Road, London N1 1RD

www.harvill-press.com

1 3 5 7 9 8 6 4 2

A CIP catalogue record for this book is available from the British Library

ISBN 1 86046 428 9

Designed and typeset in Minion at Libanus Press, Marlborough, Wiltshire

Printed and bound in Great Britain by Clays Ltd, St Ives plc

Half title illustration by Ronald Gunn

AUTHOR'S NOTE

In its own way, this book consists of many books, but two books above all. The reader is invited to choose between these two possibilities:

The first can be read in a normal fashion and it ends with chapter 56, at the close of which there are three garish little stars which stand for the words *The End.* Consequently, the reader may ignore what follows with a clean conscience.

The second can be read by beginning with chapter 73 and then following the sequence indicated at the end of each chapter. In case of confusion or forgetfulness, one need only consult the following list:

73 – 1 – 2 – 116 – 3 – 84 – 4 – 71 – 5 – 81 – 74 – 6 – 7 – 8 – 93 – 68 – 9 – 104 – 10 – 65 – 11 – 136 – 12 – 106 – 13 – 115 – 14 – 114 – 117 – 15 – 120 – 16 – 137 – 17 – 97 – 18 – 153 – 19 – 90 – 20 – 126 – 21 – 79 – 22 – 62 – 23 – 124 – 128 – 24 – 134 – 25 – 141 – 60 – 26 – 109 – 27 – 28 – 130 – 151 – 152 – 143 – 100 – 76 – 101 – 144 – 92 – 103 – 108 – 64 – 155 – 123 – 145 – 122 – 112 – 154 – 85 – 150 – 95 – 146 – 29 – 107 – 113 – 30 – 57 – 70 – 147 – 31 – 32 – 132 – 61 – 33 – 67 – 83 – 142 – 34 – 87 – 105 – 96 – 94 – 91 – 82 – 99 – 35 – 121 – 36 – 37 – 98 – 38 – 39 – 86 – 78 – 40 – 59 – 41 – 148 – 42 – 75 – 43 – 125 – 44 – 102 – 45 – 80 – 46 –47 – 110 – 48 – 111 – 49 – 118 – 50 – 119 – 51 – 69 – 52 – 89 – 53 – 66 – 149 – 54 – 129 – 139 – 133 – 140 – 138 – 127 – 56 – 135 – 63 – 88 – 72 – 77 – 131 – 58 – 131 –

Each chapter has its number at the top of every right-hand page to facilitate the search.

And moved by the hope of being of particular help to youth, and of contributing to the reform of manners in general, I have put together this collection of maxims, counsels and precepts which are the basis of those universal morals that are so much a part of the spiritual and temporal happiness of men of all ages, states and conditions, and of the prosperity and orderliness not only of the civil and Christian republic in which we live, but of any other republic or government that the most thoughtful and serious philosophers of the world might wish to contrive.

Spirit of the Bible and Universal Morals,
drawn from the Old and New Testaments
Put down in Tuscan by the Abbot Martini
with footnotes
Rendered into Castilian
by a member of the Regular Clergy of the
Congregation of San Cayetano of this Court
With permission
Madrid: Aznar, 1797

Everytime it starts to get cool, I mean in the middle of autim, I start gettin nutty ideas like I was thinkin about what was forein and diffrent, like for exsample how I'd like to turn into a swallow and get away and fly to countrys where it gets hot, or be an ant so's I could get deep into a cave and eat the stuff I stored away durin the summer or be a snake like what they got in the zoO, the ones they keep lockt up in glass cages thats heated so's they don't get stiff from the cold, which is what happens to poor human beans who cant buy no close cause the price is to high, and cant keep warm cause theys no keroseen, no coal, no wood, no fule oil and besides theys no loot, cause when you go around with bread you can go into any bar and get some booze that can be real warmin, even tho it aint good to overdo it cause if you overdos it it gets to be a bad habbit and bad habbits is bad for your body just like they is for youre selfrespeck, and when you start goin downhill cause your actin bad in everythin, they aint nobody or nothin can stop you from endin up a stinkin piece of human garbidge and they never gone give you a hand to haul you up outen the dirty muck you rollin around in, not even if you was a eaglE when you was young and could fly up and over the highest hills, but when you get old you like a highflyin bomber thats lost its moral engines and fall down outen the sky. I jes hope what I been writin down hear do somebody some good so he take a good look at how he livin and he dont be sorry when it too late and everythin is gone down the drain cause it his own fault.

CÉSAR BRUTO, *What I Would Like to Be If I Wasn't What I Am* (Chapter: "A St Bernard Dog")

From the Other Side

Rien ne vous tue un homme comme d'être obligé de représenter un pays.

JACQUES VACHÉ, letter to André Breton

1

Would I find La Maga? Most of the time it was just a case of my putting in an appearance, going along the Rue de Seine to the arch leading into the Quai de Conti, and I would see her slender form against the olive-ashen light which floats along the river as she crossed back and forth on the Pont des Arts, or leaned over the iron rail looking at the water. It was quite natural for me to climb the steps to the bridge, go into its narrowness and over to where La Maga stood. She would smile and show no surprise, convinced as she was, the same as I, that casual meetings are apt to be just the opposite, and that people who make dates are the same kind who need lines on their writing paper, or who always squeeze their toothpaste up from the bottom of the tube.

But now she would not be on the bridge. The thin glow of her face was probably peeking into the old doorways in the Marais ghetto, or maybe she was talking to a woman who sells fried potatoes, or she might be eating a hot sausage on the Boulevard de Sébastopol. In any case, I went out onto the bridge and there was no Maga. I did not run into her along the way either. We each knew where the other lived, every cranny we holed up in in our pseudo-student existence in Paris, every window by Braque, Ghirlandaio, or Max Ernst set into cheap postcard frames and ringed with gaudy posters, but we never visited each other at home. We preferred meeting on the bridge, at a pavement café, at an art movie, or crouched over a cat in some Latin Quarter courtyard. We did not go around looking for each other, but we knew that we would meet just the same. Oh, Maga, whenever I saw a woman who looked like you a clear, sharp pause would close in like a deafening silence, collapsing like a wet umbrella being closed. An umbrella, precisely. Maybe you remember, Maga, that old umbrella we sacrificed in a gully in Montsouris Park one sunset on a cold March day. We threw it away because you had found it half-broken in the Place de la Concorde and you had got a lot of use from it, especially for digging into people's ribs on the Métro or on a bus as you lethargically thought about the design the flies on the ceiling made. There was a cloudburst that afternoon and you tried to open your umbrella in the park in a proud sort of way, but your hand got all wrapped up in a catastrophe of cold lightning bolts and black clouds, strips of torn cloth falling from the ruins of unfrocked spokes, and we both laughed like madmen as we got soaked, thinking that an umbrella found in a public square ought to die a noble death in a park and not get involved in the mean cycle of dustbin or gutter. Then I rolled it up as best I could and we took it to the top of the park near the little bridge over the railway tracks, and from there I threw it with all my might to the bottom of the gully where it landed on the wet grass as you gave out a shout in which I thought I vaguely recognized the curse of a Valkyrie. It sank into the gully like a ship into green water, stormy green water, into *la mer qui est plus félonesse en été qu'en hiver*, into the treacherous wave, Maga, as we counted for a long time, in love with Joinville or with the park, embracing like wet trees or like actors in some second-rate Hungarian movie. And it stayed down there in the grass, small and black, like some trampled insect. And it did not move, none of its springs popped out as once before. Ended. Over. Oh Maga, and still we were not satisfied.

Why was I coming to the Pont des Arts? It seems to me that on that Thursday in December I had intended to cross over to the Right Bank to have some wine in the little café on the Rue des Lombards where Madame Léonie reads my palm and tells me of trips and surprises. I never took you to have your palm read by Madame Léonie, probably because I was afraid that she would read some truth about me in your hand, because you have always been a frightful mirror, a monstrous instrument of repetitions, and what we had called loving was perhaps my standing in front of you holding a yellow flower while you held two green candles and a slow rain of renunciations and farewells and Métro tickets blew into our faces. So I never took you to Madame Léonie's, Maga. You told me so and that is how I know that you did not like my watching you go into that little bookshop on the Rue de Verneuil, where a burdened old man fills out thousands of reference cards and knows everything there is to know about the study of history. You used to go there to play with a cat, and the old man let you in and didn't ask questions, content for you to get him a book from time to time from the upper shelves. You used to get warm at that stove of his with its big black chimney, and you didn't like me to know that you were going to sit next to that stove. But all of this should have been said in its proper time, except that it was difficult to know what the proper time for things was, and even now, with my elbows on the railing of the bridge, as I watched a small, must-coloured *péniche*, sparkling clean like a great big beautiful cockroach, with a woman in a white apron hanging washing on a wire strung along the prow, as I looked at its windows, painted green, with Hansel and Gretel curtains, even now, Maga, I wondered if this roundabout route made any sense, since it would have been easier to reach the Rue des Lombards by the Pont Saint-Michel and the Pont au Change. But if you had been there that night, as so many other times, then I would have known that the roundabout made sense, while now, on the other hand, I debase my failure by calling it a roundabout. I raised the collar of my lumber-jacket, and it was a matter of going along by the docks until I came to where the large shops finish at the Châtelet, passing underneath the violet shadow of the Tour Saint-Jacques, and turning into my street, thinking about the fact that I had not bumped into you and about Madame Léonie.

I know that one day I came to Paris. I know that I was living in hock for a while, doing what the others did and seeing what they saw. I know that you were coming out of a café on the Rue du Cherche-Midi and that we spoke. Everything had been going badly that afternoon because the clothes I had brought from Argentina would not permit me to cross from one pavement to the other to look at trivial items in the dimly lit shop windows on streets I don't remember any more. I followed you grudgingly then, finding you petulant and rude, until you got tired of not being tired and we went into a café on the Boul' Mich' and all of a sudden in between two croissants you told me a whole chunk of your life.

How could I have suspected that what seemed to be a pack of lies was all true, a Figari with sunset violets, with livid faces, with hunger and blows in the corners. I came to believe you later on, later on there was reason to, there was Madame Léonie, who looked at my hand which had gone to bed with your breasts, and she practically repeated your exact words: "She is suffering somewhere. She has always suffered. She is very cheerful, she adores yellow, her bird is the blackbird, her time is night, her bridge is the Pont des Arts." (A must-coloured *péniche*, Maga, and I wonder why we didn't sail off on it while there was still time.)

We had barely got to know each other when life began to contrive everything necessary for us to stop meeting little by little. Since you didn't know how to dissemble I realized at once that in order to see you as I wanted to I would have to begin by shutting my eyes, and then at first some things like yellow stars (moving around in a velvet jelly), then red jumps of humour and time, a gradual entry into a Maga world, awkward and confused, but also with ferns signed by a Klee spider, a Miró circus, Vieira da Silva ash-mirrors, a chess world where you moved about like a knight trying to move like a rook trying to move like a bishop. In those days we used to go to art movies to see silent pictures, because I had my culture, maybe not, but you, poor thing, didn't understand anything at all about that yellow and convulsed shrieking which had all taken place before you were born, that grooved emulsion in which dead people ran about. But suddenly Harold Lloyd would go by and then you would shake off the water of your dream and would finally be convinced that all was well, and that Pabst, and that Fritz Lang. You wore me out a little with your mania for perfection, with your rundown shoes, with your refusal to accept the acceptable. We used to eat hamburgers in the Carrefour de l'Odéon and we went cycling to Montparnasse, to any hotel, any pillow. Then other times we would go all the way to the Porte d'Orléans and we became more and more familiar with the vacant lots beyond the Boulevard Jourdan, where sometimes at midnight the members of the Serpent Club used to get together to talk to a blind seer, a stimulating paradox. We used to leave the bicycles on the street and go in a little way, stopping to look at the sky because it is one of the few places in Paris where sky is worth more than ground. Sitting on a pile of rubbish we would smoke for a while, and La Maga would stroke my hair or hum songs which hadn't been invented yet, absurd tunes broken with sighs or memories. I took advantage of such moments to think about useless things, a practice I had begun some years before in a hospital and which seemed increasingly richer and more necessary. With great effort, marshalling auxiliary images, thinking about smells and faces, I managed to extract from the void a pair of chestnut-coloured shoes

I had owned in Olavarría in 1940. They had rubber heels and very thin soles, and when it rained the water used to seep in up to my very soul. With that pair of shoes in the hand of my memory the rest came along by itself: the face of Doña Manuela, for example, or the poet Ernesto Morroni. But I rejected them because the game consisted in bringing back only the insignificant, the unnoticed, the forgotten. Trembling at not being able to remember, attacked by those moths suggested by postponement, an imbecile for having kissed time, I finally saw beyond the shoes a can of Sol tea that my mother had given me in Buenos Aires. And the little double teaspoon, a mousetrap spoon, where little black mice were scalded alive in the cup of water as they gave off hissing bubbles. Convinced that memory keeps everything, not just the Albertines and the great journals of the heart and kidneys, I persisted in reconstructing the contents of my desk in Floresta, the face of a girl impossible to remember named Gekrepten, the quantity of drawing pens in my pencil box in junior school, and I ended up trembling and desperate (because I had never been able to remember those pens; I know that they were in the pencil box, in a special compartment, but I cannot remember how many they were, nor the precise moment when there were two or six), until La Maga, kissing me and blowing smoke and her hot breath into my face, brought me back and we laughed, and began to walk around again among the piles of rubbish, looking for the members of the Club. It was about that time I realized that searching was my symbol, the emblem of those who go out at night with nothing in mind, the motives of a destroyer of compasses. I spoke about pataphysics with La Maga until we were both tired, because the same thing used to happen to her (and our meeting had been like that, and so many things, dark as a match), always falling into exceptions, seeing herself stuck in huts not meant for people and all this without despising anyone, without thinking we were Maldorors at the end of the trail or Melmoths privileged to wander about. I do not believe the firefly gets any great satisfaction from the incontrovertible fact that he is one of the most amazing wonders of this circus, and yet one can imagine a consciousness alert enough to understand that every time he lights his belly this light-bearing bug must feel some inkling of privilege. In just this way La Maga was fascinated with the strange mixups she had become involved in because of the breakdown of the laws governing her life. She was one of those people who could make a bridge collapse simply by walking on it, or who could sobbingly remember having seen in a shop window the lottery ticket which had just won five million. As for me, I'm already used to the fact that modestly exceptional things happen to me, and I don't find it too horrible when I go into a dark room looking for a record album and feel in my hand the wriggling body of a centipede who has chosen to sleep in the binding. That sort of thing. Or finding great grey or green tufts in a pack of cigarettes, or hearing the whistle of a locomotive coincide *ex officio* in time and pitch with a passage from a symphony by Ludwig van, or going into a *pissotière* on the Rue de Médicis and seeing a man studiously urinating then step back from the urinal and towards me as he holds in the palm of his hand as if it were a precious and liturgical object a member of incredible colours and dimensions, and my realizing at that moment that this man is the replica of another (although they are not the same) who twenty-four hours before in the Salle de Géographie had been lecturing on totems and taboos and had held up carefully in the palm of his hand ivory sticks, lyrebird feathers, ritual coins, magic fossils, starfish, dried fish, photographs of royal concubines, offerings of hunters, enormous embalmed beetles which made the inevitable ladies present quiver with startled delight.

All things considered, it's not easy to talk about La Maga, who right now must certainly be walking around Belleville or Pantin, carefully looking at the ground until she finds a piece of red cloth. If she doesn't find it she'll go on like that all night. She'll rummage in dustbins, her eyes glassy, convinced that something horrible will happen to her if she doesn't find that piece of ransom, that sign of forgiveness or postponement. I know what it's all about because I too obey these signs, and there are times when I must find a red rag. Ever since childhood, whenever I drop something I must pick it up, no matter what, because if I don't a disaster will happen, not to me, but to someone I love whose name begins with the same letter as the thing I dropped. The worst of it is that nothing can stop me when I drop something, and it doesn't work if somebody else picks it up because the curse will still be effective. People usually think I'm crazy and I really am crazy when I do it, when I pounce on a pencil or a piece of paper that I have dropped, like the night I dropped a lump of sugar in that restaurant on the Rue Scribe, a posh place overloaded with salesmen, whores with silver foxes, and well-established married couples. We were there with Ronald and Étienne, and I dropped a lump of sugar. It landed underneath a table some distance from ours. The first thing that had drawn my attention was how it had rolled so far away, because usually a lump of sugar will stay where it lands, obeying obvious geometrical principles. But this one took off like a mothball, heightening my worry, and I began to feel that it had actually been snatched out of my hand. Ronald knows me, and when he saw where it had landed he began to laugh. That caused me further anxiety, along with a touch of rage. A waiter came by and thought I had lost something of value, a Parker pen, a false tooth, and all he did was upset me even more. I didn't even excuse myself but fell to the floor to look for the lump among the shoes of people who were curious and thought (quite rightly) that something important was involved. I went under a table where there was a fat redhead and another woman, not so fat but just as whorey, and two businessmen, or so they seemed. The first thing I managed to find out was that the lump was nowhere in sight, even though I had seen it leap among the shoes which now were moving about restlessly like a flock of chickens. A carpet on the floor made things worse, and despite the fact that it was dirty from so much use, the lump had hidden itself in the pile and could not be found. The waiter was crawling around on the other side of the table and there we were, two quadrupeds making our way about among those chicken-shoes which all the while were cackling madly up above. The waiter was still looking for a Parker or a louis d'or, and when we were well under the table, with a feeling of great intimacy in the shadows, he asked me what it was and I told him the truth. His face was ready to fly off its hinges, but I was not in any mood to laugh. Fear had doubled the knot in my stomach, and I had become by then quite desperate and began to grab at the women's shoes to see if the lump might not be hiding under the arch of one, while the chickens cackled and the business-cocks pecked me on the back. I could hear Ronald and Étienne breaking up with laughter as I moved from one table to another until I found the lump ensconced behind an Empire foot. Everybody was furious and so was I, as I held the sugar tightly in my palm and felt it dissolve in the sweat of my hand, as if it were some sort of mean and sticky vengeance meant to terminate another one of those episodes that I was always getting involved in.

(–2)

2

At first it had been like a bloodletting, being here, a flogging to be taken internally, the need to feel a stupid blue-covered passport in my coat pocket, the hotel key hung securely on its rack. Fear, ignorance, bewilderment. This is the name of this thing, that's how you ask for that thing, now that woman is going to smile, the Jardin des Plantes starts at the end of that street. Paris, a postcard with a drawing by Klee next to a dirty mirror. La Maga had appeared one afternoon on the Rue du Cherche-Midi. When she came to my room on the Rue de la Tombe Issoire she would always bring a flower, a Klee or Miró postcard, and if she didn't have any money she would pick up the leaf of a plane tree in the park. At that time I used to pick up pieces of wire and empty boxes on the street early in the morning and I made them into mobiles, silhouettes which swung around the fireplace, useless gadgets which La Maga would help me paint. We didn't love each other, so we would make love with an objective and critical virtuosity, but then we would fall into terrible silences and the foam on the beer glasses would start to look like burlap, getting warm and shrivelling up while we looked at each other and figured that this was Time. La Maga would finally get up and walk uselessly around the room. More than once I saw her admire her body in the mirror, cup her breasts in her hands like a small Syrian statue, moving her eyes slowly over her body in a sort of caress. I could never resist the urge to call her over to me, to have her fall on top of me, unfold again after having been so alone and so in love for a moment, face to face with the eternity of her body.

We didn't talk much about Rocamadour those days; our pleasure was selfish and it used to come moaning over us with its narrow brow, tying us up with its salty hands. I had come to accept La Maga's disorder as the natural condition of every moment, and we would go from memories of Rocamadour to a plate of heated-up noodles, mixing wine and beer and lemonade, going to the corner to buy two dozen oysters from the old woman there, playing Schubert songs on Madame Noguet's shell of a piano, or Bach preludes, or putting up with *Porgy and Bess* along with steak and pickles. The disorder in which we lived, or the order, rather, which saw a bidet gradually and naturally changed into a storage place for records and unanswered letters, seemed to me like some sort of necessary discipline, although I didn't care to tell my feelings to La Maga. It didn't take me long to understand that you didn't discuss reality in methodical terms with La Maga. Praise of disorder would have horrified her as much as criticism of it. Disorder did not exist for her, as I discovered while I was finding out simultaneously what her purse contained (it was in a café on the rue Réaumur, it was raining and we were beginning to want each other). But I accepted it and even approved of it once I had identified it. My relations with practically all the rest of the world were based on these disadvantages, and how many times had I lain on a bed left unmade for several days listening to La Maga cry because a little girl on the Métro had reminded her of Rocamadour, or watched her comb her hair after she had spent all afternoon before a portrait of Eleanor of Aquitaine and was killing herself trying to look like the painting, and it occurred to me like a sort of mental belch that this whole alphabet of my life was painful stupidity, because it was based solely on a dialectical pattern, on the choice of what could be called non-conduct rather than conduct, on faddish indecency instead of social decency. La Maga was putting up her hair, taking it down, putting it up again. She was thinking about Rocamadour. She sang something from Hugo Wolf (badly), she kissed me, she asked me about her hairdo, she began to sketch on a scrap of yellow paper. That was all she, no doubt about it, and there was I on a deliberately dirty bed, drinking a glass of deliberately flat beer, always being myself and my life; there was I with my life face to face with other people's lives. But I was proud nonetheless to be a conscious layabout and to have lived under all sorts of moons, in all kinds of scrapes with La Maga and Ronald and Rocamadour and the Club and the streets and my moral sickness and other worse ones, and Berthe Trépat and sometimes hunger and old man Trouille, who used to get me out of trouble, under the eaves of vomity nights of music and tobacco and little meannesses and all kinds of exchanges, because underneath and on top of it all I had refused to pretend like normal bohemians that the chaos of my affairs and finances was some sort of higher spiritual order or something else with an equally disgusting label, nor had I accepted the notion that all one needed was just one split second of decency (decency, young fellow!) to crawl out from the midst of so much filthy cotton. And that's how I had met La Maga, who was my witness and my spy without being aware of it; and the irritation of thinking about all this and knowing that, since it was always easier to think than to be, that in my case the ergo of the expression was no ergo nor anything at all like it, so that we used to go along the Left Bank and La Maga, without knowing she was my spy and my witness, would be amazed at how much I knew about things like literature and cool jazz, which were great mysteries for her. And I felt antagonism for all these things when I was with La Maga, for we loved each other in a sort of dialectic of magnet and iron filings, attack and defence, ball and wall. I suppose La Maga had her notions about me and she must have thought I had been healed of my prejudices or that I was coming over to hers, more lighthearted and poetic. In the midst of this precarious happiness, this false truce, I held out my hand and touched the tangled ball of yarn which is Paris, its infinite material all wrapped up around itself, the precipitate of its atmosphere falling on its windows and forming images of clouds and garrets. There was no disorder then. The world was still something petrified and established, swinging on its hinges, a skein of streets and trees and names and months. There was no disorder to open escape-hatches, there was only filth and misery, glasses with stale beer, stockings in a corner, a bed which smelled of sex and hair, a woman who ran her small, thin hand along my thighs, holding off the stroke that would have plucked me out of this vigilance in the depths of emptiness for just a moment. Too late, always too late, because even though we made love so many times, happiness must have been something else, something sadder perhaps than this peace, this pleasure, a mood of unicorn or island, an endless fall in immobility. La Maga did not know that my kisses were like eyes that began to open up beyond her, and that I went along outside as if I saw a different concept of the world, the dizzy pilot of a black prow which cut the water of time and negated it.

During those days in the fifties I began to feel myself penned in between La Maga and a different notion of what really should have happened. It was idiotic to revolt against the Maga world and the Rocamadour world, when everything told me that as soon as I got my freedom back I would stop feeling free. A hypocrite like few others, it bothered me to spy on my own skin, my legs, my way to get pleasure from La Maga, my attempts at being a parrot in a cage reading Kierkegaard through the bars, and I think that what bothered me most was that La Maga had no idea at all that she was my witness and, on the contrary, was convinced that I was eminently master of my fate. But no, what really exasperated me was knowing that I would never again be so close to my freedom as in those days when I felt myself hemmed in by the Maga world, and that my anxiety to escape was an admission of defeat. It grieved me to recognize that with artificial blows, with Manichaean beams of light, or desiccated, stupid dichotomies I could not make my way up the steps of the Gare de Montparnasse where La Maga had dragged me to visit Rocamadour. Why couldn't I accept what was happening without trying to explain it, without bringing up ideas of order and disorder, of freedom and Rocamadour, as one sets out geranium pots in a courtyard on the Calle Cochabamba? Maybe one had to fall into the depths of stupidity in order to make the key fit the lock to the latrine or to the Garden of Olives. For the moment it surprised me that La Maga had let fantasy carry her to the point of calling her son Rocamadour. In the Club we had given up looking for reasons. La Maga had only said that her son had been named after his father, but when his father had disappeared it had seemed better to call him Rocamadour and send him to the country to be brought up *en nourrice.* Sometimes La Maga would go for weeks without mentioning Rocamadour and those would always be the same times that she was hoping to become a singer of *Lieder.* Then Ronald would sit down at the piano with his cowboy-red hair and La Maga would bellow something from Hugo Wolf with a ferocity that made Madame Noguet tremble as she sat next door stringing plastic beads to sell at a stand on the Boulevard de Sébastopol. La Maga's singing of Schumann was rather pleasant, but it all depended on the moon and what we were going to do that night, and also on Rocamadour, because no sooner did La Maga think of Rocamadour than her singing went to pot and Ronald was left alone at the piano, with all the time in the world to try out some of his bop ideas or to kill us softly with some blues.

I don't want to write about Rocamadour, at least not right now, because I would have to get so much closer to myself, to let everything that separates me from the centre drop away. I always end up talking about the centre without the slightest guarantee that I know what I'm saying, and I slip into the trap of geometry, that method we Occidentals use to try to regulate our lives: axis, centre, *raison d'être*, Omphalos, nostalgic Indo-European names. Even this existence I sometimes try to describe, this Paris where I move about like a dry leaf, would not be visible if behind it there did not beat an anxiety for an axis, a coming together with the central shaft. All these words, all these terms for the same disorder. Sometimes I am convinced that triangle is another name for stupidity, that eight times eight is madness or a dog. Holding La Maga, that materialized nebula, I begin to think that it makes just as much sense to model a doll out of crumbled bread as to write the novel I will never write or to give my life in the defence of ideas that could redeem whole peoples. The pendulum immediately changes direction and there I am again among calming notions: a worthless doll, a great novel, a heroic death. I line them up, from least to greatest: doll, novel, heroism. I think about the orders of values so well explored by Ortega, by Scheler: aesthetics, ethics, religion. Religion, aesthetics, ethics. Ethics, religion, aesthetics. Doll, novel. Death, doll. La Maga's tongue tickles me. Rocamadour, ethics, doll, Maga. Tongue, tickle, ethics.

(–116)

3

Horacio Oliveira was sitting on the bed smoking his third insomniac cigarette. Once or twice he softly stroked the skin of La Maga, who was next to him, asleep. It was just before dawn on Monday and they had already let Sunday afternoon and evening slip by reading, listening to records, getting up alternately to warm up some coffee or prepare some *mate*. La Maga had fallen asleep during the last movement of a Haydn quartet and since he did not want to listen any more, Oliveira had unplugged the record-player as he lay there on the bed. The record kept on spinning a little more, but there was no more sound from the speaker. He didn't know why, but this stupid inertia had made him think about the apparently useless movements of some insects, of some children. He couldn't sleep and he looked out of the open window towards the garret where a hunchbacked violinist was practising very late. It was not a warm night, but La Maga's body warmed up his leg and his right side; he moved away little by little and thought that it was going to be a long night.

He felt very well, as he always did when La Maga and he could get to the end of a date without quarrelling or annoying each other. He wasn't worried too much by the letter from his brother, a solid-citizen lawyer from Rosario, who had filled up four onion-skin pages with an account of the filial and civic duties that Oliveira had ignored. The letter was a real delight and he had hung it on the wall with Scotch tape so that his friends could enjoy its full flavour. The only important item was the confirmation of some money sent through the black market, which his brother delicately referred to as his "agent". Oliveira planned to buy some books he had been wanting to read and he would give La Maga three thousand francs which she could do with as she pleased, probably buy a near-life-size felt elephant to surprise Rocamadour with. In the morning he would have to go to old man Trouille's and bring the correspondence with Latin America up to date. Going out, doing things, bringing up to date were not ideas calculated to help him get to sleep. To bring up to date: what an expression. To do. To do something, to do good, to make water, to make time, action in all of its possibilities. But behind all action there was a protest, because all doing meant leaving from in order to arrive at, or moving something so that it would be here and not there, or going into a house instead of not going in or instead of going into the one next door; in other words, every act entailed the admission of a lack, of something not yet done and which could have been done, the tacit protest in the face of continuous evidence of a lack, of a reduction, of the inadequacy of the present moment. To believe that action could crown something, or that the sum total of actions could really be a life worthy of the name was the illusion of a moralist. It was better to withdraw, because withdrawal from action was the protest itself and not its mask. Oliveira lit another cigarette and this little action made him smile ironically and tease himself about the act itself. He was not too worried about superficial analyses, almost always perverted by distraction and linguistic traps. The only thing certain was the weight in the pit of his stomach, the physical suspicion that something was not going well and that perhaps it never had gone well. It was not even a problem, but rather the early denial of both collective lies and that grumpy solitude of one who sets out to study radioactive isotopes or the presidency of Bartolomé Mitre. If he had made any choice when he was young it was that he would not defend himself with the rapid and anxious accumulation of "culture", the favourite dodge of the Argentine middle class to avoid facing national reality, or any other reality for that matter, and to think of themselves as safe from the emptiness surrounding them. Thanks, perhaps, to this systematic mopiness, as his buddy Traveler had defined it, he had managed to steer clear of that order of Pharisees (many of his friends did belong to it and generally in good faith, because it was just possible and there were examples), those who plumbed the depths of problems with some sort of specialization, and who, ironically, were awarded the highest pedigrees of Argentinity for doing just that. Furthermore, it seemed slippery and facile to mix up historical problems, such as one's being Argentinian or Eskimo, with problems like the ones that deal with action or withdrawal. He had lived long enough to be suspicious of anything stuck to someone's nose that keeps falling off: the weight of the subject in the notion of the object. La Maga was one of the few people who never forgot that someone's face would always have something to do with his interpretation of communism or of Creto-Mycenaean civilization, and that the shape of someone's hands had something to do with what he felt about Ghirlandaio or Dostoevsky. That's why Oliveira tended to admit that his blood-type, the fact that he had spent his childhood surrounded by majestic uncles, a broken love affair in adolescence, and a tendency towards asthenia might be factors of first importance in his vision of the cosmos. He was middle class, from Buenos Aires, had been to an Argentinian school, and those things are not dismissed lightly. The worst of it was that by dint of avoiding excessively local points of view he had ended up weighing and accepting too readily the yes and no of everything, becoming a sort of inspector of scales. In Paris everything was Buenos Aires, and vice versa; in the most eager moments of love he would suffer loss and loneliness and relish it. A perniciously comfortable attitude which even becomes easy as it grows into a reflex or technique; the frightful lucidity of the paralytic, the blindness of the perfectly stupid athlete. One begins to go about with the sluggish step of a philosopher or a *clochard*, as more and more vital gestures become reduced to mere instincts of preservation, to a conscience more alert not to be deceived than to grasp truth. Lay quietism, moderate ataraxia, attentive lack of attention. What was important for Oliveira was to experience this Tupac Amarú quartering and not faint, not fall into that pitiful egocentrism which he heard all about him every day in every possible shape. When he had been ten years old, during an afternoon spent under some *paraíso* trees and surrounded by uncles and historico-political homilies, he had shown his first timid reaction against that so very Hispano-Italo-Argentine *¡Se lo digo yo!* punctuated with a pound on the table. *Glielo dico io! I* say so, God damn it! That *I*, Oliveira had begun to think, does it have any value as proof? What omniscience was contained in the *I* of grownups? At the age of fifteen he discovered the business of "all I know is that I know nothing"; the hemlock that went with it seemed inevitable. One doesn't challenge people that way, I say so. Later on he was amused to see how more refined forms of culture produced their own versions of "I say so!" delicately disguised even for the person using them. Now he heard, "I've always thought so," "if I'm sure of anything . . . ," "it's obvious that . . . ," almost never softened by a disinterested appreciation of the other person's point of view. As if the species in every individual were on guard against letting him go too far along the road of tolerance, intelligent doubt, sentimental vacillation. At some given point the callus, the sclerosis, the definition is born: black or white, radical or conservative, homo- or heterosexual, the San Lorenzo team or the Boca Juniors, meat or vegetables, business or poetry. And it was all right, because the species should not trust people like Oliveira; his brother's letter was the precise form of that rejection.

"The worst part of all this," he thought, "is that it always ends up in the *Animula vagula blandula.* What is there to do? With that question I'll never get to sleep. Oblomov, *cosa facciamo*? The great voices of History stir us to action: revenge, Hamlet! Shall we avenge ourselves, Hamlet, or settle for Chippendale, slippers and a good fire? The Syrian, after all, made the scandalous choice of Martha, as is well known. Will you give battle, Arjuna? You cannot deny values, reluctant king. Fight for fight's sake, live dangerously, think about Marius the Epicurean, Richard Hillary, Kyo, T. E. Lawrence . . . Happy are those who choose, those who accept being chosen, the handsome heroes, the handsome saints, the perfect escapists."

Perhaps. Why not? But it's also possible that your point of view is the same as that of the fox as he looks at the grapes. And it also might be that reason is on your side, but a lamentable and mean little reason, the reason the ant uses against the grasshopper. If lucidity ends up in inaction, doesn't it become suspect? Wouldn't it be covering up a particularly diabolical type of blindness? The stupidity of a military hero who runs forward carrying a keg of powder, Cabral, the heroic soldier covering himself with glory, is hinted to be a revelation, the instantaneous melding with something absolute, beyond all consciousness (that's a lot to ask for in a sergeant), in face of which ordinary vision, bedroom insight at three o'clock in the morning and with a half-smoked cigarette, is about as good as a mole's.

He spoke to La Maga about all this. She had woken and was snuggling up against him, mewing sleepily. La Maga opened her eyes and remained thoughtful.

"You couldn't do it," she said. "You think too much before you do anything."

"I believe in the principle that thought must precede action, silly."

"You believe in the principle," said La Maga. "How complicated. You're like a witness. You're the one who goes to the museum and looks at the paintings. I mean the paintings are there and you're in the museum too, near and far away at the same time. I'm a painting. Rocamadour is a painting. Étienne is a painting, this room is a painting. You think that you're in this room, but you're not. You're looking at the room, you're not in the room."

"This girl could leave Saint Thomas way behind," Oliveira said.

"Why Saint Thomas?" asked La Maga. "That idiot who had to see to believe?"

"Yes, sweet," said Oliveira, thinking that underneath it all La Maga had hit upon the right saint. Happy was she who could believe without seeing, who was at one with the duration and continuity of life. Happy was she who was in the room, who had the freedom of the city in everything that she touched or came in contact with, a fish swimming downstream, a leaf on a tree, a cloud in the sky, an image in a poem. Fish, leaf, cloud, image: that's it precisely, unless . . .

(–84)

4

So they had begun to walk about in a fabulous Paris, letting themselves be guided by the night-time signs, following routes born of a *clochard* phrase, of an attic lit up in the darkness of a street's end, stopping in little confidential squares to kiss on the benches or look at the hopscotch game, those childish rites of a pebble and a hop on one leg to get into Heaven, Home. La Maga spoke about her friends in Montevideo, about her childhood years, about a certain Ledesma, about her father. Oliveira listened without interest, a little sorry that he was not interested; Montevideo was just like Buenos Aires and he had to finish breaking away (what was Traveler up to, that old drifter? What kind of majestic hassles had he got into since he had left? And poor, silly Gekrepten, and the bars downtown). That's why he listened with displeasure and was making sketches in the gravel with a stick while La Maga explained why Chempe and Graciela were good girls and how it had hurt her that Luciana had not come to the ship to see her off. Luciana was a snob, which she couldn't put up with in anybody.

"What does snob mean to you?" asked Oliveira, becoming interested.

"Well," La Maga answered, lowering her head with the air of someone who senses that she is about to say something stupid, "I was travelling third class, but I think that if I had gone second class Luciana would have come to say goodbye."

"That's the best definition I've ever heard," said Oliveira.

"And besides, there was Rocamadour," La Maga said.

That's how Oliveira found out about the existence of Rocamadour, who in Montevideo had been plain Carlos Francisco. La Maga didn't seem disposed to go into very great detail about Rocamadour's origins except that she had not wanted an abortion and was beginning to regret the fact now.

"But I don't really regret it all. My problem now is making ends meet. Madame Irène costs a lot and I have to take singing lessons. All that costs a lot."

La Maga didn't really know why she had come to Paris, and Oliveira was able to deduce that with just a little mixup in tickets, tourist agents, and visas she might just as well have disembarked in Singapore or Cape Town. The main thing was that she had left Montevideo to confront what she modestly called "life". The great advantage of Paris was that she knew quite a bit of French (in the style of the Pitman School of Languages) and that she would be able to see artistic masterpieces, the best films, *Kultur* in its most eminent forms. Oliveira was moved by all this (although Rocamadour had shaken him up a bit, he didn't know why), and he thought of some of the slick girls he had known in Buenos Aires, incapable of getting any farther away than Mar del Plata, in spite of such great metaphysical desires for planetary experience. And this kid, with a child to boot, gets herself a third-class ticket and takes off to study singing in Paris without a penny in her pocket. For what it was worth, she was already giving him lessons in how to look at and see things; lessons she was not aware of, just her way of stopping suddenly in the street to peep into an entranceway where there was nothing, but where a green glow could be seen farther in, then to duck furtively into the courtyard so that the gatekeeper would not get annoyed and sometimes look at an old statue or an ivy-covered curbing, or nothing, just the worn-out paving made of round stones, mould on the walls, a watchmaker's sign, a little old man sitting in the shade in a corner, and the cats, always, inevitably the *minouche morrongos miau-miau kitten kat chat gato gatto*; greys and whites and blacks, sewer cats, masters of time and of the warm pavement, La Maga's invariable friends as she tickled their bellies and spoke to them in a language somewhere between banal and mysterious; making dates with them, giving advice and admonitions. Suddenly Oliveira felt funny walking with La Maga, but it was no use getting annoyed because La Maga almost inevitably would knock over beer glasses or pull her leg out from under the table in just the right way so that the waiter would trip over it and start to curse. He was happy in spite of being exasperated all the time with that business of not doing things the way they ought to be done, of the way she resolutely ignored the larger figures of an account to go into ecstasies over the tail of a modest 3, or would stop short in the middle of the street (a black Renault came to a halt about five feet away and the driver stuck his head out and used his Picardy accent to call her a whore). She would stop as if there was a real view to be seen from the middle of the street, as if the sight of the distant Panthéon was much better from there than from the pavement. Things like that.

Oliveira already knew Perico and Ronald. La Maga introduced him to Étienne and Étienne introduced them both to Gregorovius. The Serpent Club began to take shape at night in Saint-Germain-des-Prés. Everybody accepted La Maga's presence right away as something inevitable and natural, even though they would get annoyed with having to explain to her almost everything they were talking about, or because she would send a helping of fried potatoes flying through the air simply because she didn't know how to use a fork in the proper fashion and the potatoes would almost always land on the heads of the people at the next table, and excuses would have to be made, telling how thoughtless La Maga was. La Maga did not get along very well with them as a group. Oliveira realized that she preferred to be with them individually, to walk along the street with Étienne or with Babs, to bring them into her world, never consciously, but bringing them in all the same because they were people who only wanted to escape the ordinary routine of buses and history, and therefore, in one way or another, all the people in the Club were thankful to La Maga even though they would rain insults on her at the slightest provocation. Étienne, sure of himself as a dog or a postbox, would get furious when La Maga came out with one of her comments concerning his latest painting, and even Perico Romero had to admit that-when-it-came-to-being-a-female-La-Maga-took-the-cake. For weeks or months (keeping track of time was difficult for Oliveira, happy, *ergo* futureless) they walked and walked around Paris looking at things, letting happen whatever had to happen, loving and fighting, and all of this outside the stream of news, family obligations and physical and moral burdens of any sort.

Toc, toc.

"Come on, let's wake up," Oliveira would say from time to time.

"What for?" La Maga would reply, watching the *péniches* sail under the pont Neuf. "Toc, toc, you've got a bird in your head. Toc, toc, he picks at you all the time, he wants you to give him some Argentinian food to eat. Toc, toc."

"OK," grumbled Oliveira. "Don't get me mixed up with Rocamadour. Before we're through we'll be speaking Gliglish to some clerk or doorman and there'll be hell to pay. Look at that guy following the Negro girl."

"I know her. She works in a café on the Rue de Provence. She likes girls. The poor guy has had it."

"Did she try anything with you?"

"Naturally. But we became friends just the same. I gave her my rouge and she gave me a book by somebody called Retef, no . . . wait, Retif . . . "

"I see. So you didn't go to bed with her? It could have been fun for a woman like you."

"Did you ever go to bed with a man, Horacio?"

"Of course. For the experience, you know."

La Maga looked at him out of the corner of her eye, suspecting that he was kidding her, that all of this came from his being furious over the toc-toc bird in his head, the bird that asked him for Argentinian food. Then she threw herself at him to the great surprise of a couple strolling along the Rue Saint-Sulpice, and she mussed up his hair as she laughed. Oliveira had to hold her arms down and they began to laugh. The couple looked at them and although the husband had a hint of a smile, his wife was much too scandalized by such behaviour.

"You're right," Oliveira confessed finally. "I'm incurable. Talking about waking up when, after all, it's so nice to be asleep like this."

They stopped by a shop window to look at book titles. La Maga began to ask questions, using the colours of the covers as her guide. Flaubert had to be put in his period for her, she had to be told that Montesquieu, how Raymond Radiguet, explained to about when Théophile Gautier. La Maga listened, drawing on the window with her finger. "A bird in my head wants me to give him some Argentinian food to eat," Oliveira was thinking as he heard himself talking. "Oh, me. Oh, brother!"

"But don't you see that you can't learn anything this way," he finally told her. "You think you can get an education on the street, love, and you can't. If that's what you want, subscribe to the *Reader's Digest*."

"Oh, no. Not that crap."

A bird in his head, Oliveira was saying to himself. Not her, but him. But what did she have in her head? Air or chick-pea flour, something hard to grasp. The centre was not in the head.

"She closes her eyes and hits the bull's-eye," thought Oliveira. "The Zen method of archery, precisely. But she hits the bull's-eye because she doesn't know that it is the method. But in my case . . . Toc, toc. And that's how it goes."

When La Maga would ask about Zen (such things could happen with the Club, where they were always talking about nostalgic things, wisdom so distant that they came to think of it as fundamental, the obverse of a medal, the far side of the moon, always), Gregorovius would try to explain the rudiments of metaphysics while Oliveira would sip his pernod and watch, enjoying it. It was madness to try to explain anything to La Maga. Fauconnier was right, for people like her the mystery begins precisely with the explanation. La Maga heard the words *immanence* and *transcendence* and she opened up two big beautiful eyes which cut off Gregorovius's metaphysics. Finally she convinced herself that she had understood Zen and sighed with fatigue. Only Oliveira knew that La Maga was always reaching those great timeless plateaus that they were all seeking through dialectics.

"Don't learn any stupid facts," he would advise her. "Why wear glasses if you don't need them?"

La Maga was not quite sure. She was terribly in awe of Oliveira and Étienne, who could keep an argument going for three hours without a break. There was something like a circle of chalk around Étienne and Oliveira and she wanted to get inside, to understand why the principle of indetermination was so important in literature, why Morelli, of whom they spoke so much, whom they admired so much, wanted his book to be a crystal ball in which the micro- and the macrocosm would come together in an annihilating vision.

"It's impossible to explain to you," said Étienne. "This is Meccano number 7 and you're barely in number 2."

La Maga became sad, she picked up a leaf from the edge of the pavement and spoke to it for a while, moved it along the palm of her hand, turned it over and upside down, stroked it, and finally she took off the leafy part and left the veins exposed, a delicate green ghost was reflected against her skin. Étienne snatched it away brusquely and held it against the light.

That's why they admired her, a little ashamed at having been so brutish with her, and La Maga would take advantage by ordering another pint or, if possible, some fried potatoes.

(–71)

5

The first time had been in a hotel on the Rue Valette. They were walking along aimlessly and stopping in the doorways, drizzle after lunch is always bitter and something ought to be done about that frozen dust, against those raincoats smelling of rubber, and suddenly La Maga drew herself close to Oliveira and they looked at each other like fools. HOTEL, the old woman behind the rickety desk greeted them with an understanding air and what else was there to do in this rotten weather. She dragged one foot and it was painful to see her climb the stairs, stopping at each step to drag up her sick leg, which was thicker than the other, and go through the same manoeuvre all the way to the fourth floor. There was a smell of toilet soap, of soup, on the rug in the hallway someone had spilled a blue liquid which had taken the shape of a pair of wings. The room had two windows with red curtains, full of patches. A damp light spread out like an angel over to the bed with a yellow spread.

La Maga had thought to play the innocent, staying by the window, pretending to look at the street while Oliveira checked the bolt on the door. She must have had a system all worked out for this sort of thing, or maybe it just always happened the same way. First she put her purse on the table and looked for her cigarettes, she looked at the street, taking deep drags, she commented on the wallpaper, she waited, obviously she waited, all effort was being made so that the man could best play his role and would have all the time necessary to take the initiative. At one point they had burst out laughing, it was all too silly. Flung into a corner, the yellow bedspread looked like a shapeless doll against the wall.

They had got into the habit of comparing spreads, doors, lamps, curtains. They preferred the hotel rooms of the *cinquième arrondissement* to those of the *sixième*. In the *septième* they had no luck at all, something was always happening: pounding in the room next door or the plumbing made a lugubrious sound, and it was then that Oliveira had told La Maga the story of Troppmann. La Maga listened as she held him tight, and she would have to read the story by Turgenev. It was incredible what she would have to read in those two years (she didn't know why they were two years). Another time it was Petiot, another time Weidmann, another time Christie. It ended up with the hotel always giving them the urge to talk about crimes, but La Maga would also be engulfed by a wave of seriousness and she would ask with her eyes fixed on the flat ceiling whether Sienese painting was really as fantastic as Étienne claimed, whether they shouldn't try to save up to buy a record-player and the works of Hugo Wolf, which she would sometimes hum, breaking off in the middle, forgetful and furious. Oliveira liked to make love to La Maga because there was nothing more important to her and at the same time, in a way hard to understand, she was in a sense dependent on his pleasure, she would reach him for a moment and would therefore cling desperately and prolong it. It was as if she had woken and recognized her real name, and then she would fall back into that always somewhat twilight zone that enchanted Oliveira, fearful of perfection, but La Maga really did suffer when she returned to her memories and to everything that in some obscure way she had to think about but could not. Then he would have to kiss her deeply, incite her to new play, and the other woman, the reconciled one, would grow beneath him and pull him down, and she would surrender then like a frantic animal, her eyes lost, her hands twisted inward, mythical and terrible, like a statue rolling down a mountainside, clutching time with her nails, with a gurgling sound and a moaning growl that lasted interminably. One night she sank her teeth into him, bit him in the shoulder until the blood came, because he had fallen to one side, a little forgetful already, and there was a confused and wordless pact. Oliveira felt that La Maga wanted death from him, something in her which was not her waking self, a dark form demanding annihilation, the slow wound which on its back breaks the stars at night and gives space back to questions and terrors. Only that time, off centre like a mythical matador for whom killing is returning the bull to the sea and the sea to the heavens, he bothered La Maga in a long night which they did not speak much about later. He turned her into Pasiphaë, he bent her over and used her as if she were a young boy, he knew her and he demanded the slavishness of the most abject whore, he magnified her into a constellation, he held her in his arms smelling of blood, he made her drink the semen which ran into her mouth like a challenge to the Logos, he sucked out the shadow from her womb and her rump and raised himself to her face to anoint her with herself in that ultimate work of knowledge that only a man can give to a woman, he wore her out with skin and hair and drool and moans, he drained her completely of her magnificent strength, he threw her against a pillow and sheet and felt her crying with happiness against his face which another cigarette was returning to the night from the room and from the hotel.

Later on Oliveira began to worry that she would think herself jaded, that the play would move on to sacrifice. Above all he feared that most subtle form of gratitude which turns into dog-like love. He did not want freedom, the only suit that fit La Maga, to be lost in any strong femininity. He didn't have to worry, because as soon as La Maga was back on the level of black coffee and a trip to the toilet, it was obvious that she had fallen back into the worst of confusions. Terribly mistreated that night, opened up to an absorbent space that beats and expands, his first words when she was back on this side came like whiplashes, as they had to, and when she came back to the side of the bed she was the image of a progressive consternation which tried to soften itself with smiles and a vague hope, which left Oliveira quite satisfied. Since he did not love her, since desire would stop (because he did not love, desire would stop), he would have to avoid like the devil any kind of sacred ritualizing of their play. For days, for weeks, for some months, every hotel room and every square, every position of love, and every dawn in a marketplace café: a savage circus, subtle operation, and rational balance. That's how it came to be known that La Maga was really waiting for Horacio to kill her and that hers would be a phoenix death, entry into the council of philosophers, that is to say, the discussions of the Serpent Club. La Maga wanted to learn, she wanted to be ed-you-kay-ted. Horacio was the exalted, the chosen one, the one to fill the role of purifying priest, and since they never understood each other because when they were discussing something they would be off on different tracks and different interests (and she knew this and understood it well), therefore the only possibility of coming together would be if Horacio were to kill her while making love, where she could get together with him in the heaven of some hotel room where they would come together equal and naked and there the resurrection of the phoenix could take place after he had strangled her delightfully, dripping a string of saliva into her open mouth, looking at her ecstatically as if he had just begun to recognize her, to make her really his, to take her to his side.

(–81)

6

The technique was to make a vague date in some neighbourhood at a certain hour. They liked to challenge the danger of not meeting, of spending the day alone sulking in a café or on a park bench, reading-another-book. The another-book theory was Oliveira's, and La Maga had accepted it by pure osmosis. For her, in truth, almost all books were one-book-less; she would have liked to be overcome by an immense thirst and for an infinite period of time (calculated as between three and five years) to read the complete works of Goethe, Homer, Dylan Thomas, Mauriac, Faulkner, Baudelaire, Roberto Arlt, Saint Augustine, and other writers whose names would keep coming up in conversation in the Club. Oliveira would answer this with a sour shrug of his shoulders and talk about the distortions of the Río de la Plata, where a breed of full-time readers has developed, where libraries swarm with old maids who have forsaken love and sunshine, where the smell of printer's ink can end the joy of garlic in a home. He wasn't reading much then, too busy looking at trees, pieces of string he found on the ground, the yellowed films he saw in movie clubs, the women in the Latin Quarter. His vague intellectual tendencies had become resolved in aimless meditation, and when La Maga would ask him for help, a date or an explanation, he would only supply it grudgingly, as if it were something useless. "But you already know it," La Maga would say, resentfully. Then he would take the trouble to explain to her the difference between familiarity and knowledge, and he would ask her to try some individual research projects, which La Maga would not finish and which would drive her to her wit's end.

Since they would never normally be in certain places, they would agree to meet there and they almost always found each other. The meetings were so incredible at times that Oliveira once more brought up the problem of probability and examined the case cautiously from all angles. La Maga could not possibly have decided to turn that corner of the Rue de Vaugirard at the precise moment in which he, five blocks down the street, decided not to go along the Rue de Buci and headed for the Rue Monsieur-le-Prince for no apparent reason, letting himself go along until suddenly he saw her stopped in front of a shop window, absorbed in the contemplation of a stuffed monkey. Seated in a café they carefully reconstructed their routes, the quick changes, trying to find some telepathic explanation and always failing, and yet they had met in that labyrinth of streets, they almost always met and they laughed wildly, certain of some enriching power. Oliveira was fascinated by La Maga's store of nonsense, her calm disdain for the simplest calculation. What for him had been analysis of probabilities, choice, or simply faith in himself as a diviner, for her was simple chance. "And what if you hadn't met me?" he would ask her. "I don't know, but you're here, you see . . . " For some reason the answer made the question worthless, it showed the logical basis of ordinary common sense. After that Oliveira would feel better able to resist his bookish prejudices, and paradoxically La Maga would fight off her disdain for scholarly knowledge. Thus they went along, Punch and Judy, attracting each other and repelling, as love must do if it is not to end up as calendar art or a pop tune. But love, that word . . .

(–7)

7

I touch your mouth, I touch the edge of your mouth with my finger, I am drawing it as if it were something my hand was sketching, as if for the first time your mouth opened a little, and all I have to do is close my eyes to erase it and start all over again, every time I can make the mouth I want appear, the mouth which my hand chooses and sketches on your face, and which by some chance that I do not seek to understand coincides exactly with your mouth which smiles beneath the one my hand is sketching on you.

You look at me, from close up you look at me, closer and closer and then we play cyclops, we look closer and closer at one another and our eyes get larger, they come closer, they merge into one and the two cyclopses look at each other, blending as they breathe, our mouths touch and struggle in gentle warmth, biting each other with their lips, barely holding their tongues on their teeth, playing in corners where a heavy air comes and goes with an old perfume and a silence. Then my hands go to sink into your hair, to cherish slowly the depth of your hair while we kiss as if our mouths were filled with flowers or with fish, with lively movements and dark fragrance. And if we bite each other the pain is sweet, and if we smother each other in a brief and terrible sucking in together of our breaths, that momentary death is beautiful. And there is but one saliva and one flavour of ripe fruit, and I feel you tremble against me like a moon on the water.

(–8)

8

In the afternoon we used to go to see the fish on the Quai de la Mégisserie, in March, the leopard month, the crouching month, but now with a yellow sun which took on a little more red each day. From the pavement along the river, paying no attention to the *bouquinistes* who give nothing without pay, we would wait for the moment when we could see the fishbowls (we went along slowly, delaying), all the fishbowls out in the sun, and as if hung in the air hundreds of pink and black fish, motionless birds in their round air. An absurd joy would take us by the waist and you would sing, dragging me across the street to enter the world of fish hanging in the air.

They bring out the bowls, those great pitchers, onto the street and there among tourists and excited children and ladies who collect exotic varieties (*550 fr. pièce*) are the fishbowls underneath the sun, spheres of water which the sun mixes with the air and the pink and black birds dance around softly in a little chunk of air, slow cold birds. We would look at them, trying to bring our eyes up to the glass, touching it with our noses, annoying the old women who sell them as they go about with their nets to hunt aquatic butterflies, and we understood less and less what a fish is. We went along that path of not understanding and getting closer to those creatures that could not understand each other. We walked through the fishbowls and were as close as our friend, the woman in the second shop as you come from the Pont Neuf, who told you: "Cold water kills them, cold water is a sad thing . . . " And I remember the maid in the hotel who told me about a fern: "Don't water it, put a plate of water under the pot, then when it wants to drink it can, and when it doesn't want to, it doesn't . . . " And I thought about that unbelievable thing that we had read, that a single fish will get sad in its bowl and that all one has to do is put a mirror next to it and the fish is happy again . . .

We used to go into the shops where the more delicate species would have special tanks with thermometers and red worms. We would find out along with exclamations which used to infuriate the saleswomen – they were so sure that we were not going to buy anything at *550 fr. pièce* – all about the behaviour, the love, and the shape of the fish. The moment was delicately delicious, something like very thin chocolate or orange paste from Martinique; and we were getting drunk on metaphors and analogies, always trying to get into it. And that perfectly Giotto fish, do you remember, and those two that played about like jade dogs, or a fish which was the exact shadow of a violet cloud . . . We found out how life goes on in shapes without a third dimension, that they disappear when they face you, or at most leave a thin motionless pink line in the water. A flick of a fin and there he is miraculously again with eyes, whiskers, fins, and from his belly sometimes coming out and floating a transparent ribbon of excrement which has not come loose, ballast which suddenly puts them amongst us, which plucks them out from the perfection of their pure imagery, which compromises them, to use one of those fine words we so much liked to use around there in those days.

(–93)

9

They came into the Rue Vaneau from the Rue de Varennes. It was drizzling and La Maga clutched Oliveira's arm even tighter, pressing herself against his raincoat, which smelled like cold soup. Étienne and Perico were arguing over the possibility of explaining the world through painting and words. Oliveira put his arm carelessly around La Maga's waist. That might be an explanation too, an arm squeezing a thin, warm waist. As they walked he could feel the light play of her muscles, a sort of monotonous and persistent speech, an insistent Berlitz, I-love-you, I-love-you. Not an explanation: a pure verb, to-love, to-love. "And always following the verb, the copulative," Oliveira thought grammatically. If La Maga could only have understood how suddenly he was bothered by obedience to desire, "useless solitary obedience", as a poet had once called it, a waist so warm, wet hair against his cheek, the Toulouse-Lautrec way that La Maga used to walk snuggled up to him. In the beginning was the copulative, to rape is to explain, but not always the other way around. To discover the anti-explanatory method, so that this I-love-you, I-love-you would be the hub of the wheel. And Time? Everything begins again, there is no absolute. Then there must be feed or faeces, everything becomes critical again. Desire every so often, never too different and always something else: a trick of time to create illusions. "A love like a fire which burns eternally in the contemplation of Totality. But suddenly one breaks out into wild babble."

"Explain, explain," grumbled Étienne. "If you people can't name something you're incapable of seeing it. And this is called a dog and that's a house, as the guy from Duino used to say. You've got to show, Perico, not explain. I paint, therefore I am."

"Show what?" Perico Romero asked.

"The only reasons for our being alive."

"This creature thinks that the only sense is the sense of sight and all that can come from it," Perico answered.

"Painting is more than just a visual product," Étienne said. "I paint with my whole body. In that sense I'm no different from your Cervantes or your Tirso de What's-his-name. What I can't stand is this mania for explanations, the Logos understood exclusively as a verb."

"And so forth," Oliveira said grumpily. "Speaking of senses, the pair of you sound like a dialogue between two deaf men."

La Maga squeezed him tighter. "Now this one is going to come out with one of her asinine comments," thought Oliveira. "She has to rub first, make an epidermic decision." He felt a sort of hateful tenderness, something so contradictory that it must have been truth itself. "We ought to invent the sweet slap, the bee-kick. But in this world ultimate syntheses are yet to be discovered. Perico is right, the great Logos is watching. What a pity. We would have to have amoricide, for example, the real black light, the antimatter that troubles Gregorovius so much."

"Say, is Gregorovius coming to the recording session?" asked Oliveira.

Perico thought that he was, and Étienne thought that Mondrian.

"Think about Mondrian a minute," Étienne was saying. "Next to him Klee's magic symbols are nothing. Klee played with fate, the gifts of culture. Pure sensibility can be satisfied with Mondrian, but you need a whole bag of other tricks with Klee. A sophisticate for sophisticates. Chinese, really. Mondrian, on the other hand, paints the absolute. Stand naked in front of him and it's one thing or the other: either you see or you don't see. Pleasure, thrills, allusions, fears, delights are completely superfluous."

"Do you understand what he's saying?" La Maga asked. "It seems to me that he's not being fair to Klee."

"Fairness or unfairness has nothing to do with this," said Oliveira. "He's trying to say something else. Don't immediately turn it into something personal."

"But why does he say that such beautiful things are no good for Mondrian?"

"He's trying to say that basically a painting like one of Klee's calls for a degree *ès lettres*, or at least *ès poésies*, while all that Mondrian wants is for a person to mondrianate and that's all."

"That's not it," said Étienne.

"Of course it is," Oliveira said. "According to you a Mondrian canvas is sufficient unto itself. Therefore it calls upon your innocence more than on your experience. I mean Edenic innocence, not stupidity. Even that metaphor you used about standing naked in front of a picture has a pre-Adamite smell about it. Paradoxically, Klee is much more modest since he asks for the co-operation of the viewer and is not sufficient unto himself. The fact of the matter is that Klee is history while Mondrian is atemporality. And you're dying to find the absolute. Do I make myself clear?"

"No," said Étienne. "*C'est vache comme il pleut.*"

"You said it, *coño*," said Perico, "and that son of a bitch Ronald lives with the devil."

"Let us stiffen our pace," said Oliveira, mimicking his Spanish accent. "Let us sneak our bodies out from under this drizzle."

"There you go. I almost like your rain and your chicken better. It sure knows how to rain in Buenos Aires."

"The absolute," La Maga was saying, kicking a pebble from puddle to puddle. "What is an absolute, Horacio?"

"Look," Oliveira said, "it's just that moment in which something attains its maximum depth, its maximum reach, its maximum sense, and becomes completely uninteresting."

"There comes Wong," Perico observed. "The Chinaman's wetter than a wonton in a soup."

Almost at the same time, they spied Gregorovius coming around the corner of the Rue de Babylone, loaded down as usual with a briefcase bulging with books. Wong and Gregorovius stopped under the lamppost (and looked as if they were taking a shower together) and greeted each other with a certain solemnity. In the doorway of Ronald's building there was an interlude of umbrella-closing, *comment ça va*, who's got a match, the *minuterie* is broken, what a lousy night, *ah oui c'est vache*, and a rather confused ascent, broken at the first landing by a couple sitting on the steps and deeply engaged in the act of kissing.

"*Allez, c'est pas une heure pour faire les cons,*" said Étienne.

"*Ta gueule,*" answered a muffled voice, "*montez, montez, ne vous gênez pas. Ta bouche, mon trésor.*"

"*Salaud, va,*" Étienne said. "That's Guy Monod, an old friend of mine."

Ronald and Babs were waiting on the fifth floor, each holding a candle and smelling of cheap vodka. Wong made a sign and everybody stopped on the stairs and broke into an *a capella* version of the profane anthem of the Serpent Club. Then they ran into the apartment before the neighbours came to their doors.

Ronald was leaning against the door, redheadedly, wearing a checked shirt.

"The place is surrounded by telescopes, damn it. At ten o'clock at night the great god Silence is enthroned and woe to anyone who is irreverent. Yesterday some official came up to bawl us out. What did the gentleman tell us, Babs?"

"He mentioned 'repeated complaints'."

"So what are we going to do?" asked Ronald as he opened the door to let Guy Monod slip in.

"We'll do this," said Babs with a flawless gesture of the arm and a resonant oral fart.

"What about your chick?" Ronald asked.

"I don't know, she got lost," Guy said. "I think she's gone. We were making out fine on the stairs, and all of a sudden. Farther up she just wasn't there. What the hell anyway, she's Swiss."

(–104)

10

At night the clouds were flat and red over the Latin Quarter, the air was still damp as a listless breeze blew a few last drops against the dimly lit window, the panes were dirty, one broken and patched up with a piece of pink adhesive. Up above, under the lead gutters, the pigeons must have been sleeping, also lead, wrapped up in themselves, perfect antigargoyles. Protected by the window was that mossy parallelepiped, smelling of vodka and candles, damp clothing and leftover food, which was a kind of studio for Babs the ceramicist and Ronald the musician, the seat of the Club, wicker chairs, stained pillows, bits of pencil and wire on the floor, a stuffed owl with half his head gone, a poorly played and corny tune on an old record with a deep needle-scratch, an incessant scratch rasp scrape, a terrible saxophone that one night in 1928 or '29 had played as if it were afraid of getting lost, backed up by schoolgirl drums, a mediocre piano. But then an incisive guitar came in which seemed to signal a transition to something else and suddenly (Ronald had alerted them by holding up his finger) a cornet broke loose from the rest of the group and blew the first notes of the melody, landing on them as on a diving board. Bix took off with everything he had, and the clear sketch was inscribed on the silence as if it had been scratched there. Two corpses sparred fraternally, clinching and breaking, Bix and Eddie Lang (whose real name was Salvatore Massaro) played catch with *I'm Coming Virginia*, and I wonder where Bix is buried, thought Oliveira, and Eddie Lang, how many miles apart are their two nothings that one future night in Paris were to fight, guitar against cornet, gin against bad luck, jazz.

"I like it here. It's warm, it's dark."

"That Bix is a crazy son of a bitch. Put on *Jazz Me Blues*."

"The influence of technique on art," said Ronald, digging his hands into a pile of records, looking casually at the labels. "Before

LPs came out those guys had less than three minutes to play in. Nowadays a wild man like Stan Getz can come along in front of a mike and turn himself loose, blow anything he wants to. Poor Bix had to be satisfied with one chorus and as soon as he got warmed up, snap, it was all over. They must have got sore as hell when they cut records."

"I don't know," said Perico. "It's like writing a sonnet instead of an ode, and I don't know a damned thing about this crap. I only came because I was sick of staying in my room reading an endless essay by Julián Marías."

(–65)

11

Gregorovius let his glass be filled with vodka and began to drink with dainty sips. Two candles were burning on the mantelpiece where Babs kept bottles of beer and her dirty stockings. Gregorovius admired the listless burning of the candles through the hyaline glass, it was so foreign to all of them and so out of their time, like Bix's cornet, coming and going from a different time. He was annoyed by the feet of Guy Monod, who was on the couch either sleeping or listening with his eyes closed. La Maga came over and sat on the floor with a cigarette in her mouth. The green candles burned in her eyes. Gregorovius looked at her in ecstasy and remembered a street in Morlaix at dusk, a high aqueduct, clouds.

"This light is so much like you, something that comes and goes, always moving."

"Like Horacio's shadow," La Maga said. "His nose grows and shrinks. It's amazing."

"Babs is a shepherdess of shadows," Gregorovius said, "she works in clay, concrete shadows . . . Here everything breathes, a lost contact is established again; music helps, vodka, friendship . . .Those shadows in the cornice; the room has lungs, it palpitates. Yes, electricity is eleatic, it has turned our shadows to stone. Now they are part of the furniture and the faces. But here, on the other hand . . . Look at that moulding, how its shadow is breathing, that volute that rises and falls. In those days man lived in a soft and porous night, in a continuous dialogue. The terrors, what a luxury for the imagination . . . "

He put his palms together, keeping only his thumbs apart: a dog began to open his mouth and move his ears on the wall. La Maga laughed. Then Gregorovius asked her what it was like in Montevideo, the dog suddenly dissolved, because he wasn't sure that she was Uruguayan; Lester Young and the Kansas City Six. Shh . . . (Ronald, finger to his lips).

"Uruguay always sounded so strange to me. I picture Montevideo with lots of steeples all with bells cast after a battle. And you can't tell me that Montevideo doesn't have giant lizards along the river bank."

"Certainly," said La Maga. "All you have to do is take the bus to Pocitos."

"And do people in Montevideo really know Lautréamont?"

"Lautréamont?" asked La Maga.

Gregorovius sighed and drank more vodka. Lester Young, tenor; Dickie Wells, trombone; Joe Bushkin, piano; Bill Coleman, trumpet; John Simmons, bass; Jo Jones, drums. *Four O'Clock Drag.* Yes, tremendous lizards, trombones on the river bank, blues crawling along, *drag* probably meant a lizard in time, an endless crawling at four o'clock in the morning. Or maybe something completely different. "Oh, Lautréamont," La Maga said, suddenly remembering. "Yes, I think they know him quite well."

"He was from Uruguay, although you wouldn't think so."

"No, you wouldn't," said La Maga, coming to.

"Actually, Lautréamont . . . But Ronald's getting annoyed, he's put on one of his idols. I guess we'll have to shut up. But let's talk very low while you tell me about Montevideo."

"*Ah, merde alors,*" said Étienne, looking at them furiously. The vibes were testing the air, taking wrong steps upstairs, skipping a step, jumping five at once and coming down again on the top one. Lionel Hampton was balancing *Save It Pretty Mama,* letting it go as it fell down and spun around on the tip of his toe among pieces of glass, instant constellations, five stars, three stars, ten stars, he was extinguishing them with the tip of his slipper, he was rocking in a hammock twirling a Japanese parasol wildly in his hand and the whole band came in on the final fall, a hoarse trumpet, earth, down again, floating to a landing, *finibus,* all over. Gregorovius was listening to the whisper of Montevideo according to La Maga, and perhaps he would finally learn more about her, about her childhood, whether her name really was Lucía like Mimi in *La Bohème*; he was at that vodka level where the night began to become magnanimous and everything promised him fidelity and hope. Guy Monod had doubled up his legs and his hard soles no longer dug into Gregorovius's spine. La Maga was leaning on him a bit and he felt the soft warmth of her body, every movement she made to follow the music or the rhythm of her speech. With eyes open a crack Gregorovius managed to make out the corner where Ronald and Wong were selecting and passing records, Oliveira and Babs were on the floor, leaning against an Eskimo pelt on the wall, Horacio keeping cadence with the smoke, Babs lost to vodka, unpaid rent, and dyes that faded at three hundred degrees, a blue which melded into orangey rhombuses, something intolerable. Oliveira's lips were moving in the silence of the smoke, he was talking to himself, backwards, to some other thing that imperceptibly twisted Gregorovius's innards, he didn't know why, probably because that apparent absence of Horacio's was a fraud, which left him for La Maga to play with while he was there moving his lips in silence, speaking to La Maga through himself in the midst of the smoke and the jazz, laughing to himself inwardly at so much Lautréamont, at so much Montevideo.

(–136)

12

Gregorovius had always enjoyed meetings of the Club because it was really not a club at all in the strictest sense. He liked Ronald because of his anarchy, because of Babs, because of the way they were carefully killing themselves without worrying about anything, given over to the reading of Carson McCullers, Miller, Raymond Queneau, to jazz as a quiet exercise in freedom, to the unrestricted knowledge that they both were failures in the arts. He liked, if that's the word for it, Horacio Oliveira, with whom he had a sort of persecutive relationship in that Oliveira's presence always exasperated Gregorovius from the moment they came together, even after he had been out looking for Horacio, although he would not admit it, and Horacio would be amused by the cheap mysteries Gregorovius used to cover up his origins and way of life, by the fact that Gregorovius was in love with La Maga and did not think that Horacio knew, and the two of them would accept and reject each other at the same time in a sort of tight bullfight which in the last analysis was one of the reasons for the Club's get-togethers. They worked hard at being the knowing ones, at arranging a set of allusions to frustrate La Maga and infuriate Babs; all they had to do was mention something in passing, as now when Gregorovius was thinking that there really was a disillusioned persecution between him and Horacio, and immediately one of them would quote the hound of heaven, "I fled him," and so forth, and all the while La Maga would look at them with a kind of humble despair as one of them was in a state of I-flew-so-high-so-high-I-caught-my-prey and they would end up laughing at themselves. But it was too late because Horacio would be appalled at this exhibitionism of associative memory, and Gregorovius would feel himself touched with the annoyance that he had helped bring about, and between them both a certain resentment of accomplices would build up and two minutes later they would be at it again, and that, among other things, is what went on at meetings of the Club.

"This is one of the few times I've had such lousy vodka here," said Gregorovius as he filled his glass. "Lucía, you were about to tell me about your childhood. It's not hard for me to picture you on the river bank, with pigtails and rosy cheeks, like the girls I used to know in Transylvania, before they turned pale under the influence of this damned Lutetian climate."

"Lutetian?" asked La Maga.

Gregorovius sighed. He began to explain and La Maga was listening humbly and in a studious sort of way, just as she always did and with great intensity until rescued by some distraction. Ronald had just put on an old Coleman Hawkins record and La Maga seemed resentful that the explanation was ruining the music, and besides, it wasn't what she usually expected from an explanation, a tingling of the skin, a need to breathe deeply as Hawkins must have breathed just before taking another turn at the melody and as she would breathe when Horacio would deign to explain some really deep line of poetry for her, adding to it that other fabulous depth which could have been now if he instead of Gregorovius had been explaining this business about Lutetians, and how he would have made it blend into Hawkins's music, along with the green candles, a tickle, a deep breath which would be the only thing she could be sure of, something comparable only to Rocamadour or Horacio's lips or sometimes an adagio from Mozart that could barely be heard because the record was in such bad shape.

"Don't be like that," Gregorovius said humbly. "All I wanted was to understand your life a little better, what you are, how you happen to have so many facets."

"My life," said La Maga. "Even if I were drunk I wouldn't tell you about it. And you won't understand me any better after hearing about my childhood. Besides, I didn't have any childhood."

"I didn't either. In Herzegovina."

"Mine in Montevideo. I'll tell you one thing. Sometimes I dream about grammar school, it's so horrible I wake up screaming. And aged fifteen, I don't know whether you were ever fifteen years old."

"I think so," Gregorovius said uncertainly.

"I was, in a house with a courtyard and flowerpots where my

father used to drink *mate* and read dirty magazines. Does your father ever come back to you? His ghost I mean?"

"No, actually my mother is more apt to," Gregorovius said. "Especially the Glasgow one. My Glasgow mother comes back sometimes, but she's not a ghost, just a memory that's a little too wet, that's all. She goes away with an Alka-Seltzer, it's easy. But you . . . ?"

"How should I know," La Maga said impatiently. "It's that music, those green candles, Horacio over there in the corner, like an Indian. Why must I tell how he comes back? But a few nights ago I was at home waiting for Horacio, I was sitting near the bed and outside it was raining a little, the way it does on that record. Yes, it was something like that, I was looking at the bed and waiting for Horacio, I don't remember how the bed was made, and suddenly I saw my father lying with his back towards me and covering his face as he always did when he was drunk and beginning to fall asleep, I saw his legs and could make out his hand on his chest. I felt my hair stand on end, I wanted to scream, everything you feel at times like that, you must have been afraid sometime . . . I wanted to run away, the door was so far off, at the other end of the hallway and more hallways, the door was farther and farther away and I could see the pink bedspread going up and down, I could hear my father snoring, in a moment I would see a hand, then eyes, then his hooked nose, no, I shouldn't be telling you all this, finally I screamed so loud that the woman upstairs came down and made me some tea, and later on Horacio said I was hysterical."

Gregorovius stroked her hair and La Maga lowered her head. "Here it comes," Oliveira was thinking, and he stopped following Dizzy Gillespie's tricks as he swung on the high trapeze without a net, "here it comes, it was bound to. He's crazy about the girl and that's his way of showing it, with his ten fingers. The same game over and over. We keep falling into worn-out moulds, learning every trite role there is like idiots. But just as if I were stroking her hair, while she told me sagas of the Río de la Plata, we feel sorry for her and we have to take her home, all of us a little drunk, and put her to bed, petting her gently as we take off her clothes, slowly, button by button, every zip, and she does want to, wants to, doesn't want to, straightens up, covers her face, cries, hugs us as if suggesting something sublime, wiggles out of her slip, kicks off a shoe with a gesture that connotes protest and gets us as excited as we ever can get, how base, how base. I'm going to have to smash you in the face, Ossip Gregorovius my poor friend. No desire, no pity, exactly what Dizzy is blowing, without pity, without desire, just as absolutely without pity as what Dizzy is blowing."

"What a damned drag," Oliveira said. "Take that crap off the machine. I'm not coming to the Club any more if I have to listen to that clown."

"The gentleman doesn't like bop," Ronald said sarcastically. "Wait a minute, I'll put on something by Paul Whiteman for you."

"Let's compromise," Étienne said. "Common consent, sweet Ronald: let's hear Bessie Smith, the dove in a cage of bronze."

Ronald and Babs began to laugh for some obscure reason and Ronald looked through the pile of old records. The needle made a terrible scratch, something began to move deep down as if there were layers and layers of cotton between voice and ears, Bessie singing with a bandaged face, stuck in a hamper of soiled clothes, and her voice got more and more muffled, it came out stuck to rags and proclaimed with neither anger nor pleading, "I wanna be somebody's baby doll", it fell back to wait, a street-corner voice, one from a houseful of grannies, "to be somebody's baby doll", hotter and more yearning, panting now "I wanna be somebody's baby doll . . . "

Oliveira burned his mouth with a long drink of vodka, put his arm around Babs's shoulders, and rested against her comfortable body. "The intercessors," he thought, sinking softly into the tobacco smoke. Bessie's voice thinned out towards the end of the side, and now Ronald was flipping the Bakelite disc (if it was Bakelite) and from this piece of worn-out material the *Empty Bed Blues* would be born again, a night in the twenties in some corner of the United States. Ronald had closed his eyes, his hands on his knees, faintly keeping time. Wong and Étienne also had their eyes shut, the room was almost dark and the needle scratched on the old record; it was hard for Oliveira to believe that all of this was taking place. Why there, why the Club, those stupid rites, why did those blues come out like that when Bessie sang them? "The intercessors," he thought once more, snuggling up to Babs who was completely drunk and was crying quietly as she listened to Bessie, trembling in time to the rhythm or counterpoint, weeping inside so as not to get far away from the blues about an empty bed, tomorrow morning, shoes in puddles, unpaid rent, fear of old age, the ashen image of dawn in the mirror at the foot of the bed, the blues, life's infinite melancholy. "The intercessors, one unreality showing us another, like painted saints pointing towards Heaven. This cannot exist, we cannot really be here, I cannot be someone whose name is Horacio. That ghost there, that voice of a Negro woman killed in an automobile accident twenty years ago: links in a non-existent chain, how do we support ourselves here, how can we be meeting tonight if it is not a mere play of illusions, of rules that are accepted and agreed upon, a deck of cards in the hands of an inconceivable dealer . . . "

"Don't cry," Oliveira whispered to Babs. "Don't cry, Babs, none of this is true."

"Oh yes, oh yes it is true," Babs said, blowing her nose. "It is true."

"It could be true," said Oliveira, kissing her on the cheek, "but it isn't."

"Like those shadows," Babs said, snuffing and swallowing the mucus and moving her hand from side to side. "And it makes you sad, Horacio, because everything is so beautiful."

But all this, Bessie's singing, Coleman Hawkins's cooing, weren't they illusions, or something even worse, the illusion of other illusions, a dizzy chain going backwards, back to a monkey looking at himself in the water on that first day? But Babs was crying, Babs had said, "Oh yes, oh yes it is true," and Oliveira, a little drunk too, felt that the truth now lay in that Bessie and Hawkins were illusions, because only illusions were capable of moving their adherents, illusions and not truths. And there was more than this, there was intercession, the arrival through illusions to a plane, a zone impossible to think about because all thought destroyed it as soon as it attempted to isolate it. A hand of smoke took his hand, started him downward, if it was downward, showed him a centre, if it was a centre, put it in his stomach, where the vodka was softly making crystal bubbles, some sort of infinitely beautiful and desperate illusion which some time back he had called immortality. Closing his eyes he managed to tell himself that if a simple ritual was able to excentrate him like this the better to show him a centre, to excentrate him towards a centre which was nonetheless inconceivable, perhaps everything was not lost and some day, in different circumstances, after other proofs, arrival would be possible. But arrival where, for what? He was too drunk even to set up a working hypothesis, to form an idea of a possible route. He was not drunk enough to stop thinking consecutively, and this poor power of thought was sufficient for him to feel that it was carrying him away farther and farther from something too distant, too precious to be seen through this stupidly propitious mist, vodka mist, Maga mist, Bessie Smith mist. He began to see green rings spinning wildly about, he opened his eyes. Usually after seeing the rings he would feel like vomiting.

(–106)

13

Wrapped up in smoke Ronald was pulling out record after record, scarcely bothering to find out what the others wanted, and once in a while Babs would get up from the floor and start digging through the piles of old 78s, she would pick out four or five and put them on the table within reach of Ronald, who would lean forward and pet Babs who would twist away laughing and sit on his lap but just for a moment because Ronald wanted to be quiet while he listened to *Don't Play Me Cheap.*

Satchmo was singing:

> So what's the use
> if you're gonna cut off my juice

and Babs wiggled on Ronald's knees, excited by Satchmo's style of singing, the theme was vulgar enough to let her take liberties which Ronald would never condone when Satchmo sang the *Yellow Dog Blues,* and because in the breath that Ronald was blowing on the back of her neck there was a mixture of vodka and sauerkraut that aroused Babs fantastically. From her high outlook, a sort of delicate pyramid of smoke and music and vodka and sauerkraut and Ronald's hands marching up and down, Babs could condescend to look downward through her half-closed eyes and she saw Oliveira on the floor, his back against the Eskimo pelt on the wall, smoking and dead drunk now, with a resentful and bitter South American face whose mouth would smile from time to time between drags, Oliveira's lips which Babs had once desired (not now) were curved a little while the rest of his face looked washed-out and absent. As much as he liked jazz, Oliveira could never get into the spirit of it like Ronald, whether it was good or bad, hot or cool, white or black, old or modern, Chicago or New Orleans, never jazz, never what was now Satchmo, Ronald and Babs, "So what's the use if you're gonna cut off my juice," and then the trumpet's flaming up, the yellow phallus breaking the air and having fun, coming forward and drawing back and towards the end three ascending notes, pure hypnotic gold, a perfect pause where all the swing of the world was beating in an intolerable instant, and then the super-sharp ejaculation slipping and falling like a rocket in the sexual night, Ronald's hand caressing Babs's neck and the scratching of the needle while the record kept on turning and the silence there was in all true music slowly unstuck itself from the walls, slithered out from underneath the couch, and opened up like lips or like cocoons.

"*Ça alors,*" said Étienne.

"Yes, Armstrong's great period," said Ronald, examining the pile of records Babs had picked out. "Like Picasso's giant period, if you like. Nowadays they're both a pair of pigs. To think that doctors have invented ways to be rejuvenated . . . They'll go on screwing us for another twenty years, wait and see."

"Not us," Étienne said. "We've already shot them down and just at the right moment, and all I ask is for someone to do the same for me when my time is up."

"Just at the right moment? You're not asking for much, kiddo," said Oliveira, yawning. "But you're right, we have given them the *coup de grâce* already. With a rose instead of a bullet, if you want to think of it that way. What's left is habit and carbon paper. To think that Armstrong has just now gone to Buenos Aires for the first time and you can imagine the thousands of boobs who will think they're listening to something great while Satchmo, with more tricks than an old fighter, bobbing and weaving, tired and amortized and without giving a damn what he does, strictly routine, while some of my friends whom I respect and who twenty years ago would cover their ears if you put on *Mahogany Hall Stomp* now pay God knows how much for an orchestra seat to listen to that reheated stuff. Of course, my country itself is reheated too, with all my patriotic love I'm forced to admit it."

"Starting with you," said Perico from behind a dictionary. "You've come here in the same mould as all of your countrymen who take off for Paris to get their 'sentimental education'. At least in Spain we learn all about that in brothels and at bullfights, *coño.*"

"And from the Countess Pardo Bazán," said Oliveira, yawning

again. "Everything else you say is true, old boy. What I should really be doing is playing cards with Traveler. You didn't know him, did you. You don't know anything about all that. So what's the use of talking about it?"

(–115)

14

He came out of the corner he had been stuck in, he put one foot on a piece of floor after having examined it as if it had been vital to pick out the exact spot on which to place his foot, then he brought out the other one with the same caution, and six feet away from Ronald and Babs he began to shrivel down until he was impeccably installed on the floor.

"It's raining," said Wong, pointing at the skylight.

Wafting the smoke away with his hand, Oliveira looked at Wong with friendly contentment.

"It's best to be at sea-level where all one can see are shoes and knees all around. Where's your glass?"

"Over there," said Wong.

It turned out that it was full and within reach. They began to drink, appreciatively, and Ronald put on a John Coltrane record which made Perico snort. Then a Sidney Bechet from his Paris *merengue* period, something that seemed to be poking a little fun at Spanish prejudices.

"Is it true that you're writing a book about tortures?"

"Not exactly," said Wong.

"What is it, then?"

"In China one has a different conception of art."

"I know, we've all read Mirbeau the Chinese. Is it true that you have photographs of tortures taken in Peking in 1920 or around that time?"

"Oh, no," said Wong smiling. "They're all faded, they're not worth looking at."

"Do you really carry the worst one around in your wallet?"

"Oh, no," Wong said.

"And did you show it to some women in a café?"

"They were so insistent," said Wong. "The worst of it was they didn't understand at all."

"Let me see it," said Oliveira, putting out his hand.

Wong began to look at the hand, smiling. Oliveira was too drunk to insist. He drank some more vodka and shifted his position. A piece of paper folded four times was placed in his hand. Instead of Wong he saw a kind of Cheshire cat smiling, sort of bowing in all the smoke. The post must have been six feet high, but there were eight posts, except that it was the same post repeated eight times in four series of two photos each, which went from left to right and from top to bottom, the post was the same in spite of slight differences in focus, all that was different was the prisoner tied to the post, the faces of the people around (there was a woman on the left) and the position of the executioner, standing to the left out of deference to the photographer, some American or Danish ethnologist who had a firm hand but a bad camera, an ancient Kodak that took bad pictures, so that except for the second picture, where the choice of knives had indicated work on the right ear, and the rest of the naked body could be seen clearly, the other pictures, because of the blood which was beginning to cover the body and the poor quality of the film or the development, were rather disappointing, especially from the fourth one on, in which the prisoner appeared as a blackish mass on which one could make out an open mouth and a very white arm, and the three last pictures were practically the same except for the position of the executioner, in the sixth picture crouching next to his bag of knives, taking out one at random (but he must have been cheating, because if he was going to begin with the deepest cuts . . .), and looking more closely one could see that the victim was alive because one foot was sticking out in spite of the pressure of his bonds, and his head was thrown back, his mouth still open, on the ground Chinese gentility must have spread an abundant amount of sawdust because the pool was no bigger, it made an almost perfect oval around the post. "The seventh is the critical one," Wong's voice came out from behind the vodka and the smoke, and one had to look closely because blood was pouring out around the breasts which had been deeply excised (between the second and third pictures), but one could see in the seventh that a decisive cut had been made because the shape of the thighs which had been turned outward a bit had changed, and if one brought the picture up close one could see that the change was not in the thighs but in the groin, instead of the hazy splotch in the first picture it looked like something pouring out of a hole, something like a little girl who has been raped, with blood flowing down her thighs. And if Wong did not think highly of the eighth picture he must have been right because the victim could not have been alive any more, no one lets his head fall to the side that way. "According to what I have been told the whole operation took an hour and a half," Wong observed with ceremony. The piece of paper was folded in four, a black leather wallet opened its mouth like a crocodile and gobbled it up from amidst the smoke. "Of course, Peking is not what it used to be. I'm sorry I showed you something so primitive, but one cannot carry certain other documents in one's wallet, there have to be explanations, an initiation . . . " His voice came from so far away it seemed to be a prolongation of the images, the gloss of a ceremonious scholar. Above or below, Big Bill Broonzy had begun to chant *See, See, Rider*, and as always everything came together from the unreconcilable forms, a grotesque collage which made its adjustments with vodka and Kantian categories, those tranquillizers against any too sharp coagulation of reality. Or as almost always happened, closing one's eyes and going back, to the cottony world of any other night chosen carefully among the cards of the open deck. "See, see, rider," Big Bill was singing, another corpse, "see what you have done."

(–114)

15

It was so natural for him to remember then that night on the Saint-Martin canal, the proposition they had made him (1,000 francs) to see a film at the home of a Swiss doctor. During the war an Axis surgeon had arranged to film a hanging in all of its details. Two rolls in all, but silent. However, the photography was excellent, they swore. You could pay on the way out.

In the moment necessary to resolve it all and say no and leave the café with the Haitian girl who knew the friend of the Swiss doctor, he had had time to imagine the scene and put himself as always on the side of the victim. There was no reason to waste words on the hanging of whoever-he-was, but if that somebody had known (and the refinement could have been precisely in telling him so) that a camera was going to record every moment of his grimaces and twistings for the pleasure of future dilettantes . . . "No matter how it hurts me, I shall never be indifferent like Étienne," Oliveira thought. "What it amounts to is that I insist on the unheard-of idea that man was meant for something else. Then, of course . . . What poor tools we have to find a way out of this dungeon." The worst was that he had looked at Wong's picture with coldness only because the one they were torturing had not been his father, to say nothing of the forty years that had passed since it all took place in Peking.

"Look," Oliveira told Babs, who had come back to him after having quarrelled with Ronald, who had insisted on listening to Ma Rainey and had put Fats Waller down, "it's incredible how bastardly we can get. What did Christ think about before he fell asleep? Suddenly in the midst of a smile your mouth can turn into a big hairy spider."

"Oh, no," said Babs. "Not delirium tremens at this time of night."

"It's all superficial, baby, everything is epi-der-mic. Look, when I was a kid I used to drag them out for all the old ladies in the family, sisters and all that, the whole genealogical mess, you know why?

Well, all kinds of silly reasons, but among them because for those ladies when anyone passed on, as they would say, any kick-off which took place in their circle was much more important than a war, an earthquake which kills ten thousand people, things like that. We're cretins, but such cretins it's hard to imagine, Babs, because to come to this we've had to read Plato, the Church Fathers, the classics, without overlooking a single one, and beyond that to know everything that can be known about the knowable, and that's the precise moment that one arrives at a cretinism so incredible that he's capable of grabbing his poor illiterate mother by her shawl and blowing his top over the fact that she is upset by the death of the Jew on the corner or the girl on the third floor. And you talk to her about the earthquake in Bab-el-Mandeb or the offensive at Vardar Ingh, and you think the poor devil feels any abstract pity for the liquidation of three divisions of the Iranian army . . . ?"

"Take it easy," Babs said in English. "Have a drink, sonny, and don't be such a murder to me."

"And what it really comes down to is a case of eyes that can't see . . . Why, tell me why we must beat old ladies about the head with our puritan adolescence of shitty little cretins? Oh, brother, I'm stewed. I'm going home."

But it was hard for him to give up the warm Eskimo pelt, the distant and almost indifferent contemplation of Gregorovius as he plied La Maga with his sentimental interview. Breaking away from everything as if he were plucking a cadaverous old rooster who had resisted to the last in the name of the cock he once had been, he let out a sigh of relief on hearing the theme of *Blue Interlude*, a record he had once owned in Buenos Aires. He couldn't remember all of them, but he did know that Benny Cartel was on it and maybe Chu Berry, and hearing the difficult simplicity of Teddy Wilson in his solo, he decided to wait for the end of the record. Wong had said it was raining; it had been raining all day. That must be Chu Berry, unless it was Coleman Hawkins in person, but no, it wasn't Hawk. "It's incredible how we're cheating ourselves," thought Oliveira looking at La Maga who was looking at Gregorovius who was looking at the air. "We'll end up going to the Bibliothèque Mazarine to take notes on mandrakes, Bantu necklaces, or the comparative history of nail clippers." Think of a repertory of insignificant things, the enormous work which goes into studying them and gaining a basic knowledge of them. A history of nail clippers, two thousand volumes to acquire the certain knowledge that until 1675 these small things had never received any mention. Suddenly in Mainz someone does a picture of a woman cutting a nail. It is not exactly a pair of nail clippers, but it looks like it. In the eighteenth century a certain Philip McKinney of Baltimore patents the first nail clippers with a spring attached: the problem is solved, the fingers can squeeze with all their strength to cut toenails, incredibly tough, and the clippers will snap back automatically. Five hundred notes, a year of work. If we were to turn now to the invention of the screw or to the use of the verb *gond* in eighteenth-century Pali literature. Anything would be more interesting than to guess the conversation between La Maga and Gregorovius. To find a barricade, anything, Benny Carter, nail clippers, the verb *gond*, another drink, a ceremonial impalement conducted carefully by an executioner attentive to the smallest details, or Champion Jack Dupree lost in the blues, a better barricade than he because (and the needle was making a horrible noise)

> Say goodbye, goodbye to whiskey
> Lordy, so long to gin,
> Say goodbye, goodbye to whiskey
> Lordy, so long to gin.
> I just want my reefers,
> I just want to feel high again –

So that in all certainty Ronald would come back to Big Bill Broonzy, led by associations Oliveira knew about and respected, and Big Bill would tell them about another barricade with the same voice that La Maga was using to tell Gregorovius about her childhood in Montevideo, Big Bill without bitterness, "matter of fact",

> They said if you white, you all right,
> If you brown, stick aroun',
> But as you black,
> Mm, mm, brother, get back, get back, get back.

"I know already that nothing can come of it," said Gregorovius. "Memories only change the least interesting part of the past."

"Yes, nothing can come of it," La Maga said.

"That's why if I asked you to tell me about Montevideo it was because you're like a queen of hearts to me, all front, no substance. I put it that way so that you'll understand me."

"And Montevideo is the substance . . . Nonsense, nonsense, nonsense. What do you call the past? As far as I'm concerned everything that has happened to me happened yesterday, last night, no earlier."

"So much the better," said Gregorovius. "Now you're a queen only not of hearts."

"It wasn't so long ago for me. It's far away, very far away, but not so long ago. The arcades of the Plaza Independencia, you know them too, Horacio, that sad square with all those restaurants, knowing there had been a killing that afternoon, the newsboys selling their papers in and out of the arcade."

"The lottery and all its prizes," Horacio said.

"The woman carved up in El Salto, politics, soccer . . . "

"The boat to the racetrack, a drink of Ancap brandy. Local colour, eh."

"It must have been quite exotic," said Gregorovius, putting himself in a position so that he would block off Oliveira's view and be more alone with La Maga, who was looking at the candles and keeping time with her foot.

"There was no such thing as time in Montevideo in those days," La Maga said. "We used to live near the river, in a large house with a courtyard. I was always thirteen years old, I remember it so well. A blue sky, thirteen years old, my school teacher was cross-eyed. One day I fell in love with a blond boy who sold newspapers in the square. He had a way of saying 'paypuh' that made me feel empty somewhere here . . . He wore long pants but he couldn't have been more than twelve. My father was not working then and spent the afternoons drinking *mate* in the courtyard. I lost my mother when I was five years old, some aunts brought me up but they went to the country later on. When I was thirteen there were only my father and I at home. It was a kind of tenement, not a home. There was an Italian, two old women, and a Negro and his wife who fought at night but later on would play the guitar and sing. The Negro had red eyes, like a wet mouth. I didn't like them very much and preferred to play in the street. If my father found me playing in the street he made me come in and would spank me. One day while he was spanking me I saw the Negro peeking through his half-opened door. At first I didn't really catch on, I thought he was scratching his leg, something he was doing with his hand . . . Father was too busy hitting me with a belt. It's funny how you can lose your innocence all at once, without even knowing that you've passed into another existence. That night in the kitchen the Negro couple sang until quite late. I was in my room and I had cried so much that I was terribly thirsty, but I didn't want to leave my room. My father was drinking *mate* in the doorway. You can't imagine how hot it was because you're all from cold countries. It was the humidity that was bad there near the river, I think it's worse in Buenos Aires, Horacio has told me it's worse, I don't know. That night my clothes stuck to me, everybody was drinking *mate* that night, two or three times I went out and got a drink from the tap in the courtyard among the geraniums. I had the idea that water from that tap was cooler. There wasn't a star in the sky, the geraniums had a harsh smell about them, they're vulgar plants, very beautiful, you have to stroke a geranium leaf. The lights were out in the other rooms already and father had gone out to the bar run by one-eyed Ramos, and I went into the courtyard and there was the empty *mate* gourd he always left by the door so that the tramps from the lot next door would not steal it. I remember that when I crossed the courtyard the moon came out a little and I stopped to look at it, the moon always made me feel coldish, and I made a face that could be seen from the stars, I believed in such things, I was only thirteen. Then I drank some more from the tap and went back to my room upstairs, climbing up an iron staircase where once I had sprained my ankle when I was nine years old. When I was about to light the candle on my night-table a hot hand grabbed my shoulder, I heard the door close, another hand covered my mouth, and I began to notice Negro smell, the Negro was pawing me all over and whispering things in my ear, slobbering on my face, pulling off my clothes, and there was nothing I could do, not even scream because I knew he would kill me if I screamed and I didn't want him to kill me, anything would have been better than that, to die would have been the worst offence, the most complete stupidity. Why are you looking at me like that, Horacio? I'm telling how the Negro in the tenement raped me, Gregorovius did so want to know how I lived in Uruguay."

"Don't spare us any details," said Oliveira.

"Oh, a general idea is enough," said Gregorovius.

"There's no such thing as a general idea," Oliveira said.

(–120)

16

"When he left my room it was almost dawn and I didn't even know how to cry any more."

"The dirty bastard," Babs said.

"Oh, La Maga richly deserved that homage," said Étienne. "The only funny thing, as always, is the diabolical separation of form and content. Everything you've said is exactly the same as what happens between lovers, except for the slight resistance and the probably stronger aggression."

"Chapter 8, Section 4, Paragraph A," Oliveira said. "*Presses Universitaires Françaises.*"

"*Ta gueule,*" said Étienne.

"Let's cap it off," Ronald said. "It's about time we heard something like *Hot and Bothered.*"

"A proper title for the reminiscences we've just heard," said Oliveira, lifting up his glass. "That Negro was quite a guy."

"It's not a subject for jokes," Gregorovius said.

"You were the one who dragged it out, friend."

"And you're drunk, Horacio."

"Of course. It's the great moment, the lucid moment. You, child, should have got a job in some gerontological clinic. Just look at Ossip, your pleasant recollections have taken twenty years off him."

"He dragged it out," said La Maga resentfully. "Now he'll start saying how he didn't enjoy it. Give me a vodka, Horacio."

But Oliveira didn't seem disposed to get mixed up with La Maga and Gregorovius, who was muttering explanations that she was barely listening to. Wong got more of his attention as he offered to make some coffee. Very hot and very strong, a secret he had learned at the casino in Menton. The Club applauded unanimously. Ronald lovingly kissed the label on one record, started the turntable, put the needle on in a ritualistic sort of way. For a moment the Ellington machine obliterated them with that fabulous sparring between trumpet and Baby Cox, the subtle and easygoing entrance of Johnny Hodges, the crescendo (but the rhythm was already getting to be a little stiff after thirty years, an old tiger who could still ripple) with riffs which were both tense and loose at the same time, a difficult minor miracle: "I swing, therefore I am." Leaning against the Eskimo pelt, looking at the green candles through his glass of vodka (we used to go to look at the fish on the Quai de la Mégisserie) it was almost easy to come to the conclusion that what was called reality deserved that disparaging phrase of the Duke's, "It don't mean a thing if it ain't got that swing," but why had the hand of Gregorovius stopped caressing La Maga's hair, there was poor Ossip, sleeker than a seal, all broken up by that distant deflowering, it was pitiful to look at him, so tense in that atmosphere where the music was breaking down resistance and was weaving everything into a kind of common breathing, the peace of an enormous heart beating for all, drawing them all into itself. And now a cracked voice, making its way out of a worn-out record, suggesting unknowingly that old Renaissance invitation, that old Anacreontic sadness, a *carpe diem* from Chicago, 1922.

> You so beautiful but you gotta die some day,
> You so beautiful but you gotta die some day,
> All I want's a little lovin' before you pass away.

Every so often the words of the dead fit the thoughts of the living (if the one group is living and the other is dead). You so beautiful. *Je ne veux pas mourir sans avoir compris pourquoi j'avais vécu.* A blues song, René Daumal, Horacio Oliveira, but you gotta die some day, you so beautiful but – And that's why Gregorovius insisted on knowing about La Maga's past, so that she would die a little less from that other backward-moving death composed entirely of things dragged along by time, so as to put her in her own time, you so beautiful but you gotta, so as not to love a ghost who lets her hair be stroked under a green light, poor Ossip, and how terrible the night was turning out, everything so incredibly so, Guy Monod's shoes, but you gotta die some day, Ireneo the Negro (later on, when she had more courage, La Maga would tell him about Ledesma, about the men at carnival-time, the saga of Montevideo). And suddenly with cool perfection, Earl Hines was giving his first variation of *I Ain't Got Nobody*, and even Perico, lost in some remote reading, lifted up his head and listened, La Maga had rested her head on Gregorovius's thigh and was looking at the floor, at the piece of Oriental rug, a red strand that disappeared into the socle, an empty glass next to a table-leg. She wanted to smoke but she wasn't going to ask Gregorovius for a cigarette, without knowing why she wasn't going to ask him, and she wasn't going to ask Horacio either, but she knew why she wasn't going to ask him, she didn't want to see his eyes as he laughed and again took revenge for her lying close to Gregorovius and for not having approached him all evening. Helpless, she thought sublime thoughts, quotations from poems which made her feel that she was in the very heart of the artichoke, on one side "I ain't got nobody, and nobody cares for me," which was not entirely true, because at least two people were present who were in a bad mood over her, and at the same time a line from Perse, something like "*Tu es là, mon amour, et je n'ai lieu qu'en toi,*" where La Maga took refuge snuggling up to the sound of *lieu*, of *Tu es là, mon amour*, the bland acceptance of a fate which made her shut her eyes and made her body feel like an offering, something that anybody could have and dirty and exalt like Ireneo, while Hines's music matched the red and blue spots which danced around behind her eyelids, which for some reason were called Volaná and Valené, Volaná on the left ("and nobody cares for me") spinning madly, Valené on top, hanging like a star in a pierodellafrancesca blue, *et je n'ai lieu qu'en toi*, Volaná and Valené, Ronald would never be able to play the piano like Earl Hines, Horacio and she should really own that record to listen to at night in the dark, to learn how to make love to the phrasing, those long, nervous caresses, "I ain't got nobody" on the back, on the shoulders, fingers behind the neck, nails working in and out of the hair, one last whirlwind and Valené merges with Volaná, *tu est là, mon amour* and nobody cares for me, Horacio was there but nobody bothered with her, nobody was petting her head, Valené and Volaná had disappeared and her eyelids hurt from having squeezed them together so tightly, she could hear Ronald talking and then the smell of coffee, ah, a wonderful smell of coffee, dear Wong, Wong Wong Wong.

She got up blinking, glanced at Gregorovius who looked like something spoiled and dirty. Someone passed her a cup.

(–137)

17

"I don't like to talk about him just for the sake of talking," La Maga said.

"That's all right," said Gregorovius. "I was just asking."

"If you just want to hear talking, I can talk about something else."

"Don't get annoyed."

"Horacio is like guava jelly," La Maga said.

"What's guava jelly?"

"Horacio is like a glass of water in a storm."

"Ah," said Gregorovius.

"He must have been born during that period Madame Léonie talks about when she's a little tipsy. A time when nobody was upset, when streetcars were pulled by horses and wars took place in open country. There were no such things as sleeping pills, Madame Léonie says."

"The beautiful golden age," said Gregorovius. "They told me about times like that too, in Odessa. My mother, so romantic, with her hair down . . . They kept pineapple plants on the balconies and at night there was no need for chamber pots, it was extraordinary. But I can't picture Horacio in those royal-jelly days."

"I can't either, but he wouldn't have been so sad. In these times everything hurts him, even aspirin hurts him. Really, last night I made him take an aspirin because he had a toothache. He grabbed it and started to look at it, it was terribly hard for him to decide to swallow it. He said funny things, that it was unhealthy to use things one really knew nothing about, things invented by other people to calm other things that we also know nothing about . . . You know how he is when he goes off on a tangent."

"You repeated the word 'thing' several times," Gregorovius said. "It's rather vulgar, but it does show, on the other hand, what's wrong with Horacio. Obviously a victim of thingness."

"What is thingness?" La Maga asked.

"Thingness is that unpleasant feeling that where our presumption ends our punishment begins. I'm sorry I have to use abstract and almost allegorical language, but I mean that Oliveira is pathologically sensitive to the pressure of what is around him, the world he lives in, his fate, to speak kindly. In a word, he can't stand his surroundings. More briefly, he has a world-ache. You had an inkling of it, Lucía, and with delightful innocence you felt that Oliveira would be happier in any of the pocket-sized Arcadias manufactured by the Madame Léonies of this world, not to mention my mother, the one in Odessa. Because you probably didn't believe that business about the pineapples, I suppose."

"Or the chamber pots either," said La Maga. "It's hard to believe."

Guy Monod decided to wake up when Ronald and Étienne agreed to listen to Jelly Roll Morton; opening one eye he decided that the back outlined in the light of the green candles must belong to Gregorovius. He shuddered, the green candles seen from a bed made a bad impression on him, the rain on the skylight was strangely mixed with the remnants of his dream-images, he had been dreaming about an absurdly sunny place, where Gaby was walking around nude and feeding crumbs to a group of stupid pigeons the size of ducks. "I have a headache," Guy said to himself. He was not in the least interested in Jelly Roll Morton although it was amusing to hear the rain on the skylight as Jelly Roll sang: "Stood on a corner, an' she was soakin' wet . . . " Wong would certainly have come up with a theory about real and poetic time, but was it true that Wong had mentioned making coffee? Gaby feeding the pigeons crumbs and Wong, the voice of Wong going in between Gaby's nude legs in a garden with brightly coloured flowers, saying: "A secret I learned in the casino at Menton." Quite possible, after all, that Wong would appear with a pot full of coffee.

Jelly Roll was at the piano beating the time softly with his foot for lack of a better rhythm section. Jelly Roll could sing *Mamie's Blues* rocking a little, staring up at some decoration on the ceiling, or it was a fly that came and went or a spot that came and went in Jelly Roll's eyes. "Eleven twenty-four took my baby away-ay . . . " That's what life had been, trains bringing people and taking them away while you stood on the corner with wet feet, listening to a pianola and laughter and beating on the yellow windows of the saloon where you didn't always have enough money to go in. "Eleven twenty-four took my baby away-ay . . . " Babs had taken so many trains in her life, she liked to go by train if in the end there was some friend waiting for her, if Ronald softly put his hand on her hip the way he was doing now, sketching out the music on her skin, "Eleven-thirteen'll carry her back one day," obviously some train would bring her back again, but who knows if Jelly Roll was going to be on that platform, at that piano, that time he sang the blues about Mamie Desdume, the rain on a Paris skylight at one o'clock in the morning, wet feet, and a whore who muttered "If you can't hand me a dollar then hand me a rotten dime," Babs had said things like that in Cincinnati, every woman had said things like that somewhere, even in the bed of a king, Babs had a very special idea of what the bed of a king was like but in any case some woman must have said something like, "If you can't give me a million, gimme a lousy grand," a matter of proportions, and why was Jelly Roll's piano so sad, so much that rain that woke Guy up, that was making La Maga cry, and Wong who wasn't coming with the coffee.

"It's too much," Étienne said, sighing. "I don't know why I stand for that rubbish. It's moving, but it's rubbish."

"It's no Pisanello medallion, of course," Oliveira said.

"Or opus whatever-you-want by Schoenberg," said Ronald. "Why did you want to hear it? Besides intelligence you also lack charity. Have you ever stood with your feet in a puddle at midnight? Jelly Roll has, you can tell when he sings, it's something you learn."

"I can paint better if my feet are dry," Étienne said. "And don't come around with any Salvation Army arguments. Why don't you put on something more intelligent, like those Sonny Rollins solos. At least those modern guys make you think of Jackson Pollock or Tobey, it's easy to see that they've left the age of the pianola and the box of watercolours."

"He's capable of believing in progress in art," Oliveira said yawning. "Don't pay any attention to him, Ronald, and with that hand you have free dig out that little record of the *Stack O'Lee Blues*, when all's said and done I think it has a fine piano solo on it."

"That business about progress in art is ancient nonsense," Étienne said, "but in jazz as in any art there's always a flock of fakers. Music that can be translated into emotion is one thing, but emotion which pretends to pass as music is another. Paternal grief in F sharp, sarcastic laughter in yellow, violet and black. No, my boy, it's hard to say where art begins, but it's never that stuff."

No one seemed disposed to contradict him because Wong had quietly appeared with the coffee and Ronald, shrugging his shoulders, had turned loose Fred Waring and his Pennsylvanians and after a terrible scratching they reached the theme that fascinated Oliveira, an anonymous trumpet followed by the piano, all wrapped up in the smoke of an old record-player and a bad recording, of a corny pre-jazz band, all in all like those old records, showboats, Storyville nights, where the old only really universal music of the century had come from, something that brought people closer together and in a better way than Esperanto, UNESCO or airlines, a music which was primitive enough to have gained such universality and good enough to make its own history, with schisms, abdications, and heresies, its Charleston, its Black Bottom, its Shimmy, its Fox Trot, its Stomp, its Blues, to label its forms, this style and the other one, swing, bebop, cool, a counterpoint of romanticism and classicism, hot and intellectual jazz, human music, music with a history in contrast to stupid animal dance music, the polka, the waltz, the *zamba*, a music that could be known and liked in Copenhagen as well as in Mendoza or Cape Town, a music that brings adolescents together, with records under their arms, that gives them names and melodies to use as passwords so they can know each other and become intimate and feel less lonely surrounded by bosses, families, and bitter love affairs, a music that accepts all imaginations and tastes, a collection of instrumental 78s with Freddie Keppard or Bunk Johnson, the reactionary cult of Dixieland, an academic specialization in Bix Beiderbecke, or in the adventures of Thelonious Monk, Horace Silver or Thad Jones, the vulgarities of Erroll Garner or Art Tatum, repentance and rejection, a preference for small groups, mysterious recordings with false names and strange titles and labels made up on the spur of the moment, and that whole freemasonry of Saturday nights in a student's room or in some basement café with girls who would rather dance to *Stardust* or *When Your Man Is Going to Put You Down*, and have a sweet slow smell of perfume and skin and heat, and let themselves be kissed when the hour is late and somebody has put on *The Blues with a Feeling* and hardly anybody is really dancing, just standing up together, swaying back and forth, and everything is hazy and dirty and lowdown and every man is in a mood to tear off those warm girdles as his hands go stroking shoulders and the girls have their mouths half-opened and turn themselves over to delightful fear and the night, while a trumpet comes on to possess them in the name of all men, taking them with a single hot phrase that drops them like a cut flower into the arms of their partners, and there comes a motionless race, a jump up into the night air, over the city, until a miniature piano brings them to again, exhausted, reconciled, and still virgins until next Saturday, all of this from a kind of music that horrifies solid citizens who think that nothing is true unless there are programmes and ushers, and that's the way things are and jazz is like a bird who migrates or emigrates or immigrates or transmigrates, roadblock jumper, smuggler, something that runs and mixes in and tonight in Vienna Ella Fitzgerald is singing while in Paris Kenny Clarke is helping open a new *cave* and in Perpignan Oscar Peterson's fingers are dancing around and Satchmo, everywhere, with that gift of omnipresence given him by the Lord, in Birmingham, in Warsaw, in Milan, in Buenos Aires, in Geneva, in the whole world, is inevitable, is rain and bread and salt, something completely beyond national ritual, sacred traditions, language and folklore: a cloud without frontiers, a spy of air and water, an archetypal form, something from before, from below, that brings Mexicans together with Norwegians and Russians and Spaniards, brings them back into that obscure and forgotten central flame, clumsily and badly and precariously he delivers them back to a betrayed origin, he shows them that perhaps there have been other paths and that the one they took was maybe not the only one or the best one, or that perhaps there have been other paths and that the one they took was the best, but that perhaps there were other paths that made for softer walking and that they had not taken those, or that they only took them in a halfway sort of way, and that a man is always more than a man and always less than a man, more than a man because he has in himself all that jazz suggests and lies in wait for and even anticipates, and less than a man because he has made an aesthetic and sterile game out of this liberty, a chessboard where one must be bishop or knight, a definition of liberty which is taught in schools, in the very schools where the pupils are never taught ragtime rhythm or the first notes of the blues, and so forth and so on.

> I could sit right here and think a thousand miles away,
> I could sit right here and think a thousand miles away,
> Since I had the blues this bad, I can't remember the day.

(–97)

18

There was no use asking himself what he was doing there at that time and with that group, those dear friends strangers still yesterday and tomorrow, people who were but a fleeting episode in place and time. Babs, Ronald, Ossip, Jelly Roll, Akhnaton: what difference did it make? The same shadows from the same green candles. A binge at its highest moment. Doubtful vodka, terribly strong.

If he could have conceived of an extrapolation of all this, understanding the Club, understanding the *Cold Wagon Blues*, understanding La Maga's love, understanding every thread that would become unravelled from the cuff of things and reach down to his fingers, every puppet and every puppeteer, like an epiphany; understanding them, not as symbols of some other unattainable reality perhaps, but as agents of potency (such language, such lack of decorum), just like lines of flight along a track that he ought to follow at this very moment, disentangling himself from the Eskimo pelt which was so delightfully warm and so scented and so Eskimo that it was frightening, getting down to the level of things, down, down in a solo flight, down to the corner, the corner all by itself, Max's café, Max all by himself, the streetlight on the Rue de Bellechase where . . . where alone. And maybe from that moment on.

But all on a level that could be called me-ta-phy-si-cal. Because Horacio, words . . . That is to say that words, for Horacio . . . (a question mulled over many times in moments of insomnia). Taking La Maga's hand, taking it in the rain as if it were cigarette smoke, something that is part of one, in the rain. To make love with her again but a little bit on her side, less easy indifference, a denial that at best is swamped by the uselessness of the effort, the straw man teaching algorithms in some hazy university to grubby swots or colonels' daughters. If all this, the predawn tapioca starting to stick to the skylight, La Maga's so sad face as she looked at Gregorovius looking at La Maga looking at Gregorovius, *Struttin' With Some Barbecue*, Babs who was crying again, hidden from Ronald who was not crying but who hid his face in the sticky smoke, the vodka transformed into a truly saintly halo, Perico the Spanish ghost up on a stool of disdain and Pavlovian stylistics, if everything were able to be extrapolated, if everything just *did not exist*, if he were there just so somebody (anybody, but he at the moment, because he was the one who was doing the thinking, in any case he was the one who knew that he was really thinking, eh, Cartesius, you old fuck), so that somebody could extract from all that was going on by striving and biting and especially by delving, it was hard to say how but by delving down to the very dregs, that out of all this there might pop up some grasshopper of peace, some cricket of contentment, that a person might be able to enter any gate and come into any garden, an allegorical garden as far as the others were concerned, just as mandalas are allegorical for everyone else, and in that garden he would find a flower and that flower would be La Maga, or Babs, or Wong, but described and describing itself, reconstituted outside their appearances among the Club, back to what they were, emerged, dawning, at best this all might be just a nostalgic view of the earthly paradise, an ideal of purity, except that purity had come to be inevitably the product of simplification, the bishop moves, rooks move, the knight jumps, pawns fall away, and in the centre of the board, big as anthracite lions the kings remain flanked by the cleanest and last and purest of their armies, at dawn the deciding lances will be crossed, fate will be served, peace will reign. A pureness as of coitus between crocodiles, not the pureness of oh Mary my mother with dirty feet; a pureness of a slate roof with doves who naturally shit on the heads of ladies wild with rage and radishes, a pureness of . . . Horacio, Horacio, please.

Pureness.

(Enough. Come on. Go home, take a bath, read *Our Lady of Paris* or *The She-Wolves of Machecoul*, finish your binge. Extrapolation, what a word.)

Pureness. Horrible word. Pea-your, then ness. Think about it a bit. Brisset and his plays on words. Why are you crying? Who's crying, huh?

Pea-your, understand it like an epiphany. Damn language. To understand. Not to make sense: to understand. A hint of a paradise that can be won again: it cannot be that we are here in order not to be. Brisset? Man descends from the level of the frogs . . . Blind as a bat, drunk as a butterfly, *foutu, royalement foutu devant les portes que peut-être* . . . (An ice-cube on the back of his neck, go to bed. Problem: Johnny Dodds or Albert Nicholas? Dodds, he was almost sure of it. Note: ask Ronald.) A bad line of poetry floating down from the skylight: "*Antes de caer en la nada con el último diástole* . . ." High as a kite. The doors of perception by Aldley Huxdous. Get yourself a tiny bit of mescaline, brother, the rest is bliss and diarrhoea (all in English). But let's get serious (yes, it was Johnny Dodds, you find the proof by indirection. The drummer had to be Zutty Singleton, ergo the clarinet is Johnny Dodds, jazzology, deductive science, particularly easy after four o'clock in the morning. Hardly advisable for ladies and clerics). Let's get serious, Horacio, before we struggle up in a while and head for the street, let's ask ourselves a question while we have our soul in the palm of our hand (the palm of the hand? In the palm of our tongue, or something like that. Toponymy, anatology, descriptology, two volumes with il-lus-tra-tions), let's ask whether we should attack from above or from below (but, hey now, I'm making sense, the vodka has pinned them like butterflies onto a tray, A is A, a rose is a rose is a rose, April is the cruellest month, everything in its place and a place for every rose is a rose is a rose . . .)

Huf. Beware the Jabberwocky my son.

Horacio slid down a little more and saw very clearly everything he wanted to see. He wasn't sure whether he should attack from above or from below, with a concentration of all his forces or rather as now, dispersed and liquid, full forward to the skylight, against the green candles, or to La Maga's sad, sheeplike face, or against Ma Rainey who was singing *Jelly Bean Blues.* Better this way, spread out and receptive, spongy, the way everything is spongy as long as a person looks a lot and has good eyes. He wasn't so drunk that he didn't have the feeling that his house was a shambles, that inside nothing was in place but at the same time – to be sure, marvellously sure – on the floor or on the ceiling, under the bed or floating in a washbasin there were stars and chunks of eternity, poems like suns and enormous faces of women and cats where the fury of their species was fired up, in the mixture of garbage and jade plaques in their own language where words were woven night and day into furious battles between ants and centipedes, blasphemy existed with the pure mention of essences, the perfect image with the basest slang. Disorder was triumphant and ran through the rooms with its hair entangled in disgusting braids, glass eyes, its hands holding cards that would not meld, letters without heading or signature, and the soup was getting cold upon the table, the floor was covered with cast-off pants, rotten apples, stained bandages. And suddenly from all this there came some horrid music, it was beyond the felted order of homes where untouchable kin put things in order, in the midst of the confusion where the past was incapable of finding a button on a shirt and the present shaved itself with pieces of a broken bottle because it could not find a razor stuck away somewhere in some flowerpot, in the midst of a time which opened up like a weather vane to whatever wind was blowing, a man breathed until he could no longer do so, he felt that he had lived until he reached the delirium of the very act of taking in the confusion which surrounded him and he asked himself if any of this had meaning. All disorder had meaning if it seemed to come out of itself, perhaps through madness one could arrive at that reason which is not the reason whose weakness is madness. "To go from disorder to order," thought Oliveira. "Yes, but what kind of order can there be which does not mimic the basest, most debased, and most unhealthy of disorders? The order of the gods is called cyclone or leukaemia, the poet's order is called antimatter, firm space, flowers of trembling lips, God, I'm drunk, Jesus, I've got to get to bed." And La Maga was crying, Guy had disappeared, Étienne had left after Perico, and Gregorovius, Wong and Ronald were looking at a record that was spinning slowly, thirty-three and a third revolutions per minute, no more no less, and in these revolutions there was *Oscar's Blues*, Oscar himself on piano, of course, a certain Oscar Peterson, a certain pianist half tiger, half felt, a certain sad, fat pianist, a guy on piano and the rain on the skylight, all those things, literature, after all.

(–153)

19

"I think I understand you," La Maga said, running her hand through his hair. "You're looking for something you don't know. I've been doing the same thing and I don't know what it is either. But they're two different things. What you were talking about the other night . . . Yes, you're a Mondrian and I'm a Vieira da Silva."

"So," Oliveira said, "I'm a Mondrian after all."

"Yes, Horacio."

"You meant to say someone of a rigorous nature."

"I said a Mondrian."

"And didn't it occur to you that behind this Mondrian there might lurk a Vieira da Silva reality?"

"Yes, but up till now you haven't come out of the Mondrian reality. You're afraid, you want to be sure of yourself. I don't know . . . You're more like a doctor than a poet."

"Forget about poets," Oliveira said. "And don't try to hurt Mondrian with the comparison."

"Mondrian is wonderful, but he doesn't let you breathe. I always strangle a little bit inside. And when you start talking about the search for unity, then I start to see a lot of beautiful things, but they're all dead, pressed flowers and things like that."

"Let's see, Lucía: are you quite sure what unity is?"

"My name is Lucía but you don't have to call me that," La Maga said. "Unity, of course I know what it is. You're trying to say that everything in your life comes together so that you can see it all at the same time. Is that what you mean?"

"More or less," Oliveira conceded. "It's incredible how hard it is for you to grasp abstract ideas. Unity, plurality . . . Can't you feel them without feeling the need for examples? Can't you? Let's see, now: your life, do you think it is a unity?"

"No, I don't think so. It's pieces, things that happened to me."

"But you in turn went through those things like the string went through those green stones. And speaking of stones, where did you get that necklace?"

"Ossip gave it to me," La Maga said. "It was his mother's, the one from Odessa."

Oliveira sucked slowly on his *mate*. La Maga went over to the cot that Ronald had lent them so that they could have Rocamadour in the apartment. With the cot and Rocamadour and the complaints of the tenants there was barely any living-space left, but nobody could tell La Maga that Rocamadour would have been better off in a children's hospital. It had been necessary to go with her to the country the same day that Madame Irène had sent the telegram, wrap Rocamadour up in a bunch of rags and blankets, put him to bed, stoke up the fire in the stove, tolerate Rocamadour's wailing when the time came for a suppository or a pill or the bottle which was useless in covering up the taste of the medicine he had to take. Oliveira made himself another *mate* and out of the corner of his eye looked at the cover of a *Deutsche Grammophon Gesellschaft* that Ronald had lent him, wondering when he could listen to it without getting Rocamadour wailing and twisting. He was horrified by La Maga's laziness with Rocamadour's nappies, the way she would sing at him to distract him, the smell that emanated from his bed, cotton, wails, the stupid assurance of La Maga that it wasn't anything, that if she did what she should for her son he would be all right in a matter of days. It made no sense, it was all maybe, maybe not. What was he doing there? A month ago they both had had their places still, even after they had decided to live together. La Maga had said that they could save money this way, they only had to buy one paper a day, they wouldn't waste food. She could iron his clothes, and heat, electricity . . . Oliveira had been about to admire that brusque attack on common sense. He finally accepted because old Trouille was having troubles and owed him close to thirty thousand francs, at the time it seemed just as logical to live with La Maga as by himself, he had been walking around thinking about every detail and pondering every little thing that seemed to come upon him like a great crisis. He had come to the conclusion that the continuous presence of La Maga would stop him from speculating so much, but naturally he had not thought about the possibilities of Rocamadour. Even so, he had been able to keep to himself from time to time, until Rocamadour's howls would bring him back to a healthy grouchiness. "I'm going to end up like a character out of Walter Pater," Oliveira would think to himself. "One soliloquy after another, an endless vice. Marius the Epicurean, 'pure vice'. The only salvation left to me is the smell of that brat's piss."

"I always suspected you would end up going to bed with Ossip," Oliveira said.

"Rocamadour has a fever," La Maga said.

Oliveira made himself another *mate*. He had to watch out for his *mate*, in Paris it cost five hundred francs a kilo in chemists and it was terrible stuff, sold in the pharmacy of Saint-Lazare station next to a gaudy sign that said "*maté sauvage, cueilli par les indiens*", diuretic, antibiotic, and emollient. Luckily the lawyer from Rosario, who happened to be his brother, had sent him ten pounds of Cruz de Malta brand, but there wasn't much left. "If my *mate* runs out I've had it," Oliveira thought. "My only real conversation is with this green gourd." He studied the strange behaviour of the *mate*, how the herb would breathe fragrantly as it came up on top of the water and how it would dive as he sucked and would cling to itself, everything fine lost and all smell except for that little bit that would come up in the water like breath and stimulate his Argentinian iron lung, so sad and solitary. It had been some time now that Oliveira had been paying attention to unimportant things, and the little green gourd had the advantage that as he meditated upon it, it never occurred to his perfidious intelligence to endow it with such ideas as one extracts from mountains, the moon, the horizon, an adolescent girl, a bird, or a horse. "This *mate* might show me where the centre is," Oliveira thought (and the idea that La Maga and Ossip were seeing each other became frail and lost its strength, for a moment the green gourd was stronger, it proposed its own little petulant volcano, its smoky crater; an atmosphere which hovered over the other rather cold air of the flat in spite of the stove that had been lit around nine o'clock that night). "And just what is this centre that I don't know what it really is; can it be the coordinates of some unity? I'm walking back and forth in an apartment whose floor is tiled with flat stones and one of these stones is the exact spot where I ought to stop so that everything would come into its proper focus. The exact spot," Oliveira said emphatically, kidding himself a little so as to know that he was not just playing with words. "A shapeless quadrilateral in which we must look for the precise angle (and the importance of this example is that the angel is horribly a cute and won must have his knows right up on to the canvas so that suddenly all the senseless lines will come together to form a portrait of Francis I or the Battle of Sinigaglia, something that deflies descrumption)." But that unity, the sum of all the actions which define a life, seemed to go into hiding in the face of any previous sign that life itself could end like a played-out drink of *mate*, that is to say that only those left behind, the biographers, would recognize the unity, and all that was really not of the least importance as far as Oliveira was concerned. The problem consisted in grasping that unity without becoming a hero, without becoming a saint, or a criminal, or a boxing champ, or a statesman, or a shepherd. To grasp unity in the midst of diversity, so that that unity might be the vortex of a whirlwind and not the sediment in a clean, cold *mate* gourd.

"I'm going to give him a quarter of an aspirin," La Maga said.

"If you can make him take it you'll be better than Ambroise Paré," said Oliveira. "Come and have a *mate*, I just made some."

The idea of unity was worrying him because it seemed so easy to fall into the worst traps. When he had been a student on the Calle Viamonte around 1930, he had found out (first) to his surprise and (later) with irony, that an awful lot of people would set themselves up comfortably in a supposed unity of person which was nothing but a linguistic unity and a premature sclerosis of character. These people would set up a system of principles which had never been fundamentally proven, and which were nothing more than a concession to the word itself, to a verbal idea of strength; rejection and attraction were subjected, displaced, got out of the way, then replaced by their verbal equivalents. And in this way duty, morals, the immoral and the amoral, justice, charity, the European and the American, day and night, wives, sweethearts, and girlfriends, the army and the bar, the flag and Yankee or Moscow gold, abstract art and the Battle of Caseros came to be like teeth and hair, something accepted and inevitably incorporated, something which was not alive or capable of being analysed because *that's the way it is* and it makes us what we are, fulfils and strengthens. Man's rape by word, the masterful vengeance of word upon its progenitor, all this filled Oliveira's thoughts with bitter lack of confidence, forced to seek help from the enemy itself to open a path to the point where he might just be able to be dismissed and follow it – but with what means on what clear night or shady day? – until he could reach a complete reconciliation with himself and with the reality in which he lived. To arrive at the word without words (how far, how improbable), to grasp a deep unity without recourse to reasoning conscience, something that when all was said and done would be like sitting there sipping *mate* and looking at Rocamadour's little bottom up in the air as La Maga's fingers came and went with bits of cotton, and Rocamadour wailed because he could not stand being plucked at.

(–90)

20

"I always suspected you'd end up going to bed with him," Oliveira said.

La Maga put a clean nappy on her son, who was not bleating as much now, and wiped her hands with a piece of cotton wool.

"Please wash your hands like a civilized person," Oliveira said, "and get rid of all that crap."

"Right away," La Maga said. Oliveira was able to stand her look (which was always hard on him) and La Maga got a newspaper, opened it up on the bed, put in the cotton wool, bundled it up, and left the room to go and throw it down the toilet on the landing. When she came back her hands were red and shining; Oliveira handed her the gourd. She sat down on the low easy chair and sucked the *mate* in a deliberate sort of way. She always damaged the gourd, moving the straw around from one side to another as if she were mixing batter.

"After all," Oliveira said, blowing smoke through his nose, "the least you could have done was to tell me. Now it's going to cost me six hundred francs to hire a taxi to move my stuff. And it's not easy finding a room these days, either."

"You don't have to move out," La Maga said. "How long do you plan to go on lying to yourself?"

"Lying to yourself," Oliveira said. "You sound like a bestselling novel from the Río de la Plata. All you have to do now is laugh with all the force of your insides at my unparalleled boorishness, and we can put it all in print."

"He's stopped crying," La Maga said, looking at the bed. "Let's speak quietly, he'll go to sleep quite easily with the aspirin. I never in my life went to bed with Gregorovius."

"Oh yes you did."

"No, Horacio. Why wouldn't I have told you? Ever since I met you I haven't had any other lover but you. I don't care if I sound stupid and you laugh at the way I say it. I speak the best way I can, I don't know how to say what I feel."

"OK, OK," Oliveira said in a tired tone, having another *mate*. "Maybe your son has changed you then. For some time now you've been converted into what they call a mother."

"But Rocamadour is sick."

"All right," Oliveira said, "if that's the way you want it. But I see a different kind of change. Really, it's that we can't stand much of each other any more."

"You're the one who can't stand me. You're the one who can't stand Rocamadour."

"That's true. I hadn't thought about the boy. Three is too many for one room. And to think that with Ossip it will be four is more than I can take."

"Ossip has nothing to do with this."

"Please put the kettle on," Oliveira said.

"He has nothing to do with this," La Maga repeated. "Why do you want to make me suffer, silly? I know you're tired of me and don't love me any more. You never did love me, it was something else, some kind of dream you had. Leave, Horacio, you don't have to stay. The same thing has happened to me so many times . . . "

She looked over at the bed. Rocamadour was asleep.

"So many times," Oliveira said, putting fresh *yerba mate* into his gourd. "You have a remarkable frankness when it comes to amorous autobiography. Just ask Ossip. To meet you and hear the story about the Negro is one and the same thing."

"I have to tell it, you don't understand."

"I don't understand, but it's awful."

"I think I have to tell it even if it is awful. It's only right that a woman tell a man what her life has been like if she wants to. I'm talking about you, not Ossip. You could have told me about your girlfriends or not if you wanted to, but I had to tell everything. You know, it's the only way to get rid of a man before you start to fall in love with someone else, the only way to get them out the door so the two of us can be alone in the room."

"A kind of ceremony of expiation, and maybe propitiatory too. First the Negro."

"Yes," La Maga said, looking at him. "First the Negro. Then Ledesma."

"Then Ledesma, of course."

"And the three up the alley, on carnival night."

"Ahead," said Oliveira, sipping his *mate*, as he remembered an obscene game he played as a boy in Buenos Aires and kept it up to show his exasperation.

"And Monsieur Vincent, the hotel keeper's brother."

"Behind."

"And a soldier who was weeping in a park."

"Ahead."

"And you."

"Behind. But the idea of putting me on the list in my presence just bears out my gloomiest premonitions. You really should have recited the complete list to Gregorovius."

La Maga stirred with the straw. She had lowered her head and her hair fell over her face all at once, covering up the expression that Oliveira had been studying with an indifferent air.

Después fuiste la amiguita
de un viejo boticario
y el hijo de un comisario
todo el vento te sacó

Oliveira was singing the old tango in a low voice. La Maga sucked on the straw and shrugged her shoulders, not looking at him. "Poor thing," Oliveira thought. He reached out his hand and drew her hair back, brutally, as if opening a curtain. The straw made a dry sound between her teeth.

"It's almost as if you had slapped me," La Maga said, putting two fingers to her trembling lips. "I really don't care, but . . . "

"You just do happen to care," Oliveira said. "If you hadn't been looking at me like that I would have despised you. You're a marvel, Rocamadour and everything."

"What good is it for me for you to say that?"

"It's good for me."

"Yes, it's good for you. Everything's good for you if it helps you keep on searching."

"Sweet," Oliveira said softly, "it's a known fact that tears ruin the taste of *mate*."

"Maybe my crying is good for you too."

"Yes, it is as long as you hold me to blame."

"Go away, Horacio, that's the best thing."

"It probably is. But look, anyway, if I leave now I will be committing an act that would be awfully close to heroism, I mean, leaving you alone and with a sick child."

"Yes," La Maga said with a Homeric smile coming out from behind her tears. "Awfully close to heroism, yes."

"And since I'm by no stretch a hero, I think I'd better stay until we find out what we can adjust ourselves to, as my brother says in his elegant style."

"Stay then."

"But you do understand how and why I reject that heroic course?"

"Yes, certainly."

"Come on, explain to me why I'm not leaving."

"You're not leaving because you're just bourgeois enough to think what Ronald and Babs and your other friends would say."

"Precisely. I'm glad you see that you didn't figure in my decision at all. I'm not staying out of friendship or out of pity or because someone has to give Rocamadour his bottle. And much less because you and I still have something in common."

"You're so funny sometimes," La Maga said.

"Sure I am," Oliveira said. "Bob Hope is just a turd next to me."

"When you said that we didn't have anything in common any more, you held your mouth in a certain way."

"Sort of like this, eh?"

"Yes, it's incredible."

They had to take out their handkerchiefs and cover their faces with both hands, they let out such loud guffaws that Rocamadour might wake up, it was something terrible. Although Oliveira tried to hold her, biting his handkerchief and weeping with laughter, La Maga slowly slipped out of the chair which had the front legs shorter than the rear ones and so helped her slide down until she was on the floor caught between Oliveira's legs as he laughed with a sort of jerky hiccup and finally spit out the handkerchief in one last burst.

"Show me the face again, the one I make when I say things like that," Oliveira begged.

"Like this," La Maga said and again they rolled around until Oliveira doubled over holding his stomach, and La Maga saw his face opposite hers, and his eyes shining at her among the tears.

They kissed backwards, she face up and he with his hair hanging down like a fringe, they kissed and bit each other a little because their mouths did not recognize one another, they were kissing different mouths, trying to find each other with their hands in a devilish mess of hanging hair and *mate*, which was dripping onto La Maga's skirt from the gourd which had tipped over on the edge of the table.

"Tell me how Ossip makes love," Oliveira whispered, putting his lips hard against La Maga's. "The blood is rushing to my head, I can't do this much longer, it's frightening."

"He does it very well," La Maga said, biting his lip. "Much better than you and much longer."

"But does he retilate your murt? Don't lie to me. Does he really retilate it?"

"A lot. Everywhere, sometimes too much. It's a wonderful feeling."

"And does he make you put your plinnies in between his argusts?"

"Yes, and then we trewst our porcies until he says he's had enough, and I can't take it any more either, and we have to hurry up, you understand. But you wouldn't understand that, you always stay in the smallest gumphy."

"Me or anybody else," Oliveira grumbled, getting up. "Christ, this *mate* is lousy, I'm going out for a while."

"Don't you want me to keep on talking to you of Ossip?" said La Maga. "In Gliglish."

"I'm getting sick of Gliglish. Besides, you haven't got any imagination, you always say the same things. Gumphy, some invention that is. And you don't say 'talking to you of'."

"I invented Gliglish," La Maga said resentfully. "You come out with anything you want and sound like a million dollars, but that's not real Gliglish."

"Getting back to Ossip . . . "

"Don't be silly, Horacio, I tell you I have not gone to bed with him. Do I have to give you the sacred oath of the Sioux Indians?"

"No, I think I'm finally beginning to believe you."

"And later on," La Maga said, "I'll probably end up sleeping with Ossip, but you'll be the one who wanted it all along."

"But do you really think you could like that guy?"

"No. The fact is I owe money at the chemist's. I don't want a penny from you, and I can't borrow money from Ossip and just leave him with his illusions intact."

"I see now," Oliveira said. "Your good Samaritan side is coming out. You couldn't leave that soldier crying in the park either."

"No I couldn't, Horacio. You can see how different we are."

"Yes, pity was never one of my strong points. But I could have been crying at a time like that too, and then you would have . . . "

"I can't picture you crying," La Maga said. "You'd consider it a waste."

"I've cried in the past."

"Only from rage. You don't know how to cry, Horacio, it's one of those things you don't know how to do."

Oliveira pulled La Maga over and sat her down on his lap. He thought about the Maga smell, the back of the Maga neck, and it made him sad. It was that same smell that once before . . . "To find out what's behind something," he thought confusedly. "Yes, that's one of the things I don't know how to do, that and crying and having pity."

"We were never in love," he said, kissing her hair.

"Speak for yourself," La Maga said, closing her eyes. "You have no way of telling whether I'm in love with you or not. You don't even know how to do that."

"Do you think I'm so blind?"

"On the contrary, I think it might do you some good to be a little blind."

"Ah, yes. Touch replaces definitions, instinct goes beyond intelligence. The magic route, the dark night of the soul."

"It would do you good," La Maga insisted as she always did when she did not understand something and wanted to cover up.

"Look, I know enough to know that everybody can go his own way. I think that I have to be alone, Lucía; in all truth, I don't know what I'm going to do. It's not fair to you or to Rocamadour who I think is waking up for me to treat you so badly and I don't want it to go on that way."

"You don't have to worry about me or about Rocamadour."

"I'm not worried, but the three of us are getting under each other's feet, it's uncomfortable and unaesthetic. I may not be blind enough for you, sweetie, but my optic nerve is good enough to let me see that you are going to get along perfectly well without me. No girlfriend of mine has ever committed suicide, even though my pride bleeds when I admit it."

"Yes, Horacio."

"So if I can summon up enough heroism to run out on you tonight or tomorrow, we can say that nothing happened here."

"Nothing," La Maga said.

"You can take your kid back to Madame Irène's, and you can come back to Paris and pick up where you left off."

"That's right."

"You'll see a lot of movies, keep on reading novels, you'll take walks and risk your life in the worst neighbourhoods at the worst hours."

"Yes, all that."

"You'll pick up a lot of strange things in the street, you'll bring them home, and you'll make something out of them. Wong will teach you sleight-of-hand tricks and Ossip will follow six feet behind you with his hands clasped in an attitude of humble reverence."

"Please, Horacio," La Maga said, hugging him and burying her face.

"Of course we will meet by magic in the strangest places, like that night in the Place de la Bastille, remember?"

"On the Rue Daval."

"I was quite drunk and you came around the corner and we stood looking at one another like idiots."

"Because I thought you were going to a concert that night."

"And you had told me that you had an appointment with Madame Léonie."

"That's why we thought it was so funny meeting on the Rue Daval."

"You were wearing your green sweater and you had stopped to console a pederast."

"They had beaten him up and thrown him out of a café, and he was crying so."

"Another time I remember we met near the Quai de Jemmapes."

"It was hot."

"You never told me what you were looking for along the Quai de Jemmapes."

"Oh, I wasn't looking for anything."

"You had a coin in your hand."

"I found it on the edge of the pavement. It was shining."

"Then we went to the Place de la République where the acrobats were and we won a box of sweets."

"They were awful."

"And another time I was coming out of the movies in Mouton-Duvernet and you were sitting in a pavement café with a Negro and a Filipino."

"And you never told me what you were doing in Mouton-Duvernet."

"I was going to a chiropodist," Oliveira said. "He had a waiting room papered with violet and reddish-purple scenes: gondolas, palm trees, and lovers embracing in the moonlight. Think of it, the same thing repeated five hundred times in six-by-four-inch squares."

"That's why you went, not because of the calluses."

"They weren't calluses, my dear. I had a genuine wart on the sole of my foot. Due to a vitamin deficiency, I think."

"Did it go away?" La Maga asked, raising her head and looking at him with great intensity.

Rocamadour woke up at the first burst of laughter and began to whimper. Oliveira sighed, now they would go through the same thing all over again, for a while he would see La Maga only from behind as she leaned over the bed, her hands moving back and forth. He began to prepare some *mate* and took out a cigarette. He didn't want to think. La Maga went to wash her hands and came back. They both reached for the gourd and scarcely glanced at one another.

"The best thing about all this," said Oliveira, "is that we're not in competition with the soap operas. Don't look at me like that; if you think a little you'll figure out what I mean."

"I've figured it out," La Maga said. "That's not why I'm looking at you like this."

"Oh, you think maybe . . . "

"A little, yes. But let's not talk again."

"You're right. Well, I think I'll take a little walk."

"Don't come back," La Maga said.

"Come on, let's not carry this to extremes," Oliveira said. "Where do you expect me to sleep tonight? Gordian knots are one thing, but the wind in the street is another. It must be minus five out there."

"It would be better if you didn't come back," La Maga said. "It's easy for me to say it right now, understand?"

"Well, anyway," Oliveira said, "I think we ought to be congratulated on our *savoir faire*."

"I feel so sorry for you, Horacio."

"Oh no; hold it right there."

"You know that sometimes I really can see. I see things so clearly. To think that an hour ago I thought the best thing to do would be to go and jump in the river."

"Body of an unidentified woman found in Seine . . . But you swim like a swan."

"I feel sorry for you," La Maga repeated. "I can see now. That night we met behind Notre-Dame I also saw that . . . But I refused to believe it. You were wearing a lovely blue shirt. It was the first time we went to a hotel, wasn't it?"

"No, but that doesn't make any difference. And you taught me to speak Gliglish."

"If I were to tell you that I did it all out of pity."

"Come off it," Oliveira said, looking at her with surprise.

"You were in danger that night. It was obvious, like a siren in the distance . . . I can't explain it."

"The only dangers for me are metaphysical," Oliveira said. "They're not going to haul me out of the water with grappling hooks, believe me. I will explode from an intestinal occlusion, the Asian flu, or a Peugeot 403."

"I don't know," La Maga said. "Sometimes I think about killing myself, but then I can see that I'm not going to do it. Don't think that it's only because of Rocamadour, it was the same before he came. The idea of killing myself always makes me feel good. But you never think about it . . . Why did you say metaphysical dangers? There are also metaphysical rivers, Horacio. You're going to jump into one of those rivers."

"It would have to be the Tao," said Oliveira.

"I thought I could have protected you. Don't tell me. Then right away I saw you didn't need me. We made love like two musicians who got together to work over some sonatas."

"What you're saying is delightful."

"That's how it was, the piano on one side and the violin on the other and out of that the sonata came, but you can see now that underneath it all we never really met. I realized it at once Horacio, but the sonatas were so beautiful."

"Yes, love."

"And Gliglish."

"Sure."

"And everything, the Club, that night on the Quai de Bercy under the trees, when we hunted stars until dawn and told stories about princes, and you were thirsty and we bought a bottle of expensive champagne, and we drank it on the river bank."

"And then a *clochard* came along and we gave him half the bottle."

"And the *clochard* knew a lot of Latin and Oriental things and you were talking to him about something like . . . Averroes, I think."

"Yes, Averroes."

"And the night the soldier patted my behind in the Foire du Trône and you punched him in the face and they arrested all of us."

"Don't let Rocamadour hear," Oliveira said laughing.

"Luckily Rocamadour won't ever remember anything about you, there's still nothing behind his eyes. Like the birds who eat the crumbs you throw them. They look at you, they eat the crumbs, they fly away . . . Nothing left."

"Yes," Oliveira said. "Nothing left."

The woman who lived on the third floor was shouting on the landing, drunk as usual at that hour. Oliveira glanced vaguely at the door, but La Maga drew him to her, and she slipped down to grasp his knees, trembling and weeping.

"Why are you torturing yourself that way?" Oliveira asked. "Metaphysical rivers are flowing everywhere. You don't have to go very far to find one. Look, no one has as much right to drown as I have, dopey. I promise you one thing: I'll remember you in my last moments so that they'll be all the more bitter. A real cheap novel, with a cover in three different colours."

"Don't leave," La Maga murmured, hugging his legs.

"I just want to walk around a little, that's all."

"No, don't leave."

"Let me go. You know very well I'm going to come back, at least for tonight."

"Let's go out together," La Maga said. "Look, Rocamadour is asleep, he'll be quiet until it's time for his bottle. We've got two hours, let's go to that café in the Arab quarter, that sad little café where we feel so good."

But Oliveira wanted to go out alone. Slowly he began to extract his legs from La Maga's embrace. He stroked her head, he ran his fingers around her neck, he kissed the back of it, he kissed her behind an ear, listening to her cry as her hair hung down over her face. "No blackmail," he thought. "Let's cry face to face, but not that cheap sobbing you pick up from the movies." He raised her face up, he made her look at him.

"I'm the bastard," Oliveira said. "Let me take care of paying myself back. Cry over your son, who could be dying for all we know, but don't waste your tears on me. Jesus, I bet there hasn't been a scene like this since Zola's times. Please let me leave."

"Why?" La Maga asked without getting up from the floor, looking at him like a dog.

"Why why?"

"Why?"

"Oh, you mean why all this. You'll find out, I don't think that either you or I is too much to blame. We're not grown up yet, Lucía. It's a virtue, but it costs a lot. Children always end up pulling each other's hair when they've finished playing. That's the way it probably is. Think about it."

(–126)

21

The same thing happens to everybody, the statue of Janus is a useless waste, the *truth* is that after forty years of age we have our real face on the back of our heads, looking desperately backwards. It is what in all truth is called a *commonplace.* You can't do anything about it, that's about the strength of it, with the words that come twisting out from between the bored lips of one-faced adolescents. Surrounded by boys in baggy sweaters and delightfully dirty girls in the smoke of the *cafés-crème* of Saint-Germain-des-Prés who read Durrell, Beauvoir, Duras, Douassot, Queneau, Sarraute, here I am a Frenchified Argentinian (horror of horrors), already beyond the adolescent vogue, the cool, with an *Etes-vous fous?* of René Crevel anachronistically in my hands, with the whole body of surrealism in my memory, with the mark of Antonin Artaud in my pelvis, with the *Ionisations* of Edgard Varèse in my ears, with Picasso in my eyes (but I seem to be a Mondrian, at least that's what I've been told).

"*Tu sèmes des syllabes pour récolter des étoiles,*" Crevel kids me.

"One does what he can," I answer.

"And that female, *n'arrêtera-t-elle donc pas de secouer l'arbre à sanglots?*"

"You're unfair," I tell him. "She's just crying a little bit, it's little more than a complaint."

It's sad to reach the point in life where it's easier to open a book to page ninety-six and converse with the author, from café to grave, from boredom to suicide, while at the tables around people are talking about Algeria, Adenauer, Mijanou, Bardot, Guy Trébert, Sidney Bechet, Michel Butor, Nabokov, Zao-Wu-Ki, Luison Bobet, and in my country the boys do talk, what do the boys talk about in my country? I don't know any more, I'm so far away, but they don't talk about Spilimbergo any more, they don't talk about Justo Suárez, they don't talk about the Shark of Quillà, they don't talk about

Bonini, they don't talk about Leguisamo. *It's all quite natural.* The catch is that nature and reality become enemies for some unknown reason, there is a time when nature sounds horribly false, when the reality of age twenty rubs elbows with that of age forty and on each elbow there is a razor-blade which slashes our jackets. I discover new worlds which are simultaneous and alien, and every time I get the feeling more and more that to agree is the worst of illusions. Why this thirst for universality, why this struggle against time? I also read Sarraute and look at a picture of Guy Trébert in handcuffs, but those are *things that happen to me*, while if I must be the one who decides, it's almost always in a backward direction. My hand pokes around the bookcase, I take down Crevel, I take down Roberto Arlt, I take down Jarry. Today fascinates me, but always from the point of view of yesterday (did I say phascinate?), and that's how at my age the past becomes present and the present is a strange and confused future where boys in baggy sweaters and long-haired girls drink their *cafés-crème* and pet each other with the slow gracefulness of cats or plants.

We must fight against this.

We must establish ourselves in the present once more.

It seems that I am a Mondrian, therefore . . .

But Mondrian painted his present forty years ago.

(A picture of Mondrian looking exactly like a typical orchestra conductor (Julio de Caro, *ecco!*) with glasses and plastered-down hair and stiff collar, with the frightful air of a clerk dancing with a waterfront whore. What kind of present did Mondrian feel while he was dancing? Those canvases of his, that picture of him . . . Ab-bysses.)

You're getting old, Horacio. Quintus Horatius Oliveira, you're getting old, Flaccus. You're getting flaccid and old, Oliveira.

"*Il verse son vitriol entre les cuisses des faubourgs*," Crevel mocks.

What am I going to do? In the midst of this great disorder I still think I'm a weather vane that after every spin must show where north or south lies. It takes little imagination to call someone a weather vane: you see the spins but never the intention, the point of the arrow which tries to huddle down and hide in the river of the wind.

There are metaphysical rivers. Yes, my love, of course. And you are taking care of your son, crying from time to time, and here it is another day with another yellow sun that doesn't warm. *J'habite à Saint-Germain-des-Prés, et chaque soir j'ai rendez-vous avec Verlaine. / Ce gros pierrot n'a pas changé, et pour courir le guilledou* . . . Twenty francs in the slot and Leo Ferré will sing to you of his loves, or Gilbert Bécaud, or Guy Béart. Back in my country: *Si quiere ver la vida color de rosa / Eche veinte centavos en la ranura* . . . Better turn on the radio (the rent falls due next Monday, I thought I'd better tell you) and listen to some chamber music, probably Mozart, or have you put on some record with the volume turned low so as not to wake up Rocamadour. And I don't think you're really aware that Rocamadour is very sick, terribly weak and sick, and that he would get better care in a hospital. But I can't talk about these things with you any more, let's say it's all over and I'm wandering around here, walking up and down trying to find north, south, if I really am looking for them. If I really am looking for them. But if I'm not, what's this all about? Oh, my love, I miss you, I feel the pain of you in my skin, in my throat, every time I breathe it's as if an emptiness came into my chest where you no longer are.

"*Toi*," Crevel says, "*toujours pret à grimper les cinq étages des pythonisses faubouriennes, qui ouvrent grandes les portes du futur* . . ."

And why not, why shouldn't I go looking for La Maga, most of the time it was just a case of putting in an appearance, going along the rue de Seine to the arch leading into the Quai de Conti and I would see her slender form against the olive-ashen light which floats along the river on the Pont des Arts, we used to go along there in search of shadows, to eat fried potatoes in the Faubourg Saint-Denis, to kiss by the barges on the Saint-Martin canal. With her I would feel a new air come over me, the fantastic patterns of the sunset or the way things would put themselves in patterns when we would be together by the bars of the Cour de Rohan and the tramps would ascend into the fearful moonlit world of witnesses and judges . . . Why shouldn't I love La Maga and possess her beneath all those ceilings purchased for six hundred francs, in beds with musty and unravelled spreads, for in that crazy hopscotch, in that race of moneybags I recognized myself and called myself by name, finally and until I would escape from time and all its labelled monkey-cages, where from its show windows Omega Electron Girard Perregaud Vacheron & Constantin marked the hours and the minutes of sacrosanct castrating obligations, into an atmosphere where the last bonds were being loosed and pleasure was a mirror of reconciliation, a mirror for larks but a mirror, something like a sacrament from one being to another, a dance around the altar, a coming on of sleep with mouth to mouth, sometimes without untangling ourselves, our sexes warmly joined, our necks like twining vegetative signposts, our hands determinedly caressing thigh and neck . . .

"*Tu t'accroches à des histoires*," Crevel says. "*Tu étreins des mots . . .*"

"No, old man, that's more like what they do across the ocean, which you know nothing about. It's been a long time since I went to bed with words on. I still wear them, like you or anybody else, but I give them a good brushing before I put them on."

Crevel is distrustful and I understand why. A whole canefield of words has grown up between La Maga and me, we have only been separated by a few hours and a few blocks and my sorrow is already *called* sorrow, and my love is *called* love . . . I shall keep on feeling less and less and remembering more and more, but what is memory if not the language of feeling, a dictionary of faces and days and smells which repeat themselves like the verbs and adjectives in a speech, sneaking in behind the thing itself, into the pure present, making us sad or teaching us vicariously until one's self itself becomes a vicar, the backward-looking face opens its eyes wide, the real face slowly becomes dim as in old pictures and Janus is suddenly any one of us. I'm saying all of this to Crevel but I'm speaking to La Maga, now that we're so far apart. And I don't talk to her with the words that only used to serve to make us misunderstand each other, now that it's too late I begin to choose others, hers, the ones wrapped up in what she understands and which has no name, sparks and emanations which crackle in the air between two bodies or which can fill a room or a line of poetry with gold dust. But isn't this the way we have been living, softly slashing at each other? No, that's not the way; she might have wanted to, but once again I imposed the false order that hides chaos pretending that I was dedicated to a profound existence while all the time it was one that barely dipped its toe into the terrible waters. There are metaphysical rivers, she swims in them like that swallow swimming in the air, spinning madly around a belfry, letting herself drop so that she can rise up all the better with the swoop. I describe and define and desire those rivers, but she swims in them. I look for them, find them, observe them from the bridge, but she swims in them. And she doesn't know it, any more than the swallow. It's not necessary to know things as I do, one can live in disorder without being held back by any sense of order. That disorder is her mysterious order, that bohemia of body and soul which opens its true doors wide for her. Her life is not disorder except for me, buried among the prejudices I despise and respect at the same time. Me, inexorably condemned to be pardoned by La Maga who judges me without knowing it. Oh, let me come in, let me see some day the way your eyes see.

Useless. Condemned to be acquitted. Go home and read Spinoza. La Maga doesn't know who Spinoza is. La Maga reads tedious Russian and German novels and Pérez Galdós and forgets immediately after what she has read. She will never suspect that she has condemned me to read Spinoza. A strange judge, a judge with her hands, with her racing down the street, a judge because she can just look at me and leave me naked, a judge by being silly and unhappy and upset and dull and less than anything. By everything I have known from my bitter knowledge, with my rusty slide rule of a college graduate and enlightened man, by all of that, a judge. Fall down, swallow, with those sharp scissors with which you cut the sky of Saint-Germain-des-Prés, pluck out these eyes that look without seeing, I have quickly been condemned without appeal to those blue gallows to which the hands of the woman caring for her son have raised me, let the execution be quick, quickly back to the false order of being alone and recovering one's self-sufficiency, self-knowledge, self-awareness. And with so much knowledge a useless anxiety to pity something, to have it rain here inside, so that at long last it will start to rain and smell of earth and living things, yes, living things at long last.

(–79)

22

Opinion had it that the old man had slipped, that the car had jumped the red light, that the old man had tried to commit suicide, that things were getting worse than ever in Paris, that traffic was terrible, that it was not the old man's fault, that it was the old man's fault, that the brakes on the car were not working right, that the old man had been frightfully careless, that living was getting more expensive every day, that there were too many foreigners in Paris who didn't understand the traffic laws and were taking work away from Frenchmen.

The old man didn't seem to be hurt too badly. He was smiling weakly and stroking his moustache. An ambulance arrived, they put him on a stretcher, the driver of the car kept gesticulating and explaining the accident to the policeman and to the onlookers.

"He lives at 32 Rue Madame," said a blond boy who had been speaking to Oliveira and others who had stopped. "He's a writer, I know him. He writes books."

"The bumper hit his legs, but the driver already had the brakes on."

"It hit him in the chest," the boy said. "The old man slipped on some shit in the street."

"It hit him on the legs," Oliveira said.

"It all depends on your point of view," said an enormously short man.

"It hit him in the chest," the boy said. "I saw it with my own two eyes."

"In that case . . . Shouldn't someone tell his family?"

"He doesn't have any family, he's a writer."

"Oh," said Oliveira.

"He has a cat and lots of books. Once I delivered a package to him for the concierge and he invited me in. There were books all over the place. Something like this was bound to happen to him, writers are so absent-minded. That'll be the day, when I get hit by a car . . . "

A few drops of rain began to fall and they immediately dissolved the circle of witnesses. Putting up the collar of his lumberjacket, Oliveira turned his nose into the cold wind and began to walk in no direction in particular. He was sure that the old man had not been seriously injured, but he kept on seeing his face, which could almost be described as placid, perplexed maybe, as they carried him in the stretcher and spoke friendly comforting words to him, "*Allez, pépère, c'est rien, ça!*" from the stretcher-bearer, a redhead who must have said the same thing to everybody. "A complete lack of communication," Oliveira thought. "It's not so much that we're alone, that's a well-known fact that any fool can plainly see. Being alone is basically being alone on a certain level in which other lonelinesses could communicate with us if that were the case. But bring on any conflict, an accident in the street or a declaration of war, provoke the brutal crossing of different levels, and a man who is perhaps an outstanding Sanskrit scholar or a quantum physicist becomes a *pépère* in the eyes of the stretcher-bearer who arrives on the scene. Edgar Allan Poe on a stretcher, Verlaine in the hands of a sawbones, Nerval and Artaud facing psychiatrists. What could that Italian Galen have known about Keats as he bled him and helped him die of hunger? If men like them are silent, as is most likely, the others will triumph blindly, without evil intent, of course, without knowing that the consumptive over there, that injured man lying naked on that bed, are doubly alone, surrounded by beings who move about as if behind a glass, from a different place in time . . . "

Stopping in a doorway he lit a cigarette. It was towards the end of the afternoon and groups of girls were coming out of offices, with the need to laugh, to speak in shouts, to push each other, to soak up just this quarter-of-an-hour's worth before falling back into the world of beef and weekly magazines. Oliveira kept on walking. Without having to dramatize, the smallest bit of objectivity would bring out into the open all the absurdity of Paris, the gregarious life. Since he had been thinking about poets, it was easy to remember all of those who had denounced the solitude of man among his fellows, the comedy of greetings, the "excuse me" when people met on the stairs, the seat that is given to women on the underground, the brotherhood observed in politics and sports. Only a biological and sexual optimism is capable of covering up the isolation of some, no matter what John Donne might have felt about it. Contacts made in action in tribes in work in bed on the sports ground were contacts between branches and leaves which reached out and caressed each other from tree to tree while the trunks stood there disdainfully and irreconcilably parallel. "*Underneath it all* we could be what we are on the surface," Oliveira thought, "but we would have to live in a different way. And what does it mean to live in a different way? Maybe to live absurdly in order to do away with the absurd, to dive into one's self with such force that the leap will end up in the arms of someone else. Yes, maybe love, but that *otherness* lasts only as long as a woman lasts, and besides only as everything concerns that woman. Basically there is no such thing as otherness, maybe just that pleasant thing called togetherness. Of course, that is something . . . " Love, an ontologizing ceremony, a giver of being. And that is why he was thinking only now of what he should have thought about in the beginning: without the possession of self, there was no possession of otherness, and who could really possess himself? Who had come back from himself, from that absolute solitude which meant not even being in one's own company, having to go to the movies or to a whorehouse or to friends' houses or to get involved in a time-consuming profession or in marriage so that at least one could be alone-along-with-all-the-others? That's how, paradoxically, solitude would lead to the heights of sociability, to the great illusion of the company of others, to the solitary man in a maze of mirrors and echoes. But people like him and so many others (or those who reject themselves but know themselves close up) got into the worst paradox, the one of reaching the border of otherness perhaps and not being able to cross over. That true otherness made up of delicate contacts, marvellous adjustments with the world, could not be attained from just one point; the outstretched hand had to find response in another hand stretched out from the beyond, from the other part.

(–62)

23

Standing on a corner, fed up with the rarified atmosphere of his musing (and the fact that he kept on thinking, he didn't know why, about the injured old man lying in a hospital bed surrounded by doctors and medical students and nurses, amiably impersonal as they asked him his name, age, occupation, told him it wasn't anything, that they would take care of him right away with shots and dressings), Oliveira had begun to look at what was going on around him and how any street corner in any city was the perfect illustration of what he had been thinking and almost took his work away from him. In the café, protected from the cold (a matter of going in and having a glass of wine), a group of bricklayers were talking with the man behind the bar. Two students were reading and writing at one table and Oliveira saw them look up and look at the bricklayers, go back to their books or notebooks, look up again. From one glass cage to another, look, withdraw, look: that's all there was to it. Up above the pavement section of the café, which was closed, a young woman on the second floor seemed to be sewing or cutting out a dress by the window. Her upswept hair was moving in time to what she was doing and Oliveira tried to picture her thoughts, her shears, her children who would be coming back from school any moment now, her husband finishing work in an office or in a bank. The bricklayers, the students, the woman, and now a tramp turned the corner of the street with a bottle of red wine sticking out of his pocket, pushing a baby carriage filled with old newspapers, tin cans, torn and dirty clothes, a headless doll, a package with a fishtail sticking out. The bricklayers, the students, the woman, the tramp, and in a booth looking like someone condemned to the pillory, LOTERIE NATIONALE, an old woman with unrepatriated bits of straggly hair popping out from underneath a kind of grey bonnet, blue mittens on her hands, TIRAGE MERCREDI, waiting but not in wait for customers, a charcoal brazier by her feet, encased in her vertical coffin, motionless, half-frozen, offering good fortune and thinking God knows what, clots of ideas, senile commonplaces, the teacher who used to give her sweets when she was a girl, a husband killed on the Somme, a travelling-salesman son, at night her garret without running water, a three-day soup, *boeuf bourguignon* which is cheaper than a cut of meat, TIRAGE MERCREDI. The bricklayers, the students, the tramp, the lottery woman, every group, everybody in his glass cage, but let an old man fall under a car and right away there is a general running to the scene of the accident, an animated exchange of opinion, of criticism, disparities and coincidences until it starts to rain again and the bricklayers go back to the bar, the students to their table, the X's to X and the Z's to Z.

"Only by living absurdly is it possible to break out of this infinite absurdity," Oliveira repeated. "But Jesus, I'm going to get soaked, I've got to get under somewhere." He spotted the posters of the Salle de Géographie and took refuge in the doorway. A lecture about Australia, the unknown continent. A meeting of the disciples of the Christ of Monfavet. A piano concert by Madame Berthe Trépat. Open registration for a course on meteors. Win a black belt in judo in five months. A lecture on the urbanization of Lyons. The piano concert was going to start very soon and it didn't cost much. Oliveira looked at the sky, shrugged his shoulders, and went in. He thought vaguely about going to Ronald's or to Étienne's studio, but it was better to leave that for night-time. He didn't know why, but he thought it was funny for an artist to be named Berthe Trépat. He also thought it was amusing that he was taking refuge in a concert to get away from himself for a little while, an ironic illustration of what he had been thinking about while he was wandering about the streets. "We're nothing," he thought, as he passed 120 francs at tooth-level to the old woman caged up in the ticket booth. He got a ticket in the tenth row out of the pure perversity of the old woman, since the concert was about to start and there was nobody else except a few old bald heads, a few old beards, and some others who partook of both qualities, who had an air of being from the neighbourhood or from the family, two women between forty and forty-five with old coats and dripping umbrellas, a few young people, couples mostly and arguing strenuously with shoves and the noise of sweets being chewed and the squeaking of the old Vienna seats. Twenty people in all. It smelled like a rainy afternoon, the big theatre was cold and damp, and one could hear talking backstage behind the backdrop. An old man had lit his pipe and Oliveira was quick to dig out a Gauloise. He didn't feel too well, one of his shoes was full of water, and the musty smell and the smell of wet clothes bothered him a little. He took a deep drag, getting the cigarette hot and making it fall apart. A deaf-mute buzzer sounded outside, and one of the young people began to clap vigorously. The ancient usher, with her beret pulled to one side and make-up on that she surely must have slept in, closed a curtain at the back of the hall. At that point Oliveira remembered that they had given him a programme. It was a sloppy mimeographed sheet on which he could make out with some effort that Madame Berthe Trépat, gold medallist, would play the *Three Discontinuous Movements* of Rose Bob (première), the *Pavan for General Leclerc*, by Alix Alix (first time for a civilian audience) and the *Délibes–Saint-Saëns Synthesis*, by Délibes, Saint-Saëns, and Berthe Trépat.

"Shit," Oliveira thought. "What a fucking programme."

Somehow a double-chinned, white-haired gentleman appeared behind the piano. He was dressed in black and his pink hand fingered a chain that hung across his fancy waistcoat. Oliveira thought he noticed grease spots on the waistcoat. A young lady in a purple raincoat and gold-rimmed glasses started to applaud in a flat tone. With a croaking voice that had an extraordinary resemblance to that of a macaw, the double-chinned old man introduced the concert by explaining that Rose Bob was a former pupil of Madame Berthe Trépat and that the *Pavan* by Alix Alix had been written by a distinguished army officer who concealed himself behind that modest pseudonym, and that both pieces were written in the most rigorous observation of the most modern form of musical composition. As for the *Délibes–Saint-Saëns Synthesis* (and here the old man rolled his eyes on high), it represented for contemporary music one of the most profound innovations to which the composer, Madame Trépat, had given the name "prophetic syncretism". The term was quite precise, since the musical genius of Délibes and Saint-Saëns tended towards osmosis, towards interfusion and the interphonic approach which had become paralyzed by the excessively individualistic interpretation of Western music and thus prevented from surging forth into a higher and more synthetic creation which had been awaiting the genius and intuition of Madame Trépat. In fact, her sensitivity had discovered affinities which most listeners had missed and she had undertaken the noble but arduous task of being the mediumistic bridge by which the meeting of these two noble sons of France was to be consummated. It was pre-eminently the moment to remind everyone that in addition to her activities as a music teacher, Madame Berthe Trépat would soon be celebrating her twenty-fifth anniversary as a composer. The speaker would not take it upon himself in a simple introduction to a concert, much as he would like to, to go on at deserving length with an analysis of Madame Trépat's musical accomplishments, because the audience was growing impatient. In any case, and so that he could give the key to those who would be hearing for the first time the works of Rose Bob and Madame Trépat, he would sum up their art by mentioning antistructural constructions, that is to say, autonomous cells of sound, the result of pure inspiration, held together by the general intent of the work but completely free of classical moulds, dodecaphonic or atonal (he stressed the last two words). Thus, for example, the *Three Discontinuous Movements* by Rose Bob, one of Madame Trépat's favourite students, had their start in the reaction aroused in the spirit of the composer by the sound of a door being slammed shut, and the thirty-two chords which made up the first movement were the resulting repercussions of that sound on the aesthetic plane; the speaker did not think that he would be violating a confidence if he told his cultured audience that the technique employed in the composition of the *Saint-Saëns Synthesis* was based on the most primitive and esoteric forces of creation. He would never forget the rare privilege he had had of being present at one phase of the synthesis as Madame Trépat held a dowsing pendulum over the scores of the two masters in order to choose those passages whose influence upon the pendulum corroborated the astounding intuitions of Madame Trépat. And although he could say much more, the speaker felt that he should retire after saluting in Madame Berthe Trépat one of the beacons of French genius and a pathetic example of how the general public lives in ignorance of misunderstood genius.

His jowls were shaking and the old man, seized by a fit of coughing and emotion, withdrew behind the curtains. Forty hands gave out with a dry applause and several matches lost their heads.

Oliveira slouched in his seat as far as possible and felt better. The old man in the accident must have been feeling better too in his hospital bed, sunk in the sleepiness which follows shock, that happy interregnum in which one abdicates self-government and the bed becomes a ship, with paid vacations, any break at all with daily routine. "I'm almost capable of going to visit him one of these days," Oliveira said to himself. "But at best I would just spoil his desert island and become the footprint in the sand. God, but you're getting sentimental."

The applause made him open his eyes and observe the hard work Madame Berthe Trépat was putting into her bow of thanks. Before he had even taken a good look at her face, her shoes had stopped him in his tracks, men's shoes, incapable of disguise by any skirt. Square and heelless, with useless feminine ribbons. What followed up from them was both stiff and broad, a fat-lady stuck into a merciless corset. But Berthe Trépat was not really fat; the best you could say was that she was robust. She must have had sciatica or lumbago, something which made her move all at once, frontally now, waving with effort, and then from the side, outlined between the stool and the piano and folding herself geometrically until seated. From that position the artist turned her head around brusquely and bowed again, although the applause had stopped. "Somebody up above must be pulling strings," Oliveira thought. He liked marionettes and puppets, and he was expecting miracles of prophetic syncretism. Berthe Trépat looked at the audience once more, all the sins of the moon suddenly seemed concentrated in her face that appeared to be covered with flour, and her cherry-red mouth opened up to assume the shape of an Egyptian barge. Profile once again, her little parrot-beak nose pointed for a moment at the keyboard while her hands perched on the keys from C to B like two dried-up chamois bags. The thirty-two chords of the first discontinuous movement began to sound. There were five seconds between the first and the second, fifteen between the second and third. On arriving at the fifteenth chord, Rose Bob had decided on a pause of twenty-five seconds. Oliveira, who at first had appreciated the good Weberian use of silence that Rose Bob was making use of in her pauses, noticed that overuse was rapidly dissipating the effect. Between chords seven and eight there was coughing, between twelve and thirteen somebody struck a match noisily, between fourteen and fifteen he clearly heard the expression "*Ah, merde alors!*" contributed by a young blonde girl. Around the twentieth chord one of the more ancient ladies, a real virginal pickle, gripped her umbrella and opened her mouth to say something that was mercifully swallowed up by the twenty-first chord. Amused, Oliveira looked at Berthe Trépat, suspecting that the pianist was studying them all with what is called the corner of her eye. Out of that corner of the hook-nosed profile of Berthe Trépat a celestial grey glance seemed to come, and it occurred to Oliveira that probably the poor woman was counting the house. At chord twenty-three a man with a neat, round bald spot got up indignantly and after snorting and huffing left the hall, digging in his heels during the eight-second silence ordained by Rose Bob. After chord twenty-four the pauses began to get smaller, and between twenty-eight and thirty-two there was a rhythm like that of a dirge which could not help but have some effect. Berthe Trépat took her shoes off the pedals, put her left hand in her lap, and started on the second movement. This movement lasted for only four bars, each of three notes of equal value. The third movement consisted mainly in coming from the extreme registers of the keyboard and in approaching the middle chromatically, repeating the operation back out again, all in the midst of triplets and other adornments. At a given moment, which no one could foresee, the pianist stopped playing and stood up quickly, bowing with an air which seemed to bespeak a challenge, but in which Oliveira seemed to discern a note of insecurity or even fear. One couple applauded madly; Oliveira found himself applauding in turn and not knowing why (and when he found out why he got angry and stopped applauding). Berthe Trépat went back to her profile almost at once and ran her finger over the keyboard while she waited for them to quieten down. She began to play the *Pavan for General Leclerc.*

In the two or three minutes that followed, Oliveira had some trouble in dividing his attention between the extraordinary stew that Berthe Trépat was boiling up at full steam and the furtive or forthright way in which young and old were leaving the concert. A mixture of Liszt and Rachmaninoff, the *Pavan* was the tiresome repetition of two or three themes which then got lost in innumerable variations, bits of bravura (rather poorly played, with holes and stitching everywhere) and the solemnities of a catafalque upon a caisson, broken by sudden fireworks which seemed to delight the mysterious Alix Alix. Once or twice Oliveira was worried that the towering Salammbô hairdo of Berthe Trépat would suddenly collapse, but who knows how many hairpins were reinforcing it, amidst the rumble and tumble of the *Pavan.* The orgiastic arpeggios which announced the end came on, and three themes were successively repeated (one of which had been lifted bodily from Strauss's *Don Juan*) and Berthe Trépat let the chords rain down with growing intensity, modified by the hysterical repetition of the first theme and two chords composed of the gravest notes, the last of which came out markedly false for the right hand, but it was something that could happen to anyone and Oliveira applauded warmly; he had really enjoyed it.

The artist turned around to face the audience with one of her rare springlike motions and bowed. Since she seemed to be counting the house with her eyes, she could not have failed to calculate that there were no more than eight or nine people left. With dignity Berthe Trépat went off stage left, and the usher drew the curtain and sold sweets to the audience.

On the one hand he wanted to leave, but all during the concert there had been an atmosphere which had fascinated Oliveira. After all, poor Madame Trépat had been trying to present works in première, which in itself was a great thing in this world of the polonaise, the clair de lune, and the ritual fire dance. There was something moving about that face of a burlap-stuffed doll, of a plush turtle, of an immense nitwit stuck in a rancid world of chipped teapots, old women who had heard Risler play, art and poetry lectures in halls covered with old wallpaper, of budgets of forty thousand francs a month and furtive borrowing from friends to get through the month, the cult of au-then-tic Akademia Raymond Duncan art, and it was easy to imagine what Alix Alix and Rose Bob looked like, the base calculations before renting the hall, the mimeographed programme done by some well-meaning pupil, the fruitless lists of people to invite, the empty feeling backstage when they saw the empty hall and still had to go on, gold medal and all, she still has to go on. It was almost a chapter out of Céline and Oliveira felt himself incapable of thinking beyond the general atmosphere, beyond the useless and defeatist survival of such artistic activities among groups of people equally defeated and useless. "Of course it had to be my fate, getting stuck inside this moth-eaten set-up," Oliveira raged to himself. "An old man underneath a car, and now Madame Trépat. And let's not think about the lousy weather outside or about myself. Above all, let's not talk about myself."

Four people were left in the hall, and he thought it best to go and sit in the first row to provide a bit more company for the pianist. He was amused by this act of solidarity, but as soon as he was seated at the front he lit a cigarette. For some reason a woman decided to leave at the exact moment at which Berthe Trépat had come back on stage, and she took a strong look at her before she drew herself up to make a bow to the empty hall. Oliveira thought that the woman who had left deserved a hard kick in the arse. He suddenly realized that all of his reactions came from a certain sympathy for Berthe Trépat, in spite of the *Pavan* and Rose Bob. "It's been a long time since something like this happened to me," he thought. "I wonder if I'm getting soft with age." So many metaphysical rivers and suddenly he wants to go visit the old man in the hospital, or he is surprised to find himself applauding this madwoman in a corset. Strange. It must be the cold, his wet shoes.

The *Délibes–Saint-Saëns Synthesis* must have been going on for three minutes or so when the couple who had been the mainstay of the audience that remained got up and ostentatiously left. Again Oliveira thought he could make out a sideglance from Berthe Trépat, but now it was as if her hands had gone stiff, she bent over the piano and with tremendous effort, taking advantage of every pause to glance out of the corner of her eye at the seats where Oliveira and a peaceful-looking man were listening with what seemed to be the signs of rapt attention. The prophetic syncretism was not long in revealing its secret, even for a layman like Oliveira: three measures of *Le Rouet d'Omphale* were followed by four more from *Les Filles de Cadix*, then her left hand offered "*Mon coeur s'ouvre à ta voix*", while the right one spasmodically interspersed the theme of the bells from *Lakmé*, together they passed successively into the *Danse Macabre* and *Coppélia*, until other themes which the programme attributed to the *Hymne à Victor Hugo*, *Jean de Nivelle* and *Sur les bords du Nil* alternated showily with the better-known ones, and as far as prophetic was concerned, nothing could have been more successful, as was shown by the soft laughter of the peaceful-looking man while as a person of good breeding he covered his mouth with his glove, and Oliveira had to admit the guy was right, that he shouldn't be asked to be quiet, and Berthe Trépat must have felt the same because she kept making more and more mistakes, it seemed as if her hands had become paralysed, she kept leaning forward shaking her forearms and raising her elbows like a hen settling into her nest. "*Mon coeur s'ouvre à ta voix*," "*Où va la jeune hindoue?*" again two syncretic chords, a stray arpeggio, *Les Filles de Cadix, tra-la-la-la*, like a hiccup, several notes together (surprisingly) in the manner of Pierre Boulez, and the peaceful-looking man let out a sort of bellow and ran out holding his gloves up to his mouth, just as Berthe Trépat lowered her hands and looked fixedly at the keyboard, and a long second passed, an interminable second, something desperately empty between Oliveira and Berthe Trépat alone in the hall.

"Bravo," Oliveira said, understanding that applause would have been out of place. "Bravo, madame."

Without standing up Berthe Trépat turned a little on the stool and put her elbow on middle C. They looked at each other. Oliveira got up and went to the edge of the stage.

"Very interesting," he said. "Really, madame, I listened to your concert with real interest."

What a bastard.

Berthe Trépat looked at the empty hall. One of her eyelids was trembling a little. She seemed to be asking herself something, waiting for something. Oliveira sensed that he should keep on talking.

"An artist like you must be aware of the lack of understanding and the snobbery of the public. Deep down I know that you were playing for yourself."

"For myself," Berthe Trépat repeated in a macaw voice strikingly similar to that of the gentleman who had introduced her.

"For whom, then?" Oliveira asked, climbing onto the stage with the ease of a dreamer. "An artist can only count on the stars, as Nietzsche said."

"Who are you?" Berthe Trépat was startled.

"Oh, someone who is interested in manifestations . . ." He could have run words together the way he always did. All he could say was that he was here, looking for a little companionship without really knowing why.

Berthe Trépat was listening, still a little absent. She got up with difficulty and looked at the hall, the curtains.

"Yes," she said. "It's getting late. I've got to go home." She had said it to herself as if it were a punishment or something.

"Could I have the pleasure of accompanying you for a while?" said Oliveira as he leaned forward. "I mean if no one is waiting for you in your dressing room or at the stage door."

"There's no one. Valentin left after he introduced me. What did you think of the introduction?"

"Interesting," Oliveira said, more and more certain that he was dreaming and that he wanted to keep on dreaming.

"Valentin can do better," Berthe Trépat said. "And I thought it was nasty of him . . . yes, nasty . . . to leave the way he did, as if I were some old rag."

"He spoke of you and your work with great admiration."

"For five hundred francs he would speak about a dead fish with great admiration. Five hundred francs!" Berthe Trépat was lost in her thoughts.

"I'm playing the fool," Oliveira told himself. He bowed and got down off the stage; maybe she had forgotten about his offer. But she was looking at him and Oliveira saw that she was crying.

"Valentin is a swine. All of them . . . there were more than two hundred people, you saw them, more than two hundred. That's remarkable for a première, don't you think? And they all paid, don't think we sent out any complimentary tickets. Over two hundred, and now you're the only one left. Valentin left, I . . . "

"Some absences can mean a real success," Oliveira said in some incredible way.

"But why did they leave? Did you see them go? Over two hundred, I tell you, and prominent people, I'm sure I spotted Madame de Roche, Doctor Lacour, Montellier, the teacher whose pupil got the latest grand prize in violin . . . I don't think they liked the *Pavan* too much and that's why they left, don't you think? Because they left before my *Synthesis*, that's for certain, I saw them myself."

"Of course," Oliveira said. "You have to admit, the *Pavan* . . . "

"It isn't really a pavan at all," Berthe Trépat said. "It's a piece of shit. It's Valentin's fault, they warned me that Valentin was sleeping with Alix Alix. Why do I have to keep a queer, young man? Me, gold medallist, I'll show you my notices, hits, in Grenoble, in Puy . . . "

The tears were running down to her throat and getting lost among the withered pores of her ashen skin. She took Oliveira's hand and shook it. At any moment she was going to become hysterical.

"Why don't you get your coat and we'll get out of here," Oliveira said hurriedly. "The outside air will do you good, we can have something to drink, for me it would be a great . . . "

"Something to drink," Berthe Trépat repeated. "Gold medal."

"Whatever you want," Oliveira said incongruously. He made a motion to free himself, but the pianist gripped his arm and came closer. Oliveira could smell the sweat of the concert mixed with naphthaline and benzoin (as well as piss and cheap perfume). First Rocamadour and now Berthe Trépat, it was unbelievable. "Gold medal," she kept saying, crying and snuffling. Suddenly a great sob shook her as if a chord had burst into the air. "And it's the same old thing . . . " Oliveira finally understood as he fought in vain to get away from personal feelings, to take refuge in some metaphysical river, naturally. Offering no resistance, Berthe Trépat let herself be led back towards the curtains where the usher was looking at them, holding a torch and a feathered hat.

"Doesn't Madame feel well?"

"It's emotion," Oliveira said. "She's getting over it now. Where is her coat?"

Among easels and creaky tables, a harp and a coatrack, there was a chair with a green raincoat on it. Oliveira helped Berthe Trépat, who kept her head down but was not crying any more.

They went out through a little door and along a dark passageway and came out on the boulevard. It was drizzling.

"It'll be hard getting a taxi," said Oliveira, who barely had three hundred francs in his pocket. "Do you live far?"

"No, near the Panthéon, I'd really rather walk."

"Yes, it would be better."

Berthe Trépat moved ahead slowly, swaying her head from side to side. The hood of the raincoat gave her a martial look or something like Ubu Roi. Oliveira huddled into his lumberjacket and pulled the collar up high. The air was crisp, he was beginning to get hungry.

"You're very nice," she said. "You shouldn't bother. What did you think of my *Synthesis*?"

"I'm just an amateur, madame. Music for me, if I can say so . . . "

"You didn't like it," Berthe Trépat said.

"A première . . . "

"We worked for months with Valentin. Night and day, trying to bring the inspirations together."

"Of course you must admit that Délibes – "

"Is a genius," Berthe Trépat said. "Erik Satie admitted it one day in my presence. And no matter what Doctor Lacour says about Satie's pulling my leg . . . what would you say. Of course, you must know what the old man was like . . . But I can read people, young man, and I know full well that Satie was convinced, yes, convinced. What country are you from, young man?"

"From Argentina, madame, and I'm really not a young man, by the way."

"Ah, Argentina. The pampas . . . And do you think they would be interested in my work there?"

"I'm sure of it, madame."

"Maybe you could get me an appointment with the Ambassador. If Thibaud was able to go to Argentina and Montevideo, why not me, I play my own music. You must have noticed that, it's basic: my own music. Almost always premières."

"Do you do much composing?" Oliveira asked and felt like a mouthful of vomit.

"I'm working on my Opus 83 . . . no, let's see . . . Now that I think of it, I should have spoken with Madame Nolet before I left . . . It concerns money, of course. Two hundred people, that means . . . " It was lost in a murmur, and Oliveira asked himself whether it wouldn't really be more merciful to tell the truth outright, but she already knew, of course she knew.

"It's scandalous," Berthe Trépat said. "Two years ago I played in the same hall, Poulenc promised to come . . . Do you understand? Poulenc himself. I was at the pinnacle of inspiration that afternoon, it was too bad that a last-minute commitment stopped him from coming . . . but you know, musicians who are all the rage . . . And that was the time that Madame Nolet charged me half the take," she added angrily. "Exactly half. Of course it came out the same, counting on two hundred people . . . "

"Madame," Oliveira said, taking her softly by the arm and leading her into the Rue de Seine, "the lights were out and maybe you had trouble seeing how many people there were."

"Oh, no," Berthe Trépat said. "I'm sure I'm right, but you've made me lose track. Excuse me, I have to work out . . . " She was lost again in a dedicated whispering, and she kept on moving her lips and fingers, completely unaware of where Oliveira was taking her, and almost even of his presence. Everything she was saying aloud she could have said to herself, Paris is full of people who go along the street talking to themselves, Oliveira himself was no exception, in fact the exception was that he was playing the fool as he walked along beside the old woman seeing this tarnished puppet home, this poor blown-up balloon in which stupidity and madness were dancing the real night-time pavan. "It's repulsive, I ought to fling her down against a step and stamp on her face, squash her like an insect, make her fall apart like a piano dropped from the tenth floor. True charity would be to get her out of her world, stop her from suffering like a dog with all her illusions which even she does not believe, which she builds up so that she will not feel the wetness in her shoes, her empty room, or that dirty, white-haired old man. She repels me and I'm going to disappear at the next corner, and who will know, after all. What a day, my God, what a day."

If they could only get to the Rue Lobineau he would take off like a bat and the old woman could get on home by herself. Oliveira looked behind, he waited for the right moment, shaking his arm as if something were hanging down from it, something that had sneaked up and was hanging from his elbow. But it was Berthe Trépat's hand there, clinging with resolution. Berthe Trépat was hanging on with all her might to Oliveira's arm and he was looking out for the Rue Lobineau as he helped her cross the street and went with her towards the Rue de Tournon.

"They must have lit the stove by now," Berthe Trépat said. "It's not that the weather is so cold, really, but we artists like our warmth. Don't you think so? You must come up and have a drink with Valentin and me."

"Oh, no, madame," Oliveira said. "No indeed, it's been a great pleasure and honour just to have seen you home, besides – "

"Don't be so modest, young man. You are young, you know, isn't that so? I can tell that you're young, your arm for example . . . " Her fingers dug a little into the sleeve of his lumberjacket. "I always look older than I am. You know, an artist's life . . . "

"Of course," Oliveira said. "As for me, I'm over forty, so you've been flattering me."

That's how the words came out of his mouth and he couldn't help it, it was too much, really. Hanging on to his arm Berthe Trépat talked about other times and every so often she would stop in the middle of what she was saying and seem to be putting something back together in her mind. Sometimes she would stick a finger in her nose and look at Oliveira out of the corner of her eye; in order to stick her finger up her nose she would quickly pull off her glove, pretending that she wanted to scratch the palm of her hand (after delicately removing it from Oliveira's arm), and would raise it up with a motion worthy of a pianist to scratch one nostril for a split second. Oliveira pretended to look away, and when he looked back again Berthe Trépat was clinging to his arm again with her glove back on. They went along like that in the rain talking about many things. On passing the Luxembourg they spoke about life in Paris, more difficult every day, the pitiless competition of young people whose inexperience was matched only by their insolence, a public that was incurably snobbish, the price of beef in the Saint-Germain market or on the Rue de Buci, places where the elite go to get a good cut of meat at reasonable prices. Two or three times Berthe Trépat had asked Oliveira in a friendly sort of way what he did for a living, about his ambitions, and especially about his failures, but before he could reply everything suddenly had to do with Valentin's inexplicable disappearance, the mistake of playing Alix Alix's *Pavan* out of consideration for Valentin, but that was the last time that would happen. "A queer," Berthe Trépat muttered, and Oliveira felt her hand tighten on his lumberjacket. "Me, mind you, having to play a shapeless piece of shit for that bastard when I have fifteen pieces of my own that are waiting to be played in public . . ."

Then she would stop in the rain, peaceful inside her raincoat (but Oliveira began to feel water coming in through the collar of his lumberjacket, a collar made from rabbit skin or rat skin, which had begun to stink like a cage in the zoo, it always did that whenever it rained and there was nothing he could do about it), and stand there looking at him as if waiting for an answer. Oliveira smiled in a warm sort of way, tugging at her a little to lead her towards the Rue de Médicis.

"You're too modest, too reserved," Berthe Trépat was saying. "Tell me about yourself, let's see. I'll bet you're a poet, right? So was Valentin when we were young . . . The *Evening Ode*, a hit in the

Mercure de France . . . A card from Thibaudet. I can remember it as if it had been just this morning. Valentin was weeping in bed, whenever he had to cry he would lie face down on the bed, it was very touching."

Oliveira tried to picture Valentin crying face down on the bed but all that came to mind was a little Valentin red as a crab, he was really imagining Rocamadour crying face down on the bed and La Maga trying to give him a suppository while Rocamadour resisted and arched his back, slipping his little bottom out of La Maga's clumsy hands. They must have given the old man who had been in the accident a suppository in the hospital too, it was incredible how popular they had become, he would have to make a philosophical analysis of this surprising vindication of the anus, its elevation to a second mouth, into something that no longer limited itself to excretion but which could swallow and digest those rose green white little antiaircraft shells. But Berthe Trépat would not let him concentrate and again she wanted to know about his life and held his arm sometimes with one hand, sometimes with two, turning towards him a little bit with a girlish air which made him shiver even in the middle of the night. All right, he was an Argentinian who had been in Paris for some time, trying to . . . Let's see, what was he trying to do? It was hard to explain it all at once like that. What he was looking for was –

"Beauty, exaltation, the golden bough," Berthe Trépat said. "Don't say a word, I can make a perfect guess. I also came to Paris, from Pau, quite a few years ago, looking for the golden bough. But I was weak, young man, I was . . . What's your name?"

"Oliveira," Oliveira said.

"Oliveira . . . *Desolives*, the Mediterranean . . . I'm from the South too, we're panic, young man, we're both panic. Not like Valentin, who is from Lille. Northerners, cold as fish, like quicksilver. Do you believe in the Great Work? Fulcanelli, you understand . . . No need to answer, I can see that you're an initiate. Perhaps you haven't reached the experiences that really count yet, while I . . . Take the *Synthesis*, for example. What Valentin said is right, radiesthesia points out kindred souls to me and I think that shows through in the piece. Or don't you think so?"

"Oh, yes."

"You have a lot of karma, you can spot it in a minute . . . " her hand gripped him strongly; the pianist was ascending to a state of meditation and to do that she had to hold herself tightly against Oliveira who resisted only slightly, just enough to get her to cross the square and go up the Rue Soufflot. "If Étienne or Wong sees me they'll give me a hard time," thought Oliveira. But why should he care what Étienne or Wong might think, as if after the metaphysical rivers mixed with dirty pieces of cotton the future might have some importance. "Now it's just as if I'd never been in Paris and still here I am stupidly attentive to what is happening to me and it bothers me that this poor old woman is starting to come on with the sadness bit, the clutch of a dying man after the pavan and the complete flop of the concert. I'm worse than a kitchen rag, worse than dirty cotton, I really have nothing to do with my own self." Because this idea stayed with him, at that hour of the night and in the rain and stuck to Berthe Trépat, he began to feel like the last light in a huge mansion where all the other lights had gone out one by one, he began to get the notion that all of this was not he, that somewhere he was waiting for himself, that this person walking in the Latin Quarter hauling along an old woman who was hysterical and maybe a nymphomaniac was only a *Doppelgänger*, while the other one, the other . . . "Did you stay there in your Almagro neighbourhood? Or did you drown on the voyage, in whores' beds, in meaningful experiences, in the well-known necessary disorder? Everything seems to console me, it's comfortable to think of one's salvation even though it's just barely, the guy who is going to be hanged must keep on thinking that something will happen at the last minute, an earthquake, a noose that breaks twice so that they have to pardon him, the phone call from the governor, the uprising that will set him free. And now this old girl is just about ready to start grabbing at my fly."

But Berthe Trépat was lost in didascalic convolutions and had begun to tell with enthusiasm of her meeting with Germaine Tailleferre in the Gare de Lyon and how Tailleferre had said that the *Prelude for Orange Rhombuses* was extremely interesting and that she would speak to Marguerite Long about it so she could include it in one of her concerts.

"It would have been a success, Mr Oliveira, a triumph. But you know impresarios, little dictators, even the best artists are victims . . . Valentin thought that perhaps one of the younger pianists, someone who wouldn't worry, could do it . . . But they're just as ruined as the old ones, they're all cut from the same cloth."

"What about yourself, in another concert . . . "

"I never want to play again," Berthe Trépat said, hiding her face although Oliveira was careful about looking at her. "It's a shame that I still have to appear on stage to introduce my music when I should really be a muse, you know, the one who inspires artists; they would all come to me and beg me to let them play my things, beg me, yes, beg me. And I would give them permission, because I think my work is the spark that should ignite the sensibility of the public here and in the United States, in Hungary . . . Yes, I would give them my permission, but first they would have to come to me and ask for the honour of interpreting my music."

She clutched Oliveira's arm, and without knowing why, he had decided to go along the Rue Saint-Jacques and was walking along with the pianist gently in tow. An icy wind was blowing into their faces, filling their eyes and mouths with water, but Berthe Trépat seemed indifferent to any kind of weather, hanging on to Oliveira's arm as she began to sputter something that would be broken every few words by a hiccup or a short cackle that could have been one of spite or mockery. No, she didn't live on the Rue Saint-Jacques. No, but she didn't care where she lived either. She would just as soon keep on walking like that all night long, more than two hundred people for the première of the *Synthesis.*

"Valentin is going to get worried if you don't go home," Oliveira said, mentally grasping for something to say, a rudder to steer this corseted ball who was rolling along like a sea urchin in the wind and the rain. From out of her lengthy and disjointed rambling he was able to piece together the fact that Berthe Trépat lived on the Rue de l'Estrapade. Half-lost, Oliveira wiped the water out of his eyes with his free hand and got his bearings like a Conrad hero standing in the prow of a ship. He suddenly had a terrible urge to laugh (and it hurt his empty stomach, cramped his muscles, it was strange and painful and when he would tell Wong about it he wouldn't begin to believe it). Not at Berthe Trépat, who was going on about the honours she had received in Montpellier and Pau, with an occasional reference to the gold medal. Nor at his having been stupid enough to volunteer his company. He wasn't quite sure where the urge to laugh was coming from, it came from something previous, something farther back, not because of the concert, which should have been the most laughable thing in the world. Joy, something like a physical form of joy. Even though it was hard for him to believe it, joy. He could have laughed with contentment, pure, delightful, inexplicable contentment. "I'm going crazy," he thought. "And with this nut on my arm, it must be contagious." He didn't have the slightest reason to feel happy, water was seeping through the soles of his shoes and down his collar, Berthe Trépat was grasping his arm tighter and tighter and suddenly she began to be racked by a great sob, every time she mentioned Valentin she would shake all over and weep, it was a kind of conditioned reflex which in no way could have produced happiness in anyone, not even a madman. And Oliveira, while he wanted to burst out laughing in the worst way, carefully took hold of Berthe Trépat and was slowly leading her towards the Rue de l'Estrapade, towards Number Four, and there was no reason to think so, and much less understand it, but everything was just fine that way, taking Berthe Trépat to Number Four Rue de l'Estrapade, seeing as much as possible that she didn't step in any puddles or go under the water pouring out of the spouts on the cornices at the corner of the Rue Clotilde. The idle mention of a drink at her place (with Valentin) didn't seem bad at all to Oliveira; he would have to climb five or six floors towing the pianist after him, go into an apartment where Valentin had probably not lit the stove (but there would be a miraculous salamander, a bottle of cognac, they could take off their shoes, put their feet next to the fire, talk about art and about the gold medal). And he might even be able to come back some other night to Berthe Trépat and Valentin's place with a bottle of wine and keep them company, cheer them up. It was something like going to visit the old man in the hospital, going anywhere where until that moment it had not occurred to him to go, to the hospital, to the Rue de l'Estrapade. Before the joy there came the thing that was giving him terrible cramps in the stomach, a hand clasped underneath his skin like a delightful torture (he would have to ask Wong, a hand clasped underneath his skin).

"Number Four, right?"

"Yes, that house with the balcony," Berthe Trépat said. "An eighteenth-century mansion. Valentin said that Ninon de Lenclos had lived on the fourth floor. He's such a liar. Ninon de Lenclos. Oh, yes, Valentin lies all the time. It's almost stopped raining, hasn't it?"

"It's not raining so much," Oliveira conceded. "Let's cross here, all right?"

"The neighbours," Berthe Trépat said, looking at the café on the corner. "Naturally, the old woman from the eighth floor . . . You can't imagine how much she drinks. Do you see her there at the side table? She's looking at us, tomorrow the gossip will start . . . "

"Please, madame," Oliveira said. "Look out for that puddle."

"Oh, I know her, and the landlord too. They hate me because of Valentin. I've got to admit he has done some . . . He can't stand the old woman on the eighth floor, so one night when he came home quite drunk he daubed cat shit all over her door, from top to bottom, he made drawings with it . . . I'll never forget the uproar . . . Valentin in the tub taking the crap off, because in his true artistic enthusiasm he had got it all over himself, while I had to deal with the police, the old woman, the whole neighbourhood . . . You can't imagine what I've gone through, and me, with my standing . . . Valentin is awful, like a child."

Oliveira could see the white-haired man again, his jowls, his gold chain. It was like a path suddenly opening up in the middle of the wall: all you have to do is edge one shoulder in a little bit and enter, open a path through the stones, go through their thickness and come out into something else. The hand was clutching at his stomach so much that he was feeling nauseous. He was inconceivably happy.

"I'd like to have a *fine à leau* before I go up," Berthe Trépat said, stopping at the doorway and looking at him. "This pleasant walk has made me a little cold, and besides, the rain . . . "

"With pleasure," Oliveira said, disappointed. "But maybe it would be better if you went right up and took off your shoes, your feet are soaked."

"There's enough heat in the café," Berthe Trépat said. "I don't know whether Valentin has come home, it's just like him to be wandering around here looking for some friends. On nights like this he falls terribly in love with anyone, he's like a puppy, believe me."

"I'll bet he's home and has the stove going," Oliveira artfully suggested. "A good glass of punch, some wool socks . . . You've got to take care of yourself, madame."

"Oh, I'm like a rock. But I don't have any money to pay for anything in the café. Tomorrow I'll have to go back to the concert hall and pick up my *cachet* . . . It isn't safe to go around at night with so much money in your purse, this neighbourhood, terrible . . . "

"It would be my pleasure to buy you a drink," Oliveira said. He had managed to get her into the doorway and warm, damp air came from the hallway, musty-smelling, like mushroom sauce. His contentment was slowly going away as if it had kept on walking along alone down the street instead of staying with him in the doorway. But he had to fight against that idea, the joy had only lasted a few minutes, but it had been so new, so something else, and that moment when she had described Valentin in the bath all anointed with cat filth, the feeling had come over him that he could take a step forward, a real step, something without feet or legs, a step through a stone wall, and he could go in there and go forward and save himself from the other side, from the rain in his face and the water in his shoes. It was impossible to understand all that, as it always was with something so necessary to be understood. A joy, a hand underneath his skin squeezing his stomach, a hope – if it was possible to think of a word that way, if it was possible that something confused which he could not grasp could materialize under a notion of hope, it was just too idiotic, it was incredibly beautiful and now it was going away, it was going away in the rain because Berthe Trépat had not invited him up, she was sending him back to the corner café, re-enlisting him in the order of the day, in everything that had happened all during the day, Crevel, the docks on the Seine, the desire to go off in any direction, the old man on the stretcher, the mimeographed programme, Rose Bob, the water in his shoes. With a gesture that was slow enough to lift a mountain off his shoulders, Oliveira pointed at the two cafés which broke the darkness on the corner. But Berthe Trépat didn't seem to have any preference; suddenly she forgot her intentions, muttered something without letting go of Oliveira's arm, and was looking furtively into the darkened corridor.

"He's back," she said quickly, fixing her teary eyes on Oliveira. "He's up there, I can feel it. And somebody's with him, that's for sure, every time he introduced me at a concert he would run home to jump into bed with one of his boyfriends."

She was panting, digging her fingers into Oliveira's arm, and turning around every minute to peer into the darkness. From up above they heard a muffled mewing, like someone running along a felt path, the noise of which echoed down along the spiral of the staircase. Oliveira didn't know what to say and he took out a cigarette and lit it with some difficulty.

"I've forgotten my key," Berthe Trépat said so low that it was hard to hear her. "He never leaves a key for me when he's going to go to bed with one of them."

"But you really must get some rest, madame."

"What does he care whether I rest or explode. They've probably lit the fire and they're using up all the coal that Dr Lemoine gave me. And they're probably naked, naked. Yes, in my bed, naked, the bastards. And tomorrow I'll have to put everything in order, and Valentin has probably vomited on the pillow, he always does . . . Tomorrow like always. Me. Tomorrow."

"Don't you have any friends around here, somewhere where you could spend the night?" Oliveira asked.

"No," Berthe Trépat answered out of the corner of her eye. "Believe me, young man, most of my friends live in Neuilly. The only thing I have here are those old women and the Algerians on the eighth floor, a dirty lot."

"If you want me to, I'll go up and tell Valentin to open up," Oliveira said. "Maybe if you wait in the café we can arrange everything."

"Arrange what?" Berthe Trépat said, dragging out her words as if she were drunk. "He won't open up, I know him too well. They'll keep quiet in the dark. Why should they want light, now of all times? They'll turn on the lights later, when Valentin feels sure that I've gone to spend the night in a hotel or a café."

"If I knock on the door it will startle them. I don't think Valentin wants to have a scene."

"Nothing bothers him when he's like this, nothing bothers him at all. It wouldn't be beyond him to get dressed up in my clothes and walk into the police station on the corner singing the *Marseillaise.* He almost did it once. Robert from the warehouse caught him in time and brought him home. Robert was a good boy, he had his quirks too and he understood."

"Let me go up," Oliveira insisted. "You go to the café on the corner and wait for me. I'll fix things, you can't spend the whole night like this."

The hall light went on just as Berthe Trépat was about to give him a stronger answer. She jumped and ran out into the street, making a show of getting away from Oliveira, who stood there not knowing what to do. A couple was coming down the stairs, they passed without looking and went along towards the Rue Thouin. With a nervous glance behind, Berthe Trépat huddled back into the doorway. It was raining hard.

Not feeling like it at all, but asking himself what else he could do, Oliveira went inside looking for the stairway. He could not have taken more than three steps when Berthe Trépat grabbed him by the arm and hauled him back towards the door. She was mumbling all sorts of orders, prayers, everything got mixed up in a kind of cackling counterpoint that alternated between words and interjections and Oliveira let himself be led along, giving up to whatever might come. The light went out but it went on again in a few moments and they heard voices saying goodbye on the second or third floor. Berthe Trépat let go of Oliveira and leaned against the side of the door, pretending that she was buttoning up her raincoat as if she was getting ready to go out. She didn't move until the two men who were coming down went by her, looking at Oliveira in an incurious way and mumbling the *pardon* that goes with all hallway encounters. For a minute Oliveira considered going upstairs without any further ado, but he wasn't sure which floor she lived on. He took a heavy drag on his cigarette, back in the darkness, waiting for something to happen or for nothing to happen. In spite of the rain Berthe Trépat's sobs began to get clearer and clearer. He went over and put his hand on her shoulder. "Please, Madame Trépat, don't carry on like that. Tell me what we can do, there must be some way out of this."

"Leave me alone, leave me alone," the pianist muttered.

"You're worn out, you've got to get to bed. Anyway, let's go to a hotel, I don't have any money either, but I can make a deal with the manager, I'll pay him tomorrow. I know a hotel on the Rue Valette, it's not far."

"A hotel," Berthe Trépat said, turning around and looking at him.

"It's not good, but it is a way for you to get a good night's sleep."

"Do you really mean to take me to a hotel?"

"Madame, I will take you to the hotel, I will speak to the clerk and have him give you a room."

"A hotel, you want to take me to a hotel?"

"I don't want anything," Oliveira said, losing his patience. "I can't offer you my own place for the simple reason that I don't have any. You won't let me go up and make Valentin open the door. Would you rather I left? In that case, I'll say good night to you."

But who can tell whether he really did say all that or whether he was only thinking it. He had never been so far away from those words that at some other moment might have been the ones that came to his mind straight away. This wasn't the way to do things. He didn't know exactly what to do, but this certainly wasn't the way. And Berthe Trépat was looking at him as she huddled against the doorway. No, he hadn't said anything, he had been standing quietly beside her, and strange as it seemed, he still wanted to help, do something for Berthe Trépat who was looking straight at him and raising her hand little by little, and suddenly she let it go full force across Oliveira's face and he drew back confused, avoiding the worst of the slap but feeling the lash of her slender fingers, the instantaneous scratch of her nails.

"A hotel," Berthe Trépat repeated. "Just listen, all of you, just listen to what he said."

She was looking down the darkened hallway, moving her eyes about, her fervent painted lips were twisting around like something independent, given a life of their own, and in his upset state Oliveira thought he saw once more the hands of La Maga trying to shove the suppository into Rocamadour, and Rocamadour was clutching the cheeks of his behind together as he bellowed horribly and Berthe Trépat twisted her mouth from one side to the other, her eyes fixed on an invisible audience in the shadows of the hallway, her absurd hairdo shaking along more and more intensely with the movements of her head.

"Please," Oliveira murmured, stroking the place where she had scratched him and which was bleeding slightly, "how could you think such a thing?"

But she could think it, because (and she shouted it out and the light in the hall went on again) she knew very well what sort of degenerate followed her down the street the way they did with all decent women, but she would not permit it (and the door of the concierge's apartment began to open up and Oliveira saw the face of a monstrous rat peep out, with eyes that looked about avidly) and no monster, no drooling satyr was going to attack her in the doorway of her own home, that's what police are for and the courts – and someone came running down the stairs full speed, a boy with ruffled hair and a gypsy look was leaning on the banister to look and listen at his pleasure – and if her neighbours would not look out for her she was able to look after herself alone, because this wasn't the first time that a degenerate, a dirty exhibitionist had . . .

On the corner of the Rue Tournefort Oliveira realized that he still had the cigarette butt between his fingers, extinguished by the rain and half melted away. Leaning against a lamppost, he lifted up his face and let the rain wet it all over. That was so nobody could tell, with his face all wet in the rain nobody could tell. Then he started to walk slowly, hunched over, with the collar of his lumber-jacket buttoned up against his chin; as always, the pelt on the collar stank like something terribly rotten, like a tannery. He wasn't thinking about anything, just letting himself walk along as if he had been looking around, a big, fat-footed dog with his fur hanging down walking in the rain. Once in a while he would lift up his hand and wipe his face, but finally he let it rain, sometimes he would thrust out his lip and drink up some of the salty water running down his cheeks. When much later and near the Jardin des Plantes he picked up again the day's memories, an applied and careful retelling of every minute of that day, he said to himself that he had really not been such an idiot to have felt so happy seeing the old woman home. But that as always he had paid dearly for that foolish happiness. Now he would begin to reproach himself, put himself down little by little until the same old thing was left there, a hole where time was blowing, an imprecise continuum that had no set bounds. "Let's not get literary," he thought while he dug out a cigarette after he had dried his hands a bit with the heat of his trouser pockets. "Let's forget about bringing up those bitchy words, those made-up pimps. That's how it was and too bad. Berthe Trépat . . . It's all been too crazy, but it would have been nice to have gone upstairs and had a drink with her and with Valentin, taken off my shoes next to the fire. Actually that's all I ever wanted to do, the idea of taking off my shoes and drying my socks. I let you down, baby, what you going to do about it. Let's let things lie the way they are, I've got to get to bed. There was no other reason, there couldn't have been any other reason. If I allow myself I might go back to the apartment and spend the night being wet-nurse." From the Rue du Sommerard it would be twenty minutes in the rain; it would be better to pop into the first hotel and go to bed. One after another his matches began to go out. It was enough to make you laugh.

(–124)

24

"I don't know how to explain it," La Maga said as she dried the spoon with a towel that was not too clean. "Other people could probably do a better job of it, but I've always been that way, it's easier to talk about sad things than happy ones."

"It's a law," Gregorovius said. "Perfectly put forth, a profound truth. Raised to the level of literary skill it means that bad writing comes from good feelings, and other things along the same lines. Happiness cannot be explained, Lucía, probably because it is the ultimate moment of the veil of Maya."

La Maga looked at him perplexed and Gregorovius sighed.

"The veil of Maya," he repeated. "But let's not get things confused. You have seen very well that misfortune is, let's say, tangible, perhaps because out of it comes the separation into subject and object. That's why memory is so important, that's why it's so easy to describe catastrophes."

"What happens," said La Maga as she stirred the milk on the stove, "is that happiness belongs to only one person while misfortune seems to belong to everybody."

"A worthy corollary," said Gregorovius. "What's more, I want you to know that I'm not nosy. The other night, at the meeting of the Club . . . Well, Ronald had some vodka that was too much of a tongue-loosener. I don't want you to think that I'm any kind of prier, I just like to know my friends better. You and Horacio . . . What I mean is that there's something about you I can't explain, some kind of mystery in your core. Ronald and Babs say that you're the perfect couple, that you complement each other. I don't see that you complement each other so much."

"What difference does it make?"

"It doesn't make any difference, but you were telling me that Horacio has gone off."

"That has nothing to do with it," La Maga said. "I can't talk about happiness, but that doesn't mean that I haven't been happy. If you want I can go on telling why Horacio left, why it could have been me who left if it hadn't been for Rocamadour." She waved her hand in the direction of the suitcases, the great mess of paper and boxes and records that filled the room. "I've got to take care of all this, I've got to find some place to go . . . I don't want to stay here, it's too sad."

"Étienne could find you a place with good light. When Rocamadour goes back to the country. Something around seven thousand francs a month. In that case, if it's all right with you I'll take this place. I like it, it has an aura. One can think here, it's comfortable."

"Don't you believe it," La Maga said. "Around seven o'clock the girl upstairs begins to sing *Les Amants du Havre.* It's a nice song, but on and on . . . "

Puisque la terre est ronde,
Mon amour t'en fais pas,
Mon amour t'en fais pas.

"That's pretty," Gregorovius said indifferently.

"Yes, it has a great philosophy, that's what Ledesma would have said. No, you didn't know him. It was before Horacio, in Uruguay."

"The Negro?"

"No, the Negro's name was Ireneo."

"Then the story about the Negro was true?"

La Maga looked at him surprised. Gregorovius really was stupid. Except for Horacio (and sometimes . . .) everybody who had ever wanted her always acted like such an idiot. Stirring the milk, she went over to the bed and tried to get Rocamadour to take a few spoonfuls. Rocamadour shrieked and refused, the milk ran down his neck. "Topitopitopi," La Maga kept saying with the voice of a hypnotist giving out prizes. "Topitopitopi," trying to get a spoonful in Rocamadour's mouth as he became flushed and refused to drink, but suddenly he relented for some reason and slid down towards the foot of the bed as he took one spoonful after another to the immense satisfaction of Gregorovius, who was filling his pipe and beginning to feel a little like a father.

"Chin chin," La Maga said, leaving the pot by the side of the bed and tucking in Rocamadour who was rapidly getting drowsy. "He still has a high fever, it must be a hundred and three at least."

"Didn't you use the thermometer?"

"It's hard to get it in, then he'll cry for twenty minutes afterwards, Horacio can't stand it. I can tell by how warm his forehead is. It must be over a hundred and three, I can't understand why it doesn't go down."

"Too much empiricism, I'm afraid," Gregorovius said. "And isn't that milk bad for him when his fever is so high?"

"It's not so high for a child," La Maga said, lighting up a Gauloise. "The best thing would be to turn off the light so he'll fall asleep right away. Over there, next to the door."

A glow was coming from the stove and it seemed to get brighter as they sat opposite each other and smoked for a while without talking. Gregorovius watched La Maga's cigarette go up and down, for a second her strangely placid face would light up like a hot coal, her eyes would glisten as she looked at him, everything was wrapped up in a half-light in which Rocamadour's whimpering and clucking got softer and softer until it stopped altogether, followed by a light hiccup that came periodically. A clock struck eleven.

"He's not coming back," La Maga said. "Of course, he'll have to come for his things, but that's not the same. It's over, kaput."

"I wonder," Gregorovius said cautiously. "Horacio is so sensitive, it's difficult for him to get around in Paris. He thinks that he's doing what he wants to do, that he has a lot of liberty here, but he goes around running into barriers. All you have to do is see him on the street, once I followed him a while, from a distance."

"Spy," La Maga said in a tone that was almost friendly.

"Let's say 'observer'."

"You were really following me, even though I wasn't with him."

"Maybe I was, I didn't stop to think about it at the time. I like to see how people I know act, it's always more exciting than a game of chess. I have discovered that Wong masturbates and that Babs practises a kind of Jansenist charity, her face turned to the wall while she drops a piece of bread with something inside it. There was a time when I used to study my mother. It was in Herzegovina, a long time ago. Adgalle used to fascinate me, she insisted on wearing a blond wig when I knew very well that her hair was black. Nobody in the castle knew this; we had moved in there after Count Rossler died. When I asked her about it (I was barely ten then, it was such a happy time) my mother would laugh and make me swear never to reveal the truth. That truth I had to hide used to make me nervous, it was simpler and more beautiful than the blond wig. The wig was a work of art, my mother could comb her hair quite naturally while the maid was there and no one would suspect anything. But when she was alone, I really don't know why, but I wanted to hide under a sofa or behind the purple curtains. I decided to bore a hole in the wall between the library and my mother's boudoir – I used to work at night when they thought I was asleep. That's how I was able to watch Adgalle take off her blond wig, shake out her black hair which gave her such a different look, so beautiful, and then she took off the other wig and there was the perfect cue-ball, something so disgusting that I vomited most of my goulash on my pillow that night."

"Your childhood sounds like something out of *The Prisoner of Zenda*," La Maga said as she thought about it.

"It was a world of wigs," said Gregorovius. "I wonder what Horacio would have done in my place. We were really going to talk about Horacio, you wanted to tell me something."

"That hiccup is strange," La Maga said, looking at Rocamadour's bed. "It's the first time he's had it."

"Probably his digestion."

"Why do they insist I take him to the hospital? This afternoon again, that ant-faced doctor. I don't want to take him, he wouldn't like it. I can do everything that has to be done. Babs was here this morning and said it wasn't so serious. Horacio didn't think it was serious either."

"Horacio isn't coming back?"

"No. Horacio's gone off out there, looking for things."

"Don't cry, Lucía."

"I'm just blowing my nose. The hiccups have gone."

"Tell me about it, Lucía, if it would help."

"I can't remember anything, it's not worth it. Yes, I remember. Why? Adgalle is a strange name."

"Yes, who knows whether it was her real one. I was told . . . "

"Like the blond wig and the black wig," La Maga said.

"Like everything," said Gregorovius. "You're right, the hiccups have gone away. Now he'll sleep till morning. When did you and Horacio first meet?"

(–134)

25

She would have preferred Gregorovius to be quiet or to talk only about Adgalle, letting her smoke peacefully in the darkness, far removed from the shapes in the room, from the books and records that would have to be packed up so Horacio could take them away when he found a place. But it was no use, he would be still for a moment waiting for her to say something, and then he would ask a question, they all had something to ask her all the time, as if it bothered them that she would rather sing *Mon p'tit voyou* or make sketches with burnt matches or stroke the mangiest cats she could find on the Rue du Sommerard, or give Rocamadour his bottle.

"*Alors, mon p'tit voyou*," La Maga sang softly, "*la vie, qu'est-ce qu'on s'en fout . . .*"

"I used to adore fishbowls too," said Gregorovius, thinking back. "I lost all interest in them when I was initiated into the duties proper to my sex. In Dubrovnik, a whorehouse where I was taken by a Danish sailor who at the time was my Odessa mother's lover. There was a marvellous aquarium at the foot of the bed, and the bed too had something of an aquarium about it with its pale-blue rippling spread which the fat redhead carefully turned down before she grabbed me by the ears like a rabbit. You can't imagine the fright, Lucía, the terror of all that. We were lying on our backs, next to each other, and she caressed me mechanically, I was cold and she was talking about something or other, about the fight that had just taken place in the bar, of the stormy weather in March . . . The fish went back and forth like her hand on my legs, rising, sinking . . . That's what love-making was, then, a black fish going doggedly back and forth. An image like any other, but quite exact. The infinite repetition of an anxious desire to flee, to go through the glass and go into some other thing."

"Who can tell," La Maga said. "I don't think that fish ever want to get out of their bowls, they almost never touch the glass with their noses."

Gregorovius thought that somewhere Chestov had written about aquariums with a removable glass partition which could be taken out any time and that the fish, who was accustomed to his compartment, would never try to go over to the other side. He would come to a point in the water, turn around and swim back, without discovering that the obstacle was gone, that all he had to do was to keep on going forward . . .

"But that could be love too," Gregorovius said. "How wonderful to be admiring fish in a tank and suddenly to see them pass into the open air, fly away like doves. An idiotic hope, of course. We all draw back for fear of rubbing our noses against something unpleasant. The nose as the limit of the world, a topic for a dissertation. Do you know how they teach cats not to dirty indoors? The technique of an opportune rub. Do you know how they teach pigs not to eat the truffles? A whack on the nose, it's horrible. I think that Pascal was more of an expert on noses than one would gather from his famous Egyptian observation."

"Pascal?" La Maga asked. "What Egyptian observation?"

Gregorovius sighed. They all used to sigh when she asked a question. Horacio and especially Étienne, because Étienne not only used to sigh but would sniff, snort, and call her stupid. "It's so purple to be ignorant," La Maga thought, hurt. Every time somebody was scandalized by one of her questions a purple feeling, a purple mass would envelop her for a moment. She had to take a deep breath so that the purple mass would dissolve, would float about there like the fish, dividing up into a lot of purple rhombuses, kites in the wasteland in the Pocitos quarter, summer at the beach, purple blotches on the sun and the sun was called Ra and was also Egyptian like Pascal. Gregorovius's sigh didn't bother her much now, after Horacio she wouldn't be bothered by anybody's sighs when she asked a question, but in any case, the purple spot always came for a moment, a desire to cry, something which lasted just the time necessary to grind out her cigarette in that irresistible carpet-ruining gesture, supposing that there had been a carpet there.

(–141)

26

"When you come right down to it," Gregorovius said, "Paris is one big metaphor."

He knocked his pipe, tamped the tobacco a bit. La Maga had lit another Gauloise and was singing softly. She was so tired that she didn't even get angry at not understanding what he had said. Since she didn't hasten to ask a question as she would have normally, Gregorovius decided to explain. La Maga was listening from far off, aided by the darkness of the room and the cigarette. She heard bits and pieces, the continual mention of Horacio, Horacio's disorder, the aimless wanderings of almost all of those in the Club, the reasons behind the belief that all of this was leading towards some sense. Sometimes something Gregorovius said would become outlined in the shadows, green or white, sometimes it was an Atlan, at others an Estève, then some sound would whirl around and take shape, grow like a Manessier, like a Wifredo Lam, like a Piaubert, like an Étienne, like a Max Ernst. It was fun, Gregorovius was saying, ". . . and they're all looking out for magical Babylonian pathways, to put it that way, and then . . . ," La Maga saw a resplendent Deyrolles take shape out of the words, a Bissière, but now Gregorovius was talking about the uselessness of an empirical ontology and suddenly it was a Friedländer, a delicate Villon which made a crisscross on the half-light and made it quiver, *empirical ontology*, smoke-blues, pinks, *empirical*, a pale yellow, a hollow where whitish sparks were fluttering.

"Rocamadour has fallen asleep," La Maga said, putting out her cigarette. "I have to sleep for a while too."

"Horacio won't be back tonight, I don't imagine."

"How should I know. Horacio is like a cat, he might be sitting on the floor outside the door, and he might have taken a train to Marseilles."

"I can stay," Gregorovius said. "You go to sleep and I'll watch Rocamadour."

"But I'm not sleepy. I keep seeing things in the air while you're talking. You said 'Paris is one big metaphor', and it was like one of those designs by Sugai, lots of red and black."

"I was thinking of Horacio," Gregorovius said. "It's funny how Horacio has been changing in these months since I first met him. You wouldn't have noticed, I imagine, too close to him and too responsible for the changes."

"Why one big metaphor?"

"He walks around here the way other people look for flight in voodoo or marijuana, Pierre Boulez or Tinguely's painting-machines. He guesses that in some part of Paris, some day or some death or some meeting will show him a key; he's searching for it like a madman. Note that I said like a madman. I mean that he really doesn't know that he's looking for the key, or that the key exists. He has an inkling of its shapes, its disguises; that's why I was talking about a metaphor."

"Why do you say that Horacio has changed?"

"A question to the point, Lucía. When I met Horacio I had him down as an amateur intellectual, I mean an intellectual without rigour. You people are a little like that down there, aren't you? In Mato Grosso, places like that."

"Mato Grosso is in Brazil."

"Along the Paraná, then. Very intelligent and alert, up to date on everything. Much more than us. Italian literature, for example, or English. And the whole Spanish Golden Age, and naturally French literature on the tip of your tongues. Horacio was pretty much like that. It was only too clear. I think it's admirable that he has changed like this in so little time. Now he's turned into a real animal, all you have to do is look at him. Well, he hasn't turned into an animal quite yet, but he's trying his best."

"Don't talk nonsense," La Maga snorted.

"Understand me, what I'm trying to say is that he is looking for the black light, the key, and he's beginning to realize that you don't find those things in libraries. You're the one who really taught him that, and if he's left it's because he's never going to forgive you for it."

"That's not why Horacio left."

"There's a design to that too. He doesn't know why he left and you, the reason for his leaving, are incapable of knowing unless you decide to believe what I'm telling you."

"I don't believe it," La Maga said, sliding off the chair and lying down on the floor. "And besides, I don't understand any of it. And don't bring up Pola. I don't want to talk about Pola."

"Keep on looking at what's being drawn in the darkness," Gregorovius said pleasantly. "We can talk about other things, of course. Did you know that the Chirkin Indians, by always asking missionaries for shears, now have such a collection of them that the number of shears per capita among them far outstrips the figure for any other group of people in the world? I read about that in an article by Alfred Métraux. The world is full of strange things."

"But why is Paris one big metaphor?"

"When I was a boy," Gregorovius said, "the nursemaids used to make love to the Uhlans who were stationed in the Bozsok sector. Since I would get in their way for the performance of those duties, they used to let me play in a huge room full of rugs and tapestries which would have delighted Malte Laurids Brigge. One of the rugs showed the layout of the city of Ophir, according to the legends that have reached the West through storybooks. I used to get on my knees and with my nose or my hands push a yellow ball along, following the course of the Shan-Ten river, crossing walls guarded by black warriors armed with spears, and then after numerous dangers and after bumping my head on the legs of the mahogany table which was in the centre of the rug, I would come to the quarters of the Queen of Sheba and I would curl up like a caterpillar and fall asleep on top of the picture of a triclinium. Yes, Paris is a metaphor. Now that I think about it, you're stretched out on a rug too. What's the picture on it? Ah, lost childhood, closeness, closeness! I've been in this room twenty times and I can't remember the picture on that rug . . . "

"It's so dirty that there isn't much picture left," La Maga said. "I think it shows two peacocks kissing with their bills. It's all rather green."

They were silent, listening to the footsteps of someone coming up the stairs.

(–109)

27

"Oh, Pola," La Maga said. "I know more about her than Horacio does."

"Without ever having seen her, Lucía?"

"But I've seen so much of her," La Maga said impatiently. "Horacio carried her around in his hair, in his overcoat, he shook from her, he washed from her."

"Étienne and Wong told me about the woman," Gregorovius said. "They saw them one day at a street café in Saint-Cloud. Only the stars could tell us what all those people could possibly have been doing in Saint-Cloud, but there they were. Horacio was looking at her the way you would look at an anthill, it seems. Wong used all this later on to work out a complicated theory on sexual saturation; according to him it would be possible to advance in knowledge provided that at a given moment one would reach a certain coefficient in love (they're his words, please excuse the Chinese jargon) which would cause the spirit to crystallize suddenly on another level, become established in a surreality. Do you think that's so, Lucía?"

"I suppose that we're looking for something like that, but we almost always get swindled or do some swindling ourselves. Paris is a great blind love, we are all hopelessly in love, but there is something green, a kind of mist, I don't know. It was the same way in Montevideo, you couldn't really love anybody, strange things would turn up right away, stories of sheets or hairs, and for a woman lots of other things, Ossip, abortions, for example. So."

"Love, sexuality. Are we talking about the same thing?"

"Yes," La Maga said. "If we're talking about love we're talking about sexuality. Not so much the other way around. But sexuality is different from sex, I think."

"No theories," Ossip said unexpectedly. "Dichotomies, like syncretisms . . . Horacio was probably looking for something in Pola that you couldn't give him, I imagine. Getting down to practical matters, that is."

"Horacio is always looking for any number of things," La Maga said. "He was getting tired of me because I don't know how to think, that's all. I have the feeling that Pola thinks all the time."

"Poor love that feeds on thought," Ossip quoted.

"We've got to be fair," La Maga said. "Pola is very beautiful, I know that from the way Horacio's eyes would look at me when he would come back after being with her, he would come back like a match being struck and suddenly his hair would grow, it would only last a second, but it was marvellous, a sort of scratch, a very strong smell of phosphorus and that huge flame that would die down quickly. That's the way he would come home and it was because Pola had filled him with beauty. I used to tell him that, Ossip, and it was only right that I did. We were already a little distant although we were still in love with one another. These things don't happen all of a sudden, Pola was coming up like the sun at the window, I always have to think about things like that to know that I'm telling the truth. She was coming in slowly, breaking up the shadows around me, and Horacio was getting warmed, the same as on shipboard, he was getting tanned, he was happy."

"I never would have believed it. I thought that you . . . Of course, Pola passed on like some of the others. Because we have to talk about Françoise too, for example."

"She didn't matter," La Maga said, flicking her ash on the floor. "It would be the same as if I named people like Ledesma, for example. I'm sure you don't know anything about that any more than you know how the Pola affair finally ended up."

"No."

"Pola is dying," La Maga said. "Not from the pins, that was a joke, even though I was serious when I did it, believe me, I was very serious. She's dying of breast cancer."

"And Horacio . . . "

"Don't be dirty, Ossip. Horacio didn't know anything about it when he left Pola."

"Please, Lucía, I . . . "

"You know very well what you're saying and what you're after here tonight, Ossip. Don't be a swine, I didn't even hint at that."

"But please tell me what?"

"That Horacio knew about it before he left her."

"Please," Gregorovius repeated. "I didn't even . . . "

"Don't be dirty," La Maga said monotonously. "Why should you want to put Horacio down? Don't you know that we've split up, that he's gone away out there in the rain?"

"I'm not after anything," Ossip said, as he seemed to huddle up into the easy chair. "I'm not like that, Lucía, you're always going around misunderstanding me. Do I have to get down on my knees, like the captain of the *Graffin* that time, and beg you to believe me, and to – "

"Leave me alone," La Maga said. "First Pola, then you. All those spots on the wall and this night that never seems to have an end. I wouldn't put it past you to think that I'm killing Pola."

"It never crossed my mind."

"OK, OK. Horacio will never forgive me, even though he's not in love with Pola any more. It's laughable, a worthless little doll, made of wax from a Christmas candle, a delicate green wax, I remember."

"Lucía, it's hard for me to believe that you were capable . . . "

"He'll never forgive me, even though we didn't talk about it. He knows because he saw the doll and he saw the pins. He threw it on the floor, crushed it with his foot. He didn't realize that that made it worse, that it increased the danger. Pola lives on the Rue Dauphine, he used to go to see her almost every afternoon. Do you think he told her about the little green doll, Ossip?"

"Quite probably," Ossip said, hostile and resentful. "All of you are crazy."

"Horacio used to speak about a new order of things, about the possibility of discovering a different life. He always spoke about death when he was talking about life, it was inevitable and we would laugh a lot about it. He told me that he was sleeping with Pola and then I understood that he didn't think it was necessary for me to get upset or make a scene. I wasn't really upset, Ossip, I could go to bed with you right now if I wanted to. It's hard to explain, it's not a matter of being unfaithful and things like that, Horacio used to get furious whenever he would hear the words 'unfaithful' or 'cheating'. I must recognize that from the first time we met he told me that he didn't consider himself obligated in any way. I made the doll because Pola had got into my room, it was too much, I knew that she was capable of stealing my clothes, wearing my stockings, using my make-up, giving Rocamadour his milk."

"But you said you didn't know her."

"She was in Horacio, stupid. Stupid, stupid Ossip. Poor Ossip, so stupid. In his lumberjacket, in the fur collar, you've seen the fur collar on Horacio's lumberjacket. And Pola would be there when he came home, and in the way he would look, and when Horacio would get undressed, there in the corner, and get into that bath – you see it, Ossip? – then Pola would start coming out of his skin, I saw her like ectoplasm and I held back the urge to cry because I knew that I would never get into Pola's flat that way, that Pola would never sense me in Horacio's hair or eyes or body-fuzz. I don't know why; after all, we had been very much in love. I don't know why. Because I don't know how to think and he despises me. For things like that."

(–28)

28

There was walking on the stairway.

"It's probably Horacio," Gregorovius said.

"Probably," said La Maga. "But I rather think it's the watchmaker on the sixth floor, he always comes in late. Would you like to hear some music?"

"At this time of night? We'll wake the baby."

"No, we'll put it on very low, it would be just right to listen to a quartet. We can turn it low enough so that we'll be the only ones who can hear it, let's see."

"It wasn't Horacio," Gregorovius observed.

"I can't say," La Maga said, lighting a match and looking at some records piled in a corner. "He might have sat down outside, he does that sometimes. Sometimes he gets to the door and changes his mind. Turn on the record-player, that white button next to the fireplace."

There was something that looked like a shoebox and La Maga knelt down to put the record on, feeling around in the dark, and the shoebox hummed a little, a distant chord filled the air around her hands. Gregorovius began to fill his pipe, a little scandalized. He didn't like Schoenberg, but it was for a different reason, the time, the sick child, a kind of transgression. That was it, a transgression. An idiot idea. But sometimes he would get spells like that in which a vague sense of order would get back at him for having abandoned it. Stretched out on the floor with her head almost stuck inside the shoebox, La Maga seemed to be sleeping.

Every so often there would be a soft snore from Rocamadour, but Gregorovius was getting lost in the music, he found that he could give in and let himself be carried off without protesting, turn himself over to a dead and buried Viennese. La Maga was smoking stretched out on the floor, her face would light up in the dark, with her eyes closed and her hair over her face, her cheeks shining as if she had been crying, it was stupid to think that she could have been crying, rather she was biting her lips with rage as she listened to the dry sound of a thump from up above, the second one, the third. Gregorovius was startled and was about to shout when he felt a hand holding him by the ankle.

"Pay no attention, it's the old man upstairs."

"But we can barely hear ourselves."

"It's the pipes," La Maga said mysteriously. "Everything gets in there, it's already happened other times."

"The science of acoustics is amazing," Gregorovius said.

"He'll get tired soon," La Maga said. "The fool."

The knocking kept on upstairs. La Maga got up furiously and lowered the volume even more. Eight or nine chords, a pizzicato, and the knocking started again.

"It can't be," Gregorovius said. "It's absolutely impossible that he can hear a thing."

"He has better hearing than we do, that's the worst of it."

"This building is like Dionysus' ear."

"Whose ear? God damn him, right in the adagio. And he keeps on knocking. Rocamadour is going to wake up."

"Maybe it would be better . . ."

"No, I don't want to. Let him break the ceiling down. I'm going to put on a Mario del Monaco record and teach him a lesson, too bad I don't have one. The fool, the dirty bastard."

"Lucía," Gregorovius said softly. "It's past midnight."

"Always the time," La Maga snorted. "I'm going to get out of this place. I couldn't put the volume any lower than it is, we couldn't hear anything. Wait, I'm going to put the last movement on again. Don't worry."

The knocking stopped, for a while the quartet was moving along towards the end without even the rhythmic snoring of Rocamadour. La Maga sighed, with her head practically in the speaker. The knocking started again.

"What a fool," La Maga said. "And that's the way it is all the time."

"Don't be stubborn, Lucía."

"Don't you be a fool. I'm sick of them. I'd love to kick all of them out into the street. Just because I wanted to listen to Schoenberg, just for a while . . ."

She had begun to cry, she reached over and lifted the needle as the last notes were over and since she was next to Gregorovius, leaning over the amplifier to shut it off, it was easy for him to put his arm around her waist and set her down on one of his knees. He began to stroke her hair, clearing it away from her face. La Maga was crying with short sobs, coughing and blowing her tobacco breath in his face.

"Poor thing, poor thing," Gregorovius repeated in rhythm to his caresses. "Nobody loves her, nobody. Everybody is nasty to poor Lucía."

"You stupid arse," La Maga said as she hawked and swallowed in an unctuous sort of way. "I'm crying because I want to cry and especially to avoid anyone consoling me. My God, you've got sharp knees, they cut into me like scissors."

"Sit here a while," Gregorovius begged.

"I don't feel like it," La Maga said. "And why in the world does that idiot keep on pounding like that?"

"Don't pay any attention to him, Lucía. You poor thing . . . "

"He's still knocking, I tell you it's unbelievable."

"Let him knock," Gregorovius advised incongruously.

"You were the one who was worried before," La Maga said, laughing in his face.

"Please, if you knew . . . "

"Oh, I know everything, but be still, Ossip," La Maga said suddenly, catching on. "The guy wasn't knocking because of the record. We can put another one on if we want to."

"Oh Lord, no."

"But can't you still hear him pounding?"

"I'm going up and punch him in the nose," Gregorovius said.

"Right now," La Maga said in encouragement, getting up with a jump so that he could get by. "Tell him that he has no right to wake people up at one o'clock in the morning. Come on, get going, it's the door on the left, there's a shoe nailed to it."

"A shoe nailed to the door?"

"Yes, the old man is completely mad. There's a shoe and a green piece from an accordion. Aren't you going up there?"

"I don't think it's worth it," Gregorovius said wearily. "That all makes it so different, so useless. Lucía, you didn't understand that . . . Well, anyway, the fellow might stop knocking."

La Maga went over to the corner and took down something that in the shadows looked like a feather duster, and Gregorovius heard a tremendous blow on the ceiling. The noise stopped upstairs.

"Now we can listen to what we please," La Maga said.

"I wonder," thought Gregorovius, getting more and more tired.

"For example," La Maga said, "a Brahms sonata. How wonderful, he's got tired of knocking. Wait, I'll find the record, it's around here somewhere. I can't see a thing."

"Horacio is out there," Gregorovius thought. "Sitting on the landing with his back against the door, listening to everything. Like a tarot figure, something that has to resolve itself, a polyhedron in which every edge and every facet keeps its immediate sense, the false one, until the mediating sense is integrated, revelation. And so Brahms, me, the thumps on the ceiling, Horacio: something is slowly heading towards an explanation. But it's all so useless in any case." He wondered what would happen if he tried to embrace La Maga in the dark again. "But he's out there listening. He would be capable of enjoying what he heard, listening to us, he's repulsive sometimes." Besides, he was afraid of Oliveira and it was hard for him to admit it.

"This must be it," La Maga said. "Yes, a half-silver label with two birds on it. Who's talking outside there?"

"A polyhedron, somewhat crystallized, which takes shape little by little in the darkness," Gregorovius thought. "She's going to say this now and outside the other thing will happen and I . . . But I don't know what this is or what the other is."

"It's Horacio," La Maga said.

"Horacio and a woman."

"No, it must be the old man from upstairs."

"The one with the shoe on his door?"

"Yes, he has an old woman's voice, like a magpie. He always goes around wearing an astrakhan hat."

"Better not put the record on," Gregorovius advised. "Let's see what happens."

"So we can't listen to the Brahms sonata after all," La Maga said furiously.

"What a ridiculous subversion of values," Gregorovius thought. "There they are, about to kick each other around on the landing, in pitch dark or whatever you want to call it, and all she can think about is the fact that she won't be able to hear her sonata." But La Maga was right, as always she was the only one who was right. "I'm more prejudiced than I thought," Gregorovius said to himself. "One thinks that just because he is living the life of an *affranchi* and accepts the material and spiritual parasitism of Lutetia, he's managed to get over on the pre-Adamite side. Poor fool, what can you do."

"The rest is silence," Gregorovius said in English as he sighed.

"Silence my foot," answered La Maga, who knew English quite well. "Now watch them start in all over again. The old man will speak first. There he is, '*Mais qu'est-ce que vous foutez?*'" La Maga mimicked with a nasal voice. "Let's see what Horacio answers. I think he's laughing under his breath, when he starts to laugh he can't find the right words, it's incredible. I'm going to see what's going on."

"And we were so comfortable," Gregorovius murmured, as if he had seen the angel of expulsion approaching. Gérard David, Van der Weiden, the Master of Flemalle, at that hour all the angels for some reason seemed to be accursedly Flemish, with chubby, stupid faces, but resplendent with lace and bourgeois admonitions (Daddy-ordered-it, so-you-better-beat-it-you-lousy-sinners). The whole room full of angels, "I looked over Jordan and what did I see / A band of angels comin' after me," always the same finale, police angels, dunning angels, angel angels. Putrefaction of putrefactions, like the blast of cold air that came up the legs of his pants, the angry voices on the landing, the silhouette of La Maga in the doorway.

"*C'est pas des façons, ça,*" the old man was saying. "*Empêcher les gens de dormir à cette heure c'est trop con. J'me plaindrai à la Police, moi, et puis qu'est-ce que vous foutez là, vous planqué par terre contre la porte? J'aurais pu me casser la gueule, merde alors.*"

"Go back to sleep, old man," said Horacio, stretched out comfortably on the floor.

"*Dormir, moi, avec le bordel que fait votre bonne femme? Ça alors comme culot, mais je vous préviens, ça me passera pas comme ça, vous aurez de mes nouvelles.*"

"*Mais de mon frère le Poète on a eu des nouvelles,*" Horacio quoted with a yawn. "Have you been watching this guy?"

"A fool," La Maga said. "You put on a record turned down low and he pounds. You take the record off and he keeps on pounding. What does he want?"

"Well, it's the story of the guy who only drops one shoe."

"I don't know that one," La Maga said.

"It was predictable," said Oliveira. "Old people inspire respect in me, mixed up with other feelings, but as far as this one is concerned, I'd like to buy a bottle of formalin and stick him in it so he'd stop bugging us."

"*Et en plus ça m'insulte dans son charabia de sales métèques,*" the old man said. "*On est en France, ici. Des salauds, quoi. On devrait vous mettre à la porte, c'est une honte. Qu'est-ce que fait le Gouvernement, je me demande. Des Arabes, tous des fripouilles, bande de tueurs.*"

"Come off it with the *sales métèques*, you ought to see that bunch of Frogs pile up the loot in Argentina," Oliveira said. "What were you listening to? I just got here, I'm soaked."

"A Schoenberg quartet. Just now I wanted to listen to a Brahms sonata, turned down very low."

"The best thing would be to let it go till tomorrow," said Oliveira, sizing up the situation and sitting up on one elbow as he lit a Gauloise. "*Rentrez chez vous, monsieur, on vous emmerdera plus pour ce soir.*"

"*Des fainéants,*" the old man said. "*Des tueurs, tous.*"

The astrakhan hat could be seen in the light of the match along with a dirty bathrobe and wrathful little eyes. The hat cast a gigantic shadow on the wall of the stairwell; La Maga was fascinated. Oliveira got up, blew out the match, and went into the apartment, closing the door softly.

"Hello," Oliveira said. "I can't see anything."

"Hello," said Gregorovius. "I'm glad you handled the man upstairs all right."

"*Per modo di dire.* In truth the old man is right, and besides, he's old."

"Being old is no reason," La Maga said.

"It may not be a reason, but it is a safe-conduct pass."

"I remember your saying once that the tragedy of Argentina is in the hands of old men."

"The curtain's already come down on that play," Oliveira said. "It's been just the opposite since Perón, the young ones call the tune and it's almost worse, but what can you do. The idea of age, generation, degrees and class is a great joke. I suppose the reason that we're so uncomfortable whispering like this is because Rocamadour is sleeping his sleep of the just."

"Yes, he fell asleep before we began to listen to some music. You're soaked to the skin, Horacio."

"I went to a piano recital," Oliveira explained.

"Oh," said La Maga. "Well, that's fine. Take off your lumberjacket and I'll fix you a nice hot *mate*."

"And a glass of *caña*, there still must be half a bottle left around here."

"What's *caña*?" Gregorovius asked. "Is it the same as what they call *grappa*?"

"No, more like *barack*. Very good after concerts, especially in the case of first performances and indescribable consequences. Why don't we light a dim and timid little light which won't reach to Rocamadour's eyes?"

La Maga lit a lamp and placed it on the floor, creating a sort of Rembrandt that Oliveira found quite appropriate. The return of the prodigal, the picture of a return, even though it was fleeting and momentary, although he had not really known why he had climbed the stairs slowly to slump by the door and listen to the distant sounds of the end of the quartet and the whispered conversation of Ossip and La Maga. "They must have made love already, like a pair of cats," he thought, looking at them. But no, they must have suspected that he would be back that night, and they had all their clothes on, and Rocamadour was in the bed. If Rocamadour had been lying on a pair of chairs placed together, if Gregorovius had had his shoes and coat off . . . Besides, what the hell difference did it make, since he was the intruder there, his dripping lumberjacket, shot to hell.

"Acoustics," Gregorovius observed. "It's strange how sound gets into things and climbs from floor to floor, passing through a wall to the head of a bed, it's unbelievable. Did you two ever duck underwater in a bathtub?"

"I've thought of it," Oliveira said, tossing his lumberjacket in a corner and sitting down on a stool.

"You can hear everything the people downstairs are saying, all you have to do is put your head underwater and listen. The sounds come through the plumbing, I imagine. Once in Glasgow I discovered that the neighbours were Trotskyites."

"When I think of Glasgow I think of bad weather, a port full of sad people," La Maga said.

"Too many movies," said Oliveira. "But this *mate* is like a pardon, something incredibly conciliatory. Good Lord, look how wet my shoes got. You see, a *mate* is like a full stop and a space. You take one and then you can start a new paragraph."

"I'll never know these delights of the pampas," Gregorovius said. "But you also mentioned a drink, I believe."

"Bring the *caña*," Oliveira ordered. "I think there's over half a bottle left."

"Did you two buy it here?" Gregorovius asked.

"Why the devil does he use the plural," Oliveira thought. "They must have been rolling around here all night, it's an unmistakable sign. But then."

"No, my brother sends it to me. I have a wonderful brother in Rosario. *Caña* and reproaches, an abundance of both."

He passed his empty gourd to La Maga, who had squatted by his feet. He began to feel good. He felt La Maga's fingers on his ankle, on his shoelaces. He let her take off his shoe with a sigh. La Maga took off his wet sock and wrapped his foot in a page of the *Figaro Littéraire*. The *mate* was hot and very bitter.

Gregorovius liked the *caña*, it wasn't just like *barack* but it was similar. He went through a catalogue of Hungarian and Czech drinks, some reminiscences. They could hear the rain falling softly and they felt comfortable, especially Rocamadour, who had been sleeping for more than an hour already without stirring. Gregorovius talked about Transylvania, about some adventures in Salonika. Oliveira remembered that there was a pack of Gauloises on the table and a pair of fleece-lined slippers. Feeling his way, he went over to the table. "In Paris, any mention of something beyond Vienna sounds like literature," Gregorovius was saying, with a voice that seemed to be pleading. Horacio found the cigarettes and opened the drawer of the bedside table to take out the slippers. In the darkness he could make out the figure of Rocamadour lying on his back. Without really knowing why, he stroked his forehead with a finger. "My mother didn't like to talk about Transylvania, she was afraid that people would associate her with stories about vampires and all that . . . And Tokay, you know . . . " Horacio tried to get a better look, kneeling next to the bed. "You can imagine in Montevideo,"

La Maga was saying. "You think that people are all alike, but when you live on the Cerro side of town . . . Is *tokay* a kind of bird?" "Well, in a certain sense." The natural reaction in cases like this. Let's see: first . . . ("What does in a certain sense mean? Is it a bird or isn't it?") But all he had to do was put a finger on the baby's lips, the lack of a response. "I was taking the liberty of using a trite image, Lucía. There is a bird sleeping in all good wines." Forced breathing, idiocy. Another form of idiocy that his hands should be trembling so much, barefoot and wet (his feet would have to be rubbed with alcohol, vigorously if possible). "*Un soir, l'âme du vin chantait dans les bouteilles*," Ossip scanned. "Just like Anacreon, I think . . . " And one could almost touch La Maga's resentful silence, her mental note: Anacreon, a Greek writer no one ever reads. Everybody knows about him except me. And where was that line from, *un soir, l'âme du vin*? Horacio slipped his hand under the sheets, it was a great effort to bring himself to feel Rocamadour's tiny stomach, the cold thighs, there seemed to be a little warmth left farther up, but no, he was so cold. "Fall into the pattern," Horacio thought. "Shout, turn on the light, start the obligatory hustle and bustle. Why?" But maybe, still . . . "Then it means that this instinct is of no use to me, this thing I'm starting to discover from deep down inside of me. If I call out it will be Berthe Trépat all over again, the same stupid attempts, pity. Put the glove on, do what must be done in cases like this. Oh no, that's enough. Why turn on the light and shout if it won't do any good? An actor, a perfect fucking actor. All that can be done is . . . " He heard Gregorovius's glass tinkle against the bottle of *caña*. "Yes, it's quite like *barack*." With a Gauloise in his mouth he struck a match, taking a good look. "You'll wake him up," La Maga said as she put some fresh *yerba mate* in his gourd. Horacio blew the match out brutally. It's a known fact that if the pupils, under a bright light, etc. *Quod erat demonstrandum*. "Like *barack*, but a little less aromatic," Ossip was saying.

"The old man is knocking again," La Maga said.

"It must be a shutter,' said Gregorovius.

"This building doesn't have shutters. He must have gone crazy."

Oliveira put on the slippers and went back to the chair. The *mate* was wonderful, hot and very bitter. There was pounding upstairs, twice, weakly.

"He's killing cockroaches," Gregorovius suggested.

"No, he's got blood in his eye and he doesn't want to let us sleep. Go up and say something to him, Horacio."

"You go up," Oliveira said. "I don't know why, but he's more afraid of you than of me. At least he doesn't come out with xenophobia, apartheid, and other forms of segregation."

"If I go up there I'll tell him so many things that he'll call the police."

"It's raining too hard. Work on his moral side, praise the decorations he has on his door. Talk about your feelings as a mother and things like that. Go ahead."

"I don't feel like it," La Maga said.

"Go ahead, sweetheart," Oliveira said in a low voice.

"But why do you want me to go?"

"To please me. You'll see, he'll stop."

There were two thumps, then one. La Maga got up and went out of the apartment. Horacio followed her, and when he heard her going upstairs he turned on the light and looked at Gregorovius. He pointed to the bed. After a minute he turned out the light while Gregorovius went back to his chair.

"It's incredible," Ossip said as he grabbed the bottle of *caña* in the dark.

"Incredible, of course. Inevitable, all that. No obituaries, old man. All I had to do was leave this flat for one day and the damnedest things happened. Anyway, one thing can be the consolation for the other."

"I don't understand," Gregorovius said.

"You understand beautifully. *Ça va, ça va.* You can't imagine how little I care."

Gregorovius noticed that Oliveira was using the familiar form and this meant that things would be different, if it were still possible . . . He said something about the Red Cross, all-night chemists.

"Do what you want to do, it's all the same to me," Oliveira said. "What a day this has been, brother!"

If he could only flop on the bed and go to sleep for a couple of years. "Chicken," he thought. Gregorovius had caught his contagious immobility and was laboriously lighting his pipe. They could hear talking from far off, La Maga's voice coming through the rain, the old man answering her with his shrill voice. The door of some other apartment slammed, people going out to complain about the noise.

"Basically you're right," Gregorovius admitted. "But isn't there some legal responsibility?"

"With everything that has happened we're in it up to our necks," Oliveira said. "Especially you two, I can always prove that I arrived too late. A mother lets her child die while she takes care of her lover on the floor."

"If you're trying to say . . . "

"It doesn't really matter."

"But it's not true, Horacio."

"It doesn't make any difference to me, consummation is an after-effect. I don't have anything to do with the whole business any more, I only came up because I was soaked and I wanted a *mate*. Hey, people are coming."

"We ought to call an ambulance," Gregorovius said.

"Go ahead then. Doesn't that sound like Ronald's voice?"

"I'm not going to sit here," Gregorovius said. "We've got to do something, I tell you, we've got to do something."

"But I'm quite aware of that. Action, always action. *Die Tätigkeit*, old man. Bang, there weren't many of us left and grandmother gave birth. Keep your voices down, you'll wake the baby."

"Hello," said Ronald.

"Hi," said Babs, struggling to close her umbrella.

"Keep your voices down," said La Maga, who was coming in behind them. "Why didn't you close the umbrella outside?"

"You're right," Babs said. "The same thing always happens to me everywhere I go. Don't make any noise, Ronald. We only stopped by to tell you about Guy, it's unbelievable. Have you blown a fuse?"

"No, it's because of Rocamadour."

"Keep your voice down," Ronald said. "And put that damn umbrella down somewhere."

"It's so hard to close," Babs said. "It opens so easily."

"The old man threatened to call the police," La Maga said, closing the door. "He was ready to hit me, shrieking like a madman. Ossip, you really should see what's in his apartment, you can see a little from the stairway. A table full of empty bottles and in the middle a windmill that's so big it looks lifesize, just like the ones out in the country in Uruguay. And the windmill was turning from the draft, I couldn't help peeping through the crack in the door, the old man was frothing at the mouth he was so angry."

"I can't close it," Babs said. "I'll stick it in this corner."

"It looks like a bat," La Maga said. "Give it to me, I'll close it. See how easy?"

"She's broken two ribs," Babs said to Ronald.

"Stop fussing," Ronald said. "Besides, we'll be leaving right away, we only came to tell you that Guy swallowed a tube of gardenal."

"Poor dear," said Oliveira, who didn't care very much for Guy.

"Étienne found him half-dead, Babs and I had gone to a *vernissage* (I have to tell you about that sometime, it was fabulous), and Guy had gone up to the apartment, got into bed, and poisoned himself."

"He has no manners at all," Oliveira said in English. "*C'est regrettable.*"

"Étienne had come by to look for us, luckily everybody has a key," Babs said. "He heard someone vomiting, went in, and found Guy. He was dying. Étienne ran out to get help. They've taken him to the hospital now and he's in a critical condition. And with all this rain," Babs added, flustered.

"Sit down," La Maga said. "Not there, Ronald, there's a leg missing. It's so dark in here because of Rocamadour. Speak softly."

"Make them some coffee," Oliveira said. "Great weather, eh?"

"I'll have to be going," Gregorovius said. "I wonder where I put my raincoat – no, not there, Lucía . . . "

"Stay and have some coffee," La Maga said. "The Métro has stopped running and it's comfortable here. You can grind some fresh coffee, Horacio."

"It smells stuffy in here," Babs said.

"She always misses the pure outside ozone," Ronald said furiously. "She's like a horse, she only loves pure and unadulterated things. Primary colours, the seven-note scale. I don't think she's human."

"Humanity is an ideal," said Oliveira, feeling around for the coffee grinder. "Air has its story too. Coming from a wet street with lots of ozone, as you said, into an atmosphere whose temperature and make-up have been fifty centuries in the making . . . Babs is a kind of Rip van Winkle of respiration."

"Oh, Rip van Winkle," Babs said delighted. "My grandmother used to read me stories about him."

"In Idaho, we all know," Ronald said. "Well, what happened next was that Étienne called us at the bar on the corner a half-hour ago and told us that it would be best if we stayed away from our place for the night, at least until they know whether Guy is going to die or is going to vomit up the gardenal. It could be bad if the cops came by and found us there, they're pretty good at putting two and two together, and lately all the business with the Club has put them in a bad mood."

"What's wrong with the Club?" La Maga asked, as she dried some cups with a towel.

"Nothing, but that's precisely why we have no defence. The neighbours have complained so much about the noise, the record sessions, the coming and going at all hours . . . And besides, Babs has run-ins with the concierge and all the other women in the building, fifty or sixty of them."

"They're awful," Babs said, chewing a sweet she had taken out of her pocket. "They smell marijuana even if you're only cooking a goulash."

Oliveira was tired of grinding the coffee and passed the grinder to Ronald. Speaking softly, Babs and La Maga were discussing the motives behind Guy's attempted suicide. After fussing so much about his raincoat, Gregorovius had flopped in the easy chair and was very quiet, keeping his unlit pipe in his mouth. The rain was beating on the window. "Schoenberg and Brahms," Oliveira thought, taking out a Gauloise. "It's OK, usually under these circumstances one hears Chopin or the *Todesmusik* for Siegfried. Yesterday's tornado killed between two and three thousand people in Japan. Statistically speaking . . . " But statistics didn't stop his cigarette from tasting oily. He examined it as best he could, lighting another match. It was a perfect Gauloise, very white, with its delicate writing and shreds of its harsh tobacco coming out of the wet end. "I always wet my cigarettes when I'm nervous," he thought. "When I think about things like Rose Bob . . . Yes, it's been a mother of a day, and look what's ahead of us." The best thing would be to tell Ronald so that Ronald could pass it on to Babs in one of those almost telepathic messages that startled Perico Romero so. The theory of communication, one of those fascinating themes that literature had not gone into much until the Huxleys and the Borgeses of the new generation came along. Now Ronald was counting in time to the whispers passing between Babs and La Maga, spinning the grinder vigorously, the coffee wouldn't be ready until doomsday. Oliveira slid off the horrible art nouveau chair and made himself comfortable on the floor, with his head resting on a pile of newspapers. There was a strange glow on the ceiling which must have been more subjective than anything else. When he closed his eyes the glow would last for a moment, then great purple spheres would begin to explode, one after another, *voof, voof, voof,* each sphere evidently corresponded to a systole or a diastole, who could tell. And somewhere in the building, probably on the third floor, a telephone was ringing. An extraordinary thing in Paris at that hour. "Another death," Oliveira thought. "That's the only reason anybody calls up in this city so considerate of sleep." He remembered the time a recently arrived friend from Argentina had thought it quite natural to call him up at ten-thirty in the evening. God knows how, but he had managed to get the number of some telephone in the building from the Bottin guide and he made the call then and there. The face of the gentleman from the fifth floor in his bathrobe, knocking at the door, an icy stare, *quelqu'un vous demande au téléphone,* Oliveira confused, putting on a wrap, going up to the fifth floor, finding a steadfastly annoyed woman, learning that old buddy Hermida was in Paris and when can we get together, man, I've got news from everybody, Traveler, and the boys in the Bidú bar, etc., and the woman hiding her irritation as she waited for Oliveira to start crying when he learned of the death of somebody very close, and Oliveira without knowing why, *vraiment je suis tellement confus, madame, monsieur, c'était un ami qui vient d'arriver, vous comprenez, il n'est pas du tout au courant des habitudes* . . . Oh, Argentina, generous schedules, open house, time to throw away, the whole future in front, all of it, *voof, voof, voof,* but behind the eyes of that one six feet away there was nothing, there couldn't ever be anything, the whole theory of communication ended, no mamma, no dada, no papa, no peepee no *voof voof* no nothing, just *rigor mortis* and people hanging around who didn't even come from Salta or Mexico and so could organize a wake for the *angelito* while they still could listen to music, who couldn't find out like them a way out of the whole death business, people who had never been primitive enough to rise above the distress by means of acceptance or identification, nor yet developed enough to deny all distress and put this "one minor casualty" alongside the three thousand swept away by typhoon Veronica, for example. "But this is all cheap anthropology," Oliveira thought, conscious of a cold feeling in his stomach which was giving him cramps. It was always the solar plexus in the end. "These are the real messages, the warnings beneath the skin. And there is no dictionary for them." Who had turned out the Rembrandt lamp? He couldn't remember, a while back there had been a kind of old-gold dust on the floor, try as he could, he couldn't reconstruct what had happened since Ronald and Babs had come, nothing to do, at some moment La Maga (because it must have been La Maga) or perhaps Gregorovius, someone had turned off the lamp.

"How are you going to make coffee in the dark?"

"I don't know," La Maga said, getting out some cups. "There was some light before."

"Turn it on, Ronald," Oliveira said. "It's underneath your chair there. You have to turn the bulb, it's the classic way."

"This is all quite idiotic," Ronald said, without anyone knowing whether he meant the way the lamp had to be turned on or not. The light made the purple spheres go away, and Oliveira began to like his cigarette better. Now everything was really comfortable, it was warm, there would be coffee.

"Come on over here," Oliveira told Ronald. "You'll be more comfortable than in that chair, it has a kind of point in the middle of it that pricks your bum. Wong would include it in his Peking collection if he knew about it, I'm sure."

"I'm all right here," Ronald said, "at the risk of being misunderstood."

"You're not all right. Come here. And how's that coffee doing, ladies?"

"He's being very masculine tonight," said Babs. "Is he always like that with you?"

"Most of the time," La Maga said without looking at him. "Help me dry this tray."

Oliveira waited for Babs to start the usual comments on the job of making coffee, and when Ronald got off his chair and squatted down near him, he said something in his ear. Listening to them, Gregorovius joined in the conversation about the coffee, and Ronald's answer was lost in the praise of Mocha and how the art of making it had degenerated. Then Ronald got back up on his chair in time to take the cup La Maga was holding out to him. There was a soft pounding on the ceiling, twice, three times. Gregorovius shuddered and drank his coffee down in one gulp. Oliveira was trying not to burst out laughing, which just might have eased his cramp. La Maga looked surprised, in the shadows she looked at everybody in succession and then reached for a cigarette on the table, groping around as if she wanted to get out of something she didn't understand, something like a dream.

"I hear steps," Babs said with a marked Blavatsky tone. "That old man must be crazy, you have to watch out. In Kansas City once . . . No, it's someone coming up the stairs."

"The staircase makes a pattern in your ear," La Maga said. "I feel very sorry for deaf people. It's as if I had my hand on the stairs now and were moving it up the steps one by one. When I was a girl I got an A on a theme I wrote, the story of a little sound. It was a nice little sound, it came and went, things happened to it . . . "

"I, on the other hand . . . " said Babs. "OK, OK, you don't have to pinch me."

"My love," Ronald said, "be still a moment so we can tell whose steps those are. Yes, it's the king of pigments, it's Étienne, it's the great apocalyptic beast."

"He took it calmly," Oliveira thought. "The spoonful of medicine is for two o'clock, I think. We have more than an hour of calm left." He did not understand and he did not want to understand the reason behind the delay, that sort of denial of something already known. Negation, negative . . . "Yes, it's like the negative of reality just-as-it-ought-to-be, that is . . . But don't go getting metaphysical, Horacio. Alas, poor Yorick, *ça suffit.* I can't help it, I think it's better this way than if we turned on the light and released the news like a dove from its cage. A negative. Complete reversal . . . What's most likely is that he's alive and we're all dead. A more modest proposition: he has killed us because we are responsible for his death. Responsible, accomplices in a state of affairs, that is . . . Oh, dear boy, where are you taking yourself, you're the donkey with the carrot hanging down in front of its eyes. And it was Étienne, no less, it was the great painting beast."

"He's out of danger," Étienne said. "Son of a bitch, he's got more lives than Cesare Borgia. And what a job of vomiting . . . "

"Tell us, tell us," Babs said.

"A stomach pump, all kinds of enemas, jabs all over with a needle, a bed with springs, to keep his head down. He threw up the whole menu of the Orestias restaurant, where it seems he had lunch.

What a mess, even stuffed vine leaves. Has anyone noticed that I'm soaked?"

"We've got some hot coffee," Ronald said, "and a foul drink called *caña*."

Étienne snorted, tossed his raincoat in a corner, and went over to the stove.

"How's the baby, Lucía?"

"He's asleep," La Maga said. "He's sleeping quite soundly, fortunately."

"Let's speak quietly," Babs said.

"He regained consciousness around eleven o'clock," Étienne explained in a sort of tender way. "He was a mess, that's for sure. The doctor let me go over to the bed and Guy recognized me. 'You idiot,' I said to him. 'Go fuck yourself,' he answered. The doctor whispered to me that that was a good sign. There were other people in the ward, I got through it pretty well, and you know what hospitals do to me..."

"Did you go back to the flat?" Babs asked. "Did you have to go to the police station?"

"No, everything's been taken care of. In any case, it would be wiser if you spent the night here, you should have seen the face on the concierge when they carried Guy out..."

"The lousy bastard," Babs said in English.

"I put on a virtuous air and when I passed her I lifted up my hand and said: 'Madame, death is always respectable. This young man has tried to kill himself because he was lovesick over Kreisler.' She just hardened up, believe me, and she kept on looking at me with a pair of eyes that looked like two hardboiled eggs. And just as the stretcher was going out the door, Guy raised up a little, put his hand to his pale cheek, just like a statue on an Etruscan tomb, and puked up some green vomit in the direction of the concierge that landed smack in the middle of the doormat. The stretcher-bearers doubled up laughing, it was fantastic."

"More coffee?" Ronald asked. "And sit down over here on the floor, it's the warmest spot in the room. Give poor Étienne a good cup of coffee."

"I can't see anything," Étienne said. "And why do I have to sit on the floor?"

"To keep Horacio and me company, we're keeping a sort of knight's vigil," Ronald said.

"Come off it, you fool," Oliveira said.

"Pay attention to me, sit down here, and you will learn things that not even Wong knows about. The *Libri Fulgurales*, the writings of the ancient seers. Just this morning I was having so much fun reading the *Bardo*. They're amazing creatures, the Tibetans."

"Who initiated you?" Étienne asked, sliding down between Oliveira and Ronald and drinking his coffee down in one gulp. "A drink," Étienne said, putting his hand out imperiously towards La Maga, who put the bottle of *cana* in it. "Terrible," Étienne said after taking a swig. "Product of Argentina, I suppose. What a country, my God."

"Don't put my country down," Oliveira said. "You're like the old man upstairs."

"Wong put me through several tests," Ronald was explaining. "He says that I have enough intelligence to start destroying it profitably. We agreed that I should read the *Bardo* carefully, and from there we would go on to the fundamental phases of Buddhism. Can there really be a subtle body, Horacio? It seems that when one dies . . . A sort of mental body, you understand."

But Horacio was whispering in Étienne's ear and he was grunting and nodding, smelling of wet streets, hospitals and stuffed cabbage. Babs was telling Gregorovius, who had withdrawn into a kind of indifference, all about the innumerable faults of the concierge. Bursting with erudition, Ronald had to explain the *Bardo* to somebody and he started on La Maga, who was outlined opposite him like a Henry Moore in the darkness, a giantess seen from below, first her knees, about to burst through the black mass of her skirt, then a torso which rose up towards the ceiling, on top of it a pile of hair, darker even than the darkness all around, and on top of all this shadow among the shadows the light of the lamp on the floor which made La Maga's eyes shine as she sat in the easy chair and struggled from time to time against slipping out and falling on the floor because the front legs were shorter than the rear ones.

"Lousy business," Étienne said, taking another drink.

"You can leave if you want," Oliveira said, "but I don't think anything serious will happen, things like this happen every day in this neighbourhood."

"I'll stay," Étienne said. "This drink, what's it called? It's not bad. It smells like fruit."

"Wong says that Jung was all excited about the *Bardo*," Ronald was saying. "It's easy to see why, and the existentialists should give it a careful reading too. Look, at the moment of judgement for a dead person, the King puts a mirror to his face, but this mirror is Karma. The summation of all of the dead person's acts, you see. And the dead person sees all his actions reflected, good and bad, but the reflection doesn't correspond to any reality, it's the projection of mental images . . . Tell me why old Jung shouldn't have been a little amazed. The King of the Dead looks into the mirror, but he is really looking into your memory. Can you think of a better description of psychoanalysis? And what's even more extraordinary, my dear, is that the judgement the King pronounces is not his but your own. You judge yourself without knowing it. Don't you think that Sartre really ought to go to live in Lhasa?"

"It's incredible," La Maga said. "But this book, is it philosophy?"

"It's a book for dead people," Oliveira said.

They were silent, listening to the rain. Gregorovius felt sorry for La Maga, who seemed to be waiting for an explanation and didn't feel like asking any more questions.

"The lamas reveal certain things to dying people," he told her. "To guide them in the beyond, to help them be saved. For example . . . "

Étienne was leaning against Oliveira. Ronald was sitting with his legs crossed and humming *Big Lip Blues*, thinking about Jelly Roll, who was his favourite dead man. Oliveira lit a Gauloise, and as in a painting by La Tour, for a second the flame coloured the faces of his friends, it brought Gregorovius out of the shadows and tied the murmur of his voice to a pair of moving lips, brutally set La Maga in the easy chair, with her face that always became avid at moments of ignorance and explanations, softly bathed placid Babs, and Ronald the musician, lost in his moaning improvisations. Then there was a thump on the ceiling just as the match went out.

"*Il faut tenter de vivre*," Oliveira quoted from his memory. "*Pourquoi?*"

The line had come out of his memory just like the faces in the light of the match, instantaneously and probably gratuitously. Étienne's shoulder was warming him, was transmitting a deceptive presence to him, a nearness that death, that match that went out, was going to erase just as now the faces, the shapes, just as the silence closed in again around the knock from upstairs.

"And that is how," Gregorovius was concluding pedantically, "the *Bardo* brings us back to life, to the necessity of a pure life, precisely at the moment when escape is impossible and we are nailed to a bed with a cancer for a pillow."

"Ah, yes," La Maga said, sighing. She had understood enough, a few pieces of the puzzle were in place, although it would never be as perfect as a kaleidoscope, where each crystal, each stick, each grain of sand arranged itself in a perfect, symmetrical, boring pattern, but with no problems.

"Occidental dichotomies," Oliveira said. "Life and death, this side and that side. That's not what your *Bardo* teaches you, Ossip, although personally I haven't the slightest idea what your *Bardo* does teach you. In any case, it must be something more fluid, less categorized."

"Look," said Étienne, who was feeling remarkably well, even though the news that Oliveira had passed on to him was crawling around his insides like a crab and none of this seemed contradictory. "Look, my ball-beloved Argentine, the Orient is not so different as the Orientalists make it out to be. As soon as you start to give some serious thought to what is written there you begin to feel what you have always felt, the inexplicable attraction of intellectual suicide by means of the intellect itself. The scorpion stabbing itself in the neck, tired of being a scorpion but having to have recourse to its own scorpionness in order to do away with itself as a scorpion. In Madras or in Heidelberg it's basically the same question: there is some sort of indescribable mistake at the very beginning of things, out of which comes this phenomenon which is addressing itself to you at this moment and which you are all listening to. Every attempt at explanation comes to grief for reasons that anyone can understand, and the fact is that in order to define and understand something one would have to be outside of what is being defined and understood. *Ergo*, Madras and Heidelberg console themselves manufacturing positions, some with a rational base, others intuitive, even though the differences between reason and intuition can be far from clear, as anyone who's been to school knows. And for that reason, man only feels secure when he is on grounds that do not touch his deepest part: when he plays, when he conquers, when he puts on his various suits of armour that are products of an ethos, when he hands over the central mystery to some revelation. And on all sides the curious notion that our principal tool, the Logos that madly pulls us up the zoological ladder, is a perfect fraud. And the inevitable corollary, refuge in inspiration and babble, dark night of the soul, aesthetic and metaphysical visions. Madras and Heidelberg are different dosages of the same prescription, sometimes the Yin is in the ascendancy, sometimes the Yang, but at the two points of up and down there remain two examples of Homo sapiens, equally undefined, kicking about madly on the ground as one tries to rise at the expense of the other."

"It's strange," Ronald said. "In any case, it would be stupid to deny a reality even though we might not know what it is. Let's take the up–down axis. How is it that this axis still hasn't been of any use in finding out what goes on at its two extremes? Since Neanderthal man . . ."

"You're just using words," Oliveira said, leaning a little more on Étienne. "We like to take them out of the closet and parade them around the room. Reality, Neanderthal man, see how they play, see how they get into our ears and pull each other along on toboggans."

"That's right," Étienne said harshly. "That's why I prefer my colours: I feel sure."

"Sure of what?"

"Of their effect."

"Of their effect on you, in any case, but not on Ronald's concierge. Your colours are no more certain than my words, old man."

"At least my colours don't try to explain anything."

"And do you accept the idea that there is no explanation?"

"No," said Étienne, "but at the same time I do things that to a small degree take away the bad taste of emptiness. And that basically is the best definition of Homo sapiens."

"It's not a definition, it's a consolation," Gregorovius said, sighing. "Actually, we're like a play that we come in on during the second act. Everything is very pretty but we don't understand a thing. The actors speak and move about no one knows why or for what reason. We project our own ignorance into them and they seem like madmen to us, coming and going in a very decided way. Shakespeare has already said it anyway, and if he didn't say it he should have."

"I think he did say it," La Maga said.

"He did say it," Babs said.

"You see?" said La Maga.

"He also talked about words," Gregorovius said, "and all that Horacio has done is to raise the question in its dialectical form, in a manner of speaking. Like Wittgenstein, whom I admire very much."

"I don't know him," Ronald said, "but you all agree that the problem of reality cannot be faced with sighs."

"Who can tell," Gregorovius said. "Who can tell, Ronald."

"Come on, let's leave poetry out of this. Agreed, that we can't trust words, but actually, words come after this other thing, the fact that a bunch of us are here tonight seated around a lamp."

"Lower your voice," La Maga asked.

"Without any words I feel, I know, that I am here," Ronald insisted. "That's what I call reality. Even if that's all it is."

"Perfect," said Oliveira. "Except that this reality is no guarantee for you or for anybody else unless you transform it into a concept, and then into a convention, a useful scheme. The simple fact that you are on my left and I am on your right makes at least two realities out of this one reality, and realize that I don't want to get abstruse and point out that you and I are two entities that are absolutely out of touch with one another except by means of feelings and words, things that one must mistrust if one is to be serious about it all."

"We're both here," Ronald insisted. "On the right or on the left, it doesn't matter. We're both looking at Babs, everybody hears what I'm saying."

"But those are examples for boys in short pants, my son," Gregorovius moaned. "Horacio is right, you can't just accept like that what you think reality is. The most you can say is that you are; that can't be denied unless you want to start a row. What's wrong is the *ergo*, and what follows the *ergo*, that's well known."

"Don't turn it into a question of schools," Oliveira said. "Let's keep it on the level of a conversation among amateurs, which is what we are. Let's stick with what Ronald has so movingly called reality, and which he thinks is one by itself. Do you still think it's just one, Ronald?"

"Yes. I concede that my way of feeling it or understanding it is different from that of Babs, and that Babs's reality is different from Ossip's, and so on down the line. But it's like the different theories about the Mona Lisa or about endive salad. Reality is there and we're inside it, understanding it each in his own way."

"The only thing that matters is the business of each understanding it in his own way," Oliveira said. "You think that there is a definable reality because you and I are talking in this room and at this time, and because you and I know that within an hour or so something predetermined is going to happen here. All of this gives you a great ontological security, I think; you feel very sure of yourself, firmly planted in yourself and in your surroundings. But if at the same time you could be present in this reality from my position, or from Babs's, if you could be placed, you see, and right now could be in this same room, but from where I am and with everything I am and have been, and with everything that Babs is and has been, you would understand that your cheap egocentrism would not afford you any valid reality. All it would give you would be a belief based on terror, a need to affirm what is around you so that you would not fall into the funnel and come out God knows where."

"We're very different," Ronald said, "I'm very much aware of that. But we find ourselves in certain places outside of ourselves. You and I are looking at that lamp, maybe we don't see the same thing, but neither can we be sure that we don't see the same thing. There is a lamp there, what the hell."

"Don't shout," La Maga said. "I'm going to make more coffee."

"One has the impression," Oliveira said, "that he's following old footprints. We're unimportant little schoolboys warming over arguments that are musty and not at all interesting. And all because, dear Ronald, we've been talking dialectically. We say: you, I, lamp, reality. Take a step back, please. Go ahead, it's not hard. Words disappear. That lamp is a stimulus to the senses, nothing else. Now take another step back. What you call your sight and that stimulus take on an inexplicable relationship, because if we wanted to explain it we would have to take a step forward and everything would go to hell."

"But those steps backward are like unwalking what the species of man has already walked," Gregorovius protested.

"Yes," said Oliveira. "And right there is the great problem, to find out if what you call the species has gone forward or if, as Klages thinks, I believe, at some given point it took the wrong road."

"Without speech there's no such thing as man. Without history man doesn't exist."

"Unless there's a crime there's no such thing as a criminal. There's no proof that man could have been any different."

"We haven't done so badly," Ronald said.

"What means of comparison do you have to think that we've done well? Why have we had to invent Eden, to live submerged in the nostalgia of a lost paradise, to make up utopias, propose a future for ourselves? If a worm could think he would think that he hadn't done too badly. Man has grabbed onto science like an anchor of salvation, as someone said, and I'm not quite sure what he meant. Reason with its use of language has set up a satisfactory architecture, like the delightful, rhythmical composition in Renaissance painting, and it has stuck us in the centre. In spite of all its curiosity and dissatisfaction, science, that is to say reason, begins by calming us down. 'You are in this room, with your friends, opposite that lamp. Don't be frightened, everything's all right. Let's see, now: what is the nature of that luminous phenomenon? Do you know what enriched uranium is? Do you like isotopes, did you know that we have already changed lead into gold?' It's all very exciting, it makes you dizzy, but always from the easy chair in which we are so comfortably seated."

"I'm sitting on the floor," Ronald said, "and to tell the truth, it's not comfortable at all. Listen, Horacio: it makes no sense to deny this reality. It's here, we're part of it. The night is here for both of us, it's raining outside for both of us. How should I know what night is, the weather, the rain, but there they are and they're outside of me, they're things that happen to me, there's nothing I have to do about it."

"But of course," Oliveira said. "No one denies that. What we don't understand is why this has to happen this way, why we are here and it's raining outside. The absurd thing is not things themselves; what is absurd is that the things are there and that we think they are absurd. The relationship between me and what is happening to me escapes me at this moment, but I don't deny that it is happening to me. Of course it's happening to me. And that's what's so absurd."

"It's not very clear," Étienne said.

"It can't be clear, if it were it wouldn't be true; it might be scientifically true, perhaps, but as an absolute it would be false. Clarity is an intellectual requirement, nothing more. If only we could know more clearly, think clearly along the border of science and reason. And when I say 'if only', just try to see that I'm saying something idiotic. Probably the only anchor of salvation is science, uranium 235, things like that. But we have to live, after all."

"Yes," said La Maga, serving coffee. "We have to live, after all."

"Understand, Ronald," Oliveira said, squeezing his knees. "You are much more than your intelligence, it's obvious. Tonight, for example, what's happening to us now, here, it's like one of those paintings by Rembrandt where just a bit of light is shining in a corner, and it's not a physical light, it's not what you calmly call a lamp, with its watts and wicks. The absurd thing is to believe that we can grasp the totality of what constitutes us in this moment or in any moment, and sense it as something coherent, something acceptable, if you want. Every time we enter a crisis the absurdity is total; understand that dialectics can only set our closet in order in moments of calm. You know very well that at the high point of a crisis we always work by impulse, just the opposite of foresight, doing the most unexpected and wildest sort of thing. And at that moment precisely it could be said that there was a sort of saturation of reality, don't you think? Reality comes on fast, it shows itself with all its strength, and precisely at that moment the only way of facing it is to renounce dialectics, it's the moment for shooting somebody, jumping overboard, swallowing a bottle of gardenal like Guy, unleashing the dog, a free hand to do anything. Reason is only good to mummify reality in moments of calm or analyse its future storms, never to resolve a crisis of the moment. But these crises are like metaphysical outbursts, like a state that perhaps, if we hadn't chosen the path of reason, would be the natural and current state of *Pithecanthropus erectus*."

"It's very hot, watch out," La Maga said.

"And these crises that most people think of as terrible, as absurd, I personally think they serve to show us the real absurdity, the absurdity of an ordered and calm world, with a room where different people are drinking coffee at two o'clock in the morning, without any of this having the slightest meaning unless it's hedonistic, how nice it is to be near this stove which does its job so well. Miracles have never seemed absurd to me; the absurdity about them is what comes before and after them."

"And still," said Gregorovius, stretching, "*il faut tenter de vivre.*"

"*Voilà,*" Oliveira thought. "Another proof that I won't mention. Of all the millions of possible lines he chooses the one I was thinking about ten minutes ago. What people call chance."

"Well," Étienne said dreamily, "it's not a question of trying to live, since life is something that we have been inevitably presented with. It's been some time now since people have suspected that life and living things are two completely different things. Life lives for itself, whether we like it or not. Guy tried to deny this theory today, but statistically speaking it's incontrovertible. Which torture and concentration camps vouch for. Of all our feelings the only one which really doesn't belong to us is hope. Hope belongs to life, it's life itself defending itself. Etcetera. And with all this I'm going off to bed, because Guy's shenanigans have reduced me to ashes. Ronald, you must come by the studio tomorrow morning, I've just finished a still life that will knock you out."

"Horacio hasn't convinced me," Ronald said. "I agree that a lot of what is around me is absurd, but we probably call it that because that's what we call anything we don't understand yet. Someday we'll know."

"Charming optimist," Oliveira said. "We could also put optimism on the tab of pure life. What gives you strength is that for you there is no future, as is logical in the case of most agnostics. You're always alive, you're always present, everything is in perfect order for you as in a picture by Van Eyck. But if that horrible thing that is not to have faith and at the same time to be heading towards death were to happen to you, to be heading towards the scandal of all scandals, your mirror would fog up pretty fast."

"Come on, Ronald," Babs said. "It's very late, I'm getting sleepy."

"Wait, wait a minute. I was thinking about the death of my father, yes, there's some truth in what you say. I could never fit that piece into the puzzle, it was something that had no explanation. A happy young man, in Alabama. He was walking along the street and a tree fell on him. I was fifteen at the time and they came to get me in school. But there are so many other absurd things, Horacio, so many deaths and mistakes . . . I suppose it's not a question of numbers. It's not a total absurdity as you think."

"The absurdity is that it doesn't look like an absurdity," said Oliveira in an obscure way. "The absurdity is that you go out in the morning and find a bottle of milk on the doorstep and you are at peace because the same thing happened to you yesterday and will happen again tomorrow. It's this stagnation, this so be it, this suspicious lack of exceptions. I don't know, you see, we ought to try some other road."

"By renouncing intelligence?" asked Gregorovius, suspiciously.

"I don't know, maybe. Using it in some other way. Can it be proved beyond doubt that logical principles are part and parcel of our intelligence? There are peoples who are capable of survival within a magical order of things . . . Of course, the unfortunates eat raw worms, but that too is just a question of values."

"Worms, how awful," Babs said. "Ronald, dear, it's getting so late."

"Underneath it all," Ronald said, "what bothers you is legality in all its forms. As soon as a thing begins to function well, you feel trapped. But all of us are a little like that, a band of what they call failures because we don't have professions, degrees, and all that. That's why we're in Paris, man, and your famous absurdity is reduced once and for all to a kind of vague, anarchic ideal that you'll never be able to define in concrete terms."

"You're so very right," Oliveira said. "How nice it would be to go out on the street and put up posters in favour of a free Algeria. And along with everything there is to do in the social struggle."

"Action can give meaning to your life," Ronald said. "You must have read that in Malraux, I suppose."

"*Éditions Nouvelle Revue Française*," Oliveira said.

"But still you keep on masturbating like a monkey, turning false problems round and round, waiting for God knows what. If all of this is absurd you ought to do something to change it."

"Your words sound familiar," Oliveira said. "As soon as you think the discussion is heading towards something you consider more concrete, like your famous bit on action, you get all eloquent. You refuse to see that action, just like inaction, has to be earned. How can one act unless there is a previous central attitude, a sort of acceptance of what we call the good and the true? Your notions about truth and goodness are purely historical, based on an ethic you inherited. But history and ethics are highly dubious as far as I'm concerned."

"Sometime," Étienne said as he stood up, "I'd like to hear more details on what you call the central attitude. Right in the middle of the centre itself there's probably a perfect emptiness."

"Don't think I haven't thought of that," Oliveira said. "But even for aesthetic reasons, which are easy for you to appreciate, you have to admit that between being in a centre and fluttering around its edges there is a qualitative difference that makes you stop and think."

"Horacio," said Gregorovius, "is making great use of those very words he was so emphatically advising us against a while back. He's a man one must not ask for speeches but for other things, foggy and unexplainable things like dreams, coincidences, revelations, and above all, black humour."

"The guy upstairs knocked again," Babs said.

"No, it's the rain," said La Maga. "It's time to give Rocamadour his medicine."

"There's still some time," said Babs, crouching over hurriedly as she held her watch next to the lamp. "Ten to three. Let's go Ronald, it's quite late."

"We'll leave at five past three," Ronald said.

"Why five past three?" La Maga asked.

"Because the first quarter of an hour is always lucky," Gregorovius explained.

"Give me another shot of *caña*," Étienne asked. "*Merde*, it's all gone."

Oliveira put out his cigarette. "The knight's vigil," he thought thankfully. "They're real friends, even Ossip, poor devil. Now we shall have fifteen minutes of chain reactions which no one will be able to avoid, no one, not even by thinking that next year, at this very same hour, the most exact and detailed memory will not be capable of changing the output of adrenalin or saliva, the sweat on the palms of the hands . . . These are the truths that Ronald will always refuse to understand. What have I done tonight? Slightly monstrous, a priori. Perhaps we should have tried an oxygen balloon, something like that. Fool, really; we would only have been prolonging life the way it was in the case of Monsieur Valdemar."

"We ought to prepare her," Ronald whispered in his ear.

"Don't be foolish, please. Can't you sense that she's prepared already, that the smell is floating in the air?"

"Now you begin to speak quietly," La Maga said, "just when there's no reason to any more."

"*Tu parles*," Oliveira thought.

"Smell?" Ronald murmured. "I don't smell anything."

"Well, it'll be three o'clock pretty soon," Étienne said, shivering as if he were cold. "Make an attempt, Ronald; Horacio may not be a genius, but it's easy to sense what he's trying to tell you. All we can do is stay a while longer and go along with whatever happens.

And you, Horacio, now that I think of it, what you said about the Rembrandt painting was rather good. There's metapainting just as there is metamusic, and the old boy was sticking his arms in up to the elbows in what he was doing. Only someone blinded by logic or good manners can stop in front of a Rembrandt and not feel that there is a window there that opens onto something else, a sign. Very dangerous for painting, but on the other hand . . . "

"Painting is an art form like so many others," Oliveira said. "It doesn't need too much protection as far as being a form is concerned. Besides, for every Rembrandt there are a hundred others who are nothing but painters, so painting is quite safe from harm."

"Luckily," Étienne said.

"Luckily," accepted Oliveira. "Luckily everything is going very well in the best of all possible worlds. Turn on the big light, Babs, it's the switch behind your chair."

"I wonder where there's a clean spoon," said La Maga, getting up.

With an effort that seemed repugnant to him, Oliveira avoided looking towards the corner of the room. La Maga was dazzled by the light and was rubbing her eyes, and Babs, Ossip, and the others looked away, looked back, and looked away again. Babs had started to take La Maga by the arm, but something on Ronald's face held her back. Étienne got up slowly, pulling his trousers up since they were still wet. Ossip unfolded himself from the easy chair and was saying something about finding his raincoat. "Now is the time for them to pound on the ceiling," Oliveira thought, closing his eyes. "Several thumps in a row, and then three more, solemnly. But everything is backwards, instead of turning off the lights we turn them on, we're on the stage, there's nothing we can do about it." He got up in turn, and he felt it in his bones, walking all day, the things that had been going on all day long. La Maga had found the spoon on the side, behind a pile of records and books. She began to wipe it with the hem of her skirt, she examined it under the light. "Now she'll put the medicine in the spoon, and then she'll spill half of it before she reaches the bed," Oliveira said to himself, leaning against the wall. They were all so still that La Maga looked at them in wonder, but she was having trouble getting the bottle opened, Babs wanted to help her, hold the spoon for her, and all the while her face was all tightened up as if what La Maga was doing was some indescribable horror, until La Maga poured the liquid into the spoon and put the bottle down carelessly on the table where there was barely room for it between the notebooks and the paper, and holding the spoon like Blondin with a balancing pole, as an angel holds a saint who is about to slide off the edge of a cliff, she began to walk, shuffling her slippers, and started over to the bed with Babs at her side, whose face was twitching and who tried to look and not to look and then to look at Ronald and the others who came up behind her, Oliveira bringing up the rear with his cigarette extinguished in his mouth.

"It always spills on me when . . . " La Maga said, stopping at the edge of the bed.

"Lucía," Babs said, bringing her hands close to her shoulders but not touching them.

The liquid fell on the bedcovers and the spoon fell into it. La Maga shrieked and rolled onto the bed, face down then on her back then on her side as her hands clutched an indifferent ashen little doll who trembled and shook without conviction, uselessly mistreated and cuddled.

"Oh, shit, we should have prepared her for it," Ronald said. "There wasn't any reason, it's a disgrace. Everybody spouting nonsense and this, this . . . "

"Don't get hysterical," Étienne said sharply. "Act like Ossip, at least, he hasn't lost his head. Get some cologne if there's something like it around. I heard the old man upstairs. He's started again."

"He's got good reason," Oliveira said, looking at Babs who was struggling to get La Maga off the bed. "What a night we've been giving him, Jesus."

"He can go fuck himself," Ronald said. "I'd like to go out and smash his face in, the old bastard. If he hasn't got any respect for other people's troubles . . . "

"Take it easy," Oliveira said in English. "There's your cologne, take my handkerchief even if it's not the whitest in the world. Well, we'll have to notify the police."

"I can go," said Gregorovius, who had his raincoat over his arm.

"But of course you're a member of the family," Oliveira said.

"If you could just cry," Babs was saying, stroking La Maga on the forehead as she laid her head on the pillow and was staring at Rocamadour. "Give me a handkerchief with alcohol on it, please, something to bring her round."

Étienne and Ronald began to bustle around the bed. The thumps were coming rhythmically on the ceiling and Ronald looked up each time and once shook his fist hysterically. Oliveira had withdrawn to the stove and was watching and listening from there. He felt that he had been saddled with fatigue and that it was pulling him down, making it hard for him to breathe, to move. He lit another cigarette, the last one in the pack. Things began to get a little better. Babs had rummaged in a corner of the room and after making a sort of cradle out of two chairs and a blanket was conferring with Ronald (it was strange to watch their gestures over La Maga, who was lost in a cold delirium, in a vehement but dry and spasmodic monologue); at one point they covered La Maga's eyes with a handkerchief ("If that's cologne they're going to blind her," Oliveira said to himself), and with extraordinary quickness they helped Étienne lift up Rocamadour and carry him to the improvised cradle while they pulled the bedcover out from under La Maga and put it on top of her, speaking to her softly, caressing her, making her inhale what was on the handkerchief. Gregorovius had gone over to the door and was standing there, not having made up his mind to go out, looking furtively at the bed and then at Oliveira, who had his back turned towards him but sensed that he was looking at him. When he decided to leave, the old man was already on the landing with a stick in his hand, and Ossip jumped back inside. The stick clattered against the door. "That's the way things can keep on piling up," Oliveira said to himself, taking a step towards the door. Ronald, who had guessed what was going on, threw himself furiously towards the door while Babs shouted something at him in English. Gregorovius tried to stop him, but it was too late. Ronald, Ossip and Babs went out followed by Étienne, who glanced at Oliveira as if he were the only one who still had some common sense left.

"Don't let them do anything stupid," Oliveira said to him. "The old man must be eighty and he's crazy."

"*Tous des cons!*" the old man was shouting on the landing. "*Bande de tueurs, si vous croyez que ça va se passer comme ça! Des fripouilles, des fainéants. Tas d'enculés!*"

It was odd that he was not shouting very loudly. Through the half-open door Étienne's voice bounced back like a return shot: "*Ta gueule, pépère.*" Gregorovius had grabbed Ronald by the arm, but in the light that came from the apartment Ronald had been able to see that the old man really was very old and all he did was shake his fist in his face with less conviction each time he did it. Once or twice Oliveira glanced at the bed where La Maga was very still beneath the covers. She was sobbing heavily with her mouth plunged into the pillow, on the exact spot where Rocamadour's head had been. "*Faudrait quand même laisser dormir les gens*," the old man was saying. "*Qu'est-ce que ça me fait, moi, un gosse qu'a claqué? C'est pas une façon d'agir quand même, on est à Paris, pas en Amazonie.*" Étienne's voice became louder and swallowed up the other as he convinced him. Oliveira told himself that it would not be so difficult to go over to the bed, squat down beside it and say a few words in La Maga's ear. "But I would be doing it for myself," he thought. "She's beyond anything. I'm the one who would sleep better afterwards, even if it's just an expression. Me, me, me. I would sleep better after I kissed her and consoled her and repeated everything these people here have already said."

"*Eh bien, moi, messieurs, je respecte la douleur d'une mère*," the old man's voice said. "*Allez, bonsoir messieurs, dames.*"

The rain was slicing down on the window. Paris must be a great grey bubble in which dawn would come up little by little. Oliveira went over to the corner where his lumberjacket was looking like the torso of a quartered criminal, oozing dampness. He put it on slowly, looking all the while towards the bed as if he expected something. He thought of Berthe Trépat's arm on his, the walk in the rain. "*¿ De qué te sirvió el verano, oh rui-señor en la nieve?* " he quoted ironically. "Stinking, absolutely stinking. And I'm out of cigarettes, damn it." He would have to go all the way to the Bébert café, but in the end dawn would be just as repugnant there as anywhere else.

"What an old fool," Ronald said, closing the door.

"He went back to his flat," Étienne said. "I think Gregorovius went out to tell the police. Are you staying?"

"No, what for? They won't like it if they find so many people here at this hour. It would be better for Babs to stay, two women are always more convincing in these cases. It's more intimate, understand?"

Étienne looked at him.

"I'd like to know why your mouth is quivering so much," he said.

"Nervous tics," Oliveira said.

"Tics don't go well with the cynical air. I'll go with you, come on."

"Let's go."

He knew that La Maga had sat up in bed and was looking at him. Putting his hands in the pockets of his lumberjacket, he went to the door. Étienne made a sign as if to hold him back and then followed him out. Ronald saw them leave and shrugged his shoulders, furious. "This is all so absurd," he thought. The idea that everything was absurd made him uncomfortable, but he couldn't tell why. He began to help Babs, made himself useful, wetted compresses. The pounding on the ceiling started up again.

(–130)

29

"*Tiens*," said Oliveira.

Gregorovius was huddled by the stove, wrapped up in a black bathrobe, reading. He had hung a lamp on a nail in the wall and with a shade made out of a newspaper was guiding the light just where he needed it.

"I didn't know you had a key."

"Leftover," said Oliveira, tossing his lumberjacket in the usual corner. "I'll let you have it, now that the place is yours."

"Just for a while. It's too cold in here, and besides, I've got that old man upstairs. He pounded on the floor for five minutes this morning. Why, I don't know."

"Habit. Everything has a longer overlap than it should. Take me, for example. I climb the stairs, I take out my key, I open the door . . . It stinks in here."

"Cold as hell," said Gregorovius. "After they finished fumigating I had to keep the window open for forty-eight hours."

"And you were here all the time? *Caritas.* What kind of a guy are you?"

"That wasn't why. I was afraid somebody from the landlady might use that time to get in here and cause trouble. Lucía told me once that the landlady is an old nut and that a lot of tenants have owed her rent for years. When I was in Budapest I was reading law and things like that stick with you."

"You've made a real posh setup for yourself. *Chapeau, mon vieux.* I hope they didn't throw out my *yerba mate*."

"No, it's over there in the bedside table, among the stockings. There's lots of space now."

"So it seems," said Oliveira. "La Maga had an attack of neatness. I don't see any records or books. But now that I think of it . . . "

"She took everything," said Gregorovius.

Oliveira opened the drawer of the bedside table and took out the *yerba mate* and the gourd that went with it. He began to fill the gourd slowly, looking all around. The lyrics of *Mi noche triste* began to run through his head. He counted on his fingers: Thursday, Friday, Saturday. No. Monday, Tuesday, Wednesday. No. Thursday night, Berthe Trépat, *me amuraste / en lo mejor de la vida*, Wednesday (a wild binge; n.b., don't mix vodka and red wine), *dejándome el alma herida / y espina en el corazón.* Thursday, Friday, Ronald and a rented car, a visit to Guy Monod, like an old glove come home, buckets of green vomit, out of danger, *sabiendo que te quería / que vos eras mi alegría / mi esperanza y mi ilusión.* Saturday, where? where? somewhere near Marly-le-Roi, five days in all; no, six, a week more or less, and the room still cold in spite of the stove. Wily old Ossip, king of convenience.

"So she's gone," said Oliveira, plumping down in the easy chair and keeping the little kettle within reach.

Gregorovius nodded. He had his book open on his knees and gave the impression that he would like to keep on reading.

"And she left her place to you."

"She knew I was in delicate shape," said Gregorovius. "My great-aunt stopped sending me my allowance, she's probably dead. Miss Babington hasn't said anything, but with the situation in Cyprus . . . And you know what that can mean to Malta, censorship and all that. Since you had said you were going away, Lucía offered to share the room with me. I wasn't sure, but she insisted."

"It doesn't tie in too well with her leaving."

"But that was before all this happened."

"Before they fumigated?"

"Exactly."

"You've hit the jackpot, Ossip."

"It's all very sad, really," said Gregorovius. "It could have been quite different."

"Don't complain. A room twelve by ten for five thousand francs a month, with running water . . . "

"I want everything to be perfectly clear between us," said Gregorovius. "This room . . . "

"Doesn't belong to me. Take it easy. And La Maga has gone."

"Anyway . . . "

"Where did she go?"

"She said something about Montevideo."

"She hasn't got enough money for that."

"She mentioned Perugia."

"You must mean Lucca. Ever since she read *Sparkenbroke* she's been crazy about those things. Once and for all, tell me where she went."

"I don't have the slightest idea, Horacio. Last Friday she filled a suitcase with books and clothes, bundled a lot of things together, and then two Negroes came and took it all away. She told me I could stay here, but since she was crying all the time you can imagine how hard it was to talk to her."

"I'd like to hit you in the face," said Oliveira, sucking on his *mate*.

"It's not my fault."

"It's not a matter of fault, damn it. You're so damned Dostoevskian, repulsive and pleasant at the same time. A kind of metaphysical arse-kisser. When you put on a smile like that who in hell would ever want to hurt you."

"Oh, I'm one up on you," said Gregorovius. "The mechanics of 'challenge and response' is a bourgeois trait. You're like me, that's why you can't hit me. Don't look at me like that. I don't know what's happened to Lucía. One of the Negroes I mentioned always hangs out in the Café Bonaparte. I've seen him there. He could probably tell you. But why are you looking for her now?"

"What do you mean, 'now'?"

Gregorovius shrugged his shoulders.

"It was a very proper wake," he said. "Especially after we got rid of the police. Socially speaking, people were commenting about the fact that you weren't there. The Club was on your side, but the neighbours and the old man upstairs . . . "

"You mean to tell me that the old man came to the wake?"

"It wasn't really a wake. They let us keep the body until noon, then the authorities came. Efficient and quick, I must admit."

"I can picture the whole thing," said Oliveira. "But there's no reason for La Maga to move without so much as a word."

"She thought you'd been with Pola all the time."

"*Ça alors*," said Oliveira.

"People do get ideas, you know. It's all your fault that we're using the familiar form and that makes it harder for me to tell you certain things. It's obviously a paradox, but that's the way it is. It must be because it's a false familiarity. You started it the other night."

"I don't see any reason not to be familiar with the man who's been sleeping with my girl."

"I'm getting sick of telling you it wasn't that way. So there's no reason for us to use the familiar form. If La Maga had really drowned, I can see how in the grief of the moment, while we were embracing and consoling each other . . . But that's not how it was. At least I don't think so."

"You saw something in the paper," said Oliveira.

"The description doesn't match at all. We can still use formal address. There it is over there, on the mantel."

The description, in fact, did not match. Oliveira took the newspaper and prepared himself another *mate.* Lucca, Montevideo, *la guitarra en el ropero / para siempre está colgada* . . . And when she puts everything in a suitcase and makes up bundles one might deduce that (take care: all deductions are not necessarily proofs), *nadie en ella toca nada / ni hace sus cuerdas sonar.* Or makes music on its strings.

"Well, I'll find out where she's gone. She couldn't get very far."

"This will always be her home," said Gregorovius, "even though Adgalle is coming to stay with me this spring."

"Your mother?"

"Yes. She sent an emotional telegram in which she mentioned the tetragrammaton. It so happened that I had been reading the *Sefer Yetzirah,* trying to trace its Neoplatonic influences. Adgalle knows her kabala. There'll be some wild arguments."

"Had La Maga said anything that would make you think she'd kill herself?"

"Well, you know women."

"Anything concrete."

"No, I don't think so," said Gregorovius. "She talked a lot about Montevideo."

"She's a fool. She doesn't have a cent."

"About Montevideo and that business of a wax doll."

"Hmm, the doll. And she imagined that . . . "

"She was sure of it. Adgalle will be interested in this; what you called coincidence. Lucía doesn't think it was coincidence. You either, deep inside. Lucía told me that when you found the green doll you threw it on the floor and stepped on it."

"I hate stupidity," said Oliveira virtuously.

"All the pins had been stuck in the breasts, except for one in the organs. Did you know already that Pola was sick when you trampled on the green doll?"

"Yes."

"Adgalle will be fascinated. Do you know anything about poisoned portraits? You mix some poison with the paints and you wait for a favourable moon to paint the portrait. Adgalle tried it on her father, but there were interferences . . . In any case, the old man died of some kind of diphtheria three years later. He was alone in the castle. We had a castle in those days, and when he began to asphyxiate he tried to perform a tracheotomy in front of the mirror by inserting a goose quill or something like that. They found him at the bottom of the stairs. But I don't know why I'm telling you all this."

"Because you don't give a damn, I suppose."

"Yes, maybe," said Gregorovius. "Let's have some coffee. You can feel night coming on at this hour, even though you can't see it."

Oliveira picked up the newspaper. While Ossip put the pot on the fire he began to read the news. "Blonde, about forty-two." How stupid to think that . . . But, of course . . . *Les travaux du grand barrage d'Assouan ont commencé. Avant cinq ans, la vallée moyenne du Nil sera transformée en un immense lac. Des édifices prodigieux, qui comptent parmi les plus admirables de la planète . . .*

(–107)

30

"A misunderstanding, like everything else. But the coffee is up to the occasion. Did you drink all the *caña*?"

"The wake, you understand . . . "

"Of course, the little corpse."

"Ronald was drinking like a beast. He was really upset, nobody could figure out why. Babs was suspicious. Even Lucía was surprised at him. But the watchmaker on the sixth floor brought a bottle of brandy and it was enough for everybody."

"Did many people come?"

"Well, let's see, all the club was there, you weren't there," ("No, I wasn't there") "the watchmaker from the sixth floor, the concierge and her daughter, a woman who looked like a moth, the telegraph man stayed a while, and the police were nosing around for evidence of infanticide, things like that."

"I'm surprised they didn't talk about an autopsy."

"They mentioned it. Babs blew her top, and Lucía . . . A woman came and looked around, touching and feeling . . . There wasn't enough room for all of us on the stairway, everybody outside and it was cold. They did something, but finally they left us alone. I don't know how, but I've got the death certificate here in my wallet if you want to look at it."

"No, tell me more. I'm listening, even if I don't look like it. Come on, keep talking. I'm very upset. It doesn't show, but you can believe me. I'm listening, come on. I can picture the scene perfectly. You're not going to tell me that Ronald helped carry him downstairs?"

"Yes, he and Perico and the watchmaker. I went with Lucía."

"In front."

"And Babs brought up the rear with Étienne."

"Behind."

"Halfway between the fourth and third floors we heard a tremendous thump. Ronald said it was the old man on the fifth floor getting his vengeance. When mother comes I'm going to have her get to know the old man."

"Your mother? Adgalle?"

"She is my mother, after all, the Herzegovina one. She's going to like this place, she's quite receptive and things have happened here . . . I don't just mean the green doll."

"Come on now, let's see, explain to me why your mother is receptive and about this place. Let's talk, eh, we've got to get these pillows all stuffed. Give me the stuffing."

(–57)

31

It had been some time since Gregorovius had given up the illusion of understanding things, but at any rate, he still wanted misunderstandings to have some sort of order, some reason to them. No matter how many times the cards of the deck might be shuffled, laying them out was always a consecutive process, which would take place on the rectangle of a table-top or a bedspread. To get the *mate* drinker from the pampas willing to reveal the order behind his meanderings. In the worst moments to let him improvise for the moment; then it would be difficult for him to extricate himself from his own web. Between one and another *mate* Oliveira condescended to remember some moment from the past or answer questions. He would ask questions in turn with an ironic interest in the burial, in how people acted. He rarely referred directly to La Maga, but it was clear that he suspected some lying was going on. Montevideo, Lucca, some corner of Paris. Gregorovius told himself that Oliveira would have gone running out if he had had any idea where Lucía was staying. He seemed to be a specialist in lost causes. Lose them first, then run after them like a madman.

"Adgalle is going to enjoy her stay in Paris," Oliveira said, changing the *yerba mate* in his gourd. "If she's looking for the gates of assorted hells, all you have to do is show her some of the things that go on here. On a modest level, of course, but hell has been cheapened too. The *nekias* of today: a trip on the Métro at six-thirty, or going to the police to get your *carte de séjour* renewed."

"You would have liked to have found the main gate, eh? A dialogue with Ajax, with Jacques Clément, with Keitel, with Troppmann."

"Yes, but the biggest hole so far is the one in the bathroom. And not even Traveler understands, and that's saying something. Traveler is a friend of mine you don't know."

"You're hiding your cards," said Gregorovius, looking at the floor.

"For example?"

"I don't know, I'm just guessing. All the time I've known you, all you've done is search, but one gets the feeling that what you're looking for is right in your pocket."

"The mystics talked about that, but they didn't mention pockets."

"And in the meantime you mess up the lives of any number of people."

"They're willing, old man, perfectly willing. All I had to do was give a little shove, I walk through, and there I am. No evil intent."

"But what are you after with all that, Horacio?"

"The freedom of the city."

"Here?"

"It's a metaphor. And since Paris is another metaphor (I've heard you say so sometimes) it seems perfectly natural to me that I came here for that reason."

"But Lucía? And Pola?"

"Heterogeneous quantities," Oliveira said. "Just because they're women you think that you can add them up in the same column. Aren't they looking for their happiness too? And you, so puritanical all of a sudden, haven't you slithered in here as a result of meningitis or whatever it was they found the kid had? It's lucky that you and I are not squares because otherwise one of us would be carried out dead and the other one with handcuffs on. Something just right for Sholokov, believe me. But we don't even detest each other, it's so protective in this apartment."

"You're hiding your cards," said Gregorovius, looking at the floor again.

"Elucidate, *mon frère*, do me that small favour."

"You," insisted Gregorovius, "have an imperial notion in the back of your head. Freedom of the city? Rule of the city. Your resentment: a half-cured ambition. You came here to find a statue of yourself waiting for you on the edge of the Place Dauphine. What I don't understand is your method. Ambition, why not? You're outstanding enough in some ways. But up till now all that I've seen you do has been just the opposite of what other ambitious people would have done. Étienne, for example, and we don't even have to mention Perico."

"Ah," said Oliveira. "It seems your eyes are good for something after all."

"Just the opposite," Ossip repeated, "but without denying ambition. And that's what I don't understand."

"Oh, understanding, you know . . . It's all very mixed up. Take the bit that what you call ambition can only be productive if it's denied. Do you like the formula? That's not it, but what I want to say is something that really is unexplainable. You've got to turn round and round like a dog chasing his tail. All of this and what I said about the freedom of the city ought to satisfy you, you fucking Montenegran."

"I understand in an obscure sort of way. Then you . . . It's not a path, like Vedanta or things like that, I hope."

"No, no."

"A lay renunciation, could we call it that?"

"Not that either. I'm not renouncing anything, I simply do what I can so that things renounce me. Didn't you know that if you want to dig a little hole you've got to shovel up the ground and toss it far away?"

"But freedom of the city, well . . . "

"You've put your finger right on it. Remember the dictum: *Nous ne sommes pas au monde.* Now get the gist of it, slowly."

"An ambition to clear the table and start all over again, is that it?"

"A little bit, a touch of that, just a hair, a drop, oh stern Transylvanian, son of three witches."

"You and the others . . . " murmured Gregorovius, looking for his pipe. "What a bunch, my God. Thieves of eternity, atmospheric frauds, hounds of God, cloud-chasers. It's good we've got an education and can define them. Astral swine."

"You do me honour with those definitions," Oliveira said. "It's proof that you're beginning to understand it all fairly well."

"Bah, I prefer breathing oxygen and hydrogen in the dose the Lord prescribes. My alchemy is much less subtle than what all of you practise; all that interests me is the philosopher's stone. A trifle alongside your frauds and your bathrooms and your ontological deductions."

"It's been a long time since we had a metaphysical chat, eh? They're out of favour with our friends, they think you're a snob. Ronald, for example, finds them ghastly. And Étienne never gets out of the solar spectrum. It's nice being here with you."

"We really could have been friends," Gregorovius said, "if you had had something human about you. I suspect that Lucía must have told you that more than once."

"Every five minutes, to be exact. You've got to see what mileage people can get from the word *human*. But why didn't La Maga stay with you since you glow all over with humanity?"

"Because she wasn't in love with me. Humanity takes in all kinds."

"And now she's going back to Montevideo and she'll fall back into a life that . . . "

"She probably went to Lucca. She'll be better off anywhere without you. The same goes for Pola, or me, or the rest of us. Please excuse my frankness."

"But it fits you so well, Ossip Ossipovich. Why fool ourselves? It's impossible to live with a puppeteer who works with shadows, a moth-tamer. Someone who spends his time making pictures out of the iridescent rings the oil makes on the Seine is unacceptable. Me, with my padlocks and keys that I make out of the air, me, writing with smoke. I'll save the answer for you because I see it coming up: there is no substance more deadly than the one that can ooze in anywhere, that breathes without being aware of it, in words or in love or in friendship. It's been a long time now since I should have been left alone to me, myself and I. You've got to admit that I don't go around kissing arse. Get lost, you son of a Bosnian. The next time you run into me on the street you'd better not even know me."

"You're crazy, Horacio. You're stupidly crazy, because it suits you."

Oliveira took a newspaper clipping out of his pocket that he had kept for God knows how long: a list of all-night chemists in Buenos Aires. Ones that were open from eight o'clock on Monday until the same time on Tuesday.

"First district," he read. "446 Reconquista (Tel. 31-5488), 366 Córdoba (Tel. 32-8845), 599 Esmeralda (Tel. 31-1700), 581 Sarmiento (Tel. 32-2021)."

"What's all that?"

"Moments of reality. I'll explain: Reconquista, something we did to the English. Córdoba, a learned city. Esmeralda, a gypsy girl hanged because she was in love with an archdeacon. Sarmiento, he blew a fart and the wind carried it away. Second version: Reconquista, a street of whores and Near Eastern restaurants. Córdoba, wonderful sweetshops. Esmeralda, a river in Colombia. Sarmiento, he never missed school. Third version: Reconquista, a chemist. Esmeralda, another chemist. Sarmiento, another chemist. Fourth version . . . "

"And when I insist you're crazy it's because I don't see any way out of your famous renunciation."

"620 Florida (Tel. 31-2200)."

"You didn't go to the burial because although you renounce many things, you're still not capable of looking your friends in the face."

"749 Hipólito Yrigoyen (Tel. 34-0936)."

"And Lucía is better off at the bottom of the river than in bed with you."

"800 Bolívar. The phone number is hard to make out. If people in the neighbourhood have a sick kid they won't be able to buy him some Terramycin."

"Yes, at the bottom of the river."

"1117 Corrientes (Tel. 35-1468)."

"Or in Lucca, or in Montevideo."

"Or in 1301 Rivadavia (Tel. 38-7841)."

"Keep that list for Pola," Gregorovius said, getting up. "I'm going out, you can do what you feel like. You're not at home, but since nothing has any reality, and we have to start *ex nihil*, etc . . . Help yourself to all these illusions. I'm going out to get a bottle of brandy."

Oliveira caught up with him next to the door and put his hand on his shoulder.

"2099 Lavalle," he said, looking him in the face and smiling. "1501 Cangallo. 53 Pueyrredón."

"You forgot the telephone numbers," Gregorovius said.

"You're beginning to understand," said Oliveira, taking his hand away. "Underneath it all you've got the feeling that I can't say anything to anybody, to you, or to anybody."

The footsteps stopped when they got to the second floor. "He's coming back," Oliveira thought. "He's afraid I'll burn up the bed or cut up the sheets. Poor Ossip." But after a moment the shoes went on their way downstairs. Seated on the bed, he looked at the papers in the drawer of the bedside table. A novel by Pérez Galdós, a bill from the chemist. It was chemist night. Some pieces of paper with scribbling in pencil. La Maga had taken everything, there was a smell left over from before, the paper on the walls, the bed with the striped spread. A novel by Galdós, what an idea. If it wasn't Vicki Baum it was Roger Martin du Gard, and that brought on the strange jump to Tristan L'Hermite, hours on end repeating for any reason at all "*les rêves de l'eau qui songe*", or an artistic edition of *pantungs*, or stories by Schwitters, a kind of ransom, penitence of the most exquisite and sneaky sort, until suddenly one would fall back into John Dos Passos and spend five days swallowing enormous doses of the printed word.

The scribbling was some kind of letter.

(–32)

32

Baby Rocamadour, baby, baby. Rocamadour.

By now I know you're like a mirror, Rocamadour, sleeping or looking at your feet. Here I am holding a mirror and thinking that it's you. But don't you believe it, I'm writing to you because you don't know how to read. If you did know I wouldn't be writing to you or I'd be writing about important things. Some day I'll have to write to you and tell you to behave and keep warm. Someday seems incredible, Rocamadour. Now I can only write to you in the mirror, sometimes I have to dry my finger because it gets wet with tears. Why, Rocamadour? I'm not sad, your mother is a slob, I dropped the borscht I had prepared for Horacio into the fire; you know who Horacio is, Rocamadour, the man who brought you the velvet bunny last Sunday and who got so bored because you and I had so much to say to one another and he wanted to go back to Paris; then you started to cry and he showed you how the rabbit moved its ears; he looked beautiful then, Horacio I mean, some day you'll understand, Rocamadour.

Rocamadour, it's silly to cry like this because I spilled the borscht. The room is full of beetroot-smell, Rocamadour, you'd laugh if you could see the pieces of beetroot and the cream, all over the floor. It's not too bad because I'll have it all cleaned up by the time Horacio comes, but first I have to write to you, it's so foolish to cry like this, the pots have taken on a soft shape, there are things like halos on the windowpanes, and you can't hear the girl upstairs singing, the one who sings *Les Amants du Havre* all day long. When we're together I'll sing it for you, you'll see. *Puisque la terre est ronde, mon amour t'en fais pas, mon amour, t'en fais pas* . . . Horacio whistles it at night when he's writing or sketching. You'd like it, Rocamadour. You'd like it, Horacio gets furious because I like to use the same familiar form Perico does, but it's different in Uruguay. Perico is the man who didn't bring you anything the other day but talked so much about children and their diet. He knows a lot, you'll respect him someday, Rocamadour, and you'll be a fool if you respect him. But there I go with his familiar again.

Rocamadour, Madame Irène is upset because you're so handsome, so happy, so weepy and shouty and pissy. She says that everything is all right and that you're a charming child, but all the time she keeps her hands in the pockets of her apron the way some sneaky animals do, Rocamadour, and that frightens me. When I said so to Horacio he laughed a lot, but he didn't realize what I really meant, I can't explain it. Rocamadour, if only there was some way to read in your eyes what has happened to you in these two weeks, moment by moment. I think I'll try to get a different *nourrice* even though Horacio will get very angry and say, but you're not interested in what he thinks about me. Another *nourrice* who doesn't talk so much, I don't care whether she says you're naughty or cry at night or don't want to eat, I don't care if when she says all that I can feel that she isn't evil, that she's telling me something that won't do you any harm. It's all so strange, Rocamadour, for example, the way I like to say your name and write it down, every time I get the feeling that I'm touching the tip of your nose and that you're laughing, but Madame Irène never uses your name, she says *l'enfant*, just imagine, she doesn't even say *le gosse*, she says *l'enfant*, it's as if she put on rubber gloves every time she spoke, maybe she already has them on and that's why she puts her hands in her pockets and says that you're so good and so handsome.

There's something called time, Rocamadour, it's like a bug that just keeps on walking. I can't explain it to you because you're so small, but what I mean is that Horacio will be back any minute now. Shall I let him read my letter so that he can add something too? No, I wouldn't want anyone to read a letter that was just for me either. A big secret between the two of us, Rocamadour. I'm not crying any more, I'm happy, but it's so hard to understand things, I need so much time to understand just a little of what Horacio and the others understand right away, but they understand everything so well and they can't understand you and me, they don't understand why I can't have you with me, feed you, change your nappies, make you go to sleep or play with me, they don't understand and they really don't care, and I who care so much only know that I can't have you with me, that it would be bad for both of us, that I have to be alone with Horacio, live with Horacio, I don't know for how long, helping him look for what he's looking for and what you'll be looking for too, Rocamadour, because you will be a man and you too will be searching like a big fool.

That's how it is, Rocamadour. In Paris we're like fungus, we grow on the railings of staircases, in dark rooms with greasy smells, where people make love all the time and then fry some eggs and put on Vivaldi records, light cigarettes, and talk like Horacio and Gregorovius and Wong and me, Rocamadour, and like Perico and Ronald and Babs, we all make love and fry eggs and smoke, oh, you can't imagine how we smoke, how we make love, standing up, lying down, on our knees, with our hands, with our mouths, crying or singing, and outside there are all sorts of things, the windows open onto the air and it all begins with a sparrow or a gutter, it rains a lot here, Rocamadour, much more than in the country, and things get rusty, the leaders, the pigeons' feet, the wires Horacio uses to make figures with. We don't have many clothes, we get along with so few, a good overcoat, some shoes to keep the rain out, we're very dirty, everybody is dirty and good-looking in Paris, Rocamadour, the beds smell of night and deep sleep, dust and books underneath, Horacio falls asleep and the book ends up under the bed, we get into terrible fights because we can't find the books and Horacio thinks that Ossip has stolen them, until they show up one day and we laugh, and there just about isn't room for anything, not even another pair of shoes, Rocamadour, to set down a washbasin on the floor we have to move the record-player, but where can we put it because the table is full of books. I couldn't have you here, as small as you are there wouldn't be room for you, you'd bump against the walls. When I think about it I start to cry, Horacio doesn't understand, he thinks I'm wicked, that it's bad of me not bringing you here, even though I know he wouldn't be able to stand you for very long. No one can stand it here for very long, not even you and I, you have to live by fighting each other, it's the law, the only way that things are worth while but it hurts, Rocamadour, and it's dirty and bitter, you wouldn't like it, you see lambs in the fields, or hear the birds perched on the weather vane of the house. Horacio calls me sentimental, he calls me materialist, he calls me everything because I don't bring you or because I want to bring you, because I deny it, because I want to go and see you, because suddenly I understand that I cannot go, because I'm capable of walking for an hour in the rain if in some part of town I don't know they're showing *Potemkin* and I've got to see it even if the world comes to an end, Rocamadour, because the world doesn't matter any more if you don't have the strength to go ahead and choose something that's really true, if you keep yourself neat like a dresser drawer, putting you on one side, Sunday on the other, mother-love, a new toy, the Montparnasse station, the train, the visit you have to make. I don't feel like going, Rocamadour, and you know it's all right and you don't feel bad. Horacio is right, sometimes I don't care about you at all, and I think you'll thank me for that some day when you're able to understand, when you're able to see that the best thing was that I'm the way I am. But just the same I cry, Rocamadour, and I write this letter to you because I don't know, because maybe I'm wrong, because maybe I am wicked or sick or a little stupid, not much, just a little, but that's terrible, it makes me sick to my stomach just thinking about it, I've got my toes curled all the way under and I'm going to split open my shoes if I don't take them off, and I love you so much, Rocamadour, baby Rocamadour, little garlic clove, I love you so much, sugar-nose, sapling, toy pony . . .

(–132)

33

"There's a reason behind his leaving me alone," Oliveira thought as he opened and shut the drawer of the bedside table. "A gracious act or a dirty trick, it's all in the way you look at it. He's probably on the stairs now, listening like a half-baked sadist. He's waiting for the great Karamazov crisis, the Céline attack. Or he's tiptoed off on his Herzegovina toes and after a second glass of kirsch at Bébert's he'll raise mental hell and plan out the ceremonies for the arrival of Adgalle. Torture through waiting: Montevideo, the Seine, or Lucca. Variants: the Marne, Perugia. But then you, really . . ."

Lighting a Gauloise from the butt of the first, he looked into the drawer again, took out the novel, thinking vaguely about pity, a subject for a thesis. Pity for himself: that was more like it. "I never asked for happiness," he thought, thumbing slowly through the novel. "It's not an excuse, it's not a justification. *Nous ne sommes pas au monde. Donc, ergo, dunque . . .* Why should I pity her? Because I found a letter to her son which is really meant for me? Me, author of the complete letters to Rocamadour. No reason for pity. Out there wherever she is her hair is burning like a tower and it singes me from far away, breaks me up into pieces by nothing more than just her absence. And *patati patata.* She's going to get along fine without me and without Rocamadour. A bluebottle fly, delightful, flying towards the sun, runs into a window, bump, a bloody nose, tragedy. Two minutes later so happy, buying a paper doll in a stationery store and running out to put it in an envelope and send it to one of her strange girlfriends with Nordic names scattered about in the weirdest countries. How can you feel pity for a cat, for a lioness? Living-machines, perfect bolts of lightning. My only fault is that I wasn't combustible enough so that she could warm her hands and feet on me at her pleasure. She thought she was getting a burning bush and all she got was a pot of cold water. Poor little darling, shit."

(–67)

34

In September of 1880, a few months after the demise of my And the things she reads, a clumsy novel, in a cheap edition father, I decided to give up my business activities, transferring besides, but you wonder how she can get interested in things them to another house in Jerez whose standing was as solvent like this. To think that she's spent hours on end reading tasteless as that of my own; I liquidated all the credits I could, rented out stuff like this and plenty of other incredible things, *Elle* and the properties, transferred my holdings and inventories, and *France Soir*, those sad magazines Babs lends her. *And moved to* moved to Madrid to take up residence there. My uncle (in truth *Madrid to take up residence there*, I can see how after you swal- my father's first cousin), Don Rafael Bueno de Guzmán y Ataide, low four or five pages you get in the groove and can't stop read- wanted to put me up in his home; but I demurred for fear of ing, a little like the way you can't help sleeping or pissing, losing my independence. I was finally able to effect a compro- slavery or whipping or drooling. *I was finally able to effect a* mise between my comfortable freedom and my uncle's gracious *compromise*, a style that uses prefabricated words to transmit offer; and renting a flat in his building, I arranged matters so superannuated ideas, coins that go from hand to hand, from that I could be alone when I wished or I could enjoy family generation to generation, *te voilà en pleine écholalie. Enjoy* warmth when that became essential. The good gentleman lived, *family warmth*, that's good, shit if that isn't good. Oh, Maga, I should say we lived, in a section that had been built up on a how could you swallow this stuff, and what the hell is the charity site where the charity warehouse had once been. My uncle's flat warehouse, for God's sake. I wonder how much time she spent was the main one, 18,000 *reales* he paid, handsome and happy, reading this stuff, probably convinced that this was life, and even though it was not adequate for such a large family. I took you were right, it is life, that's why we've got to get rid of it. the ground-floor apartment, a little less spacious than the main (The main one, what's that.) And on some afternoons when one, but marvellously extensive for me alone, and I decorated I'd got the bug to cover the whole Egyptian section of the Louvre, it luxuriously and put in all the comforts to which I had become case by case, and I would come home with a taste for *mate* and accustomed. My income, thank God, allowed me to do all of this bread and jam, I'd find you stuck by the window with one of and more.

these fat novels in your hand and sometimes you'd even be

My first impressions of Madrid were surprisingly pleasant, crying, yes, don't deny it, you'd be crying because they'd just since I had not been there since the days of González Brabo. I cut somebody's head off, and you'd hug me as hard as you could was flabbergasted by the beauty and expanse of the newer sec- and want to know where I'd been, but I wouldn't tell you be- tions, the efficient system of communications, the obvious im- cause you're a burden in the Louvre, it's impossible to walk provement in the appearance of the buildings, the streets, and around there with you alongside, your ignorance is the kind that even the people; the pretty little gardens now planted where destroys all pleasure, poor girl, and it's really my fault that you once there had been dusty old squares, the magnificent homes read potboilers because I'm selfish (*dusty old squares*, that's all of the rich, the varied and well-stocked shops, inferior in no right, it reminds me of the squares in provincial towns, or the way, as was evident from the street, to those of Paris or London, streets of La Rioja in 1942, the purple mountains at sunset, that and lastly, the many elegant theatres for all classes, tastes, and feeling of happiness that comes with being alone in a particular incomes. These and other things that I later observed in my spot in the world, and *elegant theatres.* What the hell is the guy social contacts made me understand the rapid advances that talking about? He's just mentioned Paris and London some- our capital had made since 1868, advances more in the manner

where there, he talks about tastes and incomes), you see, Maga,
of whimsical leaps than in that of the solid, progressive move-
you see how these eyes of mine are being pulled along with
ment forward of people who know where they are headed; but
irony through the lines you read with great emotion, convinced
it was no less real because of all this. In a word, my nose had got
of the fact that you were getting all kinds of culture because
the scent of some European culture, of well-being, and even
you were reading a Spanish novelist whose picture is on the
riches and hard work.
fly-leaf, but right now the guy is talking about a scent of Euro-
My uncle is a well-known businessman in Madrid. In years
pean culture, you'd convinced yourself that all this reading
past he had held important positions in the government: he had
would help you understand the micro- and the macrocosm, and
been a consul general; then he had been an attaché in an em-
about all that was ever necessary was for me to come home for
bassy; subsequently his marriage demanded his presence in the
you to take out of the drawer of your desk – because you did
capital; he was with the Treasury for a while, under the protec-
have a desk, you always had to have one around even though I
tion and power of Bravo Murillo, and finally his family responsi-
never found out what kind of work you were doing on it – yes,
bilities made it necessary for him to exchange the vile security
you would take out a folio with poems by Tristan L'Hermite, for
of a salary for the adventures and hopes of work on his own.
example, or a study by Boris de Schloezer, and you would show
He was possessed of a fair amount of ambition, uprightness,
them to me with the uncertain and at the same time proud air of
activity, intelligence, good connections; he began to work as the
someone who has just bought some great things and is going to
agent in diverse commercial matters, and after running about
read them right now. There was no way to make you understand
a bit in pursuit of all this he ended up in command of every-
that you wouldn't ever get anywhere like that, that there were
thing and was able to tuck all of the accounts away in his files.
some things that were too late and others that were too soon, and
He lived off them, however, stirring up those that were dozing
you were always so close to the brink of despair in the very

in his cabinet, moving along those that had come to rest on his centre of joy and relaxation, your baffled heart was always so desk, keeping on the right track, as best he could, a few that full of fog. *Moving along those that had come to rest on his desk,* were in danger of going astray. His friendships with members no, you couldn't count on me for that, your desk was your desk of both parties were helpful to him, as was the high regard in and I didn't put you behind it or take you away from it, I simply which he was held in all branches of the government. No door watched you as you read your novels and looked at the jackets remained closed to him. One might even think that the doormen and the pictures in your folios, and you were hoping that I would of the various ministries owed their existence to him, for they sit down next to you and explain it to you, relieve your mind, do showed deep filial respect and opened doors wide for him as if what every woman hopes a man will do with her, sneak his arm they were the doors of his very own house. I had heard tell that around her waist a little and now he makes her snuggle closer, in certain periods he had made a good deal of money by putting he gives her the urge to drop her tendency to knit sweaters or his active hands on some well-known mining and railway talk, talk, talk on endlessly about everything that doesn't mean stocks; but that in other cases his timid honesty had not been anything. I'm a real beast, what have I got to be proud about, I favourable for him. When I settled in Madrid, his situation, as don't even have you any more because you were so set on losing far as could be seen, must have been comfortable but not yourself (not even losing yourself, because first you would have lavish. He had everything he needed, but he had no savings, had to find yourself), *really not a praiseworthy situation for a* really not a praiseworthy situation for a man who had worked *man who . . .* Praiseworthy, how long has it been since I heard so hard and who was now coming to the end of his days with that word, we're really losing our language in Argentina; when barely enough time in which to recoup his losses.

I was a boy I was aware of a lot more words than I am now, I

He was at that time a man who looked older than he really used to read these same novels, I built up a huge vocabulary that was, always immaculately dressed in the style of the elegant was perfectly useless for anything else, *immaculately, very dis-* young men of the time, and with a very distinguished air. He *tinguished,* yes indeed. I wonder if you really got into the plot was completely clean-shaven, this being a token of loyalty to the of this novel, or whether you used it as a jumping-off point for previous generation to which he belonged. His charm and his those mysterious countries of yours that I used to envy while joviality, always kept in delicate balance, never fell into im- you used to envy me my visits to the Louvre, that you must have pertinent familiarity or petulance. His best would come out in suspected even though you didn't say anything. And there we his conversation, as well as his worst, for knowing how good were getting closer and closer to what had to happen someday he was at speaking, he would let himself be led into the habit of when you would understand fully that I was only going to give describing every detail and his accounts would be lengthened to you part of my time and my life, *and his accounts would be* a tedious degree. Sometimes he would do this right at the very *lengthened to a tedious degree,* that's it exactly, I get boring beginning and would adorn his stories with childish minutiae to even when I reminisce. But how pretty you used to look at the such a degree that one would find it necessary to beg him, for window, with the grey of the sky hovering over your cheek, a heaven's sake, to be brief. When he would be speaking about book in your hands, your mouth always a little intense, doubt something that had happened at home (an exercise he was pas- in your eyes. There was so much lost time in you, you were so sionately fond of), so much time would elapse between the much the shape of what you might have been under different exordium and the firing of the shot, that the listener would have constellations, that taking you in my arms and making love to let his mind wander so far off the subject that the boom would you became a job that was much too tender, that bordered too give him a bit of a start. I am not sure whether I should classify much on charity, and that's where I used to fool myself, let my- as a physical ailment the chronic irritation of his tear-producing self fall into the stupid pride of an intellectual who thinks he's apparatus, which at times, mostly in winter, would make his capable of understanding (*weeping until his nose had begun to*

eyes water so that one would think that he had been weeping *run?*, but that's really too repulsive). Capable of understanding, until his nose had begun to run. I do not know of any other man it makes you want to laugh, Maga. Listen, this is just for you, with a more extensive collection of linen handkerchiefs. Because don't mention it to anyone else. Maga, I was the hollow shape, of that and because of his habit of always holding the white you used to tremble, pure and free as a flame, a stream of quick-fabric in his right hand or in both hands, a friend of mine, an silver, like the first notes of a bird when dawn is breaking, and Andalusian, a wag and a good fellow, of whom I shall speak it's nice to tell you all this in words that used to fascinate you later on, used to call my uncle *la Verónica*.
because you had thought they didn't exist outside poetry, and

He showed me real affection, and during the early days of my that we had every right to use them. Where are you now, where residence in Madrid he was continuously at my side, so that he will we be from today on, two points in an inexplicable universe, could see to it that I was getting installed without difficulties near or far, two points that make a line, two points that drift and so that he could be of help in a hundred little ways. When apart and come close together arbitrarily (*great figures who* we would talk about the family and I would reminisce about my *had made the name of Bueno de Guzmán renowned*, but how childhood or tell anecdotes about my father, a nervous discom-corny can the guy get, Maga, how did you ever get beyond page fort would come over my uncle, a feverish enthusiasm for all five . . .), but I won't explain to you the things they call the great figures who had made the name of Bueno de Guzmán Brownian movements, of course I won't explain them to you renowned, and taking out his handkerchief he would tell me and still both of us, Maga, form a pattern, you a point some-stories that were interminable. He looked upon me as the last where, me another somewhere else, displacing each other, you male representative of a stock rich in great figures, and he would probably now in the Rue de la Huchette, while I'm discovering comfort and spoil me as if I were a child, in spite of my thirty-this novel in your empty apartment, tomorrow you in the Gare de six years. Poor uncle. In these shows of affection, which would

Lyon (if you're going to Lucca, my love) and me on the Rue du cause a considerable increase in the outflow from his eyes, I Chemin Vert, where I've discovered a wonderful little wine, and found a secret and most painful sorrow, a thorn driven deep little by little, Maga, we go along forming an absurd pattern, into the heart of that excellent man. I do not really know exwith our movements we sketch out a pattern just like the ones actly how I came to make that discovery; but I was as certain flies make when they fly around a room, from here to there, that there was a wound he was covering up as if I had seen it suddenly in mid-flight, from there to here, that's what they call with my own two eyes and touched it with my own two hands. Brownian movement, now do you understand? a right angle, an It was a deep grief, overwhelming, the sorrow of not seeing me ascending line, from here to there, from back to front, up, down, married to one of his three daughters; an irremediable annoyspasmodically, slamming on the brakes and starting right up in ance, because his three daughters, alas!, were already married. another direction, and all of this is drawing a picture, a pattern, something non-existent like you and me, like two points lost in Paris that go from here to there, from there to here, drawing their picture, putting on a dance for nobody, not even for themselves, an interminable pattern without any meaning.

(–87)

35

Yes Babs yes. Yes Babs yes. Yes Babs, let's turn out the light, sweetie, see you tomorrow, sleep well, count sheep, it's all over, baby, it's all over. Everybody so nasty with poor Babs, we'll kick them all out of the Club to punish them. Everybody so nasty with poor Babs, nasty Étienne, nasty Perico, nasty Oliveira, Oliveira the worst of the lot, that inquisitor as delightful, delightful Babs had called him so exactly. Yes Babs yes. Rock-a-bye baby. Tura-lura-lura. Yes Babs yes. Something was bound to happen, in any case, there's no living with those people without something happening. Sh, baby, sh. That's the way, go to sleep. The Club's had it, Babs, that's for sure. We'll never see Horacio again, perverse Horacio. Tonight the Club took a jump like a pancake that lands on the ceiling and sticks up there. You can keep holding on to the frying pan, Babs, it won't come down again, don't knock yourself out waiting. Shh, darling, stop crying, the girl is really on a bender, even her soul smells of cognac.

Ronald slipped down a little, steadied himself on Babs, he was falling asleep. Club, Ossip, Perico, let's go back over it: everything had begun because everything had to come to an end, the jealous gods, the fried egg along with Oliveira, the real blame belonged to the god-damned fried egg, according to Étienne there was no need to throw the egg out, a marvel it was with its metallic green tints, and Babs had a kind of Hokusai hairdo: the egg had a smell of carrion that was enough to kill a person, how could the Club hold a session with that egg sitting there a couple of feet away, and suddenly Babs began to cry, the cognac was coming out of her ears, and Ronald realized that while they'd been arguing about timeless things Babs had drunk herself over half a bottle of cognac, the egg business was a way of getting it out and nobody was surprised, Oliveira least of all, that from the egg Babs would little by little get to the business of the burial, preparing herself between hiccups and a sort of fluttering around to bring up the case of the baby, the whole disgusting business. It was no use Wong trying to set up a screen of smiles between Babs and the unaware Oliveira, or making complimentary remarks about the edition of *La Rencontre de la langue d'oïl, de la langue d'oc et du franco-provençal entre Loire et Allier – limites phonetiques et morphologiques*, Wong was very emphatic – by S. Escoffier, a book of great interest, Wong was saying as he pushed Babs along in a greasy sort of way, trying to head her towards the hallway, nothing could have stopped Oliveira from hearing that business about the inquisitor and he raised his eyebrows in a look somewhere between surprised and puzzled, checking with Gregorovius along the way as if the latter could explain the epithet. The Club knew that when Babs got started she was like a catapult, it had happened before; the only solution was a circle around the recording secretary and hostess in charge of food, waiting for time to do its work, no weeping can last for ever, widows remarry. Nothing could be done, Babs was weaving drunkenly among the coats and mufflers of the Club, she came back from the hallway, she wanted to settle accounts with Oliveira, it was just the right moment to tell Oliveira about the inquisitor business, to affirm in her teary way that in all her lousy days she'd never met anyone as low, cold-blooded, bastardly, sadistic, evil, butcher, racist, incapable of the smallest kindness, trash, rotten, piece of shit, slimy, and syphilitic. Items received with infinite delight by Perico and Étienne, and with mixed reactions among the rest, including the recipient.

It was Hurricane Babs, the tornado of the *sixième*: a purée of mashed houses. The Club kept their heads down, sank into their coat collars, dragged on their cigarettes with all their might. When Oliveira managed to say something, there was a great theatrical silence. Oliveira said that he thought the little piece by Nicolas de Staël was very charming and that Wong, now that he was fucking around so much with Escoffier's work, ought to read it, give them a review of it at some other get-together of the Club. Babs called him inquisitor again, and Oliveira must have thought it was a bit funny because he smiled. Babs's hand caught him full across the face. The Club took rapid measures, and Babs went off wailing, lightly held by Wong, who got in between her and a furious Ronald.

The Club closed in around Oliveira so that Babs would be on the outside and she accepted (*a*) the idea of sitting down in an easy chair and (*b*) Perico's handkerchief. It must have been about that time that the facts about the Rue Monge had come up, along with the story of La Maga the Good Samaritan, Ronald seemed to think – he was seeing great green phosphenes in a half-asleep remembrance of the party – that Oliveira had asked Wong if it was true that La Maga was living in a *meublé* on the Rue Monge. And maybe then Wong said that he didn't know, or said that it was true, and somebody, probably Babs from where she was in the chair and with great sobs began to insult Oliveira again, throwing in his face the wonderful abnegation of La Maga the Good Samaritan at the bedside of sick Pola, and it was probably then that Oliveira began to laugh, looking especially at Gregorovius, and asked for more details concerning La Maga the nurse and her abnegation and if it was true that she was living on the Rue Monge, what number, those inevitable cadastral details. Now Ronald was stretching out his hand and putting it between Babs's legs as she grumbled as if she were far away, Ronald liked to sleep with his fingers lost in that vague warm territory, Babs the *agent provocateur* who had brought about the breakup of the Club, he'd have to bawl her out in the morning: things-like-that-are-not-done. But the whole Club had encircled Oliveira in some way or another, as at a shameful trial, and Oliveira had noticed this even before the Club itself, in the centre of the circle he broke out laughing with his cigarette in his mouth and his hands in the pockets of his lumberjacket, and then he had asked (of no one in particular, looking a bit above the heads of those who formed the circle) if the Club was waiting for an *amende honorable* or something like that, and the Club had not understood right off or preferred not to understand, except Babs who from her chair where Ronald was holding her down had started shouting the inquisitor business again, and it sounded almost tomblike at-that-hour-of-the-night. Then Oliveira had stopped laughing, and as if he had suddenly accepted the verdict (although nobody was judging him, because that's not what the Club was for) had thrown his cigarette on the floor, crushed it out with his foot, and after a moment, moving his shoulder a little to avoid the hand of Étienne, who had come forward uncertainly, had spoken in a very low voice, announcing irrevocably that he was withdrawing from the Club and that all the members of the Club, starting with himself and going on down the line, could go fuck the whore that bore them.

Dont acte.

(–121)

36

The Rue Dauphine wasn't far away, maybe it would be worth while going by to check up on what Babs had said. Of course, Gregorovius had known from the very start that La Maga, crazy as ever, would go to see Pola. *Caritas.* La Maga the Good Samaritan. Or better still, *The War Cry.* Did she ever let a day go by without doing her good deed? It was enough to make you laugh. Everything was enough to make you laugh. Or rather, there had been something like a great burst of laughter and that's what they called History. Go to the Rue Dauphine, knock softly on the door of the top-floor apartment and La Maga would appear, Nurse Lucía, to be more exact, no, it was really too much. With a bedpan in her hand or an enema bag. You can't see the patient, it's quite late and she's sleeping. *Vade retro, Asmodeus.* Or they would let him in and serve him coffee, no, worse still, and at some point they would all begin to cry, because it would certainly be contagious, all three of them would cry until they forgave each other, and then anything could happen, dehydrated women are terrible. Or they might put him to count out twenty drops of belladonna, one by one.

"I really ought to go," Oliveira said to a black cat on the Rue Danton. "A certain aesthetic requirement, complete the pattern. Number three, the Clue. But let's not forget about Orpheus. Maybe if I shave my head and cover it with ashes, go there with a tin cup, like a beggar. I am no longer he that ye once knew, oh women. Tragedian. Mime. Night of *empusae* and *lamiae,* evil shadows, the end of the great game. How tiring it gets being the same person all the time. Unpardonably. I will never see them again, it is written. *Qu'as tu fait, toi que violà, de ta jeunesse?* An inquisitor, that girl can really make them up . . . In any case, an autoinquisitor? *et encore . . .* An accurate epitaph: *Too bland.* But a bland inquisition is terrible, semolina tortures, tapioca bonfires, shifting sands, Medusa sucking sneakily. Medusa sneaking suckily. And too much pity underneath it all, me, who thought I was pitiless. It's impossible to want what I want and in the shape I want it, and share life with others besides. I had to know how to be alone and how to let so much wanting do its work, save me or destroy me, but without the Rue Dauphine, without the dead child, without the Club and everything else. Don't you think so, eh?"

The cat did not reply.

It wasn't as cold along the Seine as in the streets, so Oliveira raised the collar of his lumberjacket and went over to look at the water. Since he was not the jumping-off type, he looked for a bridge to get under and do some thinking about that business of the kibbutz, for some time now the idea of the kibbutz had been working on him, a kibbutz of desire. "Strange that all of a sudden an expression should come up like that, one that has no meaning, a kibbutz of desire, until the third time around it begins to take on some meaning little by little and suddenly the expression doesn't seem so absurd any more, like a sentence such as: 'Hope, that lush Palmyra', a completely absurd phrase, a sonorous rumbling of the bowels, while the kibbutz of desire is not absurd at all, it's a way of summing up closed in tight this wandering around from promenade to promenade. Kibbutz; colony, settlement, taking root, the chosen place in which to raise the final tent, where you can walk out into the night and have your face washed by time, and join up with the world, with the Great Madness, with the Grand Stupidity, lay yourself bare to the crystallization of desire, of the meeting. Whatch whout Whoracio," Wholiveira whobserved, sitting down on the rim along the water's edge, listening to the snoring of the *clochards* under their piles of newspapers and burlap bags.

For once in his life it wasn't hard for him to give in to melancholy. Another cigarette that warmed him up, there among the snoring that was coming out of the depths of the earth, he was in a mood to deplore the impossible distance that was separating him from his kibbutz. As long as hope is nothing but a lush Palmyra there was no reason to invent illusions for himself. Quite the opposite, take advantage of the cold of night to get that lucid feeling, with the precision of that astral system up above his head, that his vague search had been a failure and that perhaps victory was to be found in that very fact. First, because it was worthy of him (in his own moments Oliveira thought well of himself as a human specimen), because it was the search for a kibbutz so desperately far away, a citadel that could only be taken with the aid of arms contrived in fantasy, not with the soul of the West or with the spirit, those powers worn away by his own lies as they had so well pointed out in the Club, those alibis used by man the animal as he gets stuck on a road from which there is no turning back. Kibbutz of desire, not of the soul, not of the spirit. And even though desire might also be a rough definition of incomprehensible forces, he could feel it present and at work, present in every mistake and also in every forward leap, that was being a man, not just a body and a soul but that inseparable totality, that ceaseless meeting up with lacks, with everything they had stolen from the poet, the vehement nostalgia for a land where life could be babbled out according to other compasses and other names. Even though death might be waiting at the corner with his broom raised, even though hope was nothing but a lush Palmyra. And a snore, and from time to time a fart.

It was no longer so important, then, to make a mistake as it would have been had the search for his kibbutz been carried out with maps from the Geographical Society, with tested compasses, North pointing north, West west; about all that was needed was to understand, get a quick glimpse that would tell him that in the last analysis his kibbutz was no more impossible at that hour and in that cold and after those last days than if he had been searching after it according to the tribal rites, meritoriously and without earning the showy epithet of inquisitor, without getting his face slapped, without people weeping and a guilty conscience and the urge to chuck everything and go back to his enrolment-card and the protection of a slot in some spiritual or temporal budget. He would die without ever reaching his kibbutz but his kibbutz was there, far away but it was there and he knew that it was there because he was the child of his desire, it was his desire in the same way that he was his own desire and the world or what passed for the world was desire, was his desire or desire itself, it didn't make too much difference at that time of night. And then he was able to cover up his face with his hands, leaving just enough room for his cigarette, and stay there by the river, among the tramps, thinking about his kibbutz.

The *clocharde* woke up out of a dream in which somebody had been telling her repeatedly: "*Ça suffit, conâsse,*" and she discovered that Célestin had gone off in the middle of the night taking with him the baby carriage full of some tins of sardines (in bad shape) that had been given to them that afternoon in the Marais ghetto. Toto and Lafleur were sleeping like moles underneath their burlap and the new guy was sitting on a mooring post, smoking. Dawn was breaking.

The *clocharde* daintily removed the successive editions of *France-Soir* covering her, and scratched her head a bit. At six o'clock you could get hot soup on the Rue du Jour. It was practically certain that Célestin would show up to get some soup, and she could get the tins of sardines back if he hadn't already sold them to Pipon or La Vase.

"*Merde*," said the *clocharde*, beginning the complicated task of getting up. And as an encore, "*C'est cul.*"

Wrapping up in a black overcoat that reached down to her ankles, she went over to the newcomer. The newcomer agreed that the cold was almost worse than the police. When she got a cigarette from him and lit it, the *clocharde* got the idea that she knew him from somewhere. The newcomer also said that he knew her from somewhere, and both of them were pleased that they recognized each other at that hour of the morning. Sitting down on the next post, the *clocharde* said that it was still too early to go for soup. They talked about soup for a while, but the newcomer really didn't know too much about soup kitchens, she had to explain to him where the best ones were, he really was green, but he was interested in everything and maybe he would dare take the sardines away from Célestin. They talked about the sardines and the newcomer promised that as soon as he saw Célestin he would ask for them back.

"He'll pull out his hook," the *clocharde* warned. "You'll have to move fast and hit him over the head with something. They had to give Tonio five stitches, he shouted so much they could hear in Pontoise. *C'est cul, Pontoise*," the *clocharde* added, succumbing to nostalgia.

The newcomer was watching dawn break over the point of Vert-Galant, a willow tree was extricating its spider-webs out of the fog. When the *clocharde* asked him why he was shivering so much with such a good lumberjacket, he shrugged and offered her another cigarette. They smoked and smoked, talking and looking at each other sympathetically. The *clocharde* talked about Célestin's habits and the newcomer remembered the afternoons he had seen her hugging Célestin all along the benches and railings of the Pont des Arts, on the corner by the Louvre underneath the tiger-skinned plane trees, in the doorways of Saint-Germain-l'Auxerrois, and one night on the Rue Gît-le-Coeur, kissing and retching alternately, dead drunk, Célestin in a painter's blouse and the *clocharde* wearing as usual four or five dresses and some topcoats and overcoats, carrying a bundle of red material with pieces of sleeves and a broken cornet sticking out, so much in love with Célestin that it was something to see, getting his face all covered with lipstick and greasy stuff, brazenly lost in their public idyll, finally turning down the Rue de Nevers, and then La Maga had said: "She's the one who's in love, he couldn't care less," and she had looked at him for an instant before squatting down to gather up a little piece of green string and wrap it around her finger.

"At this time of the morning it's not so cold any more," the *clocharde* said, as if to encourage him. "I'm going to see if Lafleur has any wine left. Wine makes for a settled night. Célestin took two litres of mine away with him when he took the sardines. No, he hasn't got any left. You're well-dressed, maybe you can buy a litre at Habeb's. And some bread, if you've got enough money." She liked the newcomer very much, although deep down she knew that he wasn't new, that he was just well-dressed and could stand at Habeb's bar and drink one pernod after another without anybody else's complaining about his bad smell and things like that. The newcomer kept on smoking, nodding vaguely, with his head over to one side. A familiar face. Célestin would have known at once because Célestin was good at faces . . . "The cold really starts at nine o'clock. It comes from down there out of the mud. But we can go and get some soup, it's pretty good."

(And when they were almost out of sight down the Rue de Nevers, when they were coming perhaps to the exact spot where Pierre Curie had been run over by a truck ("Pierre Curie?" La Maga asked, baffled and ever ready to learn), they had turned slowly towards the steep river bank, leaning against the stall of a *bouquiniste*, although Oliveira always found that the stalls of the *bouquinistes* took on a funereal tone at night, a string of makeshift coffins lined up along a stone railing, and one snowy night they'd had fun taking a stick and writing RIP on all of the lead boxes, and a policeman had been less amused and had told them so, speaking about things like respect and tourism, they couldn't figure out why he had mentioned the last matter. In those days everything was still kibbutz, or at least the possibility of kibbutz, and walking through the streets writing RIP on the closed-up stalls of the *bouquinistes* and being amazed at the amorous *clocharde* who was a part of a confused series of against-the-grain exercises that had to be performed, approved, left behind. And that's how it was, and it was cold, and there was no kibbutz. Except for the lie of going to Habeb's and buying red wine and inventing a kibbutz like Kubla Khan's, covering the distance between laudanum and old Habeb's cheap wine.)

> In Xanadu did Kubla Khan
> A stately pleasure-dome decree.

"A foreigner," the *clocharde* said with diminishing sympathy for the newcomer. "Spanish, eh. Italian."

"A mixture," Oliveira said, making a manly effort to stand the smell.

"But you have a job, that's obvious," the *clocharde* accused him.

"Well, not exactly. I used to keep books for an old man, but I haven't seen him for quite a while."

"It's nothing to be ashamed of, as long as you don't overdo it. When I was young . . ."

"Emmanuèle," Oliveira said, putting his hand on the place where there must have been a shoulder deep down inside. The *clocharde* was startled at hearing her name; she looked at him suspiciously and then took a hand mirror out of her pocket and examined her mouth. Oliveira wondered what inconceivable chain of circumstances could have caused a *clocharde* to dye her hair. She was intent on the operation of painting her lips with the stub of a lipstick. There was plenty of time to think about himself and what an imbecile he was again. His hand on her shoulder after what had happened with Berthe Trépat. With results that were in the public domain. A self-administered kick in the arse that would flip him around like a glove. *Cretinaccio*, animal, hairy beast. RIP, RIP. *Malgré le tourisme.*

"How did you know my name was Emmanuèle?"

"I don't know. Somebody must have told me."

Emmanuèle took out a pillbox full of pink powder and began to pat it on one cheek. If Célestin had been there, he would have certainly. Surely he would have. Célestin: tireless. Dozens of tins of sardines, *le salaud*. Suddenly she remembered.

"Ah," she said.

"Probably," Oliveira agreed, surrounding himself with smoke as best he could.

"I used to see you there together many times," Emmanuèle said.

"We used to stroll around there."

"But she would only talk to me when she was alone. A nice girl, a little crazy."

"You said it," Oliveira thought. He was listening to Emmanuèle who was remembering more and more, a bundle of odds and ends, a white sweater that still had some wear, a fine girl who didn't work and wasn't wasting her time studying for a degree, a little crazy sometimes, wasting her francs to feed the pigeons on the Ile Saint-Louis, sometimes quite sad, other times breaking up with laughter. Sometimes bad.

"We would argue," Emmanuèle said, "because she told me not to bother Célestin. She never came back, but I liked her a lot."

"Did she talk to you so much?"

"You didn't like it, did you?"

"That's not it," Oliveira said, looking over at the other bank. But that's just what it was, because La Maga hadn't told him more about her dealings with the *clocharde*, and a basic generalization carried him off, etc. Retrospective jealousy, cf. Proust, subtle torture and so on. It was most likely going to rain, the willow began to look as if it was hanging there in the damp air. On the other hand, it wouldn't be so cold, not quite so cold. Perhaps he said something like: "She never spoke about you much to me," because Emmanuèle let out a satisfied and wicked laugh, and kept putting on pink powder with her blackened fingers; from time to time she would lift up her hand and give herself a pat on her matted hair which was wrapped up in a wool scarf with red and green stripes, actually a man's muffler picked up in some dustbin. Finally he had to go, go up into the city, so close by there, twenty feet above, where it began exactly on the other side of the Seine embankment, behind of the lead RIP boxes where the pigeons were talking among themselves and fluffing up as they waited for the first rays of the bland, unforceful sun, the pale eight o'clock pablum that floats down from a mushy sky because it certainly was going to drizzle the way it always did.

When he was already on his way Emmanuèle shouted something at him. He stopped and waited for her, they went up the stairs together. At Habeb's they bought two litres of red wine, they took cover in the arcade along the Rue de l'Hirondelle. Emmanuèle was so kind as to take out a bundle of newspapers from under her coats, and this made a fine cushion to put down in a corner that Oliveira had explored with the help of some timid matches. From the other side of the archway there came some snoring that smelled of garlic and cauliflower and cheap forgetfulness; biting his lip, Oliveira stumbled into the corner and settled himself as comfortably as possible against the wall, close to Emmanuèle who was already sucking on the bottle and snorting with satisfaction after every gulp. Untrain the senses, open your mouth and nose wide and take in the worst of smells, human filth. One minute, two, three, easier and easier, like any apprenticeship. Keeping his nausea under control, Oliveira grabbed the bottle, even though he couldn't see he knew the neck was anointed with spit and lipstick, the darkness sharpened his sense of smell. Closing his eyes to protect himself against something, he wasn't sure what it was, he downed half a pint of wine in one gulp. Then they started to smoke, shoulder to shoulder, satisfied. The nausea went away, not conquered but humiliated, waiting there with its crooked head, and he was able to think about other things. Emmanuèle was talking away, delivering herself of solemn discourses in between hiccups, giving a maternal scolding to a ghostly Célestin, taking inventory of the sardines, her face lighting up at every puff of the cigarette and Oliveira saw the spots of dirt on her forehead, her thick lips stained with wine, the triumphal scarf of the Syrian goddess that had been trampled on by some enemy army, a chryselephantine head rolling around in the dust, with spots of blood and gore but keeping all the while the diadem of red and green stripes, the Great Mother stretched out in the dust and trampled on by drunken soldiers who amused themselves by pissing on her mutilated breasts, until the greatest clown among them knelt down to the acclaim of all the others, his penis standing out erect above the fallen goddess, masturbating onto the marble and letting the sperm trickle into the eye-holes from which officers' hands had already plucked the precious stones, into the half-open mouth which accepted the humiliation as a final offering before rolling off into oblivion. And it was so natural that in the darkness the hand of Emmanuèle should feel along Oliveira's arm and alight there confidently while the other hand sought out the bottle and one could hear the glug-glug and a satisfied snort, so natural that everything ought to be like this with reverse and obverse, the opposite sign as a kind of survival. And even though Wholiveira might mistrust whinebriation, whastute whaccomplice of the Grand Whentrapment, something told him that there was a kibbutz there, that behind it all, always behind, there was hope for a kibbutz. Not a methodical certainty, oh no, dear fellow, never that, much as you might want it that way, nor an *in vino veritas* nor a Fichte-like dialectic or other Spinozan precious stones, only an acceptance of nausea, Heraclitus had got himself buried in a pile of manure to cure himself of dropsy, somebody had told him about it that very night, somebody who already seemed like someone out of another life, someone like Pola or Wong, people he had annoyed only because he had wanted to make contact with the good side, reinvent love as the only way ever to enter his kibbutz. In shit up to his neck, Heraclitus the Obscure, just like the two of them except without wine, and besides, he wanted to cure himself of dropsy. Maybe that's what it was, then, keeping yourself covered with shit up to the neck and also hoping, because Heraclitus certainly must have had to stay under the shit for days on end, and Oliveira was beginning to remember too that Heraclitus had said that if one did not expect he would never find the unexpected, wring the neck of the swan, Heraclitus had said, but no, of course he'd said no such thing, and while he was swallowing another long swig and Emmanuèle was laughing in the shadow as she heard the glug-glug and stroked his arm as if to show him that she was enjoying his company and his promise to take the sardines away from Célestin, there suddenly came up to Oliveira like a winy belch the double Mexican surname of the swan with the twistable neck, and he wanted to laugh so much and tell Emmanuèle, but instead he gave her back the almost empty bottle, and Emmanuèle began to sing in a scrapy sort of way *Les Amants du Havre*, a song that La Maga used to sing when she was sad, but Emmanuèle sang it with a tragic crawl, out of tune and forgetting the words as she petted Oliveira who kept on thinking that only one who expected would be able to find the unexpected, and half-closing his eyes to reject the dim light that was coming in through the entranceway, he thought that far off (across the sea, or was it an access of patriotism?) there was that pure landscape of his kibbutz. It was obvious that he had to twist the swan's neck, even if it hadn't been Heraclitus who had demanded it. He was getting sentimental, *puisque la terre est ronde, mon amour t'en fais pas, mon amour, t'en fais pas* along with the wine and the thick voice that was singing as he was getting sentimental, it would all end in tears and self-commiseration, like Babs, poor little Horacio *anclado en París*, set down in Paris, as the tango says, *cómo habrá cambiado tu calle Corrientes, Suipacha, Esmeralda, y el viejo arrabal.* But even though he put all his anger into the lighting of another Gauloise, very far away in the depth of his eyes he kept on seeing his kibbutz, not across the sea or even most likely across the sea, or there outside in the Rue Galande or in Puteaux or in the Rue de la Tombe Issoire, in any case his kibbutz was always there and it wasn't a mirage.

"It's not a mirage, Emmanuèle."

"*Ta gueule, mon pote,*" said Emmanuèle, feeling down among her innumerable skirts looking for the other bottle.

Then they got onto other things, Emmanuèle told him about a drowned girl that Célestin had seen from up on Grenelle, and Oliveira wanted to know what colour her hair had been but Célestin had only seen her legs sticking up a little bit out of the water, and he had got out of there before the police started up with their damn bit of asking everybody questions. And when they had drunk up almost all of the second bottle and were happier than ever, Emmanuèle recited a passage from *La Mort du loup*, and Oliveira gave her a quick introduction to the sestinas of the *Martín Fierro*. Now and then a truck began to cross the square, they began to hear the sounds that Delius once . . . But it wouldn't do any good to talk to Emmanuèle about Delius in spite of the fact that she was a sensitive woman, that she didn't go along with poetry and expressed herself manually, rubbing up against Oliveira in order to get rid of the cold, stroking his arm, mumbling parts of operas and obscene comments about Célestin. Biting the cigarette with his lips until it seemed to be almost a part of his mouth, Oliveira listened to her, let her rub up against him, kept repeating coldly that he was no better than she was and that if the worst came to the worst he could always cure himself like Heraclitus, it might have been that the Obscure's most penetrating message was the one he had not written down, leaving it up to anecdotes, the voice of his disciples to transmit it so that perhaps some attuned ear might come to understand it one day. He was amused by the friendly and matter-of-fact way in which the hand of Emmanuèle was going to work unbuttoning him, and at the same time he was able to imagine that perhaps the Obscure one had sunk himself up to the neck in shit without even having been sick, without having dropsy at all, simply to sketch out a pattern that his milieu would never have condoned in the shape of a message or lesson, and which he had surreptitiously carried across the border of time until it had arrived, all mixed up with theory, noting nothing but a disagreeable and painful detail, to rest alongside the earth-shaking diamond of *panta rhei*, a barbarian therapy that Hippocrates had already condemned, just as for hygienic reasons he would have condemned the fact that Emmanuèle was little by little leaning more heavily on her drunken friend and with a tongue stained with tannin was humbly licking his prick, helping to maintain its understandable abandon with her fingers and murmuring things in the language one uses when holding cats or nursing babies, completely oblivious of the meditation that was going on up above, bent on a duty that would afford her little profit, following the line of some obscure feeling of pity, so that the newcomer would feel happy on his first night as a *clochard* and maybe he would fall a little in love with her to punish Célestin, would forget about the strange things he had been muttering in his barbarian American language as he slid down a little more against the wall and let himself slide with a sigh, putting his hand on Emmanuèle's hair and imagining for a second (but that must have been hell) that it was Pola's hair, that still once more Pola had thrown herself on top of him among Mexican ponchos and Klee postcards and Durrell's *Quartet*, making him enjoy and enjoy from without, as she was attentive, analytical, and alien, before she demanded her share and stretched out against him trembling, demanding that he take her and injure her, with her painted mouth of a Syrian goddess, like Emmanuèle who was getting up, dragged to her feet by the policeman, sitting down suddenly and saying: *On faisait rien, quoi*, and all of a sudden underneath the grey that in some way was filling up the doorways Oliveira opened his eyes and saw the cop's legs next to where he lay ridiculously unbuttoned, and with an empty bottle rolling away from the gendarme's kick, the second kick on his thigh, the fierce whack right on the top of Emmanuèle's head as she hunched over and moaned, and on his knees for some reason, the only logical position in which he could put the *corpus delicti* back into his trousers as quickly as possible while it shrank prodigiously in a great spirit of co-operation and allowed itself to be closed in and buttoned up, and really now there was nothing wrong but how could you explain that to the policeman who was leading them off to the patrol van parked in the square, how could you explain to Babs that an inquisition was something else, and to Ossip, to Ossip most of all, how could you explain to him that everything still remained to be done and that the only decent thing to do was to take a step back in order to get a better start, let yourself fall down so that maybe you could get up again later on, Emmanuèle so that maybe later on . . .

"Let her go," Oliveira asked the gendarme. "The poor old girl's drunker than I am."

He ducked just in time to miss the swing. Another gendarme grabbed him around the waist, and with one shove pitched him into the patrol van. They tossed Emmanuèle in on top of him and she was singing something that sounded like *Le Temps des cerises.* They left them alone inside the truck, and Oliveira rubbed his thigh which was hurting terribly, and he joined in the singing of *Le Temps des cerises,* if that's what it was. The van started up as if it had been sprung from a catapult.

"*Et tous nos amours,*" Emmanuèle shouted.

"*Et tous nos amours,*" Oliveira said, throwing himself onto the bench and looking for a cigarette. "This bit, old girl, not even Heraclitus."

"*Tu me fais chier,*" Emmanuèle said as she began a weeping that sounded more like howling. "*Et tous nos amours,*" she sang between sobs. Oliveira could hear the cops laughing, looking at them through the grille. "Well, if you wanted tranquillity you're going to get lots of it. Better take advantage of it, forget what you're thinking about," he said to himself. It was OK to call up and tell them all what a funny dream you had had, but that's enough, don't push it. Everybody on his own side, dropsy is cured with patience, with shit, and with solitude. Besides, the Club was all over with, happily *fini,* and all that was left to get rid of would just be a matter of time. The van slammed on its brakes at a corner and when Emmanuèle started to shout *Quand il reviendra, le temps des cerises,* one of the cops opened the window and warned that if they didn't shut up he was going to kick their teeth in. Emmanuèle lay down on the floor of the truck, face down and wailing, and Oliveira put his feet on her behind and settled himself comfortably on the bench. Hopscotch is played with a pebble that you move with the tip of your toe. The things you need: a pavement, a pebble, a toe, and a pretty chalk drawing, preferably in colours. On top is Heaven, on the bottom is Earth, it's very hard to get the pebble up to Heaven, you almost always miscalculate and the stone goes off the drawing. But little by little you start to get the knack of how to jump over the different squares (spiral hopscotch, rectangular hopscotch, fantasy hopscotch, not played very often) and then one day you learn how to leave Earth and make the pebble climb up into Heaven (*Et tous nos amours,* Emmanuèle was sobbing face down), the worst part of it is that precisely at that moment, when practically no one has learned how to make the pebble climb up into Heaven, childhood is over all of a sudden and you're into novels, into the anguish of the senseless divine trajectory, into the speculation about another Heaven that you have to learn to reach too. And since you have come out of childhood (*Je n'oublierai pas le temps des cerises,* Emmanuèle was kicking about on the floor) you forget that in order to get to Heaven you have to have a pebble and a toe. Which is what Heraclitus knew, up to his neck in shit, and probably Emmanuèle too, wiping off the snot with the back of her hand in the midst of the cherry season, or the two fairies who somehow were sitting in the patrol van (but of course, the door had been opened and shut in the midst of shrieks and laughter and the toot of a whistle) and were laughing like mad as they looked at Emmanuèle on the floor and at Oliveira, who wanted a smoke but who didn't have any cigarettes and matches even though he had not remembered the police going through his pockets, *et tous nos amours, et tous nos amours.* A pebble and a toe, what La Maga had known so well and he much less well, and the Club more or less well, and who from a childhood in Burzaco or in the suburbs of Montevideo would show the straight and narrow path to Heaven without need of Vedanta or Zen or collected eschatologies, yes, reach Heaven with kicks, get there with the pebble (carry your cross? Not a very portable object) and with one last kick send the stone up against *l'azur l'azur l'azur l'azur,* crash, a broken pane, the final bed, naughty child, and what difference did it make if behind the broken pane there was the kibbutz, since Heaven was nothing but a childish name for his kibbutz.

"Let's sing and smoke for all of that," Horacio said. "Emmanuèle, get up, you weepy old woman."

"*Et tous nos amours,*" Emmanuèle bellowed.

"*Il est beau,*" one of the fairies said, looking tenderly at Horacio. "*Il a l'air farouche.*"

The other fairy had taken a brass tube out of his pocket and was looking through a hole in the end, smiling and making faces. The younger fairy snatched away the tube and took a look. "You can't see anything, Jo," he said. "Yes you can, doll," said Jo. "No, no, no, no." "Yes you can, yes you can. LOOK THROUGH THE PEEPHOLE AND YOU'LL SEE PATTERNS PRETTY AS CAN BE." "It's night-time, Jo." Jo took out a box of matches and lit one in front of the kaleidoscope. Squeals of enthusiasm, patterns pretty as can be. *Et tous nos amours*, Emmanuèle declaimed, sitting up on the floor of the van. Everything was so perfect, everything happening right on time, hopscotch and the kaleidoscope, the smaller fairy looking and looking, oh Jo, I can't see anything, more light, more light, Jo. Collapsed on the bench, Horacio greeted the Obscure one, his head of darkness sticking up through the pyramid of manure with two eyes that looked like green stars, patterns pretty as can be, the Obscure one was right, a road to the kibbutz, perhaps the only road to the kibbutz, not the world, people grabbing at the kaleidoscope from the wrong end, then you had to turn it around with the help of Emmanuèle and Pola and Paris and La Maga and Rocamadour, stretch out on the floor like Emmanuèle and from there begin to look out from the mountain of manure, look at the world through the eye of your arsehole and you'll see patterns pretty as can be, the pebble had to pass through the eye of your arsehole, kicked along by the tip of your toe, and from Earth to Heaven the squares would be open, the labyrinth would unfold like the spring of a broken clock as it made workmen's time fly off in a thousand pieces, and through the snot and semen and stink of Emmanuèle and the shit of the Obscure one you would come onto the road leading to the kibbutz of desire, no longer rising up to Heaven (rise up, a hypocritical word, Heaven, *flatus vocis*), but walk along with the pace of a man through a land of men towards the kibbutz far off there but on the same level, just as Heaven was on the same level as Earth on the dirty pavement where you played the game, and one day perhaps you would enter that world where speaking of Heaven did not mean a greasy kitchen rag, and one day someone would see the true outline of the world, patterns pretty as can be, and, perhaps, pushing the stone along, you would end up entering the kibbutz.

(–37)

From this Side

Il faut voyager loin en aimant sa maison

APOLLINAIRE, *Les mamelles de Tirésias*

37

He hated the name Traveler because he had never been outside Argentina except for trips over to Montevideo and once up to Asunción in Paraguay, cities that he remembered with sovereign indifference. At the age of forty he was still stuck on the Calle Cachimayo, and the fact that he was a sort of agent and jack-of-all-trades for a circus called Las Estrellas gave him no hope whatever of travelling around the world Barnum-style; the zone of operations of his circus extended from Santa Fe to Carmen de Patagones, with long runs in the capital, La Plata, and Rosario. When Talita, who was a reader of encyclopedias, would get interested in wandering peoples and cultures, Traveler would grumble and speak with insincere praise about a courtyard with geraniums, an army bunk, and that no place like home bit. As he sucked on one *mate* after another he would dazzle his wife with his wisdom, but it was obvious that he was trying too hard. When he was asleep he would sometimes come out with words that had to do with uprooting, trips abroad, troubles in customs, and inaccurate alidades. If Talita started to tease him when he woke up, he would start to whack her on the behind, and then they would laugh like crazy and it even seemed that Traveler's betrayal of himself did them both some good. One thing had to be recognized and it was that unlike almost all her other friends, Traveler didn't blame life or fate for the fact that he had been unable to travel everywhere he had wanted to. He would just take a stiff drink of gin and call himself an imbecile.

"Of course, I have been his best trip," Talita used to say when the opportunity would present itself, "but he's so silly that he doesn't realize it. I, my dear, have carried him off on the wings of fantasy to the very edge of the horizon."

The lady thus addressed would think that Talita was speaking seriously and would answer along the following lines: "Ah, my dear, men are so incomprehensible" (*sic* for uncomprehending).

Or:

"Believe me, that's just what happens with me and my Juan Antonio. I've always said the same thing to him, but I could just as well be speaking to the wall."

Or:

"How well I can sympathize with you, my dear. Life is such a struggle."

Or:

"Don't worry yourself about it, miss. As long as you have your health and your work."

Then Talita would tell Traveler everything that people had said and the pair of them would laugh and roll around on the kitchen floor until they had dirtied up their clothes. Traveler used to have the most fun hiding in the toilet, with a handkerchief or undershirt crammed into his mouth, and listening while Talita got the ladies from the Pensión Sobrales and some others who lived in the hotel across the street to talk. In moments of optimism, which were never for long, he would work up a soap opera which would make fun of these fat ladies without their realizing it, make them weep copiously and tune in every day. But in any case, he never had travelled, and it was like a black stone in his soul.

"A regular brick," Traveler would explain, feeling his stomach.

"I never saw a black brick," the Manager of the circus, the eventual intimate of so much nostalgia, used to say.

"It got that way from being so sedentary. And to think there have been poets who complained about being *heimatlos*, Ferraguto!"

"Talk so I can understand," the Manager said, always a little upset when he was called by name in such a dramatic sort of way.

"I can't, Boss," Traveler muttered, excusing himself tacitly for having called him by name. "Beautiful foreign words are like an oasis, stopovers. Will we ever go to Costa Rica? To Panama, where long ago royal galleons . . . ? Gardel died in Colombia, Chief, in Colombia!"

"We haven't got the cash," the Manager said, taking out his watch. "I've got to get back to the hotel. Cuca will be starting to kick up a stink."

Traveler was alone in the office and he was wondering what sunsets in Connecticut were like. As consolation he went back over the good things that had happened to him. For example, one of the good things that had happened to him was that one morning in 1940 he had gone into his superior's office in accounts carrying a glass of water. He had come back out without a job as his boss used a piece of tissue to dry off his face. That had been one of the good things that had happened to him, because that very month they had been planning to promote him, just as marrying Talita had been another good thing that had happened to him (even though they both might think otherwise), since Talita had been condemned by her pharmacy degree to grow old dispensing court plasters and Traveler had shown up looking for some suppositories to cure his bronchitis, and out of the explanation he had got from Talita love had foamed up like shampoo in a showerbath. Traveler would even insist that he had fallen in love with Talita at the precise moment when she lowered her eyes and explained how the suppository would be more effective if used after rather than before a good bowel movement.

"You devil," Talita used to say when they would reminisce. "You understood the directions perfectly well, but you played the fool so I would have to explain them to you."

"A pharmacist must serve truth, even when it turns up in the most intimate places. If you only knew my emotions when I inserted the first suppository that afternoon, right after I left you. It was a huge green thing."

"Eucalyptus," Talita said. "You were lucky I didn't sell you one of those that has a garlicky odour and can be smelled fifty feet away."

But sometimes they would turn sad and vaguely understand that once again they had been having fun as a last resort against the melancholy of Buenos Aires and a life that didn't have too much (What else could you say except "too much"? A vague uneasiness at the top of the stomach, the black brick, as always).

Talita explaining Traveler's melancholy moments to Señora Gutusso:

"It gets hold of him around siesta-time, it's like something that comes up out of his pleura."

"He must have something wrong inside," Señora Gutusso says. "It's internal pain, or whatever it is they say."

"It comes out of his soul, señora. My husband is a poet, believe me."

Shut up in the toilet with a towel around his face, Traveler is laughing so hard that his eyes are watering.

"Don't you think it might be some allergy or whatever they call it? My little boy Vítor, you can see him playing in the geraniums out there and he's really a delight, believe me, but when he gets an attack of his celery allergy it's monstrous, his dark little eyes start to close, his mouth puffs up like a toad's, and during it all he can't even bend his toes."

"Bending the toes isn't always too important," Talita says.

Traveler's muffled roars can be heard from the toilet and Talita quickly changes the subject to throw Señora Gutusso off the track. Usually Traveler will leave his hiding place feeling very sad, and Talita understands. Some mention should be made of Talita's understanding. It's an ironic, tender understanding, like something distant. Her love for Traveler is made up of dirty casseroles, long vigils, a gentle acceptance of his nostalgic fantasies and his love for the tango and a game of *truco*. When Traveler gets sad and thinks about the fact that he has never travelled (and Talita knows it's not that that bothers him, that his worries are much deeper), she has to go along with him and not say very much, prepare his *mate*, make sure that he never runs out of tobacco, do her duty as a wife alongside her husband but never casting her shadow on him, and that's what's difficult. Talita is very happy with Traveler, with the circus, grooming the counting cat before it goes on stage, keeping books for the Manager. Sometimes in her modest way she thinks that she is really closer than Traveler to those elemental depths that worry him, but metaphysical contexts upset her somewhat and she ends up convincing herself that he is the only one capable of making a puncture that will release the black and oily flow. It all floats around a little, dresses up in words or patterns, calls itself otherness, calls itself laughing or loving, and it's also the circus and life to call it by its most external and fateful names and who the hell is your aunt anyway.

But since he doesn't have this otherness, Traveler is a man of action. He calls it restricted action because it's not a question of going about knocking yourself out. For the space of four decades he has gone through various phases: football (with the Colegiales, centre forward, not too bad), pedestrianism, politics (a month in the Devoto jail in 1934), cuniculture and apiculture (a farm in Manzanares, bankruptcy within three months, smelly rabbits and ill-tempered bees), auto-racing (relief driver with Marimón, a smash-up in Resistencia, three broken ribs), artistic carpentry (turning out pieces of furniture until they piled up to the ceiling, used only once, a complete failure), marriage and cycling on the Avenida General Paz on Saturdays on a rented bike. Out of all this action he has a mental archive, two languages, a facile hand with the pen, an ironical interest in soteriology and glass balls, the attempt at creating a mandrake by planting a sweet potato in a pot of earth and sperm, the sweet potato flourishing in the wild way sweet potatoes do, invading the furnished room, growing out of the window, the surreptitious intervention of Talita, armed with a pair of scissors, Traveler inspecting the shape of the plant, suspecting something, the humiliating abandonment of the mandrake, gallows plant, *alraune*, leftovers from childhood. Sometimes Traveler talks about a double who is luckier than he, and Talita for some reason doesn't like to hear about it, and she hugs him and kisses him restlessly, does all she can to get those ideas out of his head. Then she takes him out to see Marilyn Monroe, a great favourite of Traveler's, and-slams-on-the-brakes of some purely artistic feelings of jealousy in the darkness of the Presidente Roca movie theatre.

(–98)

38

Talita wasn't so sure that Traveler was very happy about the return of a childhood friend, because the first thing that Traveler did upon learning that a certain Horacio was coming home suddenly to Argentina on the *Andrea C* was to aim a kick at the counting cat of the circus and proclaim that life was a perfect fuckup. In any case, he did go down to the dock to meet him with Talita taking the counting cat along in a basket. Oliveira was coming out of customs carrying a single lightweight suitcase, and when he spotted Traveler he raised his eyebrows in a mixture of surprise and annoyance.

"What's new?"

"Hi," Traveler said, shaking his hand with more feeling than he had expected.

"Hey," Oliveira said, "let's go to a waterfront grill and get some sausages."

"I'd like you to meet my wife," Traveler said.

Oliveira said: "Pleased to meet you," and put out his hand, barely looking at her. Then he asked immediately who the cat was and why they had brought him down to the pier in a basket. Talita, offended by the reception, found him absolutely disagreeable and announced that she was going back to the circus with the cat.

"OK," Traveler said. "Put him by the window on the tram, you know he doesn't like it in the aisle."

In the grill Oliveira began to drink red wine and eat some sausages and *chinchulines.* Since he wasn't being very communicative, Traveler told him all about the circus and how he had got married to Talita. He filled him in on politics and sports, pausing especially to talk about the rise and fall of Pascualito Pérez. Oliveira said that in Paris he had run into Fangio and that old bow-legs had seemed half-asleep. Traveler began to get hungry and ordered some chitterlings. He was pleased that Oliveira accepted his first Argentine cigarette with a smile and smoked it with appreciation. They got into another litre of red wine, and Traveler talked about his work, how he hadn't lost hope of finding something better, that is, something with less work and more cash, waiting all the time for Oliveira to tell him something, he didn't know exactly what, just some direction that could bring them together again after so much time.

"Well, tell me something," he proposed.

"The weather was very changeable," Oliveira said, "but every once in a while there would be good days. Something else: as César Bruto said so well, if you want Paris in October to move 'er, don't forget to see the Louvre. What else? Oh, yes, I went to Vienna once. They have fantastic cafés where fat women bring along their dogs and husbands to eat strudel."

"OK, OK," Traveler said. "You don't have to talk if you don't want to."

"One day I dropped a lump of sugar underneath the table in a restaurant. In Paris, not in Vienna."

"If all you're going to do is talk about cafés, you didn't have to sail across the pond."

"You understand well," Oliveira said, carefully cutting into a string of *chinchulines.* "This is something you can't get in the City of Lights. That's what all the Argentinians used to tell me. They used to weep because they couldn't get good beef, and I even knew a lady who used to think nostalgically about Argentinian wines. She used to say that French wine was no good to mix with soda."

"Jesus," Traveler said.

"And of course the tomatoes and the potatoes here are better than anywhere."

"It's obvious," said Traveler, "that you were hanging out with the upper crust."

"Once in a while. They usually didn't like the way I used to hang, to keep on with your metaphor. Boy, it's muggy."

"That's right," Traveler said. "You're going to have to get yourself acclimatized again."

They kept on along those lines for some twenty-five minutes.

(–39)

39

Of course, Oliveira was not going to tell Traveler anything about his stopover in Montevideo when he had walked through the slums, asking and looking, having a couple of drinks of *caña* to get on the good side of some toughs. And nothing, except that there was a slew of new buildings and that on the waterfront, where he spent the hour before the *Andrea C* sailed, the water was full of dead fish floating belly up, and among the fish here and there a condom softly floating in the murky water. There was nothing else to do but go back on board, thinking that maybe Lucca, that maybe it really had been Lucca or Perugia. And all so much like the divine rocket.

Before disembarking in his mother country, Oliveira had decided that everything that had passed had not been the past and that only a mental error like so many others would have allowed the easy expedient of imagining a future fertilized by games already played. He understood (only on the prow, at dawn, in the yellow fog of the harbour) that nothing would have changed if he had decided to take a stand, reject easy solutions. Maturity, supposing such a thing really did exist, was in the last analysis a kind of hypocrisy. Nothing was mature, nothing could have been more natural than for that woman with a cat in a basket, waiting for him beside Manolo Traveler, to look a little like that other woman who (but what had been the use of wandering through the slums of Montevideo, taking a taxi up to the edge of El Cerro, making use of directions assembled all over again by a restless memory). He had to keep going, either start over again or end it: there was still no bridge as yet. With a suitcase in his hand, he headed for a waterfront grill where one night somebody half-drunk had told him stories about the troubadour Betinoti, and how he used to sing that waltz: *Mi diagnostico es sencillo: / Sé que no tengo remedio.* The idea that a word like "diagnosis" should turn up in a waltz was irresistible to Oliveira, but now he was repeating the lines in a sententious sort of way while Traveler told him about the circus, about K. O. Lausse, and even about Juan Perón.

(–86)

40

He was coming to the realization that his coming back had really been his going away in more than one sense. He was already vegetating with poor, humble Gekrepten in a hotel room across from the Pensión Sobrales where the Travelers were on the rolls. Everything was going well between them, Gekrepten was enchanted, she could prepare magnificent *mates* and even though she made love and *pasta asciutta* rather badly, she had other revealing domestic qualities and she could leave him alone for all the time he needed to ponder the business of coming back and going away, a problem that used to bother him in his free moments as he went from door to door selling bolts of gabardine. At first Traveler had criticized his mania for finding fault with Buenos Aires, for treating the city like a tightly girdled whore, but Oliveira explained to him and Talita that in his criticism there was so much love that only a pair of mental defectives like them would misunderstand his attacks. In the end they realized that he was right, that Oliveira could not make any hypocritical compromise with Buenos Aires, and that at the moment he was much farther away from his own country than when he had been wandering about Europe. Only small things, old things, would make him smile: *mate*, De Caro records, sometimes the waterfront in the afternoon. The three of them used to wander around the city a lot, taking advantage of the fact that Gekrepten was working in a shop, and Traveler could spot that Oliveira was making his peace with the city, fertilizing the soil with enormous quantities of beer. But Talita was more intransigent (a definite characteristic of indifference) and she demanded quick acceptances: Clorindo Testa's painting, for example, or the films of Torre Nilsson. They got into hot arguments over Bioy Casares, David Viñas, Father Castellani, Manauta, and the policies of the YPF. Talita finally came to understand that for Oliveira being in Buenos Aires was exactly the same as if he had been in Bucharest, and that in reality he had not come back but that he had been brought back. Underneath the things they would argue about there was always a layer of pataphysics, the triple coincidence of a histrionic search for lookout points that could excentrate the viewer or the thing being viewed. Because of their battles Talita and Oliveira began to have respect for each other. Traveler would remember when Oliveira was twenty years old and his heart would ache, but it was more likely wind from all the beers.

"The trouble with you is you're not a poet," Traveler would say. "You don't have the same feeling we do for the city, a great big belly heaving slowly underneath the heavens, a huge spider with half his feet in San Vicente, in Burzaco, in Sarandi, in El Palomar, and the rest of them in the water, poor thing, you know how dirty the river is."

"Horacio is a perfectionist," Talita said with pity, for she was already becoming more sure of herself. "A gadfly on a thoroughbred horse. You ought to take a lesson from us, simple inhabitants of Buenos Aires, and still we do know who Pieyre de Mandiargues is."

"And along the streets," Traveler said, rolling his eyes, "girls pass with soft eyes and delicate faces showing the effects of rice and milk and Radio El Mundo in the pleasant foolishness of their face powder."

"Not to mention the emancipated and intellectual women who work in circuses," Talita added modestly.

"And specialists in urban folklore like myself. Remind me when we get back to the room to read you Ivonne Guitry's story of her life, old man, it's fantastic."

"By the way, Señora Gutusso wanted me to tell you that if you don't return her Gardel songbook she'll crown you with a flowerpot," Talita informed him.

"First I've got to read Horacio the life story. Let her wait, the old bitch."

"Is Señora Gutusso that species of gnu who spends her time talking to Gekrepten?" Oliveira asked.

"Yes, it's their turn to be friends this week. You'll see in a few days, that's how things go in this neighbourhood."

"Silver-plated with moonlight," Oliveira said. "It's a lot better than your Saint-Germain-des-Prés," Talita said.

"But of course," said Oliveira, looking at her. Rolling his eyes a little, perhaps . . . And the way she pronounced the French words, the way she had, and if he just squinted a little. (Pharmacist, pity.)

How they loved to play with words, making up games to play those days in the cemetery of the language, turning to page 558 in the Julio Casares dictionary, for example, and playing with *hallulla, hámago, halieto, haloque, hamez, harambel, harbullista, harca*, and *harija*. Underneath it all they were a little sad as they thought about possibilities come to nought and the Argentinian character and time's-inexorable-passage. As for the pharmacist business, Traveler insisted that it was all a matter of barbarian peoples and eminently Merovingian, and he and Oliveira dedicated an epic poem to Talita in which the Pharmaceutical hordes invaded Catalonia, spreading terror, piperine, and hellebore. The whole Pharmaceutical nation, on massive steeds. A meditation on the Pharmaceutical steppes. Oh Empress of the Pharmacists, have pity on the Mushies, the Yokies, the Lazies, and the Stuffies, all of the Runawaydies.

While Traveler was quietly working on the Manager so that Oliveira could get a job with the circus, the object of these manoeuvres was drinking *mate* in his room and catching up on Argentine literature. While he was working at this task the weather suddenly got hot and the sale of gabardine dropped off considerably. They began to get together in Don Crespo's patio. He was a friend of Traveler's and rented rooms to Señora Gutusso and other ladies and gentlemen. With the help of Gekrepten's tenderness (she spoiled him like a child), Oliveira was able to sleep as long as he could bear it and in his lucid intervals he would sometimes look at a book by Crevel that he had found in the bottom of his suitcase, and he was beginning to assume the airs of a hero in a Russian novel. No good could possibly come of this methodical laziness, and that was what he vaguely kept his faith in, in the idea that by half-closing his eyes he would be able to see things outlined more clearly, that by sleeping he would be able to clear up his meninges. Things were not going well with the circus and the Manager didn't even want to think about taking on anybody new. In the early evening, before going to work, the Travelers would go down and have some *mate* with Don Crespo, and Oliveira would come too and they would listen to records on an old phonograph that could still run, which is the way old records ought to be played. Sometimes Talita would sit across from Oliveira and they would play with the cemetery, or challenge each other by balancing questions, another game they had invented with Traveler and which they got a lot of fun out of. Don Crespo thought they were crazy and Señora Gutusso thought they were stupid.

"You never talk very much about all that," Traveler would say sometimes, without looking at Oliveira. He was stronger; when Traveler made up his mind to interrogate him he had to avoid his eyes, and he didn't know why he was never able to mention the capital of France by name, but he always said "that" the way a mother works hard at inventing inoffensive names for her children's pudenda, God's little things.

"It doesn't interest me," Oliveira would answer. "You'll find out."

It was the best way there was to enrage Traveler, a failure as a nomad. Instead of pressing the point he would tune up the horrible guitar he had bought at the Casa América and start playing tangos. Talita would glance at Oliveira, a little resentful. Without making herself obvious. Traveler had convinced her that Oliveira was an oddball, and even though that was plain to see, his oddness must have been something else, must have been off somewhere else. There were nights when everybody seemed to be expecting something. They felt very good together, but it was like the eye of a hurricane. On nights like that, if they opened up the cemetery things would come out like *cisco*, *cisticerco*, *¡cito!*, *cisma*, *cístico*, and *cisión*. Finally they would go to bed with latent ill-humour, and spend the whole night dreaming about happy and funny things, which was probably a contradiction in terms.

(–59)

41

The sun began to hit Oliveira in the face sometime after two in the afternoon. Besides the heat, it made it very hard for him to straighten out nails by hammering them on a tile on the floor (everybody knows how dangerous it is to straighten out a nail with a hammer, there is a moment when the nail is almost upright, but when you hit it with the hammer again it gives half a turn and pinches the fingers you're holding it with; there's a quick perverseness about it all), stubbornly hammering them on a tile (but everybody knows that) stubbornly on a tile (but everybody) stubbornly.

"There isn't a straight one in the lot," Oliveira was thinking as he looked at the nails scattered around on the floor. "And the hardware store is closed now, and they'll throw me out if I pound on the door and ask them to sell me thirty cents' worth of nails. I have to straighten them, there's no other way out."

Each time he managed to get a nail half-straightened, he would lift up his head and whistle in the direction of the open window for Traveler to appear. He could see part of their bedroom quite clearly from his room, and something told him that Traveler was in there, probably in bed with Talita. The Travelers slept a lot in the daytime, not so much because they were tired from working at the circus, but because of a certain principle of laziness that Oliveira respected. It was a shame to wake Traveler up at two-thirty in the afternoon, but the fingers Oliveira was using to hold down the nails were already turning purple, extravasation was setting in from the pounding the blood vessels were taking, giving his fingers the look of underdone meat, which was really repulsive. The more he looked at them, the more he felt like having some *mate* and he was all out of *yerba*: actually there was enough for half a *mate* and Traveler or Talita would have to wrap up what he needed in some paper, using some nails as ballast, and toss it through the window. With some straight nails and some *yerba*, siesta-time would be more tolerable.

"It's fantastic how loud I can whistle," Oliveira thought in amazement. From the floor below where there was a brothel with three women and a girl to run errands, someone was imitating him with a pitiful counter-whistle, something in between a boiling kettle and a toothless hiss. Oliveira was fascinated by the admiration and rivalry aroused by his whistle; he never wasted it, but would save it for important occasions. During his reading hours, which were between one and five o'clock in the morning, but not every morning, he had come to the disconcerting conclusion that whistling was not an important theme in literature. There weren't many authors who made their characters whistle. Practically none of them did. They would condemn them to a rather tiresome repertory of expression (say, answer, sing, shout, babble, mutter, pronounce, whisper, exclaim and declaim), but no hero or heroine had ever crowned the high point of one of their epics with a magnificent whistle of the type that shatters glass. English squires would whistle to call their hounds and some characters in Dickens would whistle for a cab. As far as Argentine literature was concerned, there was very little whistling, and it was a disgrace. That's why, although Oliveira had not read Cambaceres, he considered him a master because he had used "whistle" in one of his titles; sometimes he would think along subsequent lines in which whistling would insinuate itself into Argentina on the surface and underneath, would wrap it up in its glowing twine and offer up to world-wide stupefaction a tight-rolled omelette, that would have little in common with the official version put forth by embassies and what one saw in the well-digested Sunday rotogravure put out by all the Gainza Mitre Pazes, and still less with the ups and downs of the Boca Juniors and the necrophilic cults of the *baguala* and the Boedo section. "Mother-fucker" (to a nail), "they won't even let me think in peace, God damn it." Besides, these ideas were repulsive to him because they were so facile, even though he was convinced that the only way to get a hold on Argentina was to come up on it from the shameful side, find the blush hidden under a century of usurpations of all kinds, as writers had pointed out so well, and therefore the best way was to show it in some way in which it didn't have to take itself so seriously. Who could be the clown who could send such high and mighty national sovereignty off to hell? Who could laugh in its face to see it flush and maybe once in a while smile like someone who has a recognition? But, Jesus, old friend, what a way to piss away a day. Let's see now, maybe this nail won't give me as much of a hard time as the others, it seems to be more tractable.

"God, it's cold," Oliveira said to himself, because he was a great believer in autosuggestion. Sweat was pouring over his eyes out of his hair and it was impossible to hold a nail with the head up because the lightest blow of the hammer would make it slip out of his fingers which were all wet (from the cold) and the nail would pinch him again and he would mash his fingers (from the cold). To make things worse, the sun had begun to shine with full force into the room (it was the moon on snow-covered steppes, and he whistled to goad the horses pulling against their harnesses), by three o'clock the whole place was covered with snow, he would let himself freeze until he got to that sleepy state described so well and maybe even brought about in Slavic stories, and his body would be entombed in the man-killing whiteness of the livid flowers of space. That was pretty good: the livid flowers of space. Right then he hit himself full on the thumb with the hammer. The coldness that had got into him was so intense that he had to roll around on the ground in an attempt to fight off the stiffness that was coming on him from the fact that he was freezing up. When he managed to sit upright waving his hand around, he was wet from head to toe, probably from the melting snow or from that light drizzle that was mingling with the livid flowers of space and refreshed the wolves as it fell on their fur.

Traveler was tying up his pyjama bottoms and from his window he was able to get a clear picture of Oliveira's struggles with the snow and the steppes. He was about to turn around and tell Talita that Oliveira was rolling on the floor shaking his hand, but he realized that the situation was rather serious and that it would be better for him to be a stern and impassive witness.

"It's about time, damn it," Oliveira said. "I've been whistling at you for half an hour. Look what I've done to my hand."

"You didn't get that from selling bolts of gabardine," Traveler said.

"Trying to straighten out nails. I need some straight nails and a little bit of *yerba*."

"That's easy to arrange," Traveler said. "Wait a minute."

"Wrap it up and throw it to me."

"OK," Traveler said. "But now that I think of it, it's going to be hard getting into the kitchen."

"Why?" asked Oliveira. "It's not too far away."

"No, but there's a clothesline with stuff hung up to dry."

"Duck under it," Oliveira suggested. "Cut it down if you have to. The slap of a wet shirt landing on the floor is something unforgettable. If you want, I'll toss you my jackknife. I bet I can stick it right on the window. When I was a kid I could stick a jackknife wherever I wanted to and from thirty feet away."

"The trouble with you," Traveler said, "is that every problem always brings you back to your childhood. I'm sick of telling you to read a little Jung. And look how it all comes back with that jackknife, you make it sound like an interplanetary missile. It's impossible to mention anything to you without your hauling out your jackknife. Just tell me what the devil all this has to do with a little bit of *yerba* and a few nails."

"You didn't follow me," Oliveira said, offended. "First I mentioned my mangled hand, then I mentioned the nails. Then you raised the barrier of a clothesline that was stopping you from going to the kitchen, and it was logical that the clothesline should remind me of my jackknife. You ought to read Edgar Allan Poe. Clothesline and all, you can't follow the thread of anything, that's what's wrong with you."

Traveler leaned on the windowsill and looked out into the street. The little shade that there was had spread out over the pavement, and the sunny part started from the second floor up, a yellow ecstasy grasping out in all directions and literally smacking Oliveira in the face.

"The sun is really screwing you up this afternoon," Traveler said.

"It's not the sun," said Oliveira. "You ought to be able to see that it's the moon and that the cold is just too much. This hand of mine has got all purple from the cold. Gangrene is setting in, and in a few weeks you'll be bringing gladioli to me in the cemetery."

"The moon?" Traveler said, looking up. "I'll be bringing you wet towels in Vieytes, the loony bin."

"What they want most out there are cigarettes," Oliveira said. "You're full of incongruities, Manú."

"I've told you a hundred times not to call me Manú."

"Talita calls you Manú," said Oliveira, shaking his hand as if he wanted to disconnect it from his arm.

"The difference between you and Talita," Traveler said, "is something that is obvious to the touch. I don't understand why you have to pick up her vocabulary. I'm repelled by hermit crabs, symbiosis in all its forms, lichens, and all other parasites."

"My heart really bleeds for your sensitivity," Oliveira said.

"Thank you. So it's *yerba* and nails. What do you want the nails for?"

"I'm not sure yet," Oliveira said, confused. "Actually, I took down the tin of nails and found they were all twisted. I started to straighten them out, but with all this cold, you see . . . It's my idea that as long as I have straight nails I'll know what to use them for."

"Interesting," Traveler said, staring at him. "The strangest things happen to you. First the nails and then their ultimate use. It could be a tremendous lesson, old man."

"You always did understand me," Oliveira said. "And the *yerba*, you should know, I need it to brew up some good old bitter stuff."

"OK," Traveler said. "Hold on. If I take too long you can whistle. Talita likes your whistling."

Shaking his hand, Oliveira went into the bathroom and wet his head and hair. He kept on wetting himself until his undershirt was all soaked, and then he turned to the window to test the theory that if the rays of the sun fall on a wet rag a violent sensation of cold will be produced. "To think that I shall die," Oliveira said to himself, "without having read the headlines: TOWER OF PISA FALLS. It's sad, if you really take a good look at it."

He began to put headlines together, something that always helped to pass the time of day. WOOL CLOGS LOOM AND SUFFOCATES IN WEST LANÚS. He could add up two hundred possible headlines without coming upon any other one that was passable.

"I'm going to have to move," Oliveira muttered. "This room is really too small. I really have to get into Manú's circus and stay with them. *Yerba!*"

Nobody answered.

"*Yerba,*" Oliveira said softly. "Yes, *yerba.* Don't come on like that, Manú. To think that we could chat from window to window, you and Talita and maybe Señora Gutusso would join in, or the errand-girl, and we could make up games with the cemetery and other things to play with."

"After all," Oliveira thought, "I can play games with the cemetery all by myself."

He went to get the Dictionary of the Spanish Royal Academy, on the cover of which the word *Royal* stood out like an open wound, having been chipped away by a razor-blade; he opened it at random and worked out the following game from the cemetery for Manú.

"Fed up with the client and her climacteric, they clipped out her clitoris and gave her a clyster, clinically in her cloaca, and as she clucked about the clipping and the clinometric climb to get such clinkers, they sent her off to get some clerical clue to her clingy claim."

"Shit," Oliveira said with admiration. He thought that maybe shit could be a starting point, but he was mistaken because he couldn't find it in the cemetery; but on the other hand the shipworm shirked among the shirts and shivered deep within the shittim wood; the worst of it was that the shifty shingle was shimmying up and down his shin, in some Shinto shire that could be shirred for a shilling.

"It's really the necropolis," he thought. "I can't see how the binding has lasted so long on all this crap."

He began to work out another game, but it didn't come off. He decided to look into the typical dialogues and he looked for the notebook where he had been keeping them after getting inspiration in the subway, cafés, and bars. He had practically finished a typical dialogue between two Spaniards and he put down the finishing touches, but first he poured a pitcher of water over his undershirt.

A TYPICAL DIALOGUE BETWEEN TWO SPANIARDS

LÓPEZ: I had been living in Madrid for a whole year. You know, it was in 1925, and . . .

PÉREZ: In Madrid? Why, just yesterday I was saying to Dr García . . .

LÓPEZ: From 1925 to 1926. I taught literature at the University.

PÉREZ: I was saying to him: "You know, old man, anybody who has lived in Madrid knows what it's all about."

LÓPEZ: A chair was established especially for me so I could give my lectures in Literature.

PÉREZ: Precisely, precisely. Why, just yesterday I was saying to Dr García, who is a very good friend of mine . . .

LÓPEZ: Of course, as you know if you have lived there more than a year, the level of studies leaves much to be desired.

PÉREZ: He's the son of Paco García, the one who was Minister of Trade and raised bulls.

LÓPEZ: A scandal, you can be sure, a real scandal.

PÉREZ: Yes, old man, of course. Well, this Dr García . . .

Oliveira was already a little bored with the dialogue and closed his notebook. "Shiva," he thought suddenly. "Oh, cosmic dancer, how would you shine, infinite bronze, in the light of this sun? Why did I think of Shiva? Buenos Aires. You get along. Funny thing. You end up owning an encyclopedia. *De qué te sirvió el verano, oh ruiseñor.* Of course it could be worse, specializing and spending five years in the study of the behaviour of the Acrididae. But just look at this fantastic list, boy, take a look at this . . . "

It was a slip of yellow paper clipped from some document of vaguely international character. A publication of UNESCO or something of the sort, with a list of names from some Burmese council. Oliveira began to be absorbed in the list and he could not resist the temptation to take out a pencil and compose the following nonsense poem:

U Nu,
U Tin,
Mya Bu,
Thado Thiri Thudama U E Maung,
Sithu U Cho,
Wunna Kyaw Htin U Khin Zaw,
Wunna Kyaw Htin U Thein Han,
Wunna Kyaw Htin U Myo Min,
Thiri Pyanchi U Thant,
Thado Maha Thray Sithu U Chan Htoon.

"The three Wunna Kyaw Htins are a little monotonous," he said to himself as he looked at the lines. "It must mean something like 'His Excellency the Most Exalted'. But the Thiri Pyanchi U Thant is good, that's the one that sounds best. I wonder how you pronounce Htoon."

"Hi," Traveler said.

"Hi," said Oliveira. "Cold enough for you?"

"I'm sorry you had to wait. The nails, you know . . . "

"Of course," said Oliveira. "A nail is a nail, especially if it's straight. Did you wrap them up?"

"No," said Traveler, scratching his breast. "Jesus, what a day. It's like an oven."

"Look," said Oliveira, touching his completely dry undershirt. "You're like the salamander, you live in a world of perpetual pyromania. Did you bring the *yerba*?"

"No," Traveler said. "I completely forgot about the *yerba*. I only brought the nails."

"Well, go and get it, make me up a bundle, and toss it over here."

Traveler looked at his window, then at the street, and finally at Oliveira's window.

"It's going to be a close one," he said. "You know I can never hit anything even six feet away. I've fooled myself twenty times in the circus."

"But it's practically like handing it to me," Oliveira said.

"That's what you say, that's what you say, and the nails will land on top of somebody down in the street and we'll be in trouble."

"Toss me the package and then we can play some games with the cemetery," Oliveira said.

"It would be better if you came over and got it."

"Are you out of your mind? Go down three flights, cross the street through all that ice, climb up three more flights, they don't even do that in *Uncle Tom's Cabin*."

"You're not going to suggest that I undertake that bit of afternoon alpinism, are you?"

"The farthest from my mind," Oliveira said virtuously.

"Or for me to look for a board in the pantry and make a bridge with it?"

"That's not a bad idea at all," Oliveira said, "and it would give us a chance to use the nails, you on your side and me on mine."

"OK, wait a minute," Traveler said and disappeared.

Oliveira stayed there trying to think of a good insult to put Traveler down with the first chance he got. After consulting the cemetery and pouring a pitcher of water over his undershirt, he leaned on the windowsill in the sunlight. Traveler reappeared soon, dragging an enormous plank, which he shoved little by little out of the window. Just then Oliveira noticed that Talita was helping to hold the board, and he greeted her with a whistle. Talita had on a green bathrobe and had it tied so tight that it was easy to see that she didn't have anything else on underneath.

"You're such a drag," Traveler said with a snort. "You get us involved in the damnedest things."

"Shut up, you myriapod from four to five inches in length, with a pair of feet on each of twenty-one rings dividing the body, four eyes, and horny hooked mandibles which on biting exude a very active poison," he said in one breath.

"Mandibles," Traveler commented. "Listen to the words he uses. Hey, if I keep pushing this board out of the window the time will come when the force of gravity will drag Talita and me straight down to hell."

"I can see that," Oliveira said, "but don't forget that the end of the board is too far away for me to grab."

"Stretch out your mandibles a little," Traveler said.

"Don't put me on. Besides you know damned well that I suffer from *horror vacuis*. I'm a real *roseau pensant*, a *caña pensante*."

"The only *caña* I can see in you is the kind that comes from Paraguay," Traveler said furiously. "I really don't know what we can do, this board is beginning to get too heavy, you know of course that weight is a question of relativity. When we carried it out it was quite light, but of course the sun wasn't shining on it the way it is now."

"Pull it back into the room," Oliveira said with a sigh. "This is what we'll do: I have another board, not as long, but it is wider. We'll put a rope around it like a noose and tie the two boards together. I'll tie my end to my bed, you do whatever seems best with yours."

"I think we'd better tie ours onto the handle of a chest of drawers," Talita said. "You go and get yours and we'll get ours ready."

"God, but they can get involved," Oliveira thought as he went to get the board, which was in the hallway between the door of his place and that of a Levantine faith-healer. It was a cedar plank, smoothly planed but missing two or three knots that had fallen out. Oliveira stuck his finger through one of the knotholes to see what it looked like from the other side, and he wondered whether the holes could be used to tie on the rope. The hallway was almost completely dark (it was really the contrast between the sunshine in his room and the shade there) and next to the Levantine's door there was a chair on which he could make out a woman dressed in black. Oliveira nodded to her from behind the board, which he had lifted up and was holding like a huge (and ineffective) shield.

"Hello, mister," the woman in black said. "Hot enough for you?"

"Quite the contrary, madam," Oliveira said. "It's terribly cold."

"Don't be funny," the woman said. "Show some respect for people who are not well."

"But there's nothing wrong with you, madam."

"Nothing wrong? How dare you!"

"All of this is reality," Oliveira thought, grabbing the board and looking at the woman in black. "All of this that I accept as reality every minute and which can't be, can't be."

"It can't be," Oliveira said.

"Go away and don't be cheeky," the woman said. "You ought to be ashamed, coming out in your undershirt at this time of day."

"It's from Masllorens', madam," Oliveira said.

"Disgusting," the woman said.

"All of this stuff I think makes up reality," Oliveira thought, stroking the board, leaning on it. "This display window arranged and lit up by fifty or sixty centuries of hands, imaginations, compromises, pacts, secret liberties."

"Who would think that a man starting to turn grey . . . " the woman in black said.

"To get the idea that you are the centre," Oliveira thought, resting more comfortably on the board. "But it's incalculably stupid. A centre as illusory as it would be to try to find ubiquity. There is no centre, there's a kind of continuous confluence, an undulation of matter. All through the night I'm a motionless body, and on the other side of town a roll of newsprint is being converted into the morning paper, and at eight-forty I will leave the house and at eight twenty the paper will have arrived at the news-stand on the corner, and at eight forty-five my hand and the newspaper will come together and begin to move together through the air, three feet from the ground, heading towards the tram stop . . . "

"Don Bunche is certainly taking his time with that other patient," the woman in black said.

Oliveira lifted up the plank and carried it into his room. Traveler was signalling for him to hurry up, and to calm him down he answered with two shrill whistles. The rope was on top of the wardrobe, he had to bring a chair over and climb up on it.

"Can't you hurry up a little?" Traveler said.

"OK, OK," Oliveira said, going to the window. "Is your board secured?"

"We've tied it to a drawer of the dresser, and Talita has put *Quillet's Self-Teaching Encyclopedia* on top of it."

"Not bad," Oliveira said. "I'm going to put the yearly report of the *Statens Psykologisk-Pedagogiska Institut* on mine. They send it to Gekrepten, God knows why."

"What worries me is how we're going to connect them," Traveler said as he began to move the dresser so that the board started to emerge from the window little by little.

"You look like two Assyrian generals armed with battering-rams and preparing to knock down some walls," said Talita, who was not owner of the encyclopedia in vain. "Is that a German book you mentioned?"

"Swedish, stupid," Oliveira said. "It talks about things like *Mentalhygieniska synpunkter i förskoleundervisning*. Splendid words, worthy of that young man Snorri Sturluson we hear so much about in Argentine literature. Real bronze breastplates, with the talismanic figure of the falcon."

"The wild whirlwinds of Norway," Traveler quoted.

"Are you really a cultured type, or are you just putting it on?" Oliveira asked, a little surprised.

"I won't say the circus doesn't take up a lot of time," Traveler said, "but there's always a little left for me to pin a star on my forehead. This talk of the star on my forehead always comes out when I talk about the circus, pure contamination. I wonder where I got it? Do you have any idea, Talita?"

"No," said Talita, testing the strength of the board. "Probably from some Puerto Rican novel."

"What bothers me is that in my subconscious I know where I read it."

"In some classic?" Oliveira hinted.

"I can't remember what it was about any more," Traveler said, "but it was a book I'll never forget."

"So it seems," Oliveira said.

"Our board is fine," Talita said. "But I don't see how we can fasten it to yours."

Oliveira had finished unwinding the rope; he cut it in two, and with one half he tied the board to the bedsprings. Putting the end of the board on the windowsill, he moved the bed up and the board began to dip down like a lever, with the sill as its fulcrum, until little by little it came to rest on top of Traveler's, while the legs of the bed lifted up about a foot and a half. "The worst part is that it's going to keep on rising as soon as someone tries to cross the bridge," Oliveira thought worriedly. He went over to the wardrobe and began to push it towards the bed.

"Don't you have enough weight?" Talita asked as she sat on the edge of her window and looked over into Oliveira's room.

"We've got to take every precaution," Oliveira said, "so we won't have any avoidable accidents."

He pushed the wardrobe over next to the bed and slowly tipped it over on top of it. Talita marvelled at Oliveira's strength, almost as much as she did at Traveler's astuteness and his inventions. "They're really a pair of glyptodons," she thought, enraptured. The antediluvian ages had always seemed to her to be a refuge of wisdom.

The wardrobe picked up speed as it fell and landed with a thump on the bed, making the whole room shake. There were shouts from down below and Oliveira thought that the Levantine next door must have been putting together some violent shamanistic pressure. He finished placing the wardrobe and then straddled the plank, inside the window, of course.

"Now it can take any weight," he announced. "There won't be any accident to please the girls downstairs who love us so much. None of this will make any sense to them until somebody gets killed down on the street. Life, as they say."

"Aren't you going to tie the boards together with your rope?" Traveler asked.

"Look," Oliveira said. "You know very well that I get dizzy from heights. The very name of Everest makes me feel as if someone had kicked me in the crotch. I hate a lot of people, but no one the way I do Sherpa Tensing, believe me."

"In other words, we are going to have to tie the boards together," Traveler said.

"That's about the strength of it," Oliveira admitted, lighting up a 43.

"See what we've got to do?" Traveler said to Talita. "Try crawling out to the middle of the bridge and tying the rope."

"Me?" Talita said.

"That's what I said."

"Oliveira didn't say I had to crawl out to the middle of the bridge."

"He didn't say so, but he implied it. Besides it would have more style if you were the one who handed him the *yerba*."

"I won't be able to tie the knot," Talita said. "You and Oliveira know how to tie knots, but mine will come undone right away. I won't even be able to get it started."

"We'll tell you how," Traveler condescended.

Talita tightened her bathrobe and picked a thread off her finger. She needed to sigh, but she knew that sighs annoyed Traveler.

"You really want me to be the one who takes the *yerba* over to Oliveira?" she said softly.

"What are you talking about there?" Oliveira asked, leaning halfway out of the window and putting his hands on his plank. The errand-girl had brought a chair out on the pavement and was watching them. Oliveira waved at her with one hand. "A compound fracture in time and space," he thought. "The poor dear thinks we're crazy and she's waiting for a wild flight back to normality. If anyone falls she'll be splattered with blood, that's for sure. And she doesn't know that she'll be splattered with blood, she doesn't know that she put the chair there so that she would be splattered with blood, and she doesn't know that ten minutes ago she had an attack of *tedium vitae* right there in the pantry, just enough to initiate the transference of the chair out onto the pavement. And that the glass of water she drank at two twenty-five is lukewarm and upsetting for her stomach, that centre of afternoon moods, and that it had prepared her for that attack of *tedium vitae* which three tablets of Phillips milk of magnesia would have taken care of perfectly; but she couldn't have known about this last item, certain things that unleash or cut off can only be perceived on an astral plane, if one wishes to use that inane terminology."

"We're not talking about anything," Traveler was saying. "You get the rope ready."

"There it is, a magnificent knot. Come on, Talita, I'll hand it to you from here."

Talita straddled the plank and moved forward a couple of inches, leaning on her hands and picking up her behind and putting it down a little bit farther forward.

"This bathrobe isn't very comfortable," she said. "A pair of your pants or something like that would be better."

"It's too much trouble," Traveler said. "And if you fell off you'd ruin my clothes."

"Take your time," Oliveira said. "Just a little bit more and I can toss you the rope."

"This street is awfully wide," Talita said, looking down. "It's much wider than it looks from the window."

"Windows are the eyes of the city," Traveler said, "and naturally they give the wrong shape to everything they see. Right now you're at a point of great purity, and maybe you can see things the way a pigeon or a horse does, without being aware that they have eyes."

"Save ideas for the *Nouvelle Revue Française* and tie the boards up tight," Oliveira advised.

"It's just like you to blow up if anyone says something you would have loved to have said first. I can hold the board down perfectly well while I think and talk."

"I must be close to the centre," Talita said.

"The centre? You're barely out of the window. You've got at least six feet more to go."

"Not quite so much," Oliveira said by way of encouragement. "I'm going to toss you the rope right now."

"I have the feeling that the board is bending," Talita said.

"It's not bending at all," Traveler said as he straddled the plank, but from inside the window. "It's just shaking a little."

"Besides, the end of it is resting on my board," Oliveira said. "It would be mighty strange if they both broke at the same time."

"Yes, but I weigh a hundred and twenty-five pounds," Talita said. "And when I get to the centre I'll weigh five hundred at least. I can feel the board bending more and more."

"If it was bending, my feet would be off the floor, and I can still feel them firmly planted. All that can happen is that the boards might break, and that would be most unusual."

"The fibres have a lot of resistance lengthwise," Oliveira agreed. "That's the whole story behind a bunch of twigs and other examples. I suppose you've got the *yerba* and the nails."

"I've got them in my pocket," Talita said. "Hurry up and throw me the rope. I'm getting nervous, believe me."

"It's the cold," Oliveira said, twirling the rope like a gaucho. "Watch out that you don't lose your balance. Maybe I'd better rope you, that way we can be more sure that you can tie it on."

"It's funny," he thought, as he watched the lasso go over her head.

"Everything really falls into place piece by piece if you really want it to. The only thing untrue about all this is the analysis of it."

"You're getting there," Traveler announced. "Get into position so you can tie up the boards, they're a little bit apart."

"Look at the good job I did of roping her," Oliveira said. "There you are, Manú, you can't tell me now I couldn't get a job with you people in the circus."

"You hurt my face," Talita complained. "The rope is scratchy."

"I can put on a cowboy hat, come out whistling, and rope anybody or anything," Oliveira proposed with enthusiasm. "The crowd will break out cheering, a show that has few precedents in circus history."

"The sun's starting to get to you," Traveler said, lighting up a cigarette. "And I've told you not to call me Manú."

"I haven't got the strength," Talita said. "The rope is too coarse, it keeps catching on itself."

"The ambivalence of the noose," Oliveira said. "Its natural function sabotaged by a mysterious tendency towards neutralization. I think that's what they call entropy."

"It's pretty tight now," Talita said. "Shall I loop it again? There's still a little left over."

"Yes, tie it around tight," Traveler said. "I hate things that are left over and dangling; it's diabolical."

"A perfectionist," Oliveira said. "Now come on over onto my board and test the bridge."

"I'm afraid," Talita said. "Your board doesn't look as solid as ours."

"What?" said Oliveira, offended. "Can't you see that it's a fine cedar board? Are you comparing it to that piece of pine? Come on, don't worry."

"What do you think, Manú?" Talita asked, looking back.

Traveler, who was about to reply, looked at the spot where the two boards overlapped and at the poorly tied rope. Straddling his board, he could feel it vibrating between his legs in a way that was neither pleasant nor unpleasant. All Talita had to do was put down her hands, pull herself up a little and she would be over on Oliveira's side. The bridge would hold, of course; it was well built.

"Wait a minute," Traveler said doubtfully. "Can't you hand him the package from there?"

"Of course she can't," Oliveira said, surprised. "What are you thinking of? You're ruining everything."

"Like he says, I can't hand it to him from here," Talita admitted. "But I could toss it, the easiest thing in the world from here."

"Toss it?" Oliveira said resentfully. "All this trouble and you're going to end up by tossing me the package?"

"If you stick out your arm you'll only be a foot away from the package," Traveler said. "There's no need for Talita to go all the way over there. She'll toss you the package and that's that."

"She'll miss, the way women always do," Oliveira said, "and the *yerba* will spill all over the street, not to mention the nails."

"Rest assured," Talita said, quickly taking out the package. "Even if it doesn't land in your hand, it will still go through the window."

"Yes, and it'll spill all over the dirty floor and I'll have to drink *mate* that is all full of dust," Oliveira said.

"Don't pay any attention to him," Traveler said. "Go ahead and throw it and come on back."

Talita turned around to look at him, doubting whether he meant what he was saying. Traveler was looking at her in a way that she knew very well, and Talita felt a sort of caress run up over her shoulder. She clutched the package and gauged the distance.

Oliveira had lowered his arms and seemed indifferent to what Talita was or was not going to do. He was looking at Traveler over Talita's head, and Traveler returned his look fixedly. "Those two have got another bridge working between them," Talita thought. "If I were to fall into the street they wouldn't even notice it." She looked down at the cobblestones, she saw the errand-girl looking up at her with her mouth open; two blocks away she saw a woman coming along who must have been Gekrepten. Talita paused with the package resting on the bridge.

"That's the way it is," Oliveira said. "It had to happen, nobody can change you. You come right up to the edge of things and one gets the idea that finally you're going to understand, but it's useless, you see, you start turning them around to read the labels. You always get stuck in the planning stage, man."

"So what?" Traveler said. "Why do I have to play games with you, pal?"

"Games play themselves; you're the one who sticks a pole in the spokes to slow down a wheel."

"A wheel that you invented, if you want to bring that up."

"I don't agree," Oliveira said. "All I did was create the circumstances, as anyone who can understand would see. The game has got to be played clean."

"You sound like a loser, old man."

"It's easy to lose if somebody else is rolling the dice."

"Big shot," Traveler said. "Real gaucho talk."

Talita knew that somehow they were talking about her, and she kept on looking down at the errand-girl, motionless on her chair with her mouth open. "I'd give anything for them to stop arguing," Talita thought. "No matter what they talk about, it's always about me in the end, but that's not what I really mean, still it's almost what I mean." It had occurred to her that it would be very funny to drop the package so that it would fall into the errand-girl's mouth. But she didn't really think it would be funny because she could feel that other bridge stretched out above her, the words that passed back and forth, the laughs, the hot silences.

"It's like a trial," Talita thought. "Like a ritual."

She recognized Gekrepten, who had reached the next corner and was beginning to look up. "Who's judging you?" Oliveira had just said. But it wasn't Traveler they were judging, it was her. A feeling, something sticky, like the sun on the back of her neck and on her legs. She was going to have an attack of sunstroke, that's what the punishment would probably be. "I don't think you're in any position to judge me," Manú had said. Still it wasn't Manú but she who was being judged. And through her God knows what, while stupid Gekrepten was waving her left arm around and making motions as if she was the one who was about to have an attack of sunstroke and fall down into the street, condemned without appeal.

"Why are you wobbling like that?" Traveler said, holding his board with both hands. "Hey, you're making it shake too much. Watch out or we'll all be up the creek."

"I'm not moving," Talita said miserably. "All I wanted to do was toss the package and get back inside again."

"The sun's beating down right on your head, you poor doll," Traveler said. "This is really too much, damn it."

"It's your fault," Oliveira said in a fury. "There's nobody in all Argentina who can fuck things up like you."

"You insist on blaming me," Traveler said objectively. "Hurry up,

Talita. Throw the package in his face so he'll stop screwing around with us once and for all."

"It's a little late for that," Talita said. "I don't know whether I can hit the window now."

"I told you so," Oliveira muttered, and it wasn't often that he muttered and only when he was on the brink of some outrageous thing. "There comes Gekrepten loaded down with bundles. There were only a few of us, and grandmother gave birth."

"Throw him the *yerba* anyway," Traveler said. "Don't worry if you miss."

Talita lowered her head and her hair flowed down over her forehead to her chin. She had to keep on blinking because the sweat was getting into her eyes. Her tongue felt salty and covered with something that could have been sparks, little stars running back and forth and bumping into her gums and the roof of her mouth.

"Wait," Traveler said.

"Are you talking to me?" Oliveira asked.

"No. Wait, Talita. Hang on tight, I'm going to hand you a hat."

"Don't get off the board," Talita pleaded. "I'll fall down into the street."

"The encyclopedia and the dresser will hold it down fine. Don't move, I'll be right back."

The boards dipped a little and Talita hung on desperately. Oliveira whistled with everything he had as if to stop Traveler, but there was nobody in the window any more.

"What a bastard," Oliveira said. "Don't move, don't even breathe. Your life depends on it, believe me."

"I know," Talita said in a wisp of a voice. "That's the way it's always been."

"And to make matters worse, Gekrepten is coming up the stairs. She's going to balls things up, damn it. Don't you move."

"I'm not moving," Talita said. "But I think . . . "

"Yes, but don't even do that," Oliveira said. "Don't move at all, it's the only way."

"They've already passed judgement on me," Talita thought. "Now all I have to do is fall and they can get on with the circus and life."

"What are you crying about?" Oliveira asked with interest.

"I'm not crying," Talita said. "I'm sweating, that's all."

"Look," Oliveira said resentfully, "I may be stupid, but I've never confused tears with perspiration. They're quite different things."

"I'm not crying," Talita said. "I almost never cry, I swear. People like Gekrepten cry and she's coming up the stairs right now, loaded down with bundles. I'm like the swan that sings when it dies," Talita said. "That's from a record of Gardel's."

Oliveira lit a cigarette. The boards had settled together again. He took a satisfying drag.

"Look, until that fool Manú comes back with the hat, what we should do is play seesaw-questions."

"Go ahead," Talita said. "If you want to know, I put a few together yesterday."

"OK. I'll begin and we'll each ask a seesaw-question. The operation which consists of depositing a coat of metal dissolved in a liquid on a solid body by use of electric currents, isn't it an old-fashioned ship, triangular sails, hundred-ton cargo?"

"That's what it is," Talita said, throwing back her hair. "Sailing at random, wandering, missing cannon-shots, civet-scented, collecting payments according to the tithe of first fruits, and isn't it the same as any plant juice used for food, like wine, olive oil, etc.?"

"Very good," Oliveira admitted. "Plant juice, like wine, olive oil . . . It never occurred to me to think of wine as a plant juice. Splendid. But listen to this: To bloom again, turn the fields to bloom, tangle up hair, wool, get tangled in a fight or quarrel, poison water with great mullein or some similar substance to stupefy the fish so they can be taken out, isn't that the ending of a dramatic poem, particularly if it's a tragic one?"

"How beautiful," Talita said enthusiastically, "it's beautiful, Horacio. You really can squeeze the juice out of the cemetery."

"Plant juice," Oliveira said.

The door of the room opened and Gekrepten entered breathing heavily. Gekrepten was a bleached blonde, she could talk quite easily, and she was not in the least surprised to see a wardrobe flung across the bed and a man straddling a board.

"It sure is hot," she said, throwing the bundles on a chair. "It's the worst time of day to go shopping, believe me. What are you doing out there, Talita? I don't know why I always go out at siesta-time."

"Good, good," Oliveira said without looking at her. "Your turn, Talita."

"I can't think of anything else."

"Think a little, you must remember something."

"Yes, the dentist," Gekrepten said. "He always gives me the worst appointments for a filling. Did I tell you I had to go to the dentist today?"

"I remember one now," Talita said.

"And what do you think happened," Gekrepten said. "I get to the dentist's, on the Calle Warnes. I ring the bell, and the receptionist comes to the door. I say: 'Good afternoon.' She says: 'Good afternoon. Please come in.' I come in and she takes me into the waiting room."

"It's like this," Talita said. "One whose cheeks are puffed up, or a row of buckets lashed together and floated like a raft to a place where reeds grow: a storehouse for items of prime necessity, established so that certain persons can acquire them there more economically than in a shop, and everything pertaining to or relative to the eclogue, isn't it like applying the science of galvanism to a living or dead animal?"

"Such beauty," Oliveira said astounded. "It's simply phenomenal."

"She tells me: 'Please sit down for a moment.' And I sit and wait."

"I've still got one left," Oliveira said. "Just a minute, I can't remember it too well."

"There were two women and a man with a child. The minutes dragged on. I tell you I got through three whole issues of *Idilio*. The child was crying, poor thing, and his father was a little nervous . . . I'm not lying when I say that more than two hours passed from the time I had come in at two-thirty. Finally it was my turn, and the dentist says: 'Come in, madam'; I go in, and he says: 'Did the one I put in the other day bother you much?' And I tell him: 'No, doctor, how could it bother me. Besides I only chewed on one side all the time.' He says: 'Good, that's what you have to do. Please sit down.' I sit down and he says: 'Open your mouth, please.' He's very pleasant, that dentist."

"I've got it now," Oliveira said. "Listen carefully, Talita. What are you looking back for?"

"To see if Manú is coming back."

"He'll be back. Listen carefully: the action and effect of passing in opposite directions, or in tournaments and jousts, the movement of a rider to make his mount run his chest against that of his opponent's mount, isn't it a lot like the fastigium, the most critical and serious moment of an illness?"

"It's strange," Talita said thoughtfully. "Is that how they say it in Spanish?"

"Say what?"

"That business about a rider making his mount run his chest against . . ."

"In tournaments, yes," Oliveira said. "It's in the cemetery after all."

"Fastigium is a very pretty word," Talita said. "Too bad it means what it does."

"Hell, the same thing can be said about bologna and lots of other words," Oliveira said. "The Abbé Bremond has already worked on this, but what could he do. Words are like us, they're born with one face and what can you do about it. Think about Kant's face for a moment, tell me what you think. Or Bernardino Rivadavia's, to stay closer to home."

"He put in a plastic filling," Gekrepten said.

"This heat is terrible," Talita said. "Manú said he was going to get me a hat."

"It's hard to tell what that guy will bring back," Oliveira said.

"If it's all right with you, I'll toss you the package and go back inside," Talita said.

Oliveira looked at the bridge, measured the window with a vague motion of his arms, and shook his head.

"You might miss," he said. "Besides, I get a funny feeling having you out there in this freezing cold. Can't you feel icicles forming in your hair and in your nasal passages?"

"No," Talita said. "Are the icicles going to be like fastigiums?"

"In a certain way, yes," Oliveira said. "They're two things that do seem alike from the point of view of their differences, a little like Manú and me, if you think about it a little. You're probably aware that all this trouble with Manú is that we look too much alike."

"The butter has melted," Gekrepten said, spreading some on a piece of dark bread. "The butter, with all this heat, it's a battle."

"The worst difference is in all that," Oliveira said. "The worst of all worst differences. Two guys with dark hair, with the face of a Buenos Aires low-life, with practically the same disdain for the same things, and you . . ."

"Well, I . . ." Talita said.

"There's no reason to hide," Oliveira said. "It's a fact that in some sort of way when you join us the similarity and the difference come out at the same time."

"I don't think I sum up the two of you," Talita said.

"What do you know about it? How could you know? There you are in your room, living and cooking and reading the self-teaching encyclopedia, and at night you go to the circus, and then you think that you're only where you are at that moment. Didn't you ever notice latches on doors, metal buttons, little pieces of glass?"

"Yes, I notice them sometimes," Talita said.

"If you were to take a good look you would see very easily that on all sides, where you least suspect, there are images that copy all your movements. I'm very sensitive to all that foolishness, believe me."

"Come here and drink this milk before it all curdles," Gekrepten said. "Why do you people always talk about such strange things?"

"You're making me too important," Talita said.

"Oh, you can't decide things like that," Oliveira said. "There's a whole order of things you can't decide by yourself, and they're always the most bothersome, even if they're not the most important. I tell you this because it's a great consolation. For example, I was planning to have some *mate.* Now this one comes home and starts to make *café con leche* without anybody asking her. Result: if I don't drink it the milk will curdle. It's not important, but it gets under your skin. Do you know what I'm talking about?"

"Oh, yes," Talita said, looking into his eyes. "It's true that you're like Manú. The pair of you can talk so well about *café con leche* and *mate,* and one ends up realizing that *café con leche* and *mate,* in reality . . . "

"Exactly," Oliveira said. "*In reality.* So let's get back to what I was saying before. The difference between Manú and me is that we're almost exactly alike. At this level, a difference is like an imminent cataclysm. Are we friends? Yes, of course, but I would never be surprised at anything that . . . Notice how ever since we've known each other, I can tell you because you already know that, all we've done is hurt each other. He doesn't like me to be the way I am, all I have to do is try to straighten out some nails and look at the hassle he starts, and he gets you into it along the line. But he doesn't like me to be the way I am because in reality a lot of the things that come to my mind, a lot of the things I do, it's as if I've stolen them out from under his nose. Before he has a chance to think of them, zip, there they are. Bang, bang, he comes to the window and I'm straightening out the nails."

Talita looked backwards and saw the shadow of Traveler, who was listening, hidden between the dresser and the window.

"Well, but you don't have to exaggerate," Talita said. "Some of the things that occur to Manú can't always have occurred to you."

"For example?"

"The milk's getting cold," Gekrepten grumbled. "Shall I put it on the fire a little more, sweet?"

"Make a custard with it tomorrow," Oliveira advised. "Go ahead, Talita."

"No," Talita said with a sigh. "What for? I'm so hot, and I have the feeling I'm going to get sick."

She felt the bridge vibrate as Traveler straddled it by the window-sill. Lying prone and staying on his side of the sill, Traveler put a straw hat on the board. With the aid of a mop handle he began to inch it along the board.

"If it gets the least bit off course it will fall into the street and it will be a terrible drag having to go down and get it."

"I think I'd better come back inside," Talita said, looking at Traveler with a mournful expression.

"But first you've got to give Oliveira his *yerba*," Traveler said.

"It doesn't matter any more," Oliveira said. "In any case, let her throw it, it doesn't make any difference."

Talita looked back and forth at them and remained motionless.

"It's hard to understand you," Traveler said. "All this work and now it turns out that one more *mate*, one less *mate*, it doesn't really matter."

"The minute-hand has made its circle, my son," Oliveira said. "You move in the time-space continuum with the speed of a worm. Think of all that has happened since you decided to go to find that overworked Panama hat. The cycle of the *mate* came to a close without reaching fruition, and in the meantime the ever-faithful Gekrepten made her showy entrance, loaded down with cooking utensils. We are now in the *café con leche* sector, and nothing can be done about it."

"That's some argument," Traveler said.

"That's no argument, it's a proof, arrived at in a perfectly objective way. You tend to move in the continuum, as physicists say, while

I am quite sensitive to the giddy discontinuity of existence. At this very moment the *café con leche* has burst upon the scene, has installed itself, rules, is propagated, and is repeated in hundreds of thousands of homes. The *mate* gourds have been washed, put away, abolished. A temporary *café con leche* mantle now covers this segment of the American continent. Think of all that this presupposes and brings with it. Conscientious mothers lecturing their offspring on the virtues of a lactic diet, children grouped around the pantry table, all smiles on top and all kicks and pinches underneath. To say *café con leche* at this time of day means change, a friendly get-together towards the end of the working day, the recounting of good deeds, deeds to the real estate transitory situations, vague prologues to what six o'clock in the afternoon, that terrible hour of keys in the door and a race to catch the bus, will bring home with brutal concreteness. Practically nobody ever makes love at that hour, they do it either before or after. At that hour people think about a shower (but we'll take one at five o'clock) and people begin to think about something to do in the evening, whether they'll go to see Paulina Singerman or Toco Tarantola (but we're not sure, there's still time). What does all this have to do with *mate* time? I'm not talking about *mate* that's not taken properly, superimposed on the *café con leche*, but the authentic one I wanted, at just the right moment, just when the weather was coldest. And it's all these things that I don't think you understand enough."

"The dressmaker is a crook," Gekrepten said. "Do you have your clothes made by a dressmaker, Talita?"

"No," Talita said. "I know a little bit about cutting and sewing."

"Smart girl. This afternoon after the dentist I run over to the dressmaker's, it's a block away, to inquire about a skirt that should have been ready a week ago. She says to me: 'I'm awfully sorry, miss, but with my mother as sick as she's been I wasn't even able to thread a needle, you might say.' I tell her: 'But I need the skirt.' She says: 'I'm terribly sorry, miss, believe me. A customer like you. But you'll have to forgive me.' I say: 'Forgiving won't get me anything. It would have been better if you'd had it done on time and we'd all be better off.' She says: 'If that's the way you feel, why don't you go to another dressmaker?' And I say: 'Not that I don't feel like it, but since I put in an order with you it would be better if I waited, but I don't think you're very reliable.'"

"Did all that happen?" Oliveira asked.

"Of course," Gekrepten said. "Can't you hear me telling Talita all about it?"

"They're two different matters."

"There you go again."

"There's your example," Oliveira said to Traveler, who looked at him with a furrowed brow. "There's your example of what things are like. Everybody thinks he's talking about something he has in common with everybody else."

"And that's not the way it is, of course," Traveler said. "What a fresh piece of news."

"It's worth repeating, damn it."

"You repeat everything you think is a sanction against somebody."

"God put me here to watch over your city," Oliveira said.

"When you're not judging me you do it to your old lady."

"In order to prod you and keep you both awake," Oliveira said.

"Like a Mosaic mania. It came to you on the way down from Mount Sinai."

"I like things to be as clear as possible," Oliveira said. "It doesn't seem to matter to you that right in the middle of a conversation Gekrepten sticks in a completely fantastic story about a dentist and some damned skirt or other. You don't seem to realize that these outbursts, pardonable when they're beautiful or at least inspired, become repulsive as soon as they start to cut into an order of things, torpedo a structure. How I do go on, old man."

"Horacio is always like this," Gekrepten said. "Don't pay any attention to him, Traveler."

"We're so bland it's unbearable, Manú. We let reality slip through our fingers like any ordinary trickle of water. We had it right there, almost perfect, like a rainbow between our thumb and our little finger. And the work that went into getting it, the time that was required, the way we had to make ourselves deserving of it . . . Boom, the radio says that General Pisotelli has made a declaration . . . *Kaput.* Everything *kaput.* 'Something serious at last,' the errand-girl says, or this one, or maybe even you yourself. And me, because I don't want you to think that I'm infallible. How should I know where truth is? I only know that I liked the feel of that rainbow, like a little toad between my fingers. And this afternoon . . . Look, in spite of the cold I think that we were beginning to hit upon something serious.

Talita, for example, carrying out the amazing feat of not falling off into the street, and you over there, and me . . . One feels certain things, what the hell."

"I'm not sure I understand you," Traveler said. "That business about the rainbow is pretty good anyway. But why are you so intolerant? Live and let live, brother."

"Now that you've had your fun, come and get the wardrobe off the bed," Gekrepten said.

"You see?" Oliveira said.

"I see what you mean," Traveler said, convinced.

"*Quod erat demonstrandum*, old buddy."

"*Quod erat*," Traveler said. "And the worst of it is that we hadn't even got started."

"What do you mean?" Talita said, tossing her hair back and looking to see if Traveler had pushed the hat far enough along.

"Don't get nervous," Traveler advised. "Turn around slowly, put out that hand, that's the way. Wait, I'll push it a little more . . . Didn't I tell you? There it is."

Talita grasped the hat and put it on, all in one motion. Down below there were two boys and a woman who were talking to the errand-girl and looking up at the bridge.

"Now I'll toss the package to Oliveira and that'll be it," Talita said, feeling more sure of herself with the hat on. "Hold the boards tight, it'll be easy."

"Are you going to throw it?" Oliveira asked. "I bet you miss."

"Let her try," Traveler said. "If the package goofs off into the street I hope it hits old lady Gutusso on her nut, repulsive old owl."

"So you don't like her either," Oliveira said. "I'm happy because I can't stand her. What about you, Talita?"

"I'd rather toss the package to you," Talita said.

"OK, OK, but I think you're rushing it too much."

"Oliveira's right," Traveler said. "You don't want to ruin everything right at the end, after all the work that went into it."

"But I'm so hot," Talita said. "I want to come back, Manú."

"You're not so far away that you should be complaining like that. Somebody would think you were writing me a letter from Mato Grosso."

"He's thinking about the *yerba* when he says that," Oliveira explained to Gekrepten, who was looking at the wardrobe.

"Are you going to play much longer?" Gekrepten asked.

"No way," Oliveira said.

"Oh," Gekrepten said. "Just as well."

Talita had taken the package out of her bathrobe and was swinging it back and forth. The bridge began to vibrate, and Traveler and Oliveira held it down with all their strength. Tired of swinging the package, Talita began to wind up with her arm, holding it with her other hand.

"Don't do anything silly," Oliveira said. "Slower, do you hear me? Slower."

"Here it comes," Talita shouted.

"Slower, you're going to fall off."

"I don't care!" Talita shouted, letting the package go. It went full force through the window and broke open as it hit the wardrobe.

"Splendid," Traveler said, looking at Talita as if he were trying to keep the bridge in place with nothing but the strength of his look. "Perfect, my love. You couldn't have made it clearer. That's a *demonstrandum* for you."

The bridge gradually stopped moving. Talita hung on with both hands and lowered her head. Oliveira could only see her hat and her hair hanging down over her shoulders. He raised his eyes and looked at Traveler.

"If you want to know," he said. "I agree, she couldn't have made it clearer."

"At last," Talita thought, looking down at the cobblestones and the pavements. "Anything is better than being out here like this in between the two windows."

"You've got two choices," Traveler said. "Keep going forward, which is easier, and go into Oliveira's, or come back, which is harder, and save yourself going up and down the stairs and crossing the street."

"Come over here, you poor thing," Gekrepten said. "Your face is all covered with perspiration."

"Drunks and little children," Oliveira said.

"Let me rest a minute," Talita said. "I feel a little nauseous."

Oliveira lay prone over the sill and stretched out his hand. All Talita had to do was come forward two feet to touch his hand.

"A perfect gentleman," Traveler said. "It's obvious he's read Professor Maidana's manual of social graces. A real aristo. Don't miss that, Talita."

"It's because of the extreme cold," Oliveira said. "Rest a little, Talita, and then cover the distance in between. Don't pay any attention to him, you know that the snow makes one delirious before the deep sleep sets in."

But Talita had raised herself slowly, and leaning on both arms had worked her behind half a foot backwards. Another grip, another half-foot. Oliveira, still holding out his hand, looked like a passenger on a boat which is slowly pulling away from the pier.

Traveler stretched out his arms and got his hands under Talita's armpits. She didn't move, and then she threw her head back with such a quick movement that the hat went gliding down to the pavement.

"Just like at the bullfight," Oliveira said. "Señora Gutusso is going to try to steal it."

Talita had closed her eyes and was letting herself be held up, hauled off the board and through the window. She felt Traveler's lips on the back of her neck, his quick, hot breath.

"You came back," Traveler murmured. "You came back, you came back."

"Yes," Talita said, going over to the bed. "Didn't you think I would? I threw him his god-damned package and I came back, I threw him the package and I came back, I . . . "

Traveler sat down on the edge of the bed. He was thinking about the rainbow between his fingers, those things that occurred to Oliveira. Talita slipped down beside him and began to cry quietly. "It's her nerves," Traveler thought. "She had a rough time." He wanted to get her a tall glass of water with lemon juice, give her an aspirin, cover her face with a magazine, make her sleep a little. But first he had to pick up the self-teaching encyclopedia, put the dresser back where it belonged, and pull in the board. "This room is such a mess," he thought, kissing Talita. As soon as she stopped crying he would ask her to help him clean up the room. He began to caress her, say things to her.

"At last, at last," Oliveira said.

He left the window and sat down on the edge of the bed, using the space remaining next to the wardrobe. Gekrepten had finished picking up the *yerba* with a spoon.

"It was full of nails," Gekrepten said. "How strange."

"Very strange," Oliveira said.

"I think I'll go down and get Talita's hat. You know how kids are."

"A wise thought," Oliveira said, picking up a nail and twirling it with his fingers.

Gekrepten went down to the street. The children had picked up the hat and were arguing with the errand-girl and Señora Gutusso.

"Give it to me," Gekrepten said with a prim smile. "It belongs to the lady across the way, someone I know."

"Everybody knows her, child," Señora Gutusso said. "What a performance for this time of day, and with children watching."

"There was nothing wrong with it," Gekrepten said without much conviction.

"With her legs out in the air on that board, what an example for the children. You probably couldn't see, but from down here it was quite a sight, I can assure you."

"She had a lot of hair," the smallest child said.

"There you are," said Señora Gutusso. "Children tell what they see, poor things. And what in the world was she doing straddling a board, might I ask? At this hour, when respectable people are having their siesta or are busy at work. Would you straddle a board, madam, if it's not too much to ask?"

"No, I wouldn't," Gekrepten said. "But Talita works in a circus. They're all performers."

"Were they rehearsing?" asked one of the boys. "What circus is that girl with?"

"It wasn't a rehearsal," Gekrepten said. "What happened was that they wanted to give my husband a little *yerba*, and so . . . "

Señora Gutusso looked at the errand-girl. The errand-girl put her finger to her temple and made a circle with it. Gekrepten took the hat in both hands and went back into the building. The boys formed a line and began to sing to the tune of the *Light Cavalry Overture*:

> Oh, they came from behind, oh, they came from behind,
> and they stuck a pole up his aaarse-hole.
> It wouldn't come out, it wouldn't come out,
> the poor man was out of his mind.
> (Repeat)

(–148)

42

Il mio supplizio
è quando
non mi credo
in armonia.
UNGARETTI, *I Fiumi*

The job consisted of stopping kids from crawling under the tent, lending a hand with the animals when necessary, helping the man who operated the lights, writing copy for advertisements and the gaudy posters, getting them printed, dealing with the police, keeping the Manager informed of anything wrong that he should know about, helping Señor Manuel Traveler in his administrative work, helping Señora Atalía Donosi de Traveler in the box-office (if necessary), etc.

> Oh, my heart, do not rise up to bear witness against me!
> (*The Book of the Dead*, or inscription on a scarab)

During this time, Dinu Lipatti had died in Europe at the age of thirty-three. They were talking about the job and about Dinu Lipatti all the way to the corner, because Talita thought that it was also good to collect tangible proofs of the non-existence of God or at least of his incurable frivolity. She had suggested that they go out immediately and buy a Lipatti record and go to Don Crespo's to listen to it, but Traveler and Oliveira wanted to have a beer at the corner café and talk about the circus, now that they were colleagues and quite content. Oliveira had-not-failed-to-notice that Traveler had had to make a-heroic-effort to convince the Boss, and that he had convinced him more by chance than for any other reason. They had already decided that Oliveira would give Gekrepten two of the three pieces of cashmere he hadn't sold yet, and that Talita would make herself a tailored suit with the third. A matter of celebrating his appointment. Consequently, Traveler ordered the beers while Talita went to prepare lunch. It was Monday, a day off. On Tuesday there would be a performance at seven and one at nine, with the presentation of 4 BEARS 4, a juggler who had just arrived from Colombo, and, of course, the calculating cat. Oliveira's job would be all gravy at first, until the time came when he would have to pitch in. In the meantime he could watch the performance, which was no worse than any others. Everything was going very well.

Everything was going so well that Traveler lowered his eyes and began to drum on the table. The waiter, who knew them well, came over to argue about the Ferrocarril Oeste team, and Oliveira bet ten pesos on the Chacarita Juniors. As he beat out the rhythm of a *baguala* with his fingers, Traveler was telling himself that everything was perfectly all right this way, and that there was no other way out, while Oliveira was finishing up with the technicalities of his bet and drinking his beer. He had started to think about Egyptian phrases that morning, about Thoth, significantly the god of magic and the inventor of language. They argued for a while whether it wasn't a fallacy to be arguing for a while, since the language they were using, as local and slangy as it might be, was perhaps part of a mantic structure that was by no means tranquillizing. They decided that all things considered, the double ministry of Thoth was a manifest guarantee of coherence in reality or unreality; it made them happy to have left more or less resolved the continuously disagreeable problem of the objective correlative. Magic or the tangible word, there was an Egyptian god who verbally harmonized subjects and objects. Everything was really going very well.

(–75)

43

Everything was perfect in the circus, a spangled fraud with wild music, a calculating cat who reacted to cardboard numbers that had been secretly treated previously with valerian, while ladies were so moved that they made sure that their offspring noticed such an eloquent example of Darwinian evolution. When Oliveira went out onto the still-empty sawdust on the first night and looked up at the opening at the highest point of the red tent, that escape-hatch to a maybe contact, that centre, that eye like a bridge between the earth and liberated space, he stopped laughing and thought that someone else would probably have climbed up the nearest pole to the eye up there as if it were the most natural thing to do, and that that other person was not the one who was smoking and looking up at the high hole there, that other person was not the one who stayed down below smoking in the midst of all the circus shouts.

On one of those early nights he came to understand why Traveler had managed to get him the job. Talita had told him why without beating about the bush while they were counting money in the brick cubicle that served as treasury and office for the circus. Oliveira already knew why in another way, and it was necessary for Talita to tell him from her point of view so that out of the two things there could be born a new time, a present in which he felt himself placed and obligated. He tried to protest, to say that they were things that Traveler had made up, he tried to feel himself once more outside of the others' time (he, dying to agree, mix into things, be) but at the same time he understood that it was certain, that in one way or another he had transgressed the world of Talita and Traveler, without acts, without intentions even, nothing more than giving in to a nostalgic whim. Between one word and another from Talita he saw the shabby line of El Cerro become outlined, he heard the ridiculous Lusitanian phrase that had unconsciously invented a future of cold storage and *caña quemante* rum. It brought out his laugh in Talita's face, just as he had laughed that very morning at the mirror when he was about to brush his teeth.

Talita tied a piece of string around a bundle of ten-peso notes and mechanically began to count the rest.

"What did you expect," Talita said. "I think Manú was right."

"Of course he was," Oliveira said. "But he's an idiot just the same, as you know only too well."

"Not too well. I know it, or rather I knew it when I was straddling the board. You two know it only too well, I'm in the middle like that part of a scale that I never know the name of."

"You're Egeria, our nymph, our bridge, our medium. Now that I think of it, when you're present Manú and I fall into some sort of trance. Even Gekrepten has noticed it, and she told me so, using precisely the same gaudy expression."

"It could be," Talita said, entering the figures. "If you want me to tell you what I think, Manú doesn't know what to do with you. He loves you like a brother, I suppose even you have noticed that, and at the same time he's sorry that you've come back."

"He had no reason to meet me at the dock. I didn't even send him a postcard."

"He found out from Gekrepten, who had filled the balcony with geraniums. Gekrepten found out from the ministry."

"A diabolical process," Oliveira said. "When I discovered that Gekrepten had found out by diplomatic channels, I saw that the only thing left for me to do was let her throw herself into my arms like a crazy calf. Just imagine such abnegation, such extremes of Penelopism."

"If you don't feel like talking about it," Talita said looking at the floor, "we can shut the safe and go and look for Manú."

"I feel like it very much, but the complications your husband raises give me uncomfortable problems of conscience. And that, for me . . . In short, I don't understand why you yourself don't solve the problem."

"Well," Talita said, looking at him in a restful way, "it seems to me that the other afternoon anyone who wasn't stupid would have realized."

"Of course, but there's Manú the next day going to talk to the Boss and getting me this job. Precisely when I was drying my tears with a cloth sample before going out to sell it."

"Manú is a good person," Talita said. "You'll never know how good he is."

"A strange goodness," Oliveira said. "Leaving aside what I will never know, which, when all's said and done, is probably true, allow me to insinuate that Manú probably wants to play with fire. If you look closely, you'll see that it's a circus trick. And you two," Oliveira said, pointing his finger at her, "have accomplices."

"Accomplices?"

"Yes, accomplices. First me, and then someone who's not here. You think you're the pointer on the scales, to use your pretty image, but you don't know that you're leaning your body over to one side. You ought to be aware of it."

"Why don't you go away, Horacio?" Talita asked. "Why don't you leave Manú in peace?"

"I already explained to you, I was on my way out to sell cloth and that beast got me this job. Understand, I'm not going to do the dirty on him, that would be much worse. It's stupid even to think about it."

"And so you're going to hang around here, then, and Manú won't get any sleep."

"Give him some Equanil, girl."

Talita tied up the five-peso notes. When the calculating cat came on they always went out to watch him work because the animal was absolutely fantastic, twice already he had solved a multiplication before the fraud with the valerian had had time to work. Traveler was stunned, and asked his friends to watch. But that night the cat was stupid, he could barely add up to twenty-five, it was tragic. Smoking in one of the entrances to the arena, Traveler and Oliveira decided that the cat probably needed phosphated food, they would have to talk to the Manager. The two clowns, who hated the cat without anyone's really knowing why, were dancing around the platform where the feline was cleaning his whiskers under a mercury lamp. The third time around, while they were singing a Russian song, the cat put out his claws and sprang at the face of the older one. As usual, the public applauded the number madly. In the wagon of the Bonettis, father and son, clowns, the Manager got the cat back and imposed a double fine on them for having provoked the animal.

It was a strange night; looking up as he always found himself doing at that hour, Oliveira could see Sirius in the centre of the black hole and he speculated about the three days when the earth is open, when the manes ascend and there is a bridge between man and the hole on high, a bridge from man to man (because who climbs up to the hole unless it is to wish to come down changed and find one's self again, but in a different way, with one's people?). The twenty-fourth of August was one of the three days on which the earth opened up; of course, what was the use of thinking so much about that since they were only in February. Oliveira could not remember the other two days, it was strange remembering only one date out of three. Why that one precisely? Perhaps because it was an octosyllable, memory plays games like that. But then Truth was probably an Alexandrine or a hendecasyllable; perhaps the rhythms again marking the main stress and scanning the periods of the road. Some more themes for eggheads to write theses about. It was pleasurable watching the juggler, his incredible agility, the milky track on which the tobacco smoke roosted on the heads of hundreds of children from Villa del Parque, a section where luckily there are abundant eucalyptus trees to balance the scales, referring again to that adjudicating instrument, that compartment of the zodiac.

(–125)

44

It was true that Traveler was not getting much sleep, in the middle of the night he would sigh as if he had a weight on his chest and he would embrace Talita who would receive him without saying anything, squeezing herself against him so that he would be able to feel her deeply near him. In the darkness they would kiss each other on the nose, on the mouth, on the eyes, and Traveler would stroke Talita's cheek with a hand that came out from under the sheets and would go back into hiding as if it was cold, although both of them were sweating; then Traveler would murmur four or five numbers, an old habit to go back to sleep again, and Talita would feel his arms loosen, his breathing deepen, and he would settle down. During the day he went about happily and whistled tangos while he prepared *mate* or read, but Talita could not do any cooking without his appearing four or five times with various excuses and talking about something, especially about the lunatic asylum now that the negotiations seemed to be going well and the Manager was speeding up his plans to buy the madhouse. Talita didn't find the idea of the mental hospital very funny, and Traveler knew it. The two of them tried to find the humorous side, promising themselves spectacles worthy of Samuel Beckett, sneering at the poor circus which was winding up its performances in Villa del Parque and getting ready to open in San Isidro. Sometimes Oliveira would pop by to have a *mate*, although he generally stayed in his room taking advantage of the fact that Gekrepten had to go to work and he could read and smoke at his leisure. When Traveler was looking into Talita's somewhat purple eyes while he was helping her pluck a duck, a biweekly luxury that enchanted Talita, a fan of the duck in all of its culinary possibilities, he would tell himself that things were not as bad as they had been, and he even would have preferred for Horacio to come by and join in some *mates*, because they would immediately start to play a number game that they barely understood but which had to be played so that time would pass and the three of them would feel worthy of one another. They also used to read, because from a coincidentally socialist youth, a little theosophical on Traveler's side, the three of them loved reading with commentaries, each in his own way, polemics from the Hispano-Argentine pleasure in wanting to convince and never accepting contrary opinion, and the undeniable possibilities of laughing like crazy and feeling themselves above suffering humanity under the pretext of helping it come out of its shitty contemporary situation.

But it was certain that Traveler was not sleeping well, Talita would repeat it rhetorically while she watched him shave in the light of the morning sun. One stroke, another, Traveler in his undershirt and pyjama bottoms was whistling a drawn-out version of *La gayola* and then he proclaimed with a shout: "Music, moody food of us that trade in love!" and turning around he looked aggressively at Talita who had been plucking the duck that day and was very happy because the quills that came out were a delight and the duck had a benign air not often seen in those rancorous corpses, with their little eyes half open and an imperceptible band like a ray of light between the lids, unfortunate creatures.

"Why do you have such trouble sleeping, Manú?"

"*Music, moo . . . !* Me? Trouble? I don't fall asleep directly, my love, I spend the night meditating on the *Liber penitentialis* in the Macrovius Basca edition that I lifted from Dr Feta the other day when his sister wasn't looking. Of course, I'm going to give it back to him, it must be worth a lot of dough. A *liber penitentialis*, I'll have you know."

"And what might that be?" Talita asked as she now began to understand certain sleight-of-hand tricks and a drawer that had a double lock. "You've been hiding your reading from me, it's the first time that's happened since we've been married."

"There it is, you can look at it as much as you like, but always wash your hands first. I hide it because it's valuable and you're always going around with carrot-scrapings and things like that on your fingers, you're so domestic that you'd ruin any piece of incunabula."

"I don't care about your book," Talita said, offended. "Come here and cut the head off this, I don't like to, even if it is dead."

"I'll use my razor," Traveler proposed. "It'll give the whole business a truculent tone, and besides, it's always good to practise, you never can tell."

"No. Use this knife, it's sharp."

"My razor."

"No. This knife."

Traveler took his razor over to the duck and lopped off its head.

"You've got to learn," he said. "If we take over the asylum it would be good to get experience along the lines of a double murder on the Rue Morgue."

"Is that the way lunatics do their killing?"

"No, my dear, but once in a while they give it a try. Just like sane people, if you will allow me the poor comparison."

"It's cheap," Talita admitted, making the duck into a sort of parallelepiped tied together with white cord.

"As far as my not sleeping well is concerned," Traveler said, cleaning the razor with a piece of toilet paper, "you know perfectly well what's behind it."

"Let's say I do. But you also know that there's no problem involved."

"Problems," Traveler said, "are like Primus heaters, everything is fine until they blow up. I could tell you that there are teleological problems on this earth. They don't seem to exist, like right now, and what happens is that the clock in the bomb is set for twelve o'clock tomorrow. Tick-tock, tick-tock, everything's fine. Tick-tock."

"The worst part," Talita said, "is that you yourself are the one who winds it up."

"My hand, pussycat, is also set for twelve o'clock tomorrow. In the meantime, let's live and let live."

Talita covered the duck with grease, a degrading spectacle.

"Do you have any reason to reproach me?" she asked, as if she were talking to the palmiped.

"Absolutely none at the moment," Traveler said. "We'll see at twelve o'clock tomorrow, if I can prolong the image right up to its climactic outcome."

"You're just like Horacio," Talita said. "It's incredible how much the two of you are alike."

"Tick-tock," Traveler said, looking for his cigarettes. "Tick-tock, tick-tock."

"Yes, you're just like him," Talita insisted, letting go of the duck which fell to the floor with a revolting squashy sound. "He would have said tick-tock, he would have been talking in images all the time too. But are the pair of you ever going to leave me in peace? The reason I'm telling you that you're both alike is so that once and for all we can quit all this absurdity. It can't be possible that everything has changed like this just because Horacio came back. Last night I told him I couldn't take any more, that you two were playing with me, like a tennis ball, you hit me from both sides, it's not right, Manú, it's not right."

Traveler took her in his arms even though Talita was resisting, and after stepping on the duck and slipping so that both of them almost fell down, he managed to control her and kiss her on the tip of her nose.

"Maybe there's no bomb for you, pussycat," he said, smiling with an expression that softened Talita, made her try to get more comfortable in his arms. "Look, I'm not going around looking for lightning to strike me on the head, but I don't feel I should wear a lightning-rod for protection; I think I ought to go out with my head uncovered until it's twelve o'clock on some day. Only after that time, after that day, will I feel the same again. It isn't because of Horacio, love, it isn't only because of Horacio, even though he may have come like some sort of messenger. If he hadn't come, something else like it would have happened to me. I would have read some disillusioning book, or I would have fallen in love with some other woman . . . Those folds of life, you understand, those unexpected evidences of something that a person hadn't suspected and which suddenly turn everything into a crisis. You'll have to learn to understand."

"But do you really think he's after me, and that I . . . ?"

"He's not after you in the least," Traveler said, letting her go. "Horacio doesn't care a damn about you. Don't be offended, I know very well what you're worth and I'll always be jealous of everybody who looks at you or talks to you. But even if Horacio made a pass at you, even in that case, even if you think I'm crazy, I would repeat that he doesn't care a damn about you, and that therefore you've got nothing to worry about. It's something else," Traveler said, raising his voice. "It's something fucking else, God damn it!"

"Oh," Talita said, picking up the duck and wiping off the footprint with a kitchen rag. "You've caved in its ribs. So it's something else. I don't understand at all, but you're probably right."

"And if he were here," Traveler said in a low voice, looking at his cigarette, "he wouldn't understand anything either. But he'd know very well that it's something else. It's incredible, when he's with us it's as if walls collapsed, piles of things all going to hell, and suddenly the sky becomes fantastically beautiful, the stars come out on that baking dish, you can skin them and eat them, that duck is really Lohengrin's swan, and behind, behind . . . "

"Am I disturbing you?" asked Señora Gutusso as she appeared in the hallway door. "You're probably talking about personal matters, I don't want to intrude where I haven't been invited."

"Not at all," Talita said. "Come right in, señora, and look at this beautiful creature."

"Marvellous," Señora Gutusso said. "I always say that duck may be tough, but it has its own special taste."

"Manú stepped on it," Talita said. "I bet it turns out like a ball of fat."

"You said it," Traveler said.

(–102)

45

It was natural to think that he was waiting for him to appear at the window. It was enough waking up at two o'clock on a hot sticky night, with the acrid smell of the flypaper, with two enormous stars planted on the casement of the window, with the window opposite also open.

It was natural because the plank still seemed to be in the casement, and what was a negative in the bright sunlight might be something else perhaps in the middle of the night, turn into a sudden acquiescence, and then he would be there at his window, smoking to drive away the mosquitoes and waiting for sleepwalking Talita to uncouple herself softly from Traveler's body and appear and look at him from darkness to darkness. Perhaps with slow movements of his hand he would sketch signs with the lighted end of his cigarette. Triangles, circumferences, instantaneous coats of arms, symbols of the fatal love potion or of diphenilpropilamine, pharmaceutical abbreviations that she could interpret, or just a luminous back and forth from his mouth to the arm of the chair, from the arm of the chair to his mouth, from his mouth to the arm of the chair, all through the night.

There was nobody at the window. Traveler went over to the hot well, he looked into the street where a defenceless open newspaper let itself be read by a starry sky that seemed almost touchable. The window of the hotel opposite seemed even closer at night, a gymnast could have reached it in one leap. No, he couldn't have. Maybe with death at his heels, but not any other way. There was no sign of the board any more, there was no way across.

Sighing, Traveler went back to bed. He answered a sleepy question of Talita's by stroking her hair and murmuring something. Talita kissed the air, moved her hand around a little, settled down.

If he had been in some part of the black well, stuck back in the depths of the room and from there looking out of the window, he must have seen Traveler, the ectoplasm of his white undershirt. If he had been in some part of the black well waiting for Talita to appear, the indifferent appearance of a white undershirt must have mortified him thoroughly. Now he would be scratching his forearm, his usual gesture of discomfort and resentment, he would squeeze his cigarette between his lips, he would mutter some fitting obscenity, he would probably throw himself onto the bed without the least consideration for Gekrepten, who was in a deep sleep.

But if he had not been in any part of the black well, the act of getting up and going to the window at that time of night was an admission of fear, almost an assent. It was practically the same as taking for granted that neither Horacio nor he had withdrawn the boards. In one way or another there was a way across, it was possible to come and go. Any one of the three, sleepwalking, could go from window to window, walking on the thick air without fear of falling into the street. The bridge would only disappear with the light of day, with the reappearance of the *café con leche* that would bring them back to solid constructions and tear away the cobwebs of the predawn hours with the heavy hand of news bulletins on the radio and a cold shower.

Talita's dreams: She was being taken to an art exhibition in an immense ruined palace, and the pictures were hung at giddy heights, as if someone had turned the prisons of Piranesi into a museum. And so to get to the paintings one had to climb up some archways where one could secure a footing only on the carvings, go through galleries that went to the edge of a stormy sea with waves like lead, climb up spiral staircases to see finally, always poorly, always from below or from one side, the paintings in which the same whitish splotch, the same coagulation of tapioca or milk was repeated to infinity.

Talita's awakening: Sitting up suddenly in bed at nine o'clock in the morning, shaking Traveler who was sleeping face down, slapping him on the behind to wake him up. Traveler stretching out an arm and pinching her on the leg. Talita throwing herself on top of him and pulling his hair. Traveler abusing his strength, twisting her hand until Talita apologized. Kisses, terrible heat.

"I dreamed about a frightful museum. You were taking me there."

"I detest oneiromancy. Make some *mate*, animal."

"Why did you get up last night? It wasn't because you had to pee, when you get up to pee you explain to me first as if I were stupid, you tell me: 'I'm going to get up, I can't hold it any more,' and I feel sorry for you because I can hold it perfectly well all night long, I don't even have to hold it, it's a different metabolism."

"A what?"

"Tell me why you got up. You went over to the window and you sighed."

"Don't bug me."

"Idiot."

"It was hot."

"Tell me why you got up."

"No reason, to see if Horacio wasn't able to sleep either, so we could talk for a while."

"At that hour? The pair of you barely talk during the day."

"It probably would have been different. You never know."

"I dreamt about a horrible museum," Talita says, starting to put on her slip.

"You already told me," Traveler says, looking at the ceiling.

"We don't talk much any more either," Talita says.

"Of course not, it's the humidity."

"But it's as if something is talking, something is using us to talk. Don't you get that feeling? Don't you think we're inhabited in some sort of way? I mean . . . It's hard to explain, really."

"Transhabited would be better. Look, this won't go on for ever. *No te aflijas, Catalina*" – Traveler sings softly – "*ya vendrán tiempos mejores / y te pondré un comedor.*"

"Stupid," Talita says, kissing him on the ear. "This won't go on for ever, this won't go on for ever . . . This shouldn't go on for even one minute more."

"Violent amputations are bad, afterwards the stump hurts for the rest of your life."

"If you want me to tell you the truth," Talita says, "I have the impression that we're raising spiders or centipedes. We take care of them, we attend to them, and they keep on growing, at first they were insignificant little bugs, almost sweet, with so many legs, and suddenly they've grown, they jump at your face. I think I dreamed about spiders too, I remember vaguely."

"Listen to Horacio," Traveler says, pulling on his trousers. "At this hour he whistles like a madman to celebrate Gekrepten's leaving. What a guy."

(–80)

46

"Music, moody food of us that trade in love," Traveler had quoted for the fourth time, tuning up his guitar before offering the tango called *Cotorrita de la suerte.*

Don Crespo was interested in the quotation and Talita went upstairs to get all five acts in Astrana Marín's translation. The Calle Cachimayo was noisy at nightfall, but in Don Crespo's patio, except for the canary Cien Pesos, all that could be heard was Traveler's voice as he came to the part about *la obrerita juguetona y pizpireta / la que diera a su casita la alegría.* Playing the card game *escoba de quince* doesn't call for talking, and Gekrepten kept beating Oliveira time after time as he alternated with Señora Gutusso in the chore of getting rid of twenty-cent pieces. Luck's little parrot (*que augura la vida o muerte*) in the meantime had picked out a pink slip of paper: a boyfriend, long life. Which did not prevent Traveler's voice from assuming a hollow tone as he described the rapid illness of the heroine, *y la tarde en que moría tristemente / preguntando a su mamita: "¿No llegó?"* Trrang.

"Such feeling," Señora Gutusso said. "They say bad things about the tango, but as far as I'm concerned there's no comparison between it and the calypso songs and other trash they play on the radio. Can you pass me some beans, Don Horacio? I need more chips."

Traveler leaned the guitar against a flowerpot, took a deep drag on his *mate,* and got the feeling that the night was going to be a big bore for him. He almost would have preferred having to work or being sick, anything for distraction. He poured himself a shot of *caña* and drank it in one gulp, looking at Don Crespo, who with his glasses on the tip of his nose was moving suspiciously into the preface of the tragedy. Beaten, eighty cents down, Oliveira went over to sit by them and also took a shot.

"It's a fabulous world," Traveler said in a low voice. "The Battle of Actium is going to take place in a little while in there, if the old boy can last that long. And next to him those two madwomen haggling over beans on the strength of their seven-cards."

"They're occupations like any others," Oliveira said. "Do you get the sense of the word? To be occupied, have an occupation. It sends chills up my spine. But look, so we won't get metaphysical I'm going to tell you that my occupation in the circus is pure fraud. I'm earning that money without doing anything."

"Wait till we open in San Isidro, it'll be harder. In Villa del Parque we had all the problems solved already, especially that bribe that had the Boss worried. Now we've got to start all over again with new people and you'll be occupied all right, since you like the expression."

"You don't say. Great, I've really got it made. So I'm really going to have to work?"

"For the first few days, then everything will fall into place. Tell me something, didn't you ever work when you were wandering around Europe?"

"As little as I could manage," Oliveira said. "I was a clandestine bookkeeper. Old man Trouille, a character out of Céline. I'll have to tell you all about it someday if it's worth the trouble, and it isn't."

"I'd like to hear," Traveler said.

"You know, everything's so much up in the air. Anything I told you would be like a piece of the pattern in a rug. It needs a coagulant, to give it some kind of name: plunk, everything falls into its proper place and there taking shape you have a beautiful crystal with all its facets. The bad part," Oliveira said, looking at his fingernails, "is that it's probably coagulated already and I didn't notice, I stayed behind with the old men who listen to people talking about cybernetics and slowly shake their heads thinking that soon it will be time for soup with vermicelli in it."

The canary Cien Pesos gave out a trill that was more of a squeal than anything else.

"All in all," Traveler said, "it occurs to me sometimes that you shouldn't have come back."

"You think about it," Oliveira said. "I live it. Underneath it all it's probably the same thing, but let's not go into a swoon over it. What's killing you and is killing me is modesty, you know. We walk around the house naked, to the great horror of some ladies, but when it comes to talking . . . You understand, sometimes it occurs to me that I might be able to tell you . . . I don't know, perhaps right now words could be good for something, could be useful to us. But since they're not words from everyday life and *mate* in the courtyard, well-oiled conversation, one draws back, from his best friend, no less, who is the one we have most trouble telling such things to. Doesn't it happen to you, that sometimes you confide much more in just anybody?"

"It could be," Traveler said, tuning the guitar. "The worst is that with these ideas one wonders what friends are good for."

"They're good just to be there, and they might just come in handy sometime."

"Whatever you say. So it's going to be hard for us to understand each other the way we used to in the past."

"In the name of the past we carry out the greatest deceits in the present," Oliveira said. "Look, Manolo, you talk about understanding each other, but basically you realize that I also want to come to some sort of understanding with you, and *you* means much more than you yourself. The burden is the fact that real understanding is something else. We're satisfied with too little. When friends understand each other well, when lovers understand each other well, when families understand each other well, then we think that everything is harmonious. Pure illusion, a mirror for larks. Sometimes I feel that there's more understanding between two people punching each other in the face than among those who are there looking on from outside. That's why . . . Hell, I really ought to write for the Sunday supplement of *La Nación.*"

"You were doing fine," Traveler said, tuning the first string, "but you finally had one of those attacks of modesty that you were talking about before. You reminded me of Señora Gutusso when she feels obliged to mention her husband's piles."

"This Octavius Caesar says the oddest things," grumbled Don Crespo, looking at them over his glasses. "Here he's talking about Mark Antony's having eaten strange flesh on the Alps. What is he trying to tell me with that expression? Kid, I suppose."

"A featherless biped, more likely," Traveler said.

"It's hard to find anybody in this play who's not crazy," Don Crespo said respectfully. "You should see some of the things Cleopatra does."

"Queens are so complicated," Señora Gutusso said. "That Cleopatra was mixed up in all sorts of things, it was in a movie. Of course times were different then and they didn't have any religion."

"A trick," Talita said, picking up six cards from the deck.

"You're getting lucky . . ."

"I'm still losing really. Manú, I'm running out of change."

"Get some from Don Crespo who has probably reached the age of the pharaohs and will give you pieces of pure gold. Look, Horacio, what you were saying about harmony . . ."

"Well," Oliveira said, "since you insist I turn my pockets inside out and put the lint on the table . . ."

"Something besides turning your pockets inside out. My impression is that you're peacefully watching how everybody else gets all mixed up. You're looking for that thing called harmony, but you're looking for it precisely in the place where you just said it didn't exist, between friends, in the family, in the city. Why are you looking for it in social organisms?"

"I don't know. I'm not even looking for it. It's all just happening to me."

"Why should it happen to you in such a way that the rest of us can't get any sleep because of you?"

"I haven't been sleeping very well either."

"Just to give an example, why did you get together with Gekrepten? Why do you come to see me? Don't you think perhaps that Gekrepten and we are the ones who are destroying your harmony?"

"She wants to drink some mandrake!" Don Crespo shouted, stunned.

"What?" asked Señora Gutusso.

"Mandrake! She tells the slave-girl to pour her some mandrake. She says she wants to sleep. She's completely mad!"

"She ought to take some Bromural," Señora Gutusso said. "Of course in those days . . ."

"You're quite right, old man," Oliveira said, filling the glasses with *caña*. "The only thing wrong is that you're attaching too much importance to Gekrepten."

"What about us?"

"You people, well, you're probably that coagulant we were talking about a while back. It makes me think that our relationship is almost chemical, something outside ourselves. A sort of sketch that is being done. You came to meet me, don't forget."

"And why not? I never thought you would have come back with all that resentment, that they would have changed you so much over there; that you would have given me such an urge to be different . . . That's not what I mean. Hell, you don't live and you don't let live."

A *cielito* was being played on the guitar between them.

"All you have to do is snap your fingers like that," Oliveira said in a very low voice, "and you won't see me again. It wouldn't be fair that just because of me, you and Talita should . . . "

"Leave Talita out of this."

"No," Oliveira said. "I couldn't think of leaving her out. All of us, Talita, you, and I, we form a triangle that is exceedingly trismegistic. I'll tell you again: just give me a signal and I'll break it off. Don't think I haven't noticed how worried you've been."

"You won't fix anything by going away now."

"Why not, man? You don't need me."

Traveler began the prelude to *Malevaje*, stopped. It was already dark, and Don Crespo turned on the light in the courtyard so he could read.

"Look," Traveler said in a low voice. "In any case, some day you're going to beat it and there won't be any need for me to go around giving you signals. I may not be able to sleep at night, as Talita has probably told you, but underneath it all, I'm not sorry you've come back. What's more likely is that I needed you."

"Whatever you say, old man. That's the way things turn out, the best thing is to keep cool. It's not so bad for me either."

"This sounds like a dialogue between two idiots," Traveler said.

"Pure-bred mongoloids," said Oliveira.

"You think you're going to explain something, and it gets worse every time."

"Explanation is a well-dressed mistake," Oliveira said. "Make a note of that."

"Yes, it's much better to talk about other things then, about what's going on in the Radical party. It's just that you . . . But it's like a merry-go-round, it always comes back to the same thing, the white horse, then the red one, the white one again. We're poets, brother."

"Terrific troubadours," Oliveira said, filling up the glasses. "People who don't sleep well and go over to the window to get a breath of fresh air, things like that."

"So you did see me last night."

"Let me think. First Gekrepten got to be a drag and I had to temporize. Just a little, but still . . . Then I slept like a log, trying to forget. Why do you ask?"

"No reason," Traveler said, and slapped his hand across the strings. Jingling her winnings, Señora Gutusso brought a chair over and asked Traveler to sing.

"A man named Enobarbus said in here that night dampness is poisonous," Don Crespo informed them. "They're all crazy in this book, in the middle of a battle they start talking about things that have nothing to do with what's going on."

"Well, then," Traveler said, "let's do the lady's pleasure, if Don Crespo doesn't mind. *Malevaje*, a bona fide tango by Juan de Dios Filiberto. Say, old buddy, remind me to read you Ivonne Guitry's confession, it's something great. Talita, go and get the Gardel anthology. It's on the bedside table, where something like that should be."

"And give it back to me while you're at it," Señora Gutusso said. "I don't need it, but I like to have the books I like close to me. My husband is just the same, I might add."

(–47)

47

I am I, I am he. We are, but I am I, first I am I, I will defend being I until I am unable to fight any longer. I am I, Atalía. *Ego. Yo.* A professional degree, an Argentine, a scarlet fingernail, pretty sometimes, big dark eyes, I. Atalía Donosi, I. *Yo.* Yo-yo, windlass and hawser. Funny.

What a nut, Manú, going to the Casa América and renting this thing just to have some fun. REWIND. What a voice, that's not my voice. False and forced: "I am I, I am he. We are, but I am I, first I am I, I will defend . . . " STOP. Wonderful machine, but it's no good thinking out loud, or maybe you have to get used to it. Manú talks about recording his famous radio script about fine ladies; he won't do anything. The magic eye is really magical, green slits that oscillate, contract, a one-eyed cat staring at me. Maybe I should cover it with a piece of cardboard. REWIND. The tape runs so smoothly, so regularly. VOLUME. Put it on 5 or 5½: "The magic eye is really magical, green slits that osci . . . " But what would really be magic would be for my voice to have said: "The magic eye plays secretly, red slits . . . " Too much echo. I have to put the microphone closer and lower the volume. I am I, I am he. What I really am is a bad parody of Faulkner. Cheap effects. Does he dictate to a magnetic recorder or does he use whiskey for tape? Do you say magnetic recorder or tape recorder? Horacio says magnetic recorder, he was surprised when he saw the machine, he said: "What a fine magnetic recorder, old man!" The manual calls it a tape recorder, they ought to know in the Casa América. Mystery: Why does Manú buy everything, even his shoes, in the Casa América? A fixation, a touch of idiocy. REWIND. This will be funny: " . . . Faulkner. Cheap effects." STOP. It isn't very funny listening to myself again. All this should take time, time, time. All this should take time. REWIND. Let's see if the tone is more natural: " . . . ime, time, time. All this should . . . " The same thing, the voice of a midget with a cold. One thing, though, I do a good job of running it, Manú will be surprised, he doesn't trust me with machines at all. Me, a pharmacist, Horacio doesn't even notice, he looks at a person like mashed potatoes going through a strainer, mush that comes oozing out on the other side, something to sit down to and eat. Rewind? No, let's keep on, let's turn out the lights. Let's try to speak in the third person . . . Then Talita Donosi turns out the lights and there isn't anything except the little magic eye with its red slits (maybe it'll come out green, maybe it'll come out purple) and the glow of her cigarette. Hot, and Manú hasn't come back from San Isidro, eleven-thirty. There's Gekrepten at the window, I don't see her but she's there just the same, she's at the window in her nightgown, and Horacio at his tiny table, with a candle, reading and smoking. Horacio and Gekrepten's room, I don't know why, seems less like a hotel than this one. Stupid, it's enough of a hotel so that even the cockroaches must have the room number written on their backs, and they have to put up with Don Bunche next door and his tubercular patients at twenty pesos a visit, the cripples and the epileptics. And below them the brothel, and the tangos that the errand-girl sings out of tune. REWIND. A good stretch, I should go back half a minute at least. It goes against time, Manú would like to talk about that. Volume 5: " . . . the room number written on their backs . . . " Farther back. REWIND. Now: " . . . Horacio at his tiny table with a green candle . . . " STOP. Tiny, tiny. There's no reason to say tiny when you're a pharmacist. Pure corn. Tiny table! Misapplied tenderness. OK, Talita. Enough of inanities. REWIND. All of it, until the tape is ready to come loose, the trouble with this machine is that you have to judge carefully, if the tape comes loose you lose half a minute putting it back on again. STOP. Just right by an inch. I wonder what I said at the beginning? I can't remember any more but my voice sounded like a frightened little rat, the well-known mike fright. Let's see, volume 5½ so it'll be easier to hear. "I am I, I am he. We are but I am I, fir . . . " And why, why did I say that? I am I, I am he, and then talking about the tiny table, and then getting annoyed. "I am I, I am he. I am I, I am he."

Talita turned off the recorder, shut the cover, looked at it with deep disgust, and poured herself a glass of lemonade. She didn't want to think about the business of the clinic (the Manager called it "the mental clinic", which was idiotic) but if she refused to think about the clinic (besides the fact that this matter of refusing to think was more of a hope than a reality) she immediately got into another equally bothersome sphere. She thought about Manú and Horacio at the same time, in the scales simile that she and Horacio had manipulated in such an ostentatious way in the circus box-office. Then the feeling of being inhabited became stronger, at least the clinic was an idea of fear, of the unknown, a hair-raising vision of raving maniacs in nightshirts chasing her with razors and grabbing stools and bed-legs, vomiting on their temperature charts and masturbating ritually. It was going to be very amusing seeing Manú and Horacio in white lab coats, taking care of the lunatics. "I'll have a certain importance," Talita thought modestly. "The Manager will definitely put me in charge of the clinic's pharmacy. It's probably a little first-aid station. Manú is going to tease me about it as usual." She would have to review certain things, so much gets forgotten, time with its fine sandpaper, the indescribable daily battle that summer, the waterfront and the heat, Horacio coming down the gangplank with a friendless face, the rudeness of sending her off with the cat, you take the streetcar back because we've got to talk. And then a period began that was like waste ground full of twisted cans, hooks that could hurt your feet, dirty puddles, pieces of rag caught on the thistles, the circus at night with Horacio and Manú looking at her or looking at each other, the cat getting stupider every day or really more brilliant, solving problems to the delighted shrieks of the audience, the walks home with stopoffs in bars so Manú and Horacio could drink some beer, talking, talking about nothing, listening to herself talking in this heat and this smoke and the fatigue. *I am I, I am he*, she had said it without thinking, that is, it was beyond being thought, it came from a region where words were like the lunatics in the clinic, menacing or absurd entities living an isolated life of their own, jumping up suddenly without anybody being able to tie them down: *I am I, I am he*, and he wasn't Manú, he was Horacio, the inhabitant, the treacherous attacker, the shadow within the shadow of his room at night, the glow of his cigarette slowly sketching out the shapes of his insomnia.

When Talita was afraid, she would get up and make herself some tea that was half linden, half mint. She did it hoping with great longing that Manú's key would scratch on the door. Manú had said with soaring words: "Horacio doesn't care a damn about you." It was insulting but tranquillizing. Manú had said that even if Horacio had made a pass (and he hadn't, he'd never even hinted)

one of linden

one of mint

the water good and hot, first sign, of boiling, stop

not even then would she have meant anything to him. But then. But if it didn't make any difference to him, why always be there in the corner of the room smoking or reading, *be* (I am I, I am he) there as if he were needing her in some way, yes, just that exactly, needing her, hanging on to her from a distance to reach something, the better to see something, the better to be something. Then it wasn't: I am I, I am he. Then it was the opposite: I am he *because* I am I. Talita sighed, satisfied a little with her good powers of reason and the good taste of the tea.

But that wasn't all there was to it, because then it would have been too easy. It couldn't be (there's a reason for logic) that Horacio was interested and at the same time was not interested. The combination of the two things should have produced a third, something that had nothing to do with love, for example (it was so stupid to think about love when love was only Manú, only Manú until the end of time), something that was close to being a hunt, a search, or rather a terrible expectation, like the cat looking at the canary it cannot reach, a kind of congealing of time and day, a kind of crouching. A lump and a half, the soft smell of the country. A crouching without explanations, the-way-things-look-from-here, or until one day when Horacio would deign to speak, go away, shoot himself, any explanation or material on which one could imagine an explanation. Not that business of being there drinking *mate* and looking at them, making Manú drink *mate* and look at him, making the three of them dance a slow interminable pattern. "I should be a novelist," Talita thought, "marvellous ideas come to me." She was so depressed that she turned on the tape recorder again and sang songs until Traveler came home. They both agreed that Talita's voice did not come out too well, and Traveler showed her how a *baguala* should be sung. They brought the recorder over to the window so Gekrepten could be the impartial judge, and even Horacio if he was in the room, but he wasn't. Gekrepten found everything perfect and they decided to have dinner together at the Travelers', combining a cold roast that Talita had with a tossed salad that Gekrepten would make before coming over. This all seemed perfect to Talita and at the same time there was something like a bedcover about it, or a teapot cover, or some kind of cover, just like the recorder or Traveler's satisfied air, things done or decided, to be put on top, but on top of what, that was the problem and the reason that everything underneath it all was still the way it had been before the half-linden, half-mint tea.

(–110)

48

Next to El Cerro – although you never really do get next to El Cerro, you arrive all at once and never know actually whether you're already there or not, near El Cerro would be better – in a section with low buildings and arguing children, his questions got him nowhere, they would all shatter against pleasant smiles, women who wanted to be helpful but didn't really know anything, people move away, sir, there've been a lot of changes here, maybe if you go to the police they'll be able to tell you. And he didn't stay too long because the ship was going to sail, and though he kept it deep inside himself, everything had been hopeless from the start, his investigations had had their source in his doubts, like playing the numbers or working out a horoscope. Another tram back to the pier to flop down on his bunk until it was time to eat.

That same night, around two o'clock in the morning, was the first time he saw her again. It was hot, and in the steerage where a hundred-odd immigrants were snoring and sweating it was worse than sitting on the coils of a hawser underneath the dull river sky, as all the dampness of the harbour stuck to his skin. Oliveira sat down against a bulkhead to smoke, studying the few stars that were sneaking in and out of the clouds. La Maga came from behind a ventilator funnel, holding something in her hand that was dragging along the deck, and almost immediately she turned her back on him and went towards one of the hatchways. Oliveira made no attempt to follow her; he knew only too well that he was looking at something that would not let itself be followed. He thought that she was probably one of those snobs from first class who like to descend even to the filth of the forecastle, thirsting for something they would call experience or life, things like that. She did look a lot like La Maga, that was certain, but he had supplied the main part of the resemblance, so that once his heart stopped heaving like a mad dog he lit another cigarette and called himself a hopeless idiot.

To have thought that he had seen La Maga was less bitter than the certainty that some uncontrollable desire had brought her up out of the depths of that place defined as the subconscious and had been able to project her onto the silhouette of any one of the women on board. Until that moment he had believed that he could allow himself the luxury of the melancholy memory of certain things, evoke determined stories in a proper time and atmosphere, then put an end to them with the same tranquillity with which he would crush a butt in an ashtray. When Traveler introduced him to Talita on the dock, so ridiculous with that cat in a basket and an air somewhere between pleasant and Alida Valli, he again felt certain remote likenesses condensing quickly into a total false resemblance, as if from out of his apparently so well compartmentalized memory a piece of ectoplasm had suddenly emerged, capable of inhabiting and complementing another body and another face, of looking at him from outside in a way that he had thought for ever restricted to memories.

In the weeks following that were dragged along by Gekrepten's irresistible abnegation and his apprenticeship in the difficult art of selling cashmere samples from door to door, he had more than enough glasses of beer and time spent on park benches in which to dissect episodes. His explorations in El Cerro had seemed on the outside like a discharge of conscience: find, try to explain, say goodbye for ever. That tendency of man to finish cleanly what he does, without leaving any threads hanging. Now he was beginning to realize (a shadow from behind a ventilator, a woman with a cat) that this was not why he had gone to El Cerro. Analytical psychology irritated him, but it was true: this was not why he had gone to El Cerro. Suddenly he was a pit falling infinitely into himself. He scolded himself ironically, right in the middle of the Plaza del Congreso: "And you called that a search? Did you think you were free? What was that business about Heraclitus? Let's see, repeat the steps of liberation, so I can have a little laugh. But you're at the bottom of the funnel, pal." He would have liked to be sure that he had been irreparably debased by his discovery, but he was bothered by a vague satisfaction in the region of his stomach, that feline answer of contentment which the body gives when it laughs at the restless schpells of the schpirit and hunches comfortably into its ribs, its belly, and the flat soles of its feet. The worst of it was that deep down inside he was rather content to feel that way, to feel that he hadn't come back, that he was still going away even though he didn't know where. On top of the contentment he was being burned by a kind of desperation for simple understanding, a cry for something that he would have liked to make into flesh and blood, and which this vegetative contentment was sluggishly rejecting, keeping it at a distance. There were moments when Oliveira would be present like a spectator at this discord, not caring to participate, cynically impartial. That's what happened with the circus, the *mate* sessions in Don Crespo's patio, Traveler's tangos – Oliveira would look at himself out of the corner of his eye in all of those mirrors. He even wrote down some odd thoughts in a notebook that Gekrepten lovingly kept in the dresser drawer, not daring to read it. He was slowly realizing that his visit to El Cerro had been good, precisely because it had been based on other reasons than those he had imagined. To know that he was in love with La Maga was neither a defeat nor any sort of fixation in any outdated order of things; a love that could do without its object, that could find its nourishment in nothingness, that could be totalled up and come out as other strengths, defining them and bringing them together into an impulse that one day would destroy that visceral contentment of a body stuffed with beer and fried potatoes. All the words he used to fill the notebook along with great flourishes in the air and shrill whistles made him laugh like a madman. Traveler would finally come to the window and ask him to quieten down a little. But other times Oliveira would find a certain peace in manual chores, like straightening out nails or unweaving sisal threads, using the fibres to construct a delicate labyrinth which would cling to the lampshade and which Gekrepten would describe as elegant. Maybe love was the highest enrichment, a giver of being; but only by bungling it could one avoid its boomerang effect, let it run off into nothingness, and sustain one's self alone again on this new step of open and porous reality. Killing the beloved object, that ancient fear of man, was the price paid for not stopping on the stairs, just as Faust's plea to the passing moment would not have made sense if he had not abandoned it at the same time, just as one puts down an empty glass on the table. And things like that, and bitter *mate*.

It would have been so easy to organize a coherent scheme, an order of thought and life, a harmony. All that was needed was the usual hypocrisy, elevate the past to the value of experience, derive profit from the wrinkles on one's face, from the knowing look one sees in smiles and silences after forty years. Then one would put on a blue suit, comb one's greying hair, and go to art galleries, to the Sociedad Argentina de Escritores and the Richmond bar, reconciled with the world. A discreet scepticism, an air of having returned, a measured entrance into maturity, into matrimony, into the paternal sermon at carving time or on receipt of an unsatisfactory report card. I am telling you this because I have lived longer than you. I've been around. When I was a boy. They're all alike, *te lo digo yo.* I'm telling you this from my own experience, son. You don't know what life is yet.

And all of it, so ridiculous and gregarious, could have been even worse on other levels, in meditations constantly menaced by *idola fori*, words that falsify institutions, turning things to stone in the name of simplification, moments of fatigue in which one slowly takes the flag of surrender from one's vest pocket. The betrayal could have taken place in perfect solitude, without witnesses or accomplices: hand to hand, believing one's self to be beyond personal compromises and dramas of the senses, beyond the ethical torture of knowing that one is tied to a race or to a people and a language at least. In what is apparently perfect freedom, not having to render accounts to anyone, leaving the game, leaving the crossroads and following any one of the roads put there by circumstance, proclaiming it to be the necessary one or the only one. La Maga was one of those roads, literature was another (burn the notebook at once, even if Gekrepten wu-rr-inggs her hands), laziness was something else, and meditation on the sovereign kicking of the bucket was something else. Stopping in front of a pizzeria at 1300 Corrientes, Oliveira asked himself the great question: "Must one stay at the centre of the crossroads, then, like the hub of a wheel? What good is it to know or to think we know that every road is false if we don't walk with an idea that is not the road itself? We're not Buddha, and there are no trees here to sit under in the lotus position. A cop appears and asks for your identity card."

Walking with an idea that is no longer the road itself. From all that chatter (what a combination, ch, mother of chigger, cheese, and chilli beans) the only thing left was that glimpse. Yes, it was a formula that deserved meditation. In that way his visit to El Cerro would have had to have a meaning after all, in that way La Maga would cease being a lost object and become the image of a possible reunion – no longer with her but on this side of her or on the other side of her, by her, but not her – . And Manú, and the circus, and that incredible idea of the madhouse that they were talking about so much at that time, everything could have meaning just as long as it was extrapolated, the whinevitable whextrapolation at the metaphysical whour, that stately word was always on time. Oliveira took a bite of pizza, burning his gums in his usual gluttonous way, and he felt better. But how many times had he gone through the same cycle on dozens of corners and in cafés in so many cities, how many times had he reached similar conclusions, felt better, thought he could begin to live in a different way; one afternoon, for example, when he had gone in to listen to an idiotic concert, and afterwards . . . Afterwards it had rained so much, why think about it. That's the way it was with Talita, the more he thought about it the worse it was. The woman was beginning to suffer because of him, not for any serious reason, just because he was there and everything seemed to be changing between Talita and Traveler, heaps of little things like that, taken for granted and dismissed, and suddenly they start to get sharp edges and what had started out as a Spanish stew ends up as a Kierkegaardian herring, without going any deeper into the matter. The afternoon with the boards had been a return to order, but Traveler had let the chance of saying what had to be said slip by, so that on that very day when Oliveira would have ordered himself to change neighbourhoods and their lives, he not only had said nothing, but he had got him the job with the circus, proof that . . . In that case pity would have been just as idiotic as the other time: rain, rain. I wonder if Berthe Trépat still plays the piano?

(–111)

49

Talita and Traveler talked at great length about famous madmen and others less well known now that Ferraguto had decided to buy the clinic and turn the circus, cat and all, over to somebody called Suárez Melián. It seemed to them, Talita especially, that the change from circus to clinic was like a step forward, but it was hard for Traveler to see very clearly the reasons for that optimism. In hopes of understanding better they went around in great excitement and were always going over to their windows or down to the street entrance to exchange impressions with Señora Gutusso, Don Bunche, Don Crespo, and even with Gekrepten if she was within range. The worst of it was that in those days there was a lot of talk of a revolt, that the armed forces in Campo de Mayo were about to rise up, and all that seemed much more important to people than the acquisition of a clinic on the Calle Trelles. Finally Talita and Traveler set out to try to find a little normality in a psychiatry text. As usual they got excited over anything, and the day of the duck, it was hard to tell why, their arguments became so violent that Cien Pesos was going crazy in his cage and Don Crespo waited for an acquaintance to go by so he could move his index finger in a circular pattern next to his forehead. On occasions like that thick clouds of duck feathers would come flying out of the kitchen window and there would be a slamming of doors and a hand-to-hand dialectic without quarter which would barely give way to lunchtime, when the duck would disappear right down to the last tegument.

When it was time for coffee and some Mariposa *caña*, a tacit reconciliation brought them together over venerated texts, issues of esoteric reviews, long out of print, cosmological treasures that they felt they had to assimilate as a sort of prelude to their new life. They talked a lot about eccentricities, because Traveler, with Oliveira's approval, had condescended to bring out some old papers and exhibit part of his collection of phenomena, something they had begun together when they were both studying in the long-forgotten university and which they had kept up separately later on. The study of those documents was a fine dessert, and Talita had earned the right to participate thanks to her copies of *Renovigo* (*Periódiko Rebolusionario Bilingue*), a Mexican publication in the Ispamerikan tongue put out by Editorial Lumen, on which a number of madmen had collaborated with exciting results. They only heard from Ferraguto every so often, because the circus was practically in the hands of Suárez Melián already, but it seemed certain that the clinic would be turned over to them around the middle of March. Once or twice Ferraguto had shown up at the circus to watch the calculating cat, from whom he was obviously going to find it difficult to be parted, and both times he spoke about the imminence of the great transaction and the-weighty-responsibilities that would fall on their shoulders (sigh). It seemed practically assured that Talita would be entrusted with the pharmacy, and the poor girl was extremely nervous, reviewing some notes from the time of her anointment. Oliveira and Traveler amused themselves endlessly at her expense, but when they went back to the circus they would both walk around sadly and look at the people and the cat as if a circus were something unappreciably rare.

"They're a lot crazier here," Traveler would say. "There won't be any comparison."

Oliveira would shrug-his-shoulders, incapable of saying that he felt the same way inside, and he would look up at the top of the tent, losing himself stupidly in uncertain ruminations.

"Of course you have changed as you went from place to place," Traveler would grumble. "Me too, but always here, always in this meridian . . ."

He would stretch out his arm and take in the vague geography of Buenos Aires.

"Changes, you know . . ." Oliveira would say.

While they were talking that way they would choke with laughter, and the audience would look at them out of the corner of their eyes because they were distracting their attention.

In moments of confidence, the three of them would admit that they were admirably prepared for their new duties. For example, the arrival of the Sunday edition of *La Nación* would provoke in them a sadness comparable only to people lined up at the movies and reprints from the *Reader's Digest.*

"Contacts are getting cut off more all the time," Traveler would say with a note of prophecy. "You have to give great shouts."

"Colonel Flappa already gave one last night," Talita answered. "Result, a state of siege."

"That's not a shout, girl, just a death-rattle. I'm talking about the things Yrigoyen used to dream about, historic cuspidations, prophetic promissorations, those hopes of mankind that have reached such bad shape in these parts."

"You're talking just like the other one now," Talita said, looking at him worriedly but hiding her characterological glance.

The other one was still at the circus, giving Suárez Melián some last-minute help and being surprised sometimes at the fact that he was becoming so indifferent to everything. He had the feeling that he had turned over the mane he had left to Talita and Traveler, who were getting more and more excited thinking about the clinic; the only thing he really liked doing those days was playing with the calculating cat, who had taken an enormous liking to him and would do additions for his exclusive pleasure. Since Ferraguto had given instructions that the cat was not to be taken into the street except in a basket and with an identification collar like army dog-tags from the Battle of Okinawa, Oliveira understood the cat's feelings and as soon as they were two blocks away from the circus he would leave the basket in a delicatessen he could trust, take the collar off the poor animal, and the two of them would wander around inspecting empty cans in vacant lots or nibbling grass, a delightful occupation. After those hygienic walks it was almost tolerable for Oliveira to become involved in the gatherings in Don Crespo's courtyard, in Gekrepten's tender insistence on knitting him things for winter. The night that Ferraguto telephoned the boarding house to tell Traveler about the imminent date of the great transaction, the three of them were perfecting their notions of the Ispamerikan language, extracted with infinite joy from an issue of *Renovigo.* They became almost sad thinking that in the clinic seriousness, science, abnegation, and all of those things were waiting for them.

"*¿Ké bida no es trajedia?*" Talita read in excellent Ispamerikan. They went on like that until Señora Gutusso arrived with the latest radio news bulletin about Colonel Flappa and his tanks, something real and concrete at last that scattered them immediately, to the surprise of the informant, drunk with patriotic feelings.

(–118)

50

The Calle Trelles was just a step away from the bus stop, a little over three blocks. Ferraguto and Cuca were already there with the superintendent when Talita and Traveler arrived. The great transaction was taking place in a room on the second floor, with two windows that opened onto the courtyard garden where the patients took their walks and a little stream could be seen rising and falling in a concrete fountain. To reach the room Talita and Traveler had to go through several hallways and rooms on the ground floor, where ladies and gentlemen had addressed them in correct Spanish, asking for the kind donation of a pack or two of cigarettes. The male nurse who accompanied them seemed to find this interlude perfectly natural, and the circumstances did not favour any preliminary question in the nature of an orientation. Practically out of cigarettes, they reached the room of the great transaction where Ferraguto pompously introduced them to the superintendent. Halfway through the reading of an unintelligible document Oliveira appeared, and they had to explain to him with whispers and hidden gestures that everything was going along fine and that nobody understood much of anything. When Talita succinctly whispered to him about her complicated arrival shh shh, Oliveira looked at her puzzled because he had come in through an entrance that led right to that door. As for the Boss, he was dressed in black as called for by the occasion.

The heat was the kind that lowered the pitch of the radio announcers' voices as every hour they would first give the weather report and then the official denials of the uprising in Campo de Mayo and Colonel Flappa's grim intentions. The superintendent had interrupted the reading of the document at five minutes to six to turn on his Japanese transistor radio in order to keep up, as he affirmed after begging their pardon, with the news. That expression immediately brought on in Oliveira the classic look of one who has forgotten something in the hallway downstairs (and one that even the superintendent would have to recognize as another form of contact with facts), and in spite of the fierce looks from Traveler and Talita he tore out of the room by the first available door, which was not the one he had come in by.

From a couple of phrases in the document he had surmised that the clinic had five floors and in addition a summerhouse at the rear of the garden. The best thing to do would be to take a turn around the garden, if he could find his way, but he didn't get the chance because no sooner had he gone twenty feet than a young man in shirtsleeves approached smiling, took him by the hand, and led him, swinging his arm the way children do, up to a corridor where there were many doors and something that must have been the opening of a service lift. The idea of getting to know the clinic in the care of a madman was exceedingly agreeable, and the first thing Oliveira did was to offer his companion a cigarette. He was an intelligent-looking young man who accepted the cigarette and whistled with satisfaction. Then it turned out that he was an attendant and that Oliveira was not a patient, the usual misunderstandings in cases like that. The episode was cute and didn't have much to offer, but as they went from one floor to another, Oliveira and Remorino became friendly and the inside topography of the clinic was explained, with anecdotes, jibes at the rest of the personnel, and watch-out-fors between friends. They were in the room where Dr Ovejero kept his guinea pigs and a picture of Monica Vitti when a cross-eyed boy appeared, running over to tell Romorino that if the gentleman with him was Señor Horacio Oliveira, etc. With a sigh, Oliveira went down two flights and returned to the room of the great transaction where the document was dragging along to its conclusions in the midst of Cuca Ferraguto's menopausal rushes and Traveler's rude yawns. Oliveira was still thinking about the figure dressed in pink pyjamas he had glimpsed on turning the corner of the hallway on the fourth floor, a man who was getting old and who was walking along close to the wall stroking a pigeon that seemed to be asleep in his hand. It was exactly at that moment that Cuca Ferraguto let out a kind of bellow.

"What do you mean, they have to okay it?"

"Be quiet, dear," the Boss said. "The gentleman means . . ."

"It's quite clear," said Talita, who had always got along with Cuca and wanted to help her. "The transfer requires the approval of the patients."

"But that's crazy," Cuca said, very *ad hoc.*

"My dear lady," the superintendent said, plucking at his vest with his free hand. "The patients here are very special, and the Méndez Delfino Act is quite clear in this respect. Except for eight or nine who have families that have given their approval, the rest have spent all their lives between one asylum and another, if I may use the term, and no one is responsible for them. In these cases the law allows the superintendent to get from them in lucid moments their approval of the transfer of the clinic to a new owner. Here are their statements, waiting to be signed," he added, showing her a book bound in red with strips cut from the comic section sticking out. "Read them, that's all there is to it."

"If I understand correctly," Ferraguto said, "this negotiation has to be done right now."

"And why do you think I've had you all come here? You as owner and these gentlemen as witnesses: let's start bringing in the patients and we can get it all done this afternoon."

"The point," Traveler said, "is that the ones who sign have to be in what you call their lucid moments."

The superintendent gave him a look of pity and pressed a buzzer. Remorino came in dressed in a smock; he winked at Oliveira and placed the enormous register on a small table. He placed a chair in front of the table, and folded his arms like a Persian executioner. Ferraguto, who had hastened to examine the register with the air of one who understood, asked if the approval should be signed at the bottom of the document, and the superintendent said yes, so now they would call the patients in in alphabetical order and ask them to give their stamp of approval under the influence of a large, round blue fountain pen. In spite of such efficient preparations, Traveler insisted on suggesting that maybe one of the patients would refuse to sign or would throw a sudden scene. Although they didn't dare to back him openly, Cuca and Ferraguto were hanging-on-his-every-word.

(–119)

51

Remorino appeared just then with an old man who seemed rather startled, and who when he recognized the superintendent greeted him with a sort of bow.

"In pyjamas," said Cuca, dumbfounded.

"I noticed when we came in," Ferraguto said.

"They weren't pyjamas. More like . . . "

"Quiet please," the superintendent said. "Come here, Antúnez, and put your signature where Remorino will show you."

The old man examined the register closely while Remorino held the pen out to him. Ferraguto took out his handkerchief and dried his forehead with a few soft dabs.

"This is page eight," Antúnez said, "and I think that I ought to sign on page one."

"Right here," said Remorino, showing him a place in the register. "Come on, your *café con leche* is getting cold."

Antúnez signed with a flourish, bowed to everyone, and went out with little pink steps that delighted Talita. The second pair of pyjamas was much fatter, and after circumnavigating the table he went over and shook hands with the superintendent who took his hand grudgingly and pointed to the register with a curt gesture.

"You know all about it already, so sign the book and then return to your room."

"My room hasn't been swept out," fat pyjamas said.

Cuca made a mental note of the lack of cleanliness. Remorino tried to put the pen in the hand of fat pyjamas, who drew back slowly.

"It'll be cleaned right away," Remorino said. "Sign your name, Don Nicanor."

"Never," said fat pyjamas. "It's a trick."

"Don't talk to me about tricks," the superintendent said. "Dr Ovejero has already explained to you what it's all about. You people sign now and starting tomorrow you get double rations of rice and milk."

"I won't sign unless Don Antúnez agrees," fat pyjamas said.

"It so happens he signed it just before you. Take a look."

"I can't make out the signature. This isn't Don Antúnez's signature. You got him to sign with an electric cattle prod. You killed Don Antúnez."

"Go and bring him back," the superintendent ordered Remorino, who flew out and came back with Antúnez. Fat pyjamas let out an exclamation of joy and went over to shake his hand.

"Tell him you agree and that he doesn't have to worry," the superintendent said. "Let's go, it's getting late."

"Go ahead and sign, son, don't be afraid," Antúnez told fat pyjamas. "After all, it won't change you in the head in any way."

Fat pyjamas dropped the pen. Remorino picked it up with a grumble, and the superintendent got up furiously. Hiding behind Antúnez, fat pyjamas was trembling and clutching at his sleeves. There was a soft knock on the door, and before Remorino could open it there entered without further ado a woman in a pink kimono, who went straight to the register and looked it all over as if it were a pickled sucking-pig. Straightening up satisfied, she put her hand on the register.

"I swear to tell the whole truth," the woman said. "You wouldn't tell me a lie, Don Nicanor."

Fat pyjamas nodded in approval and suddenly accepted the pen that Remorino was offering him and signed just where his hand happened to fall, without taking time for anything.

"Animal," they heard the superintendent mutter. "See if it came out in the right place, Remorino. Not too bad. And now you, Señora Schwitt, now that you're here. Show her the place, Remorino."

"Unless there's some improvement in the social environment I won't sign anything," said Señora Schwitt. "Doors and windows have to be opened to the spirit."

"I want two windows in my room," fat pyjamas said. "And Don Antúnez wants to go to the Franco-Inglesa chemist to buy some cotton wool and lots of other things. This place is so dark."

Turning his head a little, Oliveira saw that Talita was looking at him and he smiled at her. Both of them knew that the other one was thinking that this was all a comedy of idiots, that fat pyjamas and the rest of them were just as crazy as they were. Not very good actors, because they didn't make any effort to appear like decent lunatics in front of people who had done a good job of reading their manual of psychiatry for the layman. For example, over there, gripping her purse in both hands with complete self-assurance and sitting stolidly in her easy chair, Cuca seemed a good deal crazier than the three signatories, who now had begun to complain about something that sounded like the death of a dog, about which Señora Schwitt spread herself around with a luxury of gestures. Nothing was too unforeseeable; the most pedestrian causality continued governing those voluble and loquacious relationships in which the roars of the superintendent served as a continuous bass to the repeated designs of complaints and demands and the Franco-Inglesa. Thus they saw successively how Remorino took away Antúnez and fat pyjamas, how Señora Schwitt disdainfully signed the register, how a skeletal giant entered, a kind of gaunt flame in pink flannel, and behind him a young man with hair gone completely white and malignantly beautiful green eyes. These last two signed without any resistance, but then they decided that they wanted to stay until the end of the ceremony. To avoid any more disputes, the superintendent sent them over to a corner and Remorino went to bring in two more patients, a girl with bulky hips and a frightened man who would not lift his eyes from the floor. More surprising mention was made of the death of a dog. When the patients had signed, the girl curtsied like a ballerina. Cuca Ferraguto replied with a pleasant nod of the head, something that brought on a monstrous laughing attack in Talita and Traveler. There were already ten signatures in the register and Remorino continued bringing people in. There were greetings and a controversy here and there that interrupted things or changed protagonists; every so often a signature. It was already seven-thirty, and Cuca took out a compact and made up her face with the gestures of the wife of the head of a clinic, something in between Madame Curie and Edwige Feuillère. More wiggling on the part of Talita and Traveler, more restlessness on the part of Ferraguto, who alternately consulted the progress in the register and the face of the superintendent. At seven-forty a woman patient declared she would not sign until they killed the dog. Remorino promised her, winking in the direction of Oliveira, who appreciated the confidence. Twenty patients had come through and there were only forty-five left. The superintendent came over to them to let them know that the most difficult cases had already been stamped (that's how he put it) and the best thing to do would be to go into the next room for some beer and news reports. During the break they talked about psychiatry and politics. The revolt had been put down by the government forces, the leaders had surrendered in Luján. Dr Nerio Rojas was at a conference in Amsterdam. The beer, delicious.

At eight-thirty, forty-eight signatures had been obtained. It was getting dark, and the room was heavy with smoke and people in the corners, with the coughing that every so often came from one of those present. Oliveira would have liked to go out into the street, but the superintendent was strict and unyielding. The last three signatories had just demanded changes in the food (Ferraguto signalled Cuca to take notes, that's all they needed, in his clinic meals would be impeccable) and the death of the dog (Cuca put the fingers of her hand together in an Italianate way and showed them to Ferraguto, who shook his head perplexed and looked at the superintendent, who was very tired and shading his eyes with a calendar from a cake-shop). When the old man with the pigeon in the hollow of his hand arrived, slowly petting it as if he wanted to make it sleep, there was a long pause while everyone stopped to contemplate the motionless dove, and it was almost a pity that the patient had to interrupt his rhythmic caresses on the pigeon's back to reach out slowly for the pen that Remorino was holding out to him. After the old man, two sisters entered arm in arm and as soon as they were in the room demanded the death of the dog and other improvements in the establishment. The business of the dog made Remorino laugh, but Oliveira finally felt as if something was getting dammed up in him all the way up to his spleen, and getting up he told Traveler he was going to take a walk and that he would be right back.

"You have to stay," the superintendent said. "You're a witness."

"I'm in the building," Oliveira said. "Check the Méndez Delfino Act, it's all provided for."

"I'll go with you," Traveler said. "We'll be back in five minutes."

"Don't leave the premises," the superintendent said.

"Don't worry," said Traveler. "Come on, old man, I think we can get down to the garden this way. Disappointing, don't you think?"

"Unanimity is boring," Oliveira said. "Not one of them has done anything distinct. Look at the way they are about the dog. Let's sit down by the fountain, the trickle of water has a lustral air about it that will do us good."

"It smells like naphtha," Traveler said. "Really lustral, as a matter of fact."

"What did we expect, really? You can see how they all sign, there's no difference between them and us. No difference at all. We're going to be stupendously comfortable here."

"Well," Traveler said, "there is one difference: they go around in pink."

"Look," Oliveira said, pointing at the upper floors. It was already almost dark, and in the windows of the third and fourth floors lights were going on and off rhythmically. Light in one window and darkness in the one next door. Vice versa. Light on one floor, darkness on the one above, vice versa.

"It's started," Traveler said. "Lots of signatures, but now they're beginning to show their worse side."

They decided to finish their cigarettes next to the lustral trickle, talking about nothing and looking at the lights that were going on and off. That was when Traveler spoke about changes, and then after a silence he could hear Horacio laughing softly in the darkness. He kept on, wanting some certainty but not knowing how to bring up a subject that would slip out of the grasp of words and ideas.

"As if we were vampires, as if a single circulatory system united us – disunited us, that is. Sometimes you and I, sometimes the three of us, let's not fool ourselves. I don't know when it started, that's the way it is and we have to open our eyes to it. I don't think we're here just because we came with the Boss. It would have been easy to have stayed on at the circus with Suárez Melián, we know the work and they appreciate us. But no, we had to come here. The three of us. I'm the first one to blame because I didn't want Talita to think . . . Well, that I was putting you aside in this business of trying to get away from you. A matter of self-respect, you realize."

"Actually," Oliveira said, "I have no reason to take this job. I'm going back to the circus, or better still, away from everything. Buenos Aires is a big place. I already told you all this once."

"Yes, but you'll be leaving after we had this conversation. I mean you'll be doing it for me and that's just what I don't want."

"In any case, explain what you mean by changes."

"How should I know? If I tried to explain, it would get even hazier for me. Look, it's something like this: as long as I'm with you there's no problem, but as soon as I'm alone I get the feeling that you're putting pressure on me, from your room, for example. Remember the other day when you asked me for the nails. Talita feels it too, she looks at me and I get the feeling that the look is meant for you; when the three of us are together, though, she can go for hours without noticing that you're around. You must have spotted that, I suppose."

"Yes. Go on."

"That's all, and that's why I don't think it would be any good for me to help you go off by yourself. It has to be something you decide alone and now since I've been stupid enough to bring the matter up with you, you don't even have the freedom to decide, because you're going to raise the question from the responsibility angle and we'll be done for. The ethical thing in this case would be to pardon the life of a friend, and I can't accept that."

"Oh," said Oliveira. "So you won't allow me to go away, and I can't do it by myself. There's a touch of pink pyjamas about a situation like that, don't you think?"

"There probably is."

"Funny, isn't it?"

"What?"

"All the lights went out at the same time."

"They must have got the last signature. The clinic belongs to the Boss, long live Ferraguto!"

"I guess now we'll have to satisfy them and kill the dog. It's incredible the way they dislike it."

"Not dislike," Traveler said. "For the moment passions don't seem to get very violent here either."

"You have a need for radical solutions, old man. The same thing used to happen to me for a long time, and then . . . "

They began to walk back, carefully, because the garden was very dark and they couldn't remember where the flowerbeds were located. When they stepped on the hopscotch, near the doorway now, Traveler laughed softly and picking up one foot began to hop from square to square. The chalk design glowed weakly in the darkness.

"One of these nights I'm going to tell you about over there," Oliveira said. "I don't want to, but it's probably the only way we can get to kill the dog, to use that image."

Traveler jumped off the hopscotch, and at the same time the lights on the third floor suddenly went on. Oliveira, who was going to say something else, saw Traveler's face come out of the darkness, and in the instant the lights stayed on before going out again, he was surprised by a grimace, a rictus (from the Latin *rictus*, the opening of a mouth: the contraction of the lips, similar to a smile).

"Talking about killing the dog," Traveler said, "did you notice that the head doctor's name is Ovejero? Sheepdog, crazy."

"That's not what you wanted to tell me."

"Look who's complaining about my silences or substitutions," Traveler said. "Of course that's not what I wanted to say, but what the hell's the difference. It's something that can't be expressed. If you want to try to prove it . . . But something tells me it's a little too late already, you know. The pizza's cooled off, you can't turn it over any more. The best thing for us would be to get to work right away, it'll be a good distraction."

Oliveira did not answer, and they went up to the room of the great transaction where the superintendent and Ferraguto were having a double shot of *caña*. Oliveira followed suit immediately, but Traveler went over and sat on the sofa where Talita was reading a novel with a sleepy face. After the last signature, Remorino had removed the register and the patients who had been witnessing the ceremony. Traveler noticed that the superintendent had turned off the ceiling light and was using instead a lamp on the desk; everything was bland and green, they were talking in low and satisfied voices. He heard them making plans to go and have some tripe *genovese* in a restaurant downtown. Talita closed her book and looked at him sleepily, Traveler stroked her hair and he felt better. In any case, the idea of tripe at that hour and in that heat was insane.

(–69)

52

Because he really was unable to *tell* Traveler anything. If he began to pull at the ball of yarn he would get a thread of wool, yards of wool, *lana*, lanadir, lanagnorisis, lanaturner, lannapurna, lanatomy, lannuity, lanativity, lanationality, lanature, *lana ad lanauseam* but never the ball of yarn. He would have had to make Traveler suspect that what he was telling him did not make any direct sense (but what kind of sense did it make?) and that it wasn't any kind of image or allegory either. The unbridgeable difference, a problem of levels that had nothing to do with intelligence or information, it was one thing to play *truco* or discuss John Donne with Traveler, everything took place in a territory of appearances in common; but the other way, to be a kind of monkey among men, to want to be a monkey for reasons that not even the monkey was capable of explaining, beginning with the fact that he had no reasons at all and his strength derived precisely from that, and so on down the line.

The first nights at the clinic were peaceful; the old employees were still doing their work and the new ones limited themselves to observing, gaining experience, and getting together in the pharmacy where Talita, dressed in white, was making the emotional rediscovery of emulsions and barbiturates. The problem was how to get out from under Cuca Ferraguto, who had installed herself in the office, because Cuca seemed to have decided to put her stamp on the clinic, and the Boss himself listened respectfully to the New Deal summarized in such terms as cleanliness, discipline, godcountryandhome, grey pyjamas, and linden tea. Continually stopping by the pharmacy, Cuca kept-her-ears-open to the supposedly professional conversations of the new team. She had some confidence in Talita because the girl had her diploma hung up there, but the husband and his buddy were suspect. Cuca's problem was that in spite of everything she found them terribly charming, which obliged her to debate like Corneille between duty and violent love, while Ferraguto organized the administration and little by little was getting used to the substitution of schizophrenics for sword-swallowers and ampules of insulin for bales of hay. The doctors, three in number, came during the morning and were not much of a bother. The resident, a great poker player, had already become friendly with Oliveira and Traveler; in his office on the fourth floor they worked on possible royal flushes, and pots from ten to a hundred pesos would change hands like-a I wanna should tell you.

The patients much better, thank you.

(–89)

53

And one Thursday, wham-bam, everybody settled at around nine o'clock in the evening. That afternoon the old personnel had left with a great slamming of doors (knowing laughs from Ferraguto and Cuca, firm on the question of severance pay) and a delegation of patients had said goodbye to the people who were leaving with shouts of "The dog is dead, the dog is dead!" which had not prevented them from presenting a petition with five signatures to Ferraguto, demanding chocolate, the afternoon paper, and the death of the dog. The new people were left behind, still a little unsure, and Remorino, who had taken charge of easing the transition, said that everything would run superbly. Radio El Mundo was feeding the sporting spirit of Buenos Aires with reports about the heat wave. A record breaker, you could sweat at your pleasure patriotically, and Remorino had already picked up four or five pairs of pyjamas discarded in the corners. Between him and Oliveira the owners were persuaded to put them back on again, at least the bottoms. Before getting involved in a poker game with Ferraguto and Traveler, Dr Ovejero had told Talita to distribute lemonade without anything to fear at all except to Numbers 6, 18 and 31. This had brought on such an attack of weeping by Number 31 that Talita had to give her a double ration of lemonade. It was already time to proceed *motu proprio*, death to the dog.

How had it been possible that one had begun to live that life so peacefully, without too much strangeness? Perhaps because there had been no previous preparation, because the manual of psychiatry acquired at the Tomás Pardo bookshop had not been exactly propedeutic for Talita and Traveler. Without experience, without any real desires, without anything: man was really the animal who gets accustomed even to not getting accustomed. The morgue, for example: Traveler and Oliveira did not know about it and heretwas Tuesday night and Ovejero sent Remorino up to get them. Number 56 on the third floor had died just as they had expected; they needed help to move him and distract Number 31 who was getting telepalpitations from it all. Remorino explained to them that the outgoing personnel had been very vindictive and had just put in the minimum of work after they found out about the severance business, so there was nothing to do but start working hard, it would get easier as it went along.

How strange that in the inventory read on the day of the great transaction there had been no mention of a morgue. But they've got to keep their cold meat somewhere until the family comes for it or the city sends its wagon. The inventory probably mentioned a storeroom, or a transfer room, or a cold chamber, euphemisms like that, or maybe it simply spoke of the eight freezers. A morgue, after all, was not a pretty thing to mention in a document, Remorino thought. And why eight freezers? Oh, that . . . Some requirement of the federal Department of Health or some arrangement the ex-superintendent had made when he was taking bids, but it hadn't been a bad idea because sometimes there were streaks, like the year San Lorenzo had won the cup (what year was that? Remorino couldn't remember, but it was the year San Lorenzo had ended up in first place), four patients suddenly kicked the bucket, all in one stroke, like nobody's business. Not very usual, of course, with Number 56 you knew in advance, what could you do. Speak low along here so we don't wake them up. What do you want at this time of night, back to bed with you, back to bed. He's a good boy, look how he takes off. He gets the notion to come out in the hall at night, but don't get the idea he's after the women, we've got that business all taken care of. He comes out just because he's crazy, that's all, just like any one of us if you really think about it.

Oliveira and Traveler thought that Remorino was great. A fellow with experience, you could see that right off. They helped the man with the cart, who when he wasn't a stretcher-bearer was simply Number 7, a curable case so that he could help out with easy jobs. They took the cart down on the service lift, a little crowded, and they felt close to Number 56's shape underneath the sheet. His family was coming for him on Monday, they were from Trelew, poor people. They still hadn't come for Number 22, it was too much. People with money, Remorino thought: the worst kind, real vultures, no feelings.

And did the city let Number 22 . . . ? The order was floating around somewhere, one of those things. So the days were going by, two weeks, you can see the advantage of having lots of freezers. For one reason or another there were three of them there now, because Number 2 was there too, she was one of the original patients. That was really something, Number 2 had no family, but the Bureau of Burials had notified them that the truck would come by within forty-eight hours. Remorino added up the hours to amuse himself, and it was three hundred and six already, almost three hundred and seven. He called her an original patient because she was a little old lady left over from the early days, before the time of the doctor who had sold out to Don Ferraguto. Don Ferraguto seems to be a nice guy, doesn't he? To think he used to own a circus, that's really something.

Number 7 opened the door of the lift, pulled out the cart, and went driving wildly down the hallway until Remorino suddenly put on the brakes and took out a key to open the metal door while Traveler and Oliveira took out cigarettes simultaneously, those reflections . . . They really should have brought their overcoats, because there was no heat wave in the morgue, which looked like a barroom with a long table on one side and a refrigerator that reached up to the ceiling on the other wall.

"Go and get a beer," Remorino ordered. "You didn't see anything, eh? Sometimes the rules here are too . . . Better not say anything to Don Ferraguto, we just have some beer once in a while."

Number 7 went to one of the doors of the refrigerator and took out a bottle. While Remorino was opening it with an opener he had on his jackknife, Traveler looked at Oliveira, but Number 7 spoke first.

"Maybe we'd better put him away first, don't you think?"

"You . . . " Remorino began, but he just stood with the open jackknife in his hand. "You're right, boy. Let's go. That one's empty."

"No," said Number 7.

"Are you going to contradict me?"

"I beg your pardon, please," Number 7 said. "But that's the one that's empty."

Remorino stood there looking at him, and Number 7 smiled at him and after a kind of salute went over to the door in dispute and opened it. A bright light came out, something like an aurora borealis or some other hyperborean phenomenon, in the middle of which could be seen the clear outline of two rather large feet.

"Number 22," said Number 7. "Didn't I tell you? I can tell them all by their feet. Number 2's in there. What do you want to bet? Take a look if you don't believe me. Convinced? Well then, let's put him in this empty one. If you would give me a hand, easy, he has to go in head first."

"He's a champion," Remorino said to Traveler in a low voice. "I really can't see why Ovejero keeps him in here. There are no glasses, so we'll have to use what we were born with."

Traveler inhaled smoke all the way down to his knees before taking the bottle. It passed around from hand to hand, and Remorino told the first dirty story.

(–66)

54

From the window of his room on the third floor Oliveira could see the courtyard with its fountain, the trickle of water, Number 8's hopscotch, the three trees shading the geranium beds, and the high wall that hid the houses on the street. Number 8 had been playing hopscotch all afternoon, he was unbeatable, Number 4 and Number 19 had tried to get Heaven away from him, but it was useless, Number 8's foot was a precision instrument, a shot at a square, the stone always stopping in the most favourable position, it was extraordinary. At night the hopscotch had a sort of weak phosphorescence about it and Oliveira liked to look at it from his window. In his bed, giving in to the effects of a cubic centimetre of hypnosis, Number 8 was probably sleeping like a stork, mentally standing on one leg, moving his stone with sharp, infallible strokes towards the conquest of a heaven that seemed to lose its charm once it had been gained. "You're an insufferable romantic," Oliveira thought to himself, preparing a *mate*. "When will you be ready for the pink pyjamas?" He had a letter from the disconsolate Gekrepten on the table, because you can only get out on Saturdays, but what kind of a life is this going to be, my love, I refuse to resign myself to being alone so much of the time, if you could just see our little room. Resting the gourd on the windowsill, Oliveira took a pen out of his pocket and answered the letter. In the first place, there was a telephone (followed by the number); second, they were very busy, but the reorganization shouldn't take more than two weeks and then they would be able to see each other at least on Wednesdays, Saturdays and Sundays. Third, he was running out of *yerba*. "I write as if I were imprisoned," he thought, signing the letter. It was almost eleven o'clock, soon it would be his turn to relieve Traveler who was doing guard duty on the fourth floor. Mixing another *mate*, he read the letter again and licked the envelope. He preferred writing, the telephone was a confusing instrument in Gekrepten's hands, she didn't understand what was being explained to her.

In the left wing the light in the pharmacy went out. Talita came out into the courtyard, locked the door (it was easy to see her in the light of the hot and starry sky) and went indecisively over to the fountain. Oliveira whistled softly, but Talita kept on looking at the jet of water, and even put out an experimental finger and held it in the water for a moment. Then she crossed the courtyard, walking across the hopscotch without any continuity, and disappeared under Oliveira's window. Everything had had something of Leonora Carrington pictures about it, the night with Talita and the hopscotch, a crossing of lines that are unaware of one another, a trickle of water in a fountain. When the figure in pink came out of somewhere and went slowly over to the hopscotch, not daring to step on it, Oliveira knew that everything was coming back into order, that of necessity the pink figure would pick a flat stone out of the several that Number 8 kept piled up next to the flowerbed, and that La Maga, because it was La Maga, would double up her left leg and with the tip of her shoe propel the marker into the first square, would push the marker into the second (and Oliveira trembled a little because the marker had been on the point of going off the hopscotch, the uneven paving had stopped it exactly on the edge of the second square), would enter lightly and remain motionless for a second, like a pink flamingo in the half-light, before bringing her foot slowly up to the marker, calculating the distance to the third square.

Talita raised her head and saw Oliveira in the window. It took her a while to recognize him, and in the meantime she was balancing on one leg, as if holding herself in the air with her hands. Looking at her with an ironical disenchantment, Oliveira recognized his mistake, he saw that the pink was not pink, that Talita was wearing an ash-grey blouse and a skirt that most likely was white. Everything (in a manner of speaking) had an explanation: Talita had come in and had gone out again, attracted by the hopscotch, and that break of a second between her passage and reappearance had been enough to trick him just as on that other night in the prow of the ship, as probably on so many other nights. He scarcely answered the gesture from Talita, who was lowering her head now, concentrating; she calculated and the marker left the second square with force and went into the third, straightened up on end, started rolling along on its edge, left the hopscotch, went one or two paving stones' distance away from the hopscotch.

"You'll need more practice if you want to beat Number 8," Oliveira said.

"What are you doing there?"

"It's hot. Guard duty at eleven-thirty. Letters."

"Oh," Talita said. "What a night."

"Magical," Oliveira said and Talita laughed briefly before disappearing under the entranceway. Oliveira heard her go up the stairs, pass by his door (but she was probably going up in the lift), reach the fourth floor. "I've already admitted that they do look a lot alike," he thought. "That, along with my being an idiot, explains it all, right down to the last detail." But just the same he stayed there looking at the courtyard for a while, the deserted hopscotch, as if to convince himself. At ten past eleven Traveler came down to get him and gave him the report. Number 5 rather restless, notify Ovejero if he got bothersome; the rest were asleep.

The fourth floor was as perfect as a glove, and even Number 5 had calmed down. He accepted a cigarette, smoked it intensely, and explained to Oliveira how the conspiracy of Jewish publishers was holding up the publication of his great work on comets; he promised him an autographed copy. Oliveira left the door half open because he was on to his tricks, and he began to go up and down the hall, looking from time to time through the magic eyes installed thanks to the astuteness of Ovejero, the superintendent, and Liber & Finkel Co.: each room a little Van Eyck, except for that of Number 14 who as always had pasted a stamp over the lens. At twelve o'clock Remorino arrived under the influence of a few glasses of gin; they talked about horses and football, and then Remorino went off to the ground floor to sleep for a while. Number 5 had quietened down completely, and the heat closed in on the silence and half-darkness of the corridor. The idea that someone might try to kill him had not occurred to Oliveira until that moment, but all he needed was an instantaneous picture, a sketch that had more of a shiver than anything else about it, to make him realize that it was not a new idea, that it did not come from the atmosphere of the corridor with its closed doors and the shadow of the service lift in the background. The same thing could have occurred to him in Roque's, or in the subway at five in the afternoon. Or much earlier, in Europe, some night when he was wandering through poor neighbourhoods, wasteland where an old tin can could be used to slit a throat almost as if the two objects were in agreement. Stopping by the shaft of the lift, he looked into the black depths and thought again about the Phlegrean Fields, the way in. In the circus it had been just the opposite, a hole up above, the opening in communication with free space, an image of consummation; now he was at the edge of the pit, the hole of Eleusis, the clinic wrapped in sulphurous vapours, the descent. Turning around he saw the straight line of the hallway to its end, with the faint purple light from the bulbs on the frames of the white doors. He did a foolish thing: picking up his left leg, he took little hops along the hall up to where he was opposite the first door. When he put his left foot down on the green linoleum again he was bathed in sweat. With each hop he had muttered the name of Manú between his teeth. "To think that I had expected a passage," he said to himself leaning against the wall. Impossible to objectivize the first fraction of a thought without finding it grotesque. Passage, for example. To think that he had expected. Expected a passage. Letting himself slide down, he sat on the floor and stared at the linoleum. Passage to what? And why did the clinic have to serve as a passage? What kind of temples did he go around needing, what intercessors, what psychic or moral hormones that could project him outside or inside himself?

When Talita arrived with a glass of lemonade (those ideas of hers, little teacher of the workers' quarter and The Drop of Milk), he brought the matter up right away. Talita wasn't surprised by anything; sitting down opposite him she watched him drink the lemonade in one gulp.

"If Cuca could see us stretched out on the floor she'd have an attack. What a way you have of standing guard. Are they asleep?"

"Yes, I think so. Number 14 covered her peephole, who knows what she's up to. For some reason I don't feel like looking in."

"You're the model of delicacy," Talita said. "But maybe I, as one woman to another . . ."

She returned almost immediately, and this time she sat down next to Oliveira, leaning against the wall.

"Sleeping the sleep of the chaste. Poor Manú had a horrible nightmare. It's always the same, he goes back to sleep but I'm so upset I end up getting out of bed. I thought you might have been warm, you or Remorino, so I made some lemonade. What a summer, and with those walls out there that shut out the breeze. So I look like that other woman."

"A little bit, yes," Oliveira said, "but that's not important. What I would like to know is why I saw you dressed in pink."

"Influence of the environment, you've assimilated her in among the others."

"Yes, that's the easiest explanation if you take everything into account. But you, why did you start to play hopscotch? Have you become assimilated too?"

"You're right," Talita said. "Why did I? I never really did care for hopscotch. But don't you go making up one of your theories about my being possessed, I'm nobody's zombie."

"You don't have to shout it."

"Nobody's," Talita repeated, lowering her voice. "I saw the hopscotch as I was coming in, there was a pebble . . . I played and I went away."

"You lost on the third square. The same thing would have happened to La Maga, she's incapable of keeping things up, she doesn't have the least sense of distance, time falls apart in her hands, she goes around bumping into everyone. Thanks to which, I might say in passing, she is absolutely perfect in her way of denouncing everybody else's perfection. But I was talking about the service lift, I think."

"Yes, you said something and then you drank your lemonade. No, wait, first you drank your lemonade."

"I was probably feeling sorry for myself; when you came I was in the midst of a shamanistic trance, on the point of jumping into the hole to put an end once and for all to conjectures, that svelte word."

"The hole ends in the basement," Talita said. "There are cockroaches, if you want to know, and coloured rags on the floor. Everything is dark and damp, and a little beyond is where the dead people start. Manú told me about it."

"Is Manú asleep?"

"Yes. He had a nightmare, he shouted something about a lost necktie. I already told you."

"It's a great night for confiding," Oliveira said, looking at her slowly.

"Very great," Talita said. "La Maga was just a name, and now she already has a face. The colour of her clothes may still be wrong, though."

"Her clothes are the least important, when I see her again who knows what she'll be wearing. She'll be naked, or she'll be walking with her child in her arms singing him *Les Amants du Havre*, a song you don't know."

"Oh yes I do," Talita said. "They used to play it a lot on Radio Belgrano. La-lá-la, la-lá-la . . . "

Oliveira sketched out a soft slap which turned into a caress. Talita threw her head back and bumped it against the wall of the hallway. She frowned and rubbed the back of her neck, but she kept on humming the tune. She heard a click and then a buzzing that seemed blue in the half-light of the hallway. They heard the service lift coming up, they looked at each other for a second before jumping up. Who could it be at that hour . . . ? Click, it passed the second floor, the blue buzzing. Talita drew back and got behind Oliveira. Click. The pink pyjamas were perfectly visible in the cube of wired glass. Oliveira ran over to the lift and opened the door. An almost cold breath of air came out. The old man looked at him as if he didn't know him and kept on stroking the pigeon; it was easy to see that the pigeon had been white once and that the continuous caressing of the old man's hand had turned it ash-grey. Motionless, with wild eyes, it was resting in the hollow of the hand that held it at chest level, while the fingers kept passing over it from neck to tail, from neck to tail.

"Go to bed, Don López," Oliveira said, breathing heavily.

"It's hot in bed," Don López said. "Look how happy she is when I take her for a walk."

"It's very late, go to your room."

"I'll bring you a cool glass of lemonade," Talita Nightingale promised.

Don López stroked the pigeon and came out of the service lift. They heard him go down the stairs.

"Everybody does what he wants around here," Oliveira muttered, closing the door to the lift. "One of these days there's going to be a general throat-cutting. You can smell it, no matter what they say. That pigeon looked like a revolver."

"We ought to tell Remorino. The old man came up from the basement, it's strange."

"Look, you stay here a while on guard, I'm going down to the basement to have a look; I hope one of the others isn't up to any tricks."

"I'm going down with you."

"OK, the ones up here are fast asleep."

Inside the lift the light was vaguely blue and it went down with a science-fiction buzz. There wasn't a living soul in the basement, but one of the doors of the freezer was ajar and a beam of light was coming out through the opening. Talita stopped in the doorway, with her hand to her mouth, while Oliveira went over. It was Number 56, he remembered very well, the family could come by any time. From Trelew. And in the meantime Number 56 had had a visit from a friend; one could imagine the conversation with the old man with the pigeon, one of those pseudo-dialogues in which the speaker doesn't care whether or not the other party speaks as long as he's there opposite, as long as there's something there opposite, anything, a face, feet sticking out of the ice. The same way as he had just been talking to Talita, telling her what he had seen, telling her that he was afraid, talking all the time about holes and passageways, to Talita or to anybody else, to a pair of feet sticking out of the ice, to any opposite appearance capable of listening and agreeing. But while he was closing the door of the freezer and for some reason holding on to the edge of the table, a vomit of memory began to take hold of him; he told himself that only a day or two before, it had seemed impossible to arrive at the point of telling anything to Traveler, a monkey couldn't tell anything to a man, and suddenly, without knowing why, he had heard himself talking to Talita as if she were La Maga, knowing that she wasn't but talking to her about the hopscotch, his fear in the hallway, the tempting hole. Then (and Talita was there, fifteen feet away, behind him, waiting) it was all like an ending, the appeal to outside pity, the re-entry into the human family, the sponge landing with a repulsive squish in the centre of the ring. He felt as if he had been going away from himself, abandoning himself so he could throw himself – the prodigal son (of a bitch) – into the arms of easy reconciliation, and from there the even easier step into the world, into the possible life, into the time of his years, into the reason that guided the actions of good Argentines, of the human animal in general. He was in his little, comfortable, refrigerated Hades, but there was no Eurydice to look for, apart from the fact that he had come down peacefully in a service lift and now, while he was opening a freezer and taking out a bottle of beer, king of the castle, anything to put an end to that comedy.

"Come and have a drink," he invited. "Much better than lemonade."

Talita took a step and stopped.

"Don't be necrophilic," she said. "Let's get out of here."

"It's the only place that's cool, you've got to admit that. I think I'll bring a bed down here."

"You're pale with the cold," Talita said coming over. "Come on, I don't like your staying here."

"Don't like it? They're not going to come out and eat me, the ones upstairs are much worse."

"Come on, Horacio," Talita repeated. "I don't want you to stay here."

"You . . ." Oliveira said, looking at her angrily, and he stopped to open the beer with a blow of his hand against the edge of a chair. He could see with great clarity a boulevard in the rain, but instead of leading somebody along by the arm, talking to her with pity, he was being led, they had given him a compassionate arm and they were talking to him so that he would be happy, they had so much concern for him that it was absolutely delightful. The past had become turned around, it was changing its sign, it was finally going to happen at last that Pity would not destroy. That woman who played hopscotch had pity on him, it was so obvious that it burned.

"We can talk some more on the third floor," Talita said by way of explanation. "Bring the bottle along and give me a little."

"*Oui madame, bien sûr madame,*" Oliveira said.

"You finally said something in French. Manú and I thought that you had taken an oath. Never . . ."

"*Assez,*" Oliveira said. "*Tu m'as eu, petite, Céline avait raison, on se croit enculé d'un centimètre et on l'est déjà de plusieurs mètres.*"

Talita looked at him with the look of one who didn't understand, but her hand rose up without her feeling it rise, and she held it for an instant on Oliveira's chest. When she took it away, he started to look at her as if from below, with eyes that looked from somewhere else.

"Who can tell," Oliveira said to someone who was not Talita. "Who can tell if you're the one who spit so much pity out at me tonight. Who can tell if after all the only thing left is to cry over love until you fill four or five buckets. Or let them cry into them for you, the way they're crying into them for you."

Talita turned her back on him and went towards the door. When she stopped to wait for him, upset and at the same time needing to wait for him because to go away at this instant would be like letting him fall into the well (with cockroaches, with coloured rags), she saw that he was smiling and that the smile was not for her either. She had never seen him smile like that, faint-heartedly and at the same time with his whole face open and front-facing, without the usual irony, accepting something that must have come to him from the centre of life, from that other well (with cockroaches, with coloured rags, with a face floating in dirty water?), going up to her in the act of accepting that thing impossible to name that was making him smile. And his kiss was not for her either, it wasn't happening there grotesquely next to a freezer full of corpses, so close to the sleeping Manú. It was as if they were coming together from somewhere else, with some other part of themselves, and it wasn't a question of themselves, as if they were paying or collecting something for others, as if they were the golems of an impossible meeting between their masters. And the Phlegrean Fields, and what Horacio had muttered about the descent, a madness so absolute that Manú and everything that was Manú and was on the level of Manú could not take part in the ceremony, because what was starting there was like the caress on the dove, like the idea of getting up to make some lemonade for the one on guard, like bending a leg and kicking a stone from the first to the second square from the second to the third. In some way they had got into another thing, into that something where one could be dressed in grey and be dressed in pink, where one could have died of drowning in a river (and she was no longer the one who was thinking about that) and appear in a Buenos Aires night to reproduce on the hopscotch the very image of what they had just attained, the last square, the centre of the mandala, the dizzy Ygdrasil through which one came out onto an open beach, an extension without limit, the world beneath the eyelids that the eyes turned inward recognized and obeyed.

(–129)

55

But Traveler was not asleep, after one or two attempts the nightmare kept circling around him and finally he sat up in bed and turned on the light. Talita was not there, somnambulist, sleepless moth, and Traveler drank a glass of *caña* and put on his pyjama top. The wicker easy chair looked cooler than the bed, and it was a good night to stay up reading. Sometimes he heard walking in the entrance hall, and Traveler twice went to the door that opened onto the administrative wing. Nobody was there, not even the wing. Talita must have gone to do some work in the pharmacy, it was incredible how enthusiastic she was about her return to science, scales, antipyretics. Traveler began to read for a while between drinks of *caña.* Still, it was strange that Talita had not come back from the pharmacy. When she did reappear, with a frightening ghostly air, the bottle of *caña* was so low that Traveler didn't much care whether he saw her or didn't see her, and they chatted for a while about many things, while Talita unfolded a nightgown and other diverse theories, almost all of them tolerated by Traveler who tended towards benevolence in the state he was in. Then Talita fell asleep on her back, a restless sleep interrupted by sharp hand movements and moans. It was always the same, it was hard for Traveler to sleep when Talita was restless, but as soon as he was overcome by fatigue she would wake up and at once become fully awake, because he would be complaining or twisting in his dreams, and that's how they would pass the night, as if they were on a seesaw. To make things worse the light had been left on and it was very complicated getting to the switch, that's why they ended up awakening completely, and then Talita turned out the light and squeezed herself a little up against Traveler who was sweating and twisting. "Horacio saw La Maga tonight," Talita said. "He saw her in the courtyard, two hours ago, when you were on guard duty."

"Oh," said Traveler, lifting up his shoulders and looking Braille system for his cigarettes. He added a confused phrase that had come out of what he had just been reading.

"I was La Maga," Talita said, snuggling closer to Traveler. "I don't know if you're aware of that."

"Most likely yes."

"It had to happen some time. What surprises me is that he's become so startled by the mixup."

"Oh, you know, Horacio gets something started and then he looks at it with the same look puppies put on when they've taken a crap and stand there amazed looking at it."

"I think it happened the very day we went to meet him at the dock," Talita said. "It's hard to explain, because he didn't even look at me and between the two of you you treated me like a dog, with the cat under my arm."

Traveler muttered something unintelligible.

"He had me confused with La Maga," Talita insisted.

Traveler listened to her talk, alluding as all women do to fate, to the inevitable concatenation of events, and he would have preferred her to shut up but Talita resisted feverishly, squeezed up against him and insisted on telling things, telling herself, and naturally, telling him. Traveler let himself be carried along.

"First the old man with the pigeon came, and then we went down to the basement. Horacio kept talking all the time we were going down, about those hollows that worry him. He was desperate, Manú, it was frightening to see how peaceful he seemed, and all the time . . . We went down in the service lift, and he went over to shut one of the freezers, it was horrible."

"So you went downstairs," Traveler said. "OK."

"It was different," Talita said. "It wasn't like going down. We were talking, but I felt as if Horacio were somewhere else, talking to someone else, to a drowned woman, for example. It comes back to me now, but he'd never said that La Maga had been drowned in the river."

"She isn't the least bit drowned," Traveler said. "I'm sure of that, although I have to admit I haven't got the slightest idea. Knowing Horacio is enough."

"He thinks she's dead, Manú, and at the same time he feels her close by and tonight it was me. He told me that he'd seen her on the ship too, and under the bridge on the Avenida San Martín . . . He doesn't say it as if he were talking about a hallucination, and he doesn't expect you to believe it either. He says it, that's all, and it's true, it's something that's there. When he closed the freezer and I was afraid and I said something or other, he began to look at me and it was the other one he was looking at. I'm nobody's zombie, Manú, I don't want to be anybody's zombie."

Traveler stroked her hair, but Talita pushed him away impatiently. She had sat down on the bed and he could feel her trembling. Trembling, in that heat. She told him that Horacio had kissed her, and she tried to explain the kiss and since she couldn't find the words she kept touching Traveler in the darkness, her arms fell like cloths over his face, over his arms, slipped down along his chest, rested on his knees, and out of all this came a kind of explanation that Traveler was incapable of rejecting, a contagion that came from farther off, from some place in the depths or on the heights or in some place which was not that night and that room, a contagion that possessed him in turn through Talita, a babbling like an untranslatable announcement, the suspicion that he was facing something that could be an announcement, but the voice that brought it was broken and when it spoke the message it spoke it in some unintelligible language, and yet it was the only necessary thing there within hand's reach, demanding recognition and acceptance, beating itself against a spongy wall of smoke and of cork, unseizable and offering itself naked between the arms but like water pouring down among tears.

"The hard mental crust," Traveler managed to think. Confusedly he heard that fear, that Horacio, that the service lift, that the dove; a communicable system was little by little entering his ear again. So the poor devil was afraid he would kill him, it was laughable.

"Did he really say that? It's hard to believe, you know how proud he is."

"It's something else," Talita said, taking the cigarette away from him and dragging on it with a sort of silent-movie eagerness. "I think the fear he feels is like a last refuge, the crossbar he holds on to before jumping. He's so happy to be afraid tonight, I know he's happy."

"That," said Traveler, breathing like a real yogi, "is something Cuca would not understand, you can be sure. And I must be in an exceedingly intelligent mood tonight, because that business of happy fear is a little hard to take, my love."

Talita slid up on the bed a little and leaned against Traveler. She knew that she was by his side again, that she had not drowned, that he was there holding her up on the surface of the water and that actually there was pity, a marvellous pity. They both felt it at the same moment, and they slid towards each other as if to fall into themselves, into the common earth where words and caresses and mouths enfolded them as a circumference does a circle, those tranquillizing metaphors, that old sadness satisfied with going back to being the same as always, with continuing, keeping afloat against wind and tide, against call and fall.

56

He wondered where he had picked up the habit of always carrying pieces of string in his pockets, of putting coloured threads together and placing them between the pages of books, of constructing all manner of figures with those things and gum tragacanth. As he wound a piece of black string around the door-knob, Oliveira wondered whether the delicateness of the threads didn't give him some kind of perverse satisfaction, and he agreed that maybe *peut-être* and who could say. The only thing certain was that the pieces of string and thread made him happy, that nothing seemed more instructive to him than to construct for example a huge transparent dodecahedron, the work of many hours and much complication, to bring a match close to it later on and watch how a little nothing of a flame would come and go while Gekrepten wr-ung-her-ha-nds and said that it was a shame to burn something so pretty. Difficult to explain to her that the more fragile and perishable the structure, the greater the freedom to make and unmake it. To Oliveira threads seemed to be the only justifiable material for his inventions, and only once in a while, if he found it in the street, did he feel like using a piece of wire or some strap or other. He liked everything he made as full of free space as possible, the air able to enter and leave, especially leave; things like that occurred to him with books, women, obligations, and he did not expect Gekrepten or the cardinal primate to understand those celebrations.

The business of wrapping a black string around the doorknob began almost a couple of hours later, because in the meantime Oliveira made various things in his room and outside it. The idea of the basins was classic and he didn't feel at all proud at having followed it, but in the darkness a basin of water on the floor works out a series of rather subtle defensive values; surprise, terror perhaps, in any case the blind rage that follows the idea of having stuck a Fanacal or Tonsa shoe into the water, and the sock a little bit beyond the shoe, and that all of this drips water while the foot completely perturbed becomes agitated in the sock, and the sock in the shoe, like a drowning rat or one of those poor guys that jealous sultans used to throw into the Bosporus inside a bag that was sewn shut (with string, naturally: everything ended up meeting, it was rather amusing that the basin of water and the threads should come together at the end of his reasoning and not at the beginning, but here Horacio permitted himself the conjecture that the order of reasoning did not have to (*a*) follow physical time, the before and the after, and (*b*) that most likely the reasoning had been unconsciously fulfilled so that it would pass from the notion of thread to that of the watery basin). In short, no sooner was it analysed a bit than it fell into grave suspicions of determinism; it would be best to keep on making barricades without paying too much attention to reasons or preferences. In any case, what came first, the thread or the basin? As execution, the basin, but the thread had been decided first. It wasn't worth the trouble to keep on worrying when life hung in the balance; obtaining basins was much more important, and the first half-hour consisted of a cautious exploration of the third floor and part of the ground floor, from where he returned with five medium-sized basins, three spittoons, and an empty can that had contained a sweet-potato preserve, all brought together under the general denomination of basin. Number 18, who was awake, insisted on keeping him company and Oliveira ended up accepting, having made up his mind to throw him out as soon as the defensive operations reached a certain stage. As far as threads were concerned, Number 18 was very useful, because no sooner was he succinctly informed of the strategic necessities than he rolled his malignantly beautiful green eyes and said that Number 6 had boxes full of coloured thread. The only problem was that Number 6 was on the ground floor, in Remorino's wing, and if Remorino woke up there would be all hell to pay. Number 18 also maintained that Number 6 was crazy, which would complicate the raid on her room. Rolling his malignantly beautiful green eyes, he suggested to Oliveira that he stand guard in the hallway while he took off his shoes and proceeded to seize the threads, but it seemed to Oliveira that this was going too far and he decided that he would assume the personal responsibility of going into Number 6's room at that time of night. It was rather amusing to think about responsibility while he invaded the bedroom of a girl snoring face up, exposed to the worst mischances; with his pockets and his hands full of balls of yarn and coloured threads, Oliveira stood looking at her for a moment, but then he shrugged his shoulders as if to make the monkey of responsibility seem a little lighter. Number 18, who was waiting for him in his room contemplating the basins piled up on the bed, thought that Oliveira had not obtained thread in sufficient quantity. Rolling his malignantly beautiful green eyes, he maintained that to complete the defensive preparations adequately what was needed was a good supply of ball bearings and a Heftpistole. The idea of the ball bearings seemed good to Oliveira, although he didn't have a clear idea of what they might be, but he rejected the Heftpistole completely. Number 18 opened his malignantly beautiful green eyes and said that a Heftpistole was not what the doctor thought it was (he said "doctor" in an obligatory tone so that anybody could see that he was saying it to be annoying) but in view of the negative response he would try to get only the ball bearings. Oliveira let him go, with the faint hope that he would not come back because he felt like being alone. Remorino would get up at two o'clock to relieve him and he had to think of something. If Remorino didn't find him in the hallway he would come looking for him in his room and that wouldn't do, unless the first test of the defences was made at his expense. He rejected the idea because the defences were conceived with a determined attack in mind, and Remorino would enter with a completely different outlook. Now he was beginning to feel more and more fear (and when he felt fear he would look at his wristwatch, and the fear would grow with the hour); he started to smoke, studying the defensive possibilities of the room, and at ten minutes to two he went out to wake up Remorino in person. He handed over a list of instructions that was a gem, with subtle alterations on the temperature entries, the time for tranquillizers, and the syndromatic and eupeptic manifestations of the guests on the second floor, to such a degree that Remorino would have to spend almost all his time with them, while the ones on the third floor, according to the same report, would be sleeping peacefully and the only thing they would need was for no one to come and bother them during the night. Remorino was interested in knowing (without much desire) if those attentions and lack of them came from the high authority of Dr Ovejero, to which Oliveira replied hypocritically with the monosyllabic adverb of affirmation suited to the circumstances. After which they separated in friendly fashion and Remorino went yawning up one flight while Oliveira went trembling up two. But by no means would he accept the help of a Heftpistole, and they ought to be thankful that he agreed to the ball bearings.

He still had a moment of peace, because Number 18 had not returned and it was necessary to go about filling up the basins and the spittoons, placing them in a first line of defence a little bit behind the first barrier of threads (still theoretical but already perfectly planned) and trying the possibilities of advance, the eventual collapse of the first line, and the efficiency of the second. In between two basins Oliveira filled the sink with cold water and put in his face and his hands, soaked his neck and his hair. He was smoking all the time, but he hadn't finished half of any cigarette and he went to the window to throw out the butt and light another one. The butts fell on the hopscotch and Oliveira calculated so that each brilliant eye would burn for a moment in a different square; it was funny. It occurred to him at that hour to fill himself with outside thoughts, *dona nobis pacem, may your patron have pesos that will last for ever*, things like that, and also suddenly strips of mental material came to him, something in between a notion and a feeling, for example, that his digging in was the last of his stupidities, that the only mad thing, and therefore the one worth trying and maybe efficient, would have been to attack instead of defending himself, besiege instead of being there trembling and smoking and waiting for Number 18 to come back with the ball bearings; but it didn't last long, almost like the cigarettes, and his hands trembled and he knew that that was all he had left, and suddenly another memory that was like a hope, a phrase where somebody was saying that the hours of sleep and wakefulness have not been joined into unity yet, and that was followed by a laugh that he heard as if it were not his, and a grimace in which he showed himself once and for all that that unity was too far away and that no part of dreams would be any good to him while he was awake or vice versa. To attack Traveler as the best defence was a possibility, but it meant invading what he felt more and more to be a black mass, a territory where people were sleeping and nobody at all expected to be attacked at that hour of the night and for non-existent causes in terms of the black mass. But while he was feeling that way, it was disagreeable for Oliveira to have formulated it in terms of a black mass, feeling was like a black mass but through his fault and not that of the territory where Traveler was sleeping; that's why it was best not to use words as negative as black mass, and simply call it territory, since one always ended up calling his feelings something. It meant that across from his room the territory began, and to attack the territory was ill-advised since the motives for the attack no longer had intelligibility or the possibility of being sensed by the territory. On the other hand, if he barricaded himself in his room and Traveler came to attack him, no one would be able to maintain that Traveler did not know what he was doing, and the one attacked was perfectly aware and had taken his measures, precautions, and ball bearings, whatever these last might be.

Meanwhile one could stay at a window smoking, studying the disposition of the watery basins and the threads and thinking about the unity so much put to proof by the conflict of territory versus room. It was always going to pain Oliveira that he could not even get a notion of that unity that other times he called centre, and which for lack of more precise dimensions was reduced to images like black shout, kibbutz of desire (so far away now, that kibbutz of dawn and red wine), and even a life worthy of the name because (he felt it while he threw his cigarette on square five) he had been just foolish enough to imagine the possibility of a dignified life coming after diverse minute indignities. Nothing at all that could be thought about, but on the other hand it could be felt in terms of stomach contraction, territory, deep or spasmodic breathing, sweat on the palms of his hands, lighting a cigarette, pulling in his guts, thirst, silent shouts that broke like black masses in his throat (there was always some black mass in that game), desire for sleep, fear of sleeping, anxiety, the image of a dove that had once been white, coloured rags at the bottom of what could have been a passage, Sirius at the top of a tent, and enough, hey, enough please; but it was good to have felt one's self deeply there for an unmeasurable time, without thinking anything, only being that which was there with tongs caught in his stomach. *That* against the territory, waking against sleep. But to say *waking against sleep* was already a return into dialectics, it was to corroborate once more that there wasn't the remotest hope of unity. That's why the arrival of Number 18 with the ball bearings became an excellent pretext to resume the preparations for defence at exactly three-twenty more or less.

Number 18 rolled his malignantly beautiful green eyes and undid a towel in which he had the ball bearings. He said that he had spied on Remorino and that Remorino was so busy with Numbers 31, 7 and 45 that he wouldn't even think of coming up to the third floor. Most probably the patients had resisted with indignation the therapeutic novelties that Remorino was trying to give them, and the distribution of pills and shots would take its own sweet time. In any event, Oliveira thought that it would be well not to lose any more time, and after telling Number 18 that he could use the ball bearings in the way he saw most fitting, he began to test the efficacy of the watery basins, to do which he went out into the hall, overcoming the fear he had of leaving his room and getting into the purple light of the hallway, and he came back in with his eyes closed, imagining himself to be Traveler and walking with his toes turned out a little like Traveler. On his second step (although he knew it) he put his left shoe into a watery spittoon, and when he quickly pulled it out he sent the spittoon flying through the air and luckily it fell on the bed so that it did not make the least noise. Number 18 was under the desk spreading out the ball bearings; he jumped up and rolling his malignantly beautiful green eyes suggested a grouping of bearings between the two rows of basins, in order to complete the surprise of the cold water with the possibility of a magnificent slip. Oliveira did not say anything but he let him do it, and when he had put the watery spittoon back in its place again, he began to wrap a black thread around the doorknob. He stretched this thread to the desk and tied it to the back of the chair; putting the chair on two legs, with the corner resting on the edge of the desk; all that was needed for it to fall on the floor was for someone to try to open the door. Number 18 went out into the hall to try it, and Oliveira held the chair so there would be no noise. He began to be bothered by the friendly presence of Number 18, who from time to time would roll his malignantly beautiful green eyes and try to tell him the story of his arrival at the clinic. Of course all that was needed was to put a finger to one's mouth so that he would be shamefully silent and stay with his back against the wall for five minutes, but at the same time Oliveira gave him a new pack of cigarettes and told him to go to bed without letting himself be seen by Remorino.

"I'll stay with you, doctor," said Number 18.

"No, go ahead. I'll defend myself perfectly well."

"You needed a Heftpistole, I told you so. It puts staples all around, and it's better to hold down the threads."

"I'll fix it myself, old man," Oliveira said. "Go to bed. Thanks just the same."

"Well then, doctor, I hope it all goes fine."

"Good night, have a good sleep."

"Watch the ball bearings, you'll see that they won't let you down. Just leave them the way they are and you'll see."

"OK."

"If it turns out that you need the Heftpistole after all just let me know, Number 16 has one."

"Thanks, see you."

At half-past three Oliveira finished placing the threads. Number 18 had taken speech away, or at least that business of looking at each other from time to time or reaching for a cigarette. Almost in the dark because he had covered the lamp with a green sweater that was slowly getting singed, it was strange to go around like a spider from one side to the other with the threads, from the bed to the door, from the bathroom to the closet, stretching out each time five or six threads and retreating with great care so as not to step on the ball bearings. Finally he was becoming fenced in between the window, one side of the desk (placed against the flat of the wall, on the right), and the bed (up against the wall on the left). Between the door and the last line were strung successively the warning threads (from the doorknob to the leaning chair, from the doorknob to a Martini vermouth ashtray placed on the edge of the sink, and from the doorknob to a dresser drawer, full of books and papers, barely held by the edge), the watery basins in the shape of two irregular defensive lines, but oriented in general from the left wall to the right one, or in other terms from the sink to the closet the first line, and from the legs of the bed to the legs of the desk the second line. There was just about a yard left between the last series of watery basins, over which hung multiple threads, and the wall where the window opened onto the courtyard (two storeys down). Sitting on the edge of the desk, Oliveira lit another cigarette and began to look out of the window;

at a given moment he took off his shirt and put it under the desk. Now he couldn't drink any more even if he was thirsty. He stayed that way, in his undershirt, smoking and looking into the courtyard, but with his attention focused on the door even though from time to time he would become distracted when throwing his cigarette end onto the hopscotch. It wasn't so bad, even if the edge of the desk was hard and the smell of the burned sweater bothered him. He ended up turning off the lamp and little by little he saw a purple beam form under the door, that is to say that when Traveler arrived his rubber-soled slippers would cut the purple band in two places, an involuntary signal that he was about to initiate his attack. When Traveler opened the door several things would happen and many others might happen. The first would be mechanistic and ordained, within the stupid obedience of effect to cause, of chair to string, of doorknob to hand, of hand to will, of will to . . . And that's where one passes to other things that might happen or not, according to whether the blow of the chair on the floor, the breaking into five or six pieces of the Martini ashtray, and the fall of the dresser drawer would have one or another repercussion in Traveler and even in Oliveira himself, because now, while he was lighting another cigarette with the stub of the previous one and threw the butt so that it would fall on the ninth square, and he watched it fall on the eighth and jump to the seventh, motherfucker, now was perhaps the moment to ask himself what he was going to do when the door would open and half the bedroom would go wild and he would hear Traveler's muffled exclamation, if it was an exclamation and if it was muffled. Basically he had been stupid to reject the Heftpistole, because aside from the lamp which didn't weigh anything and the chair, in the corner by the window there wasn't the least kind of defensive arsenal, and with the lamp and the chair he wouldn't get very far if Traveler managed to breach the two lines of watery basins and missed skating on the ball bearings. But it wouldn't happen, the strategy relied on that; defensive arms cannot be of the same nature as offensive arms. The threads, for example, they would produce a terrible effect on Traveler as he advanced in the darkness and felt a sort of subtle resistance grow against his face, on his arms and legs, and he would get that insuperable loathing of a man who runs into a spider-web. Supposing that in two jumps he knocked down all the threads, supposing that he didn't put his shoe in a watery basin and didn't skate on a ball bearing, he would finally reach the sector of the window and in spite of the darkness he would recognize the motionless silhouette on the edge of the desk. It was remotely probable that he would reach there, but if he did, there was no doubt that a Heftpistole would be of absolutely no use to Oliveira, not so much because Number 18 had spoken of staples, but because there was not going to be an encounter as Traveler might imagine it perhaps but something totally different, something that he was incapable of imagining but which he knew with as much certainty as if he were seeing or living it, a slipping of the black mass that came from outside against that which he knew without knowing, an incalculable disengagement between black mass Traveler and what was there smoking on the edge of the desk. Something like waking against sleep (the hours of sleep and wakefulness, someone had said one day, have not been joined into unity yet), but to say wakefulness against sleep was to admit until the end that there existed no hope at all for unity. On the other hand it might happen that Traveler's arrival would be like an extreme point from which to try again the jump of one into the other and at the same time of the other into the one, but that jump would be precisely the opposite of a collision, Oliveira was sure that Traveler territory could not reach him even if he fell on top of him, beat him, tore his undershirt to shreds, spit in his eyes and on his mouth, twisted his arms, and threw him out of the window. But a Heftpistole was of absolutely no use against the territory, since from what he could gather from Number 18 it might turn out to be a buttonhook or something like it, what good was a Traveler knife or a Traveler punch, poor inadequate Heftpistoles to bridge the unbridgeable distance from one body to another in which one body begins by denying the other, or the other denies the one? If in fact Traveler could kill him (and there was some reason for his mouth being dry and for the fact that the palms of his hands were sweating abominably), everything moved to deny that possibility on one plane in which its occurrence in fact would not have any more confirmation than for the murderer. But it was better yet to feel that the murderer was not a murderer, that the territory was not even a territory, to thin and minimize and underestimate the territory so that so much operetta and so much ashtray breaking to pieces on the floor would be nothing more than a noise and contemptible consequences. If he affirmed himself (by fighting against fear) in that total unattachment in relation to the territory, defence was then the best attack, the worst thrust would come from the hilt and not from the blade. Why was he winning himself over with metaphors at that hour of the night when the only sensible senseless thing to do was to leave his eyes alone to watch over the purplish lines at the bottom of the door, that thermometric ray of the territory.

At ten minutes to four Oliveira got up, moving his shoulders to get the stiffness out of them, and went over to sit on the windowsill. It amused him to think that if he had had the good luck to go crazy that night, the liquidation of the Traveler territory would have been absolute. A solution not at all in accord with his pride and his intention of resisting any form of surrender. In any case, to imagine Ferraguto inscribing his name in the register of patients, putting a number on the door and a magic eye to spy on him at night . . . And Talita preparing capsules in the pharmacy, going across the courtyard with great care so as not to step on the hopscotch again. Not to mention Manú, poor fellow, terribly disconsolate over his stupidity and his absurd attempt. Turning his back on the courtyard, reclining dangerously in the windowsill, Oliveira felt fear begin to leave him, and that was bad. He didn't take his eyes off the beam of light, but with every breath a contentment penetrated him finally without words, without anything to do with the territory, and the joy was precisely that, to feel how the territory was giving in. It didn't matter how long; with every breath the warm air of the world was reconciled with him as had already happened one time or another before in his life. He didn't even feel the need to smoke, for a few minutes he had made peace with himself and that was the equivalent of abolishing the territory, of conquering without a battle and of wanting to fall asleep finally in the moment of wakening, on that line where wakefulness and sleep first mixed their waters and discovered that there was no such thing as different waters; but that was bad, naturally, naturally all of that had to see itself interrupted by the brusque interposition of two black sectors halfway across the ray of light and a fussy scratching on the door. "You asked for it," Oliveira thought, slipping down until he was tight against the desk. "The truth is that if I had gone on another minute like that I would have dropped head first onto the hopscotch. Come right in, Manú, it all means you don't exist or I don't exist, or that we're so stupid we believe this and we're going to kill each other, brother, this time it's the payoff, that's all there is to it."

"Come right in," he repeated aloud, but the door didn't open. The soft scratching continued, probably it was a pure coincidence that down below there was someone beside the fountain, a woman with her back turned with long hair and arms hanging by her sides, absorbed in the contemplation of the trickle of water. At that hour and in that darkness it could have just as easily been La Maga as Talita or any one of the madwomen, even Pola if one really thought about it. Nothing stopped him from staring at the woman with her back towards him, since if Traveler decided to come in the defences would function automatically and there would be more than enough time to stop looking at the courtyard and face him. At any rate, it was rather strange that Traveler should keep on scratching at the door as if to ascertain whether he was sleeping (it couldn't be Pola, because Pola's neck was shorter and her hips were more well-defined), unless he too for his part had devised a special system of attack (it could be La Maga or Talita, they looked so much alike and much more so at night and from the third storey) designed to make him lose his mind, knock him off his position on the square (at least from one to eight, because he hadn't been able to get beyond eight, he would never reach Heaven, he would never enter his kibbutz). "What are you waiting for Manú?" Oliveira thought. "What good is all this doing us?" It was Talita of course, who was now looking up and stood motionless again when he stuck his bare arm out of the window and moved it tiredly from side to side.

"Come over here, Maga," Oliveira said. "You look so much alike from here that your name can be changed."

"Close that window," Talita said.

"Impossible, the heat is terrible and your husband is out there scratching on the door in a fearsome way. It's what they call a conjunction of annoying circumstances. But don't you worry, pick up a pebble and try again, who can tell but that with one . . . "

The drawer, the ashtray, and the chair all fell onto the floor at the same time. Crouching down a little, Oliveira looked blinded at the purple rectangle that replaced the door, the black shape moving around, he heard Traveler's curse. The noise must have woken everybody up.

"You simple bastard," Traveler said in the doorway. "Do you want the Boss to throw us all out?"

"He's preaching to me," Oliveira informed Talita. "He always was like a father to me."

"Close the window, please," Talita said.

"There's nothing needed so much as an open window," Oliveira said. "Listen to your husband, one can observe that he's put one foot in the water. He must have a face full of threads, he doesn't know what to do."

"You son of a bitch," Traveler was saying, lashing out in the darkness and pulling threads off himself on all sides. "Turn on the light, God damn it."

"He hasn't fallen on the floor yet," Oliveira informed. "The ball bearings are letting me down."

"Don't lean out like that!" Talita shouted, raising her arms. With his back to the window, with his head turned around to see her and talk to her, Oliveira was leaning farther and farther back. Cuca Ferraguto came running out into the courtyard, and only at that moment did Oliveira realize that it was no longer night-time, Cuca's bathrobe was the same colour as the stones of the courtyard and the walls of the pharmacy. Allowing himself a reconnaissance of the battlefield, he looked into the darkness and observed that in spite of his offensive difficulties, Traveler had decided to close the door. Between two curses he heard the sound of the latch.

"That's the way I like it, hey," Oliveira said. "Alone in the centre of the ring like two men."

"Shit on your soul," Traveler said furiously. "One of my slippers is soaked through, and that's the thing that can upset me worse than anything in the world. Turn on the light at least, you can't see a thing."

"The ambush at Cancha Rayada was something like this," Oliveira said. "You must understand that I'm not going to sacrifice the advantages of my position. Be thankful that I'm answering you, because I don't really have to do that. I had my lessons on the rifle range too, brother."

He heard Traveler breathe heavily. Outside there was a slamming of doors, Ferraguto's voice mixed in with other questions and answers. Traveler's silhouette was becoming more and more visible; everything was drawing a number and fitting into its place, five basins, three spittoons, dozens of ball bearings. They could almost see each other now in that light that was like the dove in the hands of the madman.

"Well," Traveler said, picking up the fallen chair and sitting down on it without much desire. "If you could explain a little of this mess to me."

"It'll be a little hard like. Talking, you know . . . "

"When you want to talk you always find the most unbelievable moments," Traveler said in a rage. "When we're not riding horseback on two planks at ninety degrees in the shade, you catch me with one foot in the water and these damnable threads."

"But always in symmetrical positions," Oliveira said. "Like two twins playing on a seesaw, or more simply like anybody in front of a mirror. Don't you notice it, *Doppelgänger*?"

Without answering Traveler took a cigarette out of his pyjama pocket and lit it while Oliveira took out another and lit it almost at the same time. They looked at each other and began to laugh.

"You're completely off your rocker," Traveler said. "This time there's no way to tell you to turn. To imagine that I . . . "

"Leave the word imagination in peace," Oliveira said. "Limit yourself to the observation that I took my precautions, but that you came. Not someone else. You. At four o'clock in the morning."

"Talita told me, and I thought . . . But do you really believe . . . ?"

"Underneath it all it's probably necessary, Manú. You thought that you got up to come and calm me down, give me assurances. If I had been sleeping you would have come in without any trouble at all, like anybody who goes up to the mirror without any difficulties, of course, one goes quietly up to the mirror with the brush in his hand, and suppose that instead of the brush it was that thing you have there in your pyjamas . . . "

"I always carry it," Traveler said indignantly. "Or do you think we're in some kind of kindergarten here? If you go around unarmed it's because you don't know what's up."

"So finally," Oliveira said, sitting on the edge of the window again and waving his hand at Talita and Cuca, "what I think of all this doesn't matter very much next to what has to be, whether we like it or not. It's been so long that we've been the same dog chasing his tail. It's not that we hate each other; on the contrary. There are other things that use us as playthings, the white pawn and the black pawn, something like that. Let's call it two ways, the necessity that one must be abolished in the other and vice versa."

"I don't hate you," Traveler said. "It's just that you've got me boxed into a place where I don't know what to do any more."

"*Mutatis mutandi*, you met me at the dock with something that looked like an armistice, a white flag, a sad incitement to forget. I don't hate you either, brother, but I denounce you, and that's what you call being boxed in."

"I'm alive," Traveler said looking into his eyes. "Being alive always seems to be the price of something. And you don't want to pay anything. You never wanted to. A kind of existential puritan, a purist. Caesar or nothing, that kind of radical demand. Do you think I'm not surprised at you in my own sort of way? Do you think I'm not surprised that you haven't committed suicide? You're the real *Doppelgänger*, because you're like something disembodied, you're a will in the form of a weather vane, up there. I want this, I want that, I want north and south and everything all at the same time, I want La Maga, I want Talita, and then the gentleman visits the morgue and plants a kiss on his best friend's wife. Everything because realities and memories are mixed up in him to such a non-Euclidean extent."

Oliveira shrugged his shoulders, but he looked at Traveler to make him feel that it was not a gesture of disdain. How could he transmit to him something of that thing that in the territory facing him they called a kiss, a kiss on Talita, a kiss he gave La Maga or Pola, that other game of mirrors like the game of turning his head towards the window and looking at La Maga standing there next to the hopscotch while Cuca and Remorino and Ferraguto, crowding around the door, seemed to be waiting for Traveler to come to the window and announce to them that all was well, and that a capsule of Nembutal or at best a straitjacket for a little while, until the boy got over his fit. The knocks on the door didn't contribute much to understanding either. If at least Manú were capable of feeling that nothing he was thinking made any sense from the window side, that it was only worth something on the basin and ball bearing side, and if the person beating on the door with both his fists would be quiet for just a minute, perhaps then . . . But all he could do was look at La Maga so beautiful beside the hopscotch, and wish that she would move the piece from one square to the other, from earth to Heaven.

" . . . so non-Euclidean."

"I've been waiting for you all this time," Oliveira said tiredly. "You're probably aware that I wasn't going to let myself be disembowelled just like that. Everybody knows what he has to do, Manú. If you want an explanation of what happened down there . . . just that it won't have anything to do with this, and you know that. You know that, *Doppelgänger*, you know that. What difference does the kiss make to you, and what difference does it make to her either? That's between the two of you, after all."

"Open up! Open up immediately!"

"They're taking it rather badly," Traveler said, getting up. "Shall we open up for them? It must be Ovejero."

"As far as I'm concerned . . . "

"He'll want to give you an injection. Talita must have roused up the whole loony-bin."

"Women are too much," Oliveira said. "Look at her there, so well-behaved next to the hopscotch . . . Better not open up, Manú, we're doing fine just the way we are."

Traveler went to the door and put his mouth to the keyhole. God-damned fools, why don't they stop fucking around with those shouts they pick up in horror movies. He and Oliveira were doing fine and they would open up when it was time. They would be better off making coffee for everybody, there was no living in that clinic.

It was audible enough so that Ferraguto was not convinced, but the voice of Ovejero imposed itself over his like a wise persistent rumble, and finally they left the door alone. For the moment the only sign of upset was the people in the courtyard and the lights on the fourth floor that went on and off continuously, Number 43's happy habit. Shortly afterwards, Ovejero and Ferraguto reappeared in the courtyard, and from there they looked at Oliveira seated on the window and he greeted them, excusing himself for being in his vest. Number 18 had gone over to Ovejero and was telling him something about the Heftpistole, and Ovejero seemed very interested and looked at Oliveira with professional attention, as if he no longer was his best opponent at poker, something which rather amused Oliveira. They had opened almost all the windows on the second floor, and several patients were participating with great vivacity in everything that was going on, which was not very much. La Maga had raised her right arm to attract Oliveira's attention, as if that were necessary, and she was asking him to call Traveler to the window. Oliveira explained to her in the cleverest way he could that it was impossible because the window zone belonged exclusively to the defence, but that perhaps they could arrange a truce. He added that the gesture of calling him by raising her arm made him think of actresses of the past and especially opera singers like Emmy Destinn, Melba, Marjorie Lawrence, Muzio, Bori, and why not Theda Bara and Nita Naldi, he kept spouting names with enormous pleasure and Talita lowered her arm and then raised it again in supplication, Eleonora Duse, naturally, Vilma Banky, Garbo exactly, but of course, and a photograph of Sarah Bernhardt that as a boy he had pasted in a scrapbook, and Karsavina, Baronova, women, those eternal gestures, that perpetuation of destiny although in that case it might not be possible to accede to the pleasant request.

Ferraguto and Cuca were shouting rather contradictory manifestations when Ovejero, who with his sleepy face listened to everything, motioned them to be quiet so that Talita could get through to Oliveira. An operation which was of no avail because Oliveira, after listening for the seventh time to La Maga's plea, turned his back on them and they saw him (although they could not hear him) talking to the invisible Traveler.

"They want you to come over here, you know."

"Look, in any case, just give me a minute. I can go under the threads."

"Nuts," said Oliveira. "It's the last line of defence, if you break it we'll be into hard infighting."

"OK," Traveler said, sitting down on the chair. "Keep on piling up useless words."

"They're not useless," Oliveira said. "If you want to come over here you don't have to ask my permission. I think that's clear."

"You swear you won't jump?"

Oliveira kept looking at him as if Traveler were a giant panda.

"At last," he said. "The fat's in the fire. There down below, La Maga is thinking the same thing. And I thought that in spite of everything they might know me a little."

"It's not La Maga," Traveler said. "You know perfectly well it's not La Maga."

"It's not La Maga," Oliveira said. "I know perfectly well it's not La Maga. And you're the standard-bearer, the herald of surrender, of the return to home and order. You're beginning to make me feel sorry, old man."

"Forget about me," Traveler said bitterly. "What I want is for you to give me your word you won't do anything idiotic."

"Take notice that if I jump," Oliveira said, "I'm going to land right on Heaven."

"Come on over here, Horacio, and let me talk to Ovejero. I can fix things up, tomorrow everybody will have forgotten about all this."

"He learned it all in the psychiatry manual," Oliveira said almost startled. "He's a student who has great retentive powers."

"Listen," Traveler said. "If you don't let me come to the window I'm going to have to open the door and that'll be worse."

"It's all the same to me, their coming in is one thing and their getting over here is another."

"You mean that if they try to grab you you'll jump."

"It might mean that from over on your side."

"Please," Traveler said, taking a step forward. "Can't you see it's a bad dream? They're going to think you're really crazy, they're going to think I really did want to kill you."

Oliveira leaned out a little more, and Traveler stopped at the second line of watery basins. Although he had sent the ball bearings flying with a kick, he stopped advancing. Amid the shrieks from Cuca and Talita, Oliveira straightened up and made a pacifying gesture to them. As if defeated, Traveler brought the chair up a little and sat down. They were pounding on the door again, less vigorously than before.

"Don't rack your brains any more," Oliveira said. "Why are you looking for explanations of it, old man? The only real difference between you and me at this moment is that I'm alone. That's why the best thing is for you to go downstairs and rejoin your people, and we'll keep on talking out of the window like good friends. Around eight o'clock I intend to cut out; Gekrepten agreed to wait for me with pancakes and *mate*."

"You're not alone, Horacio. Maybe you wanted to be alone out of pure vanity, play the Buenos Aires Maldoror. You spoke about a *Doppelgänger*, didn't you? Now you can see that someone is following you, that someone is like you even though he's on the other side of your damnable threads."

"It's too bad," Oliveira said, "that you have such a prissy idea of vanity. That's where it lies, making yourself an idea of something, no matter what the cost. Aren't you capable of sensing even for a single second that this might not be like that?"

"Let's say that's what I think. Just the same, there you are leaning next to an open window."

"If you really suspected that this can't be this way, if you really got to the heart of the artichoke . . . Nobody asks you to deny what you're seeing, but if you were only capable of pushing a little, understand, with the tip of your toe . . ."

"If it were only so easy," Traveler said, "if it were only a question of hanging up some idiotic threads . . . I don't say that you haven't given your push, but look at the results."

"What's wrong with them? At least we have the window open and we're breathing in this fabulous dawn, feel the freshness that comes up at this hour. And down below everybody is strolling about in the courtyard, it's extraordinary, they're getting exercise without knowing it. Cuca, take a peek, and the Boss, that type of gentle marmot. And your wife, who is laziness personified. For your part you can't deny that you were never as awake as right now. And when I say awake you understand, right?"

"I wonder if it might not be just the opposite, old man."

"Oh, those are easy solutions, fantastic stories for anthologies. If you were capable of seeing the thing from the other side you probably wouldn't want to move away from there any more. If you were to leave the territory, let's say from square one to square two, or from two to three . . . It's so difficult, *Doppelgänger*, I've spent all night tossing cigarette butts and I can't get beyond square eight. We'd all like to have the millenary kingdom, a kind of Arcadia where it would probably be much more unhappy than here, because it's not a question of happiness, *Doppelgänger*, but where there wouldn't be any more of this dirty game of substitutions that occupies us for fifty or sixty years, and where we could really hold out our hands instead of repeating the gesture of fear and wanting to know if the other person has a knife hidden between his fingers. Speaking of substitutions, it wouldn't seem strange to me at all if you and I were the same, one on each side. Since you called me vain, it appears that I've chosen the more favourable side, but who can tell, Manú. One thing I do know and that's that I can't be on your side any more, everything falls apart in my hands, I get into every kind of mess that can make you go mad, supposing it was that easy. But you're in harmony with the territory and don't want to understand this coming and going, I give a push and something happens to me, then five thousand years of rotten genes draw me back and I fall into the territory again, I splash for two weeks, two years, fifteen years . . . One day I stick my finger into habit and it's incredible how one's finger sinks into habit and comes out the other side, it looks as if I'm finally going to get to the last square and suddenly a woman drowns, let's say, or I get an attack, an attack of useless pity, because that business of pity . . . I mentioned substitutions to you, didn't I? What filth, Manú. Look up that business of substitutions in Dostoevsky. In a word, five thousand years pull me back again and I have to start all over. That's why I feel that you're my *Doppelgänger*, because all the time I'm coming and going from your territory to mine, if I really ever do get to mine, and in those weary passages it seems to me that you're my form staying there looking at me with pity, you're the five thousand years of man piled up into six feet, looking at that clown who wants to get out of his square. Amen."

"Stop fucking around," Traveler shouted at the people pounding on the door again. "Can't anybody talk peacefully in this madhouse?'

"You're wonderful, brother," Oliveira said, moved.

"In any case," Traveler said, moving his chair up a little, "you're not going to deny that you've gone too far this time. Transubstantiations and other plants are all OK but this trick of yours is going to cost us all our jobs, and I'm sorry about it especially for Talita's sake. You can talk all you want about La Maga, but I'm the one who has to feed my wife."

"You're absolutely right," Oliveira said. "One forgets he has a job and things like that. Do you want me to talk to Ferraguto? There he is over by the fountain. I'm sorry, Manú, I didn't want La Maga and you . . . "

"Do you think it's right now to call her La Maga? Don't lie, Horacio."

"I know she's Talita, but a while ago she was La Maga. She's two people, just like us."

"They call that being crazy," Traveler said.

"Everything is called something, you choose and let it go. If you'll excuse me I must attend to the people down below, because they can't take any more of this."

"I'm leaving," Traveler said, getting up.

"That's more like it," said Oliveira. "It's much better for you to leave and not bend your knees the way you are, because I'm going to explain what will happen, you adore explanations just like all the other sons of the five thousand years. As soon as you jump on me, carried away by friendship and your diagnosis, I'll move to one side, because I don't know if you remember the time I used to practise judo with the boys on the Calle Anchorena, and what will happen is that you'll continue your trip through this window and end up as a piece of mucus on square four, and then only if you're lucky because it's more likely that you won't even get beyond two."

Traveler looked at him, and Oliveira saw that his eyes were filling with tears. He made a gesture as if to stroke his hair from a distance.

Traveler waited another second, and then he went to the door and opened it. As soon as Remorino (two other attendants could be seen behind him) tried to enter he grabbed him by the shoulders and shoved him back.

"Leave him alone," he ordered. "He'll be all right in a while. We have to leave him alone, oh fuck it all."

Disregarding the dialogue that had rapidly ascended to tetralogue, hexalogue, and dodecalogue, Oliveira closed his eyes and thought that everything was so good like that, that Traveler really was his brother. He heard the noise of the door as it closed, the voices going away. The door opened again, coinciding with his eyelids which he lifted with great effort.

"Bolt the door," Traveler said. "I don't trust them."

"Thanks," said Oliveira. "Go on down to the courtyard. Talita's very upset."

He went under the few surviving threads and threw the bolt. Before returning to the window he put his face in the water in the sink and drank like an animal, swallowing and licking and snorting. Down below one could hear Remorino's commands as he ordered the patients to their rooms. When he went back, fresh and peaceful, he saw that Traveler was next to Talita and that he had put his arm around her waist. After what Traveler had just done, everything had something like a marvellous feeling of conciliation and that senseless but vivid and present harmony could not be violated, could no longer be falsified, basically Traveler was what he might well have been with a little less cursed imagination, he was the man of the territory, the incurable mistake of the species gone astray, but how much beauty in the mistake and in the five thousand years of false and precarious territory, how much beauty in those eyes that had filled with tears and in that voice that had advised him: "Bolt the door, I don't trust them," how much love in that arm that held the waist of a woman. "Probably," Oliveira thought while he answered the friendly gestures of Dr Ovejero and Ferraguto (a little less friendly), "the only possible way to escape from the territory is to plunge into it over one's head." He was aware that as soon as he got that feeling he would glimpse the image of a man taking an old woman along by the arm through rainy and freezing streets. "Who can tell," he said to himself. "Who can tell if maybe I haven't been staying on the edge, and that there probably was a passage. Manú would have found it, certainly, but the idiot thing is that Manú will never look for it and I, on the other hand . . ."

"Hey, Oliveira, why don't you come on down and have some coffee?" Ferraguto proposed to the visible displeasure of Ovejero. "You've already won the bet, don't you think? Look at Cuca, how upset she is."

"Don't get upset, señora," Oliveira said. "With your experience in the circus you're not going to go soft on me over some nonsense."

"Oh, Oliveira, you and Traveler are awful," Cuca said. "Why don't you do what my husband says? I was just thinking that we all ought to sit down together for some coffee."

"Yes, hey, come on down," Ovejero said, trying to appear casual. "I need your advice on a couple of matters that have to do with some French books."

"I can hear quite well from up here," Oliveira said.

"OK, old man," Ovejero said. "You come on down when you want to, we're going to have some breakfast."

"With nice hot croissants," Cuca said. "Shall we go and make some coffee, Talita?"

"Don't be an arse," Talita said, and in the extraordinary silence that followed her admonition, the meeting of the looks of Traveler and Oliveira was as if two birds had collided in flight and all mixed up together had fallen into square nine, or at least that was how it was enjoyed by those involved. Cuca and Ferraguto were breathing heavily during all this, and finally Cuca opened her mouth to shriek: "Why, what's the meaning of such insolence?" while Ferraguto stuck out his chest and looked Traveler up and down while the latter at the same time was looking at his wife with a mixture of admiration and censure until Ovejero found the appropriate scientific escape and said dryly: "*Hysteria matinensis yugulata*, let's go inside, I have to hand out some pills," at the same time that Number 18, violating Remorino's orders, came out into the courtyard to announce that Number 31 was upset and that there was a telephone call from Mar del Plata. His violent expulsion at the hands of Remorino helped the administrators and Ovejero to evacuate the courtyard without excessive loss of prestige.

"My, my, my," said Oliveira, teetering on the window, "and I thought that pharmacists had such good manners."

"Did you notice?" Traveler said. "She was glorious."

"She sacrificed herself for me," Oliveira said. "The other one is never going to forgive her, not even on her deathbed."

"That really worries me," Talita said. "'With nice hot croissants', get a load of that."

"And what about Ovejero?" Traveler asked. "French books! The only thing missing was for them to tempt you with a banana. I'm surprised you didn't tell them all to go to hell."

That's the way it was, the harmony lasted incredibly long, there were no words that could answer the goodness of those two down there below, looking at him and talking to him from the hopscotch, because Talita had stopped in square three without realizing it, and Traveler had one foot in six, so that the only thing left to do was to move his right hand a little in a timid salute and stay there looking at La Maga, at Manú, telling himself that there was some meeting after all, even though it might only last just for that terribly sweet instant in which the best thing without any doubt at all would be to lean over just a little bit farther out and let himself go, paff the end.

* * *

(–135)

From Diverse Sides

Expendable Chapters

57

"I'm warming up some ideas for when Adgalle arrives. What do you think about my taking her to the Club some night? Étienne and Ronald would be charmed, she's so mad."

"Take her."

"You would have liked her too."

"Why do you talk as if I were dead?"

"I don't know," Ossip said. "I really don't know. You have a look about you."

"This morning I was telling Étienne about some very pretty dreams. Right now I'm getting them all mixed up inside me with some other memories while you go on about the burial with such tender words. It really must have been a moving ceremony, eh. It's so very strange to be able to be in three places at once, but that's just what's happening to me this afternoon, it must be the influence of Morelli. Yes, yes, now I'm going to tell you about it. In four places at once, now that I think about it. I'm getting close to ubiquity, and going crazy is just one step away . . . You're right, I probably won't be able to meet Adgalle, I'll be gone to hell long before."

"Zen has a precise explanation for the possibilities of preubiquity, something similar to the feeling you've just described, if in fact you did have such a feeling."

"That's what it is. I've returned from four simultaneous points: the dream this morning, still alive and wriggling. Some interludes with Pola which I'll spare you, your gaudy description of the kid's burial, and now I realize that all at the same time I've been answering Traveler, a friend in Buenos Aires who never in his fucking life understood a few lines of poetry of mine which began like this, listen to them: 'Between sleep and wakefulness, diving into washbasins.' And it's so easy, if you think about it a little, you ought to understand it. When you wake up, with the remains of a paradise half-seen in dreams hanging down over you like the hair on someone who's been drowned: terrible nausea, anxiety, a feeling of the precarious, the false, especially the useless. You fall inward, while you brush your teeth you really are a diver into washbasins, it's as if the white sink were absorbing you, as if you were slipping down through that hole that carries off tartar, mucus, rheum, dandruff, saliva, and you let yourself go in the hope that maybe you'll return to the other thing, to what you were before you woke up, and it's still floating around, is still inside you, is you yourself, but then it starts to go away . . . Yes, you fall inward for a moment, until the defences of wakefulness, oh pretty words, oh language, take charge and stop you."

"A typical existential experience," Gregorovius said petulantly.

"Naturally, but everything depends on the dosage. In my case the washbasin really sucks me in."

(–70)

58

"You were very wise to come," Gekrepten said as she changed the *yerba.* "You're better off here at home, especially because of the environment over there, what did you expect. You should have taken two or three days off."

"I think you're right," Oliveira said. "And more important than all that, old girl. These fried cakes are sublime."

"How lucky that you like them. Don't eat too many or you'll get indigestion."

"Nothing to worry about," Ovejero said, lighting a cigarette. "Have a good nap now and tonight you'll be in prime condition for drawing a royal flush and lots of aces."

"Don't move," Talita said. "It's incredible how you can't be still."

"My wife is so upset," Ferraguto said.

"Have another fried cake," said Gekrepten.

"Don't give him anything except fruit juice," Ovejero ordered.

"National Corporation of the Learned in Suitable Sciences and their Houses of Science," Oliveira mocked.

"Seriously now, don't eat anything until tomorrow," Ovejero said.

"Here's one with lots of sugar on it," said Gekrepten.

"Try to get some sleep," Traveler said.

"Hey, Remorino, stick around the door and don't let Number 18 bother him," Ovejero said. "He's developed a terrible fixation and all he talks about is some kind of pistol."

"If you want to sleep I'll close the blinds," Gekrepten said, "then you won't hear Don Crespo's radio."

"No, leave them," Oliveira said. "They're playing something by Falú."

"It's already five o'clock," Talita said. "Don't you feel like sleeping?"

"Give him a fresh compress," Traveler said, "that seems to relieve him."

"The *mate* will be ready soon," Gekrepten said. "Do you want me to go out and pick up the *Noticias Gráficas*?"

"Fine," Oliveira said. "And a pack of cigarettes."

"It's hard for him to get to sleep," Traveler said, "but he'll be able to get through the whole night now, Ovejero gave him a double dose."

"Behave yourself, love," Gekrepten said, "I'll be right back. We're going to have steak tonight, how does that suit you?"

"With a tossed salad," Oliveira said.

"He's breathing better," Talita said.

"And I'll make you some rice and milk," Gekrepten said. "I didn't like the look on your face when you arrived."

"The tram was packed," Oliveira said. "You know what the platform is like at eight in the morning and with all this heat."

"Do you really think he'll stay asleep, Manú?"

"As far as I want to believe in something, yes."

"Then let's go up and see the Boss, he's waiting to fire us."

"My wife is so upset," Ferraguto said.

"Why, what's the meaning of such insolence?!" Cuca shouted.

"They were great people," Ovejero said.

"You don't find many like them," said Remorino.

"He refused to believe me when I told him he needed a Heftpistole," said Number 18.

"Beat it back to your room or I'll give you an enema," Ovejero said.

"Death to the dog!" Number 18 said.

(–131)

59

Then, to pass the time, they catch fish they cannot eat; to avoid the rotting of the fishes in the air, notices have been posted all along the beach telling the fishermen to bury them in the sand just as soon as they have been caught.

CLAUDE LÉVI-STRAUSS, *Tristes Tropiques*

(–41)

60

Morelli had been thinking about a list of acknowledgements which he never got around to including in his published works. It had several names: Jelly Roll Morton, Robert Musil, Daisetz Teitaro Suzuki, Raymond Roussel, Kurt Schwitters, Vieira da Silva, Akutagawa, Anton Webern, Greta Garbo, José Lezama Lima, Buñuel, Louis Armstrong, Borges, Michaux, Dino Buzzati, Max Ernst, Pevsner, Gilgamesh (?), Garcilaso, Arcimboldo, René Clair, Piero di Cosimo, Wallace Stevens, Isak Dinesen. The names of Rimbaud, Picasso, Chaplin, Alban Berg and others had a very fine line drawn through them, as though they were too obvious to be mentioned. But in the end he should have done the same to all of them, because Morelli had decided not to include the list in any of his volumes.

(–26)

61

An inconclusive note by Morelli

I will never be able to escape the feeling that there, clinging to my face, intertwined among my fingers, there is something like a dazzling explosion towards the light, an invasion of me in the direction of the other thing or of the other thing towards me, something infinitely crystalline that could coalesce and become total light outside time or space. Like a door of opal and diamond out of which one starts to be the thing one truly is and does not want and does not know and is not able to be.

There is nothing new about that thirst and that suspicion, but there is an ever greater confusion when I face the ersatz things offered me by this day-and-night intelligence, this archive of facts and memories, these passions where I go about leaving pieces of time and skin, these surmises so much underneath and far away from those other surmises there next to me, stuck to my face, prevision already mixed with vision, the denunciation of that feigned freedom with which I move through streets and years.

Since I am no more than this body which has already putrefied in some point of future time, these bones that write anachronically, I feel that the body is demanding itself, demanding from its consciousness the still inconceivable operation that would no longer be putrefaction. This body that I am has the prescience of a state in which as it denies itself as such, and as it simultaneously denies the objective correlative as such, its own consciousness would accede to a state outside the body and outside the world which would be the true accession to being. My body will be, not mine Morelli, not I, the one who in nineteen hundred and fifty has already putrefied in nineteen hundred and eighty, my body will be because behind that door of light (what can we call that besieging certainty stuck to the face) being will be something other than bodies and, than bodies and souls and, than I and the other thing, than yesterday and tomorrow. Everything depends on . . . (a sentence scratched out).

Melancholy finale: A *satori* is instantaneous and resolves everything. But in order to reach it one would have to unwind history, both the one outside and the one inside. *Trop tard pour moi. Crever en italien, voire en occidental, c'est tout ce qui me reste. Mon petit café-crème le matin, si agréable . . .*

(–33)

62

At one time Morelli had been planning a book that never got beyond a few scattered notes. It can be summed up best in this way: "Psychology, a word with the air of an old woman about it. A Swede is working on a chemical theory of thought.* Chemistry, electromagnetism, the secret flow of living matter, everything returns strangely to evoke the idea of mana; in a like manner, on the edge of social behaviour, one might suspect an interaction of a different nature, a billiard game that certain individuals play or are played at, a drama with no Oedipuses, no Rastignacs, no Phaedras, an *impersonal* drama to the extent that the consciences and the passions of the

* *L'Express*, Paris, n.d.

Two months ago a Swedish neurobiologist, Holger Hyden, of the University of Göteborg, presented to the most eminent specialists in the world, gathered in San Francisco, his theories on the chemical nature of mental processes. According to Hyden, the act of thinking, of remembering, of feeling, or of making a decision is manifested by the appearance in the brain, and in the nerves connecting it with other organs, of certain particular molecules which the nerve cells manufacture as a result of the external stimulus. (. . .) The Swedish team was able to effect the delicate separation of the two types of cell in live rabbit tissue, weighed them (in millionths of a millionth of a gram), and determined through analysis the way in which these cells utilized their fuel in various cases.

One of the essential functions of neurons is the transmission of nervous impulses. This transmission operates by means of almost instantaneous electrochemical reactions. It is not easy to surprise a nerve cell at work, but it appears that the Swedes have done so by means of the careful use of certain methods.

It has been proved that the stimulus becomes transformed in the neurons into an increment of certain proteins whose molecules will vary according to the nature of the message. At the same time, the number of proteins in the satellite cells is reduced, as if they were sacrificing their reserves for the sake of the neuron. The information contained in the protein molecule is converted, according to Hyden, into the impulse which the neuron passes on to its neighbours.

The higher functions of the brain – memory and the reasoning faculties – are explained, according to Hyden, by the particular form of the protein molecules characters cannot be seen as having been compromised except a posteriori. As if the subliminal levels were those that wind and unravel the ball of yarn which is the group that has been compromised in the play. Or to please the Swede: as if certain individuals had cut into the deep chemistry of others without having meant to and vice versa, so that the most curious and interesting chain reactions, fissions, and transmutations would result.

"Things being as they are, all that is needed is a pleasant extrapolation in order to postulate a human group that thinks it is reacting psychologically in the classic sense of that tired old word, but which merely represents an instance in that flow of animated matter, in the infinite interactions of what we formerly called desires, sympathies, wills, convictions, and which appear here as something irreducible to all reason and all description: foreign occupying forces, advancing in the quest of their freedom of the city; a quest superior to ourselves as individuals and one which uses us for its own ends, a dark necessity of evading the state of Homo sapiens towards . . . which Homo? Because *sapiens* is another tired old word, one of those that one must scrub clean before attempting to use it with any sort of meaning.

---

which correspond to each type of stimulus. Each neuron in the brain contains millions of different molecules of ribonucleic acid, which are distinguished by the disposition of their basic constituent elements. Each molecule of ribonucleic acid (RNA) corresponds to a well-defined protein, the way a key is perfectly adapted to a lock. The nucleic acids tell the neuron the make-up of the protein molecule it is to form. According to the Swedish researchers, these molecules are the chemical translation of thoughts.

Memory would correspond, therefore, to the ordering in the brain of the nucleic acid molecules, which play the same role as perforated cards in modern computers. For example, the impulse which corresponds to the note mi as it is picked up by the ear, will slide rapidly along from one neuron to another until it has reached all of those containing the molecules of RNA corresponding to that particular stimulus. The cells immediately construct molecules of the corresponding protein which that acid governs, and we have the auditory perception of the note.

The richness and variety of thought is explained by the fact that an average brain contains some ten thousand million neurons, each of which contains in turn several million molecules of various nucleic acids; the number of possible combinations is astronomical. This theory, furthermore, has the advantage of explaining why it has not been possible to discover in the brain clearly defined and special zones for each one of its higher functions; since each neuron has several nucleic acids at hand, it can take part in various mental processes, and evoke diverse thoughts and memories.

"If I were to write this book, standard behaviour (including the most unusual, its deluxe category) would be inexplicable by means of current instrumental psychology. The actors would appear to be unhealthy or complete idiots. Not that they would show themselves incapable of current *challenges and responses*: love, jealousy, pity, and so on down the line, but in them something which Homo sapiens keeps subliminal would laboriously open up a road as if a third eye* were blinking out with effort from under the frontal bone. Everything would be a kind of disquiet, a continuous uprooting, a territory where psychological causality would yield disconcertedly, and those puppets would destroy each other or love each other or recognize each other without suspecting too much that life is trying to change its key in and through and by them, that a barely conceivable attempt is born in man as one other day there were being born the reason-key, the feeling-key, the pragmatism-key. That with each successive defeat there is an approach towards the final mutation, and that man only is in that he searches to be, plans to be, thumbing through words and modes of behaviour and joy sprinkled with blood and other rhetorical pieces like this one."

*Note by Wong (in pencil): "A metaphor chosen with the deliberate intent of suggesting the direction in which he is heading."

(–23)

63

"Don't move," Talita said. "You'd think that instead of a cold compress you were getting oil of vitriol."

"It's like a kind of electricity," Oliveira said.

"Don't talk nonsense."

"I can see all sorts of phosphorescences, it's like something by Norman McLaren."

"Raise your head a minute, the pillow's too low, I'm going to change it for you."

"It would be better if you left the pillow alone and changed my head," Oliveira said. "Surgery is still in its infancy, that you've got to admit."

(–88)

64

One of the times they had met in the Latin Quarter, Pola was looking at the pavement, practically everybody was looking at the pavement. They had to stop and study the profile of Napoleon, alongside it an excellent reproduction of Chartres, and a little farther on, a mare and her foal in a green field. The artists were two blond boys and an Indo-Chinese girl. The chalk box was full of ten- and twenty-franc pieces. From time to time one of the artists would crouch down to perfect some detail, and it was easy to see that at that instant the donations would increase.

"They're using the Penelope system, but without unweaving first," Oliveira said. "That lady, for example, she didn't loosen her purse-strings until little Tsong Tsong got down on the ground to retouch the blond with blue eyes. Work produces sentiment, it's a fact."

"Is her name Tsong Tsong?" Pola asked.

"How should I know. She has nice ankles."

"So much work and tonight the women who sweep the streets will come and it's all over."

"That's precisely why it's so good. Coloured chalk as an eschatological pattern, the theme for a thesis. If the municipal waterwagons didn't put an end to all of it at dawn, Tsong Tsong would come herself with a pail of water. The only thing that really ends is what starts over again in the morning. People throw coins without knowing that they're being cheated, because those pictures are really never erased. They may change pavements or colours, but they're already there in finished form in a hand, a box of chalk, a wise system of movements; if one of those boys were to spend the morning waving his arms around he would deserve ten francs just as much as when he draws Napoleon. But we want proofs. There they are. Give them twenty francs, don't be cheap."

"I already did before you got here."

"Admirable. Fundamentally we're placing those coins in the mouth of the dead, the propitiatory obolus. Homage to the ephemeral, so that cathedral may be a chalk image that a splash of water will carry off in one second. The coin is there, and the cathedral will be reborn tomorrow. We pay for immortality, we pay for things that last. *No money, no cathedral.* Are you made of chalk too?"

But Pola didn't answer him, and he put his arm around her shoulders and they walked Boul' Mich' up and Boul' Mich' down, before wandering slowly towards the Rue Dauphine. A world of coloured chalk was spinning around them and caught them up in its dance, fried potatoes in yellow chalk, red wine in red chalk, a pale soft sky in light blue chalk with a touch of green along the riverside. They tossed another coin in the cigar box to halt the flight of the cathedral, and with that very gesture they condemned it to be erased so it could be again, disappear under the splash of water and return chalk after chalk black and blue and yellow. The Rue Dauphine in grey chalk, the staircase carefully done in tones of brown chalk, the room with its lines of flight astutely drawn in bright green chalk, the curtains in white chalk, the bed with its serape where all the chalks *¡Viva México!*, love, its chalks yearning for the fixative that would keep them in the present, love in perfumed chalk, mouth in orange chalk, sadness and surfeit of colourless chalks spinning around in imperceptible dust, settling on the sleeping faces, on the exhausted chalk of the bodies.

"Everything falls apart when you take hold of it, even if you just look at it," Pola said. "You're like some terrible acid, I'm afraid of you."

"You put too much stock in a few metaphors."

"It isn't just that you say it, it's a way you have . . . I don't know, like a funnel. Sometimes I think I'm going to slip out of your arms and fall into a well. It's worse than dreaming that you're falling in space."

"Maybe you're not entirely lost," Oliveira said.

"Oh, leave me in peace. I know how to live, you know. I live very well the way I live. Here, with my things and my friends."

"Name them, name them. That helps. Give them names then you won't fall. There's the bedside table, the curtain hasn't run away from the window, Claudette is still at the same address, DAN-ton 34 I can't remember the rest, and your mother still writes to you from Aix-en-Provence. Everything's fine."

"You make me afraid, you South American monster," Pola said, squeezing up against him. "We'd agreed that here in my place there wouldn't be any talk about . . . "

"About coloured chalk."

"About all of that."

Oliveira lit a Gauloise and looked at the folded piece of paper on the bedside table.

"Is that the appointment for the tests?"

"Yes, he wants me to have them done immediately. Feel here, it's worse than last week."

It was almost night and Pola looked like a figure out of Bonnard, stretched out on the bed which was being wrapped in a yellowish green by the last light from the window. "The street-sweeper at dawn," Oliveira thought, leaning over to kiss her on the breast, exactly where she had just pointed with a hesitant finger. "But they don't get up to the fifth floor, I've never heard of a street-sweeper or water-wagon getting up to a fifth floor. Apart from the fact that tomorrow the artist would come and do it over exactly the same way, this delicate curve where something . . . " He managed to stop thinking, for just an instant he managed to kiss her without its being anything but his own kiss.

(–155)

65

Sample entry from Club files
Gregorovius, Ossip

Stateless.

Full moon (obverse side, invisible in those yet presputnik days): craters? seas? ashes?

Tends to dress in black, grey, brown. Has never been seen wearing full suit. There are those who affirm that he owns three but will invariably combine jacket of one with trousers of another. This could easily be verified.

Age: says he is forty-eight.

Profession: intellectual. Great-aunt sends modest allowance.

Carte de séjour AC 3456923 (for six months, renewable. It has already been renewed nine times with increasing difficulty each time).

Country of origin: born in Borzok (birth certificate probably false according to declaration by Gregorovius to Paris police. Reasons for his assumption in his dossier).

Country of origin: in the year of his birth Borzok was part of the Austro-Hungarian Empire. Obvious Magyar origin. Likes to imply that he is a Czech.

Country of origin: probably Great Britain. Gregorovius was probably born in Glasgow, the son of a sailor father and landlubber mother, the result of an emergency port of call, a shifting ballast, stout, and excessive xenophilic willingness on the part of Miss Marjorie Babington, 22 Stewart Street.

Gregorovius enjoys creating a picaresque prenatal state for himself and slanders his mothers (has three, depending on type of drunkenness) by attributing licentious habits to them. The Herzogin Magda Razenswill, who appears with whiskey or cognac, was the lesbian author of a pseudo-scientific treatise on *carezza* (translated into four languages). Miss Babington, whose ectoplasm materializes with gin, ended up as a whore on Malta. Third mother is constant problem for Étienne, Ronald and Oliveira, witnesses to her hazy apparition via Beaujolais, Côtes-du-Rhône, or Bourgogne Aligoté. Depending on circumstances her name is Galle, Adgalle or Minti, she lives freely in Herzegovina or Naples, travels to the United States with a vaudeville company, is first woman to smoke in Spain, sells violets outside the Vienna Opera, invents contraceptive devices, dies of typhus, is alive but blind in Huerta, disappears along with the Tsar's chauffeur in Tsarskoie Selo, blackmails her son every leap year, practises hydrotherapy, has suspicious relations with priest from Pontoise, died at the birth of Gregorovius, who is also the son of Santos-Dumont. In some inexplicable way witnesses have noted that these successive (or simultaneous) versions of third mother are always accompanied by references to Gurdjieff, whom Gregorovius admires and despises according to the pendulum.

(–11)

66

Facets of Morelli, his Bouvard et Pécuchet side, his side as the compiler of a literary almanac (sometimes he will give the name of "Almanac" to the body of his work).

He would like to sketch certain ideas, but he is incapable of doing so. The designs which appear in the margins of his notes are terrible. The obsessive repetition of a tremulous spiral, with a rhythm similar to the ones adorning Sanchi's stupa.

He plans one of the many endings to his unfinished book, and he leaves a mockup. The page contains a single sentence: "Underneath it all he knew that one cannot go beyond because there isn't any." The sentence is repeated over and over for the whole length of the page, giving the impression of a wall, of an impediment. There are no periods or commas or margins. A wall, in fact, of words that illustrate the meaning of the sentence, the collision with a wall behind which there is nothing. But towards the bottom and on the right, in one of the sentences the word *any* is missing. A sensitive eye can discover the hole among the bricks, the light that shows through.

(–149)

67

I'm tying my shoes, happy, whistling, and suddenly unhappiness. But this time I caught you, anguish. I sensed you *ahead* of any mental organization, with the first negative judgement. Like a grey colour that might be a pain and might be my stomach. And *almost* at the same time (but afterwards, you won't fool me this time) the way was opened for the intelligible repertory, with an explicatory idea first off: "And now to live another day, etc." From which there follows: "I'm anxious *because* . . . etc."

Ideas under sail, propelled by the primordial wind blowing from underneath (but underneath is only a physical location). All that's needed is a change in the breeze (*but what is it that changes its quadrant?*) and right off, here are the happy little boats, with their coloured sails. "After all, there's no reason to complain, man," like that.

I woke up and I saw the light of dawn through the cracks in the Venetian blinds. It came from so deep in the night that I had a feeling like that of vomiting up myself, the terror of coming into a new day with its same presentation, its mechanical indifference of everytime: consciousness, a sensation of light, opening my eyes, blinds, dawn.

In that second, with that omniscience of half-sleep, I measured the horror of what astounds and enchants religions so much: the eternal perfection of the cosmos, the unending rotation of the globe on its axis. Nausea, the unbearable feeling of coaction. *I am obliged to bear the daily rising of the sun.* It's monstrous. *It's inhuman.*

Before going back to sleep I imagined (I saw) a plastic universe, changeable, full of wondrous chance, an elastic sky, a sun that suddenly is missing or remains fixed or changes its shape.

I was anxious for the dispersal of the fixed constellations, that dirty luminous propaganda put out by the Divine Watchmakers' Trust.

(–83)

68

As soon as he began to amalate the noeme, the clemise began to smother her and they fell into hydromuries, into savage ambonies, into exasperating sustales. Each time that he tried to relamate the hairincops, he became entangled in a whining grimate and had to face up to envulsioning the novalisk, feeling how little by little the arnees would spejune, were becoming peltronated, redoblated, until they were stretched out like the ergomanine trimalciate which drops a few filures of cariaconce. And it was still only the beginning, because right away she tordled her hurgales, allowing him gently to bring up his orfelunes. No sooner had they cofeathered than something like a ulucord encrestored them, extrajuxted them, and paramoved them, suddenly it was the clinon, the sterfurous convulcant of matericks, the slobberdigging raimouth of the orgumion, the sproemes of the merpasm in one superhumitic agopause. Evohé! Evohé! Volposited on the crest of a murelium, they felt themselves being balparammed, perline and marulous. The trock was trembling, the mariplumes were overcome, and everything became resolvirated into a profound pinex, into niolames of argutentic gauzes, into almost cruel cariniers which ordopained them to the limit of their gumphies.

(–9)

69

(*Renovigo*, No. 5: translated from the Ispamerikan)

ANUTHER SUISIDE

It waz a sad surprize to rede in the "Orthografik" the newz ov the demize in San Luis Potosí on march furst last of lootenant kernel (promoted to kernel on leving the surviss) Adolfo Abila Sanhes. It waz a surprize bekuz we had no newz of hiz having bin il. Furthermor, for sum time now we hav kept a katalog ov owr frends hoo wur suisides, and on won okayzhun "Renovigo" made referens too serten simtums in thoze obzervd. It iz just that Abila Sanhes did not chuze a reevolvr like the anteyklerikl riter Giyermo Delora, nor the nooss like the French esperantist Eujene Lanti.

Abila Sanhes waz a man wurthi of atenshun and apreshiayshun. An onorabl soljer, he brawt onor too hiz profeshun in theeoree and in praktiss. He had a hie ideea ov loyaltee and eevn went onto the feeld ov batl. A man ov kulchur, he tawt seyens to yung peepl and adults. A thinkr, he rote meni thingz for magazeenz and he left a fue unpublishd werks, amung them "Baraks Maxims". A poet, he versifeyed with grate fasilitee in difrent forms. An artist with pen and pensil, he ofen entertaned us with hiz kreayshuns. A lingwist, he likd too tranzlate his own produkshuns in too Inglish, Esperanto, and uther tungs.

Basikly, Abila Sanhes waz a man ov thawt and akshun, ov moralitee and ov kulchur. This is wet made up hiz being.

In the uther colum ther ar sevral entrees, and it iz nachural to hezitate befor lifting the vale on hiz prievt life. But sinse a publik man haz nun and Abila Sanhes waz just that, we wood not be tru too owrselvz if we did not sho the uther side ov the medl. In owr role as biografrz and historiunz we must abandn skruplz.

We met Abila Sanhes pursonalee arownd 1936 in Linares, N.L., and then in Monteray we vizitd him in hiz home, wich seemd prosperus and happee. Yers later wen we vizitd him in Samora the impreshun was compleetlee difrent, we realizd that hiz home waz braking up, and then wekes later, wel, it waz hiz wife hoo dezertd him and hiz childrn skatrd. Finely, in San Luis Potosí, he met a kined yung gerl hoo liked him and she agrede too maree him: that iz how he had a sekund famlee, wich waz mor tolerunt than the ferst won and nevr kame to abandn him.

Wat hapnd ferst with Abila Sanhes, hiz mentl ilness or alkoholism? We doo not no, but both thingz toogethr were the ruinayshun ov hiz life and the kauz ov hiz deth. A sik man in hiz last yers, we had expeld him noing that he waz a suiside heading toards hiz inevitabl end. Won becumz fatalistik wen won obzervz peepl so clerelee heading toards a ner and trajik deth.

The desseessed beleved in a fiucher life. If he fownd that, let him fynd happines ther, even tho with difrent karakteristiks awl ov us, awl hiumans seke it.

(–52)

70

"When I was in my first cause, I did not have God . . . ; I wanted myself and I did not want anything else; I was what I wanted, and I wanted what I was, and I was free of God and of everything . . . That is why we beseech God to free us from God, and to let us conceive the truth and to let us enjoy it eternally, there where the supreme angels, the fly, and the soul are all alike, there where I was and where I wanted that which I was and it was that which I wanted . . . "

MEISTER ECKARDT, sermon: *Beati pauperes spiritu*

(–147)

71

Morelliana

Basically, what is this story about finding a millenary kingdom, an Eden, another world? Everything written these days and worth reading is oriented towards nostalgia. An Arcadia complex, the return to the great uterus, back to Adam, *le bon sauvage* (and so it goes . . .), *Paradise lost, lost because I searched for you in my eternal darkness* . . . And so much for islands (*cf.* Musil) or gurus (if you have the cash for the Paris–Bombay flight) or simply picking up a coffee cup and looking at it all over, not like a coffee cup any more but like evidence of the immense asininity in which we all find ourselves, believing that this object is nothing but a coffee cup while even the most idiot among journalists is assigned to give us a précis of the quanta, Planck and Heisenberg, knocks himself out in three columns explaining that everything vibrates and trembles and is like a cat about to take an enormous hydrogen or cobalt leap which will leave us all with our feet sticking up in the air. An uncouth way of expressing one's self, really.

The coffee cup is white, the noble savage is brown, Planck was a formidable German. Behind all that (it's always behind, convince yourself that this is the key idea of modern thought) Paradise, the other world, trampled innocence which weeping darkly seeks the land of Hurqalyā. In one way or another everyone is looking for it, everyone wants to open the door that leads out to the playground. And not just for Eden, not so much for Eden as such, but just to leave jet planes behind, Nikita's face or Dwight's or Charles's or Francisco's, the waking up to bells, the adjustment to thermometer and weather vane, the retirement from kicks in the arse (forty years of rubbing one's behind so that it won't hurt so much, but it hurts just the same, the tip of the shoe digs in a little deeper every time just the same, and each kick dredges up for just one moment more the poor arse of the cashier or the second lieutenant or the professor of literature or the nurse), and we were saying that Homo sapiens is not seeking the door in order to enter the millenary kingdom (even though it would not be so bad, not really bad at all) but only so he can close it behind his back and wiggle his arse like a contented dog, knowing that the old whore's shoe was left behind, breaking itself against the closed door, and that one can go ahead and unbutton his poor arsehole with a sigh, straighten up, and start walking among the posies in the garden and sit down to look at a cloud for five thousand years, no less, or twenty thousand if that is possible and if nobody gets upset and if he is lucky enough to stay in the garden looking at the posies.

From time to time among the legions of people going about with their arses exposed there is one who not only might want to shut the door for protection against the kicks of the three traditional dimensions, plus the ones supplied by the categories of understanding, by that more than rotten principle of sufficient reason and other infinite drivel, but furthermore, these types believe along with other madmen that we are not in the world, that our venerable parents have set us on a course in the wrong direction and we have to get off it if we do not want to end up as an equestrian statue or transformed into an exemplary grandparent, and that nothing is lost if one maintains as his end the value of proclaiming that everything is lost and that we have to start all over again, like the famous workmen in 1907 who realized one August morning that the tunnel under Monte Brasco was off course and that they would end up by coming out more than twenty yards away from the tunnel being dug by Yugoslav workmen coming from Dublivna. What did the famous workmen do? The famous workmen left their tunnel the way it was, came out on the surface, and after several days and nights of deliberation in various Piedmont bars, began to dig on their own and at their own risk in a different part of Monte Brasco, and they kept on going without worrying about the Yugoslav workmen, and after four months and five days they came out in the southern part of Dublivna, with no small surprise for a retired schoolteacher who saw them appear in his house at bathroom level. A praiseworthy example which the Dublivna workmen should have followed (although one must recognize that the famous workmen had not communicated their intentions) instead of obstinately connecting with a non-existent tunnel, as is the case with so many poets leaning halfway out of the living-room window late at night.

And so one can laugh, and think that it is not serious, but it is serious, laughter has dug more useful tunnels all by itself than all the tears on earth, even though it may barely be known to stiff-necked people, stubborn in their belief that Melpomene is more fruitful than Queen Mab. Once and for all it would be good to arrive at a disagreement in this matter. Perhaps there is one way out, but that exit ought to be an entrance. Perhaps there is a millenary kingdom, but you don't storm a fortress by running away from an enemy charge. Until now this century has been running away from all sorts of things, it has been looking for doorways and sometimes it gets to the bottom of them. What happens afterwards no one knows; some may have managed to see and have perished, instantly erased by great black forgetfulness, others will have conformed to the small escape, the little house in the suburbs, literary or scientific specialization, travel. Escapes are planned, they become technologized, they are furnished with the Modulor or with the Nylon Law. There are imbeciles who still believe that drunkenness is a way, or mescaline, or homosexuality, anything magnificent and inane per se but stupidly elevated into a system, into a key to the kingdom. Maybe there is another world inside this one, but we will not find it cutting out its silhouette from the fabulous tumult of days and lives, we will not find it in either atrophy or hypertrophy. That world does not exist, one has to create it like the phoenix. That world exists in this one, but the way water exists in oxygen and hydrogen, or how pages 78, 457, 3, 271, 688, 75 and 456 of the dictionary of the Spanish Academy have all that is needed for the writing of a hendecasyllable by Garcilaso. Let us say that the world is a figure, it has to be read. By read let us understand generated. Who cares about a dictionary as dictionary? If from delicate alchemies, osmoses and mixtures of simples there finally does arise a Beatrice on the riverbank, why not have a marvellous hint of what could be born of her in turn? What a useless task is man's, his own barber, repeating *ad nauseam* the biweekly trim, opening the same desk, doing the same thing over again, buying the same newspaper, applying the same principles to the same happenings. Maybe there is a millenary kingdom, but if we ever reach it, if we are it, it probably will not be called that any more. Until we take away from time its whip of history, until we prick the blister made of so many *untils*, we shall go on seeing beauty as an end, peace as a desideratum, always from this side of the door where it really is not always so bad, where many people find satisfactory lives, pleasant perfumes, good salaries, fine literature, stereophonic sound, and why then worry one's self about whether the world most likely is finite, whether history is coming to its optimum, whether the human race is emerging from the Middle Ages and entering the era of cybernetics. *Tout va très bien, madame la Marquise, tout va très bien, tout va très bien.*

As far as everything else is concerned, one must be an imbecile, one must be a poet, one must have a harvest moon in order to spend more than five minutes on those nostalgias that can be handled so perfectly in just a moment. Every meeting of international tycoons, of men-of-science, each new artificial satellite, hormone or atomic reactor crushes these false hopes a little more. The kingdom will be made out of plastic material, that is a fact. And the world will not have to be converted into an Orwellian or Huxleyan nightmare; it will be much worse, it will be a delightful world, to the measure of its inhabitants, no mosquitoes, no illiterates, with enormous eighteen-footed hens most likely, each foot a thing of beauty, with remote controlled bathrooms, a different-coloured water according to the days of the week, a nicety of the national hygiene service, with television in every room, great tropical landscapes, for example, for the inhabitants of Reykjavik, scenes of igloos for people in Havana, subtle compensations that will reduce all rebellions to conformity,

and so forth.

That is to say, a satisfactory world for reasonable people.

And will any single person remain in it who is not reasonable?

In some corner, a vestige of the forgotten kingdom. In some violent death, the punishment for having remembered the kingdom. In some laugh, in some tear, the survival of the kingdom. Beneath it all, one does not feel that man will end up killing man. He will escape from it, he will grasp the rudder of the electronic machine, the astral rocket, he will trip up and then they can set a dog on him. Everything can be killed except nostalgia for the kingdom, we carry it in the colour of our eyes, in every love affair, in everything that deeply torments and unties and tricks. *Wishful thinking*, perhaps; but that is just another possible definition of the featherless biped.

(–5)

72

"It was wise of you to come home, love, if you were so tired."

"There's no place like home," Oliveira said.

"Have another little *mate*, it's fresh."

"When you have your eyes closed it tastes even more bitter, amazing. Why don't you let me sleep a little and read a magazine."

"All right, love," Gekrepten said, drying her tears and out of sheer obedience looking for *Idilio*, even though she was in no shape for reading.

"Gekrepten."

"Yes, love."

"Don't worry about all this, old girl."

"Of course not, sweet. Wait and I'll put on another cold compress."

"I'll get up in a while and we'll take a walk along Almagro. They may be showing some technicolor musical."

"Tomorrow, love, it's better for you to get some rest now. The look on your face when you came in . . ."

"It's part of the profession, what can you do about it. No need for you to worry. Listen to Cien Pesos singing down there."

"They must be cleaning out his cage, little dear," Gekrepten said. "He's showing his gratitude . . ."

"Gratitude," Oliveira repeated. "It's nice to show gratitude to the people who keep you caged up."

"Animals don't understand any of that."

"Animals," Oliveira repeated.

(–77)

73

Yes, but who will cure us of the dull fire, the colourless fire that at nightfall runs along the Rue de la Huchette, emerging from the crumbling doorways, from the little entranceways, of the imageless fire that licks the stones and lies in wait in doorways, how shall we cleanse ourselves of the sweet burning that comes after, that nests in us forever allied with time and memory, with sticky things that hold us here on this side, and which will burn sweetly in us until we have been left in ashes. How much better, then, to make a pact with cats and mosses, strike up friendship right away with hoarse-voiced concierges, with the pale and suffering creatures who wait in windows and toy with a dry branch. To burn like this without surcease, to bear the inner burning coming on like fruit's quick ripening, to be the pulse of a bonfire in this thicket of endless stone, walking through the nights of our life, obedient as our blood in its blind circuit.

How often I wonder whether this is only writing, in an age in which we run towards deception through infallible equations and conformity machines. But to ask one's self if we will know how to find the other side of habit or if it is better to let one's self be borne along by its happy cybernetics, is that not literature again? Rebellion, conformity, anguish, earthly sustenance, all the dichotomies: the Yin and the Yang, contemplation or the *Tätigkeit*, oatmeal or partridge *faisandée*, Lascaux or Mathieu, what a hammock of words, what purse-size dialectics with pyjama storms and living-room cataclysms. The very fact that one asks one's self about the possible choice vitiates and muddies up what can be chosen. *Que sí, que no, que en ésta está* . . . It would seem that a choice cannot be dialectical, that the fact of bringing it up impoverishes it, that is to say, falsifies it, that is to say, transforms it into something else. How many eons between the Yin and the Yang? How many, perhaps, between yes and no? Everything is writing, that is to say, a fable. But what good can we get from the truth that pacifies an honest property owner? Our possible truth must be an *invention*, that is to say, scripture, literature, picture, sculpture, agriculture, pisciculture, all the tures in this world. Values, tures, sainthood, a sure, society, a sure, love, pure sure, beauty, a ture of tures. In one of his books Morelli talks about a Neapolitan who spent years sitting in the doorway of his house looking at a screw on the ground. At night he would pick it up and put it under his mattress. The screw was at first a laugh, a jest, communal irritation, a neighbourhood council, a mark of civic duties unfulfilled, finally a shrugging of shoulders, peace, the screw was peace, no one could go along the street without looking out of the corner of his eye at the screw and feeling that it was peace. The fellow dropped dead of a stroke and the screw disappeared as soon as the neighbours got there. One of them has it; perhaps he takes it out secretly and looks at it, puts it away again and goes off to the factory feeling something that he does not understand, an obscure reproval. He only calms down when he takes out the screw and looks at it, stays looking at it until he hears footsteps and has to put it away quickly. Morelli thought that the screw must have been something else, a god or something like that. Too easy a solution. Perhaps the error was in accepting the fact that the object was a screw simply because it was shaped like a screw. Picasso takes a toy car and turns it into the chin of a baboon. The Neapolitan was most likely an idiot, but he also might have been the inventor of a world. From the screw to an eye, from an eye to a star . . . Why surrender to Great Habit? One can choose one's sure, one's invention, that is to say, the screw or the toy car. That is how Paris destroys us slowly, delightfully, tearing us apart among old flowers and paper tablecloths stained with wine, with its colourless fire that comes running out of crumbling doorways at nightfall. An invented fire burns in us, an incandescent sure, a whatsis of the race, a city that is the Great Screw, the horrible needle with its night eye through which the Seine thread runs, a torture machine like a board of nails, agony in a cage crowded with infuriated swallows. We burn within our work, fabulous mortal honour, high challenge of the phoenix. No one will cure us of the dull fire, the colourless fire that at nightfall runs along the Rue de la Huchette. Incurable, perfectly incurable, we select the Great Screw as a sure, we lean towards it, we enter it, we invent it again every day, with every wine-stain on the tablecloth, with every kiss of mould in the dawns of the Cour de Rohan, we invent our conflagration, we burn outwardly from within, maybe that is the choice, maybe words envelop it the way a napkin does a loaf of bread and maybe the fragrance is inside, the flour puffing up, the yes without the no, or the no without the yes, the day without manes, without Ormuz or Ariman, once and for all and in peace and enough.

(–1)

74

The nonconformist as seen by Morelli, a note clipped to a laundry bill with a safety pin: "Acceptance of the pebble and of Beta Centauri, from the pure-as-anodyne to the pure-as-excess. This man moves within the lowest and the highest of frequencies, deliberately disdaining those in between, that is to say, the current band of the human spiritual mass. Incapable of liquidating circumstances, he tries to turn his back on them; too inept to join those who struggle for their liquidation, he thinks therefore that this liquidation is probably a mere substitute for something else equally partial and intolerable, he moves off shrugging his shoulders. To his friends, the fact that he finds his happiness in the trivial, in the puerile, in a piece of string or in a Stan Getz solo indicates a lamentable impoverishment; they do not know that he is also at the other extreme, the approach towards a *summa* that denies itself and goes threading off and hiding, or that the hunt has no end and that it will not even end with the man's death, because his death will not be a death as in the intermediate band, in frequencies that are picked up by ears that listen to Siegfried's funeral march."

Perhaps to correct the exalted tone of the note, a piece of yellow paper scribbled on in pencil: "Pebble and star: absurd images. But the intimate commerce with stones that have been rolled leads one to a passage; between the hand and the stone there vibrates a chord outside time. Fulgurant . . . [an unreadable word] . . . of which Beta Centauri also partakes; names and magnitudes give way, dissolve, stop being what science thinks they are. And then one is into something that purely is (what? what?): a trembling hand that wraps up a transparent stone that also trembles." (Further down, in ink: "It is not a question of pantheism, delightful illusion, fall upward into a heaven set afire at the edge of the sea.")

In another place, this clarification: "To speak of high and low frequencies is to give way again to the *idola fori* and to scientific language, an illusion of the Western world. For my nonconformist, the happy building of a kite and its raising for the joy of children present is not a lowly occupation (low in respect to high, little in respect to much, etc.), but rather a coming together of pure elements, and out of that a momentary harmony, a satisfaction which helps him raise up the rest. In like manner the moments of estrangement, of happy alienation which hurl him into very brief touches of something that could be his paradise, do not represent for him a higher experience than the making of the kite; it is like an end, but not on top or beyond. Nor is it an end that can be understood in time, an accession in which there culminates a process of enriching despoilment; it can come to him while he is sitting on the toilet, and it especially comes between a woman's thighs, between clouds of smoke, and in the midst of reading things rarely treasured by the cultured Sunday rotogravure.

"On the level of day-to-day acts, the attitude of my nonconformist is translated into his refusal of everything that smells like an accepted idea, tradition, a gregarious structure based on fear and falsely reciprocal advantages. It would not be hard for him to be Robinson Crusoe. He is not a misanthrope, but merely accepts from men and women that part which has not been plasticized by the social superstructure; he himself is afraid of his body's getting stuck in the mould and he knows it, but this knowledge is active and not that resignation that keeps time to the rhythm. With his free hand he slaps his own face for most of the day, and in spare moments he slaps the faces of others, and they pay him back in triplicate. He spends his time, therefore, in monstrous rows brought on by lovers, friends, creditors and officials, and in the few moments he has left he makes use of his freedom in a way that startles everyone else and which always ends up in small ridiculous catastrophes, measured against himself and his attainable ambitions; another more secret and evasive freedom works on him but only he (and then just barely) is conscious of its movements."

(–6)

75

It had been so handsome, in days gone by, to feel himself installed in an imperial style of life that authorized sonnets, dialogues with the stars, meditations on Buenos Aires nights, a Goethean serenity at gatherings in the Colón, or at lectures by foreign professors. He was still surrounded by a world that lived that way, that wanted to be that way; deliberately handsome and spruced up, architectural. To sense the distance that now isolated him from that columbarium, all that Oliveira had to do was put on a wry smile and imitate the exaggerated phrases and the luxurious rhythms of yesterday, the aulic ways of speaking and keeping still. In Buenos Aires, the capital of fear, he felt himself surrounded once again by that discreet smoothing off of edges that likes to go by the name of good sense and, on top of it all, that affirmation of sufficiency which lumps together the voices of young and old, its acceptance of the immediate as the true, of the vicarious as the, as the (in front of the mirror, with the tube of toothpaste in his closing fist, Oliveira again let a laugh escape from his face and instead of putting the brush into his mouth he applied it to his reflection and carefully anointed the false face with pink toothpaste, drew a heart right over its mouth, drew hands, feet, letters, obscenities, he ran up and down the mirror with the brush and with the tube, doubling up with laughter, until desolate Gekrepten came in with a sponge, and so forth).

(–43)

76

The Pola affair was hands, as usual. There is dusk, there is the fatigue that comes from having wasted time in cafés, reading newspapers that are always the same newspaper, there is something like the top of a beer bottle that softly squeezes you at stomach level. You're ready for anything, you're capable of falling into the worst traps of inertia and abandon, and all of a sudden a woman opens her purse to pay for a *café-crème*, her fingers play for an instant with the always imperfect clasp on the purse. You get the feeling that the clasp is guarding against an entry into a sign of the zodiac, that when that woman's fingers find a way to slide down the slender golden stem and with an imperceptible half-turn the catch loosens, some outflow will dazzle the customers absorbed in their pernod and Tour de France, or maybe they'll be swallowed up, a purple velvet funnel will pull the world off its hinges, all of the Luxembourg, the Rue Soufflot, the Rue Gay-Lussac, the Café Capoulade, the Fontaine de Médicis, the Rue Monsieur-le-Prince, it will swallow up everything in one last gulp that will leave nothing but an empty table, the open purse, the woman's hands which take out a hundred-franc note and hand it to Père Ragon, while Horacio Oliveira, naturally, the gaudy survivor of the catastrophe, prepares to say what you say at moments of great catastrophe.

"Oh, you know," Pola answered. "Fear is not my forte."

She said: *Oh, vous savez*, a little like the way the sphinx must have spoken before presenting the enigma, almost excusing herself, refusing a prestige that she knew was grand. She spoke like the women in so many novels where the novelist does not wish to waste time and therefore puts the better part of the description into the dialogue, unifying in that way the useful and the pleasant.

"When I say fear," Oliveira observed, sitting on the sphinx's left on the same red plush seat, "I'm thinking especially of reverse sides. You moved that hand as if you were touching a limit and after that a world against the grain began in which, for example, I could be your purse and you Père Ragon."

He was waiting for Pola to laugh and for things to deny that they were so sophisticated, but Pola (he found out later on her name was Pola) did not find the possibility too absurd. When she smiled she showed a set of small and regular teeth against which she drew her lips a little, lips painted a vivid orange, but Oliveira was still on her hands, he was always affected by women's hands, he felt the need to touch them, pass his fingers over each joint, explore with a movement like that of a Japanese kinesiologist the imperceptible route of the veins, discover the condition of the nails, have a chiromantic suspicion of ominous lines and propitious mounds, hear the din of the moon resting against his ear the palm of a small hand a little damp from love or from a cup of tea.

(–101)

77

"You probably realize that after all this . . ."

"*Res non verba,*" Oliveira said. "It's one week at about seventy pesos a day, let's call it five hundred and fifty and you can buy the patients a coke with the other ten."

"Please remove your personal effects at once."

"Yes, sometime between today and tomorrow, more likely tomorrow than today."

"Here's your money. Please sign the receipt."

"No pleases. I'll just sign. *Ecco.*"

"My wife is so upset," Ferraguto said, turning his back and taking the cigar out from between his teeth.

"It's feminine sensitivity, menopause, things like that."

"It's dignity, sir."

"Exactly what I was thinking. Speaking of dignity, thanks for the job in the circus. It was fun and there wasn't much to do."

"My wife still can't understand," Ferraguto said, but Oliveira was already at the door. One of the two opened his eyes or closed them. There was also something about the door that was like an eye opening or closing. Ferraguto relit his cigar and put his hands in his pockets. He was thinking about what he was going to say to that unconscious lunatic as soon as he came round. Oliveira let them put the compress on his forehead (or rather it was he who had closed his eyes) and he thought about what he was going to say to Ferraguto when he was sent for.

(–131)

78

The intimacy of the Travelers. When I say goodbye to them in the doorway or in the café on the corner, suddenly it's like a desire to stay near them, watching them live, a voyeur without appetites, friendly, a little sad. Intimacy, what a word, it makes you want to stick the fateful wh in front of it. But what other word could *intimate* (in its first acceptance) the very skin of acquaintance, the epithelial reason for Talita's, Manolo's and my being friends. People think they're friends because they coincide for a few hours a week on a sofa, in the movies, sometimes in a bed, or because they happen to do the same work in an office. When we were young, in a café, how many times did the illusion of identity with our companions make us happy. Identity with men and women of whom we scarcely knew one shape of being, a shape of giving in, a profile. I remember with a timeless clarity the cafés in Buenos Aires where for several hours we would succeed in getting away from family and obligations, where we would enter a territory of smoke and confidence in ourselves and in our friends, where we would accede to something that comforted us in our precarious state which promised us a kind of immortality. And there, twenty years old, we spoke our most lucid words, we knew all about our deepest emotions, we were like gods of pint glasses and dry Cuban rum. The café a little heaven, *cielito lindo*. Afterwards the street was like an expulsion, always, the angel with the flaming sword directing traffic on Corrientes and San Martín. Homeward bound, it's late, back to lawsuits, to the marriage bed, to linden tea for the old lady, to the exam the day after tomorrow, to the ridiculous fiancée who reads Vicki Baum and whom we will marry, there's no way out.

(A strange woman, Talita. She gives the impression of going around with a lighted candle in her hand, showing a path. And the thing that is modesty itself, a rare thing in an Argentine woman with a degree, here where all one needs is the title of land surveyor to be taken seriously. To think that she used to work in a pharmacy, it's cyclopean, it's positively agglutinating. And she combs her hair in such a pretty way.)

I've just now discovered that Manolo is called Manú in moments of intimacy. It seems so natural to Talita, that business of calling Manolo Manú, she doesn't realize that for his friends it's a secret scandal, a bleeding wound. But I, what right have I . . . That of the prodigal son, in any case. Let it be said in passing, the prodigal son will have to look for work, the last digging into the coffers was absolutely speleological. If I accept the advances of poor Gekrepten, who would do anything to go to bed with me, I will have room and shirts assured, and so forth. The idea of going out to sell lengths of cloth is no more idiotic than any other, a question of trying it, but the most fun would be joining the circus with Manolo and Talita. Joining the circus, a beautiful formula. In the beginning was a circus, and that poem of Cummings where it says that at the creation the Old Man drew a circus tent of air into his lungs. You can't say it in Spanish. Yes you can, but you would have to say: *juntó una carpa de circo de aire.* We will accept Gekrepten's offer, a fine girl, and that will allow us to live closer to Manolo and Talita, since topographically we will only be separated by two walls and a thin slice of air. With a brothel close at hand, the store near by, the market just around the corner. To think that Gekrepten *has been waiting for me.* It's incredible how things like that occur to other people. All heroic acts ought to stay at least within one's family, and ere-we-ave that girl at the Travelers' keeping up to date on all my overseas itineraries, and meanwhile she weaves and unweaves the purple sweater waiting for her Odysseus and working in a store on the Calle Maipú. It would be ignoble not to accept Gekrepten's proposals, deny her her full cup of unhappiness. And from one cynicism to another / you're looking like yourself and not your brother. Whodious Whodysseus.

No, but thinking about it frankly, the most absurd thing about these lives we pretend to lead is the false contact in them. Isolated orbits, from time to time two hands will shake, a five-minute chat, a day at the races, a night at the opera, a wake where everybody feels a little more united (and it's true, but then it's all over just when it's time for linking up). And all the same one lives convinced his friends are there, that contact does exist, that agreements or disagreements are profound and lasting. How we all hate each other, without being aware that endearment is the current form of that hatred, and how the reason behind profound hatred is this excentration, the unbridgeable space between me and you, between this and that. All endearment is an ontological clawing, yes, an attempt to seize the unseizable, and I would like to enter into the intimacy of the Travelers under the pretext of knowing them better, of really getting to be the friend, although what I really want is to seize Manú's manna, Talita's elf, their ways of seeing things, their presents and their futures, different from mine. And why this mania for spiritual possession, Horacio? Why this nostalgia for annexations, you, who have just broken your moorings, just sown confusion and despair (perhaps I should have spent a little more time in Montevideo and done a better job of searching) in the illustrious capital of the Latin spirit? The fact is that on one side you've deliberately disconnected yourself from a gaudy chapter in your life, and that you won't even allow yourself the right to speak in the soft language that you liked to babble in so much a few months ago; and at the same time, oh contradictory whidiot, you're literally breaking yourself up in order to enter into the whintimacy of the Travelers, be the Travelers, whinstall yourself in the Travelers, circus whincluded (but the Manager won't give me any work, so I'll have to think seriously about dressing up as a seaman and selling gabardine samples to ladies). You fuckup. Let's see if you can sow confusion in the ranks once more, if you've put in an appearance just to ruin the lives of peaceful people. That time they told me about the guy who thought he was Judas, and how because of that led a dog's life among the best social circles of Buenos Aires. Let's not be vain. At most a loving inquisitor, as I was told one night. Look, madam, what a fine piece. Sixty-five pesos a yard, just because it's for you. Your ma . . . your husband, I beg your pardon, will be very happy when he comes back from wor . . . from business, I beg your pardon. He'll climb up the walls, believe me, on my word as a sailor off the *Río Belén*. Sure, a little smuggling to make something on the side, my kid has got rickets, my wo . . . my wife does sewing in a dress shop, I have to help out a little, you know what I mean.

(–40)

79

An exceedingly pedantic note by Morelli: "To attempt the *roman comique* in the sense in which a text manages to hint at other values and thus collaborates in that anthropophany that we still consider possible. It would seem that the usual novel misses its mark because it limits the reader to its own ambit; the better defined it is, the better the novelist is thought to be. An unavoidable detention in the varying degrees of the dramatic, the psychological, the tragic, the satirical, or the political. To attempt on the other hand a text that would not clutch the reader but which would oblige him to become an accomplice as it whispers to him underneath the conventional exposition other more esoteric directions. Demotic writing for the female-reader (who otherwise will not get beyond the first few pages, rudely lost and scandalized, cursing at what he paid for the book), with a vague reverse side of hieratic writing.

"To provoke, assume a text that is out of line, untied, incongruous, minutely antinovelistic (although not antinovelish). Without prohibiting the genre's great effects if the situation should require it, but keeping in mind the Gidean advice, *ne jamais profiter de l'élan acquis.* Like all creatures of choice in the Western world, the novel is content in a closed order. Resolutely opposed to this, we should search here for an opening and therefore cut the roots of all systematic construction of characters and situations. Method: irony, ceaseless self-criticism, incongruity, imagination in the service of no one.

"An attempt of this type comes from a rejection of literature; a partial rejection since it does depend on words, but one which must oversee every operation undertaken by author and reader. To use the novel in that way, just as one uses a revolver to keep the peace, changing its symbol. To take from literature that part which is a living bridge from man to man, and which the treatise or the essay will permit only among specialists. A narrative that will not be a pretext for the transmission of a 'message' (there is no message, only messengers, and that is the message, just as love is the one who loves); a narrative that will act as a coagulant of experiences, as a catalyst of confused and badly understood notions, which first off will cut into the one who is writing it, for which reason it will have to be written as an antinovel, because every closed order will systematically leave outside those announcements that can make messengers out of us, bring us to our own limits from which we are so far removed, while being face to face with them.

"The strange self-creation of the author through his work. If out of that magma that is a day, the submersion in existence, we wish to raise the power of values that announce anthropophany as their end, what can be done then with pure understanding, with haughty reasoning reason? From the time of the Eleatics until today dialectical thought has had more than enough time to give us its fruits. We are eating them, they are delicious, they are seething with radioactivity. And when the feast is over, why are we so sad, brothers of nineteen hundred and fifty something?"

Another apparently complementary note:

"Situation of the reader. In general every novelist hopes his reader will understand him, by participating in his own experience, or that he will pick up a determined message and incorporate it. The romantic novelist wants to be understood for his own sake or for that of his heroes; the classical novelist wants to teach, leave his trace on the path of history.

"A third possibility: that of making an accomplice of the reader, a travelling companion. Simultaneanize him, provided that the reading will abolish reader's time and substitute author's time. Thus the reader would be able to become a coparticipant and cosufferer of the experience through which the novelist is passing, *at the same moment and in the same form.* All artistic tricks are of no use in obtaining it: the only thing worth anything is the material in gestation, the experiential immediacy (transmitted through words, of course, but the least aesthetic words possible; this is where we get the 'comic' novel, anticlimaxes, irony, so many other directional arrows pointing towards the other thing).

"For that reader, *mon semblable, mon frère,* the comic novel (and what is *Ulysses*?) will have to take place like those dreams where in the margin of some trivial happening we have a presentiment of a more serious anxiety that we do not always manage to decipher. In this sense the comic novel must have an exemplary sense of decorum; not deceive the reader, not mount him astride any emotion or intention at all, but give him rather something like meaningful clay, the beginning of a prototype, with traces of something that may be collective perhaps, human and not individual. Better yet, give him something like a façade, with doors and windows behind which there operates a mystery which the reader-accomplice will have to look for (therefore the complicity) and perhaps will not find (therefore the cosuffering). What the author of this novel might have succeeded in for himself, will be repeated (becoming gigantic, perhaps, and that would be marvellous) in the reader-accomplice. As for the female-reader, he will remain with the façade and we already know that there are very pretty ones among them, very much *trompe l'oeil*, and that in front of them one can keep putting on in a satisfactory way the comedies and the tragedies of the *honnête homme*. With which everything turns out happily, and as for those who protest, they can go and boil their heads."

(–22)

80

When I have just finished cutting my nails or washing my hair, or simply now, while I'm writing, I can hear a gurgling in my stomach,

the feeling that I've left my body behind comes back (I don't retreat into dualisms but I can distinguish between myself and my nails)

and that our bodies are starting to go bad on us, that they need us or they have too much of us (it depends).

Otherwise: at this stage we ought to deserve a better machine. Psychoanalysis shows how the contemplation of the body can bring on early complexes. (And Sartre, who sees in the fact that woman has been "perforated" existentialist implications that can compromise her all her life.) It's painful to think that we're travelling ahead of this body, but that what goes before is error and obstacle and probable uselessness, because these nails, this navel,

I mean something else, almost impossible to grasp: that the "soul" (my me-not-nails) is the soul of a body that does not exist. The soul gave man a push in his corporeal evolution, perhaps, but it's tired of shoving and goes on ahead by itself. It barely takes two steps

the soul breaks up oh because its real body does not exist and lets it fall down plop.

The poor thing goes back home, etc., but that's not what I. After all.

A long talk with Traveler about madness. Talking about dreams, we realized almost at the same time that certain structures we dream could be current forms of madness if they could just continue for a while when we're awake. When we dream we give free rein to our aptitude for madness. At the same time we suspect that all madness is a dream that has taken root.

Popular wisdom: "The poor guy's crazy, a dreamer . . . "

(–46)

81

The business of the sophist, according to Aristophanes, is to invent new reasons.

Let us try to invent new passions, or to reproduce the old ones with a like intensity.

I shall analyse this conclusion once more, from a Pascalian point of view: true belief is somewhere in between superstition and libertinism.

JOSÉ LEZAMA LIMA, *Tratados en La Habana*

(–74)

82

Morelliana

Why am I writing this? I have no clear ideas, I do not even have ideas. There are tugs, impulses, blocks, and everything is looking for a form, then rhythm comes into play and I write within that rhythm, I write by it, moved by it and not by that thing they call thought and which turns out prose, literature, or what have you. First there is a confused situation, which can only be defined by words; I start out from this half-shadow and if what I mean (if what is *meant*) has sufficient strength, the *swing* begins at once, a rhythmic swaying that draws me to the surface, lights everything up, conjugates this confused material and the one who suffers it into a clear third somehow fateful level: sentence, paragraph, page, chapter, book. This swaying, this *swing* in which confused material goes about taking shape, is for me the only certainty of its necessity, because no sooner does it stop than I understand that I no longer have anything to say. And it is also the only reward for my work: to feel that what I have written is like the back of a cat as it is being petted, with sparks and an arching in cadence. In that way by writing I go down into the volcano, I approach the Mothers, I connect with the Centre – whatever it may be. Writing is sketching my mandala and at the same time going through it, inventing purification by purifying one's self; the task of a poor white shaman in nylon socks.

(–99)

83

The invention of the soul by man is hinted at every time the feeling appears that the body is a parasite, something like a worm adhering to the ego. It's enough to feel that one lives (and not only life as an acceptance, as something-that-is-good-that-it-happened) for what is even closest and most loved by the body, the right hand, for example, suddenly to be an object that participates with repugnance in the double condition of not being me and of clinging to me.

I swallow my soup. Then in the midst of what I am reading, I think: "The soup is *in me*, I have it in this pouch which I will never see, my stomach." I feel with two fingers and I touch the mass, the motion of the food there inside. And I am this, a bag with food inside of it.

Then the soul is born: "No, I am not that."

Now that (let's be honest for once)

yes, I am that. With a very pretty means of escape for the use of the finicky: "I am *also that*." Or just a step up: "I am *in* that."

I am reading *The Waves*, that cinerary piece of lace, a fable of froth. A foot below my eyes some soup is slowly moving about in my stomachic pouch, a hair is growing on my thigh, an imperceptible sebaceous cyst is coming out on my shoulder.

At the end of what Balzac might have called an orgy, a certain individual who was not at all metaphysical said to me, thinking he was making a joke, that defecation gave him an impression of unreality. I remember his words: "You get up, you turn around and look, and then you say: *But did I do that?*"

(Like the line from Lorca: "*Sin remedio, hijo mío, ¡vomita! No hay remedio.*" And crazy Swift too, I think: "But Celia, Celia, Celia shits."

On top of physical pain like a metaphysical pinprick, writing abounds. All pain attacks me with a double-edged sword: it makes me aware as never before of the divorce between my ego and my body (and its falseness, its consoling invention) and at the same time it brings my body close to me, *dresses me in it* as pain. I feel it to be more mine than pleasure or mere coenaesthesis. It is really a bond. If I could sketch I would gladly show pain chasing the soul out of the body, but at the same time I would give the impression that it's all untrue: mere characteristics of a complex whose unity lies in not having any.

(–142)

84

Wandering along the Quai des Célestins I step on some dry leaves and when I pick one up and look at it closely I see that it is full of old-gold dust, and underneath some earth profound as musty perfume that sticks to my hand. For all those reasons I bring the dry leaves back to my flat and paste them on a lampshade. Ossip comes, he stays two hours and doesn't even look at the lamp. Another day Étienne comes by, and with his beret still in his hand, *Dis donc, c'est épatant, ça!* and he picks up the lamp, studies the leaves, becomes enthusiastic. Dürer, the veins, and so forth.

A single situation and two versions . . . I keep on thinking about all the leaves I will not see, the gatherer of dry leaves, about so many things that there must be in the air and which these eyes will not see, poor bats out of novels and movies and dried flowers. There must be lamps everywhere, there must be leaves that I will never see.

And so, *de feuille en aiguille*, I think about those exceptional states in which for one instant leaves and invisible lamps are imagined, are felt in an air outside of space. It's very simple, every exaltation or depression pushes me towards a state suitable for

I will call them paravisions

that is to say (that's the worst of it, saying it)

an instantaneous aptitude for going out, so that suddenly I can grasp myself from outside, or from inside but on a different plane,

as if I were somebody who was looking at me

(better still – because in reality I cannot see myself – : like someone who is living me).

It doesn't last, two steps along the street, the time needed for

taking a deep breath (sometimes when I wake up it lasts a little longer, and then it's fabulous) and in that instant I know *what I am* because I know exactly *what I am not* (what I thereupon ignore astutely). But there are no words for a material in between word and pure vision, like a block of evidence. Impossible to objectivize, make precise that defectiveness that I caught during the instant and which was *clear absence* or clear error or clear insufficiency, but

without knowing of *what, what.*

Another way of trying to say it: When it's that, I'm no longer looking towards the world, from me towards the other thing, but for a second I am the world, the outside plane, *the rest looking at me.* I see myself as the others can see me. It's so good it can't be sensed: that's why it scarcely lasts. I measure my defectiveness, I notice everything which through absence or defect we never see in ourselves. I see what I am not. For example (I'm picking this up on the rebound, but it comes from over there): there are enormous regions where I have never been, and what one has not known is what one has not been. An anxiety to start running, go into a house, into that store, jump on a train, devour all of Jouhandeau, know German, know Aurangabad . . . Localized and lamentable examples but ones which can give an idea (an *idea*?).

Another way of wanting to say it: What is defective is felt more as an intuitive poverty than as a mere lack of experience. It really doesn't afflict me not having read all of Jouhandeau, at most the melancholy feeling of too short a life for so many libraries, etc. The lack of experience is inevitable, if I read Joyce I am automatically sacrificing another book and vice versa, etc. The feeling of lack is sharper in

It's a little like this: there are lines in the air next to your head, next to your glance

zones for the detention of your eyes, your smell, your taste,

that is to say you're going around with your limits outside

and you can't get beyond that limit when you think you've caught anything fully, just like an iceberg the thing has a small piece outside and shows it to you, and the enormous rest of it is beyond your limits and that's why the *Titanic* went down. Wholiveira whith whis whexamples.

Let's be serious. Ossip did not see the dry leaves on the lamp simply because his limits are this side of what the lamp meant.

Étienne saw them perfectly, but on the other hand his limits would not let him see that I was bitter and did know what to do about Pola. Ossip realized it at once, and made me see it. That's the way we all go.

I think of man as an amoeba who sticks out pseudopods to catch and envelop his food. There are long and short pseudopods, movements, turnings. One day this all becomes *fixed* (what we call maturity, a full-grown man). On the one side he can go farther, on the other he can't see a lamp two steps away. In this way a guy goes on living fairly well convinced that nothing interesting will escape him, until an instantaneous landslide shows him for a second, unfortunately without giving him time *to know what*,

shows him his divided being, his irregular pseudopods
the suspicion that farther on, where now I can see clear air
or in this indecision, at the crossroads of choice
I myself, in the rest of reality that I don't know,
I'm waiting uselessly for myself.

(*Suite*)

Individuals like Goethe must not have abounded in experiences of this kind. By aptitude or decision (genius lies in choosing to be a genius and *in being right*) they have their pseudopods stuck out as far as they will go in all directions. They encircle with a uniform diameter, their limit is their skin projected spiritually to great distances. It does not seem that they have need to desire what begins (or continues) beyond their enormous spheres. That's why they're classics, hey.

The unknown approaches the amoeba *uso nostro* from all sides. I can know a lot or live a lot in a given sense, but then *the other* thing moves up on the side where I have my lacks and scratches my head with its cold nail. The worst is that it scratches me when there is no itching, while just when it does itch – when I ought to want to know – everything surrounding me is so set, so located, so complete and solid and labelled, that I begin to think that I was dreaming, that I'm fine this way, that I can take care of myself all right and that I shouldn't let myself be carried away by my imagination.

(*Final suite*)

Imagination has been praised to excess. The poor thing cannot move an inch away from the limits of its pseudopods. In this direction, great variety and vivacity. But in the other space, where the cosmic wind that Rilke felt pass over his head blows, Dame Imagination does not go. *Ho detto.*

(–4)

85

Lives which end like literary articles in newspapers and magazines, so pompous on page one and ending up in a skinny tail, back there on page thirty-two, among advertisements for secondhand articles and tubes of toothpaste.

(–150)

86

The people in the Club, with two exceptions, maintained that it was easier to understand Morelli from the quotes he used than from his personal meanderings. Wong insisted until his departure from France (the police refused to renew his *carte de séjour*) that it wasn't worth the trouble champollionizing the old man's rosettes, once you found the two following quotations, both from Pauwels and Bergier:

> Perhaps there is a place in man from where the whole of reality can be perceived. This hypothesis seems delirious. Auguste Comte declared that the chemical composition of a star would never be known. The following year Bunsen invented the spectroscope.
>
> . . . .
>
> Language, just like thought, proceeds from the binary arithmetical functioning of our brain. We classify by yes and no, by positive and negative. (. . .) The only thing that my language proves is the slowness of a world vision limited to the binary. This insufficiency of language is obvious, and is strongly deplored. But what about the insufficiency of binary intelligence itself? Internal existence, the essence of things, escapes it. It can discover that light is continuous and discontinuous at the same time, that a molecule of benzine establishes between its six atoms dual relationships which are nevertheless mutually exclusive; it accepts it, but it cannot understand it, it cannot incorporate into its own structure the reality of the profound structures it examines. In order to do that, it would have to change its state, machines other than the usual ones would have to start functioning in the brain, so that binary reasoning might be replaced with an

analogical consciousness which would assume the shapes and assimilate the inconceivable rhythms of those profound structures . . .

Le Matin des magiciens

(–78)

87

In 1932, Ellington recorded *Baby When You Ain't There*, one of his least praised numbers and one to which the faithful Barry Ulanov does not give any special mention. With a curiously dry voice Cootie Williams sings the lyrics.

Why is it so necessary at certain times to say: "I loved that"? I loved some blues, an image in the street, a poor dry river in the north. Giving testimony, fighting against the nothingness that will sweep us all away. That's how in the air of the soul little things like that will linger; a sparrow that belonged to Lesbia, some blues that in the memory will fill the small space saved for perfumes, stamps and paperweights.

(–105)

88

"Hey, if you move your leg like that I'm going to stick this needle in your ribs," Traveler said.

"Keep on telling me about that business of coloured in yellow," Oliveira said. "With my eyes bandaged it's like a kaleidoscope."

"Coloured in yellow," Traveler said, rubbing the thigh with a piece of cotton, "is under the jurisdiction of the national corporation of commission agents for the corresponding species."

"Animals with yellow fur, vegetables with yellow flowers, and minerals with a yellow look," Oliveira recited obediently. "Why not? After all, Thursday is the fashionable day here, one doesn't work on Sunday, the metamorphoses between Saturday morning and afternoon are extraordinary, people so easy-going. You're hurting something awful. Is that some metal with a yellow look, or what?"

"Distilled water," Traveler said. "So you'll think it's morphine. You're quite right, Ceferino's world only appears strange to guys who believe in their own institutions to the exclusion of those outside. If you thought about everything that changes as soon as you leave the edge of the pavement and take three steps into the street . . . "

"Like going from coloured in yellow to coloured in pampa," Oliveira said. "This thing is making me a little sleepy."

"Water is a soporific. If I had my way I'd shoot you up with nebiole and you'd be more wide awake."

"Explain something to me before I fall asleep."

"I don't think you're going to fall asleep, but go ahead."

(–72)

89

There were two letters from Juan Cuevas, attorney, but the order in which they should be read was material for a polemic. The first was the poetical exposition of what he called "world sovereignty"; the second one, also dictated to a stenographer at the Santo Domingo gate, took its vengeance on the required modesty of the first:

> Make as many copies of this letter as you wish, especially for members of the UN and world officials, who are the lowest kind of swine and international jackals. If on the one hand the Santo Domingo gate is a tragedy of noise, I like it on the other because I can come here and toss the largest stones in history.

The following figured among the stones:

> The Pope in Rome is the greatest swine in history, and not by the slightest chance the vicar of God; Roman clericalism is the pure shit of Satan; every Roman clerical church should be completely razed, so that Christ's light may shine, not only in the depths of human hearts, but also shining on through God's universal light, and I say all of this because I dictated the previous letter to a most charming young lady, who looked at me with such a very languid face that I could not state certain strong items.

Oh chivalrous lawyer! The fierce enemy of Kant, he insisted on "humanizing the current philosophy of the world", to which purpose he decreed:

> And let the novel be more psychopsychiatric, by that I mean let the truly spiritual elements of the soul be set forth as scientific elements of the true universal psychiatry . . .

Abandoning for a few minutes a considerable dialectical arsenal, he peeped into the kingdom of world religion:

> But just so long as humanity follows the path of both universal commandments; and until the hard stones of the world become silken wax under the illuminating light . . .

A poet, and a good one.

> The voices of all the stones in the world will resound from out of all the cataracts and canyons in the world, with little silver threads of voices, an occasion for the endless love of women and of God . . .

Suddenly the archetypal vision invades and spreads out:

> The Cosmos of the Earth, interior just like the universal mental image of God, which would later become condensed matter, is symbolized in the Old Testament by the archangel who turns his head and sees a faint world of lights, of course, I cannot remember passages from the Old Testament word for word, but that is more or less the direction which it takes: it is as if the face of the Universe became the very light of Earth, and remained as an orbit of universal energy around the sun . . . In a like way all Humanity and its peoples must turn their bodies, their souls, and their heads . . . It is the universe and the whole Earth turning towards Christ, laying all the laws of the Earth at his feet . . .

And then,

> . . . all that remains is a sort of universal light that comes from equal lamps, lighting up the innermost heart of peoples . . .

The worst was that suddenly,

> Ladies and gentlemen: I am writing this letter in the midst of frightful noise. And, nevertheless, we shall keep right on offering what we have here to you; the fact is that you still do not realize that in order to write (?) WORLD SOVEREIGNTY in a more perfect way and for it really to arrive at universal understanding, I should at least deserve from you

> some broad help so that each line and each letter will find its proper place, and not this disorder of the sons of the sons of the son of the *chingada* mother of all mothers; fuck the mother of all noises.

But did it make any difference? Ecstasy again in the following line:

> What an excellence of universes! May they flourish like the spiritual light of delightful roses in the hearts of all peoples . . .

And the letter went on to its close in a flowery way, although with some curious last-minute grafts:

> . . . It seems that the whole universe is being brightened with the light of the universal Christ in every human flower, with infinite petals to illuminate eternally all earthly paths; and so it will remain brightened in the light of WORLD SOVEREIGNTY, they say that you no longer love me because you have other lovers. – Very truly yours. Mexico City, September 20, 1956 – . 32 Avenida 5 de Mayo, Room III. – Paris Bldg. JUAN CUEVAS, ATTORNEY.

(–53)

90

He went around thinking in those days, and the bad habit of ruminating about everything at length inevitably made things hard for him. He had been revolving about the great affair, and the inconvenience in which he was living because of La Maga and Rocamadour made him analyse with increasing violence the intersection where he felt he was stuck. In cases like that Oliveira would grab a sheet of paper and write down the grand words over which he went slipping along in his ruminations. He wrote, for example: "The great whaffair", or "the whintersection". It was enough to make him laugh and feel more up to preparing another *mate*. "Whunity," whrote Wholiveira. "The whego and the whother." He used this *wh* the way other people used penicillin. Then he would get back to the matter more slowly and feel better. "The whimportant thing is not to become whinflated," Wholiveira would say to whimself. After moments like this he would feel able to think without having the words play dirty tricks on him. Little more than methodological progress, because the great affair was still invulnerable. "Who would have told you, kid, that you'd end up as a metaphysician?" Oliveira would ask himself. "You have to resist the wardrobe with three bodies, conform to the bedside table of every day's insomnia." Ronald had come by to suggest to him that he accompany him in some vaguely political activities, and all night long (La Maga had not yet brought Rocamadour from the country) they had argued like Arjuna and the Charioteer, about action and passivity, the reasons for risking the present for the sake of the future, the blackmail side of every action that has a social end, the degree to which the risk taken serves at least to palliate an individual guilty conscience, the swinish personal behaviour of everyday life. Ronald had ended up leaving with his head bowed down, not having been able to convince Oliveira that action was needed in support of the Algerian rebels.

Oliveira had had a bad taste in his mouth all day because it had been easier to say no to Ronald than to himself. He was fairly certain of only one thing, and it was that he could not give in without betraying the passive hope by which he had lived since coming to Paris. Giving way to facile generosity and going out to paste up clandestine posters on the street seemed like a mundane explanation to him, a settling of accounts with friends who would appreciate his boldness, more than a real reply to great questions. Measuring the thing from the temporal and the absolute, he felt that he was wrong in the first case and right in the second. He was wrong in not fighting for Algerian independence, or against anti-Semitism or racism. He was right in rejecting the simple stupefaction of collective action and remaining alone once more next to his bitter *mate*, thinking about the great affair, turning it around like a ball of yarn in which you cannot see the end or where there are four or five ends.

It was all right, yes, but one also had to recognize that his character was like a foot that trampled all dialectics of action in the manner of the *Bhagavad-Gita*. Between preparing *mate* and having La Maga prepare it there was no possible doubt. But everything was fissionable and would immediately allow an opposite interpretation: to passive character there corresponded a maximum of freedom and availability, the lazy absence of principles and convictions made him more sensitive to the axial condition of life (what one calls a weather-vane type), capable of rejecting through laziness but at the same time of filling the hollow left by the rejection with a content freely chosen by conscience or by an instinct that is more open, more ecumenical, as it were.

"More whecumenical," Oliveira wisely jotted down.

Besides, what was the true morality of action? A social action like that of the syndicalists was more than justified in the field of history. Happy were those who lived and slept in history. An abnegation was almost always justified as an attitude of religious origin. Happy were those who loved their neighbour as themselves. In every case Oliveira rejected that sally of the ego, that magnanimous invasion of somebody else's corral, an ontological boomerang destined to enrich in the last instance the one who threw it, to give him more humanity, more sainthood. One is always a saint at the expense of somebody else, etc. There was no objection to that action as such, but he pushed it aside with doubts about his personal conduct. He would suspect a betrayal the moment he gave in to posters on the street or activities of a social nature; a betrayal disguised as satisfactory work, daily happiness, satisfied conscience, fulfilled duty. He was too well acquainted with certain communists in Buenos Aires and in Paris, capable of the worst villainy but redeemable in their own minds by "the struggle", by having to leave in the middle of dinner to run to a meeting or finish a job. Social action in those people seemed too much like an alibi, the way children are usually the alibi for mothers' not having to do anything worth while in this life, the way learning with its blinkers is useful in not learning that in the jail down the street they are still guillotining guys who should not be guillotined. False action is almost always the most spectacular, the kind that tears down respect, prestige and whequestrian wheffigies. It's as easy as putting on a pair of slippers, it can even become meritorious ("After all, it would be so nice if the Algerians got independence and we all ought to help a little," Oliveira said to himself); the betrayal was something else, as always it was a denial of the centre, one's installation on the periphery, the marvellous joy of brotherhood with other men who were embarked on the same action. There where a certain human type could reach fulfilment as a hero, Oliveira knew that he was condemned to the worst of comedies. So it was better to sin through omission than through commission. Being an actor meant renouncing the orchestra seats, and he seemed born to be a spectator in the first row. "The worst of it," Oliveira said to himself, "is that I always want to be an active onlooker and that's where the trouble starts."

Whactive whonlooker. He had to whanalyse the whaffair carefully. At that moment certain pictures, certain women, certain poems gave him hopes of someday reaching a position from which he could accept himself with less loathing and less doubt than at that moment. It was no mean advantage for him that his worst defects tended to be useful in that matter which was not a path but rather the search for a halt that comes at the beginning of every path. "My strength is in my weakness," Oliveira thought. "The great decisions I have always made were masks for flight." Most of his undertakings (of his whundertakings) ended not with a bang but a whimper; the great breaks, the bangs without return were the nips of a cornered rat and nothing else. Otherness was rotating ceremoniously, dissolving into time or into space or into behaviour, without violence, from fatigue – like the ending of his sentimental adventures – or from a slow retreat as when one begins to visit a friend less and less, read a poet less and less, go to a café less and less, taking mild doses of nothingness so as not to hurt one's self.

"Nothing ever really happens to me," Oliveira thought. "A flowerpot is never going to fall on my noggin." Why the unrest, then, if it was not the stale attraction of the opposites, the nostalgia for vocation and action? An analysis of this unrest, as far as is possible, would always allude to a dislocation, to an excentration in regard to a kind of order that Oliveira was incapable of defining. He knew that he was a spectator on the edge of the spectacle, like being blindfolded in a theatre: sometimes the secondary meaning of some word would come to him, or of some piece of music, filling him with anxiety because he was capable of sensing that it was the primary meaning. In moments like that he knew he was closer to the centre than many people who lived convinced that they were the axle of the wheel, but his was a useless nearness, a tantalizing instant which did not even take on the quality of torture. Once he had believed in love as an enrichment, an exaltation of interceding forces. One day he realized that his loves were impure because they presupposed that expectation, while the true lover loved without expecting anything but love, blindly accepting that the day would become bluer and the night softer and the tram less uncomfortable. "I can make a dialectical operation even out of soup," Oliveira thought. He ended up by making friends out of the women he had loved, accomplices in a special contemplation of the world around. The women started out by adoring him (they really whadored him), admiring him (a whunlimited whadmiration), then something would make them suspect the void, they would jump back, and he would make their flight easy for them, he would open the door so that they could go and play on the other side. On two occasions he had been at the point of feeling pity and letting them keep the illusion that they understood him, but something told him that his pity was not genuine, it was more a cheap trick of his selfishness and his laziness and his habits. "Pity is being auctioned off," Oliveira would say to himself and let them go; he quickly forgot about them.

(–20)

91

Papers scattered on the table. A hand (Wong's). A voice reads slowly, making mistakes, the *l*'s like hooks, the *e*'s indefinable. Notes, cards with words on them, a line of poetry in some language, the writer's kitchen. Another hand (Ronald's). A resonant voice that knows how to read. Greetings in a low voice to Ossip and to Oliveira who arrive contritely (Babs has gone to let them in, has received them with a knife in each hand). Cognac, golden light, the legend of the profanation of the Eucharist, a small De Staël. The topcoats can be left in the bedroom. A piece of sculpture by (perhaps) Brancusi. In the back of the bedroom, lost between a dressmaker's dummy rigged out as a hussar and a pile of boxes with pieces of wire and cardboard in them. There are not enough chairs, but Oliveira brings over two stools. One of those silences is produced which is comparable, according to Genet, to those observed by refined people when they suddenly perceive in a living room the smell of a silent fart. Soon thereafter Étienne opens up the briefcase and takes out the papers.

"We thought it best to wait for you before we classified them," he says. "In the meantime we've been looking over some odd pages. This bitch threw a beautiful egg into the rubbish bin."

"It was rotten," said Babs.

Gregorovius places a visibly trembling hand on one of the folders. It must be very cold outside, a double cognac then. They are warmed by the colour of the light, and the green folder, the Club. Oliveira looks at the centre of the table, the ash from his cigarette starts to join the ones that fill the ashtray.

(–82)

92

Now he realised that in his highest moments of desire he had not known how to stick his head into the crest of the wave and pass through the fabulous crash of his blood. Loving La Maga had been a sort of rite from which one no longer expected illumination; words and acts had succeeded one another with an inventive monotony, a dance of tarantulas on a moonlit floor, a viscous and prolonged manipulation of echoes. And all the time he had been waiting for a kind of awakening to come from out of that happy drunkenness, a clearer view of what was around him, whether the coloured wallpaper in hotels or the reasons behind any one of his acts, without wanting to understand that by limiting himself to waiting he had abolished all real possibility, as if he had condemned himself in advance to a narrow and trivial present. He had gone from La Maga to Pola in one fell swoop, without offending La Maga or offending himself, without getting annoyed at caressing Pola's pink ear with La Maga's arousing name. Failure with Pola was the repetition of innumerable failures, a game that ultimately is lost but was beautiful to play, while with La Maga he had begun to come out resentful, with a taste of tartar and a cigarette butt that smelled of dawn in the corner of his mouth. That's why he took Pola to the same hotel on the Rue Valette, they found the same old woman who greeted them understandingly, what else was there to do in that lousy weather. It still smelled of toilet soap, of soup, but they had cleaned the blue stain on the rug and there was room for new stains.

"Why here?" Pola asked surprised. She looked at the yellow bedspread, the dull and musty room, the pink-spotted lampshade hanging from the ceiling.

"Here or somewhere else . . . "

"If it's because of money, all you had to do was say so, love."

"If it's a question of revulsion, all we have to do is cut out, sweet."

"It doesn't revolt me. It's ugly, that's all. Probably . . . "

She had smiled at him, as if she were trying to understand. Probably . . . probable . . . Her hand found Oliveira's as they both bent over to remove the cover. All that afternoon he had again been present, another time, one of so many times, the ironical witness sorry for his own body, at the surprises, the enchantments and the deceptions of the ceremony. Habituated without being aware of it to La Maga's rhythms, suddenly a new ocean, a different set of waves shook him in his reflexes, confronted him, seemed to denounce in a vague way his solitude enmeshed in phantoms. The enchantment and the disenchantment of going from one mouth to another, of searching with his eyes closed for a neck where his hand had chastely slept, and feeling that the curve is different, a thicker base, a tendon that tightens briefly with the effort of getting up to kiss or bite. Every instant of his body was opposite a delightful lack of meeting, having to stretch out a little more, or lower his head to find the mouth that formerly was so close up there, to stroke a thinner hip, incite a reply and not get it, insist, confusedly, until he realised that everything had to be invented all over again, that the code has not been formulated, that the keys and the clues will take shape again, will be different, will respond to other things. Weight, smell, the tone in which she laughed and begged, time and precipitation, nothing coincides even if the same, everything is born again even if immortal, love plays at being invented, it flees from itself to return in its surprising spiral, the breasts tilt a different way, the mouth kisses more deeply or as if from far away, and in one moment where before there had been anger and anguish now there is pure play, an incredible frolic, or vice versa, at the moment when before one fell into dreaming, the babbling of sweet foolish things, now there is a tension, something that cannot be communicated but is present and which demands incorporation, something like an insatiable rage. Only the pleasure in his final wingbeat is the same; before and after, the world has broken into pieces and it will be necessary to rename it, finger by finger, lip by lip, shadow by shadow.

The second time was in Pola's apartment, on the Rue Dauphine. If a few phrases had succeeded in giving him an idea of what he was going to find, reality was way beyond the imaginable. Everything was in its place and there was a place for everything. The history of contemporary art was modestly inscribed on postcards: a Klee, a

Poliakoff, a Picasso (with a certain kindly condescension already), a Manessier, and a Fautrier. Hung artistically with a good sense of distance. A small signoria David did not intrude either. A bottle of pernod and one of cognac. On the bed, a Mexican serape. Pola played the guitar sometimes, the memory of a love of high plateaus. In her flat she looked like Michèle Morgan, but she was resolutely dark. Two bookshelves included Durrell's *Alexandria Quartet*, well-read and annotated, translations from Dylan Thomas stained with lipstick, copies of *Two Cities*, Christiane Rochefort, Blondin, Sarraute (uncut), and a few *Nouvelles Revues Françaises*. The rest gravitated about the bed, where Pola wept a little while she recalled a girlfriend who had committed suicide (photos, a page torn out of an intimate diary, a pressed flower). It did not seem strange to Oliveira afterwards that Pola had seemed perverse, that she had been the first to open the door to different kinds of loveplay, that night found them like two people stretched out on a beach where the sand slowly yields to the algae-laden water. It was the first time that he called her Pola Paris, as a joke, and she liked it and repeated it, and bit him on the lip whispering Pola Paris, as if she had assumed the name and wanted to be worthy of it, pole of Paris, Paris of Pola, the greenish light of a neon sign going on and off against the yellow raffia curtain, Pola Paris, Pola Paris, the naked city with its sex in tune to the palpitation of the curtain. Pola Paris, Pola Paris, every time more his, breasts without surprise, the curve of the stomach traced exactly by his caress, without the slightest fear of reaching the limits before or after, a mouth found now and defined, a smaller and more pointed tongue, less saliva, teeth less sharp, lips which opened so that he could touch her gums, enter and run over every warm ripple where it smelled a little of cognac and tobacco.

(–103)

93

But love, that word . . . Horacio the moralist fearful of passions born without some deep-water reason, disconcerted and surly in the city where love is called by all the names of all the streets, all the buildings, all the flats, all the rooms, all the beds, all the dreams, all the things forgotten or remembered. My love, I do not love you for you or for me or for the two of us together, I do not love you because my blood tells me to love you, I love you because you are not mine, because you are from the other side, from there where you invite me to jump and I cannot make the jump, because in the deepest moment of possession you are not in me, I cannot reach you, I cannot act beyond your body, your laugh, there are times when it torments me that you love me (how you like to use the verb to love, with what vulgarity you toss it around among plates and sheets and buses), I'm tormented by your love because I cannot use it as a bridge because a bridge can't be supported by just one side, Wright or Le Corbusier will never make a bridge that is supported by just one side, and don't look at me with those bird's eyes, for you the operation of love is so simple, you'll be cured before me even if you love me as I do not love you. Of course you'll be cured, because you're living in health, after me it'll be someone else, you can change things the way you do a blouse. So sad to listen to Horacio the cynic who wants a passport-love, a mountain pass-love, a key-love, a revolver-love, a love that will give him the thousand eyes of Argos, ubiquity, the silence out of which music is possible, the root out of which a language can be woven. And it's foolish because all that is sleeping a little in you, all you would have to do is submerge yourself in a glass of water like a Japanese flower and little by little coloured petals would begin to bloom, the bent forms would puff up, beauty would grow. Infinite giver, I do not know how to take, forgive me. You're offering me an apple and I have left my teeth on the bedside table. Stop, it's fine that way. I can also be rude, take note of that. But take good note, because it's not gratuitous.

Why stop? For fear of starting fabrications, they're so easy. You get an idea from there, a feeling from the other shelf, you tie them together with the help of words, black bitches, and it turns out that I want you. Partial total: I want you. General total: I love you. That's the way a lot of my friends live, not to mention an uncle and two cousins convinced of the love-they-feel-for-their-wives. From words to deeds; in general without the *verba* there isn't any *res*. What a lot of people call loving consists of picking out a woman and marrying her. They pick her out, I swear, I've seen them. As if you could pick in love, as if it were not a lightning bolt that splits your bones and leaves you staked out in the middle of the courtyard. You'll probably say that they pick her out because-they-love-her, I think it's just the siteoppo. Beatrice wasn't picked out, Juliet wasn't picked out. You don't pick out the rain that soaks you to the skin when you come out of a concert. But I'm alone in my room, I'm falling into tricks of writing, the black bitches get their vengeance any way they can, they're biting me from underneath the table. Do you say underneath or under? They bite you just the same. Why, why, *pourquoi, por qué, warum, perchè* this horror of black bitches? Look at them there in that poem by Nashe, transformed into bees. And there in two lines from Octavio Paz, thighs of the sun, corners of summer. But the same body of a woman belongs to Mary and to La Brinvilliers, eyes that cloud up looking at a beautiful sunset are the same optical instrument that gets pleasure from the twisting of a man being hanged. I'm afraid of that pimping, of ink and of voices, a sea of tongues licking the arse of the world. There's milk and honey underneath your tongue . . . Yes, but it's also been said that dead flies make the perfumer's perfume stink. At war with words, at war, keep everything that might be necessary even though intelligence must be renounced, stick with the simple act of ordering some fried potatoes, and Reuters dispatches, in letters from my noble brother and movie dialogues. Curious, very curious that Puttenham should have had a feeling for words as if they were objects, and even creatures with a life of their own. I too sometimes think that I'm engendering streams of ferocious ants that will devour the world. Oh but that the Roc could breed in silence . . . *Logos, faute éclatante!* To conceive a race that could express itself in drawings, the dance, the macramé, or abstract mimicry. Could they avoid connotations, the root of deception? *Honneur des hommes*, etc. Yes, but an honour that dishonours itself in every phrase, like a brothel of virgins, if such a thing were possible.

From love to philology, you're brilliant, Horacio. It's Morelli's fault, he's like an obsession with you, his crazy experiment makes you catch a glimpse of the lost paradise, poor preAdamite, in a cellophane-wrapped golden age. *This is the age of plastics, man, the age of plastics.* Forget about the bitches. Beat it, the pack of you, we have to think, what's called thinking, that is to say, feeling, locating yourself, and confronting yourself before you let pass the minutest main or subordinate clause. Paris is a centre, you understand, a mandala through which one must pass without dialectics, a labyrinth where pragmatic formulas are of no use except to get lost in. Then a *cogito* which may be a kind of breathing Paris in, getting into it by letting it get in you, *pneuma* and not *logos*. Argentine big buddy, disembarking with the sufficiency of a three-by-five culture, wise in everything, up to date in everything, with acceptable good taste, good knowledge of the history of the human race, the periods of art, the Romanesque and the Gothic, philosophical currents, political tensions, Shell Mex, action and reflection, compromise and liberty, Piero della Francesca and Anton Webern, well-catalogued technology, Lettera 22, Fiat 1600, John XXIII. Wonderful, wonderful. It was a little bookstore on the Rue du Cherche-Midi, it was a soft sense of spinning slowly, it was the afternoon and the hour, it was the flowering season of the year, it was the *Verbum* (in the beginning), it was a man who thought he was a man. What an infinite piece of stupidity, my God. And she came out of the bookstore (I just now realize that it was like a metaphor, her coming out of a bookstore, no less) and we exchanged a couple of words and we went to have a glass of *pelure d'oignon* at a café in Sèvres-Babylone (speaking of metaphors, I a delicate piece of porcelain just arrived, HANDLE WITH CARE, and she Babylonia, root of time, something previous, *primeval being*, terror and delight of beginnings, the romanticism of Atala but with a real tiger waiting behind the tree). And so Sèvres went with Babylonia to have a glass of *pelure d'oignon*, we looked at each other and I think we began to desire each other (but that was later on, on the Rue Réamur) and a memorable dialogue resulted, clothed from head to toe in misunderstandings, maladjustments that dissolved into vague moments of silence, until our hands began to chat, it was sweet stroking hands while we looked at each other and smiled, we lit Gauloises, each in the other's mouth, we rubbed each other with our eyes, we were so much in agreement on everything that it was shameful, Paris was dancing there outside waiting for us, we'd barely disembarked, we were barely alive, everything was there without a name and without a history (especially Babylonia, and poor Sèvres made an enormous effort, fascinated by that Babylonia way of looking at the Gothic without putting labels on it, of walking along the banks of the river without seeing the Norman ducks take flight). When we said goodbye we were like two children who have suddenly become friends at a birthday party and keep looking at one another while their parents take them by the hand and lead them off, and it's a sweet pain and a hope, and you know the name of one is Tony and the other one Lulu, and that's all that's needed for the heart to become a little piece of fruit, and . . .

Horacio, Horacio.

Merde, alors. Why not? I'm talking about then, about Sèvres-Babylone, not about these elegiac scorecards where we know that the game has been played already.

(–68)

94

Morelliana

A piece of prose can turn rotten like a side of beef. For some years now I have been witness to the signs of rot in my writing. Just like me, it has its angina, its jaundice, its appendicitis, but it is ahead of me on its way to final dissolution. After all, rotting means the end of the impurities in the component parts and the return of rights to chemically pure sodium, magnesium, carbon. My prose is rotting syntactically and is heading – with so much work – towards simplicity. I think that is why I no longer know how to write "coherent"; the bucking of a verbal bronco leaves me on foot after a few steps. *Fixer les vertiges*, how good. But I get the feeling that I should establish elements. Poems are waiting for that, and certain kinds of novel or short story or theatre. The rest is the job of stuffing and it does not work out well for me.

"Yes, but elements, are they the essential thing? Establishing carbon is not worth as much as establishing the Guermantes family."

"I think in a vague sort of way that the elements I am aiming for are a result of *composition*. The schoolbook chemistry point of view has been turned inside out. When composition has reached its extreme limit, the territory of the elemental opens up. Establish them and if it is possible, be them."

(–91)

95

In some note or other, Morelli had shown himself to be curiously explicit about his intentions. Giving evidence of a strange anachronism, he became interested in studies or nonstudies such as Zen Buddhism, which in those years was the rash of the beat generation. The anachronism did not lie in that, but in the fact that Morelli seemed much more radical and younger in his spiritual exigencies than those California youngsters getting drunk on Sanskrit words and canned beer. One of the notes referred Suzukianly to language as a kind of exclamation or shout that rises directly out of an inner experience. There followed several examples of dialogues between teachers and pupils, completely unintelligible for a rational ear and for all dualistic and binary logic, just like the answers that teachers give their pupils, consisting in the main of whacking them over the head with a ruler, throwing a pitcher of water in their faces, throwing them out of the room or, in the best cases, throwing the question back at them. Morelli seemed to move about at will in that apparently demented universe, and took it for granted that this pedagogical behaviour constituted the real lesson, the only *manner* in which one could open the pupil's spiritual eye and reveal the truth to him. This violent unnaturalness seemed *natural* to him, in the sense that it abolished the structures which made up the specialty of the Western world, the axes on which man's historical understanding rotated and which in discursive thought (including aesthetic and even poetic feeling) find their instrument of choice.

The tone of the notes (jottings with a view to mnemotechny or an end not too well explained) seemed to indicate that Morelli had gone off into an adventure analogous to the work that he had been painfully writing and publishing over the years. For some of his readers (and for himself) it was laughable to try to write the kind of novel that would do away with the logical articulations of discourse.

One ended up by divining a kind of transaction, a proceeding (even though the absurdity of choosing a narration for ends that did not seem to be narrative might remain standing).*

* Why not? Morelli himself put the question on a sheet of graph paper in the margin of which there was a list of vegetables, probably a *memento buffandi.* Prophets, mystics, dark night of the soul: the frequent use of a story in the form of an apology or a vision. Of course a novel . . . But that scandal was born more from the generic and classificatory mania of the Western monkey than from a real internal contradiction.**

** Without saying that the more violent the internal contradiction, the more efficiently it would be able to supply a technique, as it were, in the Zen manner. Instead of a whack on the head, an absolutely antinovelish novel, with the subsequent scandal and shock, and perhaps with an opening for those best alerted.***

*** As if a hope for this last item, another scrap of paper continued the Suzukian quotation in the sense that the comprehension of the strange language used by the teachers means the comprehension of one's self on the part of the pupil and not that of the sense of the language. Just the reverse of what an astute European philosopher might deduce, the language of the Zen teacher transmits ideas and not feelings or intuitions. That is why it is of no use as far as language as such is concerned, but since the choice of phrases comes from the teacher, the mystery comes to a head in the region best suited for it and the pupil opens himself up, understands himself, and the pedestrian phrase becomes a key.****

**** That is why Étienne, who had made an analytical study of Morelli's tricks (something which had seemed a guarantee of failure to Oliveira), thought he recognized in certain passages of the book, including entire chapters, a kind of gigantic amplification *ad usum homo sapiens* of certain Zen slaps on the face. Those sections of the book Morelli called "archapters" and "chaptypes", verbal nonsense in which one could deduce a mixture that was not in the least Joycean. As for what archetypes had to do with it, it was a theme of restlessness for Wong and Gregorovius.*****

***** An observation by Étienne: In no way did Morelli appear to climb the *bodhi* tree or Sinai or up to any other platform of revelation. No pedagogical attitudes were set forth by which the reader might be guided towards new and green meadows. Without servility (the old man was of Italian origin and he was quick to pick up on what came from the heart, it must be said) he wrote as if he himself, in a desperate and moving attempt, had pictured the teacher who was to enlighten him. He turned loose his Zen phrase, and one kept on listening to it – sometimes for fifty pages, the old monster – , and it would have been absurd and of little faith to suspect that those pages were directed at a reader. If Morelli published them it was partly because of his Italian side ("*Ritorna vincitor!*") and partly because he was enchanted at how gaudy they had turned out.******

****** Étienne saw in Morelli the perfect Western man, the colonizer. When his crop of Buddhist poppies had been harvested, he would return with the seeds to the *Quartier Latin*. If the last revelation was perhaps the one that he had been hoping for most, one would have to recognize that his book was before anything else a literary undertaking, precisely because it was set forth as the destruction of literary forms (formulas).*******

******* Also Western, although it should be said as praise, from the Christian conviction that there is no individual salvation possible, and that one's faults stain everyone else and vice versa. Perhaps that is why (Oliveira had a hunch) he chose the novel form for his meanderings, and published in addition what he kept on finding or unfinding.

(–146)

96

The newsspreadlikewildfire, and practically the whole Club was there at ten o'clock that night. Étienne had the key, Wong bowed down to the ground to counteract the furious reception they got from the concierge, *mais qu'est-ce qu'ils viennent ficher, non mais vraiment ces étrangers, écoutez, je veux bien vous laisser monter puisque vous dites que vous êtes des amis du vi . . . de monsieur Morelli, mais quand même il aurait fallu prévenir, quoi, une bande qui s'amène à dix heures du soir, non, vraiment, Gustave, tu devrais parler au syndic, ça devient trop con,* etc. Babs armed with what Ronald called the alligator's smile, Ronald excited and slapping Étienne on the back, pushing him so he would hurry up, Perico Romero cursing out literature, second floor RODEAU, FOURRURES, third floor DOCTEUR, fourth floor HUSSENOT, it was all too fantastic, Ronald nudging Étienne in the ribs and putting Oliveira down, the bloody bastard, just another of his practical jokes, I suppose, *dis donc, tu vas me foutre la paix, toi,* this is all that Paris is, *coño,* one fucking staircase after another, you get fed up to the fifth shit with all of them. *Si tous les gars du monde . . .* Wong bringing up the rear, Wong has a smile for Gustave, a smile for the concierge, *bloody bastard, coño, ta gueule, salaud.* On the fifth floor the door on the right opened a few inches and Perico saw a gigantic rat in a white nightgown peeking out with one eye and all of her nose. Before she could close the door again, he stuck his shoe in and recited for her that thing that among serpents, the basilisk had an organ so poisonous for all the others and so overwhelming that he frightened them just by hissing and they scattered and fled at his coming, he could kill them with his glance. Madame René Lavalette, née Francillon, did not understand much but she answered with a snort and a shove. Perico pulled out his shoe with an eighth of a second to spare, SLAM. On the sixth they stopped to watch the solemnity with which Étienne inserted the key.

"It can't be," Ronald repeated for the last time. "We're dreaming, as the princesses of Tour et Taxis say. Did you bring the drinks, Babsie? An obolus for Charon, you know. Now the door will open and the magic will begin, I expect to get something out of tonight, there's an end of the world atmosphere."

"The god-damned witch almost broke my toe," Perico said, looking at his shoe. "Open up, god damn it, man, I've had enough of staircases to last me a lifetime."

But the key wouldn't work, even though Wong hinted that in ceremonies of the initiate the simplest movements are overcome by Forces that one must conquer through Patience and Slyness. The lights went out. Who's got a lighter, *coño? Tu pourrais*

<table>
<tr><td>Babs</td><td>quand même parler français, non? Ton co-</td></tr>
<tr><td></td><td>pain l'argencul n'est pas là pour piger ton</td></tr>
<tr><td>Ronald</td><td>charabia. Give me a match, Ronald. God-</td></tr>
<tr><td>Étienne</td><td>damned key, it's all rusted, the old man kept</td></tr>
<tr><td></td><td>it in a glass of water. Mon copain, mon co-</td></tr>
<tr><td>Étienne</td><td>pain, c'est pas mon copain. I don't think he's</td></tr>
<tr><td>Wong</td><td>coming. You don't know him. Maybe you</td></tr>
<tr><td></td><td>ought. What the hell. Wanna bet something?</td></tr>
<tr><td>PERICO</td><td>Ah merde, mais c'est la tour de Babel, ma</td></tr>
<tr><td>Ronald</td><td>parole. Amène ton briquet, Fleuve Jaune de</td></tr>
<tr><td>PERICO</td><td>mon cul, la poisse, quoi. On Yin days we've</td></tr>
<tr><td></td><td>got to be patient. Two litres, but good stuff.</td></tr>
<tr><td>Wong</td><td>My God, don't fall down the stairwell. I re-</td></tr>
<tr><td>Babs</td><td>member one night, in Alabama. The stars</td></tr>
<tr><td>ÉTIENNE</td><td>were out, my love. How funny, you ought to</td></tr>
<tr><td>ÉTIENNE</td><td>be on radio. There, it's starting to move now,</td></tr>
<tr><td>Babs Ronald</td><td>it was stuck, the Yin, of course, stars fell on</td></tr>
<tr><td>Babs Babs</td><td>Alabama, my foot's all fucked up, another</td></tr>
<tr><td>Ronald</td><td>match, I can't see a thing, où qu'elle est,</td></tr>
<tr><td></td><td>la minuterie? It's not working. Somebody's</td></tr>
<tr><td>Ronald</td><td>touching me on the arse, my love . . . Shh</td></tr>
<tr><td></td><td>. . . Shh . . . Let Wong go in first to exor-</td></tr>
<tr><td>ÉTIENNE</td><td>cise the demons. Oh, by no means. Give a</td></tr>
<tr><td>& chorus</td><td>shove, Perico, he's just a Chinaman.</td></tr>
</table>

"Shut up, everybody," Ronald said. "We're in other territory, I really mean it. If somebody has come here to have a good time, he can get his arse out of here. Give me the bottles, sweetie. You always drop them when you get overcome with emotion."

"I don't like people who go around pawing me in the dark," Babs said looking at Perico and Wong.

Étienne ran his fingers slowly over the moulding of the door. They waited in silence for him to find the light switch. The apartment was small and dusty, the soft and domesticated lights enveloped it in a golden air in which the Club breathed with relief for the first time and went about looking over the rest of the place, exchanging impressions in low voices: the reproduction of the tablet of Ur, the legend of the profanation of the Eucharist (Paolo Uccello *pinxit*), the photographs of Pound and of Musil, the little picture by De Staël, the enormous quantity of books along the walls, on the floor, on the tables, in the bathroom, in the tiny kitchen, where there was a fried egg halfway between rotten and petrified, most beautiful for Étienne, garbage pail for Babs, *ergo* a sibilant argument while Wong respectfully opened the *Dissertatio de morbis a fascino et fascino contra morbos* by Zwinger, Perico up on a stool as was his speciality, running through a row of Spanish poets of the Golden Age, examining a small astrolabe of tin and ivory, and Ronald standing motionless in front of Morelli's table, a bottle of cognac under each arm, looking at the green velvet notebook, exactly the spot where Balzac would have sat down to write but not Morelli. Then it was true, the old man had been living there, a stone's throw away from the Club, and his damned publisher had declared that he was in Austria or on the Costa Brava every time they asked for his address over the phone. Notebooks to the right and to the left, between twenty and forty, all colours, empty or full, and in the middle an ashtray that was like another one of Morelli's archives, a Pompeiian pile of ashes and burned-out matches.

"She threw the still life into the bin," Étienne said furiously. "If La Maga comes she won't leave a hair on her head. But you, her husband . . ."

"Look at this," Ronald said, showing him the table to calm him down. "And besides, Babs said it was rotten, there's no reason for you to carry on. The meeting has come to order. Étienne is presiding, but how can we continue? What about the Argentinian?"

"The Argentinian and the Transylvanian are missing, Guy is in the country, and La Maga's wandering around God knows where. In any case, we have a quorum. Wong, recording secretary."

"Let's wait a while for Oliveira and Ossip. Babs, treasurer."

"Ronald, secretary. In charge of the bar. Sweet, get some glasses, will you?"

"We stand recessed," Étienne said, sitting down alongside the table. "The Club is meeting tonight to fulfil a desire of Morelli's. While we're waiting for Oliveira, if he's coming, let's drink to the old man's sitting here again one of these days. Good lord, what a ghastly spectacle. We look like a nightmare that Morelli is probably dreaming right now in the hospital. Horrible. The meeting is open for business."

"But let's talk about him in the meantime," said Ronald, whose eyes were filled with natural tears and who was struggling with the cork in the cognac bottle. "There'll never be another session like this, all these years now I've been a novitiate and I didn't know it. And you, Wong, and Perico. All of us. Damn it, I could cry. This is the way a person must feel when he gets to the top of a mountain or breaks a record, things like that. Sorry."

Étienne put a hand on his shoulder. They sat down around the table. Wong turned out the lamps, except the one that was lighting up the green notebook. It was almost a scene for Eusapia Paladino, thought Étienne, who respected spiritualism. They began to talk about Morelli's books and drink cognac.

(–94)

97

Gregorovius, an agent of heteroclite forces, had been interested in a note of Morelli's: "To plunge one's self into a reality or into a possible mode of a reality, and to feel how that which at first sight seemed to be the wildest absurdity comes to have some value, to articulate itself with other forms, absurd or otherwise, until the divergent weave (in relation to the stereotyped sketch of everyday life) appears and is defined in a coherent sketch which only by timid comparison with the former will appear mad or delirious or incomprehensible. Nevertheless, am I not sinning in the direction of an excess of confidence? To refuse to make *psychologies* and at the same time to place a reader – a certain reader, that is true – in contact with a *personal* world, with a personal existence and meditation . . . That reader will be without any bridge, any intermediate link, any casual articulation. Raw things: behaviour, results, ruptures, catastrophes, derision. There where there should be a leave-taking there is a sketch on the wall; instead of a shout, a fishing-pole; a death is resolved in a trio for mandolins. And all of that is leave-taking, shout, and death, but who is prepared to displace himself, remove himself, decentre himself, uncover himself? The outer forms of the novel have changed, but their heroes are still the avatars of Tristram, Jane Eyre, Lafcadio, Leopold Bloom, people from the street, from the home, from the bedroom, *characters*. For every hero like Ulrich (*more* Musil) or Molloy (*more* Beckett), there are five hundred Darleys (*more* Durrell). For my part, I wonder whether one day I will ever succeed in making it felt that the true character and the only one that interests me is the reader, to the degree in which something of what I write ought to contribute to his mutation, displacement, alienation, transportation." In spite of the tacit confession of defeat in the last sentence, Ronald found a presumption in the note that displeased him.

(–18)

98

And that's how blind people are the ones who light our paths. That's how someone, without knowing it, comes to show you irrefutably that you are on a path which he for his part would be incapable of following. La Maga will never know how her finger pointed towards the thin line that shatters the mirror, up to what point certain silences, certain absurd attentions, a certain scurrying of a dazzled centipede were the password for the firm establishment of my being in myself, which meant being in no place. By the way, that metaphor of the thin line . . . If you want happiness the way you say / Poetry away, Horacio, away.

Seen objectively: She was incapable of showing me anything inside my terrain, even in hers she whirled around disconcerted, touching, handling. A frantic bat, the sketch a fly makes in the air of the room. Suddenly, for me seated there looking at her, an indication, a hint. Without her knowing it, the reason for her tears or the order of her shopping list or her way of frying potatoes were *signs*. Morelli spoke of something like that when he wrote: "Reading Heisenberg until noon, notes, cards. The concierge's boy brings me my mail and we talk about a model aeroplane he is building in the kitchen of his apartment. While he tells me about it, he gives two little hops on his left foot, three on his right, two on his left. I ask him why two and three, and not two and two or three and three. He looks at me surprised, he does not understand. Feeling that Heisenberg and I are from the other side of a territory, while the boy is still straddling with one foot in each without knowing it, and that soon he will be only on our side and all communication will have been lost. Communication with what, for what? Well, let us continue reading; Heisenberg probably . . . "

(–38)

99

"It isn't the first time that he's referred to the erosion of language," Étienne said. "I could mention several places where characters lose confidence in themselves to the degree in which they feel they've been drawn through their thought and speech, and they're afraid the sketch may be deceptive. *Honneur des hommes, Saint Langage* . . . We're far away from that."

"Not so very far," Ronald said. "What Morelli is trying to do is give language back its rights. He talks about expurgating it, punishing it, changing 'descend' into 'go down' as a hygienic measure; but what he's really looking for is to give back all its glow to the verb 'descend', so that it can be used the way I use matches and not like a decorative fragment, a piece of the commonplace."

"Yes, but that battle is taking place on several planes," said Oliveira, coming out of a long silence. "In what you've just read to us, it's quite clear that Morelli is condemning in language the reflection of a false or incomplete optic and *Organum* that mask reality and humanity for us. Basically, he didn't really care too much about language, except on the aesthetic plane. But that reference to the *ethos* is unmistakable. Morelli understands that the mere writing of aesthetic is a fraud and a lie and ends up arousing the female-reader, the type that doesn't want any problems but rather solutions, or false and alien problems that will allow him to suffer comfortably seated in his chair, without compromising himself in the drama that should also be his. In Argentina, if the Club will give me permission to fall back on localisms, that kind of fraud has kept us quite content and peaceful for a whole century."

"Happy is he who finds his peers, the active readers," Wong recited. "It's on this little piece of blue paper, in notebook twenty-one. When I first read Morelli (in Meudon, a clandestine movie, Cuban friends) it seemed to me that the whole book was the Great

Tortoise turned on its back. Difficult to understand. Morelli is an extraordinary philosopher, but exceedingly stupid at times."

"Like you," said Perico, getting off his stool and elbowing his way into the group at the table. "All those fantasies about correcting language are jobs for academicians, boy, not to mention grammarians. Descend or go down, the fact is that the character beats it downstairs, and that's that."

"Perico," Étienne said, "is rescuing us from excessive confinement, from getting up into abstractions that Morelli sometimes likes too much."

"I'll tell you something," Perico said threateningly. "As far as I'm concerned, this whole business of abstractions . . . "

The cognac burned Oliveira's throat and he slid thankfully into the argument, where he could still lose himself for a while. In a certain passage (he didn't know exactly which, he would have to hunt for it) Morelli had given some keys to a method of composition. His problem to start with was always a drying up, a Mallarmean horror of facing a blank page, coincident with the necessity of opening himself up at all cost. Inevitable that a part of his work should be a reflection on the problem of writing it. He kept getting farther and farther away from the professional utilization of literature, from that type of short story or poem on which his initial prestige had been based. In some passage or other Morelli said he had reread with nostalgia and even surprise certain texts he had written years before. How could those inventions have flourished, that marvellous and yet so comfortable and simplifying unfolding of a narrator and his narration? In those days it had been as if what he was writing were already laid out in front of him, writing was running a Lettera 22 over words invisible but present, like the diamond in the groove of the record. Now he could write only with effort, examining at every turn a possible opposite, the hidden fallacy (he would have to reread, Oliveira thought, a curious passage that had delighted Étienne), suspicious that every clear idea was inevitably a mistake or half-truth, mistrusting the words that tended to organize themselves euphonically, rhythmically, with the happy murmur that hypnotizes the reader after he has found his first victim in the writer himself. ("Yes, but poetry . . . " "Yes, but that note in which he talks about the 'swing' that puts discourse on the march . . . ") Sometimes Morelli was in favour of a bitterly simple conclusion: he no longer had anything to say, the conditioned reflexes of the profession confused necessity with routine, a typical case among writers beyond the age of fifty and the important prizes. But at the same time he felt that he had never been so desirous, so urged to write. Could the delightful anxiety of doing battle with himself line by line be a mere reflection, a routine? Why then immediately a counterblow, the descending stroke of the piston, gasping doubt, dryness, renunciation?

"Hey," Oliveira said, "where's that passage about the single word you liked so much?"

"I know it by heart," Étienne said. "It's the conjunction *if* followed by a footnote, which in turn is followed by a footnote which in turn is followed by another footnote. I was telling Perico that Morelli's theories are not entirely original. It's his way of saying them that makes him intimate, the strength with which he tries to describe, as he says, to earn the right (and earn it for everybody) to enter the house of man once more with his best foot forward. I'm using his very words, or ones that are very much like them."

"We've had enough of surrealists for a while," Perico said.

"It's not a question of the job of verbal liberation," said Étienne. "The surrealists thought that true language and true reality were censored and relegated by the rationalist and bourgeois structure of the Western world. They were right, as any poet knows, but that was just a moment in the complicated peeling of the banana. Result, more than one of them ate it with the skin still on. The surrealists hung from words instead of brutally disengaging themselves from them, as Morelli would like to do from the word itself. Fanatics of the *verbum* in a pure state, frantic wizards, they accepted anything as long as it didn't seem excessively grammatical. They didn't suspect enough that the creation of a whole language, even though it might end up betraying its sense, irrefutably shows human structure, whether that of a Chinese or a redskin. Language means residence in a reality, living in a reality. Even if it's true that the language we use betrays us (and Morelli isn't the only one who shouts it to the four winds), wanting to free it from its taboos isn't enough. We have to relive it, not reanimate it."

"It all sounds most solemn," Perico said.

"It's in any good philosophical work," Gregorovius said timidly. He had been thumbing entomologically through the notebooks and seemed half-asleep. "It's impossible to relive language if one doesn't start by intuiting in a different way almost everything that makes up our reality."

"Intuit," said Oliveira, "is one of those words that can be applied to sweeping just as easily as to scrubbing. Let's not attribute to Morelli the problems of Dilthey, Husserl, or Wittgenstein. The only thing clear in everything the old man has written is that we still utilize language in its current key, with its current finalities, we shall die without ever knowing the real name of the day. It's almost stupid to repeat that life is sold to us, as Malcolm Lowry said, that it's given to us prefabricated. Morelli is also a little stupid when he insists on that, but Étienne has hit the nail on the head: the old man shows himself by the way he does it and he shows us the way out. What good is a writer if he can't destroy literature? And us, we don't want to be female-readers, what good are we if we don't help as much as we can in that destruction?"

"But afterwards, what do we do afterwards?" Babs asked.

"I wonder," said Oliveira. "Until about twenty years ago there was the great answer: Poetry, silly, Poetry. They would gag you with the great word. Poetical vision of the world, conquest of a poetical reality. But then after the last war, you must have noticed that it was all over. We still have poets, nobody can deny that, but no one ever reads them."

"Don't talk nonsense," said Perico. "I read tons of poetry."

"Of course, so do I. But it's not a question of poetry, you know, it's a question of what the surrealists were announcing and what every poet wants and searches for, that well-known poetical reality. Believe me, my dear boy, since nineteen-fifty we've been right in the middle of a technological reality, statistically speaking, at least. Very bad, a pity, it makes you want to tear your hair, but that's how it is."

"I don't give a hoot for technology," Perico said. "Fray Luis, for example . . ."

"We're in the year nineteen-fifty something."

"I'm aware of that, *coño*."

"It doesn't look like it."

"But do you think I'm about to put myself in the position of a meat-beating historicist?"

"No, but you ought to read the newspapers. I don't like technology any more than you, it's just that I feel the world has changed in the last twenty years. Any guy who's past forty has to realize it, and that's why Babs's questions back Morelli and the rest of us up against the wall. It's OK to declare war on language turned whore, literature, as it were, in the name of a reality we think is true, that we think we can reach, that we think is there somewhere in the spirit, if you'll pardon the expression. But Morelli himself sees only the negative side of his battle. He feels he has to wage it, like you and like all of us. So?"

"Let's be methodical," Étienne said. "Let's leave your 'so?' out of it. Morelli's lesson is enough as a first stage."

"You can't talk about stages without presupposing a goal."

"Call it a working hypothesis, anything you like along those lines. What Morelli is looking for is to break the reader's mental habits. Something very modest, as can be seen, nothing comparable to Hannibal crossing the Alps. Up till now, at least, there isn't much metaphysics in Morelli, except that you, Horacio Curiacio, are capable of finding metaphysics in a tin of tomatoes. Morelli is an artist who has a special idea of art, consisting more than anything in knocking over the usual forms, something all good artists have in common. For example, the Chinese-scroll novel makes him explode. The book read from beginning to end like a good child. You've probably noticed already that he gets less and less worried about joining the parts together, that business of one word leading to another . . . When I read Morelli I have the impression he's looking for a less mechanical interaction, one less caused by the elements he works with; he feels that what has already been written just barely conditions what is being written, especially since the old man, after hundreds of pages, doesn't even have a clear memory of what he's done."

"According to which," Perico said, "it turns out that a midget on page twenty is six feet tall on page one hundred. I've noticed that more than once. There are scenes that begin at six in the afternoon and end at five-thirty. A bore."

"And haven't you ever wanted to be a midget or a giant according to the state of your mind?" Ronald asked.

"I'm talking about the soma," Perico said.

"He believes in the soma," Oliveira said. "The soma in time. He believes in time, in the before and in the after. The poor fellow hasn't found some letter of his written twenty years ago in a drawer, he hasn't reread it, he hasn't noticed that nothing is sustained unless we prop it up with a crumb of time, unless we invent time so we don't go crazy."

"That's all part of a trade," Ronald said. "But behind it, behind . . ."

"A poet," Oliveira said, sincerely moved. "Your name ought to be Behind or Beyond, my dear American. Or Yonder, that's such a pretty English word."

"None of it would make any sense if there weren't a behind," Ronald said. "Any author of best-sellers writes better than Morelli. The reason we read him, the reason we're here tonight, is that Morelli has what Bird had, what all of a sudden Cummings or Jackson Pollock have, anyway, so much for examples. And why so much for examples?" Ronald shouted furiously, while Babs looked on admiringly and drinkingineveryoneofhiswordsinonegulp. "I'll quote anything I goddam please. It's easy to see that Morelli doesn't complicate life just because he likes to, and besides, his book is a shameless provocation, just like anything else that's worth something. In this technological world you were talking about, Morelli wants to save something that's dying, but in order to save it, first it has to be killed or at least given such a blood transfusion that the whole thing will be like a resurrection. The mistake of futurist poetry," Ronald said, to the immense admiration of Babs, "was wanting to comment on mechanism, believing that they'd be saved from leukaemia that way. But we won't understand reality any better by talking in a literary way of what's going on at Cape Canaveral, it seems to me."

"And it seems right," Oliveira said. "Let's keep on looking for the Yonder, there are plenty of Yonders that keep opening up one after the other. I'd start by saying that this technological reality that men of science and the readers of *France-Soir* accept today, this world of cortisone, gamma rays, and the elution of plutonium, has as little to do with reality as the world of the *Roman de la Rose*. If I mentioned it a while back to our friend Perico, it was in order to make him take note that his aesthetic criteria and his scale of values are pretty well liquidated and that man, after having expected everything from intelligence and the spirit, feels that he's been betrayed, is vaguely aware that his weapons have been turned against him, that culture, *civiltà*, have misled him into this blind alley where scientific barbarism is nothing but a very understandable reaction. Please excuse my vocabulary."

"Klages has already said all that," said Gregorovius.

"I don't pretend to hold any copyright on it," Oliveira said. "The idea is that reality, whether you accept the version of the Holy See, or of René Char, or of Oppenheimer, is always a conventional reality, incomplete and divided. The surprise some guys show in front of an electron microscope doesn't seem to be any more fruitful to me than the one concierges show at the miracles of Lourdes. Believing in what they call matter, believing in what they call spirit, living in the Emmanuel or taking courses in Zen, considering human destiny as an economic problem or as a complete absurdity, the list is long, the choice is multiple. But the very fact that there can be a choice and that the list is long is enough to show that we're still in prehistory and in prehumanity. I'm not an optimist, I doubt very much whether some day we'll find the real history of real humanity. It's going to be hard going to get to Ronald's famous Yonder because nobody will deny that the problem of reality has to be established in collective terms, not just in the salvation of a few of the elect. Accomplished men, men who have taken the leap outside time and have become integrated in a *summa*, as it were . . . Yes, I suppose they have existed and still do. But that's not enough; I feel that my salvation, supposing I can reach it, must also be the salvation of all, right down to the last man. And that, old man . . . We're no longer in the fields of Assisi, we can no longer hope that the example of a saint will sow the seeds of sainthood, that every guru will be the salvation of all of his disciples."

"Come on back from Benares," Étienne advised. "We were talking about Morelli, I think. And to connect with what you were saying, it occurs to me that this famous Yonder cannot be imagined as a future in time or in space. If we continue holding to Kantian categories, Morelli seems to say, we will never get out of this blind alley. What we call reality, the true reality that we also call Yonder (sometimes it helps to give a lot of names to a partial vision, at least it prevents the notion from becoming closed and rigid), that true reality, I repeat, is not something that is going to happen, a goal, the last step, the end of an evolution. No, it's something that's already here, in us. You can feel it, all you need is the courage to stick your hand into the darkness. I feel it when I'm painting."

"It might be the Evil One," Oliveira said. "It might be a mere aesthetic exaltation. But it might be the other too. Yes, it might be the other too."

"It's here," Babs said, touching her forehead. "I feel it when I'm a little drunk, or when . . ."

She let out a raucous laugh and covered her face. Ronald gave her a tender shove.

"Not it's here," said Wong very seriously. "It is."

"We won't get very far on this road," Oliveira said. "What does poetry give us except that partial-vision? You, me, Babs . . . The kingdom of man was not born out of a few isolated sparks. Everybody has had his moment of vision, but the worst part is falling back into the *hinc* and the *nunc*."

"Bah, you don't understand anything unless it's in absolute terms," Étienne said. "Let me finish what I wanted to say. Morelli thinks that if the lyricists, as our Perico has said, did open the way through petrified and unstable forms, whether a modal adverb, a sense of theme, or whatever you want to make it, they must have had something useful for the first time in their lives. Doing away with the female-reader, or at least severely damaging him, would help all of those who in some way are working to reach the Yonder. The narrative technique of types like that is simply an urge to get out of the rut."

"Yes, only to fall into the mud up to his neck," said Perico, who at eleven o'clock at night was against anything.

"Heraclitus," Gregorovius said, "buried himself in shit up to his neck and cured himself of dropsy."

"Leave Heraclitus in peace," Étienne said. "I'm already beginning to feel foolishly sleepy, but in any case I'm going to say the following, two points: Morelli seems convinced that if a writer keeps on being dominated by the language they have sold him along with the clothes he's wearing and his name and nationality, his work won't have any other value except the aesthetic, a value which the old man seems to despise more and more. He's rather explicit in one place or other: according to him, nothing can be denounced if the denouncing is done within the system that belongs to the thing denounced. Writing against capitalism with the mental baggage and the vocabulary that comes out of capitalism is a waste of time. Historical results like Marxism and what have you will be produced, but the Yonder is not precisely history, the Yonder is like fingertips sticking out of the surface of history, looking for something to cling to."

"Bullshit," said Perico.

"And that's why the writer has to set language on fire, put an end to its coagulated forms and even go beyond it, place in doubt the possibility that language is still in touch with what it pretends to name. Not words as such any more, because that's less important, but rather the total structure of language, of discourse."

"For all of which he uses an exceedingly clear language," Perico said.

"Of course, Morelli doesn't believe in onomatopoeic systems or in lyrics. It's not a question of substituting automatic writing or any other current fraud for syntax. What he wants to do is transgress the total literary deed, the book, if you will. Sometimes the word, sometimes what the word transmits. He works like a guerrilla fighter, he blows up what he can, the rest follows in its path. Don't get the idea that he's a man of letters."

"We should think about leaving," said Babs, who was sleepy.

"Say whatever you want," Perico insisted, "but no real revolution has ever been made against form. What counts is content, man, content."

"We've already had dozens of centuries of literature with content," Oliveira said, "and look at the results. By literature, you understand, I mean everything that can be said or thought."

"Without realizing that the distinction between form and content is false," said Étienne. "Everybody's known that for years. Let's distinguish, rather, between the expressive element, or language as such, and the thing expressed, or reality becoming awareness."

"Whatever you want," Perico said. "What I would like to know is whether the break that Morelli is trying for, I mean the breaking of what you call the expressive element the better to reach the expressible thing, really has any value at this time."

"It probably wouldn't be good for anything," Oliveira said, "but it does make us feel a little less lonely in this blind alley at the service of the Great-Idealist-Realist-Spiritualist-Materialist-Infatuation of the West, Inc."

"Do you think somebody else might have been able to open a way through language until he came to touch it at its roots?" Ronald asked.

"Maybe. Morelli doesn't have the required genius or patience. He points out a path, he takes a few digs with a pickaxe . . . He leaves a book behind. It's not much."

"Let's go," said Babs. "It's getting late and the cognac's all gone."

"And there's something else," said Oliveira. "What he's pursuing is absurd to the degree that nobody knows anything except what he knows, that is to say, an anthropological circumscription. Wittgensteinly speaking, problems link themselves together in a *backward* direction, that is to say that what a man knows can be the knowledge of a man, but he no longer knows what he ought to know about the man himself, so that his notion of reality would be acceptable. The gnoseologists brought up this problem and even thought that they had found solid ground from which they could continue the race forward, towards metaphysics. But the hygienic retreat of a Descartes appears partial and even insignificant to us today, because at this very moment there is a Mr Wilcox in Cleveland who with electrodes and other apparatus is proving that thought and an electromagnetic circuit are the same thing (things that he in turn thinks he knows very well because he knows very well the language that defines them, etc.). Add to that the fact that a Swede has just put forth a very impressive theory on cerebral chemistry. Thinking is the result of the interaction of certain acids, the name of which I do not care to recall. *Acido, ergo sum.* Put a drop on your meninges and there you are, maybe Oppenheimer or Dr Petiot, the eminent murderer. You can see then, how the *cogito*, that Human Operation *par excellence*, is nowadays located in a rather vague region, somewhere between electromagnetism and chemistry, and probably not as different as we used to think from things like an aurora borealis or a picture taken with infrared rays. There goes your *cogito*, a link in the dizzy flow of forces whose steps are called in 1950, *inter alia*, electrical impulses, molecules, atoms, neutrons, protons, positrons, microbitons, radioactive isotopes, grains of cinnabar, cosmic rays: Words, words, words, *Hamlet*, Act Two, I think. Without considering," Oliveira added with a sigh, "that it's probably just the opposite, and the result is that the aurora borealis is a *spiritual* phenomenon, and then we really are what we want to be . . ."

"Along with some similar nihilism, hara-kiri," Étienne said.

"Well of course," Oliveira said. "But getting back to the old man, if what he's after is absurd, because it's like hitting Sugar Ray Robinson with a banana, because it's an insignificant offensive in the midst of the crisis and complete breakup of the classic idea of Homo sapiens, we mustn't forget that you are you and I am I, or at least so it seems to us, and that even if we don't have the slightest certainty about everything our gigantic parents accepted as irrefutable, we still have the pleasant possibility of living and acting *as if*, choosing working hypotheses, attacking like Morelli what seems false to us, in the name of some obscure feeling of certainty, which is probably just as uncertain as the rest, but which makes us lift up our heads and count the little goats or look for the Pleiades again, those childhood animals, those bottomless fireflies. Cognac."

"It's all gone," Babs said. "Let's go, I'm falling asleep."

"In the end, as always, an act of faith," said Étienne, laughing. "It's still the best definition of man. Now, getting back to the subject of the fried egg . . ."

(–35)

100

He put the slug in the slot, slowly dialled the number. At that hour Étienne was probably painting and he hated people to call him in the middle of his work, but he had to call him just the same. The telephone began to ring at the other end, in a studio near the Place d'Italie, three miles from the post office on the Rue Danton. An old woman with the look of a rat had stationed herself in front of the glass booth; she looked furtively at Oliveira who was sitting on the little bench with his face up against the apparatus, and Oliveira felt the old woman looking at him, implacably counting the minutes. The glass in the booth was strangely clean: people were coming and going in the post office, one could hear the dull (and funereal, it was hard to say why) cancelling of stamps. Étienne said something on the other end, and Oliveira pushed the nickel button that established contact and definitively swallowed up the twenty-franc slug.

"Why do you always fuck things up," complained Étienne, who appeared to have recognized him immediately. "You know I'm always working like crazy at this hour."

"Me too," said Oliveira. "I called you because just when I was working I had a dream."

"What do you mean when you were working?"

"Yes, around three in the morning. I dreamed I was going into the kitchen, I was looking for some bread, and I cut off a slice. The bread was different from what we have around here, French bread like the bread in Buenos Aires, you know there's nothing French about it but they call it French bread. You must realize it's a much thicker loaf, light in colour, with lots of soft centre. A loaf made to be spread with butter and jam, you understand."

"I know what you mean," Étienne said. "I've eaten it in Italy."

"You're crazy. It's not like that at all. Someday I'll have to draw you a picture so you can see. Look, it's shaped like a short, fat fish, barely six inches long but quite fat in the middle. That's Buenos Aires French bread."

"Buenos Aires French bread," Étienne repeated.

"Yes, but this happened on the Rue de la Tombe Issoire, before I moved in with La Maga. I was hungry and I took out the loaf to cut off a slice. Then I heard the bread crying. Yes, of course it was a dream, but the bread started to cry when I put the knife to it. An ordinary loaf of French bread and it was crying. I woke up without knowing what was going to happen, I think I still had the knife stuck in the bread when I woke up."

"*Tiens*," said Étienne.

"Now you can see, you wake up from a dream like that, go out into the hall and stick your head under the tap, go back to bed, spend the whole night smoking . . . What could I do, the best thing was to call you, apart from the fact that we could make a date to go and see the old man in the accident I told you about."

"You did the right thing," Étienne said. "It sounds like a child's dream. Children can still dream things like that, or imagine them. My nephew told me once that he had been on the moon. I asked him what he had seen. He answered: 'There was a loaf of bread and a heart.' You realize that after bakery experiences like this you can't look at a child any more without being frightened."

"A loaf of bread and a heart," Oliveira repeated. "Yes, but I only saw a loaf of bread. So. There's an old woman out there who's starting to give me dirty looks. How long do they let you talk in these booths?"

"Six minutes. Then she'll start rapping on the glass. Is there only one old woman?"

"An old woman, a cross-eyed woman with a kid, and a travelling-salesman type. He must be a travelling salesman because besides the notebook he's thumbing through like mad, I can see the points of three pencils sticking out of his breast pocket."

"He could also be a bill collector."

"Now there are two more, a kid of fourteen who's picking his nose, and an old woman with a wild hat, like out of a painting by Cranach."

"You're feeling better," Étienne said.

"Yes, this booth isn't bad. It's a shame so many people are waiting. Do you think we've been talking six minutes?"

"Nowhere near," Étienne said. "Barely three, and not even that."

"Then the old woman has no right to rap on the glass, eh?"

"Let her go to hell. Of course she has no right. You can use your six minutes to tell me about as many dreams as you want to."

"It was just that one," Oliveira said, "but the worst is not the dream. The worst is what they call waking up . . . Don't you think that actually it's now that I'm dreaming?"

"Who can tell? But it's an overworked theme, old man, the philosopher and the butterfly, they're things that everybody knows."

"Yes, but please excuse me for insisting a little. I wanted you to imagine a world where you can cut a loaf of bread without its complaining."

"It's difficult to believe, really," Étienne said.

"No, seriously. Hasn't it ever happened to you that you've woken up sometimes with the exact feeling that at that moment a terrible mistake is beginning?"

"In the midst of that mistake," Étienne said, "I paint magnificent pictures and it doesn't matter to me very much whether I'm a butterfly or Fu Manchu."

"That has nothing to do with it. It seems that thanks to various mistakes Columbus reached Guanahani or whatever the name of the island is. Why that Greek criterion of truth and error?"

"But it wasn't me," Étienne said resentfully. "You're the one who spoke of an incredible mistake."

"That was a figure of speech too," Oliveira said. "The same as calling it a dream. It can't be catalogued, the mistake is precisely the fact that you can't even say whether or not it is a mistake."

"The old woman's going to break the glass," Étienne said. "You can hear her from here."

"Let her go to hell," Oliveira said. "The six minutes can't be up."

"Just about. But then, you have that South American courtesy one hears praised so much."

"It's not six minutes. I'm glad I told you about the dream, and when we get together . . . "

"Come by whenever you want to," Étienne said. "I'm not going to paint any more this morning, you've done me in."

"Can you hear her beating on the window?" Oliveira asked. "Not just the old rat-faced woman, but the kid and the crosseyed woman too. An attendant'll be here any minute."

"Of course you're going to punch them all in the eye."

"No reason to. My great technique is to pretend I don't understand a single word of French."

"You really don't understand very much," Étienne said.

"No. The sad thing is that this is a big joke for you, and really it's not a joke at all. The truth is I don't want to understand anything, if by understanding one must accept what we used to call mistakes. Hey, they've opened the door and there's a guy here tapping me on the shoulder. *Ciao*, thanks for listening to me."

"*Ciao*," said Étienne.

Straightening his jacket, Oliveira left the booth. The attendant was shouting the repertory of the rules in his ear. "If I only had the knife in my hand now," Oliveira thought, taking out his cigarettes, "this guy would probably start to cackle or turn into a bouquet of flowers." But things had become petrified, they were lasting a terribly long time, it was necessary to light his cigarette, being careful not to burn himself because his hand was shaking very much, and he could still hear the shouts of the guy, who was going away, turning around after every two steps to look at him and gesture, and the cross-eyed woman and the travelling salesman were looking at him out of one eye while with the other one they began to keep watch over the old woman so she wouldn't go over six minutes; the old woman in the booth looked exactly like a Quechua mummy in the Museum of Man, one of those that lights up if you push a button. But it was just the opposite as in so many dreams, the old woman was pushing a button on the inside and began to talk with some other old woman stuck away in some attic in the immense dream.

(–76)

101

Barely lifting her head Pola saw the calendar of the Postes Télégraphes Téléphones, a pink cow in a green field with a background of purple mountains underneath a blue sky, Thursday 1, Friday 2, Saturday 3, Sunday 4, Monday 5, Tuesday 6, *Saint Mamert, Sainte Solange, Saint Achille, Saint Servais, Saint Boniface, lever 4 h.12, coucher 19 h.23, lever 4 h.10, coucher 19 h.24, lever coucher, lever coucher, lever coucher, coucher, coucher, coucher.*

Putting her face to Oliveira's shoulder she kissed perspiring skin, tobacco and sleep. With a very distant and free hand she caressed his stomach, came and went along his thighs, played with the hair on his body, wrapping it around her fingers a little and tugging softly so that Oliveira got a little annoyed and bit her in play. A pair of slippers was dragging along the stairway, *Saint Ferdinand, Sainte Pétronille, Saint Fortuné, Sainte Blandine, un, deux, un, deux,* right, left, right, left, good, bad, good, bad, forward, back, forward, back. A hand went along her shoulder, playing spider, one finger, another, another, *Saint Fortuné, Sainte Blandine,* a finger here, another farther on, another on top, another below. The caresses slowly penetrated her, from a different plane. The hour of luxury, surplus, slowly biting, looking for contact with delicate exploration, with feigned hesitancy, putting the tip of the tongue against a skin, slowly digging in a nail, murmuring *coucher 19 h.24, Saint Ferdinand.* Pola raised her head a little and looked at Horacio who had his eyes closed. She wondered whether he did that with his girlfriend too, the mother of the kid. He didn't like to talk about the other girl, he required as a sort of respect that he would not refer to her except when obliged to. When she would ask him, opening one of his eyes with two fingers and kissing him wildly on the mouth that refused to answer, the only consolation then was silence, remaining there one against the other, listening to themselves breathe, with a foot or a hand travelling over to the other body, undertaking soft itineraries without consequence, leftovers of caresses lost in the bed, in the air, ghosts of kisses, little larva worms of perfumes or of habit. No, he didn't like to do that with his girlfriend, only Pola could understand, could fit so well into his whims. So well that it was extraordinary. Even when she moaned, because once she had moaned, she had wanted to free herself, but it was too late, the loop had closed and her rebellion had only served to deepen the pleasure and the pain, the double misunderstanding that they had to overcome because it was false, it could not be that in an embrace, unless yes, unless it had to be that way.

(–144)

102

Exploring like an ant, Wong turned up in Morelli's library an inscribed copy of *Die Verwirrungen des Zöglings Törless*, by Musil, with the following passage firmly underlined:

> What are the things that seem strange to me? The most trivial. Especially inanimate objects. What is there that seems strange about them? Something that I do not know. But it is precisely that! Where in the world do I get this notion of "something" from? I feel that it is there, that it exists. It produces an effect in me as if it were trying to speak. I become exasperated, as one who makes an effort to read the twisted lips of a paralytic, without managing to do so. It is as if he had an additional sense, one more than other people, but one which has not been developed completely, a sense that is there and can be perceived, but which does not function. The world for me is full of silent voices. Does that mean that I am a seer, or that I am having hallucinations?

Ronald found this quotation from *Lord Chandos's Letter*, by Hofmannsthal:

> Just as I had looked at the skin on my little finger in a magnifying glass one day, something like a field with furrows and hollows, so I looked at men and their actions now. I could no longer perceive them with the simplifying look of habit. Everything was breaking down into fragments which in turn were becoming fragmented; I was unable to grasp anything by means of a defined notion.

(–45)

103

Nor would Pola have understood why at night he held back his breath to listen to her sleep, spying on the sounds of her body. Face-up, satisfied, she was breathing heavily, and hardly if ever, out of some uncertain dream, did she move a hand or exhale by raising her lower lip and blowing the air up towards her nose. Horacio remained still, his head a little raised or leaning on his fist, his cigarette hanging down. At three o'clock in the morning the Rue Dauphine was quiet, Pola's breathing came and went, then there was something like a soft running, a minute instantaneous whirlwind, an interior agitation like a second life. Oliveira got up slowly and moved his ear close to the naked skin, rested it on the tense and warm curved drum, listened. Sounds, drops and falls, Cartesian devils and murmurs, a walking of crabs and slugs, a black and muffled world sliding out over plush, running into things here and there and covering up again (Pola breathed heavily, moved a little). A liquid cosmos, fluid, in nocturnal gestation, plasmas rising and falling, the opaque and slow mechanism moving around grudgingly, and suddenly a rumbling, a mad race almost against the skin, a flight and a gurgling of contention or leaking, Pola's stomach a black sky with fat and slow stars, glowing comets, a tumbling of immense vociferant planets, the sea like whispering plankton, its Medusa murmurings, Pola the microcosm, Pola the summing up of universal night in her small fermented night where yoghurt and white wine were mixed with meat and vegetables, centre of a chemistry infinitely rich and mysterious and remote and so near.

(–108)

104

Life as a *commentary* of something else we cannot reach, which is there within reach of the leap we will not take.

Life, a ballet based upon a historical theme, a story based upon a deed that once had been alive, a deed that had lived based upon a real deed.

Life, a photograph of the noumenon, a possession in the shadows (woman, monster?), life, pimp of death, splendid deck of cards, ring of forgotten keys that a pair of palsied hands degrade into a sad game of solitaire.

(–10)

105

Morelliana

I think about forgotten gestures, the multiple signals and words of grandparents, lost little by little, not inherited, fallen one after the other off the tree of time. Tonight I found a candle on a table, and as a game I lit it and walked along the corridor with it. The breeze stirred up by my motion was about to put it out, then I saw my right hand come up all by itself, cup itself, protect the flame with a living lampshade that kept the breeze away. While the flame climbed up again alert, I thought that the gesture had belonged to all of us (I thought *us* and I thought well, or I felt well) for thousands of years, during the Age of Fire, until they changed us over to electric lights. I imagined other gestures, the one that women make when they lift the hem of their skirts, the one that men make looking for the hilt of their swords. Like words lost in childhood, heard for the last time by old people who are heading towards death. In my home no one talks about the "camphor closet" any more, no one talks about "the triv" – the trivet – any more. Like music of the moment, 1920 waltzes, polkas that warmed grandparents' hearts.

I think about those objects, those boxes, those utensils that sometimes would turn up in storerooms, kitchens, or hidden spots, *and whose use no one can explain any more.* The vanity of believing that we understand the works of time: it buries its dead and keeps the keys. Only in dreams, in poetry, in play – lighting a candle, walking with it along the corridor – do we sometimes arrive at what we were before we were this thing that, who knows, we are.

(–96)

106

Between now and tomorrow, babe, morning, we'll have to part,
midnight to morning, babe, tomorrow we'll have to part.
Please remember just one thing about it, I've always been in your heart.

* * *

Cold feet on the kitchen floor, cold feet on the ground,
cold feet everywhere since my man left town.
Cold feet in the butcher shop, cold feet in the store
since nobody comes around to grind my meat no more.
Cold feet on the motor and cold feet on the stones
and cold feet in my bed, 'cause I'm sleeping all alone.

(–13)

107

Written by Morelli in the hospital

The best trait my ancestors have is that of being dead; I am waiting modestly and proudly for the moment when I come into my inheritance from them. I have friends who would not fail to erect a statue of me in which they would represent me face down in the act of peeping into a puddleful of authentic little frogs. By putting a coin in the slot they will see me spit in the water and the frogs will get all stirred up and croak for a minute and a half, just enough time for people to lose all interest in the statue.

(–113)

108

"*La cloche, le clochard, la clocharde, clocharder.* There's even a thesis that was presented at the Sorbonne on the subject of the psychology of the *clochard.*"

"Could be," Oliveira said. "But they don't have a Juan Filloy to write *Caterva* for them. What ever happened to Filloy?"

Naturally, La Maga was in no position to know, in the first place because she never knew he had existed. He had to explain to her why Filloy, why *Caterva.* La Maga liked the plot of the book very much, the idea that South American *linyeras* were in a class with *clochards.* She remained firmly convinced that it was an insult to confuse a *linyera* with a beggar, and her liking for the *clocharde* of the Pont des Arts had its roots in reasons that now seemed scientific. Especially in those days when she had discovered, walking along the river bank, that the *clocharde* was in love, sympathy and the desire for everything to turn out well were for La Maga something like the arch of the bridges, which always brought out her feelings, or like those pieces of tin or wire that Oliveira would pick up as they walked along.

"Filloy, shit," Oliveira said looking at the towers of the City Hall and thinking about Cartouche. "My country's so far away, damn it, it's incredible there could be so much salt water in this mad world."

"On the other hand there's not so much air," La Maga answered. "Thirty-two hours' worth, no more, no less."

"That's right. But where do you get the dough for the flight?"

"And the wish to go back, because I really don't."

"Me neither. But let's just suppose. There's no way back. Irrefutable."

"You never talked about going back," La Maga said.

"No one talks about it, wuthering heights, nobody talks about it. It's only the feeling that everything is cool for the guy without bread."

"Paris is free," La Maga quoted. "You said so the day we met.

Going to visit the *clocharde* is free, making love is free, telling you that you're evil is free, not loving you . . . Why did you go to bed with Pola?"

"A matter of perfume," Oliveira said, sitting down on the strip alongside the water's edge. "I thought that she would smell like the Songs of Songs, cinnamon, myrrh, things like that. It was a sure thing, besides."

"The *clocharde* won't be along tonight. She would have been here already, she almost never fails."

"Sometimes they arrest them," Oliveira said. "To fumigate them, I suppose, or so the city can go to sleep peacefully alongside its impassive river. A *clochard* is a worse disgrace than a thief, that's a well-known fact; basically, there's nothing that can be done about them, they have to leave them in peace."

"Tell me about Pola. We may see the *clocharde* in the meantime."

"Night's coming on, the American tourists are thinking about their hotels, their feet hurt, they bought a lot of crap, they've got their Sade, their Miller, their *Onze mille verges*, artistic pictures, pornographic snapshots, Sagans and Buffets. Look how they break up the sky on the bridge side. And leave Pola alone, that doesn't matter. So, the painter folds up his stool, there's no one to watch him any more. It's incredible how clean everything gets, the air is washed like the skin of that girl running over there, look at her, dressed in red."

"Tell me about Pola," La Maga repeated, patting him on the shoulder with the back of her hand.

"Pure pornography," Oliveira said. "You won't like it."

"But you must have told her something about us."

"No. Just generally. What could I tell her? Pola doesn't exist, you know. Where is she? Show her to me."

"Pure sophistry," La Maga said. She had learned the term in arguments with Ronald and Étienne. "She may not be here, but she's on the Rue Dauphine, that's for sure."

"And where is the Rue Dauphine?" asked Oliveira. "*Tiens, la clocharde qui s'amène.* But look, hey, she's wild."

Coming down the steps, staggering under the weight of an enormous bundle, out of which were sticking pieces of unravelled overcoats, red scarves, pairs of trousers picked out of dustbins, pieces of cloth, and even a blackened roll of wire, the *clocharde* reached dock-level below and let out an exclamation somewhere between a grunt and a sigh. On top of an indecipherable base where there probably had been accumulated skin-tight blouses and a brassière capable of holding up a pair of ominous breasts, were being added two, three, maybe four dresses, a complete wardrobe, and on top of it a man's jacket with one sleeve almost torn off, a scarf held together with a tin brooch that had one green and one red stone, and on her incredibly dyed blonde hair a kind of gauzy green clasp hanging to one side.

"She's marvellous," Oliveira said. "She's just seduced the people on the bridge."

"It's obvious that she's in love," La Maga said. "And the way she's made up, look at her lips. And the rouge, she's put on every bit she's got."

"She looks like Grock in one of his worst moments. Or some of Ensor's figures. She's sublime. How can they make love, the pair of them? Because you're not going to tell me they do it by remote control."

"I know a corner near the Hotel Sens where the *clochards* get together for that. The police leave them alone. Madame Léonie told me there's always some police informer among them, secrets come out at times like that. It seems that the *clochards* know a lot about gangsters."

"Gangsters, what a word," Oliveira said. "Yes, of course they'd know. They're on the edge of society, on the rim of fraud. They must know a lot about property owners and priests too. A scrutinizing look into dustbins . . ."

"Here comes the *clochard*. He's drunker than ever. Poor thing, the way she waits for him, see how she left the package on the ground as a signal, she's so sentimental."

"You can say all you want about the Hotel Sens, but I still wonder how they make it," Oliveira muttered. "Look at all those clothes. Because she probably only takes off one or two things when it's not so cold, but underneath she has on five or six more, not counting her underwear. Can you imagine what it must be like, and on wasteland? It's easier for the guy, pants are more manageable."

"They don't get undressed, maybe," La Maga conjectured. "The police wouldn't allow it. And the rain, give a thought to that. They hide in corners, in that bit of wasteland there are some ditches about a foot deep, with rubbish around the edges, where workmen throw rubbish and bottles. I have the feeling they make love standing up."

"With all those clothes? But that's inconceivable. You mean the guy has never seen her naked? That's a hell of a drag."

"Look how they love each other," La Maga said. "The way they look at each other."

"The guy's got wine coming out of his eyes. Eleven per cent tenderness with lots of tannin."

"They love each other, Horacio, they love each other. Her name is Emmanuèle, she used to be a whore in the provinces. She arrived on a *péniche* and stayed on the docks. We talked one night when I was feeling sad. She smells to high heaven, I had to leave after a little while. You know what I asked her? I asked her when she changed her clothes. That's a silly thing to ask. She's very good, she's quite mad, that night she thought she saw wildflowers among the cobblestones, she was naming them for me."

"Like Ophelia," Horacio said. "Nature imitates art."

"Ophelia?"

"I'm sorry, I'm being pedantic. And what did she say when you asked her about her clothes?"

"She started to laugh and drank a pint down in one swallow. She said that the last time she had taken something off she had pulled it over her legs, over her knees. It all fell apart. They get very cold in winter, they grab anything they can find."

"I wouldn't want to be a hospital orderly and have them brought in on a stretcher some night. A prejudice like any other. Pillars of society. I'm thirsty, Maga."

"Go over to Pola's," said La Maga, looking at the *clocharde* who was caressing her lover under the bridge. "Watch, they're going to dance now, they always dance a little at this time."

"He looks like a bear."

"He's so happy," La Maga said, picking up a little white stone and looking it all over.

Horacio took the stone away from her and licked it. It tasted like salt and stone.

"It's mine," La Maga said, trying to get it back.

"Yes, but look at the colour it has when it's with me. It lights up when it's with me."

"It's happier with me. Give it back. It's mine."

They looked at one another. Pola.

"So OK," Horacio said. "It means the same now as any other time. You're being silly, girl, if you only knew how peacefully you can sleep."

"Sleeping alone, that's swell. You see, don't you, I'm not crying. You can keep on talking, I'm not going to cry. I'm like her, watch her dance, she's like the moon, she weighs a ton and she's dancing, she's full of crud and she's dancing. It's an example. Give me my stone."

"Take it. You know, it's hard to say to you: I love you. It's so hard right now."

"Yes, you'd think you were giving me a carbon copy."

"We're talking like a pair of eagles," Horacio said.

"It's enough to make you laugh," La Maga said. "I'll lend it to you if you want, while the *clocharde* is dancing."

"OK," said Horacio, accepting the stone and licking it again. "Why talk about Pola? She's sick and lonely, I'm going to see her, we still make love, but that's all, I don't want to turn her into words, not even with you."

"Emmanuèle's going to fall into the water," said La Maga. "She's drunker than the guy."

"No, it'll all end up with the usual sordidness," Oliveira said, getting up from the edge. "Do you see the noble representative of authority coming this way? Let's go, it's too sad. Just because the poor girl wanted to dance . . ."

"Some old puritan dame must have raised hell up there. If we find her you can kick her in the behind."

"OK. And you can make excuses for me, saying that my leg got away from me, mortar shell, defending Stalingrad, you know."

"Then you come to attention and snap a salute."

"That I can do very well, you know, I learned it in Palermo. Come on, let's get something to drink. I don't want to look back any more, listen to the cop bawling her out. That's where the whole problem lies. Shouldn't I go back and give him a swift kick? Oh, Arjuna, counsel me. And beneath the uniform the smell of civilian ignominy. *Ho detto.* Come on, let's split once and for all. I'm dirtier than Emmanuèle, it's a crud that started collecting centuries ago, *Persil lave plus blanc*, it calls for an almighty detergent, girl, a cosmic soap. You like pretty words? *Salut, Gaston.*"

"*Salut messieurs dames,*" Gaston said. "*Alors, deux petits blancs secs comme d'habitude, hein?*"

"*Comme d'habitude, mon vieux, comme d'habitude. Avec du Persil dedans.*"

Gaston looked at him and went off shaking his head. Oliveira took La Maga's hand and counted her fingers attentively. Then he put the stone in her palm, closed the fingers over it, one by one, and to top it off gave her a kiss. La Maga saw that he had closed his eyes and seemed to be far off. "Actor," she thought tenderly.

(–64)

109

Somewhere Morelli tried to justify his narrative incoherencies, maintaining that the life of others, such as it comes to us in so-called reality, is not a movie but still photography, that is to say, that we cannot grasp the action, only a few of its eleatically recorded fragments. There are only the moments in which we are present with this other one whose life we think we understand, either when they talk about him, or when he tells us what has happened to him or projects in front of us what he intends to do. In the end there is a photograph album, with fixed instants; never the future coming about before us, the step from yesterday to today, the first prick of forgetfulness in the memory. For that reason there was nothing strange about his speaking of characters in the most spasmodic way possible; giving coherence to the series of pictures so they could become a movie (which would have been so very pleasing to the reader he called the female-reader) meant filling in with literature, presumptions, hypotheses and inventions the gaps between one and another photograph. Sometimes the pictures showed a back, a hand resting on a door, the end of a stroll through the countryside, a mouth opening to shout, some shoes in the cupboard, people walking along the Champs de Mars, a postmarked stamp, the smell of Ma Griffe, things like that. Morelli thought that the existence of those pictures, which tried to present all that with the most acuity possible, must have placed the reader in conditions ripe for taking a chance, for participating, almost, in the destiny of the characters. What he would learn from them through his imagination would immediately become hardened into action, with no trick destined to integrate them into what had already been written or was to be written. The bridges between one and another instant in those lives which were so vague and so little characterized would have to be presumed or invented by the reader, everything from the manner in which they combed their hair, even if Morelli did not mention it, to the reasons behind a behaviour or a nonbehaviour, if it seemed unusual and eccentric. The book would have to be something like those sketches proposed by Gestalt psychologists, and therefore certain lines would induce the observer to trace imaginatively the ones that would complete the figure. But sometimes the missing lines were the most important ones, the only ones that really counted. Morelli's coquetry and petulance in this field had no limits.

Reading the book, one had the impression for a while that Morelli had hoped that the accumulation of fragments would quickly crystallize into a total reality. Without having to invent bridges, or sew up different pieces of the tapestry, behold suddenly a city, or a tapestry, or men and women in the absolute perspective of their future, and Morelli, the author, would be the first spectator to marvel at that world that was taking on coherence.

But there was no cause for confidence, because coherence meant basically assimilation in space and time, an ordering to the taste of the female-reader. Morelli would not have agreed to that; rather, it seems, he would have sought a crystallization which, without altering the disorder in which the bodies of his little planetary system circulated, would permit a ubiquitous and total comprehension of all of its reasons for being, whether they were disorder itself, inanity, or gratuity. A crystallization in which nothing would remain subsumed, but where a lucid eye might peep into the kaleidoscope and understand the great polychromatic rose, understand it as a figure, an *imago mundi* that outside the kaleidoscope would be dissolved into a provincial living room, or a concert of aunts having tea and Bagley biscuits.

(–27)

110

The dream was composed like a tower of layers without end rising upward and losing themselves in the infinite, or layers coiling downward, losing themselves in the bowels of the earth. When it swooped me in its undulations, the spiralling began, and this spiral was a labyrinth. There was no vault and no bottom, no walls and no return. But there were themes repeating themselves with exactitude.

ANAÏS NIN, *Winter of Artifice*

(–48)

111

This narration was written by its protagonist, Ivonne Guitry, to Nicolás Díaz, a friend of Gardel's in Bogotá.

My family belonged to the Hungarian intellectual class. My mother was headmistress of a girls' seminary where the elite of a famous city, whose name I do not wish to mention, were educated. With the arrival of the stormy postwar period and the overthrow of thrones, social classes and fortunes, I did not know which way to head in my life. My family lost its fortune, victim of the Trianon [*sic*] borders like thousands and thousands of others. My beauty, my youth, and my upbringing would not permit me to become a humble stenographer. Then the Prince Charming of my life arrived, an aristocrat of cosmopolitan upper circles, frequenters of European resorts. I married him with all of my youthful illusion, in spite of the opposition of my family, because I was young and he was a foreigner.

Honeymoon. Paris, Nice, Capri. Then the shattering of an illusion. I did not know where to turn and I did not dare tell my family of the failure of my marriage. A husband who would never be able to make me a mother. I am already sixteen years old and I am travelling like a pilgrim without a goal, trying to make my troubles disappear. Egypt, Java, Japan, the Celestial Empire, all of the Far East, in a carnival of champagne and false happiness, with my soul in pieces.

The years pass. In 1927 we settled finally on the Côte d'Azur. I am a woman of high society, and cosmopolitan circles, casinos, balls, race tracks all render me homage.

One fine day in summer I took a definitive resolution:

separation. Nature was all in flower: the sea, the fields were opening up in a song of love and enjoyment of youth.

The mimosa festival in Cannes, the carnival of flowers in Nice, springtime in Paris. So I abandoned home, comforts, and wealth, and alone I faced the world . . .

I was eighteen at the time and living alone in Paris, without any definite direction. Paris in 1928. The Paris of orgies and the outpouring of champagne. The Paris of worthless francs. Paris, paradise of the foreigner. Full of Americans and South Americans, little kings of gold. Paris in 1928, where every day a new cabaret was born, a new sensation to make the foreigner loosen his purse.

Eighteen years old, blonde, blue eyes. Alone in Paris.

In order to soften my misfortune I turned myself completely over to pleasure. I always attracted attention in the cabarets because I was alone, squandering champagne on the chorus and tips on the waiters. I had no idea of the value of money.

Sometimes, somebody out of that element that always lives off the cosmopolitan environment discovers my secret sorrow and recommends a remedy for forgetfulness to me . . . Cocaine, morphine, drugs. Then I began to look for exotic places, strange-looking dancers, dark-hued South Americans with their long hair.

In those days a recent arrival, a cabaret singer, was collecting success and applause. He opened in the Florida and sang strange songs in a strange language.

He sang in exotic garb never seen before in those places, Argentine tangos, *rancheras* and *zambas.* He was a rather thin young man, a little dark, with white teeth that captured the attention of all the pretty women in Paris. It was Carlos Gardel. His weepy tangos that he sang with all his soul captivated the audience without anyone's knowing why. His songs at that time – *Caminito, La chacarera, Aquel tapado de armiño, Queja indiana, Entre sueños* – were not modern tangos but songs of old Argentina, the pure soul of the gaucho of the pampas. Gardel was in vogue. There was no elegant dinner party or reception to which he was not invited. His dark face, his white teeth, his fresh and luminous smile, shone everywhere. Cabarets, theatres, music halls, race tracks. He was a permanent guest at Auteuil and Longchamps.

But Gardel preferred to have a good time in his own way, among his own friends, in the circle of his intimates.

At that time there was in Paris a cabaret called Palermo, on the Rue Clichy, frequented almost exclusively by South Americans . . . That's where I met him. Gardel was interested in all women, but all I was interested in was cocaine . . . and champagne. Of course it pleased my feminine vanity to be seen in Paris with the man of the hour, with the idol of womanhood, but it did not tell my heart anything.

That friendship became established on other nights, other walks, other confidences, under the pale Parisian moon, through flowering fields. Many days of romantic interest went by. The man was getting into my soul. His words were silken, his phrases were digging at the rock of my indifference. I went crazy. My luxurious but sad little flat was now full of light. I did not go back to the cabarets. In my beautiful grey living room, by the light of electric lamps, a blonde little head became united to a firm, dark-featured face. My blue bedroom, which had known all the nostalgias of a soul without direction, was now a real love nest. It was my first love.

Time flew fast and fleeting. I can't say how much time went by. The exotic blonde who had dazzled Paris with her extravagances, with her *toiletts dernière cri* [*sic*], with her garden parties in which Russian caviar and champagne were the daily main course, had disappeared.

Months later the eternal habitués of the Palermo, the Florida, the Garon, learned in the press that a blonde ballerina with blue eyes who was now twenty years old was driving the *señoritos* of the River Plate capital mad with her ethereal dances, with her startling brazenness, with all the voluptuousness of her youth in flower.

It was IVONNE GUITRY.

(Etc.)

La escuela gardeleana, Editorial Cisplatina, Montevideo

(–49)

112

Morelliana

I am revising a story that I wanted to be the least literary possible. A despairing job from the word go, in the revision intolerable phrases start to pop up right away. A character comes to some stairs: "Raymond commenced his descent . . . " I scratch it out and write: "Raymond began to go down . . . " I turn away from the revision to ask myself again the real reasons behind this rejection of "literary" language. *Commence his descent* has nothing bad about it unless maybe it is too easy; but *begin to go down* is exactly the same except cruder, more prosaic (that is, a mere vehicle of information), while the other form seems to combine what is useful with what is pleasant to hear. In short, what repels me in "commenced his descent" is the decorative use of a verb and a noun that we almost never use in everyday speech, in short, literary language repels me (in my work, let it be understood). Why?

By persisting in this attitude that has rapidly impoverished almost everything I have written in the last few years, it will not be long before I feel incapable of setting forth the slightest idea, of undertaking the simplest description. If my reasons were those of Hofmannsthal's Lord Chandos, there would be no motive for complaint, but if this rejection of rhetoric (because basically that is what it is) is due only to a verbal withering, correlative and parallel to another one which is vital, then it would be preferable to renounce all writing completely. Rereading the results of what I have written these days bores me. But at the same time, behind that deliberate poverty, behind that "begin to go down" substituted for "commence his descent", I get a glimpse of something that encourages me. I write very badly, but something is happening through it all. The previous "style" was a mirror for lark-readers: they looked at each other, they consoled each other, they recognized each other, like those audiences that wait for, recognize and enjoy the answers of the characters of a Salacrou or an Anouilh. It is much easier to write like that than to write (to "unwrite", almost) as I would want to do now, because there is no longer any dialogue or meeting with the reader, there is only the hope of a certain dialogue with a certain and remote reader. Of course, the problem is located on a moral plane. Perhaps arteriosclerosis, the advance of age accentuates this tendency – a little misanthropic, I fear – to exalt the *ethos* and discover (in my own case it is a rather tardy discovery) that aesthetic orders are more a mirror than a passage for metaphysical anxiety.

I still thirst for the absolute as much as when I was twenty years old, but the delicate twitching, the acid and biting delight of the creative act or of the simple contemplation of beauty, no longer seem to me to be a prize, an access to absolute and satisfactory reality. There is only one beauty which can still give me that access: the one that is an end and not a means, and which is so because its creator has identified in himself his sense of the human condition with his sense of the artist's condition. On the other hand, the merely aesthetic plane seems just that to me: merely. That is the best way I can explain it.

(–154)

113

Nodules of a trip from the end of the Rue de la Glacière to the Rue du Sommerard:

"How long are we still going to date things 'AD'?"

"Literary documents seen two hundred years from now: coprolites."

"Klages was right."

"Morelli and his lesson. Sometimes repulsive, horrible, pitiful. So many words in order to cleanse himself of other words, so much filth so that Piver, Caron, Carven, AD will no longer smell. Maybe he has to go through all of that in order to recover a lost right, the original use of words."

"The original use of words (?). Probably an empty phrase."

"Small coffin, pack of cigarettes, Charon puffs a little and you cross the puddle rocking like a cradle. The boat is for adults only. Women and children free, a push and soon the other side. A Mexican death, a sugar skull, *Kindertotenlieder* . . . "

"Morelli will look at Charon. One myth facing another. An unforeseeable trip on the black waters."

"A hopscotch on the pavement: red chalk, green chalk. CIEL. The pavement, back there in Burzaco, the pebble selected with such tender care, the quick push with the tip of the shoe, slowly, slowly, even if Heaven is close by, all life in front of one."

"An infinite game of chess, so easy to imagine. But cold enters through an opening in the sole, in the window of that hotel a face like a clown's grimaces behind the glass. The shadow of a dove rubs up against the excrement a dog has left behind: Paris."

"Pola Paris. Pola? Go see her, *faire l'amour. Carezza.* Like lazy larva worms. But *larva* also means mask, Morelli wrote about it somewhere."

(–30)

114

May 4, 195 . . . (AP) In spite of the efforts by his lawyers and a final attempt at appeal on May 2, Lou Vincent was executed this morning in the gas chamber at San Quentin prison in the state of California.

. . . his hands and legs tied to the chair. The warden ordered the four jailers to leave the chamber, and after patting Vincent on the back, left in turn. The condemned man was alone in the room as 53 witnesses watched through small windows.

. . . he threw back his head and took a deep breath.

. . . two minutes later his face was bathed in perspiration and his fingers moved as if to free himself from the straps . . .

. . . six minutes, the convulsions were repeated, and Vincent pitched his head backward and forward. He began to froth at the mouth a little.

. . . eight minutes, his head fell forward on his chest after one final convulsion.

. . . At 10.12 Dr Reynolds pronounced the condemned man dead. The witnesses, who included three reporters from . . .

(–117)

115

Morelliana

Using as a basis a series of notes that were often contradictory, the Club deduced that Morelli saw in the contemporary narrative an advance towards what has been poorly termed abstraction. "Music is losing its melody, painting is losing its anecdotal side, the novel is losing its description." Wong, a master at dialectical collages, summed up this passage here: "The novel that interests us is not one that places characters in a situation, but rather one that puts the situation in the characters. By means of this the latter cease to be characters and become people. There is a kind of extrapolation through which they jump out at us, or we at them. Kafka's K. has the same name as his reader, or vice versa." And to this must be added a rather confused note in which Morelli was working up an episode in which he would leave the names of his characters blank, so that in each case the supposed abstraction would have to be resolved in a hypothetical attribution.

(–14)

116

In a passage from Morelli, this epigraph from *L'Abbé C*, by Georges Bataille: "*Il souffrait d'avoir introduit des figures décharnées, qui se déplaçaient dans un monde dément, qui jamais ne pourraient convaincre.*"

A pencilled note, almost illegible: "Yes, he suffers once in a while, but it is the only decent way out. Enough of hedonistic and premasticated novels, with *psychologies*. One must aim at the maximum, be a *voyant* as Rimbaud wanted to be. The hedonistic novelist is nothing but a *voyeur*. On the other hand, enough of purely descriptive techniques, of 'behaviourist' novels, mere movie scripts without the saving grace of images."

Relating it to another passage: "How can one *tell* a story without cooking, without make-up, without winks at the reader? Perhaps by rejecting the supposition that a narrative is a work of art. To feel it the way we would feel the plaster we put on our face to make a mask of it. But the face should be ours."

And maybe also in this odd note: "Lionello Venturi, speaking of Manet and his *Olympia*, points out that Manet did not need nature, beauty, action and moral intent in order to concentrate on the plastic image. Thus, without his knowing it, he is working as if modern art were going back to the Middle Ages. The latter understood art as a series of images, replaced during the Renaissance and the modern period by the representation of reality. The same Venturi (or is it Giulio Carlo Argan?) adds: 'The irony of history has decreed that in the very moment in which the representation of reality was becoming objective, and ultimately photographic and mechanical, a brilliant Parisian who wanted to be realistic should be moved by his formidable genius to return art to its function as the creator of images . . .'"

Morelli adds: "To accustom one's self to use the expression *figure* instead of *image*, to avoid confusions. Yes, everything coincides. But it is not a question of a return to the Middle Ages or anything like it. The mistake of postulating an absolute historical time: there are different times *even though* they may be parallel. In this sense, one of the times of the so-called Middle Ages can coincide with one of the times of the Modern Ages. And that time is what has been perceived and inhabited by painters and writers who refuse to seek support in what surrounds them, to be 'modern' in the sense that their contemporaries understand them, which does not mean that they choose to be anachronistic; they are simply on the margin of the superficial time of their period, and from that other time where everything conforms to the condition of *figure*, where everything has value as a sign and not as a theme of description, they attempt a work which may seem alien or antagonistic to the time and history surrounding them, and which nonetheless includes it, explains it, and in the last analysis orients it towards a transcendence within whose limits man is waiting."

(–3)

117

I have seen a court urged almost to the point of threat to hang two boys, in the face of science, in the face of philosophy, in the face of humanity, in the face of experience, in the face of all the better and more humane thoughts of the age.

Why did not my friend, Mr Marshall, who dug up from the relics of the buried past these precedents that would bring a blush of shame to the face of a savage, read this from Blackstone:

"Under fourteen, though an infant shall be judged to be incapable of guile prima facie, yet if it appeared to the court and the jury that he was capable of guile, and could discern between good and evil, he may be convinced and suffer death."

Thus a girl of thirteen has been burned for killing her mistress.

. . . .

One boy of ten, and another of nine years of age, who had killed their companions were sentenced to death; and the one of ten actually hanged.

Why?

He knew the difference between right and wrong. He had learned that in Sunday School.

CLARENCE DARROW, *Defence of Leopold and Loeb*, 1924

(−15)

118

How shall the murdered man convince his assassin he will not haunt him?

MALCOLM LOWRY, *Under the Volcano*

(–50)

119

Australian love-bird unable to spread wings

An inspector of the RSPCA entered a house and found the bird in a cage barely 8 inches wide. The owner of the bird was required to pay a fine of 2 pounds. In order to protect defenceless creatures we need more than just your moral support. The RSPCA needs your financial support. Contact the Offices, etc.

The Observer, London

(–51)

120

at siesta-time everybody was asleep, it was easy to get out of bed without waking up his mother, creep up to the door, go out slowly, smelling the warm earth floor avidly, escape through the door over to the grazing pen at the back; the willows were full of basket bugs, Ireneo chose a rather large one, sat down beside an anthill, and began to squeeze the bottom of the cocoon little by little until the grub popped its head out through the silky collar, then he had to take it delicately by the scruff of the neck like a cat, pull it gently so as not to hurt it, and there was the grub, naked now, twisting comically in the air; Ireneo set it next to the anthill and lay down in the shade on his stomach, waiting; at that moment the black ants were working furiously, cutting grass and hauling back living and dead insects from everywhere, a scout spotted the grub, his bulk twisting grotesquely, she touched him with her antennae as if she had to be convinced of such good luck, she ran back and forth rubbing antennae with the other ants, a minute later the grub was surrounded, climbed on, he twisted uselessly trying to free himself from the pincers that dug into his flesh while the ants pulled him in the direction of the anthill, dragging him along, Ireneo particularly enjoyed the puzzlement of the ants when they could not get the grub through the mouth of the anthill, the trick was to pick a grub that was thicker than the entrance to the anthill, ants were stupid and did not understand, they pulled on all sides trying to get the grub in but he was twisting furiously, what he was feeling must have been horrible, the ants with their feet and pincers all over his body, on his eyes and skin, he was struggling to free himself and it was worse because more ants came, some really fierce, who stuck their pincers into him and would not let go until they got the head of the grub so that it began to go into the pit of the anthill, and others who came up from down below must have been pulling from inside with all their might to drag him in, Ireneo might have wanted to be inside the anthill also, to see how the ants pulled on the grub sticking their pincers in his eyes and mouth and pulling with every ounce of strength until they got him all inside, until they took him down into the depths and killed him and ate him

(–16)

121

With red ink and manifest complacency, Morelli had copied in one of his notebooks the ending of a poem by Ferlinghetti:

Yet I have slept with beauty
in my own weird way
and I have made a hungry scene or two
with beauty in my bed
and so spilled out another poem or two
and so spilled out another poem or two
upon the Bosch-like world

(–36)

122

The nurses came and went speaking of Hippocrates. With just a small effort any piece of reality could attach itself to a famous line of poetry. But why bring up enigmas for Étienne, who had taken out his notebook and was happily sketching a flight of white doors, stretchers piled up along the walls and up to the windows where a grey and silky material was coming in, the skeleton of a tree with two doves with bourgeois crops. He would have liked to tell him about the other dream, it was so strange that all morning he had been obsessed by the bread dream, and boom, on the corner of Raspail and Montparnasse the other dream had fallen on him like a wall, or rather, as if all through the morning he had been pushed up against the wall of bread complaining and suddenly, like a movie being run backwards, the wall had come away from him, straightening up in one jump to leave him facing the memory of the other dream.

"Whenever you want," Étienne said, holding on to the sketchbook. "Whenever you feel like it, there's no rush. I still plan to live another forty years, so . . . "

"'Time present and time past,'" Oliveira recited, "'are both perhaps present in time future.' It has been written that today everything is going to end up in lines by T. S. Eliot thinking about a dream, sorry. Let's go right now."

"Yes, because it's all right about the dream. You can take that, take it, but after all . . . "

"It's really about a different dream."

"*Misère!*" said Étienne.

"I didn't tell you about it on the phone because I'd forgot."

"And the bit about the six minutes," Étienne said. "Basically, the authorities are very wise. We always shit on them, but we've got to admit they know what they're doing. Six minutes . . . "

"If I'd thought of it, all I had to do was get out of that booth and go to the next one."

"It's all right," Étienne said. "You tell me about the dream, and then we'll go down those stairs and have a little wine at Montparno. I'll swap your famous old man for a dream. Both things are too much together."

"You hit the nail on the head," Oliveira said, looking at him with interest. "The problem is knowing if those two things can be swapped. What you were telling me just today: butterfly or Chiang Kai-shek? Probably when you swap the old man with me for a dream, what you'll be swapping will be a dream for the old man."

"To tell you the truth, I don't give a damn."

"Painter," said Oliveira.

"Metaphysician," said Étienne. "And now that we're here, there's a nurse over there who's beginning to wonder whether we're a dream or a couple of tramps. What's going to happen? If she comes over to throw us out, is it a nurse who is throwing us out or a dream that throws out two philosophers who are dreaming about a hospital where among other things there is an old man and an enraged butterfly?"

"It was much more simple," Oliveira said, slipping down on the bench a little and closing his eyes. "Look, it was just my childhood house and La Maga's flat, both things together in the same dream. I don't remember when I dreamed it, I'd forgotten it completely and this morning while I was thinking about that business with the loaf of bread . . . "

"You already told me about the loaf of bread."

"Suddenly it's the other thing again and the bread can go to the devil, because they can't be compared. Maybe that's what inspired my dream about the bread . . . Inspired, that's a fine word."

"Don't be ashamed to use it, if it means what I think it does."

"You were thinking about the kid, of course. A required association. But I don't have any feelings of guilt. I didn't kill him."

"Things are not so easy," Étienne said uncomfortably. "Let's go and see the old man, we've had enough of idiot dreams for a while."

"It's really impossible for me to tell you about it," Oliveira said with resignation. "Imagine that when you get to Mars a guy asks you to describe ashes to him. Something like that, more or less."

"Shall we go and see the old man or not?"

"It doesn't make the slightest difference to me. Since we're already here . . . Bed number ten, I think. We should have brought him something, it's stupid coming here like this. In any case, give him a drawing."

"My drawings are for sale," Étienne said.

(–112)

123

The real dream was located in an imprecise zone, next to waking but without his really being awake; he would have had to make use of other references to speak about it, eliminate rotund terms like *dreaming* and *awake* that didn't mean a thing, locate himself rather in that zone where once more his childhood house would be suggested, the living room and the garden in a clear present time, with the colours as they were seen at the age of ten, reds so red, blues of tinted glass shades, green of leaves, green of fragrance, smell, and colour, a single presence at the level of nose and eyes and mouth. But in the dream, the room with its two windows that opened on the garden was at the same time La Maga's room; the forgotten province of Buenos Aires town and the Rue du Sommerard were brought together without any clash, not juxtaposed or overlapped but merged, and in the effortless removal of contradiction there was the sensation of being where one should be, in the essential place, as when one is a child and has no doubts that the living room will be there for a whole lifetime: an inalienable belonging. So that the house in Burzaco and the flat on the Rue du Sommerard were *the place*, and in the dream it was necessary to choose the most peaceful spot in the place, the reason behind the dream seemed to be just that, choosing a peaceful place. There was another person in the place, his sister, who was silently helping him choose the peaceful spot, the way a person participates in some dreams without even being there, and we take it for granted that the person or thing is there and participates; a force with no visible manifestations, something that is or does through a presence that can do without appearances. So he and his sister chose the living room as the most peaceful spot in the place, and it was a good choice because in La Maga's flat one could not play the piano or listen to the radio after ten o'clock at night, the old man upstairs would immediately start pounding on the floor or the people on the fifth floor would delegate a cross-eyed midget girl to go up and complain. Without a single word, since they didn't even seem to be there, he and his sister chose the living room that opened on the garden, rejecting La Maga's flat. In that moment of the dream Oliveira had woken up, perhaps because La Maga had put a leg between his. In the darkness the only thing he felt was that until that instant he had been in his childhood living room with his sister and also a terrible urge to urinate. Pushing La Maga's leg away unceremoniously, he got up and went out to the landing, feeling around for the dim light in the toilet, and without bothering to close the door began to piss, leaning against the wall with one hand, struggling against going to sleep and falling over in that lousy toilet, completely absorbed in the aura of the dream, watching without seeing the stream that was coming out from between his fingers and disappearing down the hole or drifting vaguely around the edges of the dirty porcelain. Maybe the real dream appeared to him at that moment when he felt he was awake and pissing at four o'clock in the morning on a sixth floor on the Rue du Sommerard and knew that the living room that opened on the garden in Burzaco was reality, knew it as only a few undeniable things are known, as one knows that he is himself, that no one but one's self is thinking that, he knew without any surprise or shock that his life as a man awake was a fantasy next to the solidity and permanence of the living room, although after going back to bed there might not be any living room and only the flat on the Rue du Sommerard, he knew that the place was the living room in Burzaco with the smell of Cape jasmine coming through the windows, the room with the old Bluthner piano, with its pink carpet and its little covered chairs, and his sister also with a cover on. He made a violent effort to get out of the aura, reject the place that was tricking him, wide awake enough to let the notion of trickery enter the notion of dream and wakefulness, but while he shook off the last drops and turned out the light, and rubbing his eyes crossed the landing to go back into the flat, everything was less, it was less signal, less landing, less door, less light, less bed, less Maga. Breathing with effort he murmured, "Maga", he murmured, "Paris", perhaps he murmured, "Today". It still sounded far away, hollow, not really alive. He went back to sleep like a person who is looking for his place and his house after a long road in the rain and the cold.

(–145)

124

It was necessary to propose, according to Morelli, a movement on the margin of all *grace*. In what he had done so far about that movement, it was easy to note the swift impoverishment of his novelistic world, not only evident in the almost simian poverty of his characters but also in the simple course of their actions and especially their inactions. He ended by not having anything happen to them, they whirled about in a sarcastic commentary on their inanity, they pretended to adore ridiculous idols which they thought they had discovered. This must have seemed important to Morelli because he had piled up notes on a supposed exigency, a final and desperate recourse to drag himself out of the rut of the immanent and transcendental ethic in search of a nakedness that he called axial and sometimes called *the threshold*. Threshold of what, to what? One could deduce the incitement to something like turning one's self inside out like a glove, as a way of receiving a brazen contact with some reality without the interposition of myths, religions, systems and reticula. It was curious that Morelli enthusiastically embraced the most recent working hypotheses of the physical and biological sciences, he presented himself as convinced that the old dualism had become cracked in the face of the evidence of a common reduction of matter and spirit to notions of energy. As a consequence, his wise monkeys seemed more and more to desire a retreat into themselves, nullifying on one hand the chimeras of a controlled reality, betrayed by the supposed instruments of cognition, and nullifying in turn their own mythopoetic force, their "soul", ending up in a kind of meeting *ab ovo* with a maximum shrinking into that point in which the last spark of (false) humanity will be lost. He seemed to propose – although he never got around to formulating it – a path that would begin with that external and internal liquidation. But he had ended up without words, without people, without things, and potentially, of course, without readers. The Club would sigh, somewhere between depression and exasperation and it was always the same thing or almost.

(–128)

125

The notion of being like a dog among men: material for an indifferent reflection that went on through two drinks of *caña* and a walk through the suburbs, the growing suspicion that only the alpha can yield the omega, that all insistence upon an intermediate period – epsilon, lambda – is the same thing as spinning around with one foot fastened to the ground. The arrow goes from the hand to the target: there's no midway in the journey, there's no century numbered XX between X and XXX. A man should be able to isolate himself from the species within the species itself, and choose the dog or the original fish as a starting point for the march towards himself. There's no passage for the Doctor of Philosophy, there's no opening for the eminent allergist. Inlaid in the species, they will be what they should be and if not they will be nothing. Very worthy men, no doubt about it, but always epsilon, lambda or pi, never alpha and never omega. The man in question doesn't accept those pseudo-fulfilments, the great decaying mask of the Western world. The guy who has wandered as far as the bridge on the Avenida San Martín and stands smoking on a corner watching a woman adjust her stocking, has a completely brainless idea of what he calls fulfilment, and he's not sorry about it because something tells him that the seed lies in brainlessness, that the bark of a dog is closer to the omega than a thesis on the gerund in Tirso de Molina. Such stupid metaphors. But he goes on doggedly, his way of putting words together. What is he searching for? Is he searching for himself? He would not be searching for himself if he had not already found himself. It means that he has found himself (but that's not brainless any more, *ergo* it cannot be trusted. As soon as you turn it loose, Reason supplies you with a special bulletin, arms you with the first syllogism in a chain that leads you nowhere except to a diploma or a ranchstyle bungalow and kids playing on the carpet to the enormous delight of mother). Let's see, let's take it slowly: What is that guy searching for? Is he searching for himself? Is he searching for himself as an individual? As a supposedly timeless individual, or as a historical entity? If it's the latter, a waste of time. If, on the other hand, he's searching for himself along the margin of all contingencies, the business of the dog is probably not so bad. But let's take it slowly (he loves to talk to himself that way, like a father to his son, so that later on he can give himself the great pleasure of all children and kick the old man in the balls), let's take it *piano piano*, let's see what this business of the search is all about. Well, search is just what it is *not*. Subtle, eh. It's not a search because he's already found himself. Just that the finding has not taken any shape. The meat, potatoes and shallots are there, but there isn't any pot. Or let's say that we're no longer with the others, that we've already stopped being a citizen (there's some reason for their weeding me out of everywhere, let Lutetia tell about it), but we still haven't learned how to get out of the dog to reach the thing that doesn't have a name, that conciliation, let's say that reconciliation.

It's a terrible job, splashing around in a circle whose centre is everywhere and whose circumference is nowhere, to use the language of scholasticism. What is being searched for? What is being searched for? Repeat it fifteen thousand times, like hammer-blows on the wall. What is being searched for? What is that conciliation without which life doesn't go beyond being an obscure joke? Not the conciliation of a saint, because if in the notion of going back to the dog, of starting over again from the dog or from the fish or from the ooze and the ugliness and the misery and any other disvaluation, there's always something like a nostalgia for sainthood, it would seem that one yearns for a non-religious sainthood (and here comes brainlessness), a state *without differentiation*, without saints (because a saint is always in some way a saint *and* those who are not saints, and that scandalizes a poor guy like the one admiring the calf of the girl absorbed in adjusting her twisted stocking), that is to say that if there is conciliation it must be something besides a state of sainthood, an exclusive state from the word go. It has to be something immanent, with no sacrifice of lead for gold, cellophane for glass, the least for the most; on the contrary, brainlessness calls for lead to be worth as much as gold, for the most to be contained in the least. An alchemy, a non-Euclidian geometry, an up-to-date indetermination for the operations of the spirit and its benefits. It's not a question of *rising*, an old mental image disproved by history, the old carrot that no longer fools the donkey. It's not a question of perfecting, of decanting, of redeeming, of choosing, of free-willing, of going from the alpha to the omega. *One is already there.* Anybody is already there. The shot is in the pistol; but a trigger has to be squeezed, and it so happens that the finger is making motions to stop a bus, or something similar.

How he talks, how he does go on, this smoking suburban tramp. The girl has already fixed her stocking, all set. You see? Forms of conciliation. *Il mio supplizio* . . . Everything is probably so simple, a pull on the mesh, a finger wet with saliva passing over the continuous part. It would probably be enough to grab one's nose and put it where one's ear is, upset circumstance a little. But no, that wouldn't do it either. Nothing easier than putting the blame on what's outside, as if one were sure that outside and inside are the two main beams of the house. But the fact is that everything is in bad shape, history tells you that, and the very fact that you're thinking about it instead of living it proves to you that it's bad, that we've stuck ourselves into a total disharmony that the sum of our resources disguises with social structure, with history, with Ionic style, with the joy of the Renaissance, with the superficial sadness of romanticism, and that's the way we go and they can turn the dogs on us.

(–44)

126

"Why, with your infernal enchantments, have you torn from me the tranquillity of my early life . . . The sun and the moon shone for me without artifice; I awoke with gentle thoughts, and at dawn I folded my leaves to say my prayers. I saw nothing evil, for I had no eyes; I heard nothing evil, for I had no ears; but I shall have my vengeance!"

Discourse of the Mandrake, in *Elizabeth of Egypt*,
by ACHIM VON ARNIM

(–21)

127

That's how the monsters would pester Cuca so she'd get out of the pharmacy and leave them in peace. Along the way and much more seriously they would discuss Ceferino Piriz's system and the ideas of Morelli. Since Morelli was little known in Argentina, Oliveira lent them his books and told them about some scattered notes he had seen at another time. They found out that Remorino, who was to stay on as an attendant and who would show up at *mate* and *caña* time, was a great initiate in Roberto Arlt, and that produced a considerable impression, so that for a whole week they spoke only of Arlt and how nobody had the right to step on his poncho in a country where carpets were preferred. But mostly they talked with great seriousness about Ceferino, and every once in a while it would occur to them to look at each other in a special way, raising their eyes at the same time, for example, and realizing that all three of them were doing it, that is to say, looking at each other in a special and inexplicable way, like certain looks in a game of *truco* or when a man who is desperately in love has to bear up under tea and pastries with several ladies and even a retired colonel who is explaining the reasons why everything is going badly in the country, and stuck in his chair the man looks at everyone the same way, the colonel, the woman he loves, and the woman's aunts, he looks at them affably because in fact it is a shame the way the country is in the hands of a band of crypto-communists, then from the cream puff, the third one on the left in the tray, and the spoon lying face up on the tablecloth embroidered by the aunts, the affable look is raised for an instant and over the crypto-communists it joins in mid-air the other look that has risen from the Nile-green plastic sugar bowl, and there's no longer anything else, a consummation outside time becomes a soft, sweet secret, and if the men of today were real men and not a bunch of god-damned fairies ("Why,

Ricardo!" "It's all right, Carmen, I just get so riled, I get so riled at what's going on in this country"), *mutatis mutandi* it was a little like the look the monsters gave when it occurred to them from time to time to look at each other with a look that was both furtive and total at the same time, secret and much clearer than when they would look at each other for a long time, but a person isn't a monster without good reason, as Cuca would say to her husband, and the three of them would let out a laugh and feel enormously ashamed at having looked at each other that way when they weren't playing *truco* and weren't illicitly in love. Unless.

(–56)

128

Nous sommes quelques-uns à cette époque à avoir voulu attenter aux choses, créer en nous des espaces à la vie, des espaces qui n'étaient pas et ne semblaient pas devoir trouver place dans l'espace.

ARTAUD, *Le Pèse-nerfs*

(–24)

129

But Traveler was not sleeping, after one or two attempts the nightmare kept circling around him and finally he sat up in bed and turned on the light. Talita was not there, somnambulist, moth of sleeplessness, and Traveler drank a glass of *caña* and put on his pyjama top. The wicker easy chair looked cooler than the bed, and it was a good night to continue his studies of Ceferino Piriz.

Dans cet annonce ou carte – Ceferino said textually – *ye reponds devant ou sur votre demande de suggérer idées pour UNESCO et écrit en el journal "El Diario" de Montevideo.*

A gallicized Ceferino! But there was no danger, *The Light of World Peace*, of which Traveler had some precious extracts, was written in admirable Spanish, the introduction, for example:

> In this announcement I wish to present some extracts from a recently written work of mine entitled *The Light of World Peace.* The aforesaid work has been or is being entered in an international contest . . . but it so happens that I cannot give you the entire work, as the Journal in which it appears will not permit for a certain length of time the aforesaid work to be supplied in its complete formation to anyone who is not in connection with said Journal . . .
>
> Therefore I limit myself in this announcement to the transmission of only some extracts from said work, which, the ones that follow, should not be published yet at this time.

Much more clear than an equivalent text by Julían Marías, for example. With two glasses of *caña* contact was established, and we're off. Traveler began to feel pleased that he had got up and that Talita was out there somewhere feeding her romanticism. For the tenth time he slowly got into Ceferino's text.

> In this book presentation is made of what we might call "the great formula on behalf of world peace". It is so much so that in this great formula there will be a Society of Nations or a UN, whereof this Society is a tendency towards values (precious, etc.) and human races; and lastly, as an undenied example of what is international, there will be a country that is truly exemplary, since it will be composed of 45 NATIONAL CORPORATIONS or ministries of the simple, and of 4 national Powers.

So-so: a ministry of the simple. Oh, Ceferino, natural philosopher, herbalist of Uruguayan paradises, nephelibate . . .

> On the other hand, this formula, great in its dimensions, is not alien, respectively, to the world of seers; to the nature of CHILD principles; from the natural measures that a formula is given entire of itself, it will not allow any alteration in the aforesaid formula given entire of itself; etc.

As always, the wise man seemed to feel a nostalgia for prophecy and intuition, but right away the mania for classification of *Homo occidentalis* raided Ceferino's little ranch and between *mates* it organized civilization into three periods:

> *First period of civilization*
>
> A first period of civilization can be conceived that goes from time immemorial in the past to the year 1940. A period which consisted in that everything was inclining towards the world war around the year 1940.
>
> *Second period of civilization*
>
> A second period of civilization can also be conceived, starting with the year 1940 up to the year 1953. A period that has consisted in everything inclining towards world peace or world reconstruction.
>
> (World reconstruction: acting so that in the world each will have what is his; reconstruct efficiently everything already undone before: buildings, human rights, universal balance of prices; etc., etc.)

Third period of civilization

A third period of civilization can also be conceived today or during the present, starting in the year 1953 until the future year 2000. A period that consists in everything marching firmly towards the efficient arrangement of things.

For Toynbee, obviously . . . But criticism turns mute in sight of Ceferino's anthropological scheme: Now then, here are human beings facing the aforementioned periods:

(A) Humans living in the second period as such, in those same days, did not manage to think very much about the first period.
(B) Humans living, or we who live in this third period of today, in these same times do not think, or we do not think very much about the second period.
(C) In the tomorrow that is to come later, or is to begin in the year 2000, the humans of those days, and in those days, they will not think very much about the third period: the one of today.

The business of not thinking very much was rather certain, *beati pauperes spiritu*, and now Ceferino went on in the manner of Paul Rivet, running down a classification that had been the high point of afternoons in Don Crespo's courtyard, to wit:

In the world one can count up to six human races: the white, the yellow, the brown, the black, the red, and the pampa.

WHITE RACE: of such race are all inhabitants of white skin, such as those of Baltic, Nordic, European, American, etc. countries.

YELLOW RACE: of such race are all inhabitants of yellow skin, such as Chinese, Japanese, Mongols, Hindus in their majority, etc.

BROWN RACE: of such race are all inhabitants of naturally brown skin, brown-skinned Russians, brown-skinned Turks, brown-skinned Arabs, Gypsies, etc.

BLACK RACE: of such race are all inhabitants of black skin, such as inhabitants of West Africa in their great majority, etc.

RED RACE: of such race are all inhabitants of red skin, such as a large part of Ethiopians of dark reddish skin, and of whom the NEGUS or king of Ethiopia is a red example; a large part of Hindus of dark reddish or "coffee-coloured" skin; a large part of Egyptians of dark reddish skin; etc.

PAMPA RACE: of such race are all inhabitants of varied or pampa-coloured skin, such as all Indians of the three Americas.

"Horacio should be here," Traveler said to himself. "He could make some good comments on this part. After all, why not? Cefe has tripped over the classic difficulties of the Gummed Label, and he does what he can, like Linnaeus or the synoptic charts in encyclopedias. The business of the brown race is a solution worthy of genius, you've got to admit."

Walking was heard in the hallway, and Traveler went to the door that opened onto the administrative wing. As Ceferino might have said, the first door, the second door, and the third door were closed. Talita must have gone back to the pharmacy, it was incredible how enthusiastic she was about her return to science, scales and antipyretic adhesives.

Alien to those trifles, Ceferino went on to explain his model Society of Nations:

> A society that might be founded in any part of the world, even if the best is in Europe. A Society that would function permanently, and therefore on all working days. A society where its main building or palace would have at least seven (7) chambers or halls that would be fairly large. Etc.
>
> Now then; of the seven mentioned chambers of the palace of the aforesaid Society a first chamber would be occupied by Delegates from countries of the white race, and its President would be of the same colour; a second chamber would be occupied by Delegates from countries of the yellow race, and its President would be of the same colour; a thir . . .

And so on all the races, or maybe one could skip over the enumeration, but it was not the same after four glasses of *caña*

(Mariposa and not Ancap, unfortunately, because patriotic homage would have been fitting); it was not at all the same, because Ceferino's thought was crystallographic, ruled by symmetry and *horror vacui*, or in other words

> . . . a third chamber would be occupied by Delegates from countries of the brown race, and its President would be of the same colour; a fourth chamber would be occupied by Delegates from countries of the black race, and its President would be of the same colour; a fifth chamber would be occupied by Delegates from countries of the red race, and its President would be of the same colour; a sixth chamber would be occupied by Delegates from countries of the pampa race, and its President would be of the same colour; and one – the – seventh chamber would be occupied by the "General Staff" of all the aforementioned Society of Nations.

Traveler had always been fascinated by that " – the – " which interrupted the rigorous crystallization of the system, like the mysterious garden in a sapphire, that mysterious spot in the gem that determines perhaps the coalescence of the system and which in sapphires irradiates its transparent celestial cross like a congealed energy in the heart of the stone. (And why was it called *garden*, unless because of the influence of gardens of precious stones that appear in Oriental fables?)

Cefe, much less deliquescent, immediately explained the importance of the question:

> More details on the aforementioned seventh chamber: in said seventh chamber of the palace of the Society of Nations will be the Secretary General of all of said Society, and the President General, also of all of said society, but such Secretary General at the same time will be the private secretary of the aforementioned President General.
>
> Still more details: well; in the first chamber will be its corresponding President, who will always preside over the aforesaid first chamber; if we speak with respect to the second chamber, *idem*; if we speak with respect to the third chamber, *idem*; if we speak with respect to the fourth chamber, *idem*;

if we speak with respect to the fifth chamber, *idem*; and if we speak with respect to the sixth chamber, *idem*.

It warmed Traveler's heart to think that this *idem* must have cost Ceferino quite a bit. It was an extraordinary acquiescence towards the reader. But now he was into the heart of the matter, and he proceeded to enumerate what he called "the skilful assignment of the model Society of Nations", *viz.*:

(1) To look after (not to say to fix) the or those values of money in its international circulation; (2) to designate the wages of workers, the salaries of employees, etc.; (3) to designate values on behalf of what is international (give or fix the price of every article for sale, and give value or merit to other things: how many weapons of war a country may possess; how many children may be born, by international convention, to a woman, etc.); (4) to designate how much monetary return as retirement pay is to be received by a retired person, a pensioner, etc.; (5) of up to how many children all respective women in the world are to bear; (6) of equitable distributions in the international sphere; etc.

Why, Traveler wisely wondered, this repetition in matters concerning freedom of the womb and demography? Under (3) it appeared as a value, and under (5) as a concrete matter of the Society's competence. Curious infractions of symmetry, of the implacable rigour of the consecutive and orderly enumeration, which meant perhaps a worry, the suspicion that the classic order was, as always, a sacrifice of truth to beauty. But Ceferino recovered from that romanticism that Traveler suspected in him, and proceeded to an exemplary distribution:

Distribution of the weapons of war:

It is already well known that each respective country in the world has its corresponding square miles of territory.

Well, then, here is an example:

(A) The country that theoretically has 1,000 square miles, will have 1,000 cannons; the country that theoretically has 5,000 square miles, will have 5,000 cannons; etc.

(By this it will be understood, 1 cannon for each square mile);

(B) The country that theoretically has 1,000 square miles, will have 2,000 rifles; the country that theoretically has 5,000 square miles, will have 10,000 rifles; etc.

(By this it will be understood 2 rifles for each square mile); etc.

This example will include all respective countries that exist: France has 2 rifles for each of its square miles; Spain, *idem*; Belgium, *idem*; Russia, *idem*; United States, *idem*; Uruguay, *idem*; China, *idem*; etc., and this will also include all types of weapons of war that exist (a) tanks; (b) machine-guns; (c) terror bombs; rifles; etc.

(–139)

130

Perils of the Zip

The British Medical Journal speaks of a new type of accident that can befall boys. This accident is caused by the use of a zip in place of buttons in trouser flies (our medical correspondent informs us).

The danger lies in the prepuce's being caught in the fastener. Two cases have already been reported. In both of them circumcision had to be resorted to in order to free the child.

The accident is more likely to occur when the child goes to the bathroom unaccompanied. In an attempt to help him, parents can make matters worse by pulling on the zip in the wrong direction, as the child will be in no condition to tell whether the accident happened when he was pulling the zip up or when he was pulling it down. If the child has already been circumcised, the damage can be much more severe.

The doctor advises that by cutting the bottom part of the zip with pliers or shears the two halves can easily be separated. But a local anaesthetic will have to be administered for the extraction of the part imbedded in the skin.

The Observer, London

(–151)

131

"What do you think about our getting into the national corporation of monks of the prayer of the sign of the cross?"

"Either that or getting into the national budget . . . "

"We'd have a heavy time of it," Traveler said, watching Oliveira's breathing. "I remember perfectly, our obligations would be those of praying for or blessing people, objects, and those very mysterious regions that Ceferino calls sites of places."

"This must be one," Oliveira said as if from far away. "It's the site of a definite place, old buddy."

"And we would also have to bless planted fields, and boyfriends badly affected by a rival."

"Call Cefe about it," said the voice of Oliveira from some site of a place. "I'd like that . . . Hey, now that I think of it, Cefe comes from Uruguay."

Traveler didn't say anything, and he looked at Ovejero who came in and took the pulse of the *hysteria matinensis yugulata.*

"Monks who are always to combat all spiritual ills," Oliveira said distinctly.

"Aha," said Ovejero by way of encouragement.

(–58)

132

And while somebody explains something as always, I don't know why I am in this café, in all cafés, in the Elephant & Castle, in the Dupont Barbès, in the Sacher, in the Pedrocchi, in the Gijón, in the Greco, in the Café de la Paix, in the Café Mozart, in the Florian, in the Capoulade, in Les Deux Magots, in the bar that puts its chairs out on the Colleone square, in the Café Dante fifty yards away from the tomb of the Scaligers and that face on a pink sarcophagus that looks as if it had been burned by the tears of Saint Mary of Egypt, in the café across from the Giudecca, with aged and impoverished marchionesses drinking scrupulous tea and getting expansive with dusty ambassadors, in the Jandilla, in the Floccos, in the Cluny, in the Richmond in Suipacha, in El Olmo, in the Closerie des Lilas, in the Stéphane (which is on the Rue Mallarmé), in the Tokio (which is in Chivilcoy), in the Chien Qui Fume, in the Opern Café, in the Dôme, in the Café du Vieux Port, in cafés anywhere where

> We make our meek adjustments,
> Contented with such random consolations
> As the wind deposits
> In slithered and too ample pockets.

Hart Crane *dixit.* But they're more than that, they are the neutral territory for the stateless of the soul, the motionless centre of the wheel from where one can reach himself in full career, see himself enter and leave like a maniac, wrapped up in women or I O U's or epistemological theses, and while the coffee swirls around the little cup that goes from mouth to mouth along the edge of days, can loosely attempt revision and balance, equally removed from the ego that came into the café an hour ago and from the ego that will leave within another hour. Self-witness and self-judge, an ironical autobiography between two cigarettes.

In cafés I remember dreams, one no man's land revives another, now I remember one, but no, I only remember that I must have dreamed something marvellous and that in the end I felt as if expelled (or leaving, but forcibly) from the dream that remained irremediably behind me. I don't know if I even closed a door behind me, I think I did; in fact a separation was established between what had already been dreamed (perfect, spherical, finished) and the present. But I kept on sleeping, that business of expulsion and the door closing I also dreamed. A single and terrible certainty dominated that instant of transition within the dream; to know that irremediably that expulsion brought with it the complete forgetting of the previous marvel. I suppose that the feeling of a door closing was just that, fateful and instantaneous forgetting. The most startling is remembering also having dreamed that I was forgetting the previous dream, and that that dream *had to be* forgotten (my expulsion from its finished sphere).

All this must have, I imagine, an Edenic root. Perhaps Eden, as some would like to see it, is the mythopoetic projection of good old foetal times that persist in the unconscious. I suddenly understand better the frightening gesture of Masaccio's Adam. He covers his face to protect his vision, what had been his; he preserves in that small manual night the last landscape of his paradise. And he cries (because the gesture is also one that accompanies weeping) when he realizes that it is useless, that the real punishment is the one about to begin: the forgetting of Eden, that is to say, bovine conformity, the cheap and dirty joy of work and sweat of the brow and paid vacations.

(–61)

133

Of course, as Traveler thought right away, what counted were results. Still, why so much pragmatism? He was doing Ceferino an injustice, since his geopolitical system had not been tested out as so many others that were equally brainless (and just as promising, one had to recognize that). Cefe intrepidly stuck to his theoretical terrain and almost immediately launched another crushing demonstration:

> Wages of workers of the world:
>
> In accordance with the Society of Nations it will be or is to be that if, for example, a French worker, let us say a steelworker, for example, earns a definite daily wage between a *minimum* base of 8 pesos and a *maximum* base of 10 pesos, then it will have to be that an Italian steelworker will also have to earn the same amount, between 8 pesos and 10 pesos a day; in addition: if an Italian steelworker earns the same aforesaid, between 8 pesos and 10 pesos a day, then a Spanish steelworker will also have to earn between 8 pesos and 10 pesos a day; in addition: if a Spanish steelworker earns between 8 pesos and 10 pesos a day, then a Russian steelworker will also have to earn between 8 pesos and 10 pesos a day; in addition: if a Russian steelworker earns between 8 pesos and 10 pesos a day, then an American steelworker will also have to earn between 8 pesos and 10 pesos a day; etc.

"What's the reason for that 'etc.,'" Traveler thought, "for the fact that at a given moment Ceferino stops and chooses that et cetera that is so painful to him? It can't just be the weariness of repetition, because it's obvious that he loves it, or the feeling of monotony, because it's obvious that he loves it (his style is rubbing off on you)." The fact was that the "etc." left Ceferino a little nostalgic, a cosmologist obliged to give in to an irritating reader's digest. The poor fellow recovered his loss at the end of his list of steelworkers:

> (For the rest, in this thesis, if we kept on speaking, there will or there should be room for all countries respectively, or rather for all steelworkers of all respective countries.)

"But," Traveler thought, pouring himself another *caña* and cutting it with soda, "it's strange that Talita hasn't come back." He should go and take a look. He was sorry to leave Ceferino's world in full process of development just when Cefe was about to enumerate the 45 National Corporations which would make up the exemplary country:

> (1) NATIONAL CORPORATION OF THE MINISTRY OF THE INTERIOR (all branches and employees in general of the Ministry of the Interior). (The ministration of all stability for every establishment, etc.); (2) NATIONAL CORPORATION OF THE MINISTRY OF THE TREASURY (all branches and employees in general of the Ministry of the Treasury). (The ministration as patronage of all goods (all property) within the national territory, etc.); (3)

And that's the way the corporations went, 45 in number, among which 5, 10, 11 and 12 stood out in their own way:

> (5) NATIONAL CORPORATION OF THE MINISTRY OF CIVIL FAVOUR (all branches and employees in general of said Ministry). (Education, Enlightenment, Love of one neighbour for another, Control, Registry (books of), Health, Sexual Education, etc.). (The ministration or Control and Registry (lawyer . . .) which will furnish "Courts of Instruction", "Civil Courts", "Council of the Child", "Judge of Minors", "Registries": births, deceases, etc.) (The Ministration which will include everything that may be part of Civil Favour: MATRIMONY, FATHER, SON, NEIGHBOUR, DOMICILE, INDIVIDUAL, INDIVIDUAL OF GOOD OR BAD BEHAVIOUR, INDIVIDUAL OF PUBLIC IMMORALITY, INDIVIDUAL WITH BAD ILLNESSES, HOME (FAMILY AND), UNDESIRABLE PERSON, HEAD OF FAMILY, CHILD, MINOR, FIANCÉ, CONCUBINAGE, etc.).

. . . .

(10) NATIONAL CORPORATION OF ESTATES (all rural establishments for the Major Breeding of animals and all employees in general of said establishments). (Major Breeding or the breeding of corpulent animals: oxen, horses, ostriches, elephants, camels, giraffes, whales, etc.);

(11) NATIONAL CORPORATION OF FARMS (all agricultural farms or large farms, and all employees in general of said establishments). (Cultivations of every respective type of plant, except vegetables and fruit trees);

(12) NATIONAL CORPORATION OF ANIMAL BREEDING HOUSES (all establishments for the Minor Breeding of animals, and all employees in general of said establishments). (Minor breeding or the breeding of noncorpulent animals: pigs, sheep, goats, dogs, tigers, lions, cats, hares, hens, ducks, wasps, fish, butterflies, mice, insects, microbes, etc.)

Touched, Traveler forgot all about the hour and how the level of the *caña* was going down. The problems came to him like caresses: Why exempt vegetables and fruit trees? Why did the word wasp have something diabolical about it? And that almost Edenic vision of a farm where goats were raised alongside tigers, mice, butterflies, lions and microbes . . . Choking with laughter he went out into the hall. The almost tangible aspect of an estate where the employees-of-said-establishment were arguing as they tried to breed a whale became superimposed on the austere vision of the night-time hallway. It was a hallucination worthy of the place and the time, it seemed perfectly foolish to wonder what Talita was doing in the pharmacy or in the courtyard, when the order of Corporations continued to offer itself as a guiding light.

(25) NATIONAL CORPORATION OF HOSPITALS AND RELATED HOUSES (all hospitals of all types, workshops for repairs and adjustments, houses for the curing of hides, stables for the curing of horses, dental clinics, barber shops, houses for the pruning of plants, houses for the arrangement of intricate legal forms, etc., and also all employees in general of said establishments).

"There it is," Traveler said. "A break that proves Ceferino's perfect central healthiness. Horacio is right, there's no reason to accept the order of things the way daddy hands them to us. Cefe thinks that the fact that something is being repaired unites a dentist and intricate legal forms; accidents are just as valuable as essences . . . But it's pure poetry, boy. Cefe is breaking the hard mental crust, as somebody or other said, and he's beginning to see the world from a different angle. Of course this is what they call being batty."

When Talita came in he was on the twenty-eighth Corporation:

> (28) NATIONAL CORPORATION OF SCIENTIFIC DETECTIVES-ERRANT AND THEIR HOUSES OF SCIENCE (all places for detectives and/or investigation police, all places for explorers (travellers) and all places for scientific explorers, and all employees in general of said same establishments). (All of the above-mentioned employees must belong to a class that is to be called "ERRANT".)

Talita and Traveler liked this part less, it was as if Ceferino were abandoning himself too soon to a persecutory worry. But perhaps the scientific detectives-errant were not mere investigators; the "errant" business invested them with a quixotic air that Cefe, probably taking it as understood, had not bothered to emphasize.

> (29) NATIONAL CORPORATION OF SCIENTIFIC DETECTIVES HAVING TO DO WITH PLEAS AND THEIR HOUSES OF SCIENCE (all places for detectives and/or Investigation police, and all places for explorers, and all employees in general of said same establishments). (All of the above-mentioned employees are to belong to a class that is to be called "PLEAS", and the places and employees of this class are to be separate from those of other classes such as the already mentioned "ERRANT".
>
> (30) NATIONAL CORPORATION OF SCIENTIFIC DETECTIVES HAVING TO DO WITH FINAL BOUNDARIES AND THEIR HOUSES OF SCIENCE (all places for detectives and/or Investigation police, and all places for explorers, and all employees in general of said same establishments). (All of the above-mentioned employees are to belong to a class that is to be called "BOUNDARIES", and the places and employees of this class are to be separate from those of other classes such as the already mentioned "ERRANT" and "PLEAS".)

"It's as if he were talking about orders of chivalry," Talita said convinced. "But the strange thing is that in these three corporations of detectives, the only thing he mentions is the places."

"That's one thing, and the other is the meaning of 'final boundaries'."

"He must be deriving *final* from *fine*. But that doesn't solve anything. What's the difference."

"What's the difference," Traveler repeated. "You're so right. The beautiful part is that there exists the possibility of a world where there will be detectives-errant, plea detectives, and final-boundary detectives. That's why it seems quite natural to me that Cefe turns now from chivalry to religious orders, with an interlude that looks like a concession to the scientifical (you've got to call it something) spirit of the times. I'll read it to you:"

> (31) NATIONAL CORPORATION OF THE LEARNED IN SUITABLE SCIENCES AND THEIR HOUSES OF SCIENCE (all houses or communal places for the learned in suitable sciences and all of the aforementioned learned men). (Learned men in suitable sciences: physicians, homoeopaths, healers (all surgeons), midwives, technicians, mechanics (all types of technicians), engineers of the second grade or architects of every branch (all executors of plans already drawn beforehand, such as would be an engineer of the second grade), classifiers in general, astronomers, astrologers, spiritualists, full doctors in every branch of the law or laws (all experts), classifiers of generic species, accountants, translators, primary school teachers (all composers), trackers – men – of murderers, pathfinders or guides, plant grafters, barbers, etc.)

"Look at this," Traveler said, taking a drink of *caña* at one gulp. "He's an absolute genius!"

"It'll be a great country for barbers," Talita said, flopping on the bed and closing her eyes. "They come pretty high on the scale. What I don't understand is why the tracers of murderers have to be men."

"I've never heard of a female tracker," Traveler said, "and probably Cefe didn't find it very appropriate. You must have noticed that he's a terrible puritan in sexual matters, it comes out all the time."

"It's hot, too damned hot," Talita said. "Did you notice how he likes to include classifiers, and even repeats the name? So let's have the mystical leap you were going to read me."

"Get ready to catalogue," Traveler said.

(32) NATIONAL CORPORATION OF MONKS OF THE PRAYER OF THE SIGN OF THE CROSS AND THEIR HOUSES OF SCIENCE (all communal houses of monks, and all monks). (Monks or men who bless, who are to remain outside all extraneous cults, uniquely and only for the world of the word and the curative mysteries of the "conquest" of the latter.) (Monks who are always to combat all spiritual ills, all harm earned or put into goods or bodies, etc.) (Penitent and anchorite monks who are to pray for and bless sometimes people, sometimes objects, sometimes sites of places, sometimes planted fields, sometimes a boyfriend badly affected by a rival, etc.)

(33) NATIONAL CORPORATION OF CHURCHGOING GUARDIANS OF COLLECTIONS AND THEIR HOUSES OF COLLECTION (all houses of collection, and *idem*, houses – deposits, warehouses, archives, museums, cemeteries, jails, asylums, homes for the blind, etc., and also all employees in general of said establishments). (Collections: example: an archive keeps files in a collection; a cemetery keeps corpses in a collection; a jail keeps prisoners in a collection, etc.)

"Even Espronceda didn't think of the cemetery bit," Traveler said. "You can't deny the analogy between the Chacarita cemetery and an archive . . . Ceferino has an intuition for relationships, and that, basically, is true intelligence, don't you think? After introductions like these, his final classification isn't strange at all, quite the contrary. A world like this should be tried."

Talita didn't say anything, but she lifted her upper lip like a festoon and let out a sigh that had its origins in what is called the first signs of sleep. Traveler took another drink of *caña* and got into the final and definitive Corporations:

(40) NATIONAL CORPORATION OF COMMISSION AGENTS FOR COLOURED SPECIES COLOURED IN RED AND HOUSES OF ACTIVE LABOUR FOR THE BENEFIT OF SPECIES COLOURED IN RED (all communal houses of

commission agents for generic species coloured in red, or the main Offices of said agents, and also all said agents). (Generic species coloured in red: animals with fur coloured in red; plants with flowers coloured in red, and minerals with the look of coloured in red.)

(41) NATIONAL CORPORATION OF COMMISSION AGENTS FOR SPECIES COLOURED IN BLACK AND HOUSES OF ACTIVE LABOUR FOR THE BENEFIT OF SPECIES COLOURED BLACK (all communal houses of commission agents for generic species in black, or the main Offices of said agents, and also all said agents). (Generic species coloured in black or simply black animals with black fur, plants with black flowers, and minerals with a black look.)

(42) NATIONAL CORPORATION OF COMMISSION AGENTS FOR SPECIES COLOURED IN BROWN AND HOUSES OF ACTIVE LABOUR FOR THE BENEFIT OF BROWN SPECIES (all communal houses of commission agents for generic species coloured in brown, or the main Offices of said agents, and also all said agents). (Generic species coloured in brown or simply brown: animals with brown fur, plants with brown flowers, and minerals with a brown look.)

(43) NATIONAL CORPORATION OF COMMISSION AGENTS FOR SPECIES COLOURED IN YELLOW AND HOUSES OF ACTIVE LABOUR FOR THE BENEFIT OF SPECIES COLOURED IN YELLOW (all communal houses of commission agents for generic species coloured in yellow, or the main Offices of said agents, and also all said agents). (Generic species coloured in yellow or simply yellow: animals with yellow fur, plants with yellow flowers, and minerals with a yellow look.)

(44) NATIONAL CORPORATION OF COMMISSION AGENTS FOR SPECIES IN WHITE AND HOUSES OF ACTIVE LABOUR FOR THE BENEFIT OF SPECIES COLOURED IN WHITE (all communal houses of commission agents for generic species coloured in white, or the main Offices of said agents, and also all said agents.) (Generic species coloured in white: animals with white fur, plants with white flowers, and minerals with a white look.)

> (45) NATIONAL CORPORATION OF COMMISSION AGENTS FOR SPECIES IN PAMPA AND HOUSES OF ACTIVE LABOUR FOR THE BENEFIT OF SPECIES COLOURED IN PAMPA (all communal houses of commission agents for generic species coloured in pampa, or the main Offices of said agents, and also all said agents). (Generic species coloured in pampa or simply pampa: animals with pampa fur, vegetables with pampa flowers, and minerals with a pampa look.)

Break the hard mental crust . . . How did Ceferino visualize what he had written? What dazzling reality (or not) showing him scenes in which polar bears moved about in a vast marble backdrop, among Cape jasmines? Or crows nesting in a pile of coal with black tulips in their beaks . . . And why "coloured in black", "coloured in white"? Shouldn't it be "in colour"? But then, why: "coloured in yellow or simply yellow"? What colours were they that couldn't be translated by Michaux's or Huxley's marijuana? Ceferino's notes, useful to lose one's self a little more (if that was useful), didn't go very far. In any case:

> Concerning the aforementioned pampa colour: pampa colour is all of that colour which is varied, or which is formed by two or more kinds of paint.

And a highly necessary clarification:

> Concerning the aforementioned or alluded agents for generic species: said agents are to be Governors, for through them none of the generic species shall disappear from the earth; the generic types, within their class, shall not cross, either one class with another, or one type with another, or one race with another, or one generic colour with another generic colour, etc.

Ceferino Piriz, a purist, a racist! A cosmos of pure colours, Mondrianesque to an intolerable degree! Dangerous Ceferino Piriz, always a possible candidate for Deputy, perhaps for President! On guard, Uruguay! And another *caña* before going to sleep while Cefe, drunk with colours, allows himself a last poem in which, as in a huge canvas by Ensor, everything explosive explodes into material for masks and antimasks. Militarism suddenly erupts in his system, and the treatment, somewhere between macaronic and trismegistical, that the Uruguayan philosopher reserved for it, had to be seen. Or in other words:

> As for the announced work *The Light of World Peace*, the question is that it includes a rather detailed explanation of militarism, but now, in a brief summary, we shall give the following version(s) dealing with militarism:
>
> *Police* ("Metropolitan" type) *for military men born under the zodiacal sign of Aries; Unions of fundamental antigovernment for military men born under the zodiacal sign of Taurus; the Direction and sponsorship of public festivities and social gatherings (dances, soirées, arrangement of betrothals: bringing fiancés together, etc.) for military men born under the zodiacal sign of Gemini; Aviation (military) for military men born under the zodiacal sign of Cancer; the Pen in support of fundamental government (military journalism, and political wizardry for the benefit of all fundamental and national Government) for military men born under the zodiacal sign of Leo; Artillery (heavy weapons in general and bombs) for military men born under the zodiacal sign of Virgo; Sponsorship and practical production of public and/or national celebrations (the use of adequate disguises on the part of military men in moments for the incorporation of either a military parade, or a festival like those called "harvest", etc.) for military men born under the zodiacal sign of Scorpio; Cavalry (regular cavalry and motorized cavalry, with their respective participation, either of fusileers, or lancers, or machete bearers: typical example: "Republican Guard", or of swordsmen, etc.) for military men born under the zodiacal sign of Capricorn; and practical military Service (couriers, orderlies, firemen, practical missionaries, servants of the practical, etc.) for military men born under the zodiacal sign of Aquarius.*

Shaking Talita, who woke up indignantly, Traveler read her the part on militarism and the two of them had to cover their heads with the pillow so they wouldn't wake up the whole clinic. But first they came to agree that the majority of Argentine military men were born under the zodiacal sign of Taurus. Traveler was so drunk, born under the zodiacal sign of Scorpio, that he declared himself ready to appeal immediately in his status as second lieutenant in the reserves for permission to make use of adequate disguises on the part of military men.

"We will organize tremendous festivals of the type called harvest," Traveler said, taking his head out from under the pillow and sticking it back again as soon as he finished the sentence. "You shall see along with all your fellows of the pampa race, because there isn't the least doubt that you're a pampa, or that you're formed by two or more kinds of paint."

"I'm white," Talita said. "And it's too bad you weren't born under the zodiacal sign of Capricorn, because I'd love you to be a swordsman. Or at least a courier or an orderly."

"Couriers are Aquarius. Horacio is Cancer, isn't he?"

"If he isn't, he deserves to be," Talita said, closing her eyes.

"Aviation touches him a bit. All you have to do is imagine him piloting one of those Bang-Bangs and there you have him crashing his plane into the Confitería del Aguila at tea and crumpet time. It would be inevitable."

Talita turned out the light and snuggled a little closer to Traveler, who was sweating and twisting, wrapped up in diverse signs of the zodiac, national corporations of commission agents who had a yellow look.

"Horacio saw La Maga tonight," Talita said. "He saw her in the courtyard, two hours ago, when you were on guard duty."

"Oh," said Traveler lifting up his shoulders and looking for his cigarettes by Braille. "We would have to place him among the churchgoing guardians of collections."

"I was La Maga," Talita said, snuggling closer to Traveler. "I don't know if you're aware of that."

"Most likely yes."

"It had to happen some time. What surprises me is that he's become so startled by the mixup."

"Oh you know, Horacio gets something started and then he looks at it with the same look puppies put on when they've taken a crap and stand there amazed looking at it."

"I think it happened the very day we went to meet him at the dock," Talita said. "It's hard to explain, because he didn't even look at me and between the two of you you treated me like a dog, with the cat under my arm."

"Breeding of noncorpulent animals," Traveler said.

"He had me confused with La Maga," Talita insisted. "Everything else had to follow as if Ceferino had enumerated it, one thing after another."

"La Maga," Traveler said, dragging on his cigarette until his face was lit up in the darkness, "is also from Uruguay. So you see there's a certain order."

"Let me talk, Manú."

"Better not. What for?"

"First the old man with the pigeon came, and then we went down to the basement. Horacio kept talking all the time we were going down, about those hollows that worry him. He was desperate, Manú, it was frightening to see how peaceful he seemed, and all the time . . . We went down in the service lift, and he went over to shut one of the freezers, it was horrible."

"So you went downstairs," Traveler said. "OK."

"It was different," Talita said. "It wasn't like going down. We were talking, but I felt as if Horacio were somewhere else, talking to someone else, to a drowned woman, for example. It comes back to me now, but he'd never said that La Maga had been drowned in the river."

"She isn't the least bit drowned," Traveler said. "I'm sure of that, although I have to admit I haven't got the slightest idea. Knowing Horacio is enough."

"He thinks she's dead, Manú, and at the same time he feels her close by and tonight it was me. He told me that he's seen her on the ship too, and under the bridge on the Avenida San Martín . . . He doesn't say it as if he were talking about a hallucination, and he doesn't expect you to believe it either. He says it, that's all, and it's true, it's something that's there. When he closed the freezer and I was afraid and I said something or other, he began to look at me and it was the other one he was looking at. I'm nobody's zombie, Manú, I don't want to be anybody's zombie."

Traveler stroked her hair, but Talita pushed him away impatiently. She had sat down on the bed and he could feel her trembling. Trembling, in that heat. She told him that Horacio had kissed her and she tried to explain the kiss, and since she couldn't find the words she kept touching Traveler in the darkness, her arms fell like cloths over his face, over his arms, slipped down along his chest, rested on his knees, and out of all this came a kind of explanation that Traveler was incapable of rejecting, a contagion that came from farther off, from some place in the depths or on the heights or in some place which was not that night and that room, a contagion that possessed him in turn through Talita, a babbling like an untranslatable announcement, the suspicion that he was facing something that could be an announcement, but the voice that brought it was broken and when it spoke the message it spoke it in some unintelligible language, and yet it was the only necessary thing there within hand's reach, demanding recognition and acceptance, beating itself against a spongy wall of smoke and cork, unseizable and offering itself naked between the arms but like water pouring down among tears.

"The hard mental crust," Traveler managed to think. Confusedly he heard that fear, that Horacio, that the service lift, that the dove; a communicable system was little by little entering his ear again. So the poor devil was afraid he would kill him, it was laughable.

"Did he really say that? It's hard to believe, you know how proud he is."

"It's something else," Talita said, taking the cigarette away from him and dragging on it with a sort of silent-movie eagerness. "I think the fear he feels is like a last refuge, the crossbar he holds onto before jumping. He's so happy to be afraid tonight, I know he's happy."

"That," said Traveler, breathing like a real yogi, "is something Cuca would not understand, you can be sure. And I must be in an exceedingly intelligent mood tonight, because that business of happy fear is a little hard to take, my love."

Talita slid up on the bed a little and leaned against Traveler. She knew that she was by his side again, that she had not drowned, that he was there holding her up on the surface of the water and that actually there was pity, a marvellous pity. They both felt it at the same moment, and they slid towards each other as if to fall into themselves, into the common earth where words and caresses and mouths enfolded them as a circumference does a circle, those tranquillizing metaphors, that old sadness satisfied with going back to being the same as always, with continuing, keeping afloat against wind and tide, against call and fall.

(–140)

134

The Flower Garden

One must be aware of the fact that a garden that is very strictly planned, in the style of "French parks", consisting of flower-beds, stone pots and trellises arranged geometrically, calls for great competence and much care.

On the other hand, in a garden of "English" type, the mistakes of the amateur are more easily disguised. A few bushes, a bed of grass, and a single flowerbed with mixed flowers that stands out neatly, in the shelter of a well-located wall or fence, are the essential elements of a very decorative and very practical combination.

If some varieties unfortunately do not yield the desired results, it will be easy to replace them by means of transplants; imperfection or lack of care in the combination will not be visible because the other flowers, arranged in patches that differ as to surface, height and colour, will always form a grouping that will be pleasant to the eye.

This type of planting, very popular in England and the United States, is called a "mixed border". Flowers set out this way, mixed in together and showing each other off as if they had grown naturally, will give your garden a rural and natural aspect, while planting done in rows, squares and circles always has an artificial character about it and requires absolute perfection.

Therefore, for practical as well as aesthetic reasons, it is proper to advise a mixed-border arrangement for the amateur gardener.

Almanach Hachette

(–25)

135

"They're delicious," Gekrepten said. "I already ate two while I was frying them, they're a real delicacy, believe me."

"Make me another bitter *mate*, old girl," Oliveira said.

"Right away, love. Wait till I change your cold compress first."

"Thanks. It's very strange eating fried cakes with your eyes bandaged. That's how they should train the guys who are going to discover the cosmos for us."

"The ones who fly to the moon in those machines? They put them in a capsule or something like that, right?"

"Yes, and they give them fried cakes and *mate*."

(–63)

136

Morelli's mania for quotations:

"It would be difficult for me to explain the publication in one single book of poems and a denial of poetry, of the diary of a dead man and the notes of a prelate friend of mine . . . "

GEORGES BATAILLE, *Haine de la poésie*

(–12)

137

Morelliana

If the volume or the tone of the work can lead one to believe that the author is attempting a sum, hasten to point out to him that he is face to face with the opposite attempt, that of an implacable *subtraction.*

(–17)

138

Sometimes La Maga and I feel like profaning our memories. It all depends on so little, an afternoon's bad mood, the anguish over what can happen if we start looking at each other straight in the eye. Little by little, along the meandering of a dialogue that's like a piece of shredded rag, we begin to remember. Two different worlds, alien, almost always irreconcilable, come into our words, and as if by common consent the joke comes into being. I usually start scornfully, remembering my old blind cult of friendship, misunderstood loyalties that gave little in return, the humble obstinacy of banners carried to political rallies, to intellectual lectures, to fervent love affairs. I laugh at a suspicious honesty that so many times caused its own or someone else's misfortune, while underneath betrayals and moments of dishonesty were spinning their webs and I could not prevent them, I could only allow others to betray or be dishonest to my face and doubly to blame could not do anything to prevent them. I make fun of my uncles and their decanted decency, stuck in shit up to their necks where the immaculate stiff collar still glows. They would fall over on their backs if they knew that they were wallowing in manure, convinced, the one in Tucuman and the other in Nueve de Julio, that they are the model of decanted Argentinity (those are the words they use). And yet I have fond memories of them. And yet I will trample on those memories on days when La Maga and I get fed up with Paris and want to do ourselves some harm.

When La Maga stops laughing and asks me why I say such things about my uncles, I wish they could be there listening behind the door like the old man on the sixth floor. I prepare a careful explanation, because I do not want to be unjust or to exaggerate. I also want it to be helpful for La Maga, because she has never been able to understand moral questions (just like Étienne, but less selfishly; just because the only responsibility she believes in is of the present, the very moment when one must be good or noble; underneath it all, for reasons just as hedonistic and selfish as Étienne's).

Then I explain that my two most honourable uncles are a pair of perfect Argentines as the expression was understood in 1915, a period in the high point of their lives that varied between ranching and business. When one talks about "Latin Americans of yesteryear", he means anti-Semites, xenophobes, bourgeoisie rooted in a nostalgia for the small ranch where Indian girls prepared *mate* for ten pesos a month, all with the bluest and whitest of patriotic sentiments, a respect for everything military and for expeditions into the frontier, with dozens of starched shirts, even though his salary isn't big enough for monthly payments to that abject being the whole family calls the "Russian", dealt with by shouts, threats, and at best with bullying phrases. When La Maga starts to share this vision (of which she personally hasn't the slightest experience) I hasten to show her that within this general panorama of my two uncles and their respective families there are people with excellent qualities. Self-sacrificing parents and their children, citizens who go to the polls and read serious newspapers, hard-working officials well thought of by their superiors and colleagues, people capable of staying up nights on end at the bedside of a person who is ill, or of doing some magnificent gauchesque sort of thing. La Maga looks at me perplexed, afraid I'm making fun of her. I have to insist, explain why I love my uncles so much, why only when we get fed up with streets and the weather it occurs to me to haul their remains out of the shadows and trample on the memories I still have of them. Then La Maga perks up a bit and starts talking about her mother, whom she loves and detests in proportions that vary with the moment. Sometimes she terrifies me with the way in which she can refer to a childhood episode that other times she has mentioned with laughter, as if it were amusing, and suddenly it becomes a sinister knot, a kind of swamp with leeches and ticks that pursue and suck. At moments like that La Maga's face looks like a fox's, her nostrils narrow, she turns pale, she speaks in jerks and starts, twisting her hands and panting and, like a huge, obscene piece of chewing-gum, her mother's pasty face begins to appear, her mother's poorly dressed body, the suburban street her mother lives on like an old spittoon on a wasteland, the misery in which her mother is a hand that scrubs a pot with a greasy rag. The worst of it is that La Maga can't go on for very long; soon she starts to cry, hiding her face against me, huddling down to an incredible degree, we have to prepare tea, forget about everything, go off somewhere or make love, make love without any uncles or mother, almost always that or going to sleep, but almost always that.

(–127)

139

The notes of the piano (la, re, mi flat, do, ti, ti flat, mi, so), those of the violin (la, mi, ti flat, mi), those of the horn (la, ti flat, la, ti flat, mi, so), represent the musical equivalent of the names of ArnoLD SCHoenberg, Anton WEBErn, and ALBAn BErG (according to the German system in which H represents ti, B ti flat, and S (ES) mi flat). There is nothing new about this kind of musical anagram. It must be recalled that Bach used his own name in a similar way and that the same procedure was common property among polyphonic composers of the 16th century (. . .) Another significant analogy with the Violin Concerto consists in the strict symmetry of the whole. In the Violin Concerto the key number is two: two separate movements, each divided into two parts, as well as the violin-orchestra division in the instrumental grouping. In the *Kammerkonzert*, on the other hand, the number three stands out: the dedication represents the Maestro and his two disciples; the instruments are grouped in three categories: piano, violin, and a combination of wind instruments; its architecture is the building up of three linked movements, each of which reveals to a greater or lesser degree a tripartite composition.

From the anonymous commentary on the Chamber Concerto
for violin, piano, and thirteen wind instruments
by ALBAN BERG (Pathé Vox recording PL 8660)

(–133)

140

In hopes of something more exciting, exercises in profanation and the far-out, in the pharmacy between midnight and two in the morning, once Cuca had gone off to get-a-good-night's-sleep (or before, so she would go: Cuca sticks it out, but she gets terribly tired from the effort of resisting with a bounteous smile and a sort of turning her back on the monsters' verbal assaults. Every time she leaves a little earlier to get some sleep, and the monsters smile pleasantly as they wish her good night. Talita, with her greater neutrality, is pasting on labels or consulting the *Index Pharmacorum Gottinga*).

The sort of thing they do: translating with Manichaean inversion a famous sonnet:

> The deflowered, dead, and fearful past,
> Can it but bring us back with sombre flap of wing?

Reading a page from Traveler's notebook: "Waiting my turn in the barber shop, spotting a UNESCO publication, and picking up on the following names: Opintotoveri/Työläusopiskelija/Työväenopisto. It seems that these are the names of some pedagogical journals from Finland. Complete unreality for the reader. Does it all really exist? For millions of blond-headed people, Opinotoveri means the Supervisor of General Education. For me . . . (Wrath). But they don't know what *cafisho* means (Buenos Aires satisfaction). Irreality multiplies. To think that specialists can foretell from the fact that one can reach Helsinki in a few hours in a Boeing 707 . . . The results of personal extrapolation. Give me a crew-cut, Pedro."

Linguistic forms of alienation. Pensive Talita, face to face with Genshiryoku Kokunai Jijo, that in no way seems to resemble the development of nuclear activity in Japan. She is just becoming convinced by superposition and differentiation when her husband, that malignant provider of material picked up in barber shops, shows her the variant Genshiryoku Kaigai Jijo, evidently the development of nuclear activities abroad. Talita's enthusiasm, convinced analytically that Kokunai = Japan and Kaigai = abroad. The confusion on the part of Matsui, the drycleaner on the Calle Lascano, when he is confronted with a polyglot exhibition by Talita, who turns away, poor thing, with her tail between her legs.

Profanations: starting with such suppositions as the famous line: "Christ's visible homosexuality," and building up to a coherent and satisfactory system. Postulating that Beethoven was a coprofage, etc. Defending the undeniable sainthood of Sir Roger Casement, as it is evident in *The Black Diaries.* The bewilderment of Cuca, confirmed and practising.

Basically it's a question of alienating one's self out of purely professional abnegation. They still laugh too much (impossible for Attila to be a stamp collector) but that business about *Arbeit macht Frei* will still have results, believe me, Cuca. For example, the rape of the Bishop of Fano must be a case of . . .

(–138)

141

It didn't take many pages to see that Morelli was aiming at something else. His allusions to the profound blanket of the *Zeitgeist*, the passages where lo(co)gic ended up by hanging itself by its own shoelaces, unable to deny the incongruity that has become a law, were evidence of the work's speleological intent. Morelli advanced and retreated in such an open violation of equilibrium and principles of space that should really be called *moral*, that it well might have happened (although, in fact, it did not happen, but nobody could be sure) that the happenings he spoke about might have all happened in five minutes that were capable of linking the Battle of Actium with the *Anschluss* of Austria (the three A's may have had something to do with his choice or, more probably, the acceptance of those historic moments), or the fact that a person who rang the doorbell of a house on the Calle Cochabamba, at number twelve hundred, would be able to open the door into a courtyard of Menander's house in Pompeii. That was all rather trivial and Buñuel, and its value as a mere incitement or as a parabola open to a deeper and more scabrous sense was not lost on those in the Club. Thanks to those exercises in flying around, so like the ones that get so showy in the Gospels, the Upanishads, and other matter loaded with shamanistic trinitrotoluene, Morelli allowed himself the pleasure of continuing to pretend a literature that he would mine, undermine and ridicule at its very inner base. Suddenly the words, a whole language, the superstructure of a style, a semantic, a psychology, and a factitiousness rushed towards hair-raising hara-kiris. *Banzai!* Even towards a new order, or no guarantee whatsoever: finally, there would always be a thread stretched out to the beyond, coming out of the book, pointing towards a perhaps, a maybe, a who knows, which would leave any petrifying aspect of the work in abeyance. And the thing that distressed Perico Romero, a man in need of certainties, made Oliveira tremble with delight, heightened the imagination of Étienne, Wong, and Ronald, and obliged La Maga to dance barefoot with an artichoke in each hand.

Along the route of arguments stained with Calvados and tobacco, Étienne and Oliveira had wondered why Morelli hated literature, and why he hated it from the standpoint of literature itself, instead of repeating Rimbaud's *exeunt* or exercising on his left temple the notorious effectiveness of a Colt ·32. Oliveira was inclined to believe that Morelli had been suspicious of the demoniacal nature of all re-creative writing (and what literature wasn't like that, even if it was something like the excipient that would make a person swallow a gnosis, a praxis, or an ethos out of all the ones that were wandering around or that could be invented?). After hefting the most inciting passages, he had ended by becoming sensitive to a special tone of Morelli's writing. The first possible description of that tone was one of disenchantment, but underneath one could sense that the disenchantment did not refer to the circumstances and happenings narrated in the book, but rather to the way they were narrated, that – Morelli had disguised it as much as possible – he was reverting definitively to what was being told. The elimination of the pseudo-conflict between content and form came up again to the degree that the old man was denouncing formal material and using it in his own way; when he doubted his tools he was at the same time disqualifying the work he did with them. What the book told about had no use whatsoever, because it was poorly told, simply because it was told, it was literature. Again one turned to the irritation of the author with his writing and with writing in general. The apparent paradox lay in that Morelli was accumulating episodes that were imagined and foe-used in the most diverse forms; trying to attack them and resolve them with every skill of a writer worthy of the name. He didn't seem to be proposing a theory, it offered no difficulty for intellectual reflection, but from everything he had written there would appear with an efficiency infinitely greater than that of any statement or analysis, the profound corrosion of a world denounced as false, the attack by accumulation and not by destruction, an almost diabolical irony that might be suspicious of the success of great passages of bravado, episodes rigorously constructed, the apparent feeling of literary happiness that for years had been building up his fame among readers of short stories and novels.

For those with a delicate sense of smell, a world sumptuously orchestrated was being resolved into nothingness; but right there the mystery began, because at the same time one was presented with the total nihilism of the work, a more careful intuition might suspect that this was not Morelli's intent, that the virtual self-destruction found in every fragment of his work was a kind of search for the noble metal among the slag. One had to pause here, for fear of mixing up the doors and going out on a limb. The fiercest arguments between Oliveira and Étienne would occur at this level of their hopes, because they feared they were making mistakes, that they were a pair of perfect cretins insisting on the belief that the Tower of Babel could not be built if in the end it was meaningless. Occidental morality at this point seemed like a pimp to them, as one by one it insinuated all the illusions of thirty centuries that had been inevitably inherited, assimilated, and digested. It was hard to deny belief in the fact that a flower could be beautiful to no end; it was bitter to accept the fact that one could dance in darkness. Morelli's allusions to an inversion of signs, to a world seen with other and from other dimensions, as an inevitable preparation for a purer vision (and all of this in a resplendently written passage, and at the same time suspicious of the farce, of icy irony before the mirror) exasperated them as it offered them the roost of an almost hope, of a justification but at the same time denied them total security, keeping them in an unbearable ambiguity. If there was any consolation left it was the thought that Morelli too moved about in that same ambiguity, orchestrating a work whose legitimate first hearing could well have been the most absolute of silences. That's how they went along through the pages, cursing and fascinated, and La Maga would always end up curling herself up like a cat in an easy chair, tired of uncertainties, looking at how dawn was breaking over the slate roofs, through all the smoke that fills in among a pair of eyes and a closed window and an ardently useless night.

(–60)

142

1. "I can't tell what she was like," Ronald said. "We'll never know. All we know about her is the effect she had on other people. We were something like her mirrors, or she was our mirror. I can't explain it."

2. "She used to be so silly," Étienne said. "Blessed be the silly, et cetera. I swear to you that I'm speaking seriously, I'm quoting seriously. Her silliness used to irritate me. Horacio insisted it was just a lack of information, but he was wrong. There's a well-known difference between ignorance and silliness, and everybody knows that, except somebody who's silly, luckily for him. She thought that by studying, her famous studying, she could get to be intelligent. She confused knowledge with understanding. The poor girl had a good understanding of so many things that we don't sense because we know so much about them."

3. "Don't fall into echolalia," Ronald said. "That whole deck of antinomies, polarizations. For me, her silliness was the price she paid for being so vegetative, so much of a snail, so stuck onto the most mysterious of things. That's it, think about it: she wasn't capable of believing in names, she had to put her finger on something and only then would she admit that it was. You don't get very far that way. It's like turning your back on the whole Western world, all of the Schools. It's no good for living in a city, having to earn your keep. That's what was gnawing at her."

4. "Yes, yes, but on the other hand she was capable of infinite moments of happiness, I used to watch her with envy. The shape of a glass, for example. What else am I looking for in painting, tell me. Killing myself, driving myself along such frightening paths, all I do is come out with a fork and two olives. Salt and the centre of the world have to be there, in that spot on the tablecloth. She'd arrive and sense it. One night she came over to my studio, I found her in

front of a painting I'd finished that morning. She was crying the way she used to cry, with her whole face, horrible and marvellous. She was looking at my painting and crying. I wasn't enough of a man to tell her I had cried that morning too. To think that it could have given her so much tranquillity, you know how much she doubted, how small she felt, surrounded by our clever brilliance."

5. "One cries for many reasons," Ronald said. "That doesn't prove anything."

6. "At least it proves a contact. How many others looking at that painting had shown their appreciation with polished phrases, a list of influences, all the possible commentaries *round about.* You see, you had to reach a level where it would be possible to join both things together. I think I'm already there, but I'm one of the few."

7. "You're probably king of the few," Ronald said. "Anything at all is enough to make you take off."

6. "I know that's how it is," Étienne said. "I know that. But it's taken me a lifetime to get my two hands to work together, the left one to its heart, the right one to its brush and canvas. At first I was someone who would look at Raphael and think about Perugino, pounce like a lobster on Leo Battista Alberti, connect, link, Pico here, Lorenzo Valla there, but look, Burckhardt says, Berenson denies, Argan thinks, those blues are Sienese, those blurs are from Masaccio. I don't remember when, it was in Rome, in the Barberini gallery, I was analysing an Andrea del Sarto, what they call analysing, and all of a sudden I saw. Don't ask me to explain anything. I saw it (and not the whole painting, just a detail in the background, a small figure on a road). Tears came to my eyes, I mean it."

5. "That doesn't prove anything," Ronald said. "One cries for many reasons."

4. "It's no good answering you. She probably would have understood much better. We're all really on the same road, except that some people start on the lefthand side and some on the right. Sometimes, right in the middle, somebody sees the piece of tablecloth with the glass on it, the fork, the olives."

3. "You're talking figures," Ronald said. "It's always the same thing."

2. "There's no other way to get back what's been lost, what's strayed away. She was closer to it and she sensed it. Her only mistake was in wanting a proof that the closeness was worth all our rhetoric.

Nobody could give her that proof, first because we're incapable of conceiving of it, and second because in one way or another we're comfortably installed and satisfied in our collective science. It's common knowledge that Fowler lets us sleep peacefully, there he is within reach, with all the answers. And it's true, but only because we're no longer capable of asking the questions that would liquidate him. When La Maga would ask why trees covered themselves in summer . . . but it's useless, man, it's better to shut up."

1. "Yes, we can't really explain any of that at all," Ronald said.

(–34)

143

In the morning, still persisting in the dozing that the hair-raising shriek of the alarm could not change into sharp wakefulness, they would dutifully tell each other about the dreams they had had that night. Head to head, caressing each other, mingling hands and feet, they tried to put into words the world they had been living in during darkness. Traveler, a friend from Oliveira's youth, was fascinated by Talita's dreams, her mouth, tight or smiling according to the telling, the gestures and exclamations with which she would accentuate it, her ingenuous conjectures about the reason and meaning of her dreams. Then it would be his turn to tell about his, and sometimes in the middle of a telling his hands would begin to caress and they would go from dreams to love, fall asleep again, be late everywhere they were going.

Listening to Talita, her voice a little sticky from sleep, looking at her hair spread out on the pillow, Traveler was startled that everything could be like that. He stuck out a finger, touched Talita on the temple, the forehead. ("And then my sister became my Aunt Irene, but I'm not sure"), he would test the barrier so few inches away from his own head ("And I was a boy naked in a pile of straw and I was looking at the raging river as it rose, a gigantic wave . . . "). They had fallen asleep with their heads touching and there, in that physical immediacy, in that almost total coincidence of attitudes, positions, breathing, the same tick-tock, the same stimuli of street and city, the same magnetic radiations, the same brand of coffee, the same stellar conjunction, the same night for both of them, tightly embraced there, they had dreamed different dreams, they had lived unlike adventures, one had smiled while the other had fled frightened by herself, one had taken an exam in algebra again while the other was coming to a city built of white stone. Talita would put pleasure or doubt into the morning retelling, but Traveler would secretly insist on looking for correspondences. How was it possible that his daytime companion would inevitably turn off into that divorce, that inadmissible solitude of the dreamer? Sometimes his image would become part of Talita's dreams, or the image of Talita would share the horror of one of Traveler's nightmares. But they did not know it, it was necessary for one to tell the other on awakening: "Then you grabbed me by the hand and told me . . . " And Traveler discovered that while in Talita's dream he had grabbed her hand and talked to her, in his own dream he had been in bed with Talita's best friend or had been talking with the manager of the Las Estrellas circus, or swimming in Mar del Plata. The presence of his ghost in an alien dream had reduced him to the status of a tool, with no precedence whatsoever over manikins, unknown cities, railway stations, stairways, all the paraphernalia of night-time reproductions. Next to Talita, wrapping up her face and head with his lips and fingers, Traveler could feel the impassable barrier, the dizzy distance that not even love could leap. For a long time he waited for a miracle, that the dream Talita was about to tell him in the morning would also be the one he had dreamed. He waited for it, incited it, provoked it, calling upon all possible analogies, looking for similarities that suddenly would bring him to a recognition. Only once, without Talita's assigning it the least importance, did they dream analogous dreams. Talita spoke about a hotel that she and her mother had gone to where everybody had to bring his own chair. Then Traveler remembered his dream: a hotel without bathrooms, which obliged everyone to take a towel and go through a railway station to take a bath in some imprecise place. He told her: "We almost dreamed the same dream, we were in hotels without chairs and without bathrooms." Talita was amused and laughed, it was already time to get up, they were shamefully lazy.

Traveler kept on hoping and waiting less and less. The dreams came back, each one on its own side. Their heads would fall asleep touching each other and in each one the curtain would rise on a different stage. Traveler thought ironically that they were like those two cinemas side by side on the Calle Lavalle, and he lost his hopes completely. He lost his faith that what he wanted could happen, and he knew that without faith it would not happen. He knew that without faith nothing that should happen would happen, and with faith almost never either.

(–100)

144

Perfumes, Orphic hymns, civets in the first and second meanings . . . Here you smell of sardonyx. Here of chrysoprase. Here, wait a minute, here it's like parsley but just a hint, a small piece lost in a chamois skin. Here your own smell starts. How strange, really, that a woman cannot smell herself the way a man can smell her. Here exactly. Don't move, let me. You smell of royal jelly, of honey in a tobacco pouch, of seaweed even though the place might make it topical. There are so many kinds of seaweed, La Maga smelled of fresh seaweed, pulled up by the sea's last surf. Of the wave itself. On some days the smell of seaweed would become mixed up with a thicker cadence, then I would have to have recourse to perversion – but it was a Palatine perversion, you understand, a Bulgaroctonous luxury, that of a seneschal surrounded by nocturnal obedience –, to bring my lips up to hers, touch with my tongue that light pink flame that fluttered surrounded by shadow, and then, as now I do with you, I would slowly separate her thighs, hold her a little to one side and breathe into her interminably, feeling how her hand, without my asking, would begin to break me up the way a flame begins to pluck its topazes out of a wrinkled newspaper. Then the perfumes would stop miraculously and everything was taste, biting, essential juices running about the mouth, the fall into that shadow, the primeval darkness, the hub of the wheel of origins. Yes, in that instant of the most crouching animality, closest to excretion and its unspeakable apparatus, there the initial and final figures are sketched, there in the viscous cavern of your daily relaxation stands the trembling Aldebaran, genes and constellations jump, everything becomes alpha and omega, *coquille, cunt, concha, con, coño*, millennium, Armageddon, Terramycin, oh shut up, don't come on with your despicable show, your easy mirrors. The silence of your skin, its abysses with the roll of emerald dice, gadflies and phoenixes and craters . . .

(–92)

145

Morelliana

A quotation:

These, then, are the fundamental, capital and philosophical reasons that have induced me to construct my work on the basis of individual parts – conceiving the work as a particle of the work – and treating man as a fusion of parts of the body and parts of the soul – while I treat all Humanity as a mixture of parts. But if someone were to make this sort of objection to me: that this partial conception of mine is not, in truth, any conception at all, but a mockery, joke, raillery and trick, and that I, instead of subjecting myself to the severe rules and canons of Art, am trying to make fun of them by means of irresponsible jests, romps and leers, I would answer yes, that it's true, that my aims are precisely that. And God knows – I do not hesitate to confess it – I want to turn away a little, gentlemen, from your Art, just as from you yourselves, because I cannot stand alongside that Art, with your conceptions, your artistic attitude, and all of your artistic milieu!

GOMBROWICZ, *Ferdydurke*, Chapter IV. Preface to the Honer lined with child

(–222)

146

LETTER to *The Observer*

Dear Sir:

Has there been any indication from your readers of the scarcity of butterflies this year? In this area which is usually quite prolific, I have seen practically none with the exception of a few flights of Fritillaries. Since March I have seen but one example of an Apantesis virgo, no Catocala cares at all, very few Swallowtails, one Quelonia, no Peacock's Eyes, no Hipposcatics, and not even a single Red Admiral in my garden, which last summer was teeming with butterflies.

I wonder if this scarcity is widespread, and if so, what is the cause of it?

M. WASHBOURN

PITCHCOMBE, GLOS.

(–29)

147

Why so far from the gods? Perhaps simply by asking.

And so what? Man is the animal who asks. The day when we will really learn how to ask there will be a dialogue. Right now questions sweep us away from the answers. What *epiphany* can we expect if we are drowning in the falsest of freedoms, the Judeo-Christian dialectic? We need a real *Novam Organum*, we have to open our windows up wide and throw everything out into the street, but above all we also have to throw out the window and ourselves along with it. It is either a case of death or a continuing flight. We have to do it, in some way or another we have to do it. To have the strength to plunge into the midst of parties and crown the head of the dazzling lady of the house with a beautiful green frog, a gift of night, and suffer without horror the vengeance of her lackeys.

(–31)

148

Concerning the etymology offered by Gabio Basso for the word person.

A wise and ingenious explanation, by my lights, that of Gabio Basso, in his treatise *On the Origin of Words*, of the word *person*, mask. He thinks that this word has its origin in the verb *personare*, to retain. This is how he explains his opinion: "Since the mask covers the face completely except for an opening where the mouth is, the voice, instead of scattering in all directions, narrows down to escape through one single opening and therefore acquires a stronger and more penetrating sound. Thus, since the mask makes the human voice more sonorous and firm, it has been given the name *person*, and as a consequence of the formation of this word, the letter *o* as it appears in it is long."

AUEIO GELIO, *Attic Nights*

(–42)

149

Mis pasos en esta calle	(My steps along this street
Resuenan	Resound
En otra calle	Along another street
Donde	Where
Oigo mis pasos	I hear my steps
Pasar en esta calle	Resound along this street
Donde	Where
Sólo es real la niebla	Only the fog is real.)

OCTAVIO PAZ

(–54)

150

Hospital Items

The York County Hospital informs us that the Dowager Duchess of Grafton, who last Sunday fractured a leg, had a restful day yesterday.

The Sunday Times, London

(–95)

151

Morelliana

It is enough to take a momentary look with everyday eyes at the behaviour of a cat or a fly to feel that the new vision towards which science seems to be heading, that disanthropomorphization urgently proposed by biologists and physicists as the only possible conjoinment with phenomena such as instinct or vegetative life, is nothing but the remote, isolated, insistent voice by which certain lines of Buddhism, Vedanta, Sufism, Western mysticism urge us to renounce mortality once and for all.

(–152)

152

The Abuse of Consciousness

This house I am living in resembles my own in every way: the disposition of the rooms, the smell of the entrance hall, the furniture, the light that slants in the morning, becomes attenuated at noon, overlaps in the afternoon; everything is the same, even the paths and the trees in the garden, and that old tumbledown gate and the paving stones in the courtyard.

The hours and minutes of the time that passes also resemble the hours and minutes of my own life. In the moment in which they spin me around, I tell myself: "They seem real. How much they resemble the real hours I am living at this moment!"

For my part, if indeed I have done away with every reflective surface in my house, in spite of it all, the inevitable windowpane insists on returning my reflection, I see someone there who looks like me. Yes, he looks very much like me, I recognize him!

But no one must think that it is I! After all! Everything is false here. When they give me back *my* house and *my* life, then I shall find my own true face.

JEAN TARDIEU

(–143)

153

"Even though you're from Buenos Aires and all that, they'll stick you with a sorrel horse if you don't watch out."

"I'll try to watch out."

"That would be wise."

CAMBACERES, *Música sentimental*

(–19)

154

In any case, their shoes were walking on linoleum-like material, their noses smelled a bittersweet aseptic powder, the old man was installed in his bed up against two pillows, his nose like a hook caught in the air holding him upright. Livid, with mortuary rings underneath his eyes. The extraordinary zigzag of his temperature chart. And why had they gone to all that trouble?

They said it was nothing, the Argentine friend had happened to be a witness to the accident, the French friend was a dauber, all hospitals, the same infinite filth. Morelli, yes, the writer.

"It's impossible," Étienne said.

Why not, stone-in-the-water-editions: plop, nothing more is known about him. Morelli took the trouble to tell them that some four hundred copies had been sold (and given away). And then this fact, two in New Zealand, a tender statistic.

Oliveira took out a cigarette with a trembling hand, and he looked at the nurse who gave him an affirmative signal and went away, leaving them hedged in between the two yellowish screens. They sat down on the foot of the bed after pushing aside some notebooks and piles of paper.

"If we had only seen it in the newspapers . . . " Étienne said.

"It came out in the *Figaro*," Morelli said. "Underneath an item about the abominable snowman."

"You know about it," Oliveira managed to murmur. "But all in all I guess it's better that way. Every fat-arsed woman would have shown up with her autograph book and a jar of homemade jam."

"Rhubarb jam," Morelli said. "That's the nicest kind. But it's better if they don't come."

"As for us," Oliveira put in, really worried, "if we're bothering you, all you have to do is say so. There'll be other times, and all that. You know what I mean?"

"You came without knowing who I was. Personally, I think you should stay a while. This ward is peaceful, and the person who was shouting the most stopped last night at two o'clock. The screens are perfect, the courtesy of a doctor who had seen me writing. On the one hand he prohibited me from continuing, but then the nurses put up the screens and nobody bothers me.

"When will you be able to go home?"

"Never," Morelli said. "My bones are going to end up here, my dear boys."

"Nonsense," Étienne said respectfully.

"Just a question of time. But I feel all right, my problems with the concierge are ended. Nobody brings me my mail, not even the letters from New Zealand, with their pretty stamps. When a stillborn book is published, the only result is a small but faithful correspondence. The lady in New Zealand, the young man in Sheffield. A sensitive freemasonry, the voluptuous feeling of being one of so few partaking of an adventure. But right now, really . . . "

"I never thought about writing to you," Oliveira said. "Some friends of mine and I are familiar with your work, we think it's so . . . But God protect me from words like that, I think I make myself understood just the same. The fact is that we've spent whole nights discussing and still we never realized that you were here in Paris."

"Up till a year ago I was living in Vierzon. I came to Paris because I wanted to do a little exploration in some libraries. Vierzon, to be sure . . . My publisher had orders not to give out my address. Who knows how those few admirers found out. My back hurts me a lot, boys."

"You'd rather we left," Étienne said. "We'll come back tomorrow in any case."

"It would hurt just as much even if you weren't here," Morelli said. "Let's have a smoke, and take advantage of the fact that they ordered me not to."

It was a question of finding a non-literary way of speaking.

When the nurse went by, Morelli drew the butt into his mouth with a diabolical deftness and glanced at Oliveira with the air of a child who was disguised as an old man that was a real delight.

* * *

. . . starting off a little from Ezra Pound's central ideas, but without his pedantry and the confusion of peripheral symbols and primordial meanings.

Thirty-eight point two. Thirty-seven point five. Thirty-eight point three. X-ray (an incomprehensible symbol).

. . . knowing that a few people can approach those attempts without thinking that they're some new literary game. *Benissimo.* Worst of all, there is so much missing and he would die without having finished the game.

"The twenty-fifth move, black resigns," Morelli said, throwing his head back. Suddenly he seemed much older. "It's too bad, the game is just getting interesting. Is it true that there is an Indian chess game with sixty pieces on each side?"

"It's possible," Oliveira said. "The infinite game."

"The one who conquers the centre wins. From that point he dominates all possibilities, and it's senseless for his adversary to insist on continuing the play. But the centre might be in some side square, or even off the board."

"Or in a vest pocket."

"Figures," Morelli said. "It's so difficult to escape from them, beautiful as they are. Mental women, really. I would have liked to have understood Mallarmé better, his sense of absence and silence was much more than just an extreme recourse, a metaphysical impasse. One day in Jeréz de la Frontera I heard a cannon-shot twenty-five yards away and I discovered another meaning of silence. And dogs that can hear a whistle inaudible to us . . . You're a painter, I believe."

His hands worked down along his sides, picking up his notebooks one by one, smoothing out some wrinkled pages. From time to time, still talking, Morelli would glance at one of the pages and slip it into the notebooks held together by paper clips. Once or twice he would take a pencil out of his pyjama pocket and number a page.

"You write, I suppose."

"No," Oliveira said. "What could I write about? In order to do that you have to have some certainty that you've lived."

"Existence precedes essence," Morelli said with a smile.

"If you want to put it that way. My case isn't exactly like that."

"You're getting tired," Étienne said. "Let's go, Horacio, you're all set to keep on talking . . . I know him, sir, he's terrible."

Morelli kept on smiling and putting pages together, as he looked at them he seemed to be identifying and comparing them. He slid down a bit, looking for a better place to rest his head. Oliveira got up.

"It's the key to my apartment," Morelli said. "I would really be very happy."

"It really will be quite a job," Oliveira said.

"No, it's not as difficult as it seems. The notebooks will help you, there's a system of colours, numbers and letters. You'll work it out at once. For example, this goes in the blue notebook, a place I call the sea, but that's marginal, a game so I can understand myself better. Number 52: all you have to do is put it in its place between 51 and 53. Arabic numerals, the easiest thing in the world."

"But you can do it for yourself in a few days," Étienne said.

"I haven't been sleeping well. I'm outside of the notebook too. Do it for me, since you came to see me. Put all of this in its place and I'll feel much better here. This is really a fine hospital."

Étienne looked at Oliveira, and Oliveira, et cetera. The imaginable surprise. A real honour, so undeserved.

"Then make a package of it all and send it on to Paku. Publisher of avant-garde books, Rue de l'Arbre Sec. Did you know that Paku is the Akkadian name for Hermes? I always thought . . . But we'll talk about that another day."

"But what if we should make a mistake," Oliveira said, "and get things all mixed up. There was a terrible complication in the first volume, this guy here and I argued hours on end as to whether there hadn't been some mistake in the printing of the texts."

"Who cares," Morelli said. "You can read my book any way you want to. *Liber Fulguralis*, mantic pages, and that's how it goes. The most I do is set it up the way I would like to reread it. And in the worst of cases, if they do make a mistake, it might just turn out perfect. A trick on the part of Hermes Paku, the winged fabricator of subterfuges and lures. Do you like those words?"

"No," Oliveira said. "Neither subterfuge nor lure. They both seem rather decayed to me."

"You've got to be careful," Morelli said, closing his eyes. "We're all chasing after purity, breaking old daubed blisters. One day José Bergamin almost fell down dead when I took the liberty of deflating two pages of his, proving that . . . But watch out, my friends, what we call purity is probably . . ."

"Malevich's perfect square," Étienne said.

"*Ecco.* We were saying that we have to think about Hermes, let him have his fun. Take all of this, put it in order, since you've come to see me. Maybe I'll be able to drop over and take a look."

"We'll come back tomorrow if you want us to."

"Fine, I'll have some more things written by then. I'm going to drive you crazy. Bring me some Gauloises."

Étienne gave him his packet. With the key in his hand Oliveira didn't know what to say. Everything was wrong, none of it should have taken place that day, it was a lousy move in a sixty-piece chess game, a useless joy in the midst of the worst sadness, having to drive it off the way one does a fly, prefer sadness when the only thing that had come into his hands was that key to happiness, a step towards something he needed and admired, a key to open Morelli's door, Morelli's world, and in the midst of happiness to feel himself sad and dirty, with his tired skin and bleary eyes, smelling like a sleepless night, like a guilty absence, like a lack of the distance necessary to understand whether he had done well all of what he had been doing and not doing during those days, listening to La Maga's gasps, the knocking on the ceiling, bearing up under the icy rain in his face, dawn on the Pont Marie, the sour belches that came from wine mixed up with *caña* and with vodka and with more wine, the sensation of carrying in his pocket a hand that was not his, a hand of Rocamadour, a piece of drooling night; wetting his thighs, joy so late or maybe too soon (a consolation: probably too soon, still undeserved, but then, perhaps, *vielleicht, tal vez, forse, peut-être,* oh, shit, shit, see you tomorrow maestro, shit shit infinite shit, yes, at visiting time, the interminable obstinacy of shit around the face and around the world, a world of shit, we'll bring him some fruit, archeshit of countershit, supershit of infrashit, shit among shits, *dans cet hôpital Laennec découvrit l'auscultation*: maybe still . . . A key, an ineffable figure. A key. Still, maybe, he could go out into the street and keep on walking, with a key in his pocket. Maybe still, a Morelli key, a turn of the key and entering into something else, maybe still.

* * *

"When you come right down to it, it was a posthumous meeting, a question of days," Étienne said in the café.

"Get going," Oliveira said. "I'm sorry if I'm letting you down, but you'd better get going on it. Tell Ronald and Perico, we'll meet at the old man's place at ten o'clock."

"The time's no good," Étienne said. "The concierge won't let us in."

Oliveira took out the key, spun it around in a sunbeam, handed it over as if he were surrendering a city.

(–85)

155

It's incredible how all sorts of things can come out of a pair of trousers, fuzz, watches, clippings, crumbly aspirins, you stick your hand in to pull out your handkerchief and you pull a dead rat out by the tail, things like that are perfectly possible. While he was on his way to pick up Étienne, still affected by the dream about bread and that other memory of a dream that had suddenly appeared like an accident in the streets, suddenly boom, nothing he could do about it, Oliveira had stuck his hand in the pocket of his brown trousers, right on the corner of Raspail and Montparnasse, all the time half-looking at the gigantic twisted toad in his dressing-gown, Balzac Rodin or Rodin Balzac, and the inextricable mixture of two lightning flashes in his wrathful helicoid, and his hand had pulled out a clipping with a schedule of all-night chemists in Buenos Aires and another one that turned out to be a list of advertisements for soothsayers and fortunetellers. It was amusing to discover that Madame Colomier, a Hungarian soothsayer (who most likely was one of Gregorovius's mothers) lived on the Rue des Abbesses and possessed *secrets des bohèmes pour retour d'affections perdues*. From there one could go on to the great promise: *Désenvoûtements*, after which the reference to a *voyance sur photo* seemed slightly laughable. It would have been of interest to Étienne, an amateur Orientalist, to find out that Professor Mihn *vs offre le vérit. Talisman de l'Arbre Sacré de l'Inde. Broch. c. 1 NF timb. B.P. 27, Cannes.* How could anyone fail to be surprised at the existence of Mme Sanson, *Medium-Tarots, prédict. étonnantes, 23 Rue Hermel* (especially since Hermel, who was probably a zoologist, had an alchemist's name), and discover with South American pride the rotund proclamation of Anita, *cartes, dates précises*, of Joana-Jopez (*sic*), *secrets indiens, tarots espagnols*, and Mme Juanita, *voyante par domino, coquillage, fleur*. He would certainly have to take La Maga to visit Mme Juanita. *Coquillage, fleur!* But not La Maga, not any more. La Maga would have liked to have discovered her fate by means of flowers. *Seule* MARZAK *prouve retour affection.* But why the need to prove anything? That you can tell right off. The scientific tone of Jane de Nys was better, *reprend ses* VISIONS *exactes sur photogr. cheveux, écrit. Tour magnétiste intégral.* When he came alongside the Montparnasse cemetery, after crumpling it into a ball, Oliveira took careful aim and sent the soothsayers off to join up with Baudelaire on the other side of the wall, with Devéria, with Aloysius Bertrand, with people worthy of having their hands examined by fortunetellers, the likes of Mme Frédérika, *la voyante de l'élite parisienne et internationale, célèbre par ses prédictions dans la presse et la radio mondiales, de retour de Cannes.* Yeah, and with Barbey d'Aurevilly, who would have had them all burned at the stake if he could have, and also of course, Maupassant too, I hope the piece of paper landed on Maupassant's grave or Aloysius Bertrand's, but those were things that one had no way of knowing from outside.

It seemed stupid to Étienne that Oliveira had come to bother him at that hour of the morning, even though he was waiting there with three paintings he wanted to show him, but Oliveira said right away that the best thing would be to take advantage of the fabulous sun hanging over the Boulevard Montparnasse, and go over to the Necker Hospital and visit the old man. Étienne gave a curse under his breath and closed up his studio. The concierge, who liked them very much, told them that their faces looked like two recently disinterred corpses, men from outer space, and from that last bit they discovered that Madame Bobet was a reader of science fiction and they thought that was great. When they got to the Chien Qui Fume they had two glasses of white wine, arguing about dreams and painting as possible answers to NATO and other nuisances of the moment. It didn't seem excessively strange to Étienne that Oliveira wanted to go and visit a guy he didn't know, they agreed it would be easier, et cetera. At the bar a woman was giving a vehement description of a sunset in Nantes, where according to what she said her daughter lived. Étienne and Oliveira listened attentively to words like sun, breeze, lawn, moon, blackbirds, peace, the lame girl, God, six thousand five hundred francs, fog, rhododendrons, old age, your aunt, celestial, I hope they don't forget, flowerpots.

Then they admired the impressive plaque: DANS CET HÔPITAL, LAENNEC DECOUVRIT L'AUSCULTATION, and both of them thought (and said so) that auscultation must have been some kind of snake or salamander hiding away in the Necker Hospital, and chased, God knows why, through strange corridors and cellars it finally surrendered panting to the young savant. Oliveira made inquiries and they sent him to the Chauffard ward, third floor on the right.

"Probably no one has come to see him," Oliveira said. "And what a coincidence that his name should be Morelli."

"He's most likely dead already," Étienne said, looking at the fountain with goldfish in the open courtyard.

"They would have told me. The guy just looked at me, that's all. I didn't want to ask him if he'd had any visitors before."

"We could have visited him just the same without going by the main desk."

Et cetera. There are moments when because of displeasure, or fear, or because one has to climb two flights of stairs and smell phenol, conversation becomes abundant, the way it does when one has to console a person whose child has died and you invent the stupidest kind of talk sitting next to the mother and buttoning up her half-open bathrobe saying: "There, now, you mustn't catch cold." The mother sighs: "Thank you." You say: "You wouldn't think so, but at this time of year it gets cool very early." The mother says: "Yes, that's true." You say: "Wouldn't you like a wrap?" No. The outer-shelter chapter over. You attack the inner-shelter chapter: "I'll make you a cup of tea." But no, she doesn't feel like one. "But you ought to have something. You can't just sit there so long without something in your stomach." She doesn't know what time it is. "A little after eight. You haven't had anything since four-thirty. And this morning you barely touched your food. You have to eat something, even if it's just some toast and jam." She doesn't feel like it. "Take some, just to please me, just try some." A sigh, neither yes or no. "Look, of course you want something. I'm going to make some tea right now." If that doesn't work there's always the business with the chairs. "These chairs are so uncomfortable, you'll get cramp." No, it's fine. "No, your back must be all stiff, you've been sitting in that hard chair all afternoon. Why don't you lie down for a while." Oh no, I couldn't do that. In some mysterious way the bed is like a betrayal. "Come on, maybe you ought to take a quick nap." A double betrayal. "You need one, it'll be a good rest for you. I'll stay with you." No, she's fine just the way she is. "All right, but I'll get you a pillow for your back." All right. "Your legs are going to get stiff, I'll bring you a footstool so you can raise them up a bit." Thank you. "And after a while you'll go and lie down. Promise me." A sigh. "All right, all right, I'm not trying to pamper you. If the doctor had said so you'd have to obey him." In short. "You have to get some sleep, love." Variations *ad libitum.*

"Perchance to dream," Étienne murmured, thinking about the variations with every step.

"We should have bought a bottle of cognac," Oliveira said. "You've got some cash."

"But we don't even know him. And he's probably dead, really. Look at that redhead, I'd like her to give me a massage. Sometimes I get fantasies about nursing and nurses. Don't you ever?"

"When I was fifteen. Something awful. Eros armed with an intramuscular hypodermic that was like an arrow, wonderful girls who would wash me from top to bottom, I used to expire in their arms."

"In short, a masturbator."

"So what? Why be ashamed of masturbating? A lesser art next to the other one, but in any case it does have its divine proportions, its unities in time, action and place, and any other rhetoric you might want to apply. When I was nine I used to masturbate under an *ombú* tree, it was really patriotic."

"An *ombú* tree?"

"It's a kind of baobab," Oliveira said, "but I'll let you in on a secret if you swear never to tell any other Frenchman. An *ombú* isn't really a tree: it's a weed."

"Well, so it wasn't so serious after all."

"How do French boys masturbate then?"

"I don't remember."

"You remember only too well. We had our own wild systems down there. Hammer-style, umbrella-style . . . You get it? I can't listen to certain tangos without remembering how my aunt used to play them."

"I don't get the relationship," Étienne said.

"That's because you can't see the piano. There was a space between the piano and the wall and I used to hide in there to jerk off. My aunt would be playing *Milonguita* or *Flores negras*, something sad like that, it used to help me with my dreams of death and sacrifice. The first time I came on the parquet it was horrible, I thought the stain wouldn't come out. I didn't even have a handkerchief. I whipped off one of my socks and rubbed like crazy. My aunt was playing *La payanca*, I'll whistle it for you if you want me to, it's quite sad . . ."

"Whistling is not allowed in the hospital. But one feels the sadness just the same. You're all screwed up, Horacio."

"I'm on the lookout for them, pal. The king is dead, long live the king. If you think that because of a woman . . . *Ombú*, woman, they're all weeds when you come right down to it."

"Cheap," Étienne said. "Much too cheap. B-movies, dialogue you can buy by the foot, you know what I mean. Third floor, stop. Madame . . ."

"*Par là*," the nurse said.

"We still haven't run into the auscultation," Oliveira informed her.

"Knock it off," the nurse said.

"Take a lesson," Étienne said. "A lot of dreaming about a complaining loaf of bread, a lot of screwing everybody up, and then your jokes don't even come off. Why don't you go to the country for a while? You've really got an expression that Soutine could use, old man."

"Basically," Oliveira said, "what bugs you is that I've pulled you away from your chromatic jerking off, your filthy daily daubs, and solidarity makes you drift along with me through Paris the day after the funeral. My sad old pal, he's got to have some fun. Friend calls, you have to adjust. Friend mentions hospital, OK, let's go."

"To tell the truth," Étienne said, "I worry less and less about you. I should have been out walking with poor Lucía. She's the one who needs it."

"Wrong," Oliveira said, sitting down on a bench. "La Maga has Ossip, she has distractions, Hugo Wolf, things like that. Basically La Maga has a personal life, even though it's taken me a long time to realize it. On the other hand I'm empty, an enormous freedom in which to dream and wander around, the toys have all been broken, no problem. Give me a light."

"You can't smoke in a hospital."

"We are the makers of manners, eh. It's good for auscultation."

"The Chauffard ward is over there," Étienne said. "We can't sit on this bench all day."

"Wait till I finish my cigarette."

(–123)

ALSO AVAILABLE IN HARVILL PANTHERS

Giuseppe Tomasi di Lampedusa

THE LEOPARD

Translated from the Italian by Archibald Colquhoun

"The poetry of Lampedusa's novel flows into the Sicilian countryside . . . a work of great artistry"

PETER ACKROYD

"Every once in a while, like certain golden moments of happiness, infinitely memorable, one stumbles on a book or writer, and the impact is like an indelible mark. Lampedusa's *The Leopard*, his only novel, and a masterpiece, is such a work"

BRUCE ARNOLD, *Independent*

Boris Pasternak

DOCTOR ZHIVAGO

Translated from the Russian
by Manya Harari and Max Hayward

"The first work of genius to come out of Russia since the Revolution"

V. S. PRITCHETT

"A book that made a most profound impression upon me and the memory of which still does . . . not since Shakespeare has love been so fully, vividly, scrupulously and directly communicated . . . The novel is a total experience, not parts or aspects: of what other twentieth-century work of the imagination could this be said?"

ISAIAH BERLIN, ***Sunday Times***

Peter Høeg

BORDERLINERS

Translated from the Danish by Barbara Haveland

"It exerts the same chill grip on the imagination as its predecessor *Miss Smilla's Feeling for Snow*, posing questions and withholding answers with the same disconcerting skill . . . The power of the novel lies in the awesome truthfulness of the child's voice" SALLY LAIRD, *Observer*

"The sustained intensity and brilliance with which the lives of these 'dark and dubious children' are captured is overpowering" JOHN MELMOTH, *Sunday Times*

Georges Perec

LIFE, A USER'S MANUAL

Translated from the French by David Bellos

"A dazzling, crazy-quilt monument to the imagination"
PAUL AUSTER, *New York Times*

"One of the great novels of the century"
GABRIEL JOSIPOVICI, *Times Literary Supplement*

Theodore Zeldin

THE FRENCH

"He opens up before us a marvellously varied landscape, not of fields and cathedrals, but of anger and passion, of love and ridicule, a subtle mosaic, patiently constructed out of the daily experiences of French people . . . Like a talented film director, he makes the masks fall" ***Quotidien de Paris***

"Highly intelligent, observant, perceptive, humorous and sympathetic" ***Spectator***

Jan Wiese

THE NAKED MADONNA

Translated from the Norwegian by Tom Geddes

"Certainly one of the finest pieces of fiction to have emerged from Norway in the last decade. Beautifully translated . . . it carves a curious niche somewhere between Umberto Eco and Hans Christian Andersen, crossing complex historical mystery with moral fable" PAUL SUSSMAN, *Spectator*

Eduardo Mendoza

THE YEAR OF THE FLOOD

Translated from the Spanish by Nick Caistor

"A magnificent short novel . . . a rural elegy and political fable and an adventure story all in one"

MICHAEL EAUDE, *Times Literary Supplement*

"All the characters and relationships are sharply and subtly drawn"

JOHN SPURLING, *Sunday Times*